Rosenbaum

D1190629

THE SHAAR PRESS

THE JUDAICA IMPRINT
FOR THOUGHTFUL PEOPLE

The Mexico File

A NOVEL BY
CHAIM GREENBAUM
best-selling author of **The Will**
TRANSLATED BY LIBBY LAZEWNIK

First edition – First impression / March 2011
Second impression / April 2011
Third impression / July 2011

Published by **SHAAR PRESS**
Distributed by MESORAH PUBLICATIONS, LTD.
4401 Second Avenue / Brooklyn, N.Y 11232 / (718) 921-9000

Distributed in Israel by SIFRIATI / A. GITLER
6 Hayarkon Street / Bnei Brak 51127

Distributed in Europe by LEHMANNS
Unit E, Viking Business Park, Rolling Mill Road / Jarrow, Tyne and Wear, NE32 3DP/ England

Distributed in Australia and New Zealand by GOLDS WORLD OF JUDAICA
3-13 William Street / Balaclava, Melbourne 3183 / Victoria Australia

Distributed in South Africa by KOLLEL BOOKSHOP
Ivy Common / 105 William Road / Norwood 2192, Johannesburg, South Africa

ISBN 10: 1-4226-1092-6 / ISBN 13: 978-1-4226-1092-3

Printed in the United States of America by Noble Book Press
Custom bound by Sefercraft, Inc. / 4401 Second Avenue / Brooklyn N.Y. 11232

PROLOGUE

The armed guard leaned over to peer into the official limousine. He was completely covered by an orange protective suit. Only his eyes were visible through the lenses of his rubber goggles as he carefully studied the car's occupants.

In the front seat sat the Israeli prime minister's regular driver, with an internal security bodyguard next to him. Behind them was the prime minister, squeezed in beside his military adjutant, his personal secretary, the minister of security, and another bodyguard — as if anyone who was able to cram into the limo in the prime minister's parking lot had done so.

The guard did not need to consult the list in his hand. All the passengers were known to him and were authorized to enter. At the wave of his arm, someone in a remote inspection booth pressed a button, and the heavy steel gates slid back with surprising speed. The limousine started forward with a screech of its tires and entered an inner area enclosed by concrete walls, wire fences, and watchtowers.

Inside, pandemonium reigned. Dozens of soldiers in gas masks raced to and fro across the wide asphalt expanse. Several of them darted toward the prime minister's car, yanked open the doors, and hustled its passengers through a door in a concrete wall built into the slope of the hill.

At that moment, two army vehicles entered through the main gate, disgorging in quick succession the head of military intelligence and four generals, along with the interior minister, who had been in the midst of conducting an official inspection of a central army base that morning. On the landing strip at the enclosure's perimeter, the Army chief of staff's helicopter made a noisy landing. Crouching, he ran from the helicopter, flanked by two aides and the head of the General Security Service (G.S.S.). Every face registered alarm, as though cognizant of the severity of the situation.

"Run! Run!" young soldiers urged their illustrious charges. "Hurry! Faster!"

But there was no need to hasten anyone along. Of their own accord, everyone sped toward a door that led into a square room that housed numerous examination cubicles. In each cubicle, an army paramedic in full protective gear quickly drew a blood sample from each newcomer's arm. Within seconds, the color green appeared in the tiny window at the top of each syringe. The medic bent the needle into a hook, inserted the syringe into the subject's lapel, and directed him to the row of elevators waiting to take them underground.

Suddenly, a cry slashed through the muted din in the big room: "Red!"

Instant silence fell. A few heads turned back for a moment. The corpulent treasury minister stood there, staring with bulging eyes at his syringe. The tiny window was colored red. Those standing nearby began to inch away, forming an ever-widening circle around him.

The portly man in the expensive suit grew very pale. He knew what that red indicator meant. Beads of perspiration formed on his forehead and his shoulders slumped in despair. His helpless gaze swept the crowd until it fell on the prime minister. He spread his hands in a mute gesture of appeal.

But not even the strong bonds of friendship between the two men — a bond going back many years — or their longstanding political ties could help him now. Painfully, the prime minister turned away and continued walking toward the elevator.

"Sir," the installation's supervisor called to the treasury minister, "you are requested to leave this area at once."

Two armed soldiers stepped up to carry out the order. Cabinet ministers and army generals watched the unfortunate man's back as he was led outside to the contaminated area — and to a world that appeared to be crumbling.

The Situation Room of the national strategy center, six flights below the entry hall built into the side of the hill, was spartan: bare concrete walls snaked with electrical cables, cold fluorescent lights, and a large, bare table in the center . This was the beating heart of the huge bunker — a small city beneath the earth built to afford protection against every form of weaponry. It was a control center capable of activating all army, security, health, and financial systems throughout the land. At the head of the table sat the prime minister, the chief of staff, the inspector general of the police, and the head of the G.S.S., with the remaining ministers and high government officials taking their places in descending order.

On the other side of the big room, a group of soldiers from Army Communications stood by to link the Situation Room of the State of Israel to the outside world — or what was left of it.

A row of oversized screens projected live broadcasts from the central news networks. Those in the room watched the screens with undisguised horror. A CNN broadcaster in a gas mask faced the camera, reporting live from a dying New York. Nor was the view from the BBC in London any more encouraging. The broadcaster for the Russian network burst into tears on camera.

The people seated around the table gazed at each other in shock. It truly looked like the end of the world. Utter catastrophe. Chaos ....

The prime minister nodded at his military adjutant, Lieutenant Colonel Uri Arbel, who stood up and began to speak.

"Well, the situation, as you see, is very bad. The east coast of the United States has been completely affected, and the epidemic is spreading westward to Pittsburgh, Cleveland, and Chicago. The death toll exceeded the million mark within a week, there are three million more who are ill, and none of the experts can estimate how many carriers are continuing to spread the plague without their knowledge. Huge areas have turned into mass graves. In New Jersey, parking lots have been turned into cemeteries, and Philadelphia is no longer bothering to bury its dead: They are simply burning them in huge pyres outside the city limits. The entire American economy has ground to a halt. Banks are closed, the stock market's crashed, and there is no one supplying food or medicine. The police and emergency services have collapsed. Stores are being looted and there is no one to put a stop to it."

"What about Washington?" the foreign minister asked.

The military officer compressed his lips gloomily. "The Americans tried to halt the plague by creating a 50-kilometer-wide 'clean band' around the capital. But the effort was futile. By this morning, some 2,000 people have died in Washington and the source of the outbreak has been traced to an office building near the Pentagon. Two White House employees have already been infected. It is very probable that we are facing — how can I put this? — a leadership crisis in the United States."

The prime minister heaved a deep sigh and sank back in his chair. The map of the United States, on the largest screen, was replaced by a map of Russia.

"The second focal point in the outbreak is in Central Asia," Uri Arbel continued. "The epidemic broke out in the city of Semipalotinsk, in northeast Khazakstan, ten days ago. We have no details about what is happening in Russia's rural districts, but within several days it had spread quickly northward, leaving whole areas strewn with what are estimated to be about 300,000 dead. Life in Russia has become completely paralyzed. People are remaining in their homes, afraid of becoming infected. There is no medicine, and the plague is continuing to exact its toll. Russia's president, as you know, died this morning. Moscow looks like a ghost town."

"How far can this go?" someone asked softly from the far end of the table.

The military man paused before replying. "Taking into consideration the fact that only thirty percent of victims recover, that the infection is airborne, and that it spreads at a high rate — we can estimate that it is likely to wipe out about half the populations of Europe and America within a few weeks."

A stunned silence enveloped the table. Averting each other's gaze, they sat enveloped in sheer terror.

"But — but what could it be?" the interior minister exploded. "A global act of terrorism? A wild mutation of some virus? A mad scientist out to destroy the world?"

"If only we knew." Uri Arbel spread his hands. "An organization calling itself the 'Sword of Mohammed' has claimed responsibility for the epidemic, but there are no indications that their claim is authentic."

"What happened this morning?" the chief of staff asked. Less than half an hour before, all those present had been summoned urgently from their homes and offices to this bunker, deep underground. Their drivers had driven at insane speeds, breaking every possible law of the road — and, as yet, no one knew why.

"Forty minutes ago, three carriers of the plague were found at Ben Gurion Airport," Uri Arbel said, to a wave of groans around the table. "The epidemic is here. In a couple of days, the State of Israel may look very different from anything we've known."

The atmosphere in the room plunged below the freezing point. Uri Arbel sat down.

"The I.D.F. and the police have quarantined the area around the airport. No one is permitted to come or go," the transportation minister reported. "As you can imagine, there's a great deal of hysteria out there. The thousands of travelers imprisoned inside are trying desperately to get away. They feel doomed."

"As of this moment, every hospital in Israel has been turned into a sealed military area," the minister of security announced. "Special elite troops have been deployed around them. Their orders: shoot to kill anyone who tries to leave or enter without authorization."

"What about the cemeteries?" the minister of religion asked. "How do we organize the mass burial of tens of thousands?"

The prime minister looked around with a pinched face, his thumb supporting his chin while his forefinger tugged at his lower lip. This isolated bunker, completely sealed against the penetration of air from the outside, now held about 200 people, including soldiers and staff workers. It had enough food, water, and energy to last several months. But what would happen to the country's millions of citizens? And what about the billions of people across the globe?

What could even the mightiest army, with smart bombs and the most celebrated air force, do against a lethal virus — a cruel and merciless germ spreading rapidly through the world while doctors and medical experts stood by helplessly?

Until now, he had been able to pat himself on the back. He had managed to bring himself and his government onto safe ground. Very commendable. But whose government were they? Would the State survive? Would its population survive?

As he scanned the faces of those seated around the table, all of them told the same story. Very similar thoughts to his own were flooding their minds.

The telephone on the table rang. The prime minister placed a hand on the receiver, as though hesitating about whether to answer. Finally, with obvious reluctance, he pressed the speakerphone button.

A childish voice filled the room. "Saba?"

A sudden smile lit up the prime minister's drawn face. With an apologetic gesture at his companions, he lifted the receiver and brought it to his ear. "Yes, Yaroni. How are you?"

"Saba, why didn't you come? Did you forget that there was a party in my *gan* today?"

The prime minister smacked his forehead and threw an accusing glare at his staff secretary. "You're right, Yaron," he said quietly. "But Saba is a little busy right now …."

The child would not back down. His voice held a hint of tears. "But Saba, you promised! Ima said that you were going to come. You always forget …."

With every eye fixed on him, the prime minister stood up. Smiling apologetically, he said, "I think we'll have to continue this later."

The sound of moving chairs filled the room. The atmosphere thawed all at once. There were broad smiles and thumps on the back. The soldiers removed their gas masks and stretched their limbs. The prime minister turned to his secretary with a smile.

"Very convincing," he said. "Even a little frightening. But, next time, try not to schedule a military exercise for me when my grandson's having a school party, okay?"

His secretary nodded, contrite.

"The timetable was excellent," the prime minister remarked to the base commander as he put on his coat. "Everyone was here within sixteen minutes. Very nice."

"Thank you, Mr. Prime Minister," the commander replied, pleased with his men.

The prime minister smiled broadly. Into the commander's ear, he whispered, "And something else. Next time, don't leave the treasury minister out. Did you see how he looked? Poor fellow. I know he's been trying to cut the military budget, but he doesn't deserve such treatment. Underneath it all, he's a good guy."

In the elevator leading up to the exit level, the prime minister was with his bodyguards and Uri Arbel. At the last moment, the vice minister of security had squeezed inside as well.

"The scenario you created is not realistic," he told Uri in his slow, tired way. "No Islamic terror group is going to unleash an uncontrollable virus, for fear that the epidemic will spread to Islamic population centers as well. It's the well-known Boomerang Effect, which keeps biological warfare off the head of the list of threats."

Uri Arbel did not answer the vice minister. Instead, he sent the prime minister a brief look, both bitter and amused. The prime minister merely tightened his lips and let out his breath disdainfully. There are things, apparently, that even the vice minister of security doesn't know.

Only the prime minister, Uri Arbel, and a few other senior people knew that, in August 2006, biological warfare had returned to the very head of the list. On a scorchingly hot afternoon, somewhere between Bnei Brak and Ramat Gan, the State of Israel had been surprised to learn that the Boomerang Effect had ceased to exist.

Tzefas — Iyar 5766 / May 2006

The heavy wooden door opened silently, and the imposing figure of the *gabbai*, R' Shammai Lederman, appeared in the doorway. The man waiting in the foyer lifted his head quickly, diverting his attention from the *sefer* he had been reading. With a slight nod, the *gabbai* invited him inside.

The man rose with undisguised excitement. He was of medium height, with a neatly trimmed beard and designer glasses. He straightened his jacket, adjusted his hat, and touched his *gartel* as if to make sure it was still there. In his right hand was a folded paper — a *kvittel* — containing some money, as is the custom among chassidim. The stern features softened into an expression of humble reverence. With his head slightly bowed, he walked to the door. R' Shammai retreated a step to let him pass into the short hallway leading to another door.

Had any of his workers or colleagues been able to see him now, they would have found it hard to believe the evidence of their own eyes. Dr. Jacob Stern, director of a department in charge of supervising agricultural toxins, was known as a hard and uncompromising man who ran his department with a firm hand. He was not one who bowed his head. When he had something to say, he said it firmly.

But here, in Tzefas, so far from Houston, Texas, he was no longer a senior official with the United States Department of Agriculture, but a chassid and admirer of the Milinover Rebbe, *shlita*. He was not Dr. Jacob Stern, but Yankel Meyer Stern. Or, as the rebbe's longtime *gabbai* had written on the *kvittel* half an hour earlier: "Yaakov Meyer ben Hinda, for good health."

Jacob Stern, watching R' Shammai write, had said quickly, almost inaudibly, as though he might regret it, "Please add: 'and protection.'"

R' Shammai had raised his brows in surprise. His twenty-five years in this position had trained him not to ask questions. Certainly not out loud ....

The scenes he had witnessed in this spot, near the Rebbe's room, had worked their way deep into his heart. He had been present at happy occasions — and sorrowful ones. He had seen Jews whose world had crumbled in a moment, and others who had left the Rebbe's room with shining eyes after a salvation. He was the recipient of deep secrets and fateful decisions, but his lips were sealed.

"The trick," the *gabbai* would tell younger men who begged eagerly for secrets from the room, "is to know when to ask, when to answer — and when to do neither."

Besides which, if Yankel Meyer Stern had caught a flight from Houston to New York and from there to Israel; if he had landed with nothing but a briefcase and the taxi fare to Tzefas, and had instructed the cab driver to wait for him and take him right back to the airport at Lod; if he had insisted on seeing the Rebbe, despite the fact that no one had been privileged to see him for weeks now, and if he was prepared to wait by the door for as long as it took — he must have a good reason.

The Rebbe's health had been precarious these past few weeks. It had been R' Shammai's suggestion that, in anticipation of the upcoming *simchah* at the summer's end, an apartment be rented on a cool hilltop in Tzefas where the Rebbe could reside for several weeks while he regained his strength.

This was slated to be an extraordinary wedding: Zalman Leib, the Rebbe's beloved young grandson, was to marry the daughter of his Rosh Yeshivah, R' Yom Tov Padlinsky, head of Yeshivas Knesses HaTorah in New Jersey.

In their heart of hearts — though no one voiced the thought aloud — the chassidim feared this might be their last chance to celebrate a *simchah* with their aged Rebbe. As his health steadily deteriorated, those with discernment could see that he was preparing to make the transition between the "corridor" to the "palace" — the leap from the material world to the world that is all good. He spent long hours immersed in holy meditations, eyes closed and lips moving as though the spiritual component within him was rapidly gaining on the little bit of the corporeal still retained in his frail frame. It was from this component that he gleaned his life force now.

When the Rebbe spoke — his words few and measured — his voice was weak and cracked. Only a chosen few were permitted to enter his room these days: his chief *gabbai*, R' Shammai Lederman; the young *hoiz bachur* who served him devotedly; R' Yoel, director of the institutions, and a few individuals who needed his guidance or blessing on critical matters that could brook no delay.

"Protection?" R' Shammai repeated, pen poised over the *kvittel*.

Jacob Stern's reply was a deep sigh that seemed be torn from the depths of his heart.

He was in dire need of protection. Someone was after him. Somebody very powerful wanted him dead. Not satisfied with the row of corpses he had left behind in Mexico City, or with those who had already been harmed in Houston, he wanted to silence Jacob Stern as well. Jacob Stern needed protection. He needed the Rebbe's blessing and prayers, so that his wife might continue to have a husband and his children a father. So that he might not go the way of those unfortunate Mexicans ....

May 6th, a week before Jacob Stern's hasty visit to Tzefas, had been a gloomy day in Mexico City. The smog that typically blanketed the city was heavier than usual, turning the air brownish-red. A sudden rain shower had left El Zócalo — the huge square in the center of the Mexican capital — wet and slippery.

At this hour, five-thirty, the square teemed with life. Government clerks hurried home after their day's work, tourists roamed in restless knots, and peddlers had their wares spread on the pavement: silver ornaments and tooled leather artifacts. Indian "medicine men" promised to chase away evil spirits and remove any sort of curse — for a price.

On the square's northeastern side, near the exit from the Palacio Nacional, the seat of Mexico's government, stood an odd-looking group of men. The one in the old checkered jacket that was just a bit too small for him was Octavio Solarz, a minor clerk in the national archive located in the Palacio Nacional. Next to him, tense with expectation, was Romero Alameda. A sparse mustache adorned Alameda's thin, tanned face, and he wore a flowered shirt over burgundy trousers.

The third man, Jorge Diaz, was tallest of the three. His good suit, expensive haircut, and full build testified to the fact that he was one of the few who had managed to free himself from the cycle of poverty in the villages. Jorge Diaz had acquired an education and obtained a steady job in the city of Juarez in northern Mexico, near the United States border — but in his heart he remained a valiant warrior like his Indian forefathers. He never forgot from where he had come. And he would never forget what the Americans had done to his people.

That was why he was here. That was why he had made the long trek from Juarez to Mexico City — a journey of hundreds of kilometers, more than twenty hours on a rickety and crowded old bus.

Dr. Jacob Stern had never heard of Jorge Diaz, Octavio Solarz, or Romero Alameda. He didn't know that those three Mexicans existed. He had never crossed the Rio Grande River that divided the United States from Mexico, and had certainly never visited Mexico City. But what was about to happen in the next few minutes would have a fateful impact on Jacob Stern's life.

Mexico City — Iyar 5766 / May 2006

C*ómo fue te viaje?* (How was the journey?)" Octavio Solarz of the government archive asked Jorge Diaz from Juarez. The question was intended as an icebreaker — something to ease the inevitable awkwardness when two strangers meet face-to-face for the first time. Their previous interactions had been via the phone.

"*Bien* (All right)," Diaz replied. "Tell me, who exactly are we going to see?"

Octavio shrugged his shoulders and gestured with his head at Romero, as if to say, "I have no idea who the man is that we're about to meet in the hotel on the other side of the square, but you can count on this skinny Indian. Romero knows what he's doing."

Actually, it had been Octavio who had uncovered the whole incident, when he stumbled upon the documents a few months earlier. In the national archive where he worked, there was little to do and therefore, a great deal of free time. After he had read the newspaper and consumed the tortilla with black beans and chili peppers that his wife had prepared for him, he was in the habit of going down to the basement level and rummaging through the files there.

Apart from the entertainment it afforded, this pastime provided him with an additional source of income that was not exactly legal: "*la mordida,*" as it was known in Mexico. Bribe money. Several hundred pesos passing from hand to hand, to smooth all manner of things.

Octavio always found someone who was ready to pay: a corrupt politician out to strike at a rival by means of a long-forgotten criminal file from the archive; a lawyer in need of information for a rich client, or a historian who wanted to know about the past but who lacked the patience to present a request through the usual snail-like channels. Octavio had developed a sixth sense about which document was worth something and which was valueless. Upon discovering, in a closed steel cabinet in a neglected storeroom, the dusty file about the Juarez affair, and reading through its yellowing pages, he had felt excitement mount to his throat. This was explosive material. A global nightmare. The U.S., the U.S.S.R., and Mexico were all involved. This stained cardboard file was worth a big *mordida*. An enormous *mordida*.

It was precisely at this juncture that Jorge Diaz had called. He had introduced himself as a clerk in the Juarez municipality, and asked for some routine service from the archive. But the fact that he had phoned from the exact area that the file dealt with had raised a red flag in Octavio's mind. *There were definite possibilities here*, he thought. But it would require several more probing conversations before he offered his wares.

The clerk from Juarez had quickly revealed his pride in being a descendant of the original Mexicans, predating the Spanish conquest. In the course of his job, he worked for the advancement of Indian youngsters, and roundly excoriated the Americans for robbing whole tribes of their ancestral lands. Though he did not state it explicitly, it was clear that he had ties to underground groups working for the restoration of rights to the village people.

This was exactly what the archivist wanted to hear. He hinted to Jorge that he had material that might interest him — something that could help a great deal in his war against America. After making some inquiries of his own, the clerk from Juarez told the archive clerk that he knew someone who was definitely interested, and who was ready to pay well for the material.

The man's name was Romero Alameda, and he lived in ... Mexico City. Octavio and Jorge laughed when they realized the turn of events. It had been necessary for Octavio to hook up with Jorge Diaz in distant Juarez, in order to conclude a deal with a man who resided right here in the capital.

The next day, when Octavio finished work, he tucked the old cardboard file under his jacket and smuggled it out of the archive building. He wandered about El Zócalo for a long time, repeatedly checking his watch. At 5:15, as per arrangement with the clerk from Juarez, a slender man with a mustache was waiting outside the bookstore near the cathedral, adjacent to the subway. Octavio approached him.

"Romero"?" he asked. "Romero Alemada?" He held out his hand.

"*Mucho gusto* (Pleased to meet you)."

The exchange had taken place without fanfare. Octavio accepted a hefty wad of cash and transferred the file to Romero. He returned home with a light step, swelled with happiness over the bulge in his jacket pocket. Forty thousand pesos! More than half his monthly salary! What a *mordida*! He had never sold information for such a huge sum before.

Months had passed since then. The money, of course, was long gone. And now, Octavio was once again meeting with Romero in the same place. However, this time they were joined by Jorge Diaz, the clerk from Juarez who had arranged their initial encounter. The three men stood at the edge of a street still slick with rain, hoping that the rain would not return as they studied the traffic on the Sixteenth of September Avenue. A slow river of cars moved along the broad street, most of them green-and-white taxicabs.

"Where's the student?" Romero asked, withdrawing a timepiece from his pocket and dangling it on its chain. "It's nearly six." Palace guards in their black uniforms were preparing for their impressive daily ritual of lowering the national flag in the center of the square. "He should have been here long ago."

"Let's give it another five minutes," Jorge suggested.

The student, Munzio Rodriguez, was the only one of the four invited guests who was a mestizo, of partly Spanish stock instead of a pureblood Indian. He was only 23, and his appearance — like that of most of Mexico's youth — was blatantly European: stylish clothes and the latest haircut, to go with a modern lifestyle. His city Spanish was more rapid than the village drawl. He was an excellent student of anthropology at the University of Mexico City, which was the reason he had been selected to assist in the study being conducted by faculty head Professor Gustavo Costa.

When Romero had brought him the stained cardboard file four months earlier, immediately after acquiring it from the national archive, the student had found it hard to conceal his excitement.

"The professor is not going to believe his eyes!" he crowed happily. "This will confirm his entire thesis. Where did you get this?"

The scrawny Indian shrugged indifferently.

The student was surprised. "You're not happy? We've been waiting months for something like this. Now we have proof!"

Romero sighed sadly and pointed his chin at the cardboard file under the student's arm. "Munzio, for you and the professor, this is just an academic study. But for me — it's the greatest crime that has been perpetrated against my people. This is what destroyed an entire Indian tribe that was innocent of any crime."

The smile on Munzio's face died at once. "I'm sorry," he said quietly.

Now, four months later, the three men stood waiting for the young student to arrive. Jorge, Romero, and Octavio eyed each passing taxi, but Munzio Rodriguez was in none of them. The informer was waiting for them in the hotel. They only hoped he would not bolt.

"Do you think that what he has to offer is serious?" Jorge asked Romero.

"Absolutely," Romero said with confidence. "He recognized all the data I showed him, and said that the crime that was perpetrated there was actually much bigger."

The man they were about to meet had contacted the Indian activist some three days before, saying that he had material and new documents that would shock him. Everything Romero already knew about the incident at Juarez, the man had said, was dwarfed by what he now held in his hand. He insisted that everyone who was involved in the matter come to a meeting, so that he might judge whether to hand this precious information over to them.

"Who is he, anyway?" Octavio asked.

"He owns an estate here in Mexico. He's originally from the States, but he 'loves' America as much as I do," Romero replied, a cynical glint in his perpetually sorrowful eyes.

Octavio glanced at the majestic hotel on the opposite side of the square, and grinned. "One thing's for sure — the man has money. A suite in that hotel is something we three couldn't afford even if we pooled all of our salaries together."

A green Volkswagen "bug" pulled up beside them. Like thousands of other Mexican taxis of its kind, it was missing its front passenger seat to make it easier for passengers to enter and exit.

The student stepped out of the taxi. "*Hola* (hello)!" he called cheerfully to the three waiting men.

"*Hola*," Romero replied in greeting. Then, to his surprise, he saw a second person emerge from the taxi. He was an older man, with a shock of white hair and a neatly trimmed goatee. He gripped a handsome leather briefcase in his hand. "I see the professor's joined you."

Professor Gustavo Costa shook Romero's hand and exchanged hurried introductions with his two friends. Romero always felt uncomfortable in the professor's company. Gustavo Costa was well fed and well dressed, with an apartment in one of Mexico City's luxury neighborhoods and, presumably, a salary to match. On the social ladder, he stood about ten rungs above Romero, and typically exuded a chilly aloofness. Romero could never quite shake the feeling that the professor's attitude toward himself and his fellow Indians was one of condescension. To him, they were nothing but research subjects — tiny creatures scurrying around beneath the microscope lens.

On the other hand, Professor Costa was the only man capable of exposing what had really happened to the unfortunate Chuma tribe, in the big valley under the black-rock mountain near the city of Juarez.

"Well? Shall we go?" the professor suggested.

He wore an air of ill-concealed excitement. Proof for his theory existed. The revelations were documented. The article he was about to write for one of the respected anthropological journals would create an international uproar.

Still, it would be interesting to hear what that estate owner had to add. Perhaps additional documentation was available, or the personal testimony of individuals suffering pangs of conscience. It was possible that he, himself, had been present when the events had transpired. As the helicopter pilot, perhaps, or one of the technicians working in the secret lab, or a survivor of the calamity at Grayston.

Whatever the case, he intended to drop the bombshell in just a few weeks' time. It was not every day that a research study capable of toppling governments was published. He would call a press conference that would spread the story to every corner of the globe — and then *everyone* would know the name Gustavo Costa, Professor of Anthropology in the University of Mexico City ....

The group, five strong now, crossed El Zócalo on the diagonal. The human throng continued to swarm throughout the square, which is one of the largest in the world and capable of holding half a million people.

"The history of Mexico City begins 700 years ago," tour guides would intone to the avid tourists around them. "Mexican legend has it that Aztec gods instructed the tribe's warriors to seek out an island in the center of a lake, on which an eagle with a snake in its beak perched on a cactus bush. When the warriors reached the place, they found the description so accurate that they decided to establish their capital on the spot. Note the drawing in the center of the Mexican flag, which commemorates the legend: an eagle on a cactus with a snake in its beak, perching on a cactus."

A group of Indians, in native costume, were putting on a folkloristic street show, in the hopes that the overturned hat beside them would quickly fill with coins. Around them, food vendors offered an assortment of popular items. The five men strode toward the hotel in near-silence. Jorge kept fingering his jacket pocket. In a cloth bag tied with a strip of leather lay the three mountain lion's teeth that the old Indian shaman had given him before the journey.

He was a little apprehensive about this meeting. The mysterious informer's insistence on meeting everyone involved in the matter aroused a vague sense of alarm. A tiny, doom-filled voice refused to stop pestering him. This could be a trap. He might have to pay for this adventure with his job. He was well aware that activity on behalf of the descendants of Indian tribes did not find favor with the Mexican government. And so, before setting out for the capital, Jorge had paid a visit to his native village, a half-hour's drive from Juarez.

The tiny village was remote and dismal. The main road was unpaved and the mud houses teetered on the brink of collapse. While the women busied themselves with shucking the ears from rotting corn stalks and feeding the hens, the men sat idly in their doorways, slowly chewing to-bacco. In a ramshackle hut near the church, he had found the shaman — an elderly Indian with a lined, leathery complexion. He lived in a single room that he shared with two goats, though none of them appeared to suffer overmuch from the arrangement.

Jorge took several coins from his pocket, and the shaman quickly trans-ferred them to his own. He went to a rickety cupboard and rummaged in a tin bowl filled with various small objects. Finally, he pulled out three mountain lion's teeth and held them in his fist. Jorge watched tensely as the shaman lifted a shriveled dried pumpkin, filled it with a foul-looking liquid from a large container, and dropped in the three teeth along with a few leaves and seeds.

Next, he stoked a small fire in the center of the hut, and threw several eagle's feathers onto the flames. The room filled with thick smoke. Jorge began to cough. The shaman commenced to dance around the flame, slowly at first, and then with gathering speed as his lips muttered strange words. From time to time he would lean over the fire and hold the gourd out to the flames. His body was bathed in sweat as he leaped higher and higher — until, suddenly, he collapsed in a heap on the floor. His eyes were closed, his body trembled, and bubbles of spittle escaped from be-tween his lips. He held out both hands, and Jorge took them in his own with a sense of revulsion. He felt dizzy, as though time was wheeling around him while he stood still.

At last, the shaman relaxed. He released Jorge's hands, opened his eyes, and sat up. He told Jorge to pick up the gourd and drink the liquid that remained inside. Then he was to remove the mountain lion's teeth. When Jorge had followed these instructions, the shaman placed the teeth into a small cloth bag, tied it closed with a strip of leather, and handed it to Jorge.

"Now you are safe and secure," the Indian medicine man said, show-ing his yellowed teeth in a big smile. "The spirit of the eagle on the black mountain will protect you. You are an eagle. You devour all other powers. No one in the world can conquer the spirit of the eagle from the black mountain."

The five-story hotel was a picture of tired splendor. The lobby offered heavy, velvet-upholstered armchairs. The elevator walls were mirrored, but the lift itself creaked and swayed. After a seemingly endless ascent, the doors opened at the top floor. In a suite overlooking El Zócalo, the informer was waiting for them.

He was slightly corpulent and strangely pale. His hair was light, and even his eyes seemed colorless.

They introduced themselves, murmuring polite greetings and shaking hands: Professor Gustavo Costa, pleased to meet you; his student and research assistant, Munzio Rodriguez; Jorge Diaz, from Juarez; government archive clerk Octavio Solarz; and Romero Alamera, activist on behalf of Indian rights.

"Please, sit down," their host invited, ushering them to a seating arrangement in a corner of the room. On a low coffee table were drinking glasses, bottles of cold water, plates of nachos — a salty Mexican treat made of corn flour — and a large tray of sliced fruit.

The professor was impatient. He longed to hear what their host had to say. But no self-respecting Mexican would ever get straight to the point.

The informer poured liberally from a bottle of tequila into a group of glasses in the middle of the table. He handed one glass to each of his guests, and raised his own with a hearty, "*Salud (L'chaim)*!"

"*Salud!*" echoed the five.

"*Viva Mexico* (Long live Mexico)! Death to America!" the estate owner cried. They responded in kind and drained their glasses in a single gulp.

The professor was the first to feel queasy. Seconds later, a horrible choking sensation filled his throat, and the pressure in his chest became unbearable. The room seemed to spin around him. He fell, unconscious.

Within two minutes, all five Mexicans were sprawled motionless on the floor. The poison in the tequila had been efficient, quick, and lethal. Their host observed the scene from the comfort of his armchair. He toyed with the idea of checking each body for a pulse, to ensure that the job had been done properly. But the scene spoke for itself.

They hardly suffered at all, he chuckled to himself. *A pity. Our materials are too efficient* .... He plucked a morsel of papaya from the fruit platter and chewed it with enjoyment. As he ate, he glanced around to make certain that he hadn't neglected anything.

His part was done. In a minute, he would leave this room and this hotel. Then the "B" crew — local mercenaries — would arrive to clear away the corpses, make the deaths look natural, and remove every clue as to what had taken place in this suite.

But first, he had to report to his superior.

He took out his cell phone and punched in a number.

A great distance away, in a different country, in a handsome and spacious office on the seventh floor of a sophisticated office building, somebody picked up the call on the first ring.

"Hello?" The voice was deep and authoritative.

"It's me," said the man in Mexico City.

"Is it finished?"

"It's finished."

"I'm writing …."

"Okay. Number 2 — Munzio Rodriguez."

From the other side of the line came the sound of a pen scratching on paper. Someone drew a firm line beneath the name.

"That's the student? The research assistant?"

"Correct."

"Who else?"

"Number 3 — Romero Alameda."

"The one with the mustache? Good. He was the most dangerous."

"Number 4 — Octavio Solarz, the archive clerk."

"The idiot who found the file. Go on."

"Number 5 — Jorge Diaz."

"From Juarez. Congratulations."

"And … I have a surprise," the "estate owner" said gaily. "We got Number 1, too."

The voice at the other end rose in excitement. "Gustavo Costa? Really?"

"Yes. Professor Costa himself decided to come. Apparently, he was curious to see what an informer might have to sell. It wasn't his wisest decision, I'm afraid."

The man at the other end of the line laughed. "The professor saved us a job. I've always said that curiosity is not too healthy."

Tzefas — Iyar 5766 / May 2006

Jacob Stern crossed the short corridor and reached the other door. The *boiz bachur* nodded with a bashful smile.

"You'll be able to go in shortly," he said. Jacob waited.

Once again, he opened the *kvittel* and read what it said. *Yaakov Meyer ben Hinda, for good health — and protection.*

It had been a good decision, coming to Israel. The Rebbe would bless him and give him the right advice. He was in a terrible bind, fighting evil forces that knew no restraint. If they had finished off five Mexicans without blinking an eye, they would have no pity on his own life.

If they could only discover where he was, they would finish him off, too.

Mexico City — Iyar 5766 / May 2006

As Angelo Morales's cell phone vibrated lightly against his shirt, he praised himself for remembering to turn on the silent mode — the appropriate mode for a funeral service.

The chapel was packed to the rafters with people who had come to pay their last respects to his partner and good friend, Romero Alameda. The weeping widow sat beside her children, all of them clad in black, and received the mourners. Angelo had been the one to purchase the casket of fine oak lined with velvet, and Romero's body, dressed in an expensive suit, was visible to all eyes, as was the local custom.

"He looks so alive," everyone said, noting his ever-present mustache and lifelike, handsome features. Only the sad eyes were closed now, as his soul wafted over the great hills to join his brave warrior ancestors.

His sudden death of a heart attack had stunned everyone who knew Romero. He had been a young man. No one — not even his wife — had known that he suffered from a weak heart. It came from taking everything to heart, everyone said, repeating the well-worn and comfortless cliche.

In his eulogy for his friend, Angelo intended to tell all those gathered something they didn't know about the departed: his battle on behalf of the Indian community and against those who had perpetrated such a horrific crime against it. He wanted to reveal to the grieving audience that Romero's final act was to attend a secret meeting with a group of activists headed by Professor Gustavo Costa, from the University — a group bent on exposing the historic wrong that had been done to the Chuma tribe decades earlier.

Just hours before his death, Romero had told him that he was on his way to the meeting. As he left the meeting, he must have been feeling ill. Our dear, departed Romero Alameda collapsed on the street and, on his arrival at the hospital, was too far gone to be helped.

That was what Angelo intended to say at the eulogy. His big heart could not endure the pain. He vowed to carry on Romero's mission in life. *I will find the professor from the university and tell him that this valiant warrior died before his time. I, Angelo Ramon Morales, swear to dedicate my life to continuing Romero Alameda's struggle.*

He felt the vibration at his waist just as he was silently rehearsing these sentences. He picked up the phone and brought it to his ear.

"Hello?" he whispered.

"Angelo?"

"*Si* (Yes)."

"Angelo Morales?"

"*Si, si.* Who is this?"

"*Un amigo* (A friend)."

"I can't talk now."

"Listen for a minute. It's about Romero. I know why he died."

Angelo Morales looked around in astonishment. "Why he died? He died of a heart attack. He collapsed in the street and was taken to the hospital."

The anonymous caller chuckled softly. "Don't be naive. The story is much more complicated than that."

Now Angelo was utterly confused. "What do you mean?"

"Not on the phone," the caller whispered. "If you want to hear, go outside. I'll be waiting behind the chapel and I'll tell you everything."

Angelo glanced uneasily right and left. Could he disappear for a few minutes? Absolutely. He must find out what that caller meant. It could make a big difference to his eulogy. He slipped through the back door and walked toward the parking lot. At the edge of the lot stood a slightly dented gray Dodge. Behind the Dodge's wheel sat a weird-looking character with a pale face and whitish hair. He motioned for Angelo to get in next to him.

The door slammed shut and the car burst from the parking lot onto the street.

"What's going on?" Angelo asked, bewildered. "Where are we going?"

At that moment, two more heads appeared in the back seat. A black bag was popped over the Mexican's head. In a flash, his incomprehension turned into panic.

"You're going to meet your friend, Romero," the pale man laughed wickedly.

Those were the last words Angelo Morales heard.

■ ■ ■

The night before, at 2 a.m., two shadowy figures had entered Professor Gustavo Costa's office in the Anthropology Department of the University of Mexico City. The men wore masks and gloves. With great dexterity and skill, they removed the hard drive from Costa's personal computer. They checked the papers on his desk, in his drawers, and in the cabinets, and made every trace of his great research project on the Chuma tribe disappear.

The professor's private residence was also broken into that night. The fact that he was divorced and childless made the job that much easier. All material pertaining to the incident at Juarez was carried away in two large boxes that were loaded into the trunk of the battered gray Dodge.

In a remote suburb of the capital, near the main highway that circled the city, a fire broke out just before dawn in an old two-story building. The building was burned down to its foundations. The police had no trouble determining that arson had been the cause of the outbreak. Office space in the building had been rented by two second-rate lawyers, a used-clothing outlet, and an organization devoted to restoring villagers' rights in the Juarez district.

Several other people lost their lives throughout Mexico that week, in a series of inventive killings. To their misfortune, the victims had known something they weren't supposed to know. Someone had been dispatched to silence them forever.

Each day, the man in the gray Dodge phoned the authoritative man in his handsome and spacious office on the seventh floor of a high-priced office building, to report on the day's progress. More than twenty lines had already been drawn on the page. More than twenty names had been crossed out.

"Good work," his boss complimented. "Good work."

And now, the pale-faced man knew, the time had come to cross the border into the United States. He had work to do there, as well. The Mexican aspect of his mission was complete. Now he must clear the field in Houston, Texas.

Jacob Stern left the conference room at a rapid clip, hurried to his office, grabbed his jacket from its hanger, and almost ran to the stairs.

"I'm leaving for a few minutes." In his haste he threw the words over his shoulder at his second-in-command, Lenny Brown. "If anyone comes looking for me, I'll be right back."

The architect who had designed the new Department of Agriculture building in Houston had taken the concept of open space seriously. Good-bye to closed doors and the blessed privacy afforded by the good old office configuration. Here, there were uniform cubicles for each employee — even if he was the head of the department — with low partitions between them. The option of hiding oneself from the eyes of the world no longer existed. At any moment, the boss could glance over the partition and ask why you were playing computer games instead of, for instance, doing some work.

"Pleasant prayers," Lenny called after him with a laugh.

Jacob grimaced as he ran. Bypassing the elevators, he took the stairs two by two on his way down. His meeting with the chief veterinarian of Texas had lasted all morning, almost making him late for Minchah. Houston boasts no *shtieblach* as do Jerusalem, Bnei Brak, or Boro Park. There was a shul two blocks from the office; anyone who missed that *minyan* would be compelled to *daven* alone.

He returned to the office half an hour later, checked to see if he had any urgent messages, and cleared a space on his desk for his lunch. He washed his hands and opened the plastic container that his wife had packed for him. Without warning, Lenny Brown darted in and collapsed into a chair. His eyes were large and wide with alarm.

"Listen," he said breathlessly. "Do you remember Professor Costa?"

"Uh-huh," Jacob nodded. He recited the blessing over bread and took a bite of his sandwich. "Gustavo Costa, the Mexican anthropologist who requested data and statistics from the fifties. What about him?"

Lenny Brown glanced around like a hunted man. He lowered his voice to a whisper. "The man's dead."

Jacob took another bite and stared at his agitated colleague over the rims of his glasses. "Did you know him personally?"

"No. But his research assistant, a young student by the name of Munzio Rodriguez, died on the same day."

"Sad." Another bite. "What happened? Traffic accident?"

"And his computer was stolen, his house broken into, and the office of an organization working on behalf of Indian rights burned to the ground in a suburb of Mexico City."

Jacob Stern put his sandwich down. This was very strange.

"... *and* several other Mexican activists involved in the issue died the same week: one in an accident, one through food poisoning, and a third of a sudden heart attack."

Jacob slowly lifted his hand and propped his chin on it. This was no longer merely intriguing. It was suspicious.

"Just a minute," he said. "How do you know all of this?"

Lenny Brown shook his head and sucked in some air as though trying to revive himself. His eyes reflected his fear. "How do I know?" he repeated. "A Mexican police detective decided to look into this series of strange deaths, and he connected the dots. Checking the professor's recent calls, he saw that he had contacted me a few weeks ago. Yesterday, the detective called me from Mexico to ask for details. We arranged to speak today ...."

"And ...?"

Lenny Brown swallowed. When his spoke, his voice shook. "A few minutes ago, I called him. At first, they told me he was unavailable. They were evasive. Then someone got on the line and told me that he was shot last night in the course of a robbery."

Jacob's jaw dropped.

After a moment's shocked silence, he remarked, "Wow. Someone in Mexico has been very busy."

"Listen," Lenny said urgently, leaning forward. "I'm scared. I gave the professor all the material. It'll take them very little time to find out that I also know about everything that happened there."

Jacob just stared at him, motionless as a rock.

"And listen," Lenny groaned. "You're involved in this thing, too."

"Why? Did you tell them that I took the material out of the archive?"

"I may have. It seems to me that I mentioned your name ... I didn't think it would be a problem."

For a few seconds, the two men sat on their opposite sides of the desk, eyes locked in alarmed speculation.

Jacob was first to recover. He snorted. "So you think the Mexican security police are going around knocking off anyone who knows details about the epidemic in the north of Mexico during the fifties? That's not logical."

"All I know is that someone talked to me yesterday — and today, he's dead."

Jacob reached across the desk to thump the other man reassuringly on the shoulder. "Go back to work, Lenny — and thank G-d that we're on the right side of the border."

"You think so?" Lenny straightened, encouraged by the fact that Jacob did not share his apprehension.

"Let me remind you, Lenny, that we are in the United States. That information is accessible to anyone. We were within our rights to pass it onto the professor, even if that made someone in Mexico uncomfortable. We did nothing wrong."

Lenny Brown nodded his thanks. He was calmer now. "You don't know how scared I was," he admitted frankly. "Okay, I've got work to do .... Hearty appetite."

He stood up and returned to his cubicle on the other side of the low partition.

■ ■ ■

An hour and a half later, Lenny's head appeared over the partition. He looked frightened.

"Someone's ... waiting for me in the lobby," he managed to choke out.

Jacob had already put their previous conversation out of his mind. He glanced up in surprise, which quickly turned to interest.

"Someone called me from downstairs," Lenny Brown explained worriedly. "He said that the guard won't let him up and he has an envelope he's got to give me."

"And you're afraid?" Jacob laughed lightly. "Your head's working overtime, Lenny. You read too many thrillers."

"Not true. I have a bad feeling about this. I've opened some kind of Pandora's box here ...."

Jacob Stern stood and walked into the adjoining cubicle. "Lenny." He placed a hand on his colleague's shoulder. "You're a serious young man. You have two academic degrees and a senior position with the Department of Agriculture. This doesn't become you. This isn't Mexico, or Argentina. People don't go around killing other people here, just like that."

Lenny thought a moment, his expression downcast. Then he raised his eyes and looked into Jacob's. "All right," he said. "If you say so .... Maybe I have been overreacting. I'll go down."

For the next twenty minutes, Jacob Stern worked as usual, forcibly pushing any anxious thoughts from his mind. But when half an hour had passed with no sign of Lenny, he began to entertain a niggling anxiety that would not go away.

They were very different, the two of them: one a mitzvah-observant Jew and the other a young black man from a broken home who, through diligence and talent, had managed to advance here in Texas, a place not known for its love for his race. But perhaps because they were both so different from everyone around them, a friendship had sprung up between them. When Jacob had been asked to choose an assistant from among the employees in his division, he had not hesitated before picking Lenny Brown.

The workday was about to draw to a close. People were saying goodbye to one another and leaving the office. Only Jacob remained. And Lenny had not yet returned.

Five minutes later, Jacob heard the elevator open and someone move in his direction. He nearly called out, "Hey, Lenny! So you're still alive?"

He stopped himself at the last minute. That was not Lenny's light tread. These footsteps were heavier, slower. A stranger was walking around his department. A person who shouldn't have been there — certainly not today, when there were no open hours for visitors.

All Jacob had to do was lift himself from his chair to see who it was. But a wave of panic swept him, freezing him in his seat.

Was Lenny right? Had someone been stalking him? Had he caught him? And how had a stranger managed to bypass the guard below and come up to this floor?

Something moved into his field of vision, beyond the partition. Jacob lifted his head in alarm. A plump face, topped by whitish hair, looked back at him from the exact spot where he was accustomed to seeing Lenny. The man had an unusually pale complexion and his eyes seemed leached of color.

"Where is Mr. Brown?" the stranger asked.

Jacob was amazed to find that he still had the power of speech. "I don't know ... maybe he left."

"Where to? Do you know?"

Jacob managed a weak smile. "I don't keep tabs on him."

The man threw him a pensive look, as though weighing the advantages of dealing with him immediately or deferring that pleasure to some later date. Finally, he retreated behind the partition and disappeared.

Jacob sat still as a mouse, afraid to move. He heard the uninvited visitor rummage through papers, open drawers, and tap on the computer keyboard. Then all sounds from behind the partition ceased.

Maybe the fact that I'm *not* reprimanding him will arouse his suspicion, Jacob thought in a panic. Anyone who heard a stranger going through his co-worker's papers would naturally get up and say something. This will tell him that I'm afraid ... that I know something ... that I'm involved in this thing, too ....

After a few long seconds, the head appeared once again on the other side of the partition. Jacob shot to his feet and stared fearfully at the intruder.

The man held up a picture. It was a family portrait that always graced Lenny's desk: himself, his wife, and their two small children in their new home in Houston Heights, a luxury neighborhood.

"Is this him?" the man asked.

"Yes," Jacob answered. "Why do you want to know?"

A fleeting expression of anger flashed across the stranger's face. His nostrils quivered and his lips thinned. Then the moment passed, and the look was replaced by a benign smile. "Never mind. I'll catch him later ...."

A cold shiver ran up Jacob's spine.

An entire hour passed. During that hour, the director of the supervisory division for agricultural toxins sat frozen in his seat, berating himself for lacking the courage to stir.

But he simply could not bring himself to move a muscle.

4

The quiet ring of the telephone roused Jacob from his paralysis of fear. With an effort, he reached for the receiver and picked it up. It was Texas' chief veterinarian, calling to thank him warmly for that morning's meeting, and to ask several questions concerning a detail or two. Jacob found it hard to concentrate on the conversation, and ended it as soon as he could. As he spoke, he rose hesitantly and scanned the department. The pale man was gone.

The anxiety in his heart was powerful, but it was leavened by a sliver of hope: If the fellow had come seeking Lenny here in the office, that must mean that he hadn't caught him down in the lobby. Who was that man? Who had sent him? One thing was certain: He was not working for himself.

Was he an agent of the Mexican secret police? I ought to report this to the building's security team, Jacob thought. Or even the FBI. Let those Mexicans murder whomever they wished to, back home; what business do they have here, in the States?

Lenny — as Jacob had surmised — *had* managed to get away. As Lenny stepped out of the elevator on the lobby level, he immediately spotted a stocky man leaning against the reception desk and eyeing the area as though waiting for someone.

There was something odd about the fellow. He seemed ... colorless. Both his skin and his hair were pale. His eyes, too, were strangely light. There was something about him that evoked fear.

The man moved away from the desk, approached Lenny, and held out his hand. "Mr. Brown? Lenny Brown?"

Working on instinct, Lenny jerked a thumb over his shoulder and said with an apologetic smile, "Oh, no. I'm Steve Jackson. If you're waiting for Lenny, I think I saw him go downstairs."

He strode briskly across the lobby, passed through the revolving doors, and went out into the street. There were few people walking around under the fierce Texas sun. Lenny paused, drawing a deep breath of air into his oxygen-starved lungs. Then he practically ran toward the nearest bus stop. He would grab a taxi, a bus, a passing car, whatever.

It would take the guy a few minutes to realize that he had been tricked. By then, Lenny would be far, far away.

Lenny Brown did not come to work the next day. At nine a.m., the bitter news spread through the office: their young and talented colleague had been grievously injured as he had walked down Main Street, between the University and Herman Park. It had been a hit-and-run accident. He was found lying on the grass near a small coffee shop.

"There have been too many accidents in Houston lately," people said, clucking their tongues. "All these wild young drivers .... Something should be done ...."

Jacob Stern sat at his desk, in a turmoil of fear. This had been no hit-and-run. Lenny had been no accidental victim, but rather the target of a chain of deliberate and cold-blooded murders. Was he, Jacob, the next in line?

Did someone in Mexico know that Lenny had shared his suspicions with him before he tried to bolt? Did they know that he, Jacob, was the one who had supplied the material that had been sent to Professor Costa? Lenny had said yesterday that the professor's computer hard drive had been stolen from his home. It was entirely possible that the name "Jacob Stern" appeared on one of the files there.

Total panic set in. His teeth rattled with fear as the image of the pale man filled his mind's eye, holding the picture of Lenny's family and saying with an evil grin, "I'll catch him later ...." Someone was conducting an uncompromising manhunt, and it had crossed the border from Mexico to the U.S. — right into the heart of Houston, Texas.

What should he do? Report this to somebody? Share the information?

With sudden resolve, Jacob grabbed his briefcase and headed to the parking lot. He could not stay in his office like a sitting duck. He had to disappear. The pale fellow could turn up at any time — and then it would be too late.

He reached his car, started the engine, and swung out of the parking lot. Jacob began driving aimlessly through the city streets, his head in a whirl. *I've got to get in touch with the police*, he thought. But that would expose the fact that he and Lenny had supplied data to a foreign entity. Though it had been done from the purest of motives, they seemed to have stepped into a minefield.

I'm to blame, Jacob berated himself. *It's my fault Lenny was killed. I dismissed his fears and sent him down to the lobby.*

On the other hand, he reflected, who could have believed that a few dry statistics that an anthropology professor requested could be sensitive enough to drive some shadowy group in Mexico to send its long arm into the United States? Or was it an *American* secret agency? The pale man had seem to be an American ....

Dr. Stern was by nature a courageous man. He had contended valiantly with stubborn farmers who stood to lose their livelihoods through his edicts. Once, he stood up to an enraged cattle rancher who brandished a rifle in Stern's office over a decision to destroy his infected herd. But this was something else. He was facing a hidden enemy that knew no limits. He was afraid.

No, he was terrified. He toyed with the idea of calling his wife, then rejected it. There was no way she could help, and the news would only cause her to panic. So what to do? What to do?

He knew what to do. He would call David, his wise younger brother. David would weigh the facts calmly. Where was he now? Jacob checked his watch. Ten-thirty. Los Angeles was two hours behind Texas, so David would already be at work. He reached for the phone and speed-dialed the number.

"Stern Winery, good morning," the secretary announced.

"Hello, Yenti. Give me David," Jacob said urgently.

"Jacob?" She recognized his voice. "David isn't here — didn't he tell you? He flew to France this morning."

The Stern family's winery was kosher *l'mehadrin*. The bulk of its output was destined for the ultra-Orthodox markets in the U.S., Europe, and Israel — but that didn't mean that it was of mediocre quality. Its high end luxury line, the "Special Reserve," vied honorably in wine competitions and had won several awards. Its Chardonnay 2004, for example, was a huge success. In writing about the Pinot Noir 2003, the *New York Times'* wine critic had opined that "the Stern family proves that it is possible to make a great wine even if the winemaker, who is a non-Jew, never touches the wine directly." The article had been framed and hung in David's office.

This time, Yenti explained, it was not a question of a competition or exhibition. David was traveling with the head winemaker to inspect some new bottling machinery. "They also plan to check out a few new barrel makers, because the barrels we tried last year were substandard. By the way, have you tasted the new Merlot?"

"Does he have his cell phone with him?" Jacob asked, the moment he could get a word in edgewise. Normally, he took an interest in the winery's business; right now, he had more important things on his mind.

"Yes. But he won't be landing for another seven hours."

Jacob kept driving aimlessly around Houston, crossing bridges, passing through intersections, moving through residential districts and commercial ones. His fear grew apace with the passing time. His mind was already busy devising schemes for escape.

He could spend the night in a motel along the highway ... or maybe it was better to sleep in his car, in some remote parking lot .... In case they could track his transactions, he must not withdraw money from a cash machine or use his credit card.

Then he would shake himself, and think, "Nonsense. No one's running after you. No one knows that Lenny shared that information with you. Go back to the office and forget about it."

And then the fears would start up again.

If the pale man *was* after him, going back to work would be a tragic mistake. He, Jacob Stern, would go the way of Lenny Brown and the list of Mexicans. There was room for caution even on the suspicion of danger.

The sun was at its zenith when his wandering brought him to Houston's police department. Jacob waited at the intersection for the traffic signal to change from red to green. The building facing him was a beehive of constant activity, as policemen congregated in the parking lot, patrol cars came and went, and a few ordinary citizens stood about on the stairs. Watching from his car window, lost and afraid, Jacob made a decision: He would lodge a complaint with the police. That was what any reasonable citizen would do.

The only parking space he found was some some distance from the door. As he walked toward the building, his steps lagged more and more. A voice in his head was buzzing an urgent warning: *Don't involve the police. Don't involve the police.*

But why not? Jacob argued with himself. His colleague had been brutally attacked, and the police were treating it as an ordinary accident. An agent of a foreign country was roaming at will through a U.S. government agency and doing whatever he pleased.

At the front desk sat a policeman, yawning tiredly.

"Yes, sir?" he inquired. "How can I help you?"

A terrible realization struck Jacob all at once. He halted in confusion. How had he been so blind? So stupid?

"Sir," the policeman repeated, with firm courtesy, "how can I help you?"

Jacob just stared.

"Sir?" The uniformed man was growing impatient.

Jacob recovered his wits and retreated a step. "No, no. It's all right," he said quietly. Turning on his heel, he left the building. It was all he could do not to break into a run.

He stood on the sidewalk, shaking. How had he not seen it at once? How had he not realized who had the biggest stake in hushing up the episode at Juarez?

That morning, shortly before hearing the news about Lenny Brown's "accident," he had taken a look at the data that had been sent to the Mexican professor. Something was strange. The data was unclear, shrouded in ambiguity — and he had just figured out what that meant.

The ones who were eager to bury the episode were not in Mexico — but in the United States.

The information that had been so innocently sent to the Mexican anthropologist pointed a serious, condemning finger directly at the United States government.

Jacob was right. The pale man did not belong to the the Mexican secret police. His boss — the one who had received the daily reports on the progress of the eliminations — was seated at his desk in the heart of the United States. In Langley, Virginia, to be exact, just kilometers away from Washington. The CIA.

The fact that his office was situated on the building's seventh floor testified that he had earned his place in the agency's upper echelons. Jacob had doubtless come across his name in news broadcasts or newspapers. He was Walter Child, the assistant director of the CIA, whom those in the know in the intelligence community had tagged as one of the agency's most powerful and influential men.

Jacob returned hastily to his car, looking around in growing alarm. He really had to decide what to do. It was all much more frightening now. He turned on the air conditioner and tilted his seat back. His heart was thudding far too rapidly, in time to the rapid pace of his thoughts.

It was one in the afternoon — time for Minchah. Just yesterday, Lenny Brown had joked around with him, wishing him "Pleasant prayers." Now Lenny lay injured and unconscious in a hospital room. Did *they* know that he, Jacob, went to shul every afternoon? He found himself considering skipping *minyan* today, for safety's sake. To change his habits, and make it harder for those tracking him.

Were *they* also listening in on all his phone calls? It was a good thing David was on his way to France, so that they hadn't had a chance to speak this morning.

He had never felt so helpless before. He had never experienced such bone-crushing fear. Where would his help come from?

Then the answer popped full blown into his brain: the Rebbe!

He would fly to the Rebbe. Only *he* could give Jacob the advice and blessing that could guide him through the horrible maze into which he had stumbled. Jacob knew only one person capable of bearing the heavy burdens of life and death: the Milinover Rebbe.

He restored his seat to its upright position and began speeding toward Houston's George Bush Intercontinental Airport. In no time at all, it seemed, he had purchased a ticket from Houston to New York, and from there a seat on an El Al flight to Israel. Fortunately, his passport was in his briefcase, as usual, since he was always prepared to travel on a moment's notice. He purchased the ticket using a department credit card, which was not in his name, vowing to repay the sum as soon as he returned. He called his wife from a public phone and told her only that he was away on an unexpected trip. There had been a serious outbreak of cattle disease in Louisiana and Arkansas, he said, which required urgent attention.

His wife believed him. She was accustomed to such last-minute, work-related jaunts. There was no reason, Jacob felt, for sharing his fears with her and making her life a nightmare as well.

Less than a day after Lenny Brown was found injured in the heart of Houston, Jacob Stern got out of a taxi in the Old City of Tzefas. He passed through a stone gate at the end of a narrow street, turned left into a small courtyard, and entered the Rebbe's house.

"Yaakov Meir ben Hinda, for good health and protection," wrote the *gabbai*, R' Shammai, on the *kvittel* Jacob gave him.

The *hoiz bachur* opened the door, rousing Jacob from his thoughts.

"Please," the *bachur* said. "You can go in now."

Texas — Iyar 5766 / May 2006

The C.I.A. agent sat in his beat-up old Dodge, eating a hamburger bought at one of Houston's many fast-food outlets. The cell phone, tossed onto the seat next to him, began ringing. Washing down the food with a gulp of diet cola, he answered it.

Walter Child's usually measured and decisive voice held a harried note. "We have a problem," he said without preamble.

"What kind of problem?"

"One of the numbers on the list has not been erased."

"Are you serious?" the pale man asked in surprise. "How is that possible?"

"How is that possible?" his boss snapped. "You can ask yourself that."

The pale man sank back in his seat.

"We're checking into it, to find out what happened," Child continued. "But one thing is certain: He knows that he's a target. He'll be doubly careful."

"Where is he now?"

"We don't know. He must have escaped somewhere," Child said. "I'm looking into it. Talk to you later."

Petach Tikvah — 5694 / 1934

The rickety coach, with its complement of passengers, entered the village's main thoroughfare in a clatter of wheels. The driver flicked his whip to extract a last effort from his tired horses. The beasts picked up their pace slightly, raising a cloud of yellowish dust in their wake.

The small settlement of Petach Tikvah was nearly deserted at this hour of the afternoon. Most of the shops were closed, and only a few wagons, horses, and trucks could be seen at the sides of the road. The passengers stretched, sighed, and parted peaceably from one another.

On the ride from Yaffo, the travelers had exchanged small talk. Only one passenger had sat huddled in his corner, eyes glued to a small volume in his hands as his lips murmured ceaselessly. His striped caftan was that of a typical Yerushalmi; on his head was a white yarmulka, topped by a low, broad-brimmed hat. Extremely thin, with a sparse beard and *payos*, he had the appearance of a sickly individual. The Yerushalmi descended from the coach and lifted his eyes to the big clock on the Bais Yaakov shul.

It was three-thirty. He had another half-hour to wait. With a sigh of resignation, he seated himself on a large rock and returned to his *sefer*.

At exactly four o'clock, an elderly figure appeared at the far end of the street. As he moved nearer, the Yerushalmi saw that he was a tall Jew wearing dusty work clothes and heavy boots. He paused near a small shop facing the shul, unlocked the door with a large key, dragged out a billboard announcing, "*Makolet*" (Grocery), and leaned it against the wall. Then he seated himself behind the counter, opened an old *Ein Yaakov*, and began to read.

The Yerushalmi stood. He crossed the street and neared the grocery store. Sensing his approach, the grocer looked up from his *sefer*. When he saw who his guest was, he smiled wholeheartedly. He stood up reverently and extended a hand in greeting. What an important visitor! What had brought R' Pinchas to the settlement? If he had left behind the holy precincts of Jerusalem, there must be a good reason.

For the span of a quarter-hour the two sat talking, until a farmer's wife came along with a shopping basket. The Jew from Jerusalem quickly stood and took his leave of the grocer, who resumed his study of the *sefer*.

R' Pinchas found a seat on the last coach to leave Petach Tikvah for Yaffo. Upon his arrival, he spent the night in the home of one of the city's *dayanim*. The two sat up into the small hours, discussing topics in Torah and *kabbalah*. In the morning, after *davening* Shacharis *kevasikin*, the *dayan* from Yaffo accompanied the Yerushalmi to the coach that would take him to Tel Aviv, and gave him instructions for finding the blind Yemenite.

Virginia — Iyar 5766 / May 2006

Walter Child was furious. The plan had hit a snag at the worst possible moment. He phoned his agent in the old Dodge. "What's happening? Where is he?"

The past few hours had shaken the assistant director out of his usual calm. Zero hour was fast approaching. In just three months, the big plan was due to be carried out. And suddenly — all because of one mistake, a single, irresponsible lapse of attention — all could be lost.

"What can I do?" the pale man asked defensively. His back was aching after sitting in his car for all those long hours, and on top of everything else the air-conditioning was on its last legs. "The guy's not at home and he's not at work. I don't have a single lead. I've been checking every hour, but still no sign of him. I've put bugs on all the lines he uses when calling out ...."

Child cut him off sharply. "Quit babbling and start working," he ordered, and slammed down the phone.

The agent disconnected his own cell phone and tossed it onto the passenger seat. His face was a picture of impotent rage. What else could he do? How was he supposed to track down one solitary man who had vanished in this gigantic country? He had gone without sleep for nearly two days and would not rest until the matter was resolved. But there were always problems that held no solution. There were always factors that were beyond his control.

He checked his tracking devices for the umpteenth time. The fellow's cell phone was still turned off and his credit card had not been used. The man was being very careful not to betray his whereabouts.

But the pale man could wait. The minute the target made a mistake — he was finished. He would never even know what hit him.

Tzefas — Iyar 5766 / May 2006

As the *hoiz bachur* quietly opened the door, Jacob Stern's heart thumped with excitement.

The room was long and narrow, with a vaulted ceiling and bow windows. The curtains moved slightly in the breeze that came through the windows, and the rays of the setting sun sent long shadows into the room. At one side of the room stood a tall bookcase and beside it a simple bed. On a low sideboard was a tray bearing numerous *yahrzeit* candles, their yellow-orange flames dancing and flickering. In the center of the room, a cloth-covered table held several holy volumes and a heavy clock. And at the head of the table, bent over a large Gemara, sat the Rebbe.

Jacob's knees felt weak. Physically, the Rebbe was small in stature, hunched and slender — but he radiated a powerful spiritual aura. Holiness wafted through the room in a kind of shining halo that cannot be described in words. The Rebbe was nearing his ninetieth year. He was ill and feeble, speaking little and rarely appearing in public. But thousands of men obeyed his lightest word and heeded his teaching. They regarded him as their guide and compassionate father, a spiritual leader and a faithful shepherd leading his flock through the wilderness.

Jacob felt a painful constriction in his heart. The Rebbe looked much frailer than he had been the last time Jacob had seen him, a number of months before. He swayed gently over his Gemara as he learned, then lifted his head. The Rebbe's eyes, Jacob saw, had not changed.

The eyes held the same penetrating and focused gaze that Jacob remembered seeing over the past 35 years, ever since his father had first brought him to the holy courtyard in Los Angeles as a child of five. His first memory of the Rebbe was those eyes. Eyes filled with softness and compassion, and at the same time sharp and probing. These were the eyes that had helped so many Jews return to their heritage across the length and breadth of America. The same eyes that saw and understood every one of his chassidim individually. The Rebbe studied the man standing before him in the doorway for a moment before smiling in welcome.

Jacob approached the table. The Rebbe held out a thin, slightly trembling hand and whispered warmly, "*Shalom aleichem*, Yankel Meyer."

Jacob grasped the hand, bent his head and kissed it. Then he straightened up and placed his *kvittel* on the table. His mouth felt dry and his muscles tense. He had been waiting for this moment for an interminable nightmarish day. This would mark the end of his inner turmoil and painful indecision. Everything would become clear now.

The Rebbe took the note and unfolded it. For a very long moment, he read the lines written there. His eyes moved from point to point until they paused, gazing into the distance as though seeing something far beyond the slip of paper. The Rebbe's brow was creased in thought, his head nodding slightly as though he had been transported to other worlds.

Jacob waited in suspense for the Rebbe to speak. In his mind, he had already formulated a few short sentences with which to answer the expected question about the nature of the danger that threatened him. He knew that the Rebbe had not been speaking much in recent months, and that chassidim who came to see him were asked to be brief and to the point in their requests. During the long flight, Jacob had rehearsed and abbreviated his words until he had it down to several dozen clear words that would summarize the situation: His life was in danger from people who were pursuing him because of a mysterious episode that had occurred in Mexico in the past. Everyone else who had knowledge of the episode had been eliminated. At first, he had thought the perpetrators were members of the Mexican secret police; now he believed it was the CIA. The question was ....

"*Vus machts du* (How are you), Dr. Stern?" the Rebbe asked suddenly. Long ago, when both the Rebbe and Jacob still lived in Los Angeles, and the Stern brothers *davened* in his shul on Shabbos — David a young bachelor and Jacob already a doctor specializing in agricultural botanics and genetics — the Rebbe would sometimes call him, fondly, "Dr. Stern."

"*Baruch Hashem*," Jacob replied, wondering if the Rebbe had missed the words "for protection" in his *kvittel*.

"*Un vus tut zich mit di kinder un de bnei bayis*? (How are the children and your wife?)"

"*Baruch Hashem, ales iz in ordenung* (Everything's in order)," Jacob said, surprised and uneasy. Was it possible that the Rebbe didn't remember that he now lived in Texas? Wasn't the Rebbe surprised to see him so unexpectedly, here in Tzefas? Was his memory, Heaven forbid, beginning to betray him?

"*Un vi azoy geit di parnassah*? (How is your livelihood?)" the Rebbe continued.

"*Baruch Hashem*."

The Rebbe asked two or three further routine questions and then, in an act that completely startled Jacob, held out his hand in parting. Jacob hastened to take it. The Rebbe's eyes closed with concentration as he blessed him at length.

Then the Rebbe lifted a silver bell from the table and rang it weakly. This was the signal for the *gabbai* to enter and escort the visitor out. Jacob heard the door open behind his back.

Stunned, he found himself unable to move. He had not received an answer. The Rebbe had not even asked him about the danger that was pursuing him, and why he needed protection. Jacob's moment was over, and the *gabbai* was here to lead him away ....

"But Rebbe!" he cried in a burst of courage. He was utterly bewildered. All the sentences he had so carefully rehearsed were a jumble in his mind. The words exploded from him in no order: "I'm in great danger ... I'm so afraid ... they've killed people ... and they're threatening me, too ...."

Though he sensed the *gabbai's* presence behind his back, he ignored it. Desperately, he wished for something from the Rebbe in these final seconds — some utterance, a promise, a reassurance. But the Rebbe merely smiled apologetically and waved a hand in dismissal. "*Fohr gezunterheit* (Go in peace)."

"But Rebbe ...."

"*Fohr gezunterheit*, Dr. Polanski," the Rebbe said, as though he had not heard a word Jacob had said. "*Fohr gezunterheit.*"

R' Shammai gently touched Jacob's shoulder. He could not remain in the room any longer. He must go. Jacob kissed the Rebbe's hand and backed out of the door, crestfallen.

R' Shammai stepped out with him for a brief moment. "*Zoltz hubben alles gut oisgepoilt* (Let everything work out for the best)," he blessed Jacob, using the time-honored phrase with which chassidim bless one another after leaving a Rebbe's presence or praying at his grave.

Filled with fear and anxiety, Jacob hardly heard the *gabbai's* words. He was disappointed and in shock — perhaps even angry at himself. He could not understand how it could be that he found himself outside the Rebbe's room without having received an answer! He had flown more than twenty hours, going from airport to airport and plane to plane; he had concealed from his wife the fact that he was leaving the country; he had disappeared from his job without explanation — all in order to see the Rebbe. He had been so certain that he would leave this room with a clear and reassuring answer. But the Rebbe had seemed to disregard the message on the *kvittel*.

He sank onto a bench with a downcast face, his eyes conveying his despair. It was only a few seconds later that the awful possibility arose in his mind and caused his heart to skip a beat. Perhaps the Rebbe had not answered because he didn't want to answer. Perhaps he had not offered his assurance because he could not do so.

He had heard of cases where the Rebbe did not offer a promise of salvation despite the most fervent entreaties. Then everyone knew that the situation was very bad. The decree had been sealed. That was what had happened fifteen years previously, when Jacob's father lay on his deathbed.

David had remained in the hospital while Jacob went to see the Rebbe. He had written his father's name on a *kvittel*, for a speedy recovery, but the Rebbe had seemed to ignore the written words. He had blessed Jacob — who had recently married — with healthy children, and David with finding a fine marriage partner in the near future. But he had not said a word about their father.

He remembered clearly what the *gabbai*, R' Shammai — fifteen years younger than he was today — had said on that occasion. "Sometimes, no answer is also an answer." Sadly, Jacob had returned to the hospital, and David had understood at once. Their father passed away on the following day.

Did this meant that his own fate had also been sealed? That the Rebbe knew that nothing could help him any longer? Jacob had hinted in his *kvittel* that he was in grave danger, but the Rebbe had paid no heed to the reference. The decree had been signed and sealed.

But something else troubled Jacob. He didn't know if R' Shammai had noticed it, but the Rebbe had mistaken his name. "*Fohr gezunterheit*, Dr. Polanski," he had said. Was the Rebbe's advanced age beginning to make itself felt? Was his mind less clear than it had once been? After all, he was an elderly man — nearly ninety. The notion frightened Jacob no less than his own fate. His despair increased. Not only had the Rebbe failed to pay attention to his request, but he had seemed — how terrible to think of it! — detached from reality.

Jacob felt as if he were being orphaned a second time. Fifteen years ago, he had lost his beloved father. Now he was losing the Rebbe to whom he was so devoted. He felt as though a lifeline had been severed. The last lifeboat had just sailed away, and towering waves were closing in. He had come to the Rebbe for advice and comfort — and found, to his deep dismay, that the Rebbe could no longer help him.

A choking sensation rose to his throat and his eyes filled with tears. A profound despair, laced with fear, slowly filled his entire being.

Tel Aviv — 5694 / 1934

Everyone in the small town of Tel Aviv of the thirties knew the blind Yemenite.

Throughout the day, he would sit on a bed of rags near the Moshav Zekeinim shul on Allenby Street, his legs swollen and his clothes torn and stained. Several thick towels were usually wound around his head.

The blind Yemenite never held out his hand for charity. He lived from the pennies that the good-hearted tossed his way of their own volition when going to and from the shul. Rumor had it that, as a young man, he had been forcibly drafted into the Turkish Army, where he lost his sight as well as a goodly portion of his sanity. Others claimed that he had made his roundabout way to this place from Yemen, where he had been a wealthy man until losing his entire fortune in one day.

R' Pinchas, in his striped caftan and broad-brimmed hat, stood out in the secular town. He drew surprised glances from passersby as he walked the streets searching for the man the *dayan* from Yaffo had told him to see. He soon located him. Within minutes, R' Pinchas was standing before the Yemenite. Reaching into his pocket, he withdrew a silver coin and pressed it into the blind man's hand as he murmured a short sentence.

The transformation that overcame the Yemenite beggar was instantaneous. He lifted his head, opened his eyes, and sent a sharp look at the Yerushalmi. A second later, he once again bowed his head and closed his eyes.

For a long moment, silence reigned between the two. Finally, the beggar lifted his head again. "But why not on erev Rosh Chodesh?" he asked in his characteristic Yemenite accent. "We always meet on erev Rosh Chodesh."

The Yerushalmi shrugged his shoulders. "I don't know," he said. "I am only a messenger. That's what R' Dovid Leib told me to say."

The Yemenite leaned back again, and the messenger from Jerusalem began to retrace his steps to the wagon stop, smiling secretly to himself as he went. Hundreds of people passed the "blind" Yemenite each day — and no one knew that he closed his eyes in order to preserve their purity and holiness. They thought he was a beggar with addled wits. No one knew that, underneath the turban of towels, he wore a pair of *tefillin* from sunrise to sunset.

Who would have believed that here, homeless and at the mercy of the elements, sat one of the great men of Yemen — a wondrous *mekubal*, outstandingly versed in the *Zohar*, who never ceased reviewing its sacred words for even a moment? A holy and exalted Jew who, on the day he turned forty, had cast himself into exile to atone for the generation's sins?

He, R' Pinchas, was no longer moved by the sight. He had seen many marvelous things since the day he had become R' Dovid Leib's messenger.

R' Dovid Leib headed a group of hidden *tzaddikim* in Jerusalem. Time after time, he would repeat that a person's external appearance was only a shell to contain his inner essence. It was the inside that was the determining factor; the more modest and concealed this was, the more exalted the person became. The "hidden Torah" meant just what its name implies: something that can be learned and used for ascension only in secret.

Very few succeeded. One, for example, did it in the guise of a grocer in Petach Tikvah. His neighbors knew him as a simple, quiet man. No one was aware that he had a powerful grasp of *Shas* and the *poskim*, and that under his shop counter he stored ancient Kabbalistic texts. Another kept a low profile by playing the part of a Yemenite beggar whom fate had dealt a harsh blow; a third — perhaps hardest of all — managed to hide his greatness in the hidden Torah, despite his renown as a *rav* and *dayan* in the city of Yaffo ....

But why was he wasting his time in thought? He still had a long way to go. He must reach the Galil: first by bus to the holy city of Teveryah and from there by wagon or donkey to Meron — and the gravesite of the holy *Tanna*, Rabbi Shimon Bar Yochai.

Tzefas — Iyar 5766 / May 2006

"Will you be returning tonight?" R' Shammai asked Jacob Stern. "Do you have a flight to the United States?"

Jacob slowly lifted sorrowful eyes to the *gabbai*. "Am I going back?" he asked heavily. "I may be going back — but without an answer from the Rebbe."

R' Shammai looked at him questioningly.

"The Rebbe didn't pay any attention to what I wrote ... 'for protection' ...." Jacob shook his head in despair.

"Yes, I noticed," R' Shammai said sympathetically. He had witnessed the odd happenings in the room, though he had not heard exactly what was being said. Perhaps the Rebbe had not wished to say anything. He did not always speak. People sometimes thought of a Rebbe as a kind of automatic salvation-machine: They came, were blessed, and were freed of their troubles. But it didn't exactly work that way. The Rebbe did not always answer as expected.

No ordinary person could understand the wide-ranging vision of the Divine angel who walked among them, the last remnant of the great rebbes of the previous generation. The Rebbe had always stood head and shoulders above the rest, lofty and hidden, a ladder with its feet on the ground and its head reaching to the heavens. In recent months, however, R' Shammai had witnessed many secret and unusual behaviors. It was obvious that the Rebbe was engaged in matters too exalted for the ordinary run of humankind.

Jacob straightened suddenly on his bench. "Tell me, R' Shammai," he demanded. "How is the Rebbe?"

The *gabbai's* brow furrowed in surprise at Jacob's tone.

"No, really," Jacob persisted. "Does the Rebbe feel well? Is he healthy?"

"Look ..." R' Shammai replied. "He's been weak lately, but, *baruch Hashem, baruch Hashem.* Why do you ask?"

Jacob's shoulders slumped again. His voice dropped abruptly. "The Rebbe spoke to me, and ... it's hard to say this ... it seemed to me that he took me for somebody else."

A cold shadow crossed R' Shammai's face. "Took you for somebody else?" he repeated anxiously. He had been serving in this capacity for more than a half-century. His entire being was devoted to the Rebbe, whose greatness he admired and whose welfare was his overriding concern. The Rebbe's mind, R' Shammai knew, was clear as crystal despite his ninety years, but the *gabbai* always nursed the worry familiar to anyone with elderly dear ones: the fear of seeing the intellect clouded — the great enemy of old age.

"Yes," Jacob said. "The Rebbe called me by another name. Didn't you hear?"

"No. Which name?"

"When he said good-bye to me, he said, '*Fohr gezunterheit*, Dr. Polanski.' "

R' Shammai considered this for a moment, eyes narrowed as he regarded Jacob solemnly. "Is that what the Rebbe said?"

"Yes, exactly that: '*Fohr gezunterheit*, Dr. Polanski.' "

The *gabbai* shook his head slowly. Then his face thawed as a smile gradually spread across it. "And you think the Rebbe did not answer your request for protection?"

"Yes," Jacob said, eyes downcast. "And I don't know what to do."

R' Shammai suddenly burst into a great shout of relieved laughter. He grabbed Jacob's right hand with both of his own and shook it enthusiastically. "Oy, Yankel Meyer. The Rebbe said, '*Fohr gezunterheit*, Dr. Polanski'? Then let's make a *l'chayim!*"

Jacob freed his hand and stared at him in stupefaction. Was the *gabbai* losing his mind?

R' Shammai's face gradually resumed its serious expression, though traces of laughter lingered in his eyes. "You know, Yankel Meyer," he began, "our holy works say that great things can be achieved in the upper worlds through stories from the lives of true *tzaddikim*. The act of recalling such a story, or a *tzaddik's* holy behavior, brings good influences down into the world and sweetens judgment. That's one of the reasons why at specific times chassidim tend to tell true stories of tzaddikim throughout the ages."

Jacob looked quizzically at the *gabbai*. He was in deep trouble, and R' Shammai was choosing this moment to teach him a lesson in Chassidus ...?

"At specific times," R' Shammai continued, ignoring Jacob's look, "the Rebbe tells stories from the lives of his holy fathers — usually at a *Melave Malkah*, and sometimes also when people come to him for help. This was a custom of his holy fathers, as well: The Rebbe does not answer directly, but tells a story that happened to a tzaddik, and through this we see the salvation — as in 'the forefathers' actions are a sign for their descendants.' Stories of tzaddikim are not like ordinary tales, Heaven forbid. They are not legends or folk tales, but treasures containing great and wonderful secrets."

Jacob leaned back in frustration, listening to R' Shammai solely out of politeness.

"I don't know why you came to see the Rebbe," the *gabbai* said, "but I can tell you the story to which the Rebbe was alluding."

"The story?" Jacob asked, a spark of interest springing into his eye.

"The story about Dr. Polanski."

"Who is that? Is there such a person?"

"There was such a person," the *gabbai* said, pouring himself a cup of tea and offering another to Jacob. "There was such a person many years ago, in the time of the Rebbe, R' Tuvia, *zecher tzaddik v'kadosh l'vrachah* — our Rebbe, *shlita's*, great-grandfather."

R' Shammai recited the blessing on the tea, positioned a cube of sugar between his lips, and took a sip of the scalding brew. Then he began his tale.

"The renowned chassid, R' Mordechai Dovid Polanski, was R' Tuvia's foremost disciple — despite the fact that, until he was thirty, he didn't even know he was Jewish. He was orphaned as a child, the son of a tavern-keeper who was thrown into prison along with the rest of the family. The *poritz* and his wife, who were childless, wanted the handsome child for themselves, and decided to adopt him as their son.

"R' Mordechai Dovid was brought to the *poritz's* estate and educated like a delicate flower by the finest tutors. When the young nobleman grew up, his adoptive father sent him to the University of Vienna to study medicine. Eventually, the young man inherited the estate and was appointed to a prestigious position in the Polish government.

"One day, Dr. Polanski met R' Tuvia — that's a story all on its own — and that meeting led Dr. Polanski to discover that he was Jewish. He became a fervent *ba'al teshuvah* and a devoted chassid. The Rebbe instructed him to retain his government position in order to help his fellow Jews. Dr. Polanski obeyed.

"Late one night, a carriage harnessed to two powerful horses came clattering into the town of Milinov, and stopped in front of the Rebbe's house. In the carriage was Dr. Polanski, who was terrified. He entered the Rebbe's room and burst into tears.

"Totally by coincidence, he had become privy to a wicked plot that several Polish ministers were weaving against the country's Jews. He tried to foil their plans through two honest officials, but the evil ministers had them murdered by hired thugs. A servant in the home of one of the ministers, whose son Dr. Polanski had once cured, sent a messenger to warn him that the same thugs were on their way to kill him. Dr. Polanski fled at once. He hired a carriage and traveled long hours until he reached Milinov and R' Tuvia's house, to cry and plead for his life ...."

As Jacob listened to the story, he gradually abandoned his indifferent stance. His eyes were fixed on R' Shammai with rapt attention. Amazingly, the tale corresponded with his own situation.

"So what did the Rebbe tell Dr. Polanski?" he asked in suspense.

The *gabbai* smiled good-naturedly and took a sip of his tea.

"The Rebbe acted as if he hadn't heard a word Dr. Polanski had told him. He simply waved his hand dismissively, and said, '*Fohr gezunterheit,* Dr. Polanski. *Fohr gezunterheit,* Dr. Polanski ....'"

Jacob felt as though an icy liquid were pouring through his veins. This was incredible! He wanted to ask what Dr. Polanski had done next. His mouth opened and closed, but he couldn't utter a word.

R' Shammai divined his question. "Dr. Polanski heard what the Rebbe said, climbed back into his carriage, and returned home. With Hashem's help, he was saved from the cabal of ministers — and even managed to foil their wicked plot against the Jews."

"Unbelievable," Jacob whispered, in shock. "Simply — unbelievable ...."

"Believe it," R' Shammai laughed. "The Rebbe told the story a number of years ago — on *Motza'ei Shabbos Kodesh, Parashas Shemos*, 5764, if I'm not mistaken. We should learn from this, he said, that *HaKadosh Baruch Hu* sometimes sends a person to a specific place in order to carry out a specific mission. Sometimes months, or even years, can go by before the time is ripe for that mission. But it would be a big mistake to abandon the race just minutes before reaching the finish line."

"That's what the Rebbe said?"

"Exactly that."

Jacob was still staring at R' Shammai, openmouthed. All at once, the *gabbai's* words penetrated fully. A sense of enormous relief spread inside him. His tense shoulders relaxed, and a trace of a smile rose to his face.

"That's why the Rebbe told me: '*Fohr gezunterheit* ....'"

He stood up and collected his coat and briefcase, moving in a daze.

"*Zolst hubben alles gut oisgepoilt*," R' Shammai said, repeating his earlier blessing. This time, the words held a special meaning.

Jacob Stern stepped into the yard and gazed at the breathtaking view. The sun, poised to set, threw a golden light onto the Galilean mountaintops. As Jacob lifted his head to the slowly darkening crimson sky and filled his lungs, he was infused with a renewed sense of peace. He felt secure and protected, as though surrounded by invisible armor. The Rebbe had indicated that he had no reason to fear. Everything was clearer now, bathed in brightness.

It was time to return to his life. First, he would call his wife and explain where he was. It would be a good idea to call his office, as well, to hear what had been happening in these last 24 hours. And he wanted to find out how Lenny Brown was doing in the hospital.

Jacob turned on his cell phone, though he wasn't sure if it would work outside the U.S. But the computerized network displayed a surprising efficiency, making the necessary connections on its own.

He noted a number of messages waiting for him. They could wait. His first priority was to call home.

"Jacob, where are you?" His wife sounded genuinely anxious. Some of the messages were doubtless from her.

"If I told you that I'm calling from Eretz Yisrael — Tzefas, to be exact — what would you say?"

The United States — Iyar 5766 / May 2006

The CIA agent in the battered old Dodge called his boss's cell phone. Assistant Director Walter Child was in his office, angry and apprehensive. When he saw the number on the screen, he quickly picked up. "Yes?"

"I found him!" the pale man crowed at the other end of the line. "He finally used his cell phone."

Meron — 5694 / 1934

It was an exhausting two-day journey before R' Pinchas reached Meron.

In the inner room of R' Shimon Bar Yochai's tomb sat a Sephardic Jew of radiant countenance. He had a long beard cascading down his chest and an open volume in front of him. R' Pinchas delivered the same message that he had given to the shopkeeper in Petach Tikvah and the Yemenite beggar in Tel Aviv: "*HaRav* Dovid Leib has instructed me to invite your honor to a special meeting this Thursday night."

Like his predecessors, the Sephardic *mekubal* reacted with anxiety. If R' Dovid Leib had summoned the secret society to meet at this extraordinary time — not one of their regular gatherings, which took place three times each year, on specific Rosh Chodesh eves — this was a sign that something had occurred requiring prayers to storm the heavens. If R' Dovid Leib was asking them to take the trouble to come to Jerusalem, a harsh decree must have befallen their nation. A decree of destruction ....

They must meet and do what they could, say their special prayers with all their hidden meanings and intentions, in the hopes that the One Above would take pity on His children.

The rest of R' Pinchas's task was easier. Next, he traveled on to pass the news to the two holy brothers, R' Zalman and R' Zeidel, who learned together in the ancient synagogue at Motzah, near Jerusalem; to another Torah scholar who sat day and night in the Yeshuos Yaakov shul in Meah Shearim; to a Moroccan scholar who studied the Torah's secrets in the attic of Machaneh Yehudah's Zaharei Chamah *beis midrash;* to a man known as *"der Poilisher melamed,"* who taught young children their *alef-beis* in the Eitz Chaim *cheder* by day and — unbeknownst to all — spent his nights delving into the hidden Torah; to R' Zelig, a Chortkover chassid who prepared tea and coffee for those who came to learn in the *shtiebel,* tidying and putting away *sefarim* in return for permission to sleep in an adjoining hovel, but who devoured whole tractates of the Talmud by night, along with their commentary; and to a regular member in the Karliner *beis midrash* who carried on a private but fervent correspondence with the greatest rebbes of Poland and Russia.

On Wednesday night, R' Pinchas returned home to inform R' Dovid Leib that he had carried out his mission. All of them had been given the information. All of them would be attending.

Langley, Virginia — Iyar 5766 / May 2006

The assistant director of the CIA exhaled in silent relief. Everything was much simpler now. If the subject had activated a cell phone, he could be traced, followed, and — most important of all — eliminated. Cell phones were one of the most important tools of intelligence agencies. The electronic signals they emitted and received made it possible to pinpoint their locations to within mere meters.

"Where is he?" Walter Child asked carefully. "Inside or out?"

The man in the beat-up Dodge was a veteran agent and needed nothing spelled out. The meaning was clear: "Inside" meant within the borders of the United States; "outside" was anywhere else on the globe.

Operations carried out on the inside were much more dangerous. Lenny Brown's accident, for example, had slightly muddied the waters. The Houston police had begun sniffing around. Someone had apparently noticed the Dodge hit Brown and send him flying. Fortunately for the eyewitness, he had not been able to make out the license-plate number, since the plates had been deliberately coated with mud.

Outside operations, on the other hand, were a breeze. In Mexico City, in the guise of an informer, he had managed to knock down a whole row of pins without a hitch. *Viva Mexico!*

"Just a second, I'm checking," the agent said. He tried to keep one hand on the wheel while listening to the phone tucked between his cheek and his shoulder and, at the same time, pressing keys on the laptop computer keyboard beside him. The Dodge wove between the lanes, causing other drivers to blare their horns in annoyance. Abandoning the computer, he concentrated on the road.

"I'm on the highway," he told his boss. "Let me find someplace to stop so I can check."

"Get back to me the minute you know something," the assistant director ordered.

"Sure." Wearing a broad smile, the agent took a long sip of the drink perched in the holder between the seats. "This time, he's finished."

■ ■ ■

Tzefas — Iyar 5766 / May 2006

R' Shammai stepped out into the Rebbe's front yard just as Jacob Stern was concluding his call to his wife in Houston. He had told her, briefly, what had brought him to Israel on such short notice, and had calmed her fears. If the Rebbe said there was nothing to be afraid of, he was completely calm. In any case, he said, he was returning on an El Al flight that very night, and would be home by Friday.

R' Shammai smiled with pleasure. Yankel Meyer Stern now looked the way a Jew ought to look: content.

"I'll see you at the wedding, eh?" the *gabbai* asked, though he already knew the answer.

"What a question! *B'ezras Hashem*," Jacob replied. "Are you getting ready for a big crowd? Lots of guests will probably be coming from the *mechutan's* yeshivah."

"Certainly," R' Shammai said. Suddenly, he remembered something. "By the way, what about the wine?" R' Shammai was not involved in the logistical side of the affair — that was being handled by a committee under the leadership of R' Yoel, the energetic director of the Milinov institutions. But Stern family wine was a longstanding tradition. Without it, no Milinov wedding was complete.

"There'll be wine, there'll be wine," Jacob assured him. "Next week, I make a special trip to the winery to choose the wine with David."

"It's important that it not be too dry," R' Shammai said. "The type we had at Yisrael Moshe's wedding was excellent."

Jacob nodded in agreement. At one previous wedding, they had sent a wine whose credentials were outstanding in professional circles — an unfiltered Petite Sirah that had been allowed to age in new barrels for eighteen months. Though the wine had won several international awards, its bitter, unfamiliar flavor had not suited the Chassidic palate. Since then, the Stern brothers had chosen lighter, half-dry wines that everyone could enjoy. The Emerald Riesling they had provided for the most recent wedding — that of Yisrael Moshe — had been delicate and tasty, and everyone had taken great pleasure in it.

"But you know what I always say," R' Shammai added with a smile. "You're just wasting fine raw material."

Jacob laughed out loud, though he had heard the joke many times before. R' Shammai's family for a very long time owned a vinegar business. He had inherited it from his mother and ran it himself for years. Recently, his sons had entered the business, changed the name of the firm to "Lederman and Sons," and begun marketing an assortment of additional products.

Each time the venerable *gabbai* met Jacob or David Stern, he would remind them that, from his perspective as a purveyor of fine vinegar, their wine business was an outrageous waste of potential raw material. They took something that had the potential to be transformed into the best vinegar, and simply drank it before its time ....

Langley, Virginia — Iyar 5766 / May 2006

Assistant Director Child's cell phone vibrated in his pocket. He checked the number on the readout screen and took the call immediately.

"Good news," said the voice at the other end of the line. "He's outside."

It was the agent in the beat-up Dodge. He was parked on the shoulder of the highway. The moment he parked, he had bent over his computer and begun tapping its keys. Noting the target's exact location, a broad smile appeared on his face. He had called his boss at once.

"He's outside," the agent repeated. The target was not within the United States. That meant it was going to be that much simpler to eliminate him.

"Okay," said Walter Child. "Take care of it. I'm can't wait to cross that name off the list."

Israel — Iyar 5766 / May 2006

The cab driver promised to reach the airport on time — and he kept his word. At ten minutes past midnight, he dropped Jacob Stern at the terminal entrance. Jacob had enough time to catch a *minyan* for Maariv before boarding his plane.

Over the course of the day his cell phone battery had lost its charge, and he had not found a way to recharge it. In his last call before the phone died, he had received painful news. A co-worker told him that Lenny Brown had succumbed to his injuries. The funeral was scheduled for the following Sunday.

Jacob stepped aboard the plane in a depressed frame of mind. Lenny had definitely been a fine human being. His young life had been cut off in its prime, his death a terrible waste. Jacob's earlier fears flooded back. He was on his way back to the States; was the pale man still searching for him? Would he track him down the way he had tracked Lenny?

Then Jacob remembered the Rebbe's words: *"Fohr gezunterheit,* Dr. Polanski." He could feel secure. *HaKadosh Baruch Hu* would protect him from all harm. He would return to his home and his workplace and his shul, in complete confidence that the Guardian of Israel did not slumber.

After the mad tempo of the past two days, Jacob was exhausted. He placed a mask over his eyes and quickly fell into the deep sleep of a carefree baby.

Neither the assistant director of the CIA nor his pale-faced agent were calm at all. They had seen the light at the end of the tunnel — and it had suddenly blinked out.

Walter Child's car emerged from the underground parking lot at Langley and headed toward Washington. He was due to meet with two

Democratic senators, William T. Johnson and Roy Franklin. Neither man had done a thing in his life but loll around in a leather armchair ordering his assistants to do his thinking for him. Child loathed the "Hill" and its swarm of slick politicians. But these were the men and women who determined the CIA's budget. They oversaw the dedicated work of the good people who safeguarded America against those who wished her ill. And so, he would play the game.

He would smile at them, and say all the right things. He would tell them a few good spy stories to flatter their egos — and, if he was lucky, he would get the nod from them at their next budget meeting. But soon ....

Soon, all that was going to change. In just three months' time, everything would look different. Three months from now, the CIA would have no problems, budgetary or otherwise.

Three months from now, the world would be a far better place.

His phone beeped in his pocket. The text message comprised just a few words: "His phone is off again."

Walter Child slammed his fist into the passenger seat next to him. The guy was playing games with them. They had to get him, wherever he was. He could cause the agency irreversible damage.

"I'm on my way to a meeting," he texted back. "The minute he surfaces, he must be disposed of."

Houston, Texas — Iyar 5766 / May 2006

The Stern dining room gleamed with an air of festivity and light.

On the table was a pristine white cloth on which the silver Shabbos candlesticks gleamed. The three Stern children sat at the table singing *zemiros* in pleasant harmony. Jacob hummed along, but his thoughts had wandered. It had been a week of turmoil and change, starting with a panicked bolt in fear of his life. But he was home now, back in his warm nest, safe and secure. His wife came from the kitchen carrying a plate of steaming chicken soup. Jacob leaned back in his chair, content. *Shabbos kodesh*. A restful day.

The jangle of the telephone startled the adults and amused the children. It must be a non-Jew who had mistakenly dialed a wrong number, they guessed. Who else would be calling on a Friday night?

The caller appeared to be not only mistaken, but stubborn as well. Only after ten rings did the phone fall silent. Jacob attached no special significance to the minor disturbance — until the phone rang again an hour and a half later, and then a third time near midnight. By then, a definite uneasiness had crept into his heart.

"It must be a wrong number," his wife said soothingly. But at seven the next morning, as Jacob wrapped himself in his *tallis* preparatory to leaving for shul, the ringing started again. It echoed through the quiet house. Jacob shot his wife a doubtful look. She was no longer as certain as she had been the night before.

"It's probably your office," she suggested. "Maybe there's some emergency."

Jacob waved this away. His staff knew not to call him on Shabbos, even if a lethal epidemic was decimating every herd of cattle in Texas.

On his return from shul later that morning, his wife met him at the door wearing a troubled look. The phone had rung every ninety minutes or so. It was driving her crazy. She had placed pillows and blankets over the instrument to stifle the ring .... But who could it be?

Jacob didn't like this. He sat down at the table and opened a *siddur*, determined not to let some anonymous individual ruin his Shabbos. Filling his goblet to the brim with wine, he remembered something. "By the way," he told his wife, "this week I'll be going to David to choose wines for the Rebbe's wedding."

This tradition had not begun with Jacob, or even with Jacob's father. Five generations of Sterns had been sending Stern Family wines to Milinover celebrations — as the Rebbe himself had informed Jacob and David when he came to pay a *shivah* call when their father had passed away.

The brothers had been stunned and grief stricken. They were still very young, in their early twenties. Until two months before, not a single cloud had marred their futures. Their father had been hale and hearty. And then, with tragic suddenness, he had fallen ill and faded before their eyes. The mourning was deep and anguished, and there was an urgent question waiting to be answered: What to do with the family business?

Wine had always played a role in their home. Expensive bottles appeared on their table on Shabbos and at family occasions, and their father's personal cellar held a liquid fortune worth thousands. But not everyone who knows how to drink wine or appreciate it is capable of running a winery that produces tens of thousands of bottles a year.

Their competitors did not wait for the week of mourning to end before tendering their bids. All wanted to acquire the winery. On paying his *shivah* call, the Rebbe heard the brothers' ambivalence about selling. He sank into thought for a long moment, and then said that he wished to tell them a story that had happened to one of his holy fathers.

"When my holy great-grandfather, R' Tuvia," the Rebbe began, as all those present listened attentively, "was preparing for his oldest son, R' Azriel's, wedding, your great-grandfather, R' Naftali Tzvi Stern, sent a barrel of fine wine in honor of the occasion. R' Naftali Tzvi's winery was known throughout Galicia and Austro-Hungary, and his wines were featured on the tables of kings and princes. His custom was to send wine to the Rebbe's weddings, to be distributed at the meal for the poor that takes place before the *chuppah*. The older chassidim would say that this barrel of wine benefited R' Naftali Tzvi immeasurably. In the glass of wine that he received from the Rebbe at that meal, he fulfilled whatever obligations of poverty he might have — and 'bought' himself wealth until the next wedding."

Jacob and David, on their low mourners' stools, nodded in understanding. They remembered a large wedding in New York that the Rebbe had held for his son several years earlier. Jacob, already a bar mitzvah, and David, eleven, had dressed in their best and traveled to the wedding with their father, feeling strange in their suits and ties amid the sea of chassidim in their long coats and *shtreimels*.

The meal for the poor was a sight they would never forget: All the impoverished of Boro Park and Williamsburg sat at beautifully set tables as older, respected chassidim served them their food. The two boys had stared, curious and amazed.

At the head of one table sat the Rebbe and his *mechutanim*; around them, entranced, stood a sea of chassidic men and youths. At the conclusion of the meal, the *gabbaim* had placed numerous bottles of wine on the Rebbe's table. The boys' father whispered to them that this was the wine he had sent. The invitees lined up before the *mechutanim's* table — but the *gabbai* called up their father first. The Rebbe poured the first glass of wine for Mr. Stern. Then one by one, each of the men, rich and poor alike, received his glass of wine along with a gift of money.

Mr. Stern had hurried back to his sons, taking care not to spill his wine. He had taken a sip, then passed the glass to Jacob and to David.

The rest, he said, he would save for their mother. It was a great *segulah* to drink from wine that the Rebbe had dispensed.

"The barrel that your great-grandfather sent was kept in the cellar," the Rebbe continued his story. "But before the meal for the poor, when they wanted to bring the wine up to the *beis midrash*, they discovered that the barrel was open. One of the gentile workers had drunk from it. Of course, this made the wine forbidden for Jews to drink. Your great-grandfather, R' Naftali Tzvi, nearly fainted in his distress, and it took time to revive him. A different barrel of wine was found to distribute to the crowd, but the incident had cast a shadow over the *simchah*. Everyone viewed it as a bad omen.

"The next morning, the employee who had drunk from the wine was found dead in his bed. We discovered that a Jew-hating priest from the monastery near Milinov had intended to poison the town's Jews. Knowing that all the wedding guests would be drinking from the wine in that barrel, he had found a means to slip some poison inside. The intoxicated gentile who drank some of the wine and disqualified the rest for the Jews was an agent of Divine Providence, sent to save the wedding guests from a terrible tragedy. What had appeared to be an evil omen turned out to be their salvation!"

The Rebbe lingered in the house of mourning for a long time, and his visage left an indelible impression on both brothers. They had known him, of course, and had prayed in his shul from time to time. The Rebbe had served as *mesader kedushin* at Jacob's wedding, and David had gone to him for a blessing before undergoing complicated surgery on his foot. But this was the first time they had ever had a long and meaningful discussion with the Rebbe. His wisdom and radiance restored their spirits.

On that day, they became bound to the Rebbe with total devotion, and became his devoted chassidim.

When they sat down to their sorrowful supper that evening, their mother told them that, in her opinion, it would be wrong to sell the winery. This, she believed, had been the message embedded in the Rebbe's words. Besides, their father would undoubtedly have wanted the name "Stern Wineries" to continue to thrive.

Her two sons agreed with her. On the Rebbe's advice, Jacob — who had already been accepted for a position in Houston's Department of Agriculture — would keep his government job, while David, despite his youth, would try his hand at winemaking. David had planned to attend business school; he would now become a student in the university of life.

Fifteen years had elapsed since then. David had flourished in his new role. After a few early, inevitable mistakes, he had quickly learned the business and been instrumental in the winery's move forward. Apart from simple *kiddush* wines and grape juice — products that were unglamorous but decidedly profitable — he began making inroads in the area of luxury wines. His wisest decision had been made when, several years earlier, he hired a talented young vintner, a recent graduate of Davis University. The new man had brought about a virtual revolution in the winery. The Emerald Riesling sent to the previous wedding had been one of the vintner's more successful experiments.

This time, as well, it was to be hoped that he would find an interesting wine to honor the *simchah* and continue the longstanding family tradition.

The Stern family's daytime *seudah* and afternoon rest were marred by the telephone's periodic and disturbing ringing. The silences in between were no less jarring on the nerves. Would it ring again? When? And who was the caller? *Who* could it be?

Jacob did not confide his fears to his wife. In her presence, he evidenced a quiet, confident demeanor. Inside, however, an anxious question had crept into his consciousness: Could this be connected to the deaths of Lenny Brown and all those Mexicans?

Was it the pale man, searching for him?

On the other hand, the Rebbe had said that he was safe from all harm. The Rebbe had said, "*Fohr gezunterheit*, Dr. Polanski ...."

The last sequence of rings came at 5 p.m. After that, a blessed silence descended on the Stern home.

It lasted until Jacob returned from Maariv.

The spices and candle were ready on the table. His wife and children gathered around as he prepared to pour wine into the goblet. Suddenly, his eye caught a furtive movement in the yard.

The hand holding the bottle went rigid. Jacob stared out. A dark figure was crossing the lawn, from the front gate to the bushes.

A wave of fear swept through him. Who was that? Was it the man who had chased Lenny? Maybe he had phoned all Shabbos to check whether anyone was home. Now he had come to finish the job ....

Jacob's heart thudded wildly. His nightmare was coming true, right before his eyes. They were coming for him — not at his office, on the fourth floor of the Agricultural Department building ... but at home. Where his wife was, and his three children.

With a sharp motion, Jacob set down the bottle of wine and shot into the bedroom. In a small safe in his closet he kept a gun and a box of bullets. He grabbed them and raced back to the dining room. Pushing aside the drapes, he threw open the large glass door.

The figure ducked behind the swing set on the far left edge of the yard. Jacob leveled his gun. "Who's there?" he shouted.

The man straightened up. The corner where he stood was dark, making it hard for Jacob to distinguish his features.

"Dr. Stern?" Jacob heard from the shadows. "Oh! At last, I've caught you."

Get away from there — *now!*" Jacob yelled.

The man in the corner of the yard stepped slowly forward, hands raised to show that he was not armed. Jacob's heart beat rapidly, but the hand holding the gun was steady.

"You are Jacob Stern?" the man asked.

"Get out of there now!" Jacob cried. "Or I'll shoot!"

"I've been trying to call you all day. There was no answer."

"Who are you? What do you want?"

"You worked with Lenny Brown, right?"

Jacob felt as though someone had kicked him in the solar plexus. His fears were realized. The Mexican episode had cast its long arm in his direction.

"I told you, get out of there or I'll shoot!" he shouted again.

"And you know what he was working on before he was murdered," the man continued.

Jacob's heart skipped a beat. Those long arms were beginning to squeeze him. He began to beat a cautious retreat into the house. "I don't know what you're talking about," he said hoarsely. "Lenny was working on a lot of things. Anyway, he was injured in a traffic accident. He wasn't murdered."

"If only that were true," the man replied. "Someone wanted to get rid of him because he knew what happened in the 50's to the Mexican Indians near Juarez."

Mustering his courage, Jacob gestured with the gun toward the front gate. "I have no idea what you're talking about," he said. "And in any case, this conversation is over."

The man didn't move. "All the information that he gave Professor Costa in Mexico was provided by you," he stated. "Do not deny it. He mentioned your name several times."

"I don't know what you're talking about!" Jacob's voice rose. "*Get out of here!*"

From beyond the gate came the sudden flash of whirling red and blue lights. A patrol car on its routine rounds was inching slowly up the street.

The uninvited visitor stirred uneasily. He glanced around as though seeking an escape route. "Did you call the police?" he called softly. "Are you crazy? They'll kill you, too."

"Get out of here before the cops come," Jacob shouted, seizing his opportunity.

The man did not head for the front gate. Instead, he broke into a run in the direction of the neighboring house. Vaulting the fence, he continued straight ahead at a rapid sprint, parallel to the street.

Jacob ran into the middle of the lawn to watch him go. The man was moving quickly across the neighbor's yard. He leaped over the next fence and raced across another yard before escaping into the street. Jacob kept his gun pointed at the intruder's back, his hand shaking with rage and frustration. Only after a long moment did he slowly lower his arm and lean exhaustedly against the fence.

He closed his eyes and breathed deeply. Finally, he turned his head to look at his home, where his wife and children stood in the brightly lit living room, staring fearfully out at him.

Jacob headed inside on leaden legs. Returning to his bedroom, he took a holster out of his safe, strapped it around his waist, and slipped the gun inside. He had been deeply frightened tonight and wanted to be ready for whatever might come next. The passing patrol car had frightened away the intruder, but he might be back — and even more insistent than before.

"Come. Let's make *Havdalah*," he told his family, when he was certain that his voice would not betray his fear.

The children were too young to really comprehend what had just happened. In their minds, a bad man had entered their yard and their father had chased him away with a gun; now they could go back to their games. Jacob and his wife were left quiet and shaken. The protective shield around their home had been breached. A hostile stranger had invaded their territory. The long shadow of Juarez had managed to disrupt their daily lives. For all he knew, that shadow might threaten more than just their serenity. It might pose a menace to their very lives.

Jacob's wife went into the kitchen to turn on the loaded dishwasher. Then she sank into a chair, in the grip of half-formed fears. Her nerves were already stretched taut, after a Shabbos spent listening to the phone ring at close intervals. And then that man had entered their yard ....

Jacob sat on the sofa, immersed in the thousand-and-one thoughts flying through his brain. The intruder had alarmed him to an extraordinary degree. He had hoped the episode was behind him; he knew now that he had been mistaken. He had returned from his visit to the Rebbe feeling calm and tranquil — only to find that the danger had not disappeared.

What bothered him most was the troubling question of whether he had missed an opportunity. Perhaps he should not have chased the stranger away. He should have listened to what the man had to say. Thinking back, he realized that the fellow had not seemed to pose a real threat. Jacob was not at all certain that tonight's visitor was the same man who had come to his office looking for Lenny Brown.

Jacob strained to remember what the pale man had looked like, but all he had had was a brief glimpse of him over the office partition. Tonight, he'd seen nothing more than a dim figure lurking near the bushes in a dark corner of the yard. The stranger's face had been shrouded in darkness. His body language had not been menacing. On the contrary — the fellow had seemed frightened, and had scurried away at the sight of the the patrol car. He hadn't behaved like a cool, professional assassin. Maybe Jacob shouldn't have chased him off. He should at least have heard him out.

Then again, he thought, maybe the whole thing had been an act. Perhaps the intruder *was* Lenny's killer, and had acted that way in order to draw Jacob out — to get him into a dark corner and harm him. Maybe he was out to get as much information out of him as possible, before killing him in cold blood ....

What to do if the stranger came back? Fire at him? Call the police? It might be a good idea to send his wife and children away to safety. For greater security, he lowered the metal shutter over the large French door, locked the front door, and wore the gun tucked into its holster.

And tomorrow .... Tomorrow was Lenny Brown's funeral. Jacob would attend the nondenominational service to say good-bye to his unfortunate friend. Such a pity. Such a needless death. What kind of evil could prompt someone to do away with such a promising young man merely because he had spoken with someone in Mexico about a murky episode from the past?

Jacob rose to make another tour of the house, to make sure that no one was lurking in the yard. In addition to his fear, he was also angry. He couldn't say a word of this at tomorrow's funeral, he realized. People believed that Lenny had died as a result of a random traffic accident. But how could he remain silent? How was it possible to close his eyes to the truth?

He knew the truth. He knew that somebody had chased Lenny down — and caught him. He knew that several hours before that car struck him, someone had been searching Lenny's office. Someone who had looked at Lenny's picture and said with a chilling smile, "I'll catch him later ...."

An alarming thought crossed Jacob's mind: Was that why the man had come here tonight? To warn him to keep his mouth shut at the funeral?

No, he decided. The man had not seemed threatening. On the contrary — he'd seem to be in some sort of distress.

What a pity he hadn't dropped a hint as to why he had come.

The children went to bed and the house grew quiet. When the telephone rang shortly after midnight, Jacob realized that he'd been expecting it. The caller ID indicated it was the same number that had called throughout Shabbos.

"It's him," Jacob told his wife. He lifted the receiver and motioned for her to listen in on the extension in the kitchen.

"Dr. Stern. This is ... the person who was at your place tonight," the voice said.

"Yes," Jacob said curtly.

"Sorry about the intrusion," the voice continued. "I didn't mean to scare you."

"Thanks for your consideration," Jacob said sarcastically.

"No, really. I called all day long, and no one answered. I wanted to leave you a note. Then I saw that you were home, so ...."

"What do you want from me?" Jacob broke in.

"I must meet with you," the man said. "I must talk with you about Lenny Brown, and the epidemic in Mexico."

"Listen to me," Jacob said, his voice hard. "I don't know who you are or why you came. I have no idea what you're talking about. I don't think I can help you."

The man sounded on the edge of despair. "If you are Jacob Stern from the Agricultural Department, in charge of overseeing the use of poisons in farming, you know very well what I'm talking about." He started talking faster. "You're the only one who can help me. If you don't want me to come to your house, I'll respect that. Let's meet in a neutral location."

"I told you. There's nothing for us to talk —"

"Please, sir. I have no one else to turn to. Do you know the Nature and Science Museum?"

"Excuse me. It's very late."

"The Nature and Science Museum," the man pleaded. "Let's meet there tomorrow morning."

Jacob was silent. He glanced at his wife, his eyes reflecting his doubts.

"I'll be there at ten o'clock," the man said, sounding as if he were on the verge of tears. "Please, come talk with me."

"Not a chance," Jacob said firmly. "I'm hanging up now, and if you call again or try to come here, I'll call the police."

"I'll be there at ten," the man shouted. "Please come!"

"Good night." Jacob hung up.

Jacob and his wife looked at one another in silence.

"What are you planning to do?" his wife asked.

"I don't know. But I'm certainly not going."

"He didn't sound threatening. He sounded like ... a victim."

"Or maybe it was all an act, to get me exactly where he wants me," Jacob said.

"I was just thinking … about what the Rebbe said."

Jacob thought this over, weighing what she had said. "A person is not allowed to put himself in danger," he mused. "We can't rely on miracles."

"He didn't sound dangerous," his wife said again. "Maybe he needs help."

"Or he wants to sound that way …."

Jacob did not sleep well that night. Every sound startled him. He checked and rechecked that the gun was in the drawer of his nightstand, that all the windows were closed, that the children were safe in their beds. When he finally managed to drop off, hours after he had gone to bed, he knew that he would be meeting the stranger in the morning.

Washington — Iyar 5766 / May 2006

A visit by the head of Spain's security service in Washington was arranged with little notice. There was no shortage of topics to discuss after the series of terror attacks in Madrid and the exposure of an Al-Queda sleeper cell in the southern half of the peninsula.

But not all meetings take place in offices or conference rooms. Even heads of intelligence organizations are still human, to be swayed by a bit of flattery and attention. Walter Child took the Spaniard and his entourage to dinner at a gourmet Japanese restaurant in one of the American capital's more upscale neighborhoods. It was the kind of place where a table had to be reserved a week in advance and confirmed the afternoon before — that is, for everyone except a prominent government official.

As the Asian waiter bowed and collected the remains of their sushi and sashimi, the assistant director's phone vibrated in his pocket. Excusing himself politely, he moved a few steps away. "What happened?"

"I've got him."

The old Dodge was parked at the edge of Houston Heights, not far from Jacob Stern's home. The agent was sprawled in his seat, surrounded by a sea of take-out containers and empty Coke cans. His grin stretched from ear to ear.

"Are you sure?" Child asked.

"Absolutely. He'll be at the Museum of Nature and Science at ten a.m. tomorrow. This is where the story ends."

Jerusalem — 5694 / 1934

At a few minutes past midnight on a cold night in Shevat, several figures could be seen walking slowly through the Jerusalem's Shaarei Chesed neighborhood.

The darkness was dense. Heavy clouds blanketed the sky, propelled by a chilling wind. One by one came the men whom R' Pinchas, R' Dovid Leib's faithful messenger, had summoned: the shopkeeper from Petach Tikvah, the blind Yemenite from Tel Aviv, and the *dayan* from Yaffo. The holy brothers, R' Zalman and R' Zeidel, arrived from Motzah, as well as the *"Poilisher melamed"* and the other invitees.

Here, far from strangers' eyes, at an hour when the rest of humankind was asleep, they would gather at designated intervals to delve into the hidden Torah and to pray in unison. Their prayers penetrated the Heavenly gates and had the power to rescind evil decrees: prayers with special intentions, combinations, and Names known only to a select few.

R' Pinchas studied them reverently: some of them so elderly that walking was difficult, and others only in their fifties or sixties. But they were all — as R' Dovid had told him on occasion — holy and pious men worthy of wearing the mantle of leadership in Israel.

The youngest of the group was R' Tzvi Hirsch HaLevi, known in Jerusalem as a fundraiser for Kollel Tzidkas Yerushalayim. From time to time, he traveled abroad to knock on doors and collect money for the *kollel* members' support. The city boasted many who were well versed in Torah and in fear of Heaven; among them, R' Tzvi Hirsch did not stand out in any way. Only R' Dovid Leib, head of the secret group, knew that here was a giant of a man, an exalted tzaddik who worked hard to conceal himself. Under the mask of a simple *gabbai tzedakah* was a monumental scholar in both the revealed and the hidden Torah, a man scrupulous in halachic observance who detached himself from all the empty pleasures of this world.

R' Pinchas, the messenger, also served as R' Dovid Leib's *gabbai* when the occasion arose. He was the one who brought the special *siddurim* with the holy Names and intentions to the *beis midrash*, and made sure there was an ample supply of hot tea and biscuits. R' Pinchas was also the one who went that night to a certain Rosh Yeshivah in the Old City, with R' Dovid Leib's regular request: a minyan of *talmidei chachamim* to learn Torah throughout the night. They must be totally diligent and not stop learning for even one moment.

The Rosh Yeshivah was surprised. Usually, R' Dovid Leib made this request only on a Rosh Chodesh eve. This was the middle of the month of Shevat.

Asking no questions, he did as he had been told. He knew that when R' Dovid Leib requested something, one did it.

When the last of the group had entered the *beis midrash*, R' Pinchas closed the doors from the outside and sat down to serve as watchman. No one generally walked the streets at this late hour, but some eager Torah student might take it into his head to continue his studies in a quiet place. R' Pinchas stood guard to make sure no one disturbed the prayers of the tzaddikim inside.

He had often wanted to ask R' Dovid Leib to explain these mysterious gatherings — but had never dared. Only once had the rebbe hinted to him that these prayers were capable of nullifying harsh decrees, and that the earthly *beis din* had a definite influence on the one above. And once, when his spirit was mellow at a Purim *seudah*, R' Dovid Leib had remarked that he had merited what so many others had not: to see, with his own eyes, some of the 36 hidden tzaddikim in whose merit the world existed.

R' Pinchas fixed himself a cup of tea and opened a *Tehillim*. Though he was not on the exalted level of those inside, this was certainly a propitious time to pray on behalf of himself and his family.

Through the closed door he could hear only a quiet murmuring. A stifled groan reached his ears from time to time, and very occasionally R' Dovid Leib's voice rose as he recited a particular verse. After about an hour, he heard the shuffling of many feet, as though the men inside were making a circuit around the *bimah*. Then silence returned, punctuated as before by the murmuring voices and muffled cries.

Three hours passed. The darkness intensified and a hard rain began to fall. R' Pinchas huddled inside his coat. The voices in the shul grew louder and more animated. In the east, the sky began to pale. Just seconds before dawn, he heard the sound of a shofar: a thin, muted cry, like the wail of a newborn baby. Two additional shofars joined in, these more vigorous than the first — until the combined blasts echoed in the dark street, rolling through the slumbering neighborhood and out to the surrounding hills.

The rain intensified, a bolt of lightning ripped the darkness, and a great drumbeat of thunder sounded in the heavens. At that moment, a line of light appeared in the east. Total silence reigned.

R' Pinchas waited.

At long last, three faint knocks sounded from inside the room. R' Pinchas hurried inside. On a chair near the *bimah* sat R' Dovid Leib, utterly spent. His eyes were closed, his face was pale, and one hand supported his forehead as his lips continued to whisper. The other men in the room were already donning their prayer shawls and *tefillin*.

R' Pinchas had known R' Dovid Leib a long time, and could sometimes read his face. Every other time the secret gathering had completed their prayers, his face had been radiant with joy. This time, it was anxious and drawn. The other tzaddikim appeared equally melancholy. There was a sense of sorrow in the room, as though they knew that they not received the response they had been seeking.

R' Pinchas handed R' Dovid Leib his *tallis* and *tefillin*. The leader of the secret group opened his eyes and gave his helper a sad look. He nodded briefly as a heavy sigh escaped his lips.

Houston, Texas — Iyar 5766 / May 2006

The funeral parlor was filled to capacity with Lenny Brown's relatives, colleagues, and friends. The atmosphere was sorrowful. Lenny's widow and his elderly mother wept continuously, while his small children looked on, lost and frightened.

Jacob remained at the ceremony for just a quarter of an hour. He shook some hands and murmured a few words of consolation to the family. As the minister began to deliver a prayer, Jacob slipped out, got into his car, and drove to the center of town. The rest of the mourners would linger for a while, swapping memories and bewailing the young life cut off before its time. They would say that Lenny had had a bright future ahead of him and would undoubtedly have gone far. People would wonder if there had been any progress in the investigation into finding the hit-and-run driver who had killed him.

But Jacob had no time for small talk. He was the only one who was doing something to help. He was on his way to the Museum of Nature and Science, to meet the man who had tried to see him the night before. He had a feeling he was going to hear some very interesting things.

Amazingly, he found an empty parking space right outside the museum. He locked his car, checked that his gun was in its holster, and began walking toward the entrance. He did not notice the old gray Dodge parked across the street.

Had he glanced in that direction, he would have seen a familiar and alarming face: that of the pale man who had prowled through his department, searching for Lenny Brown.

The Museum of Nature and Science is housed in a handsome building, low and broad. The area in front is a maze of pleasant walks landscaped with flower beds, manicured bushes, and shade trees.

Jacob stood on Herman Street and looked around. There were many visitors, but no one appeared to be waiting for him.

Jacob had an eerie feeling, as though someone were secretly watching him. He entered one of the paths and began walking. He felt less exposed here, more protected. After a glance at his watch, he took a seat on a stone bench. An uneasy feeling began to steal into his heart. The sense of urgency he had felt as he left Lenny's funeral had all but dissipated. He was about to meet a total stranger, someone about whose character and intentions he was completely in the dark. Coming here might have been a mistake. Maybe he had been a little too hasty ....

After several minutes of internal debate, Jacob stood up and began pacing nervously to and fro. He went over to a nearby stand and bought a can of soda, then resumed his seat and took a long drink, his eyes darting continually over the rim of the can.

He never sensed the man approaching from behind, and he was startled when a sudden shadow fell over him.

"Dr. Stern?"

Jacob jumped up in confusion. The man behind him offered a smile and his hand to shake. "Thanks for coming to meet me."

Jacob returned the handshake and exhaled with relief. This was not the pale fellow after all. He was clearly of Mexican-Indian descent: broad nose, brown skin, straight black hair. He did not appear threatening. On the contrary, the man seemed tired and harried, his clothing stained and his hair disheveled.

"My name is Jorge Diaz," the man introduced himself. "I'm the assistant director of the municipal lighting department in Juarez, Mexico. Or rather," he corrected himself with a grimace, "that's what I was until a week ago." He met Jacob's eye. "I'm sorry I trespassed on your property yesterday."

"You scared us," Jacob admitted as the tension in his body drained away. "We are religious Jews — Orthodox — and we don't use the telephone on our Sabbath. That's why we didn't answer the phone all day. But we were all on edge — believe me, I have no idea why I didn't shoot you immediately."

"Sorry," Jorge said again. "But I had no choice. I think they're looking for me. Just to make sure you know — Lenny Brown did *not* die in a random traffic accident."

"Listen, Mr ... Diaz," Jacob said, though he was actually in complete agreement with the Mexican. "I simply do not believe that here, in the United States, a person can be murdered in the streets. Forgive me, but this isn't Mexico!"

Jorge's friendliness vanished. He pointed a finger at Jacob, his black eyes blazing. "Dr. Stern, Lenny Brown was killed because he knew too much about the epidemic near Juarez in the 50s. I was meant to have died, too. If not for ..." He fell silent, glancing down at his hand, which grasped something soft and concealed. "If not for ... I have something that protects me." His voice resumed its harsh tone. "They will kill you, too, the minute they find out that you gave Lenny the information."

"Leave me out of this," Jacob said, nervously playing with the Coke can. In his nervousness, he dented the metal. "I didn't give Lenny anything."

Jorge gave him a bitter smile. "I know that you'd love to be out of the picture. I, too, would like to be home right now, going to work and getting on with my life. Does that help me? For the past week I've been on the run: sleeping in the streets, washing up in public restrooms, stealing food in order to survive."

Though the Texas sun blazed with all its might, a shiver ran up Jacob's spine. "Can you tell me what's going on? Who's against whom? And ... who are you, anyway?"

The Mexican pulled a pack of cigarettes from his pocket and lit one slowly. "Okay." He sat down on the bench beside Jacob and emitted a puff of acrid smoke. "A group of us are fighting on behalf of restoring rights to the villagers. Mexico's corrupt governments have mistreated the tribal Indians for generations. They've stolen their land, abolished their rights, and tried to eradicate their culture and language.

"All along, it was the Mexican government that was blamed. Then came the incident at Juarez — the mysterious epidemic that wiped out the Chuma tribe some decades ago — and turned the spotlight on the U.S.

"Until recently, the episode was just an unconfirmed rumor, a folk legend that circulated among the villages. A sad tale that the village elders would tell around the fire on cold nights. Then Professor Gustavo Costa, the well-known anthropologist from the University of Mexico City, decided to investigate the story.

"He traveled to the small villages near Juarez, talking to the old people and recording their testimony. He also studied the wall drawings on the mysterious tribal cave that was discovered in the jungle not long ago. But he had not yet succeeded in finding any proof against the United States."

Jacob had never heard of the Chuma tribe or its mysterious cave in the jungle. He did not interrupt the Mexican's narrative with his questions.

"The connection," Jorge Diaz continued, "was made by a man named Octavio Solarz, an employee of the government archives in Mexico City. A few months ago, he found a cardboard file in the basement. The file had all the proofs about the Juarez incident: names, places, dates, the number of dead — everything. The Soviet KGB had sent the file to the Mexican government in order to undermine the U.S. — but, for some reason, Mexico decided to do nothing with it. The file was buried in the archive basement.

"Octavio shared the secret of the file's existence with five or six people: myself, an Indian activist by the name of Romero Alameda, Professor Costa, and a research assistant of his, plus a few other friends. The file had all the proofs the professor needed to publish his article. He said it was a discovery that would stun the world.

"And then, one day, a man phoned and claimed that he had additional information regarding the incident. He arranged to meet us all in a hotel near El Zócalo. We all put in an appearance. The man welcomed us warmly, poured us glasses of tequila, and raised his glass to wish us long life ...."

Jorge was silent for a long moment, his dark eyes brimming with tears. "My friends never knew it," he said, "but the drinks had been poisoned. Within seconds, they all began to feel sick, and to writhe on the floor until they died."

The Mexican was crying openly now. Jacob was rigid with shock. A cold thread of fear trickled up his spine. Lenny Brown had said something about those who had paid with their lives. But with such cruelty?

"What about you?" he asked Jorge. "How did *you* survive?"

The Mexican glanced again at the object in his hand. "I had luck," he said. "I had something to protect me. But my friends ..." He shook his head, took a deep breath, and added, "I ... I'm not sure why ... I was suspicious of the informer from the start. There was something strange about him ... cruel ... that scared me. He was very pale. His hair was very light and his eyes were pale and watery. There was something ... lifeless ... about him."

Jacob's throat constricted. Terror gripped him. He recognized the description very well. That was the man who had entered his office seeking Lenny — now being interred in the cemetery on the other side of town ....

"While they'd all had their drinks," Jorge continued, "I pretended to take a sip from my glass. But I didn't put any of it into my mouth. As they began to collapse, I realized that we had made a huge mistake. I dropped under the table, where I lay without moving, almost without breathing, as if I were dead. Believe me, Dr. Stern, those were the most frightening moments of my life. Then the informer made a call to someone, and told him that 'all the numbers were erased.' Do you understand, Dr. Stern? In their eyes, we're not people, but numbers. A list of unnecessary objects to be gotten rid of.

"After that, luckily, the killer left the room. I used the opportunity to run down the emergency staircase."

The CIA agent sat in his Dodge across the street from the museum, a pair of binoculars to his eyes. He spoke excitedly into the phone. At last, he had tracked down his target: the number that hadn't been erased. He was finally looking at Jorge Diaz, who had managed to escape his clutches one week ago.

"I see the Mexican!" he reported to the deputy director. "And guess who he's talking to?"

"Who?"

"The Jew who worked next to the black guy."

This managed to surprise even Walter Child. "Are you serious?"

"Absolutely. I'm looking at them right now."

"Think you can get rid of them both?"

"With pleasure," the pale man said. "With pleasure."

Many people frequented the shul because of the *ba'al koreh*, R' Zisha.

On weekdays, R' Zisha earned his livelihood from a pocket-sized grocery store, where he sold his fellow Jerusalemites a loaf of bread, some halvah, or broken biscuits at a discount. But it was his Shabbos *laining* that was his glory. It made him a king — and the weekly portion was his kingdom.

He would pronounce each word with great feeling, lowering and raising his voice according to the subject matter, sometimes imbuing the verses with a festive air and sometimes with a sad or stern one. The worshipers not only *heard* the weekly portion, they seemed to see it, too, and experience it with their own bodies.

When the Israelites crossed the Red Sea, the men in shul felt the waters rising up on either side; when the *parashah* discussed sacrificial offerings, they could hear the Levites singing in the *Azarah*; and when R' Zisha reached the part about the willful son whose parents testified that he ate and drank like a glutton, the worshipers could practically catch the sound of chewing. The Heavenly Hosts gathered to hear R' Zisha's *laining*, they would say, quoting a holy Jerusalem personality.

This week's portion was *Parashas Mishpatim*, which deals with laws and mitzvos. For R' Zisha, it was a celebration of riches: the *eved Ivri*, the goring ox, an eye for an eye and a tooth for a tooth. He had reached the fourth *aliyah* and his enthusiasm was growing. *"Kol almanah v'yasom lo sa'anun* (You shall not cause pain to any widow or orphan)," he chanted, swaying vigorously, with one hand gripping the *atzei chayim* (posts) of the *Sefer Torah* and the forefinger of the other pointed Heavenward. He raised his voice in rebuke, like an angry prophet: *"Im aneh sa'aneh oso ki im tza'ok yitz'ak eili, shamoa eshma es tza'kaso* (If you [dare to] cause him pain —- for if he shall cry out to Me, I shall surely hear his outcry)!"

He paused briefly, then raised a clenched fist. *"V'charah api v'haragti eschem becharev, v'hayu nesheichem almanos u'beneichem yesomim* (My wrath shall blaze and I shall kill you by the sword, and your wives will be widows and your children orphans)!"

Before R' Zisha could go on, the shul was rent by a shrill scream from the women's section. Then came the thud of a falling body, and excited, feminine cries. Someone had fainted! Help!

Several men ran upstairs to the women's section. Others summoned the pharmacist from the next street, who came quickly with his bag of medicines.

"It's Chaikeh, the *almanah*," came the report from the women's section. The others shook their heads in distress and compassion. Just a few weeks earlier, Chaikeh had buried her husband. And now, on top of that, a fresh tragedy had occurred: Her daughter's engagement was broken. *Ai, ai, ai*, the people clucked with compassion. *What a pity, what a pity*. It was hard to know who was in the right in that situation. Had the Levingers — the *chasan's* family — been correct in canceling the match? Was Chaikeh's daughter really a heretic, who visited foreign places of worship and bowed before the cross? Who knew. Who knew .... It was very hard to judge. But how could Chaikeh the widow hear these verses and not feel her heart tearing to shreds?

The pharmacists' soothing concoctions did Chaikeh no good at all. Neither did treatment at the so-called Wallach Hospital — Shaarei Tzedek Hospital, under the leadership of Dr. Moshe Wallach. The moment Shabbos was over, the streets of Meah Shearim rang with the announcement of her demise. *"Gait tzu di levayah fun ha'ishah hachashuvah, Maras Chaikeh Lederman* (Go to the funeral of the honorable woman, Mrs. Chaikeh Lederman)."

Houston, Texas — Iyar 5766 / May 2006

Jacob Stern stared at the Mexican in open shock. If he'd had any lingering doubts about Lenny Brown's death, Jorge had just dissolved them.

"I spent the next few days wandering around Mexico City," Jorge continued. "I didn't go home. I stayed away from my office and didn't call anyone I know. I, Jorge Diaz, a senior bureaucrat in the Juarez municipality, became a homeless person.

"I was sure the killer was still after me, so I was careful about anything that might lead him to me. I didn't take money out of the ATM machine and didn't use my credit card. I turned off my cell phone and turned it on again only when I tried to call you. With the help of good people, I traveled north across Mexico, crossed the border and ... here I am."

"Aren't you afraid that he's still looking for you?" Jacob asked, looking anxiously around.

"How? Do you think he followed me on those mountain paths? Smuggled across the border with me in a truck loaded with corn? Calm down. If he's looking for me, he's doing it in Mexico."

"I hope so," Jacob said soberly. "For both of our sakes."

"Anyway, I've got something protecting me." Jorge opened his hand. Jacob saw a cloth bag tied with a strip of leather. "The shaman of my tribe gave this to me. It's the spirit of the eagle of the black mountain. It watches over me. It turns me into an eagle that devours all its enemies."

Jacob ignored the last statement, which smacked of idol worship. "But if you claim that the killer is trying to prevent the publication of information that would harm the United States," he said, "why cross the border? Why walk into the lion's den?"

"Because the proof is here, in the U.S.— and I have to find it. I'm the only one left alive of our group, and I have a mission. The world has to know about what happened in Juarez — and I'm going to tell them.

"I come from a family of warriors, Dr. Stern. My ancestors, the Aztecs, fought the rival tribes who wanted to conquer their territory, fought the

Catholic Spaniards who came from Europe, and fought the Americans who wanted to defeat Mexico. We Indians never lay down our weapons. I do not intend to give up."

As Jacob looked at the other man, a suspicion began to grow in his mind. "How did you find me?"

"You?" The Mexican smiled. "I didn't find you, Dr. Stern. I wanted to meet with Lenny, but when I reached Houston I was told that he'd been in an 'accident.' "

Jacob grimaced. The reference to Lenny's death only increased the bad vibes that were overwhelming him.

"And what do you want of me?" he asked.

"Not much. I just want you to get me the material that Lenny sent to the professor."

"*What?*" Jacob yelped. "The material?"

Jorge nodded. "Of course. Why not? You work in the Department of Agriculture and have access to the information. It's only about five or six pages."

Instinctively, Jacob inched away from the man beside him on the bench. Did this Mexican really expect him to provide incriminating evidence against the United States? Was he crazy?

"Listen to me," he said, quietly but decisively. "I very much admire your fighting spirit, but we're not on the same side. I feel terrible about my friend, Lenny. I feel terrible about your friends. But I have a family — a wife and kids. All I want is to go home in peace."

Jorge stopped him with a wave of his hand. "All I need from you is one small favor. I won't involve you in the affair."

"Just one small favor?" Jacob repeated mockingly. "Someone already died because of that small favor."

"I must reach the media," Jorge said. "Professor Costa said that newspapers are the only weapon that can help justice prevail. I'll tell the story of Juarez to the whole world — but I need proof."

"Let me make myself perfectly clear," Jacob reiterated. "You won't get any help from me in that direction."

Jorge leaned forward, elbows on his knees. He spoke without looking at Jacob. "Dr. Stern, I want to tell you something. You're already in deep. If they killed Lenny Brown and my friends, they won't hesitate to add you to the list. Get me the material — and I'll forget who you are. I never heard your name and never met you in my life. All I want is those five pages from the archives. I have no desire to see anyone else hurt. Understand?"

Jacob's throat went dry. He tilted the soda can to his mouth and drank down the last sip. The Mexican had spoken quietly, but his meaning was clear. *Blackmail. He's threatening me ....*

"I need time," he said, after a moment's thought. "I need to think over the possibilities."

"What's there to think about?" Jorge raised his voice. "You just go into your office, photocopy a few pages, and you'll never see me again."

"There's nothing I can do today. It's Sunday. The office is closed."

Anger clouded Jorge's face. "You can enter your office any time you want. You're the director! I've been hiding out for a week. I was nearly killed. Can't you make this one small effort?"

Jacob stood up, signaling that the conversation was about to end. "Let's talk again tomorrow. Okay? I need to think. Maybe I can find a way to help you."

Jorge Diaz got to his feet as well. He stepped close to Jacob and brought his face menacingly close. "You're trying to wriggle out of this," he said in a hard voice. "You won't bring me the pages. You plan to go straight to the police. But remember this: If they catch me, I'm going to give them your name."

Jacob placed a calming hand on the Mexican's shoulder, trying to dispel the tension. "You have nothing to worry about," he said, looking directly into Jorge's eyes. "I am not going to the police. I am not trying to get away. Today, it's simply impossible. Accept that as a fact. Let's meet tomorrow and see what can be done."

Jorge sat back down on the stone bench. The look he sent Jacob was angry and confused. "It's not right," he mumbled. "It's just not right." His shoulders slumped and his eyes filled with despair. "They'll catch me and kill me, too. They'll finish the job." He gazed at a small group sitting nearby. Two children, Jacob saw, were munching on sandwiches. There was something about the way Jorge looked at them that caught Jacob's attention. The look spoke of one thing: hunger.

"Tell me," Jacob said, suddenly overcome with pity. "Have you eaten anything today?"

The Mexican turned out his jacket pockets. They held a few coins that did not add up to a dollar. "This is all I have. But I'll get by ...."

"And where will you sleep?"

"I found a place in a public park." Jorge sounded resentful. "Why the sudden interest? I'm sure to sleep in a jail cell tonight. You're on your way to the police, aren't you?"

Jacob checked his wallet. It contained some small change and a fifty-dollar bill.

"I already told you: I'm not going to the police," he said. "Wait here. I want to get you some money so you can sleep somewhere reasonable and eat like a human being. Tomorrow we'll talk again and decide on the next step."

Jorge's face held a mixture of gratitude and distrust. "I can manage," he said, not very convincingly.

"I insist," Jacob said. "I can't see a person starving to death right in front of me. Wait a minute while I go over to the cash machine. I'll be right back."

The ATM on the corner was not working. Jacob went into a bank across the street and waited patiently while the elderly woman in front of him managed, on the third try, to punch in her PIN number and withdraw some cash, a businessman used four different debit cards to withdraw a large sum of money, and two teenagers, foiled in their attempt to withdraw ten dollars, kicked the machine and cursed the whole elitist banking world. By the time Jacob left the bank with one hundred dollars in his hand, ten minutes had passed since he had left the Mexican in front of the museum.

All along, he had been pondering if he was doing the right thing. His innate compassion did not allow him to abandon Jorge to his fate. On the other hand, Jorge might perceive the gesture as a softening on his part, and step up the pressure for the documents he wanted. Then again — on the third hand — perhaps gratitude would impel the Mexican to drop his demand.

Lost in thought, Jacob did not hear the wail of sirens close by. It was only as he was nearing the museum that he noticed something odd. On the street fronting the museum was an impressive array of no less than four police cars and two ambulances.

He approached cautiously, caught up in the stream of curious onlookers. Snatches of conversation reached his ears: "... shot him ..." "... some Mexican ..." "... at short range ...."

For a second, Jacob's legs felt incapable of supporting him. Was it Jorge Diaz? Had somebody tried to hurt him? Jacob froze in shock and terror as he saw Diaz's body sprawled on the grass.

A tall officer, clad in the uniform of a Texas state trooper strolled past him. From his fingers dangled a plastic evidence bag. Inside lay a motley collection of objects: a small cloth bag with a leather tie, three mountain lion's teeth, and a single eagle feather.

"An Indian amulet," the policeman said, leaning into the window of a patrol car to speak to a fellow officer seated inside. "The guy was holding an Indian amulet — the kind their magic men put together. Looks like it wasn't much help ...."

In his other hand the officer held a second evidence bag, with a familiar object inside. It was a red soda can. *My can*, Jacob thought in rising horror. He recognized it by the dent he had made in it as he had nervously listened to Jorge's story.

The plump officer handed the two bags to his colleague, then leaned against the patrol car and spoke into his radio. "Shots fired at close range. One casualty — a Mexican. There are witnesses who saw the killer talking with the victim and drinking a can of Coke. We've got the can. I'm sending it to the crime lab to check for fingerprints."

12

Jerusalem — 5694 / 1934

The funeral of the widow Chaike Lederman was not well attended. It was a wintry *Motza'ei Shabbos*. A cold, wind-driven rain had been falling since noon and the paths were slick and muddy. The members of the *Chevrah Kaddisha* held kerosene lanterns in their frostbitten hands to light their way to the Mount of Olives.

They were surprised to see two unexpected figures following behind them: R' Dovid Leib and the fund-raiser of Kollel Tzidkas Yerushalayim, R' Tzvi Hirsch HaLevi. *What were those two doing in this company?* they wondered. *Why had they seen fit to attend the funeral of this simple woman?*

Their astonishment grew as the two men — along with R' Dovid Leib's faithful helper, R' Pinchas — continued to accompany the body out of the neighborhood, even after most of the other attendees walked the traditional four cubits and dropped away to seek the warmth of their homes.

R' Dovid Leib's head was bowed, and bitter sighs escaped him now and then. Ever since the nighttime prayers earlier in *Shevat*, his soul had known no peace. How many tears had he shed; how many chapters of

Tehillim had he recited; how many supplications had he made? But his heart told him that he and his group had not succeeded in nullifying the harsh decree.

With his delicate sensibilities, he knew that they had succeeded, perhaps, in postponing it — but not in canceling it entirely.

And now — calamity. Iniquity heaped upon iniquity. The terrible wrong had not only distressed an orphan, but had brought her mother in sorrow to the grave. Who knew the depth of the judgment to be rendered? The soul of the Jewish woman was now rising to the Heavenly Court, to bring her complaint before the Throne of Glory and demand justice for her mortification. *"If you cause him pain …. If he shall cry out to Me, I shall surely hear his outcry."*

R' Dovid Leib shuddered with fear as the rest of the verse flashed through his mind: *"My wrath shall blaze and I shall kill you by the sword, and your wives will be widows and your children orphans!"*

The two tzaddikim walked a long way, with R' Pinchas following at a discreet distance. Near the walls of the Old City, R' Tzvi Hirsch suddenly halted. He raised his eyes to R' Dovid Leib and said in a trembling voice, *"Men darf mesirus nefesh — nohr mesirus nefesh* (We need self-sacrifice — only self-sacrifice)."

R' Dovid Leib, head of the society of hidden tzaddikim, shook his head slowly from side to side. He did not agree.

R' Tzvi Hirsch, he knew, meant one specific thing: *mesirus nefesh* on behalf of the nation. When a tzaddik beseeches Hashem to take his life as an atonement for his generation, in order to save that generation from a harsh decree. A communal offering ….

"Korban tzibbur," R' Tzvi Hirsch murmured, confirming R' Dovid Leib's thoughts. "What we need is a *korban tzibbur.*"

The members of the *Chevrah Kaddisha* strode rapidly along with the bier. R' Dovid Leib quickened his pace, motioning for his friend to do the same.

"R' Tzvi Hirsch," he said on a note of pleading. "Do we, in our time, have a notion of what a *korban tzibbur* is? Who can know the depth of the judgment?"

"Korban tzibbur …. That's what we need," R' Tzvi Hirsch insisted.

"Would a single death suffice?" R' Dovid Leib continued. "Or would that tzaddik lose both this world and the next? What if his soul is forced to wander without rest, and to undergo terrible suffering until its *tikkun* comes ...."

R' Tzvi Hirsch, caught up in an emotional storm of his own, seemed not to hear his friend's words at all. *"Korban tzibbur ... korban tzibbur,"* he kept repeating.

"Sometimes the death of the righteous is not enough," R' Dovid Leib said in a whisper. "Sometimes the sacrifice of a person of high spiritual standing is not sufficient. It has happened that, to complete the true rectification, what is required is self-sacrifice by a simple Jew. An ordinary Jew, with no special spiritual accomplishment. *Mesirus nefesh* in its most basic sense. Sometimes, R' Tzvi Hirsch, *that* is what can tear up a harsh decree ...."

R' Tzvi Hirsch nodded. He knew this. He knew it well ....

Houston, Texas — Iyar 5766 / May 2006

Jacob Stern stumbled wild-eyed into his kitchen. With shaking hands he poured himself a glass of water and slumped into a chair to drink it. His heart was racing as though he had just run a marathon. The image of Jorge Diaz, lying on the ground, kept returning to him over and over, bearing a fresh burden of horror each time.

How had he made it home? He had no idea. Whole segments of the past hour had vanished from his memory. He felt as though he had been sucked out of his own body and was floating above it while someone else went through the motions in his place. It had been his inborn instinct of self-preservation that had taken him away from the danger zone and seen to it that he arrived home safely.

He recalled that, despite his absolute terror, he had walked slowly in order not to arouse suspicion. He remembered heading toward his car. It was only after he was seated behind the wheel that he had begun to shake.

Angels had watched over him on the drive home. He had gripped the wheel, his eyes glazed and unseeing. More than once, irate drivers had honked at him as he strayed out of his lane or disregarded a traffic signal.

He was just a short step away from prison. All that was needed was one eyewitness to identify him as the man who had spoken with the slain Mexican, and he would be under arrest. Once his fingerprints were matched with those on the Coke can, it would be a hop, skip, and a jump to arrest, trial, and Heaven only knew what else. Go explain to the judge that he had gone to take money out of the ATM machine for a Mexican stranger — who, a moment before, had tried to blackmail him with threats.

The house was empty. The children were in school and his wife was attending a *chesed* meeting. Jacob lowered the blinds and drew the draperies. Then he sat in the kitchen, pistol in hand. His fingers trembled. His teeth chattered. He had never been so afraid in his life.

The Texas police were not his main problem. They would not delve too deeply into Jorge Diaz's murder. Who really cared about some illegal immigrant from Mexico? No, the one who really frightened Jacob was his pursuer: the pale man. There was no doubt in his mind that it was he who had shot Jorge Diaz. And if he had seen Jacob conversing with the Mexican, it was only a matter of time before he came after him, as well.

"I couldn't approach them from the front, the CIA agent tried to justify himself to Walter Child. "You should have seen the place. It was too open and there were too many possible witnesses."

He was sitting in his Dodge, outside the museum, watching as the Mexican's body was loaded onto an ambulance. His boss, at the other end of the line, was apoplectic.

"Under other circumstances," Child exploded, "I'd kick you out of the service right now! I've never seen such unprofessionalism!"

From the snippets of information he had managed to catch on Diaz's phone the previous night, the agent had known that he was due to meet someone at the Museum of Nature and Science. Who? That was the big question. Because of the special nature of this business, they did not have the CIA's full investigative powers at their disposal. After all, their activities were being carried out along rather unconventional lines ....

But it didn't really matter whom Diaz was meeting, Walter Child had stressed. He was to be taken out before the two had a chance to speak. The Mexican must not be allowed to pass anything to the person he was meeting.

And then, at ten this morning, as the agent sat parked across from the museum, he had seen an unexpected figure: the Jew who worked in the Department of Agriculture, side by side with Lenny Brown.

The pale man was taken totally by surprise. He did not immediately realize that Jacob Stern was the person Diaz intended to meet. In his mind, Stern was nothing more than an annoying hitch in the plan. Someone who could point a finger at him and raise a commotion.

By the time he realized that the Jew had come here to meet with the Mexican, it was too late. The two had sat down to talk on a bench at the edge of the plaza, not far from where the agent was waiting. Had he attempted a frontal approach. Diaz would undoubtedly have recognized him as the "informer" who had met with him and his friends in Mexico City. And the Jew would have known him as the man who searched Lenny Brown's office on the day before his "accident." They might have cried out, attracting the attention of other museum-goers. He had no choice but to detour around the back of the museum and approach the pair from the rear.

By the time he had made the roundabout trip and come up behind the bench, breathless and cursing under his breath, the Jew was gone. Only the Mexican remained on the bench. The agent had dealt with him at once.

The question was: How much information had Diaz managed to pass on to the Jew — and what did the Jew intend to do with it?

"This entire operation has been one comedy of errors," the asssistant director said furiously.

It had begun in Mexico City. The agent had been certain that all the participants in his little meeting had drunk their poisoned tequila and could be crossed off the list. But Jorge Diaz, Number Five, had been far too suspicious. When the "B" crew had come to clear away the bodies, they found one body too few and one tequila glass too full.

In the ensuing days, the Mexican had proved extremely wily. He had refrained from all the usual things that could have helped the CIA agent track him down. Only once had he activated his cell phone while still across the border in Mexico — somewhere between Mexico City and Juarez. The next time his electronic footprint appeared had been in Houston.

The pale agent had managed to listen in on the conversation as Diaz arranged a meeting at the museum this morning. Had they only known in advance whom he was intending to meet, this complication could have been prevented.

"Do you know who the Jew is?" the assistant director asked. "What's his name? Where does he live?"

"I only know that he works at the Department of Agriculture, on the same floor where Brown had his office. Next cubicle, in fact. I don't know his name."

"Find out, and take care of him," Child snapped, and slammed down the phone.

The Jew brought this on himself, Child thought, after he had listened several times to the recording of Stern's late-night telephone conversation with Jorge Diaz. He was not involved in this business. Initially, he hadn't wanted to meet with the Mexican at all. He surely wasn't part of the conspiracy that had been hatched in Mexico City.

But people pay the price for the decisions they make. By agreeing to meet Jorge Diaz at the museum, he had stepped into the circle of fire.

The Jew would die for that — and he had only himself to blame.

Amere two months before that nighttime funeral, no one had been calling her "Chaikeh the widow." She'd been Chaikeh Lederman, wife of Chatzkel Lederman, the quiet man who owned the small vinegar shop in the Meah Shearim *shuk*.

It was less a shop than a dim niche distinguished by a rickety wooden door and the ever-present smell of aged vinegar. In the rear stood two large barrels filled to the brim. From time to time, a customer would come in to buy a *rotel* (3 liters) or half a *rotel*. When one of the barrels became empty, Chatzkel would bring a new one from his storeroom — located in the cellar of his family home on the other side of the *shuk*.

Chatzkel Lederman was a very simple Jew, short and stout. Nor was his wife, Chaikeh, an educated woman. Still, between them they ran the shop with integrity, though it provided only the most meager of incomes. There were seven children at home, apart from three who had died of illness before reaching the age of five. They must all be fed, not to mention shod and dressed. Their shoes were full of holes and their clothes boasted patches on top of patches. And it was high time they bought several thick down quilts with which to face the approaching winter.

But what was all of this, in comparison to the family's *real* problem? Toivy, the eldest girl, was already sixteen and still at home.

Ribono shel Olam, what is to become of her? Chaikeh would wail silently over her small *Tehillim*. Would Toivy remain single until her hair turned white? Most of her friends were already married, or at least engaged. At the age of fourteen, their parents had begun looking around, and they had quickly found their matches. Why, young Shaindel Dorfman, the neighbors' daughter who still played with the children on the streets of Meah Shearim, had barely turned thirteen when shiduch proposals began pouring in. While Toivy — so capable, so responsible, so diligent, such a little *balebusta* — had not yet found her proper match.

Every time she saw the bent form of Shimshon *der shadchan* hurrying through the *shuk*, Chaikeh's heart would twist inside. There he was, with his tiny notebook and the pencil between his teeth, on his way to propose another shiduch. There he raced, with his small, rapid steps, to bring joy and blessing to some other home in Jerusalem. But who wanted to marry into a family of lowly shopkeepers? Who, in all the city, would take the daughter of an *am ha'aretz* who hardly knew how to open a *sefer*? Who would introduce his son into a world where he would never be rid of the smell of vinegar?

But one day — the miracle happened. Shimshon *der shadchan* came to a stop in front of the store, paused, looked around, and went inside.

"*Vu iz Reb Chatzkel* (Where is Chatzkel)?" he called.

Chaikeh Lederman was almost too excited to speak. "He's in the storeroom under the house, at the far end of the *shuk*," she managed with difficulty. R' Shimshon set out at once. Chaikeh clapped her hands together joyously. *Baruch Hashem* — a shiduch! Toivy's salvation was near.

Chaikeh walked around as if in a dream. She could not settle down to anything. Everything slipped right out of her hands. Every few minute she peeked outside until, an interminable quarter of an hour later, she caught a glimpse of R' Shimshon disappearing down a side street. Chaikeh locked the shop — something she had never before done in the middle of the day — and ran through the *shuk* in the direction of home.

"*Nu?*" she burst out even before she reached the cellar steps.

Her husband looked up in surprise. "What do you mean, '*Nu*'?"

She nearly danced down the curved stairs. "What did R' Shimshon have to say?" She was tense with expectation. "Shimshon *der shadchan!*"

Her husband was concentrating on pouring vinegar from a large barrel into several smaller containers. "He suggested a shidduch for Toivy."

"I know he didn't come to buy vinegar!" Chaikeh cried gaily. "Who?"

Chatzkel shrugged. "Kalman Levinger's son."

Chaikeh Lederman clasped her hands together and cast a grateful look heavenward. Then her face grew sober. "Do you think they'll want us?" she asked fearfully. The Levingers were a good family — one of the oldest in Shaarei Chesed. Would they agree to a shidduch with a simple family of vinegar-sellers?

"They've already agreed," Chatzkel said. And he went on pouring vinegar from the big barrel.

Binyamin Levinger, the designated *chasan*, was, like his namesake, the youngest child in his family. Like all the boys in the city, he had learned in a *cheder*, gone on to yeshivah, and was now, at nearly seventeen, ready to build his own *bayis ne'eman b'Yisrael*. When the matchmaker asked why they had waited so long, instead of marrying him off at fifteen or sixteen, they had responded immediately: His mother had found it very difficult to part from him, her youngest child.

But the boy was a veritable gem, R' Shimshon had assured R' Chatzkel, as were his ten older brothers and sisters, all of whom had married into beautiful and respectable families. Money, too, was not lacking. It was no secret that they had a rich uncle in far-off America, a generous philanthropist who shared his wealth with the poor of Jerusalem. All the charity collectors knew of him and found their way to his door. Rumor had it, R' Shimshon had concluded his remarks, that his own relatives were not forgotten.

Chaikeh returned to the shop, floating above the old tiles and smiling for all she was worth. Such a family could only produce a boy of sterling character, and her Toivy deserved exactly that. She was a wonderful girl, pious and modest and good. So, if the match was *bashert*, all should go smoothly. Not like the Reiferman shidduch, which dragged on for weeks and drove everybody to the point of madness. How she longed to see her Toiveleh in a white dress under the *chuppah!*

A few days later, the boy's parents met the girl's. The Lederman home had been vigorously scrubbed and polished in honor of the guests. On the floor was a dusting of clean sand; the walls had been freshly whitewashed, and the windows had been left open for hours on end to get rid of — or at least weaken — the stubborn smell of vinegar.

At the second meeting, Toivy was given a chance to see her proposed *chasan*. She sat in the front room and watched as he and his parents passed through to the inner room. He was tall and thin, wearing a broad-brimmed hat. His face was the face of a child, and the long, curly *peyos* dangled beside cheeks that did not yet show signs of a beard.

He, too, threw a bashful look her way — and that was the extent of their encounter, in fulfillment of the Talmud's edict that one should not marry a woman until he has seen her. They glimpsed each other again briefly at the *vort,* when their mothers emotionally broke a plate and all the guests shouted, "Mazel tov!" The next time they were due to meet would be under the *chuppah*.

This, their parents decided, would take place no later than the end of the year, at a time agreed upon by both sides.

Long months passed. Preparations for the wedding were moving at a snail's pace. On Chol HaMoed Succos, the *mechutanim* met for the traditional visit and began thinking about a wedding date. After Shavuos, probably, or at the start of Elul.

The Yom Tov ended, and a stormy winter settled over Jerusalem. It was intensely cold, with freezing, howling winds and snow that covered the streets and houses. One day, Chatzkel Lederman climbed the stairs from his storage cellar burning with fever. He was shivering uncontrollably, and had a deep, hacking cough.

The neighborhood pharmacist dosed him with medicine, but the fever continued to climb. The next night, a doctor was summoned to the house. He entered the patient's room, examined him thoroughly, then stepped out to face the frightened family. "Pneumonia," he said.

Chaikeh paled. Pneumonia! That terrible, fearsome illness. A wagon was hastily brought around and Chatzkel was taken to Dr. Wallach's hospital in the hope that something could be found to help him and ease his suffering. Six years hence, scientists would make penicillin, the first antibiotic, available to the public. Until then, pneumonia continued to be an illness of great suffering and almost no cure.

All night long, Chaikeh sat at her husband's bedside, praying fervently, pressing damp washcloths to his burning forehead, and crying bitter tears. In the morning, his condition seemed slightly improved. His breathing was quieter and less ragged. He gestured for his wife to go. If the shop was closed, there would be no food at home.

Toivy remained with her father. Her heart ached at the sight of him, lying motionless on the white sheet, eyes half-closed and mind clouded. Chatzkel's chest rose and fell rapidly as he tried to inhale the oxygen he needed, and the breaths whistled out through his bluish lips. Every now and then he succumbed to an attack of wracking coughs, which tore at his chest and felt like knives cutting into him. When the attack subsided, he lay limp as a rag, mouth open in a futile effort to bring some air into his starving lungs.

Chatzkel lay burning with fever in his hospital bed for three days. On the afternoon of the fourth day, he gestured for his daughter to come sit beside him.

"Toivy," he whispered in a voice hoarse from coughing. "I want you to do something."

Toivy nodded obediently.

"Go to Tzipporah, the cook in the orphanage for Sephardic children. Tell her that I'm sick, and that's why I'm sending you this time ...." He could say no more. A terrible spate of coughing seized him. His eyes bulged and filled with blood. His oxygen-starved chest felt seared. *Go, go,* he motioned to his daughter. *Don't delay.*

Anxious and tearful, Toivy hurried to the orphanage, wondering if the request had not been the product of a fever-driven hallucination. The cook was, indeed, named Tzipporah. When she heard that the girl was Chatzkel Lederman's daughter, and that he was ill, she sighed sympathetically. Then she pointed to a corner of the big kitchen. "It's ready."

In the corner stood a large straw basket covered with a cloth napkin. Toivy gasped at its weight. After she had passed through the orphanage gates and was sure that the cook couldn't see her, she lifted the napkin. The basket held a veritable feast: three cooked chickens, a quantity of fruits and vegetables, two large loaves of bread, and other foodstuffs. For whom was this food intended? Who was the lucky person who could look forward to a kingly banquet in poverty-stricken Jerusalem? And what connection did her father have to this basket?

Her father had told her to tell the cook that he had sent her *this time*. In other words, there had been other times. Why? Since when? Why did no one at home know about this? And most of all — what was she supposed to do with the basket?

A thousand questions raced through her mind; a thousand answers surfaced and were rejected. Curiosity and worry lent her feet wings, and she made her way back to the hospital in record time. Her father was lying restlessly in his bed, his face flushed with fever as he mumbled incoherently through parched lips.

When she entered the room, he opened his eyes. A fleeting smile crossed his face when he saw the basket in her hands. Then his eyes clouded again. He motioned for her to come closer. After another violent coughing fit, he spoke. "I never thought I would have to tell you this. But now, with my days numbered —"

"Abba, don't say that!" Toivy cried. "You're going to get better. *B'ezras Hashem*, you're going to dance at my wedding!"

A feeble smile of resignation rose to Chatzkel's lips. "My Toiveleh, what wouldn't I give to dance at your wedding. But now I have to tell you something. Something very important. Something that not even your mother knows …."

Houston, Texas — Iyar 5766 / May 2006

Jacob felt like a man on death row waiting for the executioner to come. He remained locked inside his house. Every noise made him jump. Every few minutes, he checked out the surrounding area: first, a peek through the peephole in the front door, then a glance through the window blinds at the side of the house. Last of all, he moved aside the kitchen curtain to catch a glimpse of the backyard.

The gun never left his hand. It bothered him that he had only a handful of bullets. What if he needed more? *I have to stock more ammunition*, he told himself.

The hands of the big kitchen clock seemed to crawl. Right now all was quiet, but that told him nothing. He kept hearing sounds from the yard, but couldn't see anything suspicious. Was someone waiting for him to step outside? The pale man, perhaps, waiting patiently …. Too bad the house didn't have closed-circuit video surveillance covering the entire yard. If he got out of this in one piece, he intended to have such a system installed.

It was the silence that drove him mind. Strange, disconnected thoughts flew through his head. He tried to say *Tehillim*, but was too restless even for that.

An hour passed.

Jacob grew somewhat calmer. Gradually, his thinking became more coherent. Actually, he told himself, he was not at all certain that the pale man was looking for him. He didn't know for sure that the fellow had seen him talking to Jorge Diaz. It had taken him ten minutes to go to and from the ATM. Maybe this was all in his imagination.

He made another round of the doors and windows. No one was standing by the front door or stalking him in his backyard. The lawn was bare. He studied the street; no unfamiliar car was parked there.

It was already noon. In another half-hour, his wife and children would be coming home. What to do with them? What to tell his wife? It sounded so terribly odd — a grown man hiding in his darkened house for two hours, taking off his shoes so that his footsteps would not make a sound, and even turning his cell phone to vibrate. Was he being paranoid? Losing his mind?

And why was he so worried, anyway? Where was his *emunas chachamim*? He had traveled to see the Rebbe to ask for his blessing for protection, and the Rebbe had said, "*Fohr gezunterheit*, Dr. Polanski." Had he forgotten already? The meaning had been clear: He had nothing to be afraid of. There was no danger on his horizon. Why, then, was he sitting here, shaking with fear? What kind of chassid was he?

At 12:30, Jacob heard the garage door slide open as his wife drove the car inside. He heard his children chattering as they entered through the porch. Hastily, he restored the house to its usual state: blinds open and kitchen curtains pushed aside.

From force of habit, Jacob checked the backyard again. To his dismay, he saw someone climbing over his fence into the neighboring yard. The climber had his back to Jacob, but there was another man beside him, still standing on the far side of the fence. The blood in Jacob's veins turned to ice.

In the noonday sun, there was no mistaking that face. It was the pale man.

14

Jerusalem — 5694 / 1934

A nurse in white came into the room, straightened the pillow under Chatzkel's head, and gave Toivy a sad smile.

"Abba, what did you want to tell me?" Toivy asked, when the nurse had left.

Chatzkel closed his eyes. His voice was very weak, almost inaudible, but his first words struck his daughter like a thunderbolt.

He spoke to her for a number of minutes, pausing to cough and then to cough again. The girl's face had turned pale as death. She had been prepared for anything but a story like this.

Gradually, Chatzkel's voice faded. At last, he fell silent in mid-sentence. It was unclear whether he had lost the strength to move his lips, had decided that the rest wasn't that important, or had sunk into unconsciousness. He lay motionless, each shuddering breath whistling softly through his lips. Toivy's helpless gaze traveled from her father's face to the basket of food ... back to her father ... and back again to the basket.

What was she to do? She must obey her father — but she couldn't! She was simple incapable of performing such a task.

She burst into bitter tears. *Oy, Abba, what have you done?* she wailed silently. The food basket lay at her feet, emitting a tantalizing aroma. If only it would disappear. If only her father had not given her this terrible task. If only she could turn back the wheel of time ....

The bout of weeping cleared her mind. Toivy faced the facts: There was no way out. Tears were useless. She must get up and act. As the eldest daughter, the responsibility was hers. Her father had chosen to share his secret with her. He was counting on her. She would not let him down.

She dried her eyes and stood up. With a steady hand she straightened her father's blanket, replaced the damp cloth on his forehead, and turned to go. She passed through the hospital gates and, basket in hand, circled behind Meah Shearim in the direction of the Jaffa Gate.

She knew this route well, having gone often to the Old City with her mother and brother. She soon came to an intersection near an old fig tree. Here — on her father's instructions — she turned right and began climbing a dirt path that led toward the village.

Almost immediately, several dogs raced up to her, barking madly. Toivy nearly passed out from fright. An old Arab woman, picking vegetables in the field, lifted her head and spat in her direction, muttering imprecations. Toivy quickened her step.

Ten minutes later, her eyes beheld a fearsome and imposing building, the focus of many stories heard throughout her childhood.

It crouched on its stony hill like a creature of old, supported by enormous boulders and surrounded by a turret-topped wall. Toivy did not allow her fears to overwhelm her. She packed them tightly into a ball, as it were, and crammed them into a distant corner of her mind. Then, without pause or hesitation, she strode briskly forward.

Within minutes, she reached the small gate set into the formidable wall. From this point on, there was no turning back.

Two days later, Chatzkel Lederman died without ever returning home and was buried on the Mount of Olives.

He left his widow, the engaged Toivy whose joy had turned to bereavement, and six other young orphans. During the week of mourning, the house hummed with comforters. The Lederman family came, accompanied by an impressive array of in-laws and cousins and nephews.

But the world did not cease turning. The *shivah* ended, as did the *shloshim,* and life went on as usual. Chaikeh — now referred to by one and all as "Chaikeh *der almanah* (Chaikeh the widow)" — reopened the vinegar shop and sent her sons back to *cheder* and yeshivah. Toivy resumed her preparations for the wedding.

It would be a dolorous affair, with no father to escort the *kallah* to the *chuppah*, the mother of the bride newly widowed, and her brothers and sisters orphaned. Still — it would be a wedding.

The first one to notice the approaching storm was Chaikeh *der almanah*. Shimshon *der shadchan* passed her vinegar shop several times, and peeked inside. When he saw her, he bowed his head. It was said that R' Shimshon knew everything that happened in Jerusalem even before those who were actually involved. His sniffing around got on Chaikeh's nerves.

On her return home, she noticed two women, her neighbors, avert their faces and quickly disappear into their homes. They had looked at her the way one looks at the victim of a tragedy. Chaikeh felt suddenly cold. Her earlier uneasiness turned into genuine apprehension. Something bad had happened. Everyone knew, but nobody wanted to be the one to tell her.

Fear gripped the widow as she opened the door of her house and walked in. To her surprise, all was quiet. The younger children were in bed and the older ones were eating their evening meal. Her Toivy, like a diligent young housewife, had completed all her chores and had gone to see Rebbetzin Margolis, to learn how to establish a true Jewish home.

Chaikeh's bad feeling eased slightly. She must have been imagining things. That sort of thing had been happening more frequently since Chatzkel died. All was in order at home. She would fix herself a cup of tea and calm down.

Then came the sound of running footsteps, hard breathing, and a rapid knocking at the door. Before Chaikeh could move, the door burst open and her sister, Sara Perel, charged in.

"Why?" she cried, raising her hands heavenward as she threw the question into the air. "Why did she do it? Where is she? Where's Toivy?"

Toivy's aunt began to move from room to room, her movements furious and her expression grim. Chaikeh was seized with panic. "What happened?" she asked shakily.

Sara Perel stopped suddenly. She whirled around, incredulous. "You don't know?"

"Know *what*?" Chaikeh screamed.

Her sister's eyes filled with compassion. "They want to break the shidduch," she said gently. "Haven't you heard?"

"Who?" Chaikeh cried. "Who wants to break the shidduch?"

"The *mechutanim*. The Levingers. Toivy's *chasan*."

"But — why? Why?" Covering her face with her hands, Chaikeh broke into a wail. "What have we done to them?"

Sara Perel lowered her eyes and struggled with her own tears. So many misfortunes were collapsing onto her poor sister all at once. First her husband fell ill and died, and now her daughter had gone out of her mind.

"She went to the Christian mission," Sara Perel said quietly. "People said they saw her returning from the monastery near the Old City."

Astonishment dried Chaikeh's tears. "The Christian mission? What was she doing there?"

"That's what all of Yerushalayim wants to know."

"All of Yerushalayim." Chaikeh's face went back into her hands. "They all know .... "

"And they won't stop talking about it," her sister whispered.

"But *you* know it's not true," Chaikeh burst out. "You know that Toivy is a good girl — a girl filled with *yiras Shamayim*, a girl who *davens* every day!"

Sara Perel spread her hands helplessly. What difference did it make what she knew, if the entire city was convinced that the mission had been supporting the Lederman family since Chatzkel's death? What did it matter what she thought, if everyone else was saying that Toivy planned to transfer her young brothers to the mission school?

Who knew for sure? she thought sadly. *There was no smoke without fire. Maybe the Church had dug its claws into Toivy.* Such things had happened before. Who could ever forget the terrible episode of the family from Nachlat Shivah, on whom the Russian missionary Sergei Nikolev had showered money and gifts, and who had ended by converting, one and all?

And who didn't remember the young woman, Rochel Turkowitz, who had come here with her husband from Poland, became widowed shortly afterward, and was left with two hungry orphans? Today, with the mission providing money and food, both children were attending the Christian school.

Or the young boy from the Even Yisrael neighborhood who loved to read secular books, and became friendly with a priest he had met in the library, until he moved slowly away from his faith? He had been given a job in the church library and was today a member of the Christian community ….

The two sisters sat in mournful silence for a long time. The lamp burned out and darkness enveloped the room, but neither woman stood up to add kerosene and light it again.

It was nearing ten o'clock when hurried footsteps were heard outside. The door opened and Toivy walked in, smiling. But the smile quickly faded as she took in the sight of her mother and aunt sitting in the darkness, watching her.

"Has something happened?" she asked in alarm.

"Where have you been?" Chaikeh demanded, standing up.

"N-nowhere," Toivy said in confusion. "I went to Rebbetzin Margolis."

"Not true!" Chaikeh screamed. "Tell me the truth: Where are you coming from? The mission? The Church? What are you looking for there?"

Toivy went pale as a sheet. "I have not become a Christian. You have nothing to worry about," she said in a trembling voice.

"It doesn't matter what *I* think," Chaikeh said, slumping back into her chair. "The question is what the *mechutanim* think. What your precious *chasan* thinks."

Toivy went rigid with shock. "They know?"

"They know. They know! They want to cancel the wedding."

The shriek that emerged from the *kallah's* mouth shattered the stillness. She ran into her room, where she collapsed on the bed, hid her face in the pillow, and let out a great wail.

Houston, Texas — Iyar 5766 / May 2006

All of Jacob's fears came rushing back at once — redoubled.

The pitiless killer had found him, and it had happened at the worst possible moment: when his wife and children were home. It had apparently taken him the past two-and-a-half hours to discover where Jacob lived. But here he was, determined to eliminate anyone and everyone who knew about Juarez. Jorge Diaz had paid the price this morning. It was Jacob's turn now.

Jacob was mistaken. It had taken the agent in the beat-up Dodge and Walter Child no more than a few minutes to learn his name and address. Even before the ambulance bore the Mexican's body away to the city's forensic morgue, the pale man had phoned his boss to report that the Jew's name was Dr. Jacob Stern, and that he was an expert in botanics and genetics who served as director of the Department of Agriculture's poison-supervision division. On the agent's screen were also Jacob's phone number as well as that of his wife; their passport, driver's license, and credit-card numbers; the names of their children; and every other detail that existed in any database in the United States.

"He must have headed for home," the agent said. "I'll follow him there."

"No," Child said. "Don't go."

"Why not?"

"He was Lenny Brown's direct superior. Imagine what would happen if both of them were killed within three days of each other."

"What would happen?"

"Simple. The FBI would take the investigation into its own hands and begin sniffing around everywhere. That would be extremely dangerous for us."

"But we can't let him live," the agent protested.

"Put a tail on him. That should be enough," Child said. "He's already terrified. He won't talk to anyone."

"It's a mistake to leave him alive," the agent insisted.

The assistant director was enraged. "Don't talk to *me* about mistakes! It was a mistake to leave anyone alive in that hotel in Mexico City. It was a mistake to kill the Mexican only after he'd managed to talk to the Jew. So far, *you're* the one who's made all the mistakes."

"You're the boss." The pale man was angry but resigned.

"That's right. I am the boss," Child said in a hard voice. "And you will do exactly as you're told."

"Okay."

"You are to stick to him until you receive new orders. I want taps on all his phones: at work, at home, his cell — everything. Is that clear?"

"Perfectly clear."

"Someone will be in touch with you soon, with instructions." Child hung up, frowning deeply. He felt as if he were regressing to the old days, when he had been a lowly agent covering the Baltimore area. He shouldn't have to deal with the nitty-gritty at this stage. But what choice did he have? In an ordinary operation, he would have ordered dozens of agents to cover the museum. He would have had the use of sensitive microphones and sophisticated cameras. Every CIA lab would have been open to him.

Instead, with everything taking place outside official channels, all he had was one field agent who hadn't risen very high in the agency ranks. Even the wiretapping equipment would have to be borrowed from an old friend who owed him a favor.

The battered Dodge drove slowly through a decrepit industrial area, looking for the sign that indicated that he had reached his destination. There it was: a flashing neon sign in the shape of an electric bulb.

The store was large and messy. Suspended from pegboards on the walls and heaped in baskets was an assortment of electronic components: bulbs, fuses, transformers, and anything else that an electronics-lover's heart might desire. A few customers were picking through the merchandise and discussing its merits between themselves. Behind the counter stood a very corpulent, red-faced man wearing a baseball cap from which a profusion of gray-white hair stuck out on all sides.

"Hey," he called to the agent standing by the door. "Are you Walter's guy?"

The agent nodded and approached the counter. The storekeeper, with a grunt, picked up a large bag and gave it to him. He motioned for one of his employees to join them.

"Walter's a good kid," the storekeeper said with a wink. "Tell him I said 'hi.' "

It was 11:30 a.m. when the CIA agent and the electronics-store employee reached the street behind the Stern home. The employee slipped into the yard and began installing sophisticated wiretapping equipment. Within the hour, all the machinery was in place.

The pale man, in his car, could now hear everything that was happening inside the house. If there was a phone call, whether on the house line or a cell phone, he'd be able to listen in on that, too. Every now and then, the agent looked around uneasily. Surveillance in broad daylight was not ideal, but so far luck had smiled on them.

The job was completed by 12:30. The electronics worker collected his tools, checked to make sure there was no trace of his presence, and retreated cautiously toward the adjoining yard. As he tried to climb the fence with his bag of equipment, the agent came to give him a hand. The agent glanced at the kitchen window at the exact moment when the curtain was unexpectedly moved aside. He was eye to eye with Jacob Stern. And, judging by the terror in his eyes, Stern had definitely recognized *him*.

The pale man didn't waste a second. Tugging urgently at the other man's arm, he raced back to his car. They tumbled inside. He started his engine, and the Dodge sped away with a screech of its tires.

What a stupid idea, he fumed, *leaving the Jew alive! I ought to just kill him and be done with it.*

Jerusalem — 5694 / 1934

Toivy's storm of weeping did not last long. She did shed some more tears when her mother and her aunt came into the room and tried to talk to her, but this was merely a ruse to get them out of the room. Recent events had matured her beyond her years, and taught her to set aside her emotions. This was no time for weeping. She had to make decisions that no girl her age should have to make.

Her aunt gave up and went home. Chaikeh did not go to bed. She sat at the table and poured tears like rain onto her *Tehillim*. Now and then she would doze off; then, starting up with a jerk, she resumed her crying and praying. Once, as she awoke, she saw Toivy slip out the front door, dressed in a warm coat and scarf.

"Where … ?" Chaikeh mumbled. She went to the door and peered out, but her daughter had hurried down the stairs and out of sight.

Throwing a thin blanket around her shoulders, Chaikeh hurried after her. Toivy was almost running across the expanse of the *shuk*. Where was the child going in the middle of the night? The gates of Meah Shearim were closed and the streets beyond the neighborhood were desolate. Did the accursed missionaries who had bewitched her daughter live *inside* the neighborhood? Did those who snared good Jewish girls in their trap live right here in Meah Shearim?

While Chaikeh entertained this horrific possibility, Toivy managed to disappear. With a heavy sigh torn from her heart, Chaikeh returned home in tears. What else could she do? If she continued standing there in the cold, she was liable to contract pneumonia, like her husband, of blessed memory.

Oy, Chatzkel, do you see what your daughter is doing? From your place up above, do you know how low she's fallen? Please, Chatzkel, go before the Throne of Glory and plead for your daughter's soul! Please, Chatzkel, beg for mercy for Toivy bas Chaikeh, that she should do a full teshuvah and never abandon her faith — if she has not taken that terrible step already ....

The hour was very advanced when the knocking began on the peeling wooden door. The sound was hesitant but urgent. At first, no one responded. When the knocking grew louder and more insistent, it finally elicited the sound of weary legs dragging themselves to the door.

"*Ver iz dorten* (Who's there)?" called Rebbetzin Margolis.

There was no reply from the other side of the door — just the gasping of a sobbing girl. The rebbetzin lifted the metal latch and opened the door. "Who's there, so late at night?" Then, catching sight of her anguished visitor's crumpled face, she softened. "Toivy! Toiveleh, what happened?" She ushered the girl quickly inside and seated her in a chair by the oven.

Only now, as she sat near the fire gazing at the rebbetzin's lined face and wise eyes, did Toivy abandon herself to the full force of her tears. The daunting secret that her father had handed her before his death threatened to be exposed to the world — and would destroy her life. The appalling mistake made a decade earlier was poised to turn her own future into a pile of rubble ....

Long minutes passed before her sobs abated enough to allow her to speak. After a few sentences, the rebbetzin realized that the situation was too complex for her to handle on her own. She went into the next room and spoke briefly with her husband, Rav Margolis. She returned at once.

"Come, Toivy," she said gently. "The rav wants to hear what you have to say."

Toivy gave her a doubtful look. The rebbetzin said, "The rav promises that he will not tell this to anyone without your permission."

She would remain in the room, as her husband always asked her to do when speaking to women. She, too, promised to keep Toivy's secret forever.

Rav Margolis sat at a table, one hand supporting his high forehead as he learned from the large *sefer* open in front of him. Toivy stood at the table's edge, nervous and frightened, but comforted by the rebbetzin's supportive presence. Here, she felt, was a place where she might unburden herself of the terrible weight that rested on her heart. Here were two loyal people who could safely share her secret and offer wise counsel.

"It all started two days before my father, *zichrono livrachah*, was *niftar*," she began her story. She spoke in a whisper, eyes downcast. "His condition had grown worse, and he sensed that he was about to leave this world. He asked me to sit down beside him and told me that he wished to reveal a great secret that no one else knows. It began, he said, in the terrible winter of 5684 — ten years ago. There was a big snowfall, and ice covered the streets. And that was the night it was my mother's time to give birth .... "

Houston, Texas — Iyar 5766 / May 2006

Irritably, Walter Child picked up the phone. It was his agent in Houston again, and he sounded agitated.

"There's been a glitch," the agent gasped. He had dropped his accomplice a few blocks away and given him fifty dollars to catch a cab back to work.

The assistant director fought hard to contain his annoyance. "You mean, with the number that was not eliminated?"

"That's right. We had finished the job, but as we were leaving, the subject glanced out the window."

"Where are you now?"

"On the road. I made tracks, fast."

"Is the wiretap working?"

"Yes. I can pick up everything said in the house. He's nervous and scared."

The agent paused and listened. "I was recognized," he reported. "He told his wife that the guy who killed Lenny Brown was in their backyard. Just a second ...." He listened a few seconds longer. "He told her to head to the garage with the kids."

"He's planning to flee," Child said angrily.

"There's a call from the house right now," the agent reported, eyes on his computer screen. "To a cell phone."

"Whose?"

"I'm checking ...."

The members of the Stern family in California had been seated around the table, the atmosphere relaxed and pleasant. They had just finished lunch. The children told their mother that everything had been delicious, Moishy went to get the *bentchers*, and they all recited the *Birkas HaMazon* in unison.

A cell phone in the next room rang. David continued peacefully *bentching*. That's what voice mail was for, right?

After a few rings, the device fell silent. "Rivky, bring Daddy his phone," David's wife said.

The seven-year-old jumped up and went into her father's office. "It's Uncle Jacob," she said, reading the screen.

David continued *bentching*. He would get back to Jacob later.

"Who is he calling?" Walter Child asked. "Quickly!"

"It's taking a few seconds .... Hold on .... Here it is. He's trying to call David Stern, in Los Angeles. A relative, probably. His father or brother."

Child calculated rapidly. "He's planning to run," he said. "He intends to let someone know that there's a problem. And he's not going to take his cell phone with him so that we won't be able to trace him."

"I told you I should have knocked him off."

The assistant director did not respond.

"I could finish the job now," the agent offered. "I can eliminate the whole family."

Child maintained his silence.

"He's trying to call again," the agent reported.

"Can you disconnect the call?" Child asked suddenly.

"Sure." The pale man in Houston sounded surprised. "But why?"

Disconnecting calls, as any fledgling technician knows, is simple enough. But one did not usually cut off calls that one wanted to listen to. It made no sense. Such a move would only arouse suspicion and cause the target to behave more circumspectly than before.

"Disconnect the call to Los Angeles," ordered Child. "And give me the suspect's number. I want to talk to him."

David did not answer on the second try, either. Discouraged and at a loss, Jacob replaced the receiver. He wanted to *talk* to his brother — not leave him messages. Why wasn't David answering his cell phone? Maybe he should try David's home number. He didn't know it by heart. Maybe it was listed in his cell phone's memory. In his confusion, he didn't even remember the area code for Los Angeles. Maybe he should just leave the house and try calling again later from a public phone.

I'll try one more time, Jacob decided. But before he could act on this decision, the phone rang.

At last! He snatched up the receiver. "David? Where are you?"

It wasn't David. It was a man with a deep, authoritative voice. "Good afternoon, Mr. Stern."

"Who is this?" Jacob demanded, as his heart began to dance crazily in his chest.

"A friend," said the stranger.

Jerusalem — 5684 / 1924

With great difficulty, Chatzkel Lederman managed to find a wagon driver to take his wife to the hospital. The distance was not great, but on such a snowy night the trip took quite some time. More than once, the wagon slipped backward, and Chatzkel and the driver were forced to get out and help the horse by pushing at the back of the vehicle.

On their arrival at the hospital, it seemed at first to be deserted. A flurry of urgent knocking finally elicited a compassionate nurse with a lantern in her hand. The building was intensely cold. They had run out of coal for heating; only the maternity ward had a kerosene stove that gave out a bit of heat.

Chatzkel waited in the anteroom for good news, but for a long time nobody came to wish him "mazel tov." Instead, he became aware of a great deal of bustle behind the closed door. He heard urgent voices and hurried footsteps.

Chatzkel was overwhelmed with anxiety. What was happening? Was everything all right? He began pacing nervously to and fro, picturing the worst-case scenarios. The baby had been born alive, he knew, because he'd heard the distant wail. *So maybe Chaikeh ...? Oy, Ribono shel Olam,* bring us salvation!

After an eternity, the midwife emerged from the room, twisting her fingers helplessly. It was hard for her to find the words. She had never seen anything like this .... It was no baby, but a grotesque creature ... Defective .... It might not be a good idea for Mr. Lederman to see him. In any case, the doctor had said that the infant was going to die within minutes.

The father insisted on seeing his child. He walked into the room — and screamed.

"What can I tell you?" Chatzkel told a stunned Toivy on his deathbed, ten years later. "He was my son, my flesh and blood, but there are no words to describe what he looked like. Terrible. Simply horrible. A monstrosity in the form of a human being."

After a few seconds, Chatzkel sent a suffering glance at the midwife. She nodded in understanding and compassion. "He won't survive the night," she said quietly. "To preserve your wife's sanity, simply tell her that the baby died."

Chatzkel would, in later months and years, soundly berate himself for heeding this advice. Sorrowfully, he told his wife that the child had died just moments after birth. Hashem gives, and Hashem takes away, may the Name of Hashem be blessed .... The important thing now was for her to regain her strength. There were other children at home who needed a strong, healthy mother.

Chaikeh cried all night. As he tried to comfort her, Chatzkel was busy planning: Tomorrow morning he would summon the *Chevrah Kaddisha* to bury the baby, and the matter would be ended.

In the morning, however, the midwife greeted him in confusion. "Did you tell her that the baby died?" she asked. Against all expectations, the unfortunate infant had lived through the night. The midwife had hidden him in a side room and had been checking hourly on his progress. Though weak and drowsy, barely clinging to life, his breathing was stable. Still, the doctor assured her, the baby would not last past noon.

Three days later, the child was still living, to the astonishment of both the doctor and the midwife. Chatzkel was beside himself. He walked the hospital's corridors like a madman, gnawed by remorse and guilt for wishing his son dead. His wife had resigned herself to the tragedy. Despite the snow, her sister, Sara Perel, who had arrived to stay devotedly at her side, urged her to seek consolation and strength. *HaKadosh Baruch Hu* would send her other, healthy children. Everyone believed that the baby was dead and buried. Only Chatzkel carried the awful weight of the truth in his heart.

The great freeze ended. Huge mounds of snow were pushed to the sides of the roads and the city began slowly to return to normal. The bereaved mother was due to return home — and the newborn baby still showed no signs of releasing his hold on life. The only one who agreed to tend to the grotesque infant was the midwife, who felt guilty over her part in the deception. It was she who came to Chatzkel with a solution to the problem.

There was a place, she said, that was prepared to accept the baby; a place where he could end his short, sad life. A place where good angels did their work, without asking for any recompense.

Chatzkel, caught in the pincers of a terrible dilemma, was glad to hear it. In a dim way, at the edge of his consciousness, he was aware of the nature of that place, and of who those devoted caretakers were. But he didn't ask. Just let the child be taken away. Then Chatzkel would deal with whatever came next.

"You must have guessed by now that that poor baby — the little brother that you've never seen — did not die," Chatzkel told his daughter as he lay burning with fever in his hospital bed a decade later. "He went on living, for months, and then years. In fact, he is still alive today. He is severely retarded, his face is deformed, and he looks frightening. The monks — for I am sure you realize, my dear Toivy, that the institution where your brother lives is a Christian monastery — agreed to keep him without pay. They insisted on just one thing: that I provide him with food. He has grown quickly and requires large quantities of sustenance daily.

"I did not argue with this demand, even though I knew that they did not make it of everyone. Perhaps I am a fool, but I thought that, although he is not of sound mind and therefore not obligated in the mitzvos, at least he would not eat forbidden foods. It was the least I could do for him. He is a Jewish *neshamah*, I thought, though his body is flawed and his mind defective. It is my fault that he has spent his miserable life among crosses and statues, surrounded by Christian prayers all day long. Once, one of the nuns innocently told me that he'd made a little progress: He knew how to make the sign of the cross .... Those words were like a white-hot knife in my heart. Only Hashem Above, before Whom I will soon be standing to pay for my wicked deeds, knows how much I have suffered, how much I have regretted, how many tears I have shed. But I cannot undo what was done. Your mother has accepted her baby's death. She has found comfort in the children that were born to her later: Moishele, Yenty, and Esther Malka.

"I'd always worked hard to support the family, and now there was another child, a secret child, whom I was obligated to feed. I never thought I'd have to ask you to take over for me and hide your brother's existence from your mother. She would not be able to bear it: neither the shame, nor the suffering, nor the knowledge that she gave birth to such a deformed creature. But I'm afraid I have no choice. My days are numbered.

"You, my oldest daughter, must take my place. That is the only way I can die in peace, knowing that I've done at least one good thing: I kept this awful knowledge from your mother. You are the only one who can continue bearing this burden."

Total silence reigned in Rav Margolis's room.

"So you started going to the monastery?" the rebbetzin asked quietly.

Toivy nodded, pressing her lips tightly together to prevent herself from succumbing to tears again.

The first time had been the hardest, Toivy told the rav and rebbetzin. All the way from the hospital to the monastery, her heart had pounded like a drum. In her terror, her legs had nearly given way beneath her. How was it possible that she, a modest Jewish girl who had always moved aside when passing a priest or nun, could now be walking straight into the lion's den?

As she knocked on the iron gate, she'd murmured chapters of *Tehillim* from memory. A small peephole opened in the gate, and an elderly nun looked out. Her face was surrounded by a black wimple. Upon catching sight of Toivy, a look of astonishment had crossed her face — quickly changing to a honeyed smile. "What can I do for you?" the nun inquired.

"I'd l-like to speak to Sister Mary," Toivy had answered, without meeting her eye.

"Just a moment." The elderly nun disappeared, to be replaced some minutes later by a younger one.

"I'm Chatzkel Lederman's daughter," Toivy had said, as the nun's eyes widened in surprise. "He's ill, and ... he asked me to bring the food in his place. His condition is very serious ... I don't know if he'll be able to come any time soon."

The nun took the basket from her and then, with a gracious gesture, invited her inside.

"No, no — I can't come in," Toivy exclaimed. Fishing in her pocket, she produced the coin as her father had told her to.

She left the monastery with tears blurring her vision.

On her return to the hospital, she was told that her father had lost consciousness. Two days later, he passed away. No one knew of the secret he had bequeathed to his eldest daughter before he died.

"And since then, you've gone there every week?" Rav Margolis asked. Toivy nodded, stifling a sob. For a period of time, she had managed to keep her visits a secret. She had stolen out at night, rigid with fear as the wolves howled in the wadi. More than once she had passed Arabs who glared at her with hatred. All the way to the monastery she would murmur *Tehillim* and repeat to herself, "Those who are messengers to do a mitzvah are not harmed." But someone had seen her.

Perhaps it was the day Sister Mary had said that she had to go down to the city, and would accompany her. They had walked a short distance together before Toivy managed to get away by pretending to stumble over a rock and saying that she had to rest a little. The nun had offered to stay with her, but Toivy sent her on her way. Perhaps someone had seen them in the distance on that occasion; or it may have happened a different time. The important thing was that the news had made its way to the *mechutanim* and now they now wanted — understandably — to break the shidduch.

Rav Margolis stood up and put on his coat. "I'm going to talk to them," he said.

"But — it's so late!" the rebbetzin protested. It was also cold and rainy outside. "Can't the rav go in the morning?"

"No. This matter can brook no delay."

"I'm sorry, rebbetzin," Toivy said in an urgent undertone. "But I can't let the rav go to them!"

Both the rav and the rebbetzin stared at her in disbelief. "Are you prepared to give up the shidduch?" the rebbetzin demanded. "The rav is willing to explain to the Levingers that they've made a mistake."

Toivy lowered her moisture-filled eyes, but her voice was steady. "If the story comes out," she said, "my father's memory will be blemished and my mother will never be able to withstand the shame. If they want to break the shidduch — let them."

"I must speak to them," Rav Margolis insisted, as though Toivy hadn't spoken. "One may not remain silent in the face of such a wrong." He picked up his stick and started for the door.

Toivy seized the rebbetzin's hand pleadingly. "The rav promised that no one would know," she cried. "The rav promised not to tell!"

Rav Margolis halted in the middle of the room and exchanged a quick glance with his wife. Then he turned to Toivy and asked gently, "Do you know what this means? Not only will they cancel the match — but the reason will soon become known everywhere. Who will want to marry a girl who appears to have left the faith?"

Toivy breathed hard, once again on the verge of tears. "I don't care," she said finally. "I will not tarnish my father's memory."

"Do you think this is what your father would have wanted?"

"*HaKadosh Baruch Hu* is my Father now," Toivy whispered. "He will take care of me. He is the Father of all orphans. He will find me a shidduch. I will not walk to the *chuppah* on my father's blood."

Tears of emotion gathered in both the rav's and the rebbetzin's eyes. With a sigh, the rav returned to his seat. He would not break his promise. He would not give away Toivy's secret without her permission.

However, he did have a suggestion to make. He would go to the *chasan's* family and assure them that the girl was a fine, pious Jewess. Once she was married, of course, she would have to reveal the secret to her husband. Until then, the rav would undertake to hire someone to bring food to the poor child instead of Toivy, and all would be well.

Toivy agreed to his proposal, and went home with a feeling of relief.

The next morning, Rav Margolis sent word to the Levingers that he wished to speak with them. On his arrival, he was greeted by a noisy contingent made up of the entire family.

"Yesterday," he began, after being respectfully welcomed and seated at the head of the table, "I spent a long time speaking with your *kallah* .... "

"*Former kallah*, you mean," a daughter muttered.

Ignoring her, the rav continued. "And I want to tell you this: I have not met a girl with such *yiras Shamayim* and modesty in a long time. I can promise you faithfully that she has not been drawn into Christianity; on the contrary, she is a performer of *chesed* on a par with Rivkah Imeinu, a"h."

R' Margolis was a noble figure, with a long white beard, penetrating eyes, and deeply lined forehead. His words made an impression on R' Kalman, the *chasan's* father. He stared down at the tabletop, digesting the rav's words and — mostly — awaiting his wife's reaction.

Mrs. Levinger asked the inevitable question. "So what was the big *tzaddekes* doing at the mission?"

R' Margolis sighed sadly. "She told me the reason after I promised her not to tell anyone. A strange request, perhaps, but you can depend on me. Believe me, I would not allow your son to marry a girl who had even a trace of apostasy in her."

Mr. Levinger was inclined to agree. If Rav Margolis was prepared to accept full responsibility, and if he guaranteed that everything was all right, that was fine with him.

Then his wife, daughters, and daughters-in-law stepped in. They had a very different opinion.

"We can't let Binyamin marry such a sinner!" one of his sisters screamed. "If she has a good reason for her actions — let her speak up. She shouldn't hide behind rabbanim."

"If you ask me, anyone who is seen coming out of the mission is a Christian until proved otherwise," stated a daughter-in-law who believed herself to be an intellectual.

"Who's going to marry the young couple — a priest?" another sister asked sarcastically.

"The whole city is talking. She's embarrassed all of us," yet another sister declared. "She should be thrown out of the house as fast as possible!"

Rav Margolis quickly saw which way the winds were blowing. His words had fallen on deaf ears. Standing up, he parted with the father and son by begging them to seriously rethink their decision. Toivy Lederman was a fine, good girl — and, apart from this, causing pain to an orphan and a widow was no small matter.

Even as this comment made its mark, a daughter-in-law sniffed. "Orphan? Widow? When we took her, her father was very much alive. Who was talking about an orphan then?"

That afternoon, Rav Margolis was pained to hear that his efforts had not borne fruit. The shidduch was called off, and the women of the Levinger clan spared no ammunition in hurling abuse at the girl who had been slated to be their sister-in-law. Toivy remained in her home — which, according to rumor, had already been fitted with all the symbols of the Christian religion.

Chaikeh did not open her shop. She could not bear the whispers, the speculative eyes, or the regular customers who sidled past the store and did their shopping elsewhere. Her family's fortunes seemed to have turned with startling suddenness. First her husband had died, and now this terrible slander about her daughter.

But *was* it mere slander? Chaikeh lost sleep at night, wondering and suffering. Toivy had refused point-blank to tell her what she'd been doing at the mission. The mother kept asking, but the daughter would not say a word. Though Rav Margolis, in his goodness, had tried telling the Levingers what a good girl Toivy was, Chaikeh didn't know what to think. Why couldn't the girl tell her why she'd gone to the monastery? What could she possibly have to hide from her own mother? Why had she seen fit to tell the rav, and not her?

Meanwhile, Toivy was wasting away before her eyes. The girl spent whole days lying in bed and crying. What would become of her? The stronger the rumors grew, the weaker became any chance of her ever getting married. R' Shimshon *der shadchan* had undoubtedly drawn a thick black line through her name in his little notebook — and through those of her sisters and brothers, too.

Oy, Chatzkel, Chatzkel, do you see what's happening? Why did you have to go? Why did you leave us? If you were alive, you would have been able to do something. I have no strength left. I can't take it any longer. My heart is so full of pain, it's about to explode. Enough!

On Shabbos morning, after days of seclusion at home, Chaikeh pulled Toivy out of bed. She must go to shul and *daven*, or everyone would be certain that she had indeed converted to Christianity.

Chaikeh felt the other women's eyes on her, cutting into her like dagger thrusts. She sensed them all whispering about her and Toivy. Her suffering increased from moment to moment. More than anything, she longed for the release of tears — but she would not cry in front of them. She must be strong. All she could do was sit in her corner, bend her head over her *siddur*, and hope that the *davening* would pass quickly.

But the *ba'al koreh* seemed to feel he had all the time in the world. R' Zisha read slowly and with emphasis, as though to provide her with enough time to understand that each verse was directed specifically at *her*.

"If you buy an eved ivri, six years shall pass and on the seventh he goes free ...." But she would never go free. Chatzkel had managed to do it. He had risen to the Next World — while she, brokenhearted, remained behind to suffer.

"If [the girl] is bad in her master's eyes ...." Like Toivy. She had made such a bad impression, wandering about among monasteries and church-es and befriending nuns and priests ....

The Torah reading continued. The Kohen stepped down and the Levi stepped up; then came *shlishi* and *revi'i*. None of the women near her turned to Chaikeh; they treated her as though she were invisible. "Mother of an apostate!" she thought she heard someone whisper from a back bench. Her heart constricted. Another whisper floated her way. It was Toivy's new nickname: Toivy the Nun.

R' Zisha's voice rose. *"Kol almanah v'yasom lo s'anun* (You shall not oppress the widow and orphan)!" *Oy, Chatzkel, Chatzkel, you went away and left me a widow, and our children orphans.*

"If you oppress him and he screams to Me .... " *Oy, oy, oy!* This was the worst oppression of all — to know that the entire city was pointing at her. She sat in the women's section as it rustled with whispers, skewered by scornful glances, and her suffering heart tore to shreds.

Suddenly, everything went black. The pressure in her chest was hor-rible — terrifyingly strong — as though all the pain and anguish had gath-ered together into a single point of unbearable pain. Darkness engulfed her. The *ba'al koreh's* words, *"V'charah api v'haragti eschem becharev* (My wrath shall blaze and I shall kill you by the sword)" became mixed in her fading consciousness with Toivy's heartrending cry: "Mama!"

As though from a distance, she heard someone scream down to the men below for help. Then she sank into a bottomless void, lower and ever lower ... down, down, down.

The funeral procession of Mrs. Chaikeh Lederman, a"h, left Meah Shearim for the Mount of Olives on *Motza'ei Shabbos*. The skies themselves seemed to be weeping tears for the unfortunate widow.

It was late at night by the time the members of the *Chevrah Kaddisha* returned home, after burying her near her husband's grave. Along with them came the hidden tzaddikim, R' Dovid Leib and R' Tzvi Hirsch HaLevi, trailed by the *shamash*, R' Pinchas.

Not a word was spoken all the way back from Har HaZeisim to Meah Shearim.

But R' Pinchas was not easy in his mind over what he had heard on the way there. He had not been meant to overhear it, but in the quiet of the night fragments of sentences had reached his ears. At first, he had not believed what he was hearing. Then, realizing that he had heard all too well, he had broken out in goose bumps.

He knew that R' Dovid Leib had been very distressed over the widow's death and the orphan's suffering. Several times, he had heard him muttering something about a terrible *kitrug* (indictment). But it was the words of R' Tzvi Hirsch Halevi, that had frightened him most of all: "We need *mesirus nefesh*. Only *mesirus nefesh* .... " And then the *meshulach* had repeated several times, "*Korban tzibbur*." A communal offering ....

The two tzaddikim had walked in silence for a time, and then R' Dovid Leib had answered. R' Pinchas had heard snatches of that reply: "The death of tzaddikim is not enough .... It requires the complete sacrifice ... of a simple Jew ... with no pretensions .... That will be ... a true and complete *tikkun*."

Houston, Texas — Iyar 5766 / May 2006

Jacob Stern gripped the receiver with a shaking hand as terror invaded every cell of his being.

"A friend?" he babbled. "What friend?"

"A friend who wants to protect your life — and the lives of your family," the anonymous voice replied.

Jacob's legs refused to bear his weight. He leaned against the wall to prevent himself from collapsing.

"Let's speak openly," the voice said, in a courteous tone that sent chills up Jacob's spine. "I know who you are; I know where you work; I know where you live. A moment ago, you saw one of my men on your fence."

Jacob was on the verge of fainting.

"And you know what? He insists that we have to kill you," the caller continued pleasantly, as though they were discussing putting down a diseased steer. "But I think we may be able to make a deal. What do you say?"

Jacob didn't answer. He couldn't manage a single word.

"Listen, Mr. Stern. I know that you are a good American citizen, a government employee and the head of your division. You have no part in the Mexican conspiracy. Your involvement in this whole affair was purely accidental. All you have to do is forget everything that's happened these past few days. You have no idea what happened in Juarez, no one ever threatened you, you never met a Mexican in front of the museum. I'll get out of the picture and you'll go on with your life. What do you say?"

"I ... I .... " In his confusion, Jacob was finding it nearly impossible to string together the simplest sentence.

The caller chuckled. "I know what you're thinking. 'Someone's threatening me? I'll go to the police.' Well, let me tell you something, Mr. Stern: I'm above the police. Way above them. But just a second .... It seems to me that there was some sort of shooting near the museum this morning. True, the victim was only an illegal immigrant from across the river. A 'wetback,' as you Texans call them. Mexican trash. The police have apparently already closed the file on him. Who'd be interested in someone like that?

"But what do you think would happen if they received a tip saying that the fingerprint found on that Coke can belongs to a senior employee of the U.S. Department of Agriculture? Specifically, to Dr. Jacob Stern, director of supervision of agricultural toxins?"

Jacob shuddered. How had he ever gotten himself into this mess?

"But we're friends," the caller went on in his convivial way. "We can help one another: You forget about Juarez, and I forget to call the police. Do we understand each other?"

Jacob's wife came in from the garage to see what was delaying her husband. Jacob shushed her with a gesture.

"Just one question," he said into the phone. "Why did you people kill Lenny Brown?"

The caller's voice grew sorrowful. "An unfortunate mistake. I'm going to personally see to it that his family is compensated. But there's no need to reach the point where *your* family will need compensation, too. Is there?"

"N-no."

"Then we have a deal?"

"Yes."

The caller's smile came clearly through the phone. "Nice doing business with you, Mr. Stern."

Jacob hung up, his face white as chalk and his breathing coming with difficulty. Before his wife could ask what had happened, the phone rang again. He snatched it up.

"You were looking for me?" It was his brother, David, calling from his home in Los Angeles.

"No," Jacob lied, shrugging as if to say, *What choice do I have?*

"Someone called me twice from your house."

"I don't know .... Maybe one of the kids pressed the speed-dial."

"Jacob, are you all right?" David asked. "You sound strange."

"Yes, yes. I'm fine. I'm just on my way out .... We'll talk later, okay?"

Jerusalem — 5694 / 1934

Once again, the Lederman children sat *shivah* for a parent.

There was no time for Toivy to feel sorry for herself. She now bore the full burden of responsibility for her seven younger siblings: the six at home, and the seventh at the monastery.

The number of people who came to comfort them that week was significantly fewer than the time before. People were confused; they did not know what to say to these unfortunate double orphans — and especially to their oldest sister, whose conscience was doubtless troubling her terribly. After all, it was because of her that her mother had died in her prime. The Levinger family, which had come out in full force during the week of mourning for Chatzkel Lederman, were understandably absent this time. However, their absence did not prevent them from sharpening their claws on Toivy.

"We *would* have gone to be *menachem avel*," one of the Levinger girls said viciously, "but we don't exactly know the mourning customs of Christians .... "

Rav and Rebbetzin Margolis came every day. The rav sat with Toivy's brothers and his wife with the girls — encouraging, consoling, listening, and doing their best to fill the vacuum that the children's mother had left behind.

On the last day of the week, Rebbetzin Margolis drew Toivy aside and said she had something to tell her that, while it could not precisely be called "happy," was nevertheless likely to lessen Toivy's pain.

Binyamin Levinger, she said — Toivy's former *chasan* — was not the model young man the Ledermans had believed him to be. In fact, on closer scrutiny, it was hard to find a single positive quality that he possessed in any measure. The Levingers were a fine family, but this particular apple had fallen far from the tree.

For fear of speaking *lashon hara*, the rebbetzin refrained from going into detail. All she said that her husband, Rav Margolis, had learned things about Binyamin that would certainly have sufficed as reason enough to break the *shidduch*.

"No one knows why Hashem makes things come about the way they do," the rebbetzin said, stroking Toivy's head, "but this thing ended for the best. You would have learned the bitter truth only after the wedding, when it was too late." And she added her blessing: that *HaKadosh Baruch Hu*, the Father of orphans and the Judge of widows, would soon turn Toivy's agony to happiness and find her a proper match — a husband who would respect her and take joy in her.

Somehow, Toivy was not too surprised. Had her parents really thought that a family like the Levingers would want the daughter of poor vinegar merchants — unless their "merchandise" was flawed?

Still, when word came several weeks later that her erstwhile *chasan* had become engaged to another girl, she could not prevent a pang.

Her name was Devorah Rothstein. Toivy recognized the name. Devorah had once been suggested as a match for Toivy's cousin, Aunt Sara Perel's son, but her aunt wouldn't hear of it. "A girl who lost both her parents and is living with her older sister?" Toivy had heard her aunt say to her mother in the next room. "Not for us."

And what's wrong with an orphan? Toivy thought bitterly. *Am I not one myself?*

Rebbetzin Margolis had spoken with her about forgiveness. Her husband, the rav, said that when a couple breaks an engagement, it is proper for them to forgive each other. This was not obligatory by Jewish law, and there were those who demanded payment in exchange for their forgiveness. But she — a good, G-d-fearing girl — knew the reward for those whose actions went beyond the letter of the law. What nobility of spirit she would demonstrate, if she acceded to the Levingers' request for *mechilah*! What an awesome merit she would accrue up Above, and what *nachas* she would bring to her parents in Gan Eden, if she forgave the Levingers with all her heart for the bad turn they'd done her.

But Toivy wasn't asked to display her nobility. Binyamin Levinger became engaged, and soon afterward married Devorah Rothstein, without either he or any member of his family asking his former *kallah* — alone, rejected, and humiliated — for forgiveness.

It was not long before Devorah Rothstein Levinger realized just whom she had married.

The first clue came during the week of their *sheva berachos*, when he launched into a glowing description of the way things were done in America. Eyes shining, he described an American-style wedding to his new wife. Over there, he said, a wedding feast was not merely a matter of herring and crackers, the way the poor celebrated here. In America, a guest was served a proper meal on a table set with china plates and cloth napkins — just like in the big restaurants that the British officers patronized on King George Street.

In America, the *chasan* and *kallah* came to the hall in a car decorated with ribbons, or in a horse-drawn carriage, and the wedding did not take place on Friday afternoon but on a weeknight, just like high-society fetes that one could read about in books. And the young couple did not live in a hovel with blackened walls and a cracked floor, but in a spacious, whitewashed apartment, in a building with elevators.

Devorah did not feel comfortable with her husband's enthusiasm for the niceties of this world. She had never heard such stories in her parents' home, may their memories be a blessing. Her mother and father had been satisfied with a bit of dry bread dipped in sesame oil, and a little boiled milk. The family had crowded into a single narrow room and no one had complained.

At her sister's house, too, where she had lived since her parents' deaths, poverty was rampant and food scarce, but they all had been happy with their lot. Devorah had to admit that Binyamin's stories were interesting.

The books he brought home from the Zionist library had a certain fascination — but it was all so different from everything she had ever known before.

And Binyamin was so different from her sister's husband. Her brother-in-law was a saintly person who kept a *sefer* propped open in front of him even when he was eating, while Binyamin mumbled the words of the *Birkas HaMazon* rapidly, said his *berachos* in a rush, and was not at all scrupulous in his mitzvah-observance. On Shabbos, he rose late and went to *daven* in one of the *shtieblach* — but even the little time he spent there, Devorah could see from the women's section, was mostly spent in energetic conversation with his friends.

Money, on the other hand, was never lacking. They did not live luxuriously, but Binyamin seemed to have additional and mysterious sources of income. The money certainly did not come from the kollel's *chalukah* (stipend) .... Devorah quickly pushed the thought aside. It was none of her business. Her husband ran the home, and she must be grateful for that. She saw her young friends, girls her own age, painfully scraping their shillings together just to buy food for Shabbos. If she had a little more, she mustn't complain.

But Jerusalem was too small for Binyamin Levinger. Everyone knew him here. Anyone might run into him as he came out of the bookstore near the Hebrew high school, or find him sitting in a coffee house, or emerging from a meeting of one of the Zionist organizations. Jerusalem was no better than a village. In America, he told Devorah, everything was much bigger. Why, the pastures his uncles used for grazing his flocks were larger than all of Jerusalem — maybe even all of Eretz Yisrael! Did she know that it took a full week to drive around the perimeter of his spread?

"If his farm is so big," Devorah asked innocently, "where does he find a *minyan* for *davening*?"

Binyamin hid a smile.

Once, when Binyamin was a child, his uncle had visited them in Eretz Yisrael. He had arrived at the Levinger home in a carriage driven by an Arab hired at the port in Yaffo. Binyamin recalled the visit clearly: It had been a big event in the city. He remembered charity collectors knocking on the door at all hours, and his mother protesting that if Shmiel gave all his money to *tzedakah*, there would be nothing left for his family. Uncle Shmiel's Yiddish had had a strange lilt, making it sound like a foreign language.

"It's a Texas accent," someone said. Binyamin had rolled the word around his tongue, as though it held an enchantment: Texas ... Texas.

His uncle had repeatedly remarked on how small everything was in Jerusalem. He wasn't used to such narrow streets or such low-ceilinged houses. What a smart move he had made, leaving the crowded Holy City for the wide-open spaces of America. Little Binyamin had sat on his uncle's knees and tried on his hat, and his uncle had grinned and said that, one day, he must come to visit him in America, and he would show him the farm and his enormous herd of cattle, the Indians riding around on unbroken horses, and the cowboys roping steer with their lassoes.

"Want to go to America, Devorah?" Binyamin asked his wife.

The idea terrified her. She would never travel abroad. Heaven forbid! Her father had never left Eretz Yisrael; near the end of his life he had not even passed beyond the walls of the Old City. America? What did she lack in Jerusalem? Her family was here, and all her friends and neighbors. Here was where her mother and father were buried.

At the last minute, Binyamin bit back a mocking retort. The little fool needed time to get used to the idea. Slowly, slowly .... A pity about that apostate he had previously been engaged to .... What was her name? Toivy Lederman. *She* would have understood. She had already spoken to nuns and hobnobbed with priests — things that even he lacked the courage to do. It would not have been difficult to persuade *her* to fly off to America.

Los Angeles — Nissan 5766 / April 2006

Professor Barry Majdi, the popular lecturer, stood at the window of his office in the Biology Department of the University of California and looked out at the campus quadrangle. He was happier than he ever remembered being before. The single page that the fax machine had just spit into his hands represented the peak of his achievement. He had worked toward this piece of paper for many years. And now, here it was, in his hands.

He read the lines again and again, and studied the three seals ranged at the bottom of the page. His heart swelled with emotion.

Five minutes earlier, his secretary had taken a call for him and transferred it to his office. "Professor Majdi?" the caller had asked. Barry Majdi had identified the voice immediately. He also knew from where the call had originated.

"This is Brian, from BioSystems, London branch," the man introduced himself, before the professor could say a word. "I am happy to be able to inform you that we've finally received confirmation of your patent. If you have a fax machine handy, I can send you a copy. The document is highly classified and for your eyes only. Please read it immediately and then destroy it. You must be aware of our company's strict policies with regard to privacy and information security."

The professor had given the caller the number of his personal secure fax machine on his desk. He locked the door and stood tensely beside the machine, heart pounding, jaw clenched, and breathing in gasps. The fate of long years of work was about to be decided. The fate of the grand plan in which tens, if not hundreds, of thousands of dollars had been invested.

The moment the page shot out of the machine, he snatched it and scanned it rapidly. What he read at first glance was enough — but he conquered his emotions until he had read it again, more closely this time, from the first word to the last. Only then did he let his happiness explode within him. It couldn't have been better. This was final confirmation from the highest authority. Nothing could stop the program now.

There was no question of shouting with joy, of course. His academic secretary of sober mien sat right next door, and the rest of the floor was filled with the offices of his learned colleagues, lecturers and researchers in the field of biology. An exultant yell would not sit well in this restrained and elegant atmosphere. And he certainly would not have been able to explain the reason for his jubilation.

It was terrible, not having a soul with whom to share his feelings. The professor wanted to celebrate, to break into dance, to call someone and shout out the wonderful news. But all that was impossible. He could only grip the paper and read it over and over. And then over again ....

He stood near the door reading the fax for the seventh or eighth time, rejoicing over every word and committing each line to memory. He had no need of warnings from "Brian of BioSystems." He was well aware that the page must be destroyed at once. Such a thing must not remain lying about, not in such turbulent times. If someone knew that Professor Barry Majdi, the well-known biology expert, had a document like this .... If anyone even suspected that the man with the precise haircut, trimmed goatee and tailored blazer, who filled every lecture hall to capacity, held a bombshell of this magnitude in his hands — it would spell not only his own professional demise, but the end of the divine plan as well.

Just before he turned from the window, the professor reread the lines one last time, imprinting them on his mind to review in coming days, and drawing from them the strength he would need. Oh, how much he was going to need it ....

Someone knocked at his office door, and then turned the knob.

"Professor Majdi?" his secretary called in surprise. Almost immediately, the surprise turned to anxiety. "Barry, are you all right?" The professor never locked his door.

"Just a minute," he said, loudly enough to send her scurrying back to her desk.

He inserted the page into the shredder that would turn it into confetti. First to be swallowed up were the three signatures at the bottom of the page. The first two belonged to men who were still alive; the third and most senior of them had died and been buried only that morning. Within seconds, the rest of the page was shredded.

But this was not enough for him. The professor opened the compartment that held the shredded remains, collected them in his hands and went to the men's room. He mustn't take any chances. A janitor, emptying the shredder, might become suspicious. Someone could rearrange the shredded paper and read what it said. Or someone could even make the horrifying discovery that the person who had called the professor was not named Brian, did not work for BioSystems and had not called from London. Someone could learn that the fax did not contain confirmation of a new patent, but something very, very different.

Barry Majdi looked at the shreds of paper in his hand. No, he was not paranoid. These were not empty fears. The shredded paper had to be flushed down the toilet.

Three months after Binyamin and Devorah Levinger's wedding, an envelope reached them from America. Binyamin's uncle had sent a generous gift. As he had done for his other nieces and nephews, he had given them a crisp ten-dollar bill. A fortune.

Mr. Levinger wrote his brother a thank-you letter, but this wasn't enough for Binyamin. He sat down and wrote a long letter of his own, in which he described his wedding, the numerous guests, and his fine bride. He ended by once again expressing his gratitude for the present, and wished his uncle success in all his future endeavors.

Long weeks later — Binyamin had nearly stopped hoping — a reply came. Binyamin's uncle had been very moved by his nephew's letter. Of course he remembered him! How could he ever forget little Binyamin'l, who had played on his lap when his Uncle Shmiel visited the Holy Land. And now that little boy was all grown up and married! Binyamin must continue writing those nice letters to him, telling him what was happening in Jerusalem and how the British were building up the place. When he'd last been there, in the time of the Turkish rule, the city had been in a state of sorry disrepair.

And how was the family? Here in America, it was work, work, work, from morning to night. If only he had had the sense, when he was young, to marry a nice girl and raise a family .... He was enclosing an additional five dollars — an advance gift for the *bris* that would no doubt be taking place in due course. And what if it was a girl, eh? They would definitely name her Shaina, after her grandmother — his mother, and that of Binyamin's father, Kalman. He impatiently awaited the next letter. Regards to the whole family!

Devorah had never seen her new husband so excited. His eyes sparkled as they rested on the letter from America. First he touched the envelope as though he couldn't believe it really existed. Then he passed a finger over the English words on the outside — words that symbolized the first step in realizing his big dream. Finally, he opened the envelope and read the letter aloud, word for word.

He sat right down to pen a reply. He thanked his uncle profusely for the present — though, unfortunately, despite the months that had passed since the wedding, they were not yet expecting a baby .... All was the same in the city, except that Her Majesty's exalted representative, Sir Arthur Grenfell Wauchope, had paid a visit to Meah Shearim and been received with great honor. The Jews said that he was a righteous gentile, though the Arabs, naturally, didn't like him much .... Yesterday, a British soldier had gone mad and begun shooting over the Old City wall toward the wagons and automobiles coming from Yaffo .... Three immigrant families from Austria had moved into the neighborhood, and were in temporary *"Hachnassas Orchim"* quarters until housing could be found for them .... The Jerusalemites laughed at them, but they insisted that Eretz Yisrael, for all its bloodthirsty Arabs, was still safer for Jews than civilized Europe. What did his uncle think of that fellow, Adolf Hitler, who had risen to power in Germany? Had they heard of him over there in America?

After that, letters between uncle and nephew flowed back and forth. Sometimes months could elapse between letters; at other times, the tempo increased, and the letters came more frequently. For Binyamin, locked away inside the walls of Jerusalem, his uncle's letters were like a window on the world. For his uncle, they were a walk down memory lane to the fine and ancient world that he had left behind: Jerusalem, his family, *Yiddishkeit*.

Years ago, when he had immigrated to Eretz Yisrael from Poland together with his brother, Kalman, he was Shmuel. Shmuel Levinger. Their father spent his days and nights toiling over the Torah and in service to his Creator, just as he had done back in Warsaw. Kalman, Binyamin's father, followed in his footsteps. But young Shmuel needed only two years to make up his mind: He wanted a different kind of life.

Jerusalem was a poor city, where children walked around barefoot and swollen with hunger. A city where Turkish officers, rendered even crueler by poverty, ripped young boys from their mothers' arms and sent them to fight a war that was not theirs. Against his father's objections, Shmuel departed on a tour of Europe, via Turkey, Greece, and Italy. He did any sort of work, saving his money for fare to cross the Atlantic and reach a new continent — a place where the possibilities were unlimited. A place where one worked hard seven days a week, fifty-two weeks a year, but was rewarded by a pot of gold at the end of it all.

When he finally realized his dream and landed on American shores, Shmuel Levinger continued as full as energy as before. He did any and all kinds of work: selling newspapers and matches on the streets of New York City, toiling nights in a clothing factory along with dozens of other immigrants, working as a trainman. And when he could not find a regular job, he joined the city's criminal underworld and sold stolen goods. Only on Sundays, after carefully counting up the week's earnings, did he permit himself any relaxation. He would visit one of the taverns in Brooklyn, to refresh himself with a meal and several whiskeys, and weave his dreams of quick riches with two friends — red-cheeked Texas Tom, whose wallet never seemed to empty, and Sean the Irishman, with his thatch of sandy hair and a stomach that seemed capable of holding enormous quantities of beer.

It was Tom who, the worse for drink one day, provided Shmuel Levinger with the opportunity that was to change his life forever.

Tom's father owned a huge cattle ranch in Texas. Now that he was aging, the father wanted Tom to come home and take over the family business. A grown man of thirty, his father wrote repeatedly, should not be wasting money on whiskey in New York when the herd needed him.

Tom, however, was perfectly satisfied with the present arrangement. He very much enjoyed living in New York on the allowance his parents provided. He had spent his entire childhood and youth in the Southwest, and had no intention of going back.

To free himself of his obligation to his family, Tom decided, all he had to do was find a fine young man or two with good heads on their shoulders — strong fellows who could ride a horse and rope a bucking steer with a lariat. Brave ones, who would not hesitate to shoot a trespassing Indian or Mexican out to steal his cattle. The boys would earn a good paycheck from his father, learn a profitable trade, and build themselves a nice financial future. He — Tom concluded, with the aid of another bottle — did not intend to bury himself in Texas, where there were more cows than people.

To his two friends, it all sounded like quite an adventure. Within days, they embarked on the long journey across America. Only one of them reached Texas. Sean managed to get himself killed in a drunken brawl at a roadside bar somewhere between Mississippi and Louisiana. A hotheaded Southerner did not give Sean a chance to explain just what he'd meant by the term, "redneck," but put a bullet in him for all the "foreigners" he believed were contaminating his beautiful country.

Three days later, Shmuel Levinger, tired and dusty, reached his destination: the sleepy, sun-baked town of Grayston.

He stood facing Tom's parents' house with his suitcase in his hand and a great many hopes in his heart. They welcomed him with a hearty meal. An hour later, he was working on the ranch.

Years passed. Tom, in New York, had cut off communication with his family. Rumor had it that he was in the employ of the Mob, that he had been shot several times, and might even have done some jail time. His parents grew older and passed away. And that was how a Jewish boy from Poland, by way of Jerusalem, found himself the owner of a large cattle ranch spreading down to the Mexican border, along the Rio Grande.

No one in Texas called him Shmuel Levinger. His original Jewish name had given way, back in New York, to the name Sam Lowinger. Only his brother Kalman, in faraway Jerusalem, still called him Shmuel — or, in Yiddish, Shmiel.

His father had long since left this world, and Sam's connection with his brother vacillated. From time to time, on holiday eves or family *simchahs* he became aware of through the invitations they sent him, he would mail a gift. The money always drew a heavy sigh from his brother. Kalman Levinger said that it was money earned through the desecration of Shabbos and other grave transgressions, and must be returned so that Shmiel would not think that supporting his family was an atonement for his sins. But, each time, he never quite mustered the strength to send the money back.

Each time, he would leave the envelope on the table as though he refused to touch the money inside. And, each time, the envelope somehow disappeared, to find its way into his wife's purse for household expenses. She, at any rate, did not suffer from pangs of conscience. If the charity collectors of Jerusalem did not turn their backs on Sam Lowinger and his generous checkbook; if their institutions all sent letters filled with flattery, posters to hang in the succah he probably never built, and calendars full of pictures of orphans and widows enjoying a good meal in a charitable institution; if *they* were allowed to happily accept his checks and to send him thank-you letters brimming with gratitude — well, her husband Kalman didn't have to be a bigger tzaddik than they were.

Through Binyamin's long, descriptive letters, Sam Lowinger was reintroduced to Yiddish — that lively, colorful language that he had not heard for decades.

At first, it was hard for him to read the Yiddish, and even harder to write it. He'd forgotten some of the words. Deciphering his nephew's first letter, two pages long, had required two solid hours of effort. Then he had remembered an old English-Yiddish dictionary that he had bought many years before, on his arrival in America. At that time, his goal had been to learn English; now, he would use it to go back to the *"mama lashon."* He went up to the attic room were he had stayed when the former owners were still alive, turned on the light, and rummaged among the old boxes and bundles until he found the dictionary. That made it easier to read and write future letters.

Sam Lowinger was no longer young. He had passed his sixtieth birthday and was the owner of the largest ranch north of the Mexican border. He employed dozens of workers, both permanent and temporary, who lived in quarters on his spread. But his own home was quiet and empty.

He had neither wife nor children. His meals were cooked by a Mexican woman who came each day from nearby El Paso. The meals themselves were silent affairs. He could have chatted with the antlered buck's head mounted on the dining-room wall, but the buck just gazed back at him with its lifeless eyes and never answered. Now he understood why Tom had refused to return to his parents' place — to the enormous, lonely spread and the knowledge that only several hundred people lived within a radius of many miles, most of them interested mainly in cattle and horses.

Every day was just like the day before. The seasons chased one another without pause. Birthing season ended and the herd migration began; the hot season passed and the rainy one was upon them. There were people who envied Sam Lowinger his great wealth, but he was a sad and lonely man.

That was the situation until Binyamin's letters began coming from Jerusalem, to breathe a breath of life into the sun-baked routine of Sam's existence. The correspondence was like a refreshing breeze in the endless, dull heat of southwest Texas. The long hours he spent reading and writing the letters lent new meaning to his life.

There was no word in any letter about an upcoming happy event. The couple had been married for five years, and were still childless. While Devorah did not give up hope, much of her joy in life had leached away, and her smiles were few and far between.

Binyamin did what he could to make things easier for her. They moved to an apartment in a newer neighborhood — not one where, as in Meah Shearim, the neighbors were crowded together and forever asking slyly when they might hear some "good news," but a more modern area with people who were more to Binyamin's taste. People who went to the cinema and the theater, who patronized the coffee shops of Rehavia and the German colony. People who belonged to the big world. People after Binyamin's own heart.

The couple also consulted numerous doctors to seek help for their infertility — in vain. Binyamin's mother and sisters urged them to use the tried-and-true methods: Asking rebbes and *rabbanim* for a blessing, visiting the graves of tzaddikim, praying at the *Kosel HaMa'aravi* and at *Kever*

Rachel. Binyamin firmly rejected them all. He was a modern, progressive fellow. A rationalist. He didn't do those kinds of things.

When they'd been married ten years, his mother tried to hint that, by Jewish law, he could divorce his wife — who, in any case, spent much of her time moping around the house in a depressed state of mind — and marry someone else. A woman who would bring joy and the laughter of children into his home. Binyamin wouldn't hear of it. Not because his marriage was particularly successful, but because he was not the sort of man who would divorce his wife even though halachah said that he could.

What his mother did not tell him was that she had secretly sent messengers to Toivy Lederman, asking her forgiveness.

Toivy was by now an older spinster, no longer the timid girl she had been a decade earlier. The tiny shop she had inherited from her parents had flourished under her management into a not-inconsiderable business that supplied quantities of vinegar to the British Army as well as to hotels, restaurants, and factories.

First, Mrs. Levinger sent her sister — a woman with pleasant manners and a persuasive tongue — to see Toivy. When Toivy realized who she was, she said firmly that only a sense of respect prevented her from physically throwing her out of the shop. It was preferable that she leave quietly and quickly, and never come back.

When a second messenger — a *talmid chacham* who was a friend of the family — came back with a similar answer, Binyamin's mother sat down and wrote a letter soaked in tears. She knew now that they had perpetrated a terrible misdeed. She was now persuaded that Toivy had not been an apostate and had not befriended nuns as the rumors had said. She wished — oh, how she wished! — that things had turned out otherwise. How she longed to turn back the clock!

From the day she and her daughters had stubbornly refused to heed Rav Margolis's advice and had rejected Toivy, Mrs. Levinger's life had been one long round of suffering. Her husband had died young, and she herself was ill and did not know how much longer she had to live. Her youngest daughter-in-law was barren, and Binyamin himself was hardly mitzvah-observant anymore, being fatally drawn to the secular Zionists and the freethinkers and their abandoned lives. He was dragging his wife after him, too, though she came from a good and pious family.

Mrs. Lederman wept and pleaded: "Please, please, forgive me ...." There were no words to describe how sorry she was, how deeply she regretted her actions. "Please forgive a foolish woman, and forgive her family for its arrogance and wickedness; forgive Binyamin, who had been hardly more than a callow youth, led by his mother and sisters."

"Please," she begged, "go beyond the letter of the law and forgive us our iniquities." And, in this merit, she blessed Toivy from the depths of her heart that Hashem should send her a complete and speedy salvation. It would be the happiest day of her life, the mother concluded her painful letter, to hear that Toivy, too, had married and was building her own Jewish home.

Toivy Lederman received Mrs. Levinger's letter on Erev Rosh Hashanah. The lines, written from the depths of a remorseful heart, did not leave her indifferent. She *did* need a personal salvation. Though she was marrying off her younger siblings, one after another, she had not yet found her own match. What would Rebbetzin Margolis, now in Gan Eden, have said? What would Rav Margolis, *zichrono livrachah*, have advised her to do?

They would certainly have urged her to forgive — but she couldn't. She lacked their greatness of spirit. Besides, what had her mother done to deserve having her heart broken, and to be lying under a slab of stone these past ten years instead of raising her children and walking them down to the *chuppah*?

After several days of soul-searching, she sent her answer by messenger. If *he* asked her forgiveness, she said, she would acquiesce. If Binyamin himself understood that he had done her wrong and wanted to seek atonement, she would not harden her heart.

Binyamin's mother welcomed this answer with a fresh bout of hot tears. She was well aware that it was tantamount to a refusal. Binyamin would never ask his rejected *kallah's* forgiveness — not because he did not feel that he had done any wrong, but out of contempt for the very notion that such an insult to a Jewish girl could be the reason he had not yet merited a child. Day by day, he was moving further away from his spark of *Yiddishkeit*. Recently, he had begun associating with members of the Zionist underground, and was deeply influenced by their lifestyle. He once let drop a remark to the effect that he and his wife were considering moving to a kibbutz. He was learning English, despite the fact that foreign languages were not studied in his circles.

She would not even tell him that she had appealed to his former *kallah*, lest he retort that he did not believe in such things, that he was a rational, progressive person — all the things that made her glad her husband was no longer alive to see the change in his sweet little boy.

Binyamin was not much interested in maintaining a close connection with his religious brothers and sisters. Of all the family, he had chosen to embrace the black sheep — secular Uncle Shmiel, in America. The two of them seemed to have found a common language. Like will always be drawn to like.

Germany — 5705 / 1945

The American prisoner-of-war camp in occupied West Berlin was located in a large valley. Long rows of military tents were surrounded by barbed-wire fences and watchtowers manned by armed soldiers. The stench of death still hung in the air. Surrounding towns and villages had been reduced to rubble under the Allied bombing. The Second World War was over, leaving behind a crippled, bleeding Europe.

The German winter was a brutal one. Nonstop rains turned the prison camp into a muddy quagmire. The mood of the Wehrmacht officers and troops was equally sullen. They had been trained over the course of years to believe that the Third Reich was invincible. Throughout the war, they had been convinced that Nazi Germany's victory was assured. But the Allies had brought them to their knees and vanquished the Fatherland. The Fuhrer, Adolf Hitler, had taken his own life in a Berlin bunker, and American and Soviet tanks had taken possession of Germany's cities in a triumphant victory march.

There were more than a few troops who had breathed a sigh of relief at their defeat. They felt lucky to have survived the difficult war years, and impatiently anticipated a prisoner exchange and restarting their civilian lives. Many others felt degraded and hopeless, unable to absorb the bitter reality that saw Germany defeated and torn into pieces by the Allied conquerors.

There was one thing they all agreed on: Being a prisoner of the Americans was many times preferable to falling into Soviet hands. They had heard horror stories of cruel interrogations, torture, and Siberian exile as the Red Army handed over its prisoners to the notorious KGB.

In one tent lay a lone German soldier. He was not young, and his untrimmed beard added years to his age. He spent most of the hours of the day prone on his field cot, not joining in the conversations around him or in the endless card games with which the prisoners whiled away their time. His tentmates believed that the horrors of the war had confused his mind. The only times he left the tent was to stand in line for meals, which he swallowed hurriedly before returning to his cot.

In the routine questioning, the soldier did not offer many personal details. He said that he had lived in a small German village with his elderly mother, and that he had been drafted into the army despite the fact that he was an only child. He had had no ambition to advance within the military hierarchy, only a desire to get through the war alive and whole. When he was released from this prison camp, he told his interrogators, he planned to return to his village and his old mother, his chickens and his pigs.

One morning, two soldiers entered the prisoner's tent, ordered him into their jeep, and brought him to another tent at the camp's perimeter.

There, behind an army-issue table, sat a man in civilian clothes. He put on a pair of round spectacles to scan a thick dossier. After a few minutes, he lifted his eyes and broke into a smile.

"*Herr Doktor* Heinrich von Reiner." He stood up. "I am glad to finally meet the illustrious scientist I've been trying to track down for the past four years."

The older soldier shrugged. "You are mistaken," he said quietly. "My name is Max Heidelberg."

The American offered an apologetic smile. "There's no need to dissemble any more, sir." He rounded the table and began pacing the tent, hands behind his back. "You can open that dossier" — he pointed at the

binder on the table — "and you'll find everything: pictures, documentation, tokens of honor from the Fuhrer, certificates of excellence from the
heads of the Institute."

The prisoner did not move a muscle.

"Did you think the beard would disguise your identity?" the American
asked mockingly. "Did you really think we would not figure out who you
were?"

The German stood still, eyes cast down.

"I am just a simple soldier," he said in a low voice. "My name is Max
Heidelberg."

The American returned to his seat behind the table and opened the
dossier. "What we have here," he said, "is enough to send you straight to
the scaffold. The disease research you conducted in that military institute, Dr. von Reiner, constitutes a war crime of the severest caliber. You
will stand trial and you will be hanged."

"I don't know what you're talking about," the soldier repeated in a
monotone. "I am just a simple soldier."

Over the course of the next quarter-hour, the American attempted
to convince the soldier to admit that he was the noted German scientist Heinrich von Reiner. He mentioned the names of other scientists
who had worked at the Institute, displayed a thorough knowledge of von
Reiner's life dating back to his childhood, dropped his parents' names
and those of his siblings — to no avail. The man continued to deny any
connection.

The American spread his hands with a sigh. He closed the dossier with
a bang and fixed his eye on the German.

"Okay. There's someone I'd like you to meet who might be able to
clear up the confusion."

The soldier bowed his head submissively.

"I'll be right back," the American said, and left the tent.

Five minutes later, he returned, leading a dog on a leash. It was a tall
greyhound. The moment he dropped the leash, the dog raced toward the
German. Barking with joy, he licked the soldier's face over and over.

"Looks like he recognizes you," the American observed. "What's his
name? Rudy, right?"

The German began to look distressed. His eyes darted from the dog to
the American, and back to the dog.

"Rudy was Dr. von Reiner's beloved pet," the American said, retrieving the greyhound's leash and pulling out a gun. "When we took the Institute, we found him sitting and howling at the scientist's door. If you are … what name did you say? Max Heidelberg? … you certainly won't mind if I kill the dog, would you?"

Beads of perspiration dotted the German's forehead. His lips quivered. He tried unsuccessfully to hide his agitation.

"Shall I shoot?" the American asked. He placed the barrel of the gun against the dog's head.

The soldier didn't move.

A gunshot rang out.

The German shot forward with a scream. Hearing the dog's excited barking, he realized that the American had tricked him. With a muttered curse, he looked back down at the ground.

The American was holding the leash as the still-barking greyhound strained toward the German, trying to reach him. He pointed the pistol at the dog's head. "This is your last chance," he said curtly. "This time, I'll really kill him."

The German met his eyes. "What do you want?"

"What is your name?"

"Heinrich von Reiner," the German replied. "Dr. Heinrich von Reiner."

"What have you been doing these past few years?"

"You already know that."

The American seemed not to hear the answer. "What have you been doing these past few years?" he repeated, in exactly the same tone as before.

"I worked in the military institute for disease research near Berlin."

"Do you admit that you are guilty of war crimes, including the murder of prisoners and participating in genocide?"

"I only carried out orders that I was given by my superiors," the Nazi scientist said.

"Were those orders to torture and murder American and Soviet prisoners? Were your orders to cruelly murder hundreds of Jews — supplied by the concentration camps — through scientific experimentation? Were the orders to use human guinea pigs?"

Dr. von Reiner did not drop his eyes. "My orders," he said clearly, "were to find the ultimate weapon to win the war. I did my best for my Fatherland."

The American threw him a withering glance. "Sometimes I think it a pity that a person can't be killed more than once," he said. "*You* had no pity on thousands of prisoners and soldiers. Only on one dog."

He released the leash, and the greyhound bounded eagerly to his master, wagging his tail as he licked the German's hand. Von Reiner stroked the dog's head lovingly, whispering, "Rudy ... Rudy .... " The charade was over, he thought in despair. His hope was gone.

Dr. Heinrich von Reiner had planned his escape for months. He had sensed that Germany was about to go under, and he did not intend to drown with her. Secretly, he obtained the uniform of a private in the Wehrmacht, which he hid in the Institute's attic. When the conquering army reached the outskirts of Berlin, he put on the uniform, slipped out through the Institute's back door, and began walking toward the forest. He walked until he found a squad of American soldiers. Then he raised his arms in surrender and was brought to this camp, a prisoner of war.

He had managed to conceal his identity for weeks by remaining shut up in his tent playing the role of a simple villager suffering from depression or shell-shock. Patiently he awaited release with the other prisoners. Then, he hoped, he would make his way to South America or some other remote location.

But the Americans, somehow, had identified him. Now he would undoubtedly be transferred to a prison, then tried and executed. Perhaps it would be better to finish it now. He would attack the American in civilian clothes; soldiers would burst into the tent and shoot him.

The American continued pacing the tent until he was standing behind the German scientist.

"On the other hand," the American said, "I sometimes think: Wouldn't it be a loss for humanity to lose a scientist of the caliber of a Heinrich von Reiner?"

The German's head lifted slightly. Was he hearing correctly?

The American continued pacing, and stopped facing von Reiner. "Sometimes, I wonder: Maybe the man would want to atone for his terrible deeds by using his talents for the good of humanity."

Von Reiner's eyes opened wide. "Wh-what are you saying?"

"I am authorized by my government to offer you refuge — in exchange for your placing the results of your research at the disposal of the United States."

The American returned to his table, where he removed a sheaf of papers from his briefcase. "You can sign these documents now," he said. "And, within a hour, you will be on a plane — en route to America."

Heinrich von Reiner hesitated. He looked at his dog, and then at the American.

"Can I take Rudy with me?" he asked.

Dr. Heinrich von Reiner was removed from the P.O.W. camp in a U.S. military car that had been waiting outside the command tent. No one saw him leave.

In the car were a number of American officers. He directed them to a small cave in the mountains, near an abandoned mine, where he had hidden the plans and formulas he had succeeded in spiriting away from the Institute. The notebooks and papers made a fairly small bundle, wrapped in brown paper and held together with a rubber band. There were some slight signs of water damage, but by and large the material had held up well. On his arrival in America, he would be able to pick up the thread of his research exactly where he had left off a few days before Berlin fell.

Two hours later, an almost-empty cargo plane lifted off from an American airstrip. Apart from the pilot and several soldiers, there were only three passengers: Dr. Heinrich von Reiner, the American with the round spectacles and civilian clothes, and Rudy, the scientist's beloved greyhound.

"By the way," the American held out his hand. "I forgot to introduce myself. My name is Colin Baron."

"Which agency do you work for?" asked von Reiner, who had begun to regain some of his self-confidence.

Colin Baron smiled. "This may sound a little strange. I work for the United States Department of Agriculture."

Los Angeles — Nissan 5766 / April 2006

Barry Majdi returned to his office only after he had made certain that every last shred of paper had been flushed away. With a reassuring word to his secretary, he went to stand at the window. He closed his eyes and, with a contented smile, tilted his face up to the California sun and let its rays warm him.

The campus below swarmed with students. Some were relaxing on the grass, others were studying their lecture notes, while still others sat at small round tables drinking coffee. Beyond the lawn were several booths where carefree young people urged their fellow students to sign up for one worthy cause or another: peace on earth, anti-globalization, or a volunteer project in one of Los Angeles's poverty-stricken neighborhoods. A large sign invited all comers to the annual Student Union "Happening," slated to take place in just a few days' time and featuring outstanding stars, humorous contests, limitless beer, and plenty of fun.

That's exactly how it all started, the professor thought suddenly. He smiled nostalgically. At the annual Happening, in the year .... Had it been a decade ago? Eleven years? His neat goatee had been free of the silver strands it showed now, he had not yet needed reading glasses, and the tiny paunch he kept trying to hide had not yet made its appearance. It had been 1995 — or was it 1996? Several years, in any case, after he had left his government job in Atlanta.

Back then, he had been an ambitious young university lecturer eager to prove himself. He had tried to ignore the excitement on campus and to focus instead on completing his scientific article, "Chemical Reactions in Multi-Cellular Organisms." But the powerful loudspeakers robbed him of his concentration.

"And now," a lively voice had shouted, "a tasting competition! Who can tell the difference between Coke and Pepsi? Between Diet Sprite and Diet Seven-Up? Miller Beer and Budweiser? Step right up and show us what you can do!"

Ten years had passed since then, but he remembered it vividly. That announcement had triggered his interest in the event. Hot dog-eating or balloon-blowing contests filled him with nothing but contempt. A taste-testing competition, in his opinion, was far more interesting.

The young Professor Majdi had abandoned his desk and his article, and had gone to the window to watch — just as he was doing now. The campus lawn had been teeming with thousands of merry students. The emcee — an energetic and perspiring young man in a baseball cap — repeated his invitation to anyone who thought he could tell the difference between tastes. Step up and join the contest!

A few brave contestants climbed onto the stage — only to descend again in embarrassment after they were unable to tell the difference between even vodka and a mild herbal tea. The competition quickly dwindled to three contestants who demonstrated a high level of discernment in determining, time after time, what it was they were drinking.

The audience was divided three ways. Most of the minority students shouted themselves hoarse for their favorite: an African-American psychology major. Another group — primarily white — supported a New Yorker in stylish horn-rimmed glasses who closed his eyes to concentrate and was seemingly able to identify nearly every alcoholic beverage invented by man. The third contestant, a nondescript fellow with only a fraction of the New Yorker's charisma, had few followers, mostly friends.

Professor Majdi moved closer to the window and squinted at the stage below. The last contestant seemed familiar. He had been in the professor's biology course, though by no means one of the more brilliant students. He belonged to the group that habitually occupied the rear of the lecture hall, paying scant attention but always managing to get a copy of the lecture notes from a more diligent classmate. What was his name ...?

The professor had no idea. How typical of the student to waste his time in silly competitions instead of doing some studying in the library or toiling in the lab to complete his end-of-term project.

"And now, for the final round! Here we have two bottles of Scotch," the emcee screamed, waving the bottles above his head for the audience's benefit. "Johnny Walker Blue and a 21-year-old Glenfiddich. Each of these bottles is valued at $200. The contestant who can tell the difference between the two, and who can tell us which one he's drinking, will receive them both!"

The audience went wild. Applause and whistles filled the air. Liquid from each bottle was poured into marked glasses behind the contestants' backs. The judges took their seats. The contestants' eyes were covered, and two glasses set down before each of them.

Professor Barry Majdi found himself straining to watch the three figures as they sipped their drinks, heads tilted back to taste the full flavor, foreheads wrinkled in concentration. Three times, each contestant was asked to drink and to identify the whiskey in his glass. The emcee did his best to draw out the suspense, but it soon became clear that the one who would emerge the victorious winner of the two prize bottles was the third contestant.

As he stepped off the stage, triumphant, his friends greeted him with cries of joy, hugs, thumps on the back — and an eagerness to help him empty the two bottles of Scotch as quickly as possible.

The professor, still at his window, grimaced. He could understand the need for a shot of whiskey now and then. But to waste $200 on an orgy of unrestrained drinking?

He returned to his desk and his nearly finished article in a thoughtful frame of mind. The past few minutes had been extremely edifying. The victor of the taste-testing contest would no doubt find himself sitting bored at the rear of the lecture hall one day soon. That would provide the professor with an excellent opportunity to have a little talk with him. A most surprising talk ....

That talented drinker didn't know it yet, but today's silly competition was going to change his life.

20

Jerusalem — 5607 / 1947

The idea of a trip to America came up in one of Binyamin's letters to his uncle.

In the letter, which breathed an ardent Zionism, Binyamin told his uncle about the new Jewish state poised to come into existence, about the Arabs' threat to destroy it the moment the British Army evacuated the country, and about the Hagganah and Etzel's plans to defend against such an attack. Near the end of his missive, he asked if his uncle thought it was a good idea for him and his still-childless wife to come to America to consult physicians there.

An enthusiastic reply arrived almost at once. He had long been thinking about inviting the couple to Texas to visit, Uncle Sam wrote; the only thing that had held him back was the memory of how strongly his father and brothers had felt about leaving Eretz Yisrael. If dear Binyamin and his wife were prepared to come, he would send them first-class tickets this very day.

His part of the country, he admitted, did not boast many sophisticated hospitals, many of its doctors being more prone to expertise in horse and cattle ailments. But there were big hospitals in New York, and highly respected doctors there. He would be happy to help them find the right people.

Devorah was immediately infected by her husband's excitement. Her neighbors, the wives of professors and engineers, traveled abroad from time to time and returned with wonderful stories. She longed to see the amazing America that Binyamin was always talking about. It would be nice to get away for a while, far from the fear and uncertainty bred by the Arab threat to the Jewish settlement. Most of all, if she could return from America with a baby, she would be the happiest woman in the world.

Binyamin told his mother and siblings about the plan just days before he and Devorah were due to sail. They were not pleased that the uncle of doubtful lifestyle would be funding the trip, but Binyamin didn't care what they thought. He was an independent adult; and anyway, he added with a smirk, according to halachah one was permitted to leave Eretz Yisrael for medical reasons, wasn't that so?

He did not allow any family members to accompany them to the port at Haifa. This was because he did not wish them to see the new clothes he had purchased in honor of the trip. In place of the long Yerushalmi coat and flat-brimmed hat he had long-since begun to despise, he had bought a modern suit and a snap-brimmed felt hat.

Another surprise awaited Devorah on board the ship. Binyamin went into the bathroom in their private cabin, and emerged long minutes later with his cheeks clean shaven. There was no need for a beard in America, he explained with a broad smile. They were now citizens of the wide world. Now they could do whatever they pleased, without worrying about what their fanatic and old-fashioned families would have to say about it.

Devorah found it hard to get used to her husband's new look. Suddenly, Binyamin looked like an immature youth, round faced and pink cheeked. He hurried out of their cabin to investigate the various pleasures and recreational activities that the ship offered its esteemed passengers in first class. He was told that there was an elegant dining room, a ballroom for special events, and even a large orchestra. He planned to enjoy these next two weeks on board as he had never enjoyed himself before.

Apart from all of this, he wanted to stand on deck and watch Haifa grow tiny in the distance, until there was nothing but sea to be seen on every side. An open sea that held no restrictions, prohibitions, or customs such as the ones he had chafed under in the Jerusalem they had left behind.

The Jerusalem that — though his wife did not know it yet — he intended never to see again.

The trip took two full weeks. Fourteen consecutive days on the waves, pleasurable at first but tedious toward the end. Binyamin and Devorah Levinger landed on the shores of America on the first day of the year 1948. The city was all dressed up in honor of the new year, and the couple was filled with the same sense of expectation. Binyamin was waiting impatiently to meet his uncle and see the ranch he had heard so much about, while Devorah looked forward to the promised visit to renowned doctors, who would finally free her from the prison of her barrenness.

Binyamin's basic English, which he had practiced seriously during the voyage, proved sufficient to get them a taxi ride to an inexpensive hotel at the edge of the Bronx. The reception clerk showed him how to obtain a railroad ticket and how to send a telegram informing his uncle of their scheduled arrival time.

But first, they spent three days touring the huge metropolis. It was one thing to read about America or even to look at pictures in the newspaper, and quite another to actually walk into the Empire State Building, the tallest building in the world, to take the elevator up to the observatory on the 86th floor and gaze breathlessly in every direction.

The train trip from New York to Texas was no less exhausting than the journey by ship had been. They traveled on a long train pulled by a locomotive that belched clouds of black smoke. The wheels chugged across the huge expanse of the country, gradually leaving behind the Eastern Seaboard with its big, sophisticated cities to make its way across the country into the dusty Southwest.

After some days, the train finally neared Sam Lowinger's ranch — or rather, small, remote Grayston, the town closest to it. The depot was nothing more than a wooden shack beside the platform, beyond which ran a deteriorating asphalt road. Along this road stood several stores and businesses, and then a network of smaller streets.

Binyamin and Devorah descended from the train hesitantly, casting apprehensive glances around them. On the other side of the road, leaning on the hood of an old Ford pickup truck, was a sunburned man of medium height, wearing a wide cowboy hat, overalls with a checked flannel shirt underneath, and a pair of muddy boots. The man puffed at a cigarette as he squinted at the platform. Catching sight of the Levingers, his face lit up. He tossed away the cigarette, straightened up, and strode toward them with a broad smile.

"Ben!" he called when he was within earshot. "Ben — hello!"

Uncle Sam looked very different from the picture Binyamin carried around in his mind from that long-ago visit to Jerusalem. His tousled hair was whiter and his face redder. Back then, he had worn a tourist's wardrobe; now he was dressed in stained work clothes. Then, he had been well groomed and wearing cologne; now he reeked of manure, cigarette smoke, and alcohol.

If Binyamin was surprised, Devorah was stunned. Was this the uncle about whom Binyamin had spoken of with pride and a tinge of envy all these years? He looked like a *goy* in every respect!

"So we meet at last!" Sam gave his nephew a powerful hug, then bowed lightly to Devorah and touched his fingers to the brim of his hat. "And howdy to the missus," he added. "How was the trip over? The train? I sure hope you'll enjoy Texas. I simply cannot believe you're here! ... Well, why am I chattering away like an old fool? You must be tired and hungry."

Sam strapped their luggage into the bed of the pickup, open to the skies. Ben sat in the front passenger seat while Devorah squeezed into the space behind the driver. The truck began moving — and then screeched to a halt.

"Hey, Sheriff!" Sam called to a tall, thin man in a cowboy hat, who had a silver star pinned to the front of his suit. "I'd like you to meet my nephew, Ben Levinger."

Sheriff Jack Abrams, the local lawman, grinned and shook Binyamin's hand warmly. "You're the nephew from Jerusalem?" he asked. "Nice to meet you. Sam never stops talking about you. I threatened to lock him up in a cell if he mentions your name one more time."

Smiling, Sam pressed the gas pedal and the truck roared to life. "Okay, Sheriff. I'll be getting back to the ranch now. My guests are tired and hungry. Maybe you'll drop by tomorrow evening?"

The sheriff nodded. "The wife'll like that."

"Bring the kids, too, of course."

"Sure."

"His kids," Sam said with friendly envy as the truck moved away. "He's got three strapping sons, all of them workhorses, one taller than the next — and stronger, too! They have a ranch ... what can I tell you?" He glanced at the slender, short-statured Binyamin. "Believe me, you'd never guess they were one of us."

"One of us?" Binyamin repeated in surprise.

"The sheriff of Grayston is a full-fledged Jew," Sam chuckled. "And so are his kids. I tell you, Ben, his three are the strongest Jews I've ever seen in my life!"

The truck left Grayston's main street and made for the open road. Binyamin's eyes drank in the sights. The low hills were lush with grass, and from time to time he saw a large herd of cattle. Devorah, meanwhile, was in a near panic. She had just noticed the rifle.

It was propped up on the front seat, right between Binyamin and his uncle. A real rifle, capable of killing someone! She gaped at the driver's neck with open fear. She would never have thought of him as that kind of man. She had no idea that Binyamin's uncle looked like one of the gentile farmers her mother used to tell stories about when she was a little girl. And now — a rifle? What was he, a murderer? Where was Binyamin taking her?

Binyamin had discovered the rifle, too. He studied it, fascinated.

"It's a hunting rifle," his uncle said proudly, noting his interest. "A Remington. Want to see it in action?"

"Sure," Binyamin said excitedly. They were bumping along a narrow road between green fields set off by wooden fences.

Sam applied the brakes and picked up the rifle. He stuck his head out the window, aimed the rifle upward, closed one eye, and fired. A passing bird fell with a flapping of wings, to land with a thud on the grass on the other side of the fence.

"Did you see that shot?" Uncle Sam chuckled. Drawing himself back into the truck, he started the engine again. "Too bad that bird didn't fall onto the road. We could have taken it home for dinner."

"Are — are you allowed to shoot, just like that?" an astounded Binyamin asked.

His uncle laughed. "Sure. This is Texas. Go ahead — try it for yourself." He thrust the still-smoking firearm toward Binyamin.

Binyamin hesitated, then took the rifle into his own trembling hands. He touched the barrel and recoiled. "It's boiling hot!"

"It's also capable of killing someone." His uncle moved the muzzle aside. "Don't point it at people."

"I like the decorations," Ben remarked, examining the carved wooden stock.

"I've got lots of rifles at home. This is one of my best," Sam Lowinger said. "It was manufactured in 1920 and works to this day. I inherited it — along with the farm — from the previous owners. And I'll leave it to the next owner."

Binyamin picked up the rifle, aimed it out his window, and peered through the sight as though preparing to shoot. He wondered if Sam was thinking the same thing that had just occurred to him: If he had no children, who would the ranch's next owner be? Could it be ... him? Binyamin — or Ben, as he would be known from now on?

Sam Lowinger cautiously plucked the rifle from his nephew's hands. If Ben was interested, he said, he could take him to see a shooting competition that targeted clay dishes — a favorite Texas sport. Clay saucers were hurled skyward and men tried to shoot them out of the air. Did Ben think he would enjoy that?

"Sure," Ben replied, with an eager glance at his wife behind him. He was surprised to see how pale and frightened she looked.

"Enough talk about guns. My wife's trembling," he said mockingly.

"She'll get used to it," his uncle grinned. "We'll buy her a little pistol and teach her how to shoot. Here in Texas, the ladies shoot, too."

After this pronouncement, Sam concentrated on driving, listening with half an ear as Ben described the ocean voyage, the days spent in New York, and the long train ride. He spoke enthusiastically, oblivious to his wife's agitation. In the past few weeks, Devorah had seen her husband turn into another person, right in front of her eyes: starting with his new clothes and shaving off his beard on their first day on board ship, through his behavior during the voyage, up until now, as he hastened to embrace his uncle's free-for-all lifestyle, joining in his wild laughter and enjoying every minute spent in his company.

The longer they drove, the more depressed she became. She realized that she could not expect to find much congenial company in this place. The road was a narrow dirt strip winding between broad pastures. An endless row of electric poles marched parallel to the road, strung with tired, drooping wires. Around them all was lush and green, but devoid of any sign of humanity.

Ben noticed this, too. "Doesn't anyone else live around here?" he asked.

His uncle explained that this part of Texas was dominated by huge cattle ranches. The ranch houses were usually set far back and were not always visible from the main road. The sole sign of human habitation was a lone mailbox perched at the edge of the road, often accompanied by an iron gate opening into a long lane. These indicated that, somewhere behind the trees or beyond the open field, stood a house where people lived.

A few miles later, Sam Lowinger reached his own mailbox. He turned right, onto a gravel road. He waved to several ranch hands who greeted him as he drove along. The gravel stretched for several hundred yards and ended before a large house. Behind the house, pastureland stretched to the horizon.

"All this is yours?" Ben asked in awe.

"All mine," Sam answered with satisfaction. "And this is only a small part of it. The ranch stretches all the way down to the Mexican border."

As they moved closer, the house rose up in all its glory: a spacious, wooden, two-story building. A wraparound porch was covered by a handsome slanted roof. On either side of the house rose two square towers, which had once been manned by sharp-eyed guards. Sam parked his truck near the steps.

"We're here!" he announced.

Ben jumped out and looked around with interest. A low wooden fence surrounded a square area with the house in its center. Several sheds and outbuildings stood some distance to the rear. To the right of the house was a fruit orchard backed by a cornfield. The stables were on the left, abutting a large corral where several horses roamed.

Sam instructed a pair of ranch hands to remove the luggage from the back of the truck. An older woman in an embroidered apron emerged from the front door to welcome them.

"This is a house with a history," Sam told his nephew proudly. "It was built in the year 1834, when Texas was still an independent republic. This is where General Sam Houston — Texas' great liberator — and his senior officers convened to prepare for war with Mexico. Come on in and take a look at my gun collection. There's nothing like that in Jerusalem, now is there?"

The Mexican housekeeper, Manuela, had already set the massive dining-room table, and presently she served a meal whose tantalizing aromas permeated the house. Sam invited several of his ranch hands to join them. The men were devout Catholics who were excited to hear that Ben hailed from Jerusalem, in the Holy Land.

Devorah looked at her husband with stricken eyes. She did not taste a morsel or utter a word. She simply could not believe how everything had deteriorated. She had understood that Binyamin's uncle was not particularly pious, but it had never entered her mind that he could be completely detached from everything having to do with *Yiddishkeit*.

And Binyamin — he was eating the non-Jewish housekeeper's cooking with no qualm in the world. How was it that the food was not sticking in his throat?

Back on the ship, she had attempted to remonstrate with him. In fact, even before they had left home she had suggested that they bring dried provisions with them for the voyage. But Binyamin had insisted that they could make do with what they found on board. Which was true … if you wanted to eat *treife* meat and drink nonkosher wine.

Her heart constricted with pain as she recalled the way her husband had talked and laughed with the other passengers, sharing in their vulgar humor. She realized now that the fear she had entertained in the past had turned into a reality. Binyamin had not come here for a visit. He had come to America intending to stay forever.

Ben spent the next few weeks making friends with the ranch hands. He learned how to ride a horse, shoot a rifle, and drive a pickup truck. He tried to learn how to drink whiskey, and caused an eruption of giggles among the Mexicans as he grimaced under the drink's fiery onslaught.

At first, he tried to include his wife in these exciting new experiences, but she was totally disinterested. In fact, she was not interested in much of anything. She spent hour upon hour sitting in the rocking chair in their room, enveloped in anguished silence. Because she did not speak English and made no effort to learn the language, she could converse only with her husband. But when he returned home, hungry and tired, she was the last thing on his mind. His world had moved very far from hers. He was living the life of the ranch and trying to turn himself into a real cowboy, while her head was filled only with the thought of the expert doctors and hospitals in New York.

At first, she would remind him that this had been their purpose in coming to America — as he had explicitly promised her. But he dismissed her claims. "What's the rush?" he asked. "Let's relax a little first. The doctors won't run away." Only now did she realize that the distance between Texas and New York was like that between two different countries. She hadn't known this back in Jerusalem. Binyamin hadn't bothered to tell her.

"Ben," Uncle Sam would say, glancing at Devorah from afar. "If there's a woman in the house, she should at least cook. Let her do something! She can't just sit around the house all day, crying."

But Devorah continued to rock monotonously and silently in her chair by the window. She barely ate or drank, and never smiled. Time crawled by. Winter gave way to summer, and then summer moved over for winter. And still Devorah sat by the window, quiet and sad.

■ ■ ■

The year was 1952. Nearly five years had passed since Binyamin and Devorah Levinger had arrived in Texas, and had anyone from their old Jerusalem neighborhood seen the pair, they would never have recognized them.

Ben had become Sam Lowinger's right-hand man. He had grown no taller, but had filled out and was now a sturdy and muscular young man. He knew how to rope a horse and how to throw a cow on its side and brand it with a white-hot branding iron. He knew how to chase away cattle thieves and how to bargain with cattle merchants to sell a herd at a good price. From time to time he made the trip into Grayston to visit the Drunken Ox saloon opposite the bank. He would return to the ranch swaying on his feet, with a thinner wallet but plenty of alcohol in his system. His uncle watched him with a contented smile. *A fine boy,* he thought.

Over the years, Devorah had become a shadow of her former self. She became so thin that she resembled a skeleton more than anything else. The window no longer interested her. Neither did the rocking chair. She spent whole weeks in bed, the shades down in the darkened room. The housekeeper pleaded with her to eat something and gain some strength, but Devorah would look at her with sad eyes and say nothing.

There were other days — few and far between — when she got up and went down to the kitchen to help Manuela. Though they did not speak each other's language, they shared a common domestic tongue: the language of pots and pans, of brooms and mops. On these rare occasions,

Devorah was happier. Immediately afterward, however, she would sink back into her depression.

"A child — that's the medicine for her," Sam would tell his nephew. "Ben, take two weeks' vacation and go to New York with Debbie. Take her to the big hospitals and the medical specialists. You promised her."

But some reason always came up to postpone the trip. Ever since the ranch manager had been caught engaging in long-standing thievery of Sam's cattle, "Mr. Ben," as he was known to the hands, was acting manager. He kept the ranch's books and supervised registration of the herd. He hired the ranch hands, paid them their salaries, and even persuaded his uncle to mortgage a portion of his land to obtain a bank loan for the ranch's development.

Besides, he was by no means certain that he wanted to raise a family with this woman. She didn't belong here. It was a pity he had brought the depressed creature to America in the first place. She should have stayed in Jerusalem, with her sister, her brother-in-law, and their ten children, living in a room-and-a-half in the Old City and subsisting on dry bread dipped in oil.

Here, she had unlimited food, a gigantic house, and enormously spacious grounds. If she wished, she could travel to Grayston, El Paso, or even Houston, and buy anything her heart desired: clothes, jewelry, a small horse to ride on. Whatever she wanted. His whole marriage was a big mistake. He had made a fatal error in breaking off his first match. He should have married that girl — what was her name? — the Christian, the apostate, the one they had caught visiting the convent. *She* wouldn't have been as much trouble. *She* would doubtless have enjoyed Texas from the very first minute.

The years had passed for Toivy Lederman in Jerusalem, too, and they were no less difficult. She had passed her thirtieth birthday and was still single. Her younger siblings were married. At each wedding, everyone blessed her, saying, "Your turn should be next — soon!" The blessings, though sincere, pierced Toivy's heart like arrows. She didn't feel blessed; on the contrary, there were moments when she felt decidedly cursed. At her age, she should already be marrying off her own children. But it was only her brothers and sisters that she walked down to the *chuppah*, the focus of pitying glances and compassionate whispers. In the first few years, she had still received occasional suggestions for a match with a widower or a divorced man, an older bachelor, or a fellow who had some sort of defect. With time, however, even these proposals dried up and she was left alone.

The neighborhood women couldn't understand why she didn't marry. The old rumors had long since dissipated, and she was such a nice girl, so pious, and so devoted to her family. One of the neighbors whispered that a well-known *mekubal* had placed a terrible curse on her after she had refused to forgive her former *chasan*.

"She doesn't lack for money," said Malka the Washerwoman, regaling the other women as she scrubbed stains from dirty clothes. "Her vinegar business, *baruch Hashem,* provides enough livelihood for three families. The boy would have to bring nothing to the marriage. He could come *mit leidige hent* — with empty hands. So why can't she find a reasonable shidduch ... or even a slightly less than reasonable one, but at least a husband!"

For once, Malka the Washerman was actually correct in the first part of her assertion: Chatzkel Lederman's vinegar shop had, under Toivy's management, flourished into a thriving business. A vinegar factor in Haifa turned out a large quantity of the product for her several times a year. Trucks brought the barrels to warehouses that she rented in an industrial area, from which they were distributed throughout the country. On the list of customers buying from Lederman's Vinegar were hotels and guest houses, restaurants and public kitchens.

Nor did Toivy turn her back on her veteran customers, the neighborhood women who still remembered the days when Toivy's mother ran the tiny shop in Meah Shearim. They continued to arrive at the new premises, carrying glass bottles or tin cans to fill with one quantity or another of vinegar. And even though a single factory sale provided a much larger profit, and the women sometimes appeared at her door in the middle of an important meeting with a supplier or significant buyer, Toivy would invariably rise to pour out the required amount of vinegar, asking the women how they and their families were faring and parting from them with friendly warmth.

There was only one type of customer with whom she absolutely refused to do business: convents, monasteries, and Christian institutions. She had suffered enough at their hands. Perhaps not everybody in Jerusalem remembered the story — she certainly spoke of it to no one — but there was no point in feeding gossip. The last thing she wanted to see was a man in a cassock walking into her shop and greeting her. The last thing she needed was to provide fodder for the slanderers and gossipmongers who had already caused her so much suffering.

In eighteen years, she had never climbed the winding path leading to the monastery. In eighteen years, she hadn't knocked with pounding heart on the iron door until the peephole slid open. In eighteen years, she had not waited outside for Sister Mary to step out in her black robe and gold cross, to take the basket that Tzipporah, the cook at the Sephardic orphanage, had prepared.

After Toivy's shidduch was broken, Rav Margolis had undertaken to tend to the matter of Toivy's brother in her stead. After his death the job passed to his son, the younger Rav Margolis. They paid the monastery for keeping the retarded child, who was no longer a child but a man of nearly thirty — a baby's mind in a grown-up body. Later, when Toivy had the means, Rav Margolis hired a man to take her brother for walks in the courtyard several times a week. He taught him how to say a blessing and "*Shema Yisrael*," put a *kippah* on his head, and treated him like a human being. The hired man did not know for whom he was caring. The younger Rav Margolis kept the secret as carefully as his father had. No one but himself, Toivy, and a few nuns knew the truth, not even Toivy's other brothers and sisters.

Eighteen whole years has passed since then. Her brother Moishele married, and then Yenty; finally, even Esther Malka, the youngest, took her turn beneath the *chuppah*. It was a joyous occasions, tinged with sadness. The *kallah* did not remember her parents at all. Her father had died when she was just one year old, her mother three months later. It had been her oldest sister who fed her cereal from a spoon, who braided her hair, took her to the doctor, and helped her with her homework. And it was Toivy who walked her to the *chuppah*.

A year after Esther Malka's wedding, she gave birth to a son. Eight days later his *bris* was celebrated, and he was named — like many of his cousins had been before him — Yechezkel, after Chatzkel, his long-departed grandfather. It was Toivy, as always, who paid for the *seudah* and made sure that the *mohel* received his due. Once again, she endured the heartfelt blessings that were thrown at her head, to the effect that she should soon merit building a home in Israel and bear children of her own. The smile with which she received these good wishes did not betray the pain that the words caused her. If only, if only, *HaKadosh Baruch Hu* would see her suffering and hasten her salvation! Had she not already paid, over and above, enough for the pain she had caused her mother? Was her cup of anguish not overflowing? Wasn't it time for her, too, to be granted forgiveness and atonement — and redemption and salvation?

That afternoon, Toivy returned to the business. One last worker, lingering later than the others, said good-bye and went home. Toivy locked the door and sat down at her desk to go over her accounts. She tried to concentrate. An unexpected order was due to be shipped the next day, and she must increase production for the coming month. She must add up the customer accounts and urge them to make their payments .... But her thoughts carried her to other times and places.

The lines of figures blurred before her filling eyes. Uninvited images began floating through her mind. Toivy let the tears fall, and was soon sobbing. *Ribono shel Olam, what is to become of me? How long am I to be alone? How long must I be an object of pity to other people? All of my brothers and sisters are married and have borne children.*

The last one — Esther Malka, the baby of the family — had just celebrated her son's *bris milah*. Only she, Toivy, was spending her time with vinegar shipments and account books, trying to push aside her thoughts and ignore her feelings of guilt.

The sobs subsided after a few minutes, but she sat for a long time afterward, staring into space and torturing herself with her reflections. Only when dusk began to darken her office windows did she wash her face and go back to her desk, ready to return to her rows of figures.

There was a knock at the door.

Toivy looked up, startled and curious. Who could it be at this hour? The opaque glass showed her only the blurred outline of a short, thin woman dressed in black. Toivy did not rise to answer the knock. The woman would understand that the store was closed and she would come back the next day.

But the knocking continued, intensifying, as though the woman knew, or at least hoped, that someone was inside. Toivy remained seated, trying to focus on her account books. Then she heard the woman call through the door, "Toivy! Toivy!"

The voice had a strange accent, as though from foreign parts. The woman certainly did not live in Meah Shearim. Toivy strained her mind for a moment — and then froze. She knew who it was.

She hurried to the door, feeling the rage rise up inside her. Opening it, she saw that she hadn't been mistaken. It was Sister Mary, from the convent. The nun who had taken the food basket from Toivy for her brother. She stood on the doorstep in her black robe, the gold crucifix glittering on her bodice.

"What are you doing here?" Toivy hissed. She had not seen Sister Mary in eighteen years, and now here she was, appearing as if out of thin air.

The nun gestured tranquilly. "May I come in?"

Toivy moved aside. Bringing her inside was undoubtedly better than talking to her in plain view of the whole street.

Los Angeles — Nissan 5766/April 2006

Professor Barry Majdi still stood at his window, gazing nostalgically down at the campus quadrangle. Memories washed over him. He had to plan his next steps in the light of the long-awaited document that had just arrived by fax, but his thoughts persisted on dragging him back to the year 1996.

The winner of the tasting competition was George Bellini, a Biology major. Professor Majdi gleaned these details from the student newspaper, which had devoted a full page to the yearly "Happening." Checking Bellini's file in the university office, Majdi learned that he was the son of Italian immigrants living in one of the less prosperous neighborhoods of Los Angeles. His father was an independent truck driver, his mother a housewife, and he had no wealthy relatives to speak of. How had George Bellini come to be enrolled in this expensive university?

He was here on a scholarship he had received for academic excellence in high school. However, the grades he had earned this past semester — some of them from Professor Majdi himself — did not justify continuing the scholarship into the next term. No wonder the boy was trying to bury his problems in drink. By every reasonable estimation, he would not be able to continue in this university next semester …. But life holds many surprises.

George was absent from Majdi's next lecture. The professor scanned the rear rows of the large hall and then, just to be sure, checked the front ones as well. George Bellini was not among those present. Which, Majdi thought, was to have been expected. After the back-thumping victory he had just enjoyed, dropping down from the heights to dull routine would seem especially galling. This would provide fertile soil for the little chat the professor intended to have with his student.

George put in an appearance at the next class — coming late as usual — and took a seat at the very back of the lecture hall, trying to conceal his yawns. Professor Majdi, also as usual, walked up and down the aisles while lecturing, forcing his students to twist their necks when he was behind them. Normally, he ventured only as far as the center of the hall, not too far from the blackboard and slide projector. Today, he moved on to the rear of the large room. He stood near the door — and George.

"On this bright, sunny morning, let's talk a bit about chlorophyll, anthocyanins, and carotenoids," the professor announced. He paused to allow his students to lean over their notebooks and scribble down what he said. He used the brief interval to lean over an astonished George Bellini and whisper, "Wait outside my office after class."

A second later, he raised his voice and continued his lecture: "Every first-year biology student knows that these are pigments — nature's own food coloring. Without them, my dear students, California's oranges and grapefruits would be white or gray, and no one would buy them. And then our great state would have no money with which to build this beautiful campus of ours ...."

The professor was delayed at the end of his lecture by several students who, as usual, lingered to ask a host of inane questions. He arrived at his office to find George waiting for him, his knapsack over his shoulder and worry clearly stamped on his features. Why did the professor want to see him? Was he going to be booted out of the course? To be honest, he had not kept up with the course work. His project was gathering dust in the student lab and the pages from the resource books he had photocopied in the library remained largely unread.

To his relief, the professor was relaxed and smiling. There was no sign of an impending rebuke. Majdi placed a hand on George's shoulder and asked if he had any special plans for the next two or three hours.

"No," George answered. "No plans." *And even if I had*, he thought, *they have just been canceled.*

"Then let's go," Majdi said.

His decrepit Oldsmobile was waiting in the parking lot. Today, a decade later, with Biologic Systems holding several of his patents in the fields of biology and medicine, Majdi was driving a gleaming Jeep Cherokee. But in those long-ago days at the cusp of his academic career, after having recently left his government job in Atlanta, the Olds was all he could afford. He drove out of the campus, headed for the beach.

The car left behind the skyscrapers and the luxury suburbs of Los Angeles, with their verdant gardens and private swimming pools, and was soon speeding along the coast with the Pacific stretching endlessly off to the left and, on the right, California's fields and vineyards.

Conversation flowed between the two, irrespective of the immense stature gap between failing student and popular university lecturer. George was entranced by the professor, who fed him tidbits of gossip from the college faculty room. Majdi expressed an interest in the tasting contest and in George's highly developed sense of taste, and casually grilled him about his family and his past.

Not a word was said about George's dismal academic record. If the question crossed George's mind as to the purpose of this little jaunt, he quickly banished it. He felt as if he was speaking with a peer rather than with someone who had the power to decide his fate — to determine his project grades and influence the decision of the scholarship committee.

"Hungry?" the professor asked suddenly, as they approached one of the restaurants dotted along the highway. "There's a good place coming up. Let's go in."

Even now, from his vantage point ten years later, Barry Majdi's mouth began to water at the memory of what they ate that day: braised veal and onions, stuffed with ginger, chili, and garlic. They knew how to cook at this restaurant, and they knew how to pair each dish with the appropriate wine. He'd only eaten in that place five times in all ... the last time, with George Bellini.

Actually, it was six times. On the first occasion, he had come alone, to scout out the place before bringing a guest there. After that, on the average of once every month or two, he would visit the restaurant in the company of a new student candidate. By the time he came with George, the waiter already knew what Majdi would order, and even what he would drink: Pinot Noir 1992, of course.

George was the fifth student he had brought here. And the last. From the very start, the professor sensed that this candidate stood head and shoulders above the other five. And now, a decade later, it was clear that he had not been mistaken. George had proved a most profitable investment. He had justified every dollar of the tens of thousands that had been poured into him.

How are you?" Sister Mary asked in a friendly tone, as though they were old friends.

Toivy answered with a stiff nod. She was fine, *baruch Hashem* — but she would be happier if Mary would explain the reason for this strange visit.

The nun paid no attention to the hint that her presence was unwanted. "Shall we sit?" she suggested in the same pleasant tone. She moved toward the desk.

The two sat facing each other. Toivy looked at the nun in silence, waiting for her to speak. Before his death, her father had told her more than once that he often wondered if Sister Mary was not really a Jew who had somehow ended up among the gentiles — or a righteous gentile who did all she could to help Jewish patients within the convent walls. It was more than eighteen years since Toivy had last laid eyes on her. Sister Mary had aged, but she still remained an unsolved riddle.

"I won't keep you long," the nun began. "But I have a duty to tell you something."

The conversation between the two women lasted only minutes. It was punctuated by lengthy silences, tears, and sighs. Then Sister Mary departed, leaving Toivy feeling stunned, confused, and helpless. The storm of weeping that had overtaken her earlier returned, redoubled. She sat at the desk for a long time, sobbing unabashedly. Finally, she wiped her tears and carefully weighed the situation. After consulting with an adviser, she formed her decision.

Only four hours were needed to gather together all her brothers and sisters in the old house in Meah Shearim. It wasn't easy: One had gone to shul and had lingered there; a second was in his regular *Daf Yomi shiur*; a sister had gone to the *shuk* and was not back yet; and Esther Malka's newborn baby, little Yechezkel, was very cranky since his *bris* and she couldn't leave him. They were all very curious and tense, and pleaded with Toivy to tell them why she had summoned them so urgently. Trying for a humorous approach, one of them jokingly asked if she was planning to surprise them all by announcing an engagement. But they quickly discerned her agitated spirit and realized that Toivy was in no mood for jokes.

It was near ten by the time the new mother, Esther Malka, put in a belated appearance, her infant having finally been soothed to sleep. The three brothers and three sisters crowded together in the tiny kitchen. The older siblings appropriated the chairs, where they sat drinking cups of tea, while the younger ones leaned against the counters or the ancient refrigerator.

"Listen," Toivy began, her face solemn. "We … have to talk about something. Something extremely important. You all know about my … broken shidduch, many years ago."

Her siblings surreptitiously exchanged surprised glances. Their sister *never* broached this painful subject. She never referred to that difficult period in her life.

"It's no secret that there were rumors that I went to the convent," Toivy continued. "That I hobnobbed with priests and nuns and so on. The time has come to tell you the truth."

She took a deep breath, and sipped from the cup of water that Esther Malka had poured for her.

"Well, the truth is that I *did* visit the convent. I went there each week for a period of three months — but not, of course, in order to convert. We had a brother there. A brother who had been born more than thirty years ago, before Moishele, Yenty, and Esther Malka. He was born defective — extremely retarded ...."

Toivy proceeded to reveal to her stunned siblings the terrible secret she had heard from their dying father in his final days. The secret that he had kept from his wife, the mother of his children, for so many years. "Someone told the Levingers that I'd been seen coming out of the convent, but I couldn't reveal the reason. Believe me, I've spent plenty of time torturing myself since then, wondering if I did the right thing. Wondering if I wasn't responsible for shortening our poor mother's life. But what could I do? It was Abba's wish. His private instruction to me. He didn't want Ima to know that her husband had done such a thing."

Total silence filled the room. No one said a word or looked at anyone else.

"You must be wondering why I've decided to share the story with you now. Well, it wasn't my decision. A few hours ago, Sister Mary — the nun who was in charge of our brother — came to see me at the shop. She told me that our brother passed away this morning. The convent staff wanted to bury him in their own graveyard, but she insisted on consulting me first. This evening, I went to young Rav Margolis and he says that our brother must be buried in a Jewish grave and that we must mourn him properly."

Toivy concluded her story with tear-filled eyes. Her brothers and sisters were shocked to the core. So many things had been dropped on them at once: their father's incredible behavior; their mother's ignorance until her dying day; and their oldest sister's noble — there was no other word for it — self-sacrifice.

As per Jerusalem custom, the funeral took place that same night, and by dawn it was the talk of the town. The week of mourning saw the Lederman home packed with visitors. All of Toivy's siblings were married; each of them had relatives, neighbors, and friends who all wanted to hear, firsthand, the amazing story, hidden so long and so well, that had been suddenly exposed to the light of day.

There were those who lauded Chatzkel and others who reviled him, but about Toivy, opinion was unanimous: she was a heroine. She had forfeited her happiness and her future for the sake of her father's honor. A terrible wrong had been perpetrated upon her, yet she had maintained her silence for years. Toivy modestly rejected the praise that was heaped upon her. Anyone would have done the same, she protested. Anyway, she had had no choice. Her siblings noted the curious apathy that seemed to envelop her all that week. She was distant, as though an invisible screen divided her from everyone around her.

Late on the last night, a bent old woman entered the house. Her face was crosshatched with lines and her entire bearing spoke of anguish. She sat in a remote corner and took no part in the lively conversation that Toivy's sisters were conducting with several of the comforters. Toivy sat huddled in her low chair, eyes downcast and lips trembling. For nearly a week she had scarcely spoken. But how much — oh, how much! — she had looked forward to seeing this visitor.

They did not exchange a word. After a few minutes, the old woman stood up, moved toward the line of mourners, and quietly intoned the customary sentiment: "*HaMakom yenacheim eschem b'soch sh'ar aveilei Tzion ve'rushalayim.*" She paused briefly, as though deciding whether or not to say something else. Then she bowed her head submissively and began moving toward the door.

Near the door, she stopped again. Toivy was now right in front of her. The old woman appeared extremely agitated. She twisted her fingers tightly together, and her chin wobbled the way it does when one is trying her hardest not to cry. Finally, she mustered her courage and leveled a glance into Toivy's eyes.

"We did not deserve a precious *kallah* like you," she whispered — and hurried out the door.

"Who was that?" one of Toivy's sisters asked. "What did she say?"

Toivy didn't respond. She did not seem to have heard the question. Burying her face in her hands, she burst into bitter tears.

The old woman was Mrs. Levinger — Binyamin's mother. All that week, ever since the news had reached her about the brother in the convent, she had known no peace. Day after day, she had not stopped crying. She tried to persuade her daughters to visit the house of mourning with her, but they lacked the courage to look Toivy in the face. Why bring up that whole story again, one of the daughters said. So many years had passed since then ....

But their mother could not let the matter rest. On the last night of the *shivah*, she wrapped herself warmly and walked from Shaarei Chesed to Meah Shearim. She went simply to say that she knew, that she regretted, and that she was suffering to the depths of her soul. Toivy had been in the right, and she had been in the wrong. Toivy had been righteous; she and her daughters were the wicked ones.

Texas — 5713 / 1953

"Ben!" came the faint call, accompanied by a slow shuffle of slippers. "Ben, where are you?"

Ben sighed, and kicked the table in frustration.

"Just a second," he told the insurance agent in his office. "It's the old man. Let me put him in his place."

The man nodded sympathetically. He, too, had an aged father. He understood the problem.

The insurance agent was a man of massive proportions, with a car to match. He was here to urge Mr. Lowinger to acquire an insurance policy to cover natural disasters — unfortunately, three months too late.

"If you'd been insured before the epidemic struck," he had told Ben bluntly, "If you'd signed up even one day before nearly one-third of your herd was wiped out, you would have been holding a fat check from our company right about now."

Tall Willy, who owned the ranch down the road, had also bought himself an insurance policy the day before, the agent told Ben. As had Bobby Fault, from the ranch up the river — after losing a majority of his cattle to the plague. The only lucky ones were the three Abrams brothers, the sheriff's sons. They had taken out a policy half a year ago. When their cattle began to drop, one after the other, they hadn't panicked. In fact, they had already received an advance on their insurance and were going to use it to buy a new herd.

Ben rose from his swivel chair with a sigh, and rounded the large desk, moving toward the office door.

"Ben!" The old man's face lit up at the sight of his nephew. "Who's in there with you?"

Ben led his uncle back to the wraparound porch in front of the house. "Relax a little," he said, seating Sam Lowinger in the rocking chair and throwing a glance at Manuela, who had just materialized in the doorway. How many times did he have to tell her to keep an eye on the old man, especially when he, Ben, was in a meeting? It was impossible to work with his uncle wandering about and getting in the way.

"Sorry about that," Ben said, returning to his office and the insurance agent. "That's my uncle. He has his good days but he can get a little confused."

"What's the matter with him?"

"He's starting to get senile. And when he *is* clear in his mind, he tends to get drunk ...."

"How old is he?"

"He hasn't hit eighty yet," Ben said. He grinned. "In my book, when they reach seventy, they all ought to be shot."

"Absolutely," the agent chuckled. "But not before you take out a life-insurance policy on them!"

Less than seven years after he had arrived at Sam Lowinger's ranch, Ben was in charge.

In his first years there, his uncle had taught him the ropes involved in various aspects of running a ranch. It had been clear from the start that his abilities would never come close to matching those of the Texas-born ranch hands — cowboys from birth. He would never equal the sheriff's three boys, for example, all of them expert riders who could compete honorably against all comers in roping a rampaging steer or moving a herd.

On the other hand, Sam knew, no Texan with a "*goyische kupp*" could run the financial end of things like Ben, that seasoned Yerushalmi. Ben purchased stud bulls on easy terms, sold herds at the best price, made the stables run more efficiently, and in general had substantially increased the ranch's profits.

At first, Ben was afraid of the responsibility. He had never given orders to others nor managed a large enterprise. But his early successes built his confidence. As Sam transferred more and more authority onto his nephew's shoulders, the big north room was turned into Ben's office. This looked the way a ranch manager's office ought to look: a big wooden desk, a tall executive chair upholstered in leather, an antlered buck's head mounted on one wall and the flag of Texas draped across another. There was even a coiled lasso, hanging from a nail in the wall — as though the manager was about to step outside at any moment to deal with some unruly beast.

Ben Lowinger — no Texan called him Binyamin Levinger — resembled a Texas rancher in every respect. He boasted a luxurious mustache and sideburns, and sported a broad-brimmed cowboy hat and hand-tooled riding boots. But his preferred method of locomotion was not on horseback; it was in the big Ford pickup truck he had purchased for his own use.

Sam Lowinger was thrilled. "I'm not getting any younger," he told his friend Jack Abrams. "Now there's someone to take over for me, after they put me in the ground."

No one, of course, broached the taboo topic of returning to Eretz Yisrael. For his part, Ben was prepared to completely forget the city of his birth — but Jerusalem insisted on reminding him of her existence in her usual stubborn fashion.

Every six months, before the High Holy Days and Pesach, the ranch's mailbox was piled high with envelopes bearing Hebrew lettering. Ben would open them with an expression of long-suffering disgust: *Kollel Polin, Kollel Ungarin, Kollel Shomrei HaChomos, Kollel Tzidkas Yerushalayim.* They all sent Sam letters requesting a donation — and he, the old fool, responded to them all with a lavish hand, sending generous checks that generated a slew of grateful thank-you letters.

Had it been up to Ben, these institutions would not have received one red cent. But Sam insisted on continuing his charitable donations, and even increasing them. "Ben, there's nothing left of my *Yiddishkeit*," he would say. "This is the last thing, and I won't give it up. Who's going to say *Kaddish* for me? Who'll learn *Mishnayos*? You?"

Devorah's situation had also undergone a change. Her husband had, at long last, found the time to keep his promise, and they spent a period of time in New York. When the medical establishment gave up on them, they returned to Texas without the good news they had hoped for. Devorah sank again into her depression, finding comfort only in the company of the housekeeper and maids, and in pottering around in the vegetable garden behind the house. She was the only one who treated the Mexicans like human beings, and they reciprocated by supplying her with strange herbs and seeds that they had brought with them from the other side of the river. They ground these up into pungent concoctions and promised her that, if she drank them faithfully, she would bear a child.

Maybe it was the herbs and maybe not, but the summer of 1954 was the happiest in Devorah's life. After nearly twenty years of marriage, the long-awaited salvation arrived. Devorah was expecting her first child.

The housekeeper and maids — her only friends — clustered around, preventing her from exerting herself in any way and carrying out her every wish. The only one who remained untouched by all the excitement was her husband.

"Aren't you happy, Ben?" Sam asked him during one of his lucid moments. "I'm surprised at you. If I had a wife and she hadn't had children for so many years, I don't think I'd be walking around with such a sour face right now."

Ben glanced at him briefly, then dropped his eyes to his papers. What could he say? That he regretted the many years he had wasted with her? That right now, as he was about to become a father, he understood just how much he longed to be rid of Devorah forever? From his point of view, she was a nonentity.

Once, he had despised her; now he could not even muster that emotion. As far as he was concerned, she could sit around idly all day or socialize with the servants in the kitchen or garden. She was just a lingering bad smell left over from his past — a mistake that he was paying for to this day.

He was neither happy nor sad. He was completely indifferent. He didn't care if his wife gave birth or not, if she lived or died, if she was exultant or miserable. To him, she was of less significance than a ranch hand or a stable boy. They, at least, served a purpose, while she did nothing but eat and cry. He could fire them at any time, and send them back across the river from where they had come. But she was bound to him, a thorn in his side for the rest of his life.

Los Angeles — Nissan 5766 / April 2006

Barry Majdi chuckled. He was still standing at his office window, looking out at the lovely day, but his thoughts continued to dwell in the past. They were still locked in place on the day ten years ago, in the summer of 1996, when he had spoken with George, his failing biology student. He remembered the way the smile had vanished from George's face as Majdi leaned back at the end of the meal and asked, "What do you plan to do next year?"

George felt as though the restaurant was spinning around him. "I ... er ... was hoping to continue studying biology," he said. At the look on the professor's face — half-skeptical, half-mocking — he faltered.

The look said, "With marks like yours, forget about a scholarship. Your parents can't afford the tuition. And as for working your way through college, we both know that you're far too lazy for that."

"I really have to spend more time studying," George said earnestly. "I'll complete all my projects and get better grades ...."

The professor cut him off with a sharp gesture. "Let's be frank with each other," he said. "Next year, you have no place to go." Even if the boy made a monumental effort, he would not be able to bridge the grade gap. In any case, it was he, Professor Barry Majdi, who determined the grades. And he would make certain that George would not pass.

It was time for dessert. The professor chose a cherry sherbet, smothered in a mound of whipped cream, and attacked it with gusto. George declined. He was in no mood for desserts.

"Do you know the biggest mistake that people make?" Majdi asked between spoonfuls. "They don't take advantage of the gifts that nature has bestowed on them."

George looked at the professor angrily.

"Take yourself, for example," Majdi continued. "You have a very rare talent — and you squander it on beer and diet cola."

There was a question in George's eye.

"I'm talking about your sense of taste. About your phenomenal memory and discernment for different tastes and smells. I saw you win that tasting contest. In my opinion, you ought to leave Biology. That's not the field for you."

George leaned closer, interested. "And ...?"

"And," the professor said, "study Oenology."

"Oenology? What's that?"

"The science of winemaking."

"Wine?" George was the picture of astonishment.

"Wine, George. Wine. You were born to be a winemaker. You're wasting your talents on microbes and bacteria."

"But I hate wine!" George grimaced. The professor shook his head with a forgiving smile.

"Yes, I saw you drown that magnificent braised veal in Coke just now. I thought I was going to explode .... That's like sprinkling several spoonfuls of sugar on the meat. Why spoil the taste? Why not complement it with a glass of red wine that goes marvelously with it and brings out the full flavor of the dish?"

"I like how Coke tastes," George protested.

"Take the Pinot Noir that I just drank, for example." The professor lifted the bottle, put on his reading glasses, and focused on the back label. "It says this wine has the bouquet of ripe sour cherries and a touch of tobacco, with a hint of peeled oak in the background. Did you know that?"

George poured a small amount into his glass and sipped.

"It's obvious," he said after a few seconds. "I didn't need to read that. You can taste it."

"You can taste it?" The professor laughed incredulously. "Do you know that most people are convinced that vintners make all that up? Where, they say, does a Cabernet Sauvignon have 'an aroma of wild strawberries, raspberries, and cherries'? Where does a Chardonnay have 'a hint of melon and pineapple, and a delicate, buttery taste'? *I've* never tasted any of that. Only great experts can sense these faint aromas and flavors. If you're able to sense them, then you have an extraordinary sense of taste and you must take advantage of it."

"I thought everyone was like me," George said in surprise.

"You really don't understand what you have," the professor smiled warmly. "A sense of taste like yours is extremely rare. Winemakers study for years to achieve half your discernment. Even though you're on the verge of failing Biology — in Oenology you'd be a young genius. At the head of the class. If you study hard, in a few years you'll be one of the most famous winemakers in this country. And it'll earn you plenty of money, too. Let's not forget that."

"Where do you study such a thing?" George asked. That last bit, about the money, had piqued his interest.

"Winemakers study in three places in the world. In France, for example, in the Agropolis Institute in Montpelier."

"France sounds amazing."

"Only if you speak French," the professor said dryly. He continued: "You can also study winemaking in southern Australia, which has a thriving wine industry, at either the Perth or Adelaide Universities ...."

"They do speak English there."

"True. But there, you'd have to finance your studies on your own. The third place to study Oenology is right here in California — at Davis University."

"And here ... it's free?"

"No. But you might be able to win a scholarship from the Fine Wine Foundation."

"The what?"

"The Fine Wine Foundation. It's a public foundation that provides scholarships to talented young people, with the aim of promoting wine-making in California."

"But I hate wine," George objected suddenly, as he belatedly realized what he was getting into.

"So start liking it." The professor spoke with a trace of anger. "Because that's your future. It's your only chance not to end up like your father — a truck driver who sleeps at the side of the road and sees his home once a week."

"Sorry," George muttered. "I didn't mean to put it down. It's all just so new and surprising, that's all."

"Then grab the chance with both hands." Majdi spoke harshly, as though he hadn't heard George's apology, and he accompanied the words with a decisive blow with his open hand on the table. "Don't reject this golden opportunity. Very few people have been privileged to have what you have, without any effort on their part."

On the drive back to Los Angeles, the professor took care to restore the earlier friendly atmosphere. The world of wine was an amazing world, he told George. But that world was sealed and shuttered to those on the outside. To get in, all you had to do was pop a cork and sniff the bouquet. Once you started sipping the wine — rolling it on the tongue and letting its aroma tickle the nostrils — it was impossible to stop.

Before dropping George at the student dormitory, the professor reminded him to stop in at his office the next day to pick up the foundation's application form. It would be a good idea to fill it out as soon as possible, he urged, because the committee's annual meeting was scheduled to take place at the end of the month.

George nodded gratefully, threw his knapsack over his shoulder, and walked away with a cheerful step. Majdi stayed where he was for a moment, both hands on the wheel and a secret smile on his face. "The Fine

Wine Foundation" was a brilliant idea. George was the fifth "applicant" about to receive generous funding for the study of winemaking. None of those naive young students ever dreamed that the foundation existed only in Majdi's imagination. The "committee" met whenever he wanted it to — inside his head. It was a committee of one, a foundation of one, a philanthropic enterprise of one man with big and far-reaching plans.

But since then? Ten years had passed since those early days. It was now 2006. For ten years, he had been waiting for the document that had arrived by fax today. The document that he had just shredded and carefully flushed away.

The document that gave the green light for his great plan to be carried out at last.

23

Jerusalem — 5713 / 1953

It was during the week of mourning for her brother that Toivy Lederman's shidduch began to take shape.

One of those who came to the house to comfort the mourners was Yochanan Lederman, a cousin on their father's side, who had come to Eretz Yisrael from Poland just months earlier. His wife and children had perished in the Holocaust; he had survived the death camps only through a miracle. He told his cousins that he had been planning to visit for some time, and what a pity it was that his first encounter with his flesh and blood should take place under such sad circumstances.

None of Toivy's siblings viewed him in the light of a potential match for their sister. He limped slightly, was penniless, and had to be at least ten years older than she. It was R' Shimshon *der shadchan*, the man who had proposed the first shidduch some nineteen years earlier, who raised the possibility. Two days after the *shivah* week was over, he entered Toivy's place of business — older, slower, but still clutching his eternal notebook and pencil — and asked if he might propose a match for Toivy.

Despite the fact that the truth of the old rumors had come to light and everyone now knew that her former broken shidduch had had its source in a terrible slander, Toivy was no longer young or, despite her thriving business, particularly desirable. The new proposal took its course and was satisfactorily concluded. Yochanan Lederman was found to be a good-hearted man, and he made Toivy a devoted husband. He joined her in the business and set aside times for Torah study. Peace and joy reigned in the home that Yochanan and Toivy Lederman built, and it was not very long before their only son was born.

A difference of opinion arose between them: Yochanan wanted to name the son after Toivy's father, or at least after his own. But she claimed that each of them already had numerous children named after them. She was the only one who could name her baby after her poor brother.

"It won't bring *berachah* to the child, to name him after a person who was mentally deficient and who lived among Christians all his life," Yochanan Lederman tried to explain to his wife. But the new mother recruited Rav Margolis to her side. The *rav* said that his father, the elder Rav Margolis, used to say that *HaKadosh Baruch Hu* sometimes sends exalted souls down into this world wrapped in broken vessels — defective bodies and minds. Only then did Toivy's husband agree to accede to his wife's wishes.

At the *bris milah*, the guests were stunned. Toivy's brothers and sisters had not known of her decision, and had been certain that she would name the child Yechezkel, after their father. But when Rav Margolis was honored with reciting the blessings, he lifted up his voice and cried, "And his name shall be known in Israel as ... Shammai ben R' Yochanan!"

Grayston, Texas — 5714 / 1953

Sam Lowinger's ranch house was ablaze with light. Apart from the family, several of the ranch hands had been invited to Thanksgiving dinner. A huge roasted turkey had pride of place in the center of the table, in accordance with best American tradition. Just one day earlier, that turkey had been running around the yard. Then Manuela had seized it, wrung its neck, and turned it into the ultimate Thanksgiving fare.

"Ben," Sam handed the knife to his nephew, "carve the turkey."

Ben began to carve the succulent bird and placed the slices on each plate. Last year, Sam had insisted on distributing the turkey with his own trembling hands, and had nearly cut himself in the process. This year, he had prudently decided to delegate the task to the man who actually ran the ranch.

"Ben — did any letters come?" he asked suddenly.

Ben shrugged angrily. When the old man said "letters," he meant one thing only: receipts from Jerusalem. Sam collected them and guarded them like precious treasure. Ben had tried explaining to him that the good times were over, that their financial situation was worsening from year to year, but Sam continued writing checks liberally: Two hundred dollars to the Romanian Kollel, two-fifty to the Zibenbergen Kollel, three hundred dollars to the Diskin Orphan Home ....

Let him at least decrease his donations, give more reasonable sums! The epidemic that had run rampant through the herd had nearly decimated it, competition with nearby ranches was cutting into the profits, and insurance was expensive. Thieves continued stealing horses and cattle and, on top of all that, there was the new law about to go into effect in January.

When Ben heard about the law poised to be passed in Washington, he felt that he was mired in a nightmare. It was as if someone had concocted the law especially to harm them, as though the two members of Congress who had proposed the law had had no one but Sam and Ben Lowinger in mind.

Sheriff Jack Abrams said it was a draconian law and must be fought tooth and nail. He suggested that all the ranch owners who would be hurt by the new law travel to Austin, the state capital, to meet with the governor.

What the sheriff could not know, Ben thought sourly, *was that the only place that would be hurt was the Lowinger ranch.*

Weeks passed. The summer was nearly over. One morning, Ben climbed into his truck and set out for Grayston, planning to go from there to El Paso. Behind him swayed an empty trailer used for transporting horses. There was to be a public auction of stud horses today; maybe he would find one at a good price.

As he turned from the gravel lane onto the main road — just as he was passing the mailbox — he suddenly noticed one of the ranch hands racing after him on horseback.

Ben slowed down until the horse was galloping parallel to him.

"Sam wants you to go back!" the man shouted, gesturing dramatically as he strained to make himself heard above the roar of the engine and the wind. Ben motioned that he understood, and the Mexican started back for the ranch by way of the pastures. Ben continued on to Grayston.

He had no intention of turning around. That senile old man had played this trick a number of times before. He would warn Ben — shaking a tremulous finger for emphasis — that he must not pay more than seven hundred dollars for a horse. Not one dollar more! Who was running this place anyway, he or Sam? Let the old man decide: Did he trust him or not? Ben Lowinger was well aware of how much a horse was worth. Ben Lowinger had not been born yesterday.

It was close to evening when he drove back toward the ranch. This time, the horse trailer was filled to capacity. He had bought two stud horses, both of them healthy, handsome, and a bargain at the price. Bobby Fault's ranch manager had intended to bid against him, but he hadn't shown up at the auction and the prices had remained reasonable.

As he parked the truck in front of the house and crossed the front porch, he thought Manuela was looking at him strangely. It was almost a hostile look. He opened the door and walked inside. Sam was sitting at the big table.

"Where were you?" he asked with an accusing glare.

"It's all right," Ben said placatingly. "The two horses — both together — cost us under a thousand dollars."

"You idiot." His uncle's face creased into a broad smile. "You get a 'mazel tov.' "

Ben froze for a second. Then his eyes found the housekeeper at the door. "I'm hungry," he announced. "Is there anything to eat?"

Sam drew a breath. "You have a son," he said slowly. "Don't you understand?"

Ben looked at the old man as if he had just noticed him. "I haven't eaten a thing since this morning," he said, and glanced again at the housekeeper. "Is there any food in this house?"

Sam stood up, enraged. The chair he had been sitting in tumbled backward. Manuela placed a bowl of soup before Ben, her face shuttered.

A few minutes later, as she served him the main course, she ventured in a small voice, "He's a lovely boy, Mr. Ben. Looks just like you."

Ben did not answer. He bent over his steak, plying knife and fork. When he was done, he leaned back in his chair and pulled out a cigar.

Sam moved across the room, breathing hard in visible anger. *What a heartless dog*, he thought furiously. If he could, he would throw him straight back to Eretz Yisrael. But he had no choice. Ben carried the entire ranch on his shoulders. He himself was old and sick, and his dry bones didn't even let him ride horseback anymore. But — such behavior? Such detachment? Where did it come from? The Levinger family had never possessed such a stony, wicked character as this.

A week went by. Ben had deigned to take a look at his son, and had even promised to take the new mother into Grayston to buy a crib, diapers, and other necessities. Sam would hardly talk to him. He was furious over his nephew's behavior. Ben found that he preferred the hours when Sam was detached from reality; he had a little peace then.

Sunday dinner was a lavish affair. Several of the ranch hands joined them at the table. At the meal's conclusion, Sam snapped at Ben, "Your son will be eight days old tomorrow. You have to get hold of a *mohel*."

Ben was startled. Then, with a dismissive laugh, he stood up. "Tomorrow, my dear Sam, I'll be at the big horse race in El Paso."

Sam turned his head, elbows on the table, and glared balefully at his nephew. "What did you say?" he roared.

Ben laughed out loud, enjoying the spectacle of his uncle's anger. "I told you, I'm going to El Paso. I bet a large sum on Dennis Half-Tooth's black horse. He's going to win, and I'm going to clean up."

The ranch hands were silent, sensing that a power struggle beyond their understanding was taking place. A very big, dark shadow was passing between the ranch owner and his nephew.

"If there's no *bris* here tomorrow," Sam said, "then you won't be here either." And he punctuated the threat with a slam of his fist on the table.

The next morning was hot and humid. Devorah stood at the window, rocking her screaming infant in her arms in an effort to soothe him to sleep. Sam sat in his rocking chair on the porch. Ben came downstairs and walked over to his truck.

"Are you going to fetch a *mohel*?" his uncle called from the porch.

Ben turned to him with an impatient sigh. "Maybe tomorrow, okay? I'm busy today. I'm going to the race in El Paso and stopping in at the feed store on the way home. Tony says the new vaccines have come in."

Sam stood up without a word and went into the house. Ben began emptying some old harness tackle from the back of his truck. Devorah started crying soundlessly.

Suddenly, the front door opened with a bang and Sam appeared in the doorway. In one hand he held the old double-barreled hunting rifle that he had inherited from the former owner of the ranch and that he would bequeath to its next owner; in his other hand he grasped a number of bullets. Slowly, he returned to his rocking chair and sat down. He placed the bullets on the table and inserted one into the rifle. Ben, busy at the back of the truck, had not yet noticed what was happening. Sam lifted the rifle in a leisurely way and pressed the trigger. The thunder of gunfire filled the air.

Ben leaped up in alarm and spun around. Sam was inserting another bullet into the barrel. Then he lifted the rifle and aimed at his nephew.

"My hands may shake, Ben, but I know how to hit my mark," he said hoarsely. "If you come back without a *mohel*, the next bullet will get you right between the eyes."

Ben moved away from the truck, white with rage, and walked menacingly over to his uncle. The old man still had his rifle pointed directly at him. When he was two steps away, the rifle nearly grazed his chest. But Sam did not lower it.

"You want to kill me?" Ben asked mockingly. "Go ahead — shoot. He's my child, and I'll decide what to do with him."

"Your child?" Sam almost spat. "It doesn't look like you have any connection to him at all. It doesn't look like you feel any sense of obligation toward his mother. A stallion treats its mare better than you treat your wife."

Ben turned even paler. "Don't you tell me how to treat my wife!" he yelled.

Sam was unmoved. The ghost of a smile touched his lips.

"You're going to Grayston," he said, looking directly into Ben's eyes, "and you're coming back with a *mohel*, you hear? Otherwise, the boy will be an orphan before nightfall."

Uncle and nephew squared off for a long moment, holding each other's eyes. It was Ben who looked down first. He spat furiously on the ground and stalked toward his truck. Something in Sam's face had frightened him. He saw the same rock-hard stubborness that Sam had possessed years ago, when he had been in his prime. The old man was serious.

But Ben was not about to forfeit his horse race. He had high hopes for Dennis Half-Tooth's black horse. He had bet a considerable sum on him, had followed his training schedule, and had even slipped some cash to the right person to make sure that the competing horse with the best chances — Star, a chestnut with a white forehead — would be absent from the race. Today he was going to clean up in a big way. He was not about to lose his big chance because of a senile old man's whim.

Sam Lowinger sat on the porch all day, dozing and waking by turns, his old rifle between his knees and the four bullets on the table at his elbow. In the late afternoon, he saw a cloud of dust in the distance. He sat up straight and shaded his eyes with his shaking hand. Yes, it was Ben's green Ford. With a measured movement, he picked up one bullet and sat back again.

The engine's roar grew louder by the second. Old Sam waited tensely. The truck pulled into the small square in front of the house. There was only one figure in the front seat: Ben's. The seat beside him and the one in back held piles of wooden boxes — the vaccines, no doubt. Sam opened the rifle's chamber, slipped the bullet inside, and snapped it shut again.

The truck stopped right in front of the porch. Ben opened the door and got out, threw a brief glance at his uncle, and walked around to the rear of the truck.

Old Sam lifted his rifle. "You didn't listen to me," he said in a hard voice, pointing the gun at his nephew. "Did you think I was joking?"

Ben reached the rear compartment and unlatched the door. Out came a small, rotund figure carrying a small suitcase. He had a short-cropped beard and wore an odd, narrow-brimmed hat beneath which strawlike hair peeped out. His three-quarter-length coat was no less strange.

"Here's your *mohel*," Ben said mockingly. He leaped up all three porch steps in a single bound. "I'm hungry. Is there any food?" he shouted at the housekeeper, who hurriedly set a brimming plate of meat and beans on the table.

The old man ushered in their guest, who resembled a jester more than a *mohel*, and led him to the new mother's room.

"Is that the father?" the *mohel* whispered. Ben, it seemed had not treated him very considerately during the trip. In Grayston, he had tossed him into the back of the truck like a trussed steer; judging by the man's bruises, Ben had driven with excessive abandon to make the ride as unpleasant as possible.

Sam snorted with open contempt. Some father ....

The *mohel* checked the baby and found him healthy and strong. "A little cowboy," he announced jovially. He opened his suitcase, extracted a goblet and a bottle of wine, and made the necessary preparations for the circumcision. Then he looked around the room and spoke the words he generally found himself saying at the *bris milah* ceremonies that he conducted: "So, I understand that there's no *minyan*."

Very few Jews lived in Southern Texas, and even fewer in the Grayston area. No one knew how the *mohel* had wandered into this region some thirty years earlier, but his status as the local holy man was well-established. From time to time he would be summoned to perform a *bris* on a Jewish child — such as, for example, Sheriff Abrams' three sons. So far, there had never been a quorum of ten kosher Jews present at these ceremonies. In the majority of the cases, the attendees had included only the father, mother, and the newborn guest of honor ....

The *mohel* himself, to be honest, was not overly scrupulous in his mitzvah observance. His two former wives — one had divorced him and the other had made him a widower — had not exactly been kosher Jewish women, and his present wife was no different. Still, he knew how to conduct a *bris milah*, and it provided him with a livelihood. In addition, he would appear at any Jewish funeral that was taking place — often, this would be the first time the dead man's friends became aware of the fact that he was Jewish — recite the "*Keil malei rachamim*" and *Kaddish*, and take his fee in cash. On Yom Kippur, the *mohel* put on his cantor's high hat and gathered together a few old men for "*Kol Nidrei*." One could purchase matzos from him near Pesach time. All this religious activity had crowned him with the humorous title that Sheriff Jack Abrams had provided: "Chief Rabbi of the Greater Grayston Area."

Ben was still having his meal and the *mohel* did not want to wait. Old Sam was honored with the role of *sandek*. Devorah, overcome with emotion, was supported by her friend, Manuela. The other ranch hands gathered in the room to witness the ceremony. When the baby started wailing, the Mexicans muttered various words and phrases under their breath.

The ceremony was nearly over when Ben appeared. He leaned negligently against the doorjamb.

"Are you finished here?" he asked. He was ready to drive the *mohel* back to Grayston. It was nearly sunset.

The *mohel* poured the wine into the goblet and began to recite the blessings. Sam, moved to the point of tears, held a wine-soaked corner of a diaper to the baby's mouth. Devorah wept, and the Mexicans continued their strange muttering.

"*V'yikarei shemo b'Yisrael* ...?" The *mohel* said the words in the form of a question, lifting his eyes to Sam.

The old man shrugged, and turned to Devorah.

She returned his gaze with a questioning one of her own. A name? On this crazy day, she had not even had a chance to think about it.

"Have you decided what you're going to call him?" the *mohel* repeated, this time in explicit terms.

"John," Ben suddenly spoke up from the doorway. "We'll call him John."

The *mohel* grimaced uncomfortably. *John* was no name for a *bris milah*. Later on, they could call the boy whatever they wished; right now, he needed a Jewish name. "Is your father alive?" he asked Devorah.

She shook her head. "No."

"What was his name?"

"Yaakov."

"So, shall we name the baby after him?"

"I *said*, we're calling him John," Ben called into the room.

"Debbie will decide the name. Don't interfere," Sam snapped. Ben retreated a step.

The *mohel* returned to his goblet and raised his voice: "*V'yikarei shemo b'Yisrael* Yaakov ben Binyamin ...."

Five minutes later, Ben set the *mohel* on a crate in the back of the truck and set out at breakneck speed for Grayston. Sam clapped his hands three times and invited all those present to a party. The ranch hands clustered gleefully around the big table, which was laden with food. Manuela had toiled all morning to prepare a rich meal. Exotic aromas spread throughout the house. The whiskey flowed.

Three ranch hands pulled out a mandolin, a fiddle, and a clarinet and began playing Mexican music. As the whiskey, tequila, and rum began to leave their mark, circles of dancers formed in the big room. The women embraced Devorah and her beautiful baby, while the men politely tipped their hats to her and offered their heartfelt good wishes. Sam moved from person to person with a bottle in his hand, making sure that every glass was full. The celebration was merry despite the absence of the baby's father, who was then making his way into Grayston with the sorely battered *mohel* in the back of his truck.

That was how dozens of drunken gentiles, eating to repletion, drinking to excess, and dancing or staggering about on unsteady feet, welcomed a new Jewish child into the covenant of Avraham Avinu.

24

Sam Lowinger's condition continued to deteriorate. In addition to his addled wits and increasing memory loss came physical weakness. It became harder and harder for him to walk, and the once-sturdy physique turned thin and twisted. Sam spent long days rocking on the front porch, holding his hunting rifle and gazing vacantly ahead. Sometimes he would, with great effort, lift the rifle and terrify everyone around him with feeble attempts to shoot at a passing bird. The house-keeper consistently confiscated bullets from his pockets, but the old man always contrived to get hold of fresh ones.

The ranch was not flourishing either. Its profits dwindled and its burden of debt grew. While the land itself was worth a great deal, nearly all of it was mortgaged to the bank. But it would have been possible to cope with all of this — if not for the new law. That law, Ben knew, spelled the ranch's death knell.

Every ranch with 200 miles or more of its borders running adjacent to an international border — meaning, of course, the border with

Mexico — was required to pay a special tax, to be assessed annually at a rate of a certain percentage of the price of every head of cattle. The two Democratic members of Congress who were the initiators of the law, Sheriff Abrams explained to Ben, were longtime opponents of the oversized Texas ranches. This time, surprisingly, the lawmakers from the Republican Party, who were supposed to staunchly defend the Texas cattle ranches, did not stand in their way.

Perhaps the reason for this, the sheriff speculated aloud, was that only a handful of ranches were slated to suffer under the new law. How many ranches owned 200 miles of land adjoining the Mexican border? There were great, sprawling ranches that did not run along the border, and there were others that were close to Mexico but did not attain the requisite size.

In effect only one ranch stood to pay the price of this new law: Sam Lowinger's place. The news spread on wings throughout the region. The Grayston bank manager hinted to Ben that he was worried about an expected drop in the ranch's profits, and said that the main branch in Houston was likely to demand payment of some of the collateral if there were delays in repayment of its loans. Ben replied, smiling, that the bank could rest easy: January was still half a year away, and he had no doubt that the law would be voted down. He and the sheriff intended to travel to Austin to meet with a congressman who supported the law. When they had explained the situation to his satisfaction, he would surely not allow those accursed Democrats in Washington to rob an upright American citizen in this unjust way.

Still, the atmosphere around the ranch was dismal. No one knew what to expect. The workers clustered together and whispered anxiously. Frankie, the veteran stable manager, came into "Mr. Ben's" office one morning, shifted his weight from foot to foot, and finally blurted his news: Several of the hands were seeking work elsewhere.

The Lowingers cut corners wherever possible and tightened their belts and their budget to the bare minimum. Some of the usual preparations for winter were bypassed this year. The house would have to get by without its usual maintenance, the pastures and fields would have to struggle harder to produce crops from cheaper seeds. They would buy no new horses and might even sell the big John Deere tractor that had been purchased just the winter before.

There was only one substantial expense that could not be avoided, despite the difficult economic climate. Ben decided to build an additional access lane from the main road to the back of the house — in order to be able to come and go without running the risk of being shot by Sam from the porch.

At first, his old uncle had shot only at strangers; more recently, he had begun to shoot at anyone who came close to the square in front of the house. Once, he even took a potshot at Frankie. Luckily, his shaking hands could no longer aim the way they once had — otherwise, half the ranch hands would no longer be among the living.

One day, Ben returned from Grayston upset and angry. Tony from the supply store had refused to sell him coils of barbed wire on credit. He had demanded cash because, he said uncomfortably but firmly, "There are rumors flying, Ben, and I have a wife and four kids to feed." Reeling from this blow, Ben entered the Drunken Ox and downed half a bottle of Black and White Scotch, his favorite liquor.

He clambered aboard his truck afterward on slightly wobbly legs. As he turned off the main road, he saw an unfamiliar car. It was not the usual truck or jeep common to the area, but a white Plymouth sedan. *A bureaucratic car*, Ben thought. The car was crawling along behind a big lumbering truck hauling calves, but made no attempt to pass it. Ben drove closer to the white car, peering over the steering wheel to see who was inside. He saw two men wearing business suits and narrow-brimmed hats. They bore no similarity to anyone who belonged in the area.

The truck with the calves turned into the Abrams' ranch, and the Plymouth continued slowly on. In a burst of curiosity, Ben decided not to pass it, but to follow and see where the car was going. An uneasy feeling began to creep into his heart. The feeling grew as they passed the entrance to each successive farm. The next entrance led to the Lowingers' place. His heart thudded in his chest. As they neared the mailbox, his fears grew. The car slowed down and turned toward the ranch house. Ben caught his breath. Something bad was happening. What did these strangers want?

He hurried after the Plymouth, hoping that the old man wasn't sitting on the porch, his rifle aimed at intruders. As the white car glided toward the small open square in front of the house, he honked his horn to direct it toward the bypass road at the rear. But the men in the Plymouth either didn't hear him or pretended not to. Ben heard the crack of a gunshot, and the squawking of birds as they scattered in every direction.

The two men got out of the car, alarmed and shaken, hands in the air. Frankie burst out of the house, darted over to Sam, and grabbed the rifle from him. He made soothing, apologetic gestures at the newcomers.

Seen up close, the men certainly didn't look like locals. Their faces were pale, as if they spent most of their time indoors. One of them carried a leather briefcase and wore round spectacles. They approached Ben, who was still seated in his truck.

"Are you Benjamin Lowinger?" the round-spectacled one inquired, extending his hand.

Apprehensively, Ben leaned out and shook the proffered hand. "And you are ...?"

"My name is Colin Baron," the man introduced himself. "I represent the United States government. We're interested in buying your ranch."

Old Sam, who had sunk back into his rocking chair, suddenly sat up alertly. His hand sought his rifle and he was angry when he couldn't find it. "This ranch is not for sale," he said with momentary firmness. Then he fell back into his customary limp position.

"The United States government?" Ben repeated incredulously.

"Well, not the president himself," the spectacled man chuckled. "We're from the Department of Agriculture."

Ben recovered from his initial shock. "And why does the Department of Agriculture want this ranch in particular?" he asked.

"We heard you might be selling."

"You heard my uncle." Ben gestured at Sam in his rocking chair. "This ranch is not for sale."

Colin Baron glanced at his companion, then leaned closer to Ben and lowered his voice. "In January, or maybe earlier, the bank is going to put the ranch up for sale. So why not make a deal right now?"

Ben could not hide his surprise. "This ranch is not for sale," he repeated, a little less firmly than before. The difference was not lost on the two men.

In the same friendly tone — as if he had nothing but Ben's benefit in mind — the government agent continued speaking. "Mr. Lowinger, the economic picture here in Texas is not a promising one. Maintaining a ranch is becoming more expensive, competition is fierce, and in January, as you know, your taxes are about to double. Unless you have an oil well or a gold mine on your property, I'd strongly urge you to seize this opportunity with both hands."

"Because if we don't do business with *you*," the second man put in nonchalantly, "we'll find another location."

"But I think that you know that you really have no choice," the first man went on. "In January, the bank is going to foreclose on the ranch and sell it for a fraction of its value. Much better to sell it now ..."

"... while you're still up on the horse," the second completed the sentence, with a condescending smile. "As the cowboys say."

Ben said nothing. He was confused. What was behind the offer? Who were these two bureaucrats? Whom did they represent, and why were they so confident that the bank intended to foreclose on the ranch in January?

"You heard my uncle," he repeated finally. "He owns this place, and he says that it's not for sale. We're going to hold on."

Colin Baron looked at old Sam. "He's the owner?" He grinned. "Does he even know what's happening to him? He's finished. Tomorrow he'll be gone, and the ranch will be yours."

"In any case, there's nothing to talk about," Ben said. "We're not selling the land."

One of the men withdrew a business card from his inside jacket pocket and handed it to Ben. "If you change your mind, call me."

"Unless we find a better buy in the neighborhood," the second warned, spurning the gravel with his shoe.

Ben crumpled the card in his fist and tossed it contemptuously onto the seat beside him. "You know your way out?" he asked coolly.

The two men grinned at each other, got into their car, and drove away.

■ ■ ■

Ben watched the Plymouth depart in a cloud of dust. He tossed a glance at Sam, snoring in his rocking chair, and then let his eyes rove around the ranch.

Colin Baron was right — but only partly. Sam was incapable of thinking clearly, and it would probably not be long before he closed his eyes forever. When he did, the ranch would not pass on to any bank or Department of Agriculture. On that day, it would belong to him. The enormous tract of land, the huge herds of cattle, the dozens of ranch hands, the pastures and the stables — all his.

Someone, it didn't matter who, had cast an eye on his ranch because of Sam's weakened state, but Ben did not intend to give in. He would fight to the bitter end.

The ranch was not for sale. And this time, it was no senile old man saying it. It was he, Benjamin Lowinger — future owner of the Lowinger Ranch.

Several days passed peacefully, and Ben thought he was rid of the government men. Then, on the third day, a telegram arrived at the ranch house. The bank manager in Grayston invited Mr. Benjamin Lowinger to see him in his office — urgently.

Ben climbed into his truck, his heart weighed down with foreboding.

The bank manager's fixed smile was nowhere in evidence. Likewise, his customary small talk about rodeo personalities and horse-race gossip was absent. The banker appeared distressed, and his teeth chewed uncomfortably on his lower lip.

"Mr. Lowinger," he said with a sigh. "As you are undoubtedly aware, your uncle's ranch owes the bank a total of $530,000."

"But the next payment isn't due for two weeks," Ben pointed out.

"We … are forced to demand payment of the loan in full," the banker said, almost inaudibly.

Ben blanched.

"The entire amount? In January?" His voice shook. "You know that we can't arrange such a sum on such short notice."

"The entire thing, Ben." The banker paused, casting his eyes down and then looking up at him sadly. "Immediately."

Ben was speechless. He felt as though he were suffocating. "But … why?" he managed to croak.

The banker spread his hands in a true gesture of helplessness. "Believe me, this was not my decision. I received a direct order from our main branch in Houston. I have no control over this."

"*I* know who's behind this!" Ben slammed his fist on the table in sudden rage. "They're trying to force me to sell. Well, it won't work!"

The banker looked at him, lips compressed in compassion and empathy. "Ben, take some advice from a man of experience," he said gently. "There are powers stronger than we are. Some forces are simply …

unbeatable. If the United States Government wants your property — it doesn't matter why — then it will get it."

The man knows what he's talking about, Ben thought.

"I've known Sam for over thirty years," the banker continued. "And I've known you ever since you came to Grayston. I've always liked and respected both of you, and I've tried to meet you halfway. This time, unfortunately, I don't have the power to do that any more. My orders are to move things along quickly. If you do not repay the loan in full within fourteen days, the ranch will be in foreclosure and will be put up for sale."

"But that's impossible," Ben burst out angrily. "A man can't be thrown off his own land, just like that!"

"Impossible?" the banker repeated with a sorrowful smile. "Be thankful they're at least offering you money. Once upon a time, here in Texas, they would come into your house, shoot the whole family, and take the land. And they could invoke the law of eminent domain and just move you out at pennies on the dollar. You have no choice, Ben. You're also running out of time. I'm speaking as a friend."

In turmoil, Ben stood up and left the bank manager's office. His entire being revolted at the injustice being perpetrated upon him. He was a mere step away from owning the ranch — and now they were trying to steal it from him. No! He wouldn't let it happen.

He went out into the street and sat in his truck, sad and frustrated. Was this America? It was a dictatorship! What was the difference between the United States and the Soviet Union? Between Eisenhower and Stalin? Why did everyone condemn the Communists, when the American government oppressed its own innocent citizens, too?

After half an hour, he stopped cursing and started thinking. The question was: What to do now? He was caught in a genuine bind. If the bank put the ranch into foreclosure, the price it fetched would not even cover his debts. Maybe it was worth his while to check out the options. On the floor of the truck he found the discarded business card that the two bureaucrats had given him. It was soiled and creased.

With a sigh, he picked it up.

Ben sat in a corner of the Drunken Ox, staring down at the scarred wooden table. The bartender gave him his usual bottle of Black and White and he tried not to drink too much of it.

The two government agents, as arranged by phone, arrived thirty minutes later. They joined Ben at his table, declining his offer of a drink. In the time that had elapsed since his meeting with the bank manager — with, perhaps, some help from the whiskey — Ben had come to terms with his bitter dilemma. The ranch was going to be sold. All that was left now was to negotiate the price.

"Okay," he said angrily. "What do you want?"

"What is the ranch's total debt?" Colin Baron asked.

"Why are you asking? I'm sure you already know. It's $530,000."

"We are prepared to purchase the land along with all the debt ...."

"But the land is worth much more than that!" Ben protested hotly. "It's worth $800,000 or more."

"... plus one million dollars."

Ben froze. His eyes darted in disbelief from one man to the other.

"A million dollars?" he managed to say, when he'd found his voice.

"A million dollars," Colin affirmed.

"The Department of Agriculture must really want that land," Ben said with bitter sarcasm. The government men neither agreed nor disagreed. They simply watched him, stone faced.

"You know something?" he said suddenly. "You two don't look like ranchers to me. What exactly are you planning to do with that property? Why are you willing to pay so much for it?"

Colin Baron leaned across the table and brought his face close to Ben's. His expression was suddenly menacing. "Mr. Lowinger," he said in a hard voice. "You are going to get a lot more than you ever dreamed of for that land. The deal includes not asking questions, not opening your mouth, not being too interested in what doesn't concern you. Understand?"

Ben swallowed and lowered his gaze.

"The problem is the old man," he muttered. "Sam will never agree to sell the land."

"Does he ever go out on the property?" Colin asked.

"No. He's holed up at home all day, mostly sitting on the porch and shooting at anyone who approaches."

"If he's not clear in his mind, you can be appointed his legal guardian, with power of attorney to act as you see fit and to dispose of the property as you wish."

Ben looked at him for a moment, digesting this information. "Okay," he said. "But try and get him out of that house. He's lived there for decades. He'll never agree to leave."

"Don't worry about that. We've thought of everything," Colin said. "We'll make this arrangement: During his lifetime, you can all go on living in the house. We'll also let you have a few hundred yards around the house: the orchard, the stables, and part of the pastureland. As soon as he passes on, you'll all leave."

"As long as Sam lives, we can stay?"

"Certainly."

Ben thought this over for a few more seconds, and then slowly nodded his head. There was no other option open to him.

Colin held out his hand across the table. "Do we have a deal?"

What happened over the next few hours confirmed Ben's suspicions that he was not dealing with Department of Agriculture bureaucrats at all, but with agents of a much more powerful body.

The three men left the tavern and in the white Plymouth drove to El Paso's central courthouse. A man was waiting for them near the rear entrance. He led them down a corridor and up an elevator to an airy, spacious office.

Five minutes later, a large man with an intellectual appearance hurried into the room. He wore a black robe. The robed man sank into his chair and studied his visitors.

"Good morning, Your Honor," the fellow who had let them into the building said with a slight bow. "Judge Fitzgerald, with your permission ...."

"I'm in the process of hearing a case," the judge cut in. "Make this quick and just tell me what you need."

The man handed him a form to sign. The judge's eyes raced briefly over the printed lines, even as his hand pulled out a pen. Five seconds later, his signature was scrawled across the bottom of the page.

"Thank you, Your Honor," the man said. The judge rose and, without a word, returned to his courtroom.

"You are now Sam Lowinger's legal guardian," Colin told Ben with a hint of mockery. "Simple, wasn't it?"

They told Ben that they would be heading to the Department of Agriculture next. To his surprise, they passed right by the big department building and parked in the lot of a smaller structure next door.

"Our division isn't located in the main building," Colin Baron explained, noting Ben's puzzlement. He winked at his partner.

They rode up to the second floor where, in a handsome, well-lit room, a lawyer waited for them with a mass of close-typed pages. Although Ben had planned to study the contract very carefully, the sight of the check clipped onto it befuddled him completely. The name on the check was his own — Benjamin Lowinger — and the sum was for one million dollars. He found himself signing wherever the lawyer told him to: his full name here, his initials there ... Another one here, please ... Now, just once more ... And they were done.

Colin Baron and his partner brought Ben back to Grayston, where he could deposit the check in the bank and drive his truck back to the ranch. On the way, they agreed on the following: All the cattle would remain on the ranch. They were included in the price of the sale and had become government property. However, the ranch hands were Ben's responsibility. He was to fire them, without mentioning a word regarding the conditions of the sale or the identity of the buyer.

The family could stay on in the ranch house, as they had arranged, until the old man breathed his last. Until that time, a tall fence would be constructed, separating the Lowinger property from the land now owned by the United States Government.

25

The changes on the Lowinger ranch were felt immediately.

Early in the morning on the day after the signing, the main road brought a long convoy of trucks and tractors to the ranch. A new concrete road was poured, running behind the house, with a tall barbed-wire fence stretched alongside. The family was left with a plot of land that included the house, barn, stables, orchard, and a portion of the pasture.

Old Sam, the owner of the ranch though presently detached from reality, continued sitting on the front porch staring at a fixed point: the small clearing in front of the house, with the road running across the horizon and Tall Willy's pasture beyond that, remained untouched. But behind him, without his being aware of it, his whole world was disappearing.

Cement mixers moved to and fro, along with cranes, bulldozers, and trucks laden with asphalt. The cattle were loaded onto trucks and taken off the ranch. There, on the land into which Sam had poured his life for so many years, a small town of huts sprouted, to serve as living quarters for the workforce and as offices for their managers. With lightning speed, rows of trees were uprooted and deep holes dug in the ground. Someone seemed to be in an extreme rush to build something on the Lowinger ranch, and that someone apparently had an unlimited budget.

The house became an empty, quiet place. The ranch hands were fired and sent on their way. Only two employees remained: Manuela, the housekeeper, to cook their meals and help Devorah with the baby, and Frankie, the veteran stableman, whose current responsibility was to handle not horses, but old Sam.

Ben spent the next two weeks selling off his equipment. Tony from the supply store bought most of his stable equipment, neighboring ranchers purchased the tractors and other agricultural tools, and what was left went to the sheriff's three sons, Dennis Half-Tooth, Bobby Fault, and Tall Willy.

With the equipment gone and the ranch no longer requiring his management, Ben's days stretched before him, long and tedious. At home he had a wife he despised, a bawling infant, and a witless old uncle. Ben sought escape in his green Ford pickup. He spent hours sitting in the truck's cabin, switching stations on the radio, chain-smoking, and guzzling down endless beers.

People in Grayston were curious to know what was being constructed behind his house. The sheriff asked him point-blank what he knew about the mysterious project, but Ben had no answers. He would sit for long hours watching the activity, he told the sheriff, but was no closer to understanding what it was all about than he had been at the start. Cement mixers worked nonstop at a spot about a hundred yards from the ranch house, but as far as he could see there was no building going up there. The workers were also pouring a broad road leading southward, and quickly erecting a concrete wall around the entire area.

"Find out what's going on, Ben," the sheriff urged. "There's something about this I don't like."

The sheriff did not tell Ben that he, too, had tried to investigate. He had friends in high places. But he was told in no uncertain terms that if he had plans to be voted in again in the coming election, it would be a good idea for him to stop poking his nose into business that wasn't his.

One morning, Ben turned off the main road and drove down the newly paved one that led into the depths of the ranch. Driving slowly, he approached the building site. Now he understood why he hadn't been able to see anything going up. Most of the building was being constructed below ground level.

He got out of the truck and walked over to the workmen. From this vantage point, he could count at least four subterranean levels. Suddenly, one of the foremen, red-faced and perspiring beneath his construction helmet, spotted him. He hurried over to Ben, looking stern.

"Get out of here. This is private property," he yelled.

"This was my ranch," Ben said. "I just want to see what you people are building here."

The foreman was unimpressed. To him, Ben was just another of the many Texas troublemakers who repeatedly stopped their big trucks, stuck their heads out their windows in those ludicrous cowboy hats, and asked too many questions in their strange, drawling accent.

"Get out of here before I call Security," he shouted, raising his walkie-talkie to his lips.

Ben beat a hasty retreat and drove, defeated, back home.

In the evenings, Ben regularly drove into town to drown his sorrows. Some nights he would end the evening dead drunk; on others, slightly less so. The bank manager, an old friend of Sam's, watched in dismay as Sam's nephew, who held the legal power of attorney, withdrew more and more money from the bank and proceeded to fritter it away on drink, rodeo competitions, and the like.

Ben was welcome in the Drunken Ox, as well as in every other saloon in the area, but beneath the hospitable veneer was profound contempt. A true Texan, they said, spitting on the ground, would never sell his land — not for all the money in the world. If Sam had been the way he once was, he would have shot those two city men before he even listened what they had to say. But the old man was senile and confused. A longtime friend, come to pay Sam a visit, heard him mumble something about being about to leave Jerusalem and sail away to America. In New York, the friend reported, Sam said that he could make a lot of money and throw off the onerous burden of his overly strict father. The old man had apparently returned to the days of his youth; everything that had happened since then was erased from his memory. Better for him to be dead, the folks at the Drunken Ox said. It was time for the good L-rd to gather Sam Lowinger to his final rest.

Ben did not share in these sentiments. With all his heart, he hoped his uncle would live to a ripe old age. The ranch house was his to live in only as long as Sam was alive and breathing. On the day he was laid to rest in the old cemetery, Colin Baron and his partner from the "Department of Agriculture" would throw Ben and his family out into the road without the slightest compunction.

Little John had grown into a chubby, healthy baby. His presence helped lift his mother at least partially out of her depression. If she did not become a contented, jolly woman, she was at least able to function. She fed and dressed the child, took him to the doctor, and washed his diapers. From time to time, she and Manuela went to Grayston, or even as far as El Paso, to buy the boy clothing and toys. Once in a very long while, Devorah even bought a little something for herself.

Ben remained remote. Though both women tried more than once to interest him in his son, their efforts were in vain. He was as indifferent to the boy as he was to the boy's mother. The childish laughter that filled the house, the first prattled words, the first staggering steps — none of these things found their way into his sealed and distant heart.

Late one winter morning, Ben stepped onto his porch with creased clothes and bleary eyes. There was a familiar car parked in front of the house: a spacious black Chevrolet with the word "Sheriff" along with a five-pointed white star stenciled on the door. The sheriff himself stood beside Sam's rocking chair, his face drawn and sad. Seeing Ben, he turned to him with a sigh and a brief nod in greeting.

"He's completely gone." Abrams pointed at the old man in the chair. "He doesn't recognize me anymore."

Ben shook his head and rubbed his eyes in an effort to come fully awake. "He doesn't recognize anyone, if that's any comfort to you," he said. "A few old-timers from the neighborhood used to stop by once in a while. Now even they no longer visit."

The sheriff walked back to his car, lost in thought, his boots kicking up a spray of gravel. Ben accompanied him silently.

When they reached the car, the sheriff gestured at the tall concrete wall enclosing the area behind the house. Construction had been concluded some time ago, and the sealed-off area hummed with life. No one in town knew what was inside, but no one could miss the intense activity taking place there. There was a steady stream of private cars, big trucks, and military vehicles — the latter, no doubt, bringing personnel to man the watchtowers that had been built above the concrete wall at regular intervals. At first, some attempt was made to conceal this fortress on the U.S.–Mexico border: camouflage nets were draped over the towers, and large tree branches were inserted into the netting. But the pretense quickly fell away, and the sight of armed soldiers on the watchtowers was clearly evident.

"I have no idea what that is," the sheriff said worriedly. "They've erected a no-man's-land right under my nose, and no one's willing to talk to me."

Ben waved a dismissive hand. "What are you getting so excited about? They're not hurting anyone."

"Not hurting anyone?" the sheriff repeated indignantly. "They shot at Willy Junior yesterday. Didn't you hear?"

Willy Jr., Tall Willy's 11-year-old son from the ranch across the road, was a deaf-mute. Although feeble minded, he was physically very strong. His father had warned him not to go near the big wall, but when Tall Willy left for a cattle sale the day before, his son had seized his chance. He crossed the road and approached the wall. The soldiers on the watchtower shouted warnings at him, and gestured with their rifles, but Willy Jr. just laughed and kept moving until the soldiers had no choice but to shoot.

"Luckily, he was only lightly grazed," the sheriff said. "But when I was summoned to the scene, the soldiers refused to talk to me. An arrogant officer — a black man, do you believe it? — opened the gate a crack and yelled that it was none of my concern. He said that I and everyone in Grayston should just mind our own business. Hear that, Ben? I've been sheriff of this region for upward of twenty years, elected by the people time after time. I was bearing arms in the First World War before that black boy was born — and he refused to talk to me! We give those folks civil rights, and they go and stick their noses in the air .... By the way, when they bought the land from you, what did they say? Who are they? *What* are they?"

"Department of Agriculture," Ben answered, with blatant skepticism. "They said they belong to some division within the Department of Agriculture."

"Agriculture?" the sheriff murmured, half to himself. "Far as I know, the Department of Agriculture is not subservient to the CIA."

"The CIA?"

"That's what that black officer said. He said, 'This is federal property. if you have any problems, take them to the CIA.' Then he slammed the gate shut in my face."

Ben laughed. "Listen, Sheriff. One thing's certain: They're not from the Department of Agriculture. There's nothing growing and no livestock. It's anything *but* agriculture."

The Sheriff's eyes narrowed with suspicion. "How do you know what's in there?"

Ben turned toward the house and pointed, grinning, at the southern tower. An expression of surprise crossed the sheriff's face. Why hadn't he realized till now that the tower stood nearly a meter and a half higher than the wall?

"You can see from there?" he asked.

"You can see just fine," Ben said with pleasure. "I guess they didn't think of that. Want to take a peek, Sheriff Abrams?"

Sam Lowinger's ranch had been built in the year 1834, when Texas was still an independent republic. It had broken away from Mexico, but had not yet joined the Union. All land from the Mississippi to the Pacific was known as the "Wild West" — with some justification. An assortment of interesting characters and outlaws roamed that vast region: Indians, independent cattlemen, adventurous gold-seekers, and drifters, all of whom bred fear in the hearts of the area's few settlers. An isolated ranch like this one was a magnet for the kind of men who didn't balk at crime or violence. To protect his home and provide a good view of the surrounding land, two structures had been built, one at either side of the house, both stretching a story and a half above it. A narrow wooden staircase led from the house to the tops of these towers.

Time had passed, conditions had changed, and there was no longer any need to protect the ranch from invaders. No one had bothered climbing those steps for decades. The stairwells had become storage areas for all sorts of unwanted objects and rubbish, work tools, and broken furniture.

The northern tower had been badly damaged in one of the periodic tornados that swept the region, years before young Shmuel Levinger had arrived from Jerusalem and had evolved into Sam Lowinger. The powerful wind had plucked off the pointed roof, making the tower appear to have been beheaded. Instead of repairing it, the former owners had simply sealed off the roof and the entrance to the tower with sheets of plywood, and left it strictly alone.

The southern tower also did not suffer from too much human contact. In the year 1934, when Sam was still in the full flower of his strength and his young nephew, Binyamin, had just begun writing to him from Jerusalem, an excited Sam had begun searching for the old English-Yiddish dictionary that he had purchased in his first days in America. Surmising that it must still be in the suitcase he had brought with him from New York to Texas, he had climbed up to the small room where he had lived in his first months at the ranch house — the southern tower's topmost room — found the dictionary, and climbed down.

Since then, the tower had deteriorated badly. Several of the roof shingles were broken and the room had turned into a favorite nesting place for the local birds. The wooden floorboards were strewn with grass, bits of hay, and dried leaves. An old straw mattress, its stitching unraveling at the edges, lay at an angle across a metal frame with broken legs; ancient suitcases filled with equally ancient rags were strewn about; and spiders had woven their webs across everything. Just one week earlier, a new visitor had come to the tower — a visitor who discovered, quite by accident, that the tower was a bit taller than the concrete wall of the sealed-off compound, and that its windows provided a view of what was taking place behind that wall.

Ben and the sheriff went into the house. Sheriff Abrams tipped his hat politely to the two women in the kitchen — Manuela, slicing vegetables for a salad, and Devorah, silently watching her. Little John crawled on the wooden floor. Abrams paused for a moment to lift him in his strong arms and toss him fondly in the air.

"Ho, ho, ho! You've got a fine little cowboy here!" he told Devorah with a smile. "How old is he?"

Devorah didn't answer. "One year," the Mexican answered for her.

"Coming, Sheriff?" Ben asked impatiently.

The sheriff put the baby down and followed Ben to a heavy door, beyond which rose a rickety wooden staircase that led directly up to the top of the tower.

The door at the upper end of the stairs hung from a single rusty hinge. Opening it with caution, they found themselves in a small room. Most of the window panes had been replaced by wood over the years, and what little glass remained was filthy. The heavy curtains smelled of mildew.

"You can see from here," Ben whispered. "But be careful. If they see any movement, they won't hesitate to shoot."

The sheriff twitched a dusty curtain slightly to one side — and then quickly dropped it in alarm. Not ten meters away, literally facing him, stood one of the watchtowers. He felt that he could almost touch the two armed soldiers standing guard in the booth. Neither of them had noticed him. They sat on makeshift chairs made of ammunition crates, their weapons leaning against the wall of the booth while they drank their morning coffee.

Sheriff Abram's eyes opened wide in amazement as he peeked through a narrow gap in the curtains. "They've built a whole city out there," he whispered.

From his vantage point, he could take in the entire enclosed area at a glance. It was shaped like an isosceles triangle, with the ranch house at its apex and the two walls on either side of the triangle stretching down toward the Mexican border until they disappeared from view behind a rolling rise in the landscape.

The building that Ben had seen was several hundred yards away. Long and narrow, and only two stories high, this was clearly the beating heart of the compound. The building was surrounded by a second tall fence and under greater security than any other part of the compound. Scattered here and there were other buildings, all of them several stories high and each with its complement of lawn and garden. Some of them, at least, appeared to be designated as living quarters.

Another fenced-in area gave the impression of a military base, with a number of huts and a drill clearing. This, the sheriff surmised, was where the guards lived.

There were at least ten private cars in the parking lot. A long road stretched beyond the horizon; closer, near the secure building, stood a large hangar with an adjacent asphalt area for helicopters to land.

The sheriff stood scanning the sealed compound for a long time. At first, nothing happened. The soldiers on the watchtower finished their coffee and began a game of cards. Other guards patrolled the inner pe-rimeter. A few people emerged from one of the buildings and entered the central structure.

Ten minutes later, two closed trucks drove in through the front gate. A bevy of workers unloaded numerous wooden crates and carried them into the central building. The sheriff watched with interest, but the mystery was not solved. Indeed, it had only deepened.

What, exactly, was going on in the enclosed area? Why had it been built? And what was it that called for such constant and strict protection?

26

Moscow — 5713 / 1953

The minor KGB bureaucrat — a novice in the Technology Department — knocked respectfully at General Sergei Petroshov's door. He was holding a coarse sheet of paper, folded in quarters and stapled shut. The document had been enlarged from a tiny strip of microfilm that the general had sent to the developing lab shortly before.

"*Da* [Yes]!" came the impatient roar from inside the room.

The underling entered the room and handed the general the page.

"*Spasiba* [Thank you]," Sergei Petroshov said, in a rare show of courtesy, waving his subordinate out of the room .

When he was alone, he removed the staple, unfolded the sheet of paper, bent his head, and began to read what was written there. After a few words, he felt as if his heart were about to explode. The message that his agent, "Black Sheep," had sent from America held bad news this time — very bad news, indeed. For all intents and purposes, Black Sheep wrote, the Soviet Union had fallen into the pit and would be as putty in the hands of the United States for many long years to come.

From line to line, the general's fears grew. He shook his head in disbelief, as though trying to prevent the harsh news from becoming reality. But the words mercilessly thrust the truth on him. He dropped the page onto his desk and held his head in his hands, his expression stricken.

"Black Sheep" was the code name for the top Soviet spy in the U.S. He held a strategic position in Washington's Department of Defense and, idealistically, refused to accept payment for his work on behalf of the Communist Party. He had ties to all the American elite. His information was always accurate and precise.

This morning, word had come from him that was likely to start a figurative earthquake. General Petroshov slowly lifted the page to his eyes and read the message again:

> June 25'. Black Sheep informs us that he has learned with certainty that the infamous Nazi scientist, Dr. Heinrich von Reiner — previously presumed dead — is still alive. Dr. von Reiner was captured by the U.S. Army immediately after Nazi Germany surrendered in the year 1945, and was flown to the United States. Since then, he has continued his scientific work in the service of the American military.

The KGB general rose to his feet in helpless fury. Then he sat down again, slamming both fists on his desk. This was more than just a triumph of America over Russia. It was a personal defeat for him.

It was he, Sergei Petroshov, whom the Soviet leadership had entrusted at the war's end to locate and capture Dr. von Reiner — the Nazis' secret card in the manufacture of German weapons. Petroshov had been given every assistance he required. All his requests had been filled at once. A special branch of the Soviet secret police had been established behind the lines. Hundreds of fresh troops were brought in from the now-quiet fronts to enter his service, as well as investigators, secret agents, and vehicles. Even as the determining battle for Berlin drew near, when every man who could hold a weapon was desperately needed, hundreds of troops were allocated to one purpose: capturing Heinrich von Reiner.

The campaign had begun auspiciously. The KGB had succeeded in obtaining accurate intelligence on what was taking place inside the military Institute for Disease Research outside Berlin, and knew that the atmosphere there was one of near-despair. General Petroshov had managed to pass a message to the scientist himself, inside the institute, saying that the Soviet Union was ready to offer the best possible conditions for completing his research. If he wished to communicate with the Russians, a planted Soviet spy told him, he could do so at any time. All he had to do was send a letter to Zurich, Switzerland, addressed to P.O. Box 1766, postal code 8002.

But when Soviet troops finally reached the institute on the day Berlin fell, they found the building burned to the ground. There was no one there. The offices and labs had been consumed in the fire; nothing was left. No bodies were found. It was concluded that the institute staff had managed to escape.

Moscow's instructions were unequivocal: Find Heinrich von Reiner at any cost. Sergei Petroshov's men interrogated captured German soldiers, burst into homes in nearby villages, threatened and murdered village residents, searched through caves in the hills, and combed the prisoner-of-war camps. But all their efforts were in vain. No one was found. No one had heard a word about Heinrich von Reiner.

And now — the general again slammed his fists onto his desk — now they had learned that the United States had gotten to him first. The disappointment and degradation were multiplied by the fact that the Americans had managed to keep the fact a secret for eight whole years. From 1945 until 1953, Heinrich von Reiner had been working for them! Who knew what he had accomplished in that time? Who knew how far he had developed his work?

Who knew how great was the danger that now threatened the Soviet Union?

The next message from Black Sheep arrived seven months later, at the beginning of January.

They had not been restful months for General Petroshov. He had activated every spy he had planted in the United States in an effort to obtain information by any means. His efforts were futile. Von Reiner's capture — and his recruitment to serve U.S. interests — were shrouded in the utmost secrecy. Public opinion would have found it hard to digest the rehabilitation of a war criminal on such a massive scale — apart from the fact that the nature of the work von Reiner was doing was of the hush-hush variety in any case.

The only one who managed to dig up a modicum of information was Black Sheep. He sent his message, as usual, coded and on microfilm that had been smuggled from West Germany to East Germany, and from there to Moscow.

Dr. Heinrich von Reiner was, indeed, continuing the work he had begun in Berlin, the spy wrote to his Russian controller. He was engaged in the field of biological warfare and focusing on ways to control the spread of an epidemic in order to turn it into an effective weapon that would not turn around and bite the hand that had set it loose.

All this time, said the spy, Dr. von Reiner had been working in El Paso, near the Department of Agriculture building. More recently, the U.S. Government had purchased a broad and isolated stretch of land in the small Texas town of Grayston, near the Mexican border. A large complex of sophisticated laboratories had been built there, to provide the scientist with optimal conditions for completing his work. Within this complex would also be stored the lethal germs that he produced.

Northern Mexico — 5714 / 1953

The Indian village, situated in a clearing in the jungle, had no official name. The place — consisting of huts made of mud and tree branches — appeared on no map, and no road led to it. Hundreds of kilometers of dense forest separated the village from the nearest civilized habitation.

This did not bother the primitive village children. The village and its environs constituted their whole world. As far as they were concerned, this was where they would stay as long as fruit grew on the trees, as long as there were monkeys to be hunted, as long as there were fish in the stream. Here was where they had been born, and here they would live in tranquility as long as the Black Mountain — the volcano that soared above the green valley — did not explode in searing fury; as long as no powerful storm came along to destroy their modest huts; as long as the giant white hornet, that consumer of human flesh, did not return to sow disease and death among the tribe's warriors.

The members of the Chuma tribe had never set eyes on a white man. They spoke in their ancient tribal tongue and lit fires by striking two stones together. These Indians had never been drawn into Western civilization. The missionaries who had roamed their land since the seventeenth century had yet to make their way to this clearing to urge their children to take shelter beneath the wings of the church, as they had done to most of the Indian nation. The Chuma tribe continued to worship their pagan gods: the spirit of the water snake and the eagle spirit of the Black Mountain.

It was seven in the evening. The chief who ruled the tribe sat on a large rock beside the stream, a worried expression on his granite features. Near him sat the tribe's old shaman, or magic-maker, with his long, wild white hair and draped in the animal skin he wore on his skinny frame. The two gazed silently at the flowing water, thinking about the new and dangerous enemy that had just arisen to threaten the tribe.

Both men were offspring of an ancient and venerable lineage. The chief was the son of the tribe's previous leader, the grandson of the leader before that, and a descendant of the Chuma tribe's first great chief. The shaman, too, was the son of the previous magic-man and the last of an old and honored family of shamans who had come, according to Indian legend, from the land of fire on the other side of the Black Mountain. During that golden era, many years ago, the Chuma tribe had numbered in the hundreds of thousands, and its brave warriors had triumphed over all rival tribes.

The legends had passed from generation to generation. The shamans would sit by the fire and regale the youngsters with tales of the brave exploits of Fire Serpent, Fasting Coyote, and all the other heroes — the immortal sons of the first chief who lived in the enchanted city in the heart of the great forest.

In those far-off days, they said, the Chuma kingdom had covered vast tracts of land: from the high mountains where fallen warriors went to the vast sea that extinguished the sun at the end of each day. They erected ornate pyramids on which to bring sacrifices: large clusters of bananas and jungle fruit, and animals with their hearts torn out while they were still alive. They brought human sacrifices as well.

Today, the tribe numbered no more than a few hundred. Disease had ravaged it mercilessly, and wild beasts occasionally attacked the village — but they had never had to deal with what had happened four suns ago. The sun had stood high in the sky when a frightening buzzing had sounded among the trees, moving inexorably closer to the village. The sound came from the biggest hornet that the chief or the shaman had ever seen.

It was bigger than a jaguar or a mountain lion. It circled above the huts, eyes shining eerily and fixed wings turning oddly above its head while alarming noises sounded from its throat. The monstrous sight filled the natives with terror.

As the women and children were sent into hiding in the huts, the shaman began muttering incantations and the tribe's warriors donned their frightening war masks and dipped their arrows in the lethal poison that the shaman had mixed in his hut.

In a single concerted rush, the warriors burst out of the trees and raced toward the monster. They began shooting arrows at it to persuade it to move away from the village. The huge hornet circled the village several times, flying lower each time. The tribesmen had succeeded in forcing it away from the huts, when one of the arrows seemed to pierce an eye or a wing. With a prolonged, high-pitched wail, the giant hornet emitted a plume of liquid that turned into tiny droplets falling like rain on the tribal warriors. For a minute the hornet hovered in place, as though poised to fall. Then it turned around and began flying away as though afraid for its life.

A cry of triumph burst from the warriors' throats. The women, the children, and the elderly emerged from the huts and joined in the celebration. The shaman thanked the tribal gods for rescuing their children from the terrible hornet, and added an appropriate gift: several bunches of ripe bananas and a monkey that had been found impaled on one of the trees.

By the next sunrise, however, the warriors began to fall ill, one by one. These strong young men lay in their huts, burning with fever, writhing in pain, and watching their bodies erupt in reddish boils. The shaman concocted his remedies and ran from hut to hut, but the warriors' condition only worsened. Two sunsets later, three of the warriors were dead. The mourning tribesmen piled the bodies in a spot close to the village and covered them with branches and leaves. After another sunset and a sunrise, they would burn the bodies, to permit their spirits to soar up to the high mountains where the eternal warriors rested.

Now the chief and the shaman sat by the stream, filled with helpless dread. The events of the last few days were beyond their understanding. In all the tribe's history, since the days of the first chief and the shaman from the valley of the springs where the water snake was born, nothing like this had ever happened before. The tribe had been called upon to cope with all sorts of threats and dangers — but never with a homicidal hornet.

For when the shaman had risen with the dawn to pour banana oil on the warriors' bodies and set them on fire, he had not been able to believe his eyes. The giant hornet had returned. In front of the shaman's terrified eyes, the hornet was clutching the bodies and swallowing the corpses. When it saw the shaman it began to flee in alarm — with yet another of the bodies gripped in its claw. It took the body away to its nest, over the mountain of black rock, where it doubtless devoured it with gusto.

All that evening, the Chuma tribesmen kept their eyes fixed on the heavens. The water snake — so the shaman explained — bit off another small piece of the moon every night, until the night came when it had swallowed it all and the sky was dark. The natives now waited for the new moon to be born in the night sky. That was when the shaman would begin the parting ceremony.

The natives would sip mescal, an intoxicating liquid fermented from the peyote cactus, causing visions and hallucinations. They would dance wildly all through the night, floating on clouds of alcohol until, near sunrise, they collapsed on the ground. Only then would the shaman disappear from sight, as he started the journey to the ancient tribal cave in the Black Mountain.

The shaman had prepared enough food to last several days. His bag of animal skins was also packed with the things he would need for the ritual in the cave: a dry gourd to hold the intoxicating mescal drink, bundles of grasses and special seeds, flint stones for lighting the fire, pitch torches, and other items. He left the village at first light, while his fellow tribesmen lay sprawled on the ground, physically exhausted and mentally confused, and began trudging along the path that led toward the Black Mountain.

He walked slowly, bent over his ancient stick with the head of a water snake engraved on it. Ahead of him was a journey of at least two suns. It was the same journey that his forefathers — the tribe's previous shamans — had made after every significant event in the tribe's history. He must reach the river and, from there, make his way up to the ancient cave on the road to the land of fire.

The second sunset was almost upon him when the shaman reached the cave. He passed through the secret entrance behind the great waterfall.

The cave was spacious and dark, except for a trickle of light that penetrated the curtain of falling water. The air was humid and the sound of the waterfall deafening. The shaman knelt on the hard ground and, using his flints, made a small fire fueled by the grasses he had brought with him. Fetid smoke began to fill the cave. The flames illuminated the shaman's lined face and lent it an odd tinge. His white hair took on a reddish cast and his black eyes shone with a strange, mysterious light.

The shaman lit several torches and set them in the center of the cave. In their light, the many pictures on the cave walls sprang to life. This was the secret history book of the Chuma tribe.

Every significant event that had taken place in the tribe over the course of the centuries had been recorded on the walls by generations of shamans. Every victory over a rival tribe, every conquest, every epidemic or tragedy — all of them were commemorated on these walls. The death of every chief and the consecration of every new sacrificial pyramid; the heroic exploits of Royal Crown and Flying Jaguar, those immortal warriors who had galloped on wild horses and dominated the entire continent — all these were depicted on the stone wall, from floor to ceiling.

Strangers, the Chumas believed, would never find the history wall. Members of rival tribes could not pass behind the waterfall that guarded the cave's entrance. Jaguars would devour anyone who dared try; snakes would bite him; the trees would lash him with their branches, and the water would drown him. Only the shaman could enter the cave and add to the tribe's ongoing artistic saga.

Despite his fatigue, the shaman did not linger. Taking a sip of the fiery drink, he picked up a sharp stone and began etching feverishly on the soft stone. The lines he drew quickly turned into a large new picture. This drawing was different from every other picture before it. It showed a hornet with burning eyes and a strange tail. A giant hornet, larger than any jaguar or mountain lion that had ever been sighted in the forest. A weird hornet whose wings did not sprout from its sides, like its fellow insects, but rotated rapidly overhead. In all the wall pictures that had been carved into the stone over the course of centuries by dozens of shamans, there was not a single image like this one. Never before had the tribe been attacked by such a powerful and terrifying enemy.

When he finished the hornet, the shaman began drawing many images of warriors lying beneath it with outstretched arms and legs, their arrows bent and their bows broken. Then he drew a picture of three dead tribesmen. His body dripped with perspiration. From time to time he drank a little mescal as he continued etching on the stone wall without pause. Then he drew the huge hornet again — this time the warriors' bodies in its belly and gripped between its legs.

The old shaman worked throughout the night, interspersed with periods of nightmare-filled sleep. Only when sunlight began peeking behind the waterfall did he complete the task. The shaman straightened up, his old body aching from crouching for hours and sleeping on hard rock. He studied his wall drawing. A sad page had been added to the Chuma history book. Here was the great white hornet arriving in the village; here were the warriors, fighting it off in vain; here the hornet managed to escape without a scratch, killing three warriors and taking them off to its nest for dinner.

The shaman placed a bunch of bananas into a large stone bowl near the history wall — a gift to appease the gods of the jungle, so that they might continue to guard the cave entrance and not permit any stranger to enter. Leaving the torches burning, he left the cave. Hungry and drained, he began walking the paths that ran along the great riverbank. His fingers were raw and bleeding and his entire body ached.

Ahead of him lay a long journey of two full suns, to the jungle clearing where his ancient tribe had its home.

Grayston, Texas — 5714 / 1954

Two days after he first went up to the tower and looked out over the sealed compound, Sheriff Jack Abrams returned to the ranch house — this time, with a pair of binoculars. Telling Ben that he had to check something out, he climbed the narrow stairs to the topmost room in the tower and spent a long time looking through the window.

The fact that such a large tract of land was being used for purposes unknown to him troubled the sheriff. He felt a compelling drive to discover what was being done in such secrecy behind the wall. Until now, he had been forced to subdue his curiosity. It was beneath his dignity to ask what was going on behind Sam Lowinger's ranch house, like any Grayston gossip. But the moment he learned that there was a way to observe the secret area for himself, he knew no rest. After his second visit, he made a third, and then a fourth, at weekly intervals.

The sheriff soon became a regular visitor at the Lowingers. He would greet Devorah and the housekeeper, thump Sam's shoulder as the old man gazed vacantly into space, tickle little John as he crawled on the floor, and then climb to the top of the tower. At first, Ben always joined him there. He soon grew bored, however, and let the sheriff go up alone.

Abrams knew that he was taking a risk. At any time, the armed guards on the watchtower could spot the gleam of his binocular lens through a slit in the curtain. That haughty black officer was liable to wonder why the sheriff's Chevrolet was parked in front of the ranch house for hours on end. But he couldn't control the impulse to maintain his vigil in the tower. He would start the day in his office, make his regular appearance at the Port Stockton courthouse, and perform his usual street patrols. But at least once or twice a week found him drawn, as if by a magnet, to the road that led to the Lowinger place.

It was obvious to him that something fishy was going on. The entire story, from start to finish, was one big puzzle: beginning with the Lowinger family being forced to sell their land to the government, through the lightning construction taking place in the compound, all the way to the tight guard and total secrecy that were maintained in the enclosed area. What, in heaven's name, were they doing in there?

Jack Abrams had a private theory of his own. It was a frightening theory — a hair-raising theory — a theory that robbed him of his sleep. There was a good reason why the government had chosen such a remote and sparsely populated spot, he thought. They must be working on a project that had to be kept away from populated areas.

But what about Grayston? Were the lives of its residents not to be considered at all? Weren't there enough wide-open spaces in the United States? The government could have established its project in the desert reaches of New Mexico or Nevada, or even on a remote island somewhere — places where there was no living creature within a 100-mile radius. Why had it chosen to set up its project near Grayston?

Who, exactly, had made that decision?

And who would stand in judgment if a catastrophe occurred?

One day, Sheriff Abrams was once again driving along the road that led to the ranch. Near Tall Willy's gate, as he was about to turn in the direction of the Lowinger place, Abrams suddenly heard a loud, clattering noise. He parked his car, got out and looked questioningly around.

A few seconds later, the mystery was solved. Rising from behind the wall was a large white helicopter. It hovered in place for a moment or two and then, turning southward, flew off into the distance and vanished from sight.

The sheriff stood riveted in place, trying to figure out what he had just seen. A young ranch hand — one of Tall Willy's — drove up on a small tractor and paused near the obviously bemused sheriff.

"That's been happening every few weeks or so," the worker said. "That helicopter always goes off in the direction of Mexico, and comes flying back an hour or two later."

Jack Abrams half-turned to face the young man, taking pains to hide his burning curiosity. "What might they be looking for?" he asked nonchalantly.

"They say it's the border patrol," the worker shrugged. He threw a hostile glance at two Mexican laborers standing some distance away. "Believe me, Sheriff — if they manage to get those bean-eaters to stop taking away our jobs, then good luck to them, I say!"

"Just a minute. You don't happen to be Norman Chambers' son, do you?" the sheriff asked in sudden recognition. There was no one in the region who wasn't familiar with Norman Chambers' fine bakery shop on Grayston's main street, between the feed store and the Drunken Ox. His incredible donuts attracted customers from miles around.

The young man extended his hand. "Sure am. Steven Chambers. Nice to meet you."

"I take it you're not planning to follow in the bakery trade, eh, Steve?" The sheriff shook the proffered hand with a smile.

Chambers pointed with his chin at a herd of cattle grazing in the pasture on the other side of the fence. "As a proud Texan, I prefer steak," he said with a grin. It was clearly a witticism he had repeated often.

Northern Mexico — 5714 / 1954

Cries of terror and the pounding of fleeing footsteps echoed through the Indian village. The Chuma tribe's forest clearing was a scene of pandemonium. Panicked men raced feverishly in every direction, seeking shelter. Fearful women grabbed their children's hands and ran with them into the nearest hut. The hornet was back!

The terrible, giant hornet with the searing eyes — the hornet that swallowed men whole — had returned to attack the tribe again.

A few peaceful months had passed since the hornet's last visit, and the tribe had settled back into its normal routine. There was plenty of food and water. Old people passed on, new babies were born, and the dead warriors were gradually forgotten. A new group of young men underwent rigorous training and then submitted to the tribal ritual calling upon them to demonstrate their courage and daring and turning them into warriors.

Now, everyone came running in terror. The hornet's horrifying thrumming sounded throughout the forest. A few of the children glimpsed the winged creature flying in the sky, turning this way and that, rising and falling as it hunted its prey.

The young warriors gathered quickly near the shaman's hut, filled with the brazen spirit of youth and eager to fight. They donned their war masks, adorned with jaguar teeth and vulture feathers. One by one, they sipped the mescal that the shaman offered them, and dipped their arrows in the poison he had concocted. The women and the elderly watched hopefully from the safety of their huts, hoarsely shouting their encouragement.

As though drawn by the war cries, the white hornet suddenly appeared above the trees and hovered above the village clearing. The children shrieked in terror. There it was — the giant hornet with the eerie, burning eyes and the strange, monstrous wings that did not emerge from the sides of its body but stretched above its head, whirling with lightning speed.

The shaman threw some grasses onto his small fire, and thick black smoke began coiling upward. He gave the signal for the warriors to surge toward the hornet, bellowing for all they were worth. They raced to meet the enemy, leaping ecstatically, waving their bows and loosing a rapid succession of arrows.

The hornet sank lower for a moment, as though it intended to land on them. Dozens of poisoned arrows were shot directly at it. The hornet had not expected such a concerted attack. It began slowly to fall, tilted forward with its head down and its tail pointed at the sky. Then, recovering, it righted itself and remained suspended in the air, brushing the treetops. The hornet hovered precisely above the stream and the tribe's water pool. The thrumming changed into a deafening roar, drowning out even the cries of the women and children, as its whirling wings caused the branches to flail wildly in their wind and made the mud huts tremble.

The Indian warriors were seized with terror, but they would not surrender. Undeterred, with courage and self-sacrifice, they continued to loose a barrage of poisoned arrows at their gigantic winged enemy.

Near his hut, the shaman danced madly around the fire, shouting a string of unintelligible syllables. He was summoning the forest gods to come to the warriors' aid. He called on the eagle spirit from the Black Mountain and the spirit of the water snake to rescue the Chuma from the terrible white hornet.

At that moment, a victory cry went up from the warriors. The hornet had begun to flee. Turning around, it began to make its way back in the direction of the Black Mountain.

The children were ecstatic. They streamed from the huts and began cheering. The young warriors broke into the Chuma's special victory dance. They leaped high into the air, brandishing their bows. Then they removed the masks from their faces and tossed them at one another, yowling with joy.

The old shaman stood soberly in the doorway of his hut. He did not take part in the general rejoicing. He remembered, if the others did not, that in the previous attack the warriors had also seemed to triumph — only to fall sick the next day. That giant hornet seemingly had its own, invisible, poisoned arrows. Who knew what would happen to the young tribesmen now celebrating their victory? Who knew how they would be feeling in two or three suns? Who knew how many dead warriors he would have to draw on the wall of the secret cave behind the waterfall?

Could the already bruised and battered tribe survive the deaths of scores of young warriors?

The hornet with the searing eyes and the wings above its head rose to a great height. Then it made its way, not to its nest on the other side of the Black Mountain, but in the direction of the United States border. More specifically, to the helipad near the central laboratory buildings in the secret compound behind the Lowinger house.

The pilot of that "hornet" turned a knob and reported into the microphone in his helmet: "Thirteen to base: Operation 'Mexican B Fever' was successfully carried out at 12:46, local time. Target point: 2906/3658. I repeat, Operation 'Mexico B Fever' was successfully carried out at 12:46, local time. Target point: 2906/3658. Returning to base."

There were a few seconds of silence, broken only by the helicopter's whirring. Then a voice with a heavy German accent came on the air. The voice belonged to Dr. Heinrich von Reiner, the Nazi scientist who had been granted safe haven in the United States.

"Received. Have a safe flight."

Los Angeles — Iyar 5766 / May 2006

"George, call the office," came the announcement from the loud-speaker in the winery's courtyard. When the head winemaker had not responded to the secretary's repeated rings on his office phone, she assumed that he was somewhere outside. "George Bellini, call your office."

George's office was located in a small room off the winery's courtyard, between the fermentation building and the bottling plant. Given his senior standing, he could have chosen one of the handsome rooms in the adminis-tration building at the winery's entrance. But he preferred to live and work among the wine itself. He had the aroma of fermenting grapes on one side, the assembly-line hiss of bottles being filled on the other, and the sight of forklifts loading the filled crates of wine to complete the picture.

George Bellini was considered the California wine country's *wunder-kind*. Writers of wine columns, especially, enjoyed his riveting life story. Until ten years ago, George had been an average student, majoring in Biology at UCLA. It was then that his extraordinarily developed senses of taste and smell were discovered, through the medium of a tasting compe-tition on campus. He was simply born to be a winemaker — and he had had no clue as to his innate talent.

He had easily been accepted into an oenology program at Davis University, where he completed his studies with distinction. After two seasons in France and one in southern Australia, George had returned to the States to work for a small winery in the Napa Valley. Then he was of-fered a job at the Stern Family Winery. This offer was particularly attrac-tive to him because one of the owners, David Stern, had recently decided to begin creating wines worthy of the name, to penetrate the luxury wine market. For George, this was an exciting challenge: to begin establishing a high-end winery, literally from the bottom up. Indeed, the process had given him an opportunity to prove himself. The Stern Family Winery soon found its place on the map with its line of prestigious wines.

When interviewed, George always glossed over Professor Barry Majdi's pivotal role in thrusting him into the wine business. This was not from any lack of gratitude, but rather at Majdi's explicit request. They had kept in touch all through the years, and George often consulted his former teacher on topics related to his chosen field. He introduced the professor to David Stern — an introduction that would prove of immense benefit to the winery.

Several months earlier, stores and restaurants had started shipping cases of wine back to the winery, after the bottles had begun to emit a moldy odor reminiscent of wet cardboard. This phenomenon was caused by a bacterium known as T.S.A. in the bottle's cork, which made the cork rot and spoiled the wine. The professor permitted George and David to try a special, experimental disinfection agent, without taste or smell, that he had personally developed. Later, he said, when the method had proved itself and the bottles were no longer returned, they could talk further. In the meantime, George was asked to keep a precise list of the wine shipments whose corks had been disinfected at the winery. Professor Majdi visited the winery to supervise the process on a number of occasions.

"David asked if you could step into his office," the secretary said, when George called to ask what she wanted. "His brother has just arrived from Houston."

Jacob Stern was sitting in David's office, feeling wonderful.

It was only a week since he had traveled halfway around the world in a terrified attempt to save his life from ending at the hands of the pale man, but he had recovered and was feeling like himself again. Ironically, it was his phone conversation with the CIA agent — he had not introduced himself that way, but that was the clear impression the caller had given — that had calmed him. After his initial panic, Jacob had understood that he was actually safer now. As long as he kept his end of the bargain and forgot that he had ever heard of Juarez, the pale man and his minions would leave him alone.

And that was exactly what he had done. The next day, Jacob returned to work and resumed his usual routines. He told no one — including David — about his hair-raising experiences. Seven whole days had gone by and, so far, all was well.

"Hello, Jacob," George greeted him. "How are you?" From their few previous meetings, he knew Jacob Stern to be a true connoisseur of wines, perhaps even more so than his brother, who ran the winery.

Right now, several wineglasses and three bottles of unlabeled wine stood on the desk. Only a handwritten adhesive note on each bottle listed the ingredients in the respective wines. These were pilot wines; a decision had to be made as to whether or not to put them on the market. David wanted his brother to taste them and give his opinion. When George entered the office, both brothers had already tasted one of the wines: a white with a rich, golden hue.

"Congratulations, George," David called, holding up his wineglass. "My brother likes your Chardonnay."

"It's perfect," Jacob said, as David poured another glass and handed it to George.

"I must admit," David said, "that I wanted to bottle this wine three months ago. It was George who insisted that we leave it in the barrel a bit longer. And he was absolutely correct. The wine has a much better blend now."

Jacob agreed fully with his brother. "Without a doubt. It's buttery and rich. You can sense just the right amount of wood, and there are hints of melon, pear, and tropical fruit. An excellent wine."

George placed a hand over his heart and bowed theatrically, like an actor acknowledging his audience's applause.

"All right, George," David said. "Have a seat. There are a few things that need to be decided."

The winemaker took a chair, still holding his wineglass.

"As I told you this morning," David continued, "we are planning to send our Rebbe, in Israel, some wine in honor of his grandson's wedding. If we want it to get there on time, we need to make arrangements now."

"We have to bear in mind that this wine is intended for use by those who are accustomed to drinking fine wine. It has to be of good quality, but light," said Jacob.

"What kind of quantity are we talking about?" asked George.

"No more than three hundred bottles," David told him.

George scratched the back of his neck, thinking.

"I may have something suitable," he said at last. "There's one barrel, 225 liters, of a Zinfandel 2004. I stopped the fermentation right at the start and left the wine on the sediment. It was an experiment, and it produced something very interesting: a red wine, half-dry but sweet, and very fruity and aromatic. Even someone who doesn't know a thing about wine will enjoy it."

The brothers glanced at one another. This definitely sounded interesting.

"Please get some for us to taste," David said.

Naturally, he did not mean that the winemaker himself should tap the barrel. When George had begun working for the Stern winery, it was explained to him that since he was a non-Jew, there would be strict rules preventing him from being in physical contact with the wine.

He could not, for example, go down into the wine cellar by himself. He could not wander alone around the fermentation equipment or turn a spigot to taste a wine. He was to roam the winery as though his hands were tied. Not even opening or closing a tap leading to a pipe that carried wine was permitted. The kashruth supervisor, or some other Jewish employee, always accompanied him and was always the one to pour wine for him or to open any barrel or bottle from which he might wish to taste.

George phoned down to Avrumi, the *mashgiach*, and asked him to go down to the basement where he would find three lone barrels. He was to draw a bit of wine from Barrel 627 — the one marked "Zinfandel 2004, Experimental: George Bellini" on it — and bring it up to David's office. He would find the barrel easily. If not, he could phone up to the office and George would guide him right to it.

Northern Mexico — 5714 / 1954

The first hours after the giant hornet's second attack were very anxious ones for the shaman. At any moment, he expected the symptoms of their earlier illness to reappear: the reddish boils, the terrible headaches, the weakened muscles, and uncontrollable trembling.

But the sun set and rose, and then repeated the cycle again. By noon of the third day, faint hope began to beat in the shaman's chest. None of the young warriors felt ill. They continued their work of rebuilding the huts that had been destroyed in the heat of the battle, and then energetically went out to hunt for food while the women hauled water from the pool near the stream.

By sunrise of the fourth day, the shaman allowed himself a slight easing of his anxiety. The night had passed in peace. He stood erect in the doorway of his hut, listening to the night sounds gradually fade and the merry chirping of birds replace them. As the sun's rays illuminated the forest clearing, a great feeling of relief filled his being. This time, he believed, the forest gods had stood by the tribe. The Chuma warriors had triumphed over the great hornet — permanently. It had fled to its nest, licking its wounds, and would never be back again.

This had been a very significant event. An event that must be memorialized on the tribe's secret cave wall. Over the course of the next few evenings, the Chumas gazed up at the heavens and saw the water snake take another bite out of the moon each night. When the sky was completely dark, they launched the parting ritual for their shaman.

All night long, the natives smoked the peyote cactus and sipped the mescal drink. They danced wildly, moving in a frenzy of endless ecstasy, eyes closed, arms waving, and lips shouting unintelligibly. With first light, the shaman slung his bag over his shoulder and disappeared along the trail that led to the Black Mountain.

Once again, the magic-man toiled up the slope of the great river, following in the footsteps of his forefathers, the shamans of old. He had made this trip several times before over the course of his life — the last one only months before, after the great hornet's first attack.

Near the second sunset, he reached the secret cave. Nothing had changed since his previous visit. There was the same darkness, the same oppressive odor, the same sheet of falling water that sounded like the roar of a wounded jaguar. Once again, the shaman crouched on the hard cave floor and lit a fire by striking stone on stone. Again he lit a few pitch torches, which cast a reddish light on the etched images that covered the walls from floor to ceiling.

The shaman did not delay. He was eager to begin his drawing depicting the tribe's great victory against the gigantic white hornet. He took a long swallow of his herbal drink, picked up a stone, and began etching lines and shapes into the cave wall. Once again, he drew the great hornet, with its burning eyes and its upright wings. This time, however, the warriors were standing erect, their heads raised and their hands wielding taut, unbroken bows. The last segment of his drawing showed the great hornet fleeing in terror, a score of arrows stuck in its side.

He worked on his drawing all night, etching sketch after sketch in a continuous line. Now and then he dropped into a fitful doze, filled with nightmarish visions. When the job was done, he straightened up and studied his handiwork with satisfaction. He was tired and hungry, but today he had added a joyous chapter to the tribe's archives. A chapter in which the Chuma warriors had triumphed over a cruel and bitter enemy.

A chapter that would nourish the tribe and keep it strong for many years to come.

As he lifted the heavy stone bowl to fill it with fresh bananas, a gift to the gods of the forest, his hands inexplicably shook. Leaving the torches burning in the cave, he walked slowly to the hidden entrance, his head spinning in dizzy waves.

It took the shaman two full suns to walk back to his tribe along the forest trails. Despite his joy and his elevated spirits, he was terribly weak and ached all over. The muddy ground was difficult to traverse, and he was exhausted, hungry, and aching. These were no ordinary hardships of the trail. This fatigue was something out of the ordinary. His legs grew weaker and scarcely obeyed his command to move. His hands found it hard to grip his walking stick. Beads of perspiration dripped from his face as his uncontrolled trembling increased from hour to hour.

At sunrise on the second day, the shaman plucked several leaves from a healing plant he came upon on the trail. He put them in his mouth and chewed them as they were, without squeezing or pulverizing them. The plant revitalized him slightly, and he continued on his way — until, several hours later, the pain came back, redoubled. This time, the medicinal leaves did not help. As the noonday sun beat down mercilessly on his head, his mind grew confused and he began to hallucinate. He thought he heard jaguars roaring in his head and imagined thousands of insects crawling along his body.

With his last remaining strength, the shaman kept putting one foot in front of the other. The sun's powerful rays blinded him, and tree branches whipped him as he passed. The closer he came to the village, the worse he felt. After every few steps he was forced to lean on a tree and rest, breathing heavily, and knowing full well that he could not lie down lest he never get up again. There was still a small amount of the herbal extract in a gourd inside his pouch. He drank it down at a gulp, then mustered his strength to advance a little farther on tottering steps.

He reached the patch of land where the peyote plant grew. From this point there was only a single path, narrow and straight, that led to the forest clearing. Tribesmen occasionally walked here. He would go on a little farther, in the hope that he would meet someone who could summon a pair of strong young men to carry him home. Each time he returned from a visit to the cave, he needed a few days' respite. But he had never felt as weak as he did now. He was literally at the end of his strength.

No one appeared in the lane. There was only the rustle of the wind in the trees, the murmuring of the stream, and the more distant sounds of forest creatures. By now, he should have heard the voices of the tribesmen at their carving and the women chattering as they sat spinning and weaving. He should have heard children playing and warriors practicing their martial arts. But only an eerie silence met his ears. A silence that froze his blood and raised the hair on the back of his scalp. A deathly silence.

The shaman crawled down the sloping path, feeble and shivering, his breath rattling in his chest. Every cell in his body hurt, his forehead burned, his eyes were glassy, and his vision was blurred.

Three more steps brought him into view of the village in the clearing.

A terrible scream rose inside him. A silent, wordless cry, to which his weakened body was unable to give voice. The old shaman collapsed on the ground, shaking violently, and knowing that these were his final moments on earth. He had nothing left to live for. He had nothing left to fight for.

With the last of his fading awareness, the shaman, last of the Chumas, gazed on the tragic scene.

The ancient tribe had been completely destroyed. Scores of bodies lay sprawled around the clearing, near the huts or the stream: young and old, men, women, and children. Of the entire tribe, there were no survivors.

Then, as his consciousness dimmed, he heard strange voices. With a mighty effort, the shaman lifted his head slightly and tried to focus his eyes for a brief moment. He saw several of the tribe's warriors lying on the ground, either dead or in the final stages of dying. Among them roamed strangers, dressed in white from head to toe and drawing blood from the warriors with strange implements.

The shaman's eyes blurred again. Exhaling in despair, he let his head sink back onto the ground. His eyes remained open as his heart beat its last. The last thing he saw was the great white hornet — the tribe's terrible enemy. It had returned. It landed with calm triumph behind the shaman's hut. Its wings no longer turned and its eyes no longer burned as, from its belly, stepped more strange men in white clothing.

The last shaman of the Chuma tribe died in the knowledge that no one would draw the last picture on the wall of the secret cave. No one would etch the sad end of the famed Chumas. No one would tell the gods of the forest that the tribe had been vanquished. No one would tell the spirits of the water snake or the Black Mountain that a gigantic hornet had beaten them.

With his last breath, the shaman knew that his gods had let him down. They had let his tribe down. The spirits of the forest had not protected the Chumas. The giant white hornet had cruelly destroyed them, down to the last native.

Grayston, Texas — 5714 / 1954

It was Sunday, and once again Sheriff Abrams had driven over to the Lowinger place. As he climbed the stairs to the tower, he heard a distant clatter approaching from the south. He hurried to the topmost room and peeked through the gap in the curtains. This was the first time that he had seen the white helicopter returning from the Mexican border. It approached the compound slowly, looking like a huge white hornet. The headlights in the cockpit resembled a pair of gleaming, malicious eyes.

When the helicopter landed, the sheriff saw four workers waiting for it at the central building's exit. His brow creased in surprise. These men were not dressed in the usual overalls, but in sealed rubber suits that covered them from head to toe. They wore gas masks and carried tanks of oxygen on their backs. The four opened the helicopter door and leaned into it, moving something from side to side.

Abrams rapidly scanned the rest of the area. There was no other figure to be seen anywhere inside the wall. When he returned his attention to the helicopter, the four workers were already on their way back to the central building. He swiveled his binoculars in that direction — and his heart skipped a beat.

There was no mistaking what he was seeing. The four men were carrying two stretchers, and on those stretchers lay the burden that the helicopter had brought with it: the corpses of two young men.

The stretcher-bearers had nearly reached the building. A new figure — similarly dressed in protective garb — came out to meet them and opened the door. The sheriff gazed through the binoculars. No one had bothered to cover the bodies, and they were borne along with a frightening lack of respect, but that was not what troubled him. The veteran Texas lawman had seen other dead men in his life. There was something different about these corpses — something very strange. He fixed his eyes on the bodies, and his jaw dropped.

There was no question about it. Judging by the characteristic facial structure, he was looking at a pair of dead Mexican-Indian natives.

Los Angeles — Iyar 5766 / May 2006

One week after David and Jacob Stern met with winemaker George Bellini to decide which wine to send to Israel for the Milinover Rebbe's grandson's wedding — and two weeks after Jacob's phone conversation with CIA assistant director Walter Child, in which Child offered Jacob his life in exchange for his total silence about the Juarez episode — another meeting took place. This one was between two other men, and it took place in the faculty room of the Biology Department at UCLA.

At that hour of the evening, the building was virtually deserted. The senior faculty had gone home and their secretaries had completed their day's work. The lecture halls were empty, the corridors darkened. Only in the labs on the basement level did a few students still hunker over their bubbling test tubes or study the growth of cultured bacteria.

In Professor Majdi's office on the third floor, a light still shone. He was waiting tensely for a very important visitor. A few moments earlier he had sent his research assistant down to the parking lot to meet the visitor and guide him through the maze of corridors. The younger man had been visibly excited to carry out Majdi's request.

At long last, the expected knock came. The professor stood up with a sense of relief, opened the door, and welcomed his guest with a hearty handshake.

The newcomer was an impressive-looking man. He boasted a neatly trimmed beard and a high forehead that rose majestically above his firm-featured face. His eyes were dark and penetrating. They held a latent intensity that was impossible to disregard.

"Please, sit down," the professor invited, gesturing at an arrangement of armchairs in a corner of the room. He smiled with amusement at his visitor's elegant suit. He couldn't remember when he had ever seen his old friend, Imam Bashir Abdul Aziz, clad in such an outfit. Still, under the circumstances, he had to admit it had been a wise choice. The traditional white robe that the imam normally wore in his mosque might have stood out a bit in this academic setting ....

The professor took a chair facing Aziz. Yousuf, his research assistant — almost speechless with excitement at finding himself in the presence of the two most important men in his life — poured them each a cup of black coffee.

The imam sipped slowly as he scanned the room. He had never been here before, in this workplace of his friend Barry Majdi — just as the professor had never set foot inside the imam's mosque. The shelves and cabinets around the office were packed with a jumble of paper-filled binders, glass bottles, and tubes and vessels of varied shapes and sizes, all filled with various strangely colored liquids. The office held a great deal of lab equipment, including a sophisticated new microscope and two cages in which a number of white mice scurried incessantly.

The small talk rolled on in a leisurely fashion, waiting for the night's main topic to be broached. There was nothing new in the mosque, the imam related. The *madrasa*, the school for Arabic and Islamic studies, was progressing nicely, with classes taking place each evening. Several neighbors, upset at the vehicle congestion near the mosque on Fridays, had been invited to a relaxed getting-acquainted meeting in Aziz's office. At the meeting, he had explained to them in his precise English that Islam had much in common with Christianity. "You must understand that not every mosque in America is a branch of Al-Qaeda," he had told them with a pleasant smile, "and not every imam is Osama bin Laden." Since then, the cars that filled the block every Friday no longer annoyed the neighbors.

The popular Biology professor and the charismatic imam of the largest mosque in Los Angeles were the same age. Both had been born 45 years earlier in the same poverty-stricken section of Cairo. Both had played in the same mud puddles among the rickety hovels. And both had studied the Koran at the feet of the same imam, Mohammed Taheh Abu-Samir.

When they were thirteen, more than thirty years ago, the two went their separate ways. Barry Majdi's parents decided to try their luck in the United States, saving their pennies to give their child the opportunities that they had never had. They sent Barry to the best schools in Los Angeles and encouraged him to embark on what proved to be a flourishing academic career.

Bashir Abdul Aziz's parents stayed in Egypt and sent their son to the Islamic University at Alexandria, where he became an imam and was sent to America by his teachers to spread the faith. His fluent English and exquisite manners, along with his innate intelligence and charisma, had brought him to his present eminence: head of the fast-growing Moslem community in Los Angeles, that archetypical Western metropolis.

Aziz's marvelous talent for fund-raising had formed an inseparable part of his success. Bashir Abdul Aziz knew how to pluck at the heartstrings of the Moslem immigrants who settled in the United States, built homes, started businesses, and watched in dismay as their children were sucked into a valueless American culture. He reminded them of their roots and aroused their Islamic consciousness. He railed against the younger generation's lack of morals and translated their parents' dissatisfaction into fat checks that he used to build and expand his mosque.

Above all, Bashir Abdul Aziz was careful never to engage in anti-American incitement or to express his support of any terrorist operation. The imam of the largest mosque in Los Angeles never appeared at any function sponsored by the "Committee for the Holy Lands" or any other fringe organization. He was considered a middle-of-the-road Islamic leader — much to the disgust of the radical jihadist militant organizations.

The first time the two childhood friends met again had been fourteen years earlier, in the summer of 1992. That was when Barry Majdi returned from a special mission to Russia, which earned him lavish praise and his appointment as a full professor at UCLA. While out celebrating with some friends at a Los Angeles restaurant, his attention was drawn to a nearby table. Only two people sat at that table: Daoud Hativi, a well-known Lebanese-American hotelier, and another man who seemed familiar to Majdi. When the pair finished their meal, they passed near Majdi's table. He stood up, and saw a look of surprise cross the other man's face.

"Bashir?"

"Barry?"

The two old friends exchanged a warm hug.

"What are you doing in America?" Barry Majdi asked. He learned that his childhood chum had become an imam back in Egypt, and was now in the process of establishing a mosque in Los Angeles.

Majdi told Bashir that he, too, would be returning to Los Angeles after a long period of working in Atlanta, Georgia. He had just been appointed a professor at UCLA — which was the reason for the present celebration.

"In which field?" Aziz asked.

"Biology," Majdi replied.

"Biology? Very interesting …. Is that what you were involved with in Atlanta, too?"

"Yes. I did research there. Here in L.A., I'll be teaching."

"What kind of research?" Aziz asked.

"I worked for the CDC — the Centers for Disease Control. But I got tired of living with viruses and microbes all the time. I want to work with people!"

The two made a date to meet the next day. At that meeting, they reminisced about the old days in Cairo, spoke of their parents and siblings, and caught each other up on the stories of their lives from the age of thirteen.

Their childhood bond was renewed and evolved into a firm friendship. They quickly came to realize that they shared similar views on a number of important topics. The unique philosophy and worldview that Imam Mohammed Taheh Abu-Samir had instilled in them long ago still energized them both. Barry Majdi and Bashir Abdul Aziz met frequently to talk. Both felt that their running into each other again had been no coincidence. The merging of their paths in the same city, after so many years, could have only one purpose: To allow them to carry out the old imam's grand vision.

The professor had never cultivated close friendships among his own brethren in America; now he deliberately refrained from any identification with them. From time to time, some Islamic organization, discovering that there was a senior professor teaching at UCLA, would try to recruit him to their politics. He always said "no." Barry Majdi was a loyal American citizen, he would reiterate firmly — an immigrant who had become fully involved in his new country. Coming from Egypt, he was no different from all the others who had arrived at these shores from Italy, Ireland, or Japan. He never set foot in a mosque and did not appear publicly in Aziz's company. All their activity aimed at actualizing the old imam's far-reaching vision took place under wraps. Only the two of them were privy to the great secret.

It was the professor who handled the practical end of things, while the funding was supplied by the imam. Though Majdi, over the years, became a prosperous man in his own right due to his scientific and medical advances, his income could not be compared to the millions of dollars that flowed through the mosque's bank account.

Bashir Abdul Aziz put down his coffee cup and leaned back in his armchair. "So what do you say about London?" he asked the professor with a chuckle.

Majdi's research assistant, Yousuf Nadir, caught his breath in excitement. Did the imam mean what Nadir thought he meant? Was he referring to what had happened in Great Britain two months before? No — it couldn't be. Yousuf had been attending the mosque for two years now and never once had he heard the imam speak on *those* subjects. The imam never talked about Islamic terrorism, either in praise or in condemnation.

Yousuf had avidly devoured every scrap of information that was printed about the series of terrorist incidents that Al-Qaeda had inflicted on the London Underground system. Fifty-two British heretics had been killed in those heroic acts, and another 700 injured. It had been, beyond a doubt, a feather in Al-Qaeda's cap. Maybe not as grand as the much-vaunted episodes in Madrid the year before, in which no less than 200 Spanish citizens lost their lives ... but 52 heretics was something, too.

The professor grimaced in open contempt. "A herd of Afghan boors."

"I've never believed in that gang of primitive farmers," Aziz agreed. "So they knocked down the Twin Towers — big deal. They sent some envelopes filled with anthrax germs. Wow!" His voice dripped with sarcasm.

The professor's young assistant gazed at the two men in deep disappointment. This was the first time he had heard them speak about matters that went to the heart of true Islam — and it was certainly not what he had hoped to hear. The professor had never expressed any religious or political views in his assistant's presence before, and the imam was also careful to avoid the subject. In his speeches at the mosque, he would speak about the five commandments incumbent on the Moslem individual, but he had never offered any sort of opinion, positive or negative, about the glorious actions of their *shahid* brothers. He never mentioned the suffering of the Palestinians under the Zionist oppressors' rule, or remarked on the sacrifice of the 9/11 martyrs.

Yousuf had always wondered what the imam's views were on these things, and the answer he had just heard was extremely disappointing. The imam had called Al-Qaeda a gang of primitive farmers, and the professor referred to them as "Afghan boors." Did they really think that the Prophet Mohammed had opposed the use of the sword? Had they fallen prey to the twisted commentary of American Islamic "experts" — men who were labeled "moderate," but who were actually devoid of a single shred of religious pride? Were they, too, dining at the rotten table of the West and eating out of its hand? Had they bought into the mind-set of those who regularly distorted the Koran's meaning?

The professor, maybe. He had sunk deeply into the indulgent lifestyle of Los Angeles. He taught at the university, drove an expensive car, and made big bucks from his scientific discoveries.

But not the imam. Yousuf could not believe that the esteemed Imam Aziz had become blinded by the false American glitter. It was impossible that he, too, was one of the Muslims who lacked a backbone — those weak, miserable men who so badly misinterpreted the messages implicit in the Koran.

Grayston, Texas — 5714 / 1954

On the day the tragedy occurred, Ben was away from home.

The secret compound behind the Lowinger place had become part of the background of Grayston's life. Although its workers were officially prohibited from mingling with the local populace, the men could often be seen whiling away an evening at the Drunken Ox or dropping into Norman Chambers' confectioner's shop. A few of them moved into the town or its environs, and in time several Grayston youths took jobs in what was locally referred to as "the Project." One of these was Norman's son, Steve Chambers, who worked there in the capacity of groundskeeper.

Sheriff Abrams, too, grew accustomed to the presence of the mysterious "Project" and eventually returned to his normal activities: catching cattle- and horse-thieves, locking up drunks at night, and releasing them the next morning. While he did not abandon his surveillance of the walled enclosure, it became far less obsessive. He had learned to recognize several faces regularly seen around the compound: its director, Colin Baron of the round spectacles; the haughty black officer who had threatened the sheriff's men; a tall, thin man with a trimmed beard who often strolled through the compound accompanied by a dog, and others.

On the day the tragedy occurred, Ben had gone to the big rodeo at Lubbock. Contestants had to keep their seat on a wild bronco for eight full seconds without being tossed to the ground and trampled on by the 2,000-pound beast. The rodeo's managers appreciated spectators like Ben, who showed up each week in his cowboy hat, wide sideburns and mustache, opened a bottle of whiskey — tossing away the cork, as he saw no need to hold onto it — and gathered a group of noisy, congenial companions who raucously cheered on the contestants along with him.

On that day, the sheriff decided to stop in at the Lowinger house. He was driving slowly along the road when he suddenly saw a hysterical female figure running at him, waving her arms. He pressed on the gas, filled with trepidation when he realized that the woman was the Lowingers' housekeeper. She was screaming and crying. Her hands were covered with blood; every time she touched her clothes or face, she left another red mark.

The sheriff pulled up alongside her. Gasping for breath, the woman shrieked, "Devorah! Devorah!" She pointed at the house. "She's dead!"

The sheriff told her to get in the car and sped toward the ranch. He stopped with a screech of his brakes and jumped out.

The front door gaped open. In the front hall he saw Devorah lying on the floor, which was awash in blood, while the stableman, Frankie, tried to stanch the flow with wads of cloth. When he saw the sheriff, he compressed his lips and shook his head, as if to say, "It's too late ...."

"What happened?" Abrams demanded. His trained eyes scanned the room and noticed bloodstains leading from the door to the tower room.

Briefly, Frankie told what he knew. Devorah had decided, for some reason, to go up to the tower room — from curiosity, perhaps, or else a desire to clean and organize the place. Opening the window wide, she had leaned out and viewed the compound. One of the soldiers, seeing her, lifted his rifle and fired instinctively at the figure that had unexpectedly appeared just meters away. The bullet struck her shoulder and she fell to the floor.

Many precious minutes had passed before her absence was noted. The housekeeper had gone in search of her. As she passed the open door leading to the narrow staircase, she had heard weak groans from above. Heart pounding, she climbed the stairs — and broke into piercing shrieks at the sight of her mistress lying on the floor in an ever-expanding puddle of blood.

An ambulance was quickly dispatched to the ranch house. On the front porch stood the sheriff, Frankie, and the weeping housekeeper, holding little John in her arms. They watched in silence as two paramedics lifted a very pale Devorah onto a stretcher and bore her off to the hospital. No one said a word. Old Sam sat in his rocking chair, staring into space, completely detached from reality.

"We have to let Ben know," Frankie said, as the wail of the ambulance receded into the distance. He spoke in a tone that made no attempt to hide his disgust. "Let him go to the hospital and see to his wife. You'll probably find him hanging around the Drunken Ox or some place like that."

Devorah died the next day.

Grayston boiled over with raw emotion. Feeling ran high against the guards at the compound. Everyone remembered Willy Jr., Tall Willy's deaf-mute son, who'd also been fired on without posing any danger. Why did they need that accursed Project, if its men were going to be shooting and killing people?

That evening, as the local workers returned from the compound and descended one by one from the shuttle bus, they were greeted by the full strength of the townspeople's pent-up anger. In the streets, in the shops, everywhere, they were met by accusing stares. Hard words were thrown at them in the Drunken Ox, to the slam of whiskey glasses on tables. The workers maintained a confused silence, eyes downcast.

Earlier that day, as word of Mrs. Lowinger's death began to circulate, the black officer had gathered all the local workers near the truck unloading zone, and reminded them in a harsh tone that they had signed an official document forbidding them to speak to outsiders about anything that went on behind these walls. Anyone who dared make a peep, he warned, would not only be fired immediately, but he and his whole family would rue the day they had been born.

Angriest of all was Sheriff Abrams. The moment the ambulance drove off with the wounded Devorah, he had stalked furiously around the back of the ranch house and straight over to the main gate, where he demanded a meeting with the director.

The arrogant black officer had once again peered out at him through a high slit. This time, he had refused to even listen to what Sheriff Abrams had to say.

"Anyone who comes sniffing around this place will be shot like a dog," he yelled through the slit. "Tell your people that they had better keep their long noses away from this compound. This is federal property and spies will be executed."

The sheriff was shaking with rage. "What spies?" he shouted back. "She was a just a simple woman."

"Man, woman, spy — it's all the same."

"We're not going to let this pass," the sheriff bellowed. "I'll make sure you people are thrown out of here!"

A small smile touched the officer's lips. "Listen up, Sheriff," he hissed. "If it comes to a choice between this compound and your measly town — *you're* going to be the ones moving, not us. Is that clear?"

Many of Grayston's residents attended Devorah's funeral in the old cemetery. Ben appeared unemotional at the funeral. The housekeeper, Manuela, in contrast, could not stop crying or hugging poor, motherless little John. Frankie pushed old Sam in his wheelchair.

The local priest moved closer to the plain wooden coffin, resting on a platform surrounded by wreaths and flowers, and gazed in some confusion at the crowd. The deceased woman's husband had said that he didn't care what sort of ceremony she had, as long as it was brief. The priest had no objection to rushing the soul of this female Jewish sinner into the grave, but there was someone who usually took care of this sort of thing. Where in heaven's name was he? Why was he always late ...?

The priest heaved a sigh of relief as he spotted an urgent movement at the cemetery gate. A short, plump man in a narrow-brimmed hat and a strange three-quarter coat rolled through the crowd in his direction, holding a small suitcase as he skipped over the headstones in his way. The two men exchanged a brief nod. Then the priest stepped back to let the other conduct the ceremony.

Ben hid a grin. He recognized this character: It was the *mohel* whom old Sam had forced him to bring for little John. The rabbi apparently had his own means of learning about every birth and death in the county.

The "Chief Rabbi of Greater Grayston" was not the most proficient of cantors. The problem was, he didn't know it. He warbled the "*Keil Malei Rachamim*" in such a distorted fashion that even had those attending the funeral been born-and-bred Jews, it is doubtful whether they would have recognized the words. Then he recited the *Kaddish* and a few additional verses, and gave the signal to lower the coffin into the ground.

The priest delivered some parting words. A local ranch owner — in cowboy hat, jeans, and mud-splattered boots — offered a few hoarse sentences to comfort the bereaved family, and the ceremony was over.

Everyone filed past Ben, shook his hand, and murmured their condolences. The more courageous bent over the wheelchair to shake Sam's limp hand as well. The cemetery gradually emptied, until the only one left apart from the Lowinger household was the *mohel-chazzan-*"Rabbi," hat in hand and expectation in his eyes. No one had invited him here — but then, no one ever did invite him, and yet he was always paid something in the end. A few dollars for his trouble; especially since the priest, when no one was looking, always demanded his share.

For a moment, Ben stood facing him with an insolent stare. Then he turned and walked toward his truck.

"Mr. Lowinger!" The *mohel* ran after him. "Mr. Lowinger!"

Ben continued striding toward his pickup. He opened the door, and turned back mockingly.

"What do you want? Money?" he asked. He pointed at Devorah's fresh grave. "Go ask her."

Though feelings still ran high against the Project, other voices began gradually to make themselves heard.

The day after the funeral, the project director, Colin Baron, called a town hall meeting in Grayston and spoke to the local residents, saying that the administration was very sorry about the death of an innocent American citizen. At the same time, he stressed, they must understand that the people on this compound were the ones working to keep America safe from those who wished her ill. Barely ten years had passed since the U.S. had beaten down the Nazi monster, he said, and she was now threatened by the evil Soviet empire, with its nuclear-tipped ballistic missiles pointed at New York, Washington, Chicago, Philadelphia, and other great American cities. Here, in your small, patriotic town, he insisted, permanent answers to the Kremlin's threat were being devised. It had been Grayston, of all other towns, that had been selected to safeguard American supremacy and give those Red rats what they had coming to them. "You can tell that to your friends and neighbors," the director urged them. "It's time for Grayston to feel proud about what's happening right here."

Two months later, Ben remarried.

Despite his surly personality, he was considered prime marriage material in the Grayston area. He was healthy, not that old, living in a nice ranch house and — rumor had it — the owner of a very respectable bank account.

The lucky bride was ten years younger than he. Her name was Barbara. She was the rather loud sister of Tony, from the supply store. For some years, she had been absent from Grayston, having married a Mississippi man and moved with him to Livingston, in western Texas. Her husband came home only on the weekends, ostensibly spending the rest of his time on the job at a big drilling rig. But when the police came knocking on her door one day with an arrest warrant, she learned to her shock that her husband preferred drilling holes in bank vaults and then emptying them of their contents. Her brother, Tony, found her an inexpensive lawyer and she divorced her husband in a hastily arranged proceeding that took place in front of the holding cell at the Houston courthouse.

Little John was not yet two when his new stepmother joined the family. By the end of the following year, he had a baby brother named Eddie. The two boys did not resemble each other at all. John had olive skin and dark hair, while Eddie was extremely fair and had pale blond hair. Tony, their uncle, dubbed them "Black and White." It was unclear whether he was referring to their coloring, or their father's favorite alcoholic beverage ....

The differences between Ben's first and second wives soon became all too apparent. Barbara was anything but quiet and submissive. She did not spend her time in the kitchen with the housekeeper, Manuela, or tend to the vegetable garden. She demanded, and received, a big new truck of her own, and informed her husband that she planned to work in her brother's store and keep the money that she made for her own use.

Tony's wife was not enamored of their new employee, but she could not argue with a cash register that began ringing energetically all day long. Cattlemen are not known for being easy customers, but sharp-tongued Barbara was not afraid of them. She was no less coarse or hardheaded than they were.

She rapidly took matters into her own hands, curtailing purchases on credit and refusing to allow the ranch owners to accrue overly large debts. She taught her brother to sell them harness and tackle of slightly inferior quality, to increase profits. She reminded him that his store was the only one of its kind in the area. Anyone who didn't like how it was run could, for all she cared, travel to El Paso for every padlock or tin of brass polish they needed. Barbara Lowinger's domineering personality soon became an inseparable part of Tony's store — and of Grayston.

John and Eddie grew up like typical Texas children — ranch kids who learned to ride before they learned to read. They grew up wild, their clothes more likely than not torn and dirty, their arms and legs scratched. Manuela wielded no control over them. They raced through the house, overturning furniture, throwing everything that was not bolted down, and perpetrating pranks on poor old Sam in his rocking chair. Now and then, Barbara took them with her to Grayston. There, in the room behind the shop, they could play among the bales of hay, spools of wire, farm tools, and riding tackle.

All the way from the ranch, the two boys would bicker in the back seat, pinching and kicking each other until they almost drove Barbara out of her mind. She was no shrinking violet. Ben Lowinger's second wife — as the people of Grayston soon learned — did not distinguish between her own son and John, her stepson. She shouted at them both and rained blows down on them with equal force.

Los Angeles — Iyar 5766 / May 2006

Two years before that meeting, Yousuf Nadir, Professor Majdi's research assistant, had been a typical American teenager. A serious student, he had completed high school with excellent grades and went on to college as a matter of course, selecting Biology as his major.

Yousuf's father was the embodiment of the American dream. As a young man, he had emigrated from Pakistan and opened a small appliance shop in the United States. This business had steadily expanded until it had developed into a successful chain with fifteen branches. He owned a large house with a swimming pool in Beverly Hills; he drove a new Lexus; he had an American wife who managed to spend much of what he earned; and he had an only son named Joe, who like all boys his age loved baseball, loud music, and electronic games.

The change began when young Joe was sent to visit the family's native Pakistan. His father wanted him to see the hole from which he had crawled and how far he had risen through the toil of his own two hands. When the teenager returned two weeks later, he was a different person. He refused to answer to the name of "Joe" any longer, but only to "Yousuf." In Pakistan he had discovered his Muslim roots, visited mosques, and read portions of the Koran. His relatives had brainwashed him, explaining that the America he had so admired was the Great Satan. According to Islamic faith, infidels must not be allowed to dominate true believers. Something must be done to change the situation.

Joe-Yousuf searched Los Angeles — and, to his surprise, discovered a mosque there, too. It was the large, beautiful mosque headed by Imam Bashir Abdul Aziz. Every Friday, the young man removed his shoes, knelt on a prayer rug, and piously murmured verses from the Koran. Then he attended a class in the *madrasa*, where he studied Arabic and deepened his knowledge of the faith from which his father had strayed.

Sharing his feelings with the imam, he stated that he no longer wished to attend university. He wanted to return to Pakistan and study in the Islamic University there.

"And how do your parents feel about that?" asked Imam Bashir Abdul Aziz. As he had expected, he saw the enthusiasm drain from the boy's face.

On the following Friday, after receiving his personal invitation, Joe's parents came to meet with the imam in his home. The father participated in the private Muslim prayer service after years of abstention. His son knelt on the prayer rug beside him, excited and happy — while his mother, a well-brought-up Catholic, watched them both in distress. She had opposed the idea of Joe's traveling to Pakistan in the first place. She would have preferred him to tour classical Europe and visit several renowned museums. The trip had roused sleeping demons in their family. Her husband seemed fully absorbed in what he was doing: bending, bowing, straightening up …. Standing where she was, behind them, she realized to her chagrin that it was virtually impossible to distinguish between her husband and the other men praying in the mosque.

When she married him, she had paid scant attention to his Pakistani origins. He was just a rich young man with a nice car. As a couple they had navigated the post-9/11 period peacefully, though some of her husband's friends had fallen prey to a surge of Arabic nationalistic fervor. Her husband always denounced the terrorists and those who had sent them. And now — this business with Joe.

As they chatted in the imam's office immediately after the prayer service, she was favorably impressed. Contrary to her fears, the imam strove to cool her son's religious ardor. Bashir Abdul Aziz was sly enough, and smooth enough, to trap far more sophisticated people in his net. Yousuf's naive American mother was easy prey for him.

"You must honor your parents," he told the boy. "If your mother and father want you to go to college, you must listen to them. At the same time, you can continue coming here to the mosque on Fridays. But do not reject all the good that your parents have given you. Mohammed does not admire ingrates."

"I was pleasantly surprised," the mother later told her friends. The imam, she said, was an understanding and feeling person. He had advised against Joe's changing his name to Yousuf, for example, but the boy stubbornly insisted. "Teens go through a terrible stage," she declared. "Kids get all sorts of crazy ideas in their heads, and you have simply no idea where they came from …."

If Joe intended to major in Biology at UCLA, the imam remarked, he had a good friend there — a professor by the name of Barry Majdi. Aziz would drop a word in Majdi's ear and ask him to look out for the boy. They had nothing to worry about. They could call him, Aziz, whenever they chose — day or night. He gave them his direct numbers, for his cell phone and at the mosque.

Joe-Yousuf did well in his studies and continued to hone his Muslim faith. Two years later — no longer a boy now, but a young man of twenty and an outstanding student in his third year at the university — the professor appointed him his research assistant.

Yousuf never heard Majdi refer to his Egyptian roots; it was as though he were an American from birth. He never saw the professor pray or visit a mosque. More than once, he wondered why the imam had told his parents that Majdi was a good friend of his when he, Yousuf, had never heard them exchange a word. Today was the first time he had witnessed a meeting between the two men.

And now, to his dismay, he had just discovered that they were against the attack on the Twin Towers. They were contemptuous of Yousuf's personal heroes: the *shahids* he so admired, such as Mohammed Atta, Ramzi Abu-Yousuf, and their cohorts, who had succeeded in bringing the infidel America to its knees. The men who, more than anyone, he longed to emulate ....

Yousuf was deeply disappointed. He wished he could learn that the professor and the imam shared his views. He longed for the day when they would tell him that it had all been a gigantic farce, and that they believed America was the Satan incarnate.

"Our brother Osama is dragging the masses of fanatic Muslims along with him," the imam continued. He glanced at Yousuf. "He is completely distorting Mohammed's intentions."

Yousuf's face fell. He was in crisis.

"Is this Islam?" the imam went on. "Is this what Mohammed wanted? Doesn't the Koran promise that he would 'purify the believers of their sins and wipe out the infidels'?"

Aziz paused for a moment to let his message sink in, the way he did during his discourses at the mosque. "Wipe out the infidels," he repeated. "Wipe out the infidels! Two thousand, nine hundred dead? Would Mohammed have been satisfied with that? No! What about the millions of other Jews and Christians? Why are *they* still controlling the world and degrading the Muslim nation? Why do Democracy and Leisure — the two new religions the infidels have created — continue to dominate the younger generation and distance them from the true faith?"

Yousuf lifted his head slowly. Total astonishment was written on his face.

"Osama was satisfied with too little," the imam said. "That is not what Mohammed intended."

Yousuf's heart missed a beat. He had been mistaken. The imam had not bowed his head to the West. On the contrary, he was firm and resolute.

And the professor, though milder of temperament, agreed with every word. "If the old sheik were here to see what was happening today, he'd go crazy," he said with a sigh.

The imam compressed his lips and nodded in vigorous assent.

"Something must be done," declared Bashir Abdul Aziz. He turned to Yousuf. "What do you say?"

Yousuf was infused with a powerful excitement. Was he dreaming? Was this no more than a sweet illusion from which he was about to wake?

Were the imam and the professor about to do *something* — and planning to include him?

KGB General Sergei Petroshov often entertained a mental picture of his old mother. She would sit over her embroidery for hours, softly humming sad Russian melodies under her breath. Beneath her skillful fingers, the white cloth sprouted colorful images of snowcapped mountains, green forests, beautiful flowers, and blue skies.

Young Sergei would sit at her feet, enchanted by the needlework. He was mesmerized by the way another spot of color, another strand, another swoop of the needle all combined to form one big picture. That was exactly the way he felt now. He was embroidering a large, complicated tapestry made up of thousands of tiny details. Each in itself was just a single strand, a spot of color. But when looked at all together, a complete picture emerged. Intelligence work was just like his mother's needlework. One needed endless patience and diligence, because every tiny detail, every scrap of information had its part to play in the whole.

It was in this way, through the slow accumulation of many small details, that the Soviet general in Moscow had come to know what only a handful of people in Washington were privy to. Only thus was he able to report to his superiors about a secret chapter of modern-day history known only to a few in Washington's upper echelons: the story of Juarez.

Word of the great fire in the forests of northern Mexico reached him in the year 1957, two full years after the fact. It appeared on an inside page of one of the American newspapers available in Moscow. The American Army claimed that the episode was nothing but an unfortunate accident. A bomb dropped from a military plane, they said, had caused the forest fire in the large valley near the city of Juarez. The Mexican government, on the other hand, angrily declared that it had been a deliberate act of genocide by the United States government, intended to destroy the local populace.

It was just another item in the overabundance of information that came under the general's scrutiny each day. At first, it appeared to be a random tidbit. Then he devoted an extra moment of thought to the episode. There was something interesting here. The accident had occurred not far from the laboratories of Dr. Heinrich von Reiner in the small town of Grayston, Texas.

Eighteen months later, early in 1959, "Black Sheep" — the senior Soviet spy burrowed deep in the United States Department of Defense — added a sentence regarding the subject of his report. The secretary of state, he wrote, was furious with bureaucrats from the Department of Agriculture who had met with a senior Mexican official and pledged to pay a substantial sum as compensation for the rehabilitation of a forest burned because of American activities in the air. Defense Department officials announced that more than just trees were burned in the fire; an Indian tribe indigenous to the region had also been destroyed. An adviser to the secretary of state claimed in closed session that he suspected the Department of Agriculture of trying to cover up a different kind of activity. This, he declared, must be investigated.

Another strand, another blob of color, and the tapestry began to take shape. General Petroshov began putting the pieces together: Black Sheep's two reports, several years apart; an item in an American newspaper, and his knowledge of the German scientist's personality.

Together, these disparate strands allowed him to weave a picture of what he believed had really taken place in the big valley near Juarez.

Heinrich von Reiner needed human guinea pigs to test the biological weapon he had developed. The Jews and prisoners of war who had served in this capacity against their will during the Second World War were no longer available. He had turned, therefore, to the Indian natives dwelling in the forests of northern Mexico.

The United States Government had not wished to leave any trace of the event. Therefore, it had concocted an "accident" in which a military plane dropped a bomb on the forest, destroying it with fire.

When the matter aroused diplomatic criticism, the U.S. agreed to pay Mexico a stupendous sum. This payment was ostensibly for the rehabilitation of the forest, but actually intended to put an end to the incident once and for all, and to close the chapter on a heinous crime: the murder of the Chuma tribe by American germ warfare — under the guidance of Nazi scientist Heinrich von Reiner.

Grayston, Texas — 5720 / 1960

Dinnertime in the Lowinger household closely resembled a no-holds-barred fight between two roosters. Eddie and John were big boys now, ages five and seven, and they rampaged continuously. They raced around the dining-room table, under it, or even — if they deemed it necessary — on top of it.

It was one of the hottest days in memory. The air in the dining room was thick and humid, and not even the ceiling fan succeeded in lowering the temperature. Everyone was listless and irritable, except for the two boys, who ran around and quarreled as if the appalling heat had injected them with an extra dose of energy.

"Ben!" Barbara yelled from the kitchen. "Shut them up!"

Manuela and Frankie sat silently in the kitchen, trying to avoid both the sharp edge of Barbara's tongue and the youngsters' flailing fists. Old Sam, completely detached from reality, sat in his wheelchair and stared into space.

"Stop running around. You're making my head spin!" Barbara screamed, as she walked into the dining room bearing a platter of food. "Can't you calm them down?" This last question was addressed to Ben — but her husband was no longer at the table. He had moved into the living room, absorbed in a baseball game being broadcast live.

"Are you coming to the table?" Barbara called impatiently.

"Bring the food here," Ben replied in the same snappish tone.

Barbara didn't even bother answering. This was an argument that played itself out nearly every evening. He knew what she would say, and she knew what he would say, so why waste their words? Family harmony did not reign in the Lowinger household. He was sick and tired of his shrew of a wife who thought she was something special; she was fed up with the lazy bum who did nothing all day but sprawl in the living room drinking one beer after another. No, she would not bring his meal to the sofa. If he wanted to eat, let him come to the table!

Barbara set down the platter, scowling. She distributed portions of meat and carrot pudding to the various plates, including one for the absent Ben, and sat down angrily. The boys ran outside to continue their fight — ignoring the expected bellow from their mother, to the effect that they had better eat now or they would go to bed hungry.

She herself ate rapidly, then stood up and stepped out onto the porch to light a cigarette. She knew what would happen next. Her dear husband would not budge until the game was over. He would remain in the living room even if the game bored him, just to show her who was boss. Then he would amble over to the table, roar that the food was cold, tell Manuela to throw it into the garbage, and announce that he was going out to eat in Grayston or Port Stockton. He would return much later, half-drunk, after stuffing himself at one restaurant or another and washing the meal down with several large whiskeys at the Drunken Ox. Ben Lowinger ....

It wasn't as if she hadn't been warned. Her brother, Tony, had told her that Ben would not be a model husband — but he did say that she would have plenty of money. If she was lucky, a tractor would run him over and she would be left with the big house and a substantial bank account. The problem was that Ben played his cards very close to the chest. They had been married for nearly six years, and despite all her efforts she had yet to ascertain just how much money he had, or how she could get her hands on it.

The only things she did manage to lay hands on were the envelopes.

Barbara, as opposed to Ben, got up early each morning. She — again, in contrast to her husband — went to work. By nine a.m. she had to be in the store to open its doors. Each morning she would turn on the radio, drink a cup of coffee, and set off for Grayston.

"Do you need anything at the post office or the pharmacy?" she would ask.

Dazed with sleep, Ben in his sloth soon turned the mail over to her. She was the one who sent out the store's mail in any case; she could add an envelope or two to pay their electric bill or their insurance premium, or send a letter from Manuela to her family back in Mexico.

Twice a year, her husband would drowsily mutter that there were "some envelopes on the desk" before turning over in bed. She would smile smugly to herself as she fetched the letters from the desk in his office and slipped them into her purse. She knew all about those envelopes. She also knew to whom they were addressed.

Once, when they had still been capable of conducting a civil conversation, Ben had told her that he had promised old Sam one thing: As long as Sam lived, Ben must continue sending out the donations that the old man had sent all his life to the orphanages, organizations for the needy, and *yeshivos* in Jerusalem. She had learned the routine: Twice a year, around September and April, the postman would deliver mail bearing strange, square lettering from Israel. Ben would roundly curse the old man, but in the end he felt compelled to write out the checks and send them off to Jerusalem. Sam had apparently not placed all his trust in his nephew; he had told him that he had appointed his bank manager in Grayston to check to see whether Ben was keeping up the donations. While Ben was not sure whether or not his uncle was to be believed, he didn't dare take a chance.

But she was perfectly willing to take the chance. So far, it had gone extremely smoothly.

She did not drop the envelopes into the mailbox near the Grayston Bank. Instead, she tore them open and removed the checks. Tony, her brother, would whistle at the sight of the huge sums. Ben Lowinger, it seemed, could be quite generous when he wasn't dealing with his own wife.

Tony would travel to El Paso, where he knew someone who agreed to cash the checks in exchange for a modest fee of ten percent. Old Sam was completely senile, Barbara would say. He neither knew nor cared if the money ever reached the Holy Land, so Ben might as well stop wasting his cash on faraway orphanages and charities. If he didn't have the sense to give money to his wife, she would take what she deserved — in her own way.

As Eddie was approaching his sixth birthday, his mother heaved a sigh of relief. Next year, she would enroll the boys in the regional school in Port Stockton. For at least half the day, someone else would have to cope with those two barrels of energy. Meanwhile, they roamed restlessly through Grayston's streets with nothing to do. Most of their day was occupied with developing and implementing new and innovative kinds of mischief.

Once, they hid in a secluded corner of the bank at the end of the workday, and then set off the alarm. Another time, they tied the deaf-mute, Willy Jr., to the cemetery gate. The poor boy couldn't shout for help, and hours passed while his frantic parents searched for him. From time to time, the boys "forgot" to pay for something at Norman Chambers' bakery. Nor were they above stealing small odds and ends — or even a few coins from the cash register — at their uncle's store.

Ben fulfilled his fatherly duties by showing the boys how to down a shot of whiskey at a single gulp and by taking them to the rodeos he loved. John and Eddie fired their first shots from their father's gun when they were barely big enough to pull the trigger. When they were old enough, he promised, he would take them on a real hunting trip. They would be able to shoot at small animals, which Manuela would then turn into a tasty meal.

On registration day, Barbara put both boys into the back of the pickup truck and warned them to behave politely and make a good impression on the principal. At the start of the trip they were still dressed presentably, in pale linen suits and matching ties. But they squabbled and fought the whole way down. By the time they arrived at the school their clothes were creased and dirty, and their cheeks bright red from the slaps that Barbara had given each of them in an effort to bring their bickering to a halt.

The principal, Mr. Gardiner, was a tall, broad man with a pair of half-spectacles perched on his nose. He greeted Barbara jovially; he had been *her* principal many years earlier. "He looks exactly the way you did at that age!" he said, pointing at Eddie. "Like two peas in a pod. The other boy looks less like you."

"You're right at that …. Can we sign them up?" Barbara asked uneasily. "I have to get back to work." Neither she nor Ben had ever told John that he was not her biological son. He had no recollection that he'd been born to a different mother — a mother who had died when he was about one year old. Maybe they would tell him one day …. In the meantime, every reminder of the fact that John didn't look like her made Barbara uncomfortable.

"Are they twins?" the principal asked, as he rounded his desk and sat down behind it.

"No. Just brothers," Barbara said, grasping John's hand tightly after he kicked Eddie under the desk. "They're two years apart. John will be eight at the beginning of the year." She lifted him to his feet, and the principal held out a huge hand that swallowed the boy's for a moment. "And Eddie's six."

The principal shook Eddie's hand, too. Then he pulled out two registration forms and began filling them out. His eyes, above the spectacles, went from one brother to the other as they sat side by side.

"And where has John been studying until now?" he asked as he wrote.

Barbara squirmed uneasily. "Well …. He hasn't exactly studied anywhere."

"That's against the law, you know." The principal stared at her in rebuke. "A six-year-old must go to school. Texas is no longer a land of uneducated cattlemen. A boy must learn not only how to ride a horse, but also reading, writing, and arithmetic. He needs to know science and geography."

Barbara shrugged apologetically. What could she say — that she had no interest in John? That, from her point of view, he was nothing but a burden? That she loathed him, and was under no obligation to care about him at all? That, as far as she was concerned, the kid could go join his Jewish mother?

"We'll put them both in the first grade." The principal added a few more lines to the page in front of him. Then he looked up again at the two brothers. "You boys will be quiet and well behaved, right? I remember when your mother was a pupil here. She was an excellent student."

This, of course, was an outright lie. The faculty at the Port Stockton School still shuddered with horror at the memory of young Barbara Scott. She had been anything but an excellent student.

The two boys nodded their heads obediently, blushing pink. But under the desk, where the principal couldn't see, each one reached out and pinched the other's leg with all his might.

Neither of them grimaced or made a sound. Neither of them would be the first to let go of his brother's leg. Neither John nor Eddie would give up. If his brother stopped pinching him, then he would stop, too. But *he* would not be the first to give in — however much it might hurt.

Los Angeles — Iyar 5766 / May 2006

Until they were thirteen, Imam Mohammed Taheh Abu-Samir had been the dominant figure in the lives of young Barry Majdi and Bashir Abdul Aziz. He taught them in the old Islamic *madrasa* in Cairo. Every Friday, when they returned from the mosque, they would sit at the old sheik's feet along with the other neighborhood children, listening to him reciting chapters from the Koran and telling the tales of Mohammed's exploits.

Even thirty years later, his image and the sharp scent of tobacco that had filled his room were still vivid in their memories. They remembered his voice, hoarse from smoking: a voice that both inspired fear and drew them as though with magnets. He had strong opinions and was not afraid to express them.

As children, they hadn't understood what the police and security men were looking for in the imam's mosque, or why he disappeared now and then, for weeks at a time. Only when they grew older did they understand that the Egyptian authorities had been suspicious of his extremist religious views. They called him a fundamentalist and a provocateur; they persecuted him and arrested him at every opportunity. But youngsters from all across Egypt continued to flock to him, to thirstily drink in his words and to receive justification for their nationalistic fanaticism. Most of the criticism leveled at Imam Abu-Samir came from the more moderate streams of Islam. He would roundly curse all those who claimed that the spread of Islam need not come about through bloodshed, but rather through "*daweh*" — persuasion, education, and explanation.

They vividly recalled the way Abu-Samir would open his old Koran and with blatant hatred begin reciting Mohammed's words: "*When you meet the infidels in battle, you shall strike at every neck until you overpower them, and safeguard the prisoners well ....*"

It was well that the imam couldn't see what had become of Islam in America, Aziz and Majdi would tell each other in the course of private and highly secret conversations that no one but they knew were taking place. The distortion had reached unprecedented dimensions. American Islamic theology experts constantly sought and found new interpretations that would sound sweet to the Western ear.

Aziz had undertaken to maintain strict silence so as not to tarnish his image as a moderate Muslim — but, if he could, he would have heaped fiery scorn on their heads. What counterfeit rubbish they spouted! What outright lies! Those academics were trying to win the West's praise for their progressive interpretation of the Koran. But the falsity reached to the heavens. *Jihad* was *jihad* was *jihad*! And *jihad* could take place only amid bloodshed.

"*When you meet the infidels in battle, you shall strike at every neck until you overpower them,*'" the old imam would thunder at his young audience, who listened openmouthed. "Every Jew and every Christian is doomed to death!" His words reverberated through a smoky pall, thrilling the hearts of the barefoot, hungry children, inflaming their imaginations and sowing the seeds of a burning hatred against anyone who did not attend the mosque five times a day and bow in the direction of Mecca.

"*When you meet the infidels in battle, you shall strike at every neck until you overpower them.*" For the old imam, Imam Bashir Abdul Aziz had often thought, this had been an impossible vision. Abu-Samir knew how to fan the flames of hatred in innocent children, but he had never held any real hope that the true believers would ever succeed in destroying all the infidels, down to the last man.

Aziz had been of the same opinion — until he ran into his old friend, Barry Majdi.

It didn't happen at their first meeting, nor even at their second. It was months before Majdi trusted Aziz enough to share his great secret. A full year after their first encounter, after hundreds of hours of conversation, Barry Majdi finally told Bashir Abdul Aziz the information that he had personally dubbed "The Mexico File," and conveyed to him the two lethal options it contained.

For long seconds, Aziz had gaped at his old friend, thunderstruck. What he felt was neither surprise nor excitement, but much more: He had a tangible sense of human history changing before his very eyes. Even more: He felt as though a lightning bolt had struck him, proclaiming that he had been selected as one of the two men who would change the face of the world.

Only after two full minutes did Aziz manage to utter a word.

"And you can lay hands on the two ... Mexico things?" he had asked.

"Not only can I lay my hands on them," Majdi had answered, equally aware of the significance of the moment. "I have them in my possession: Mexico A and Mexico B."

Ten years had passed since that day. Now they were seated in Barry Majdi's office, along with the young research assistant who — though he might not know it yet — was slated to play a significant role in the great plan.

"All right. We didn't come here to talk about Osama bin Laden," the imam said. The professor nodded. Yousuf sat up eagerly, acutely conscious that he was being included in fateful events.

"Well, then," Professor Majdi said. Opening a desk drawer, he took out a folded newspaper. He flipped through it until he found the page he wanted. He put on his reading glasses and read aloud, "'The wedding of the year is expected to take place this summer: The elderly Milinover Rebbe's grandson is to wed the daughter of the Rosh Yeshivah (dean) of Yeshivas Knesses HaTorah.'

"This is the opportunity we've been waiting for," he said, handing the paper to Aziz. "The perfect set-up."

The imam took the newspaper and scanned the body of the article, although there were a few words he didn't understand. "'The wedding of the elderly Milinover Rebbe's grandson — the son of the rav of the Milinover chassidim in the United States — to the daughter of HaGaon HaRav Yom Tov Padlinsky, *shlitah*, Rosh Yeshivah of Yeshivas Knesses HaTorah in New Jersey, will take place *iy"H* on 29 Av at the Ganei HaSimchah wedding hall in Ramat Gan ....'"

Aziz looked up. "When does that Hebrew date fall on the Gregorian calendar?"

"August 23rd," Majdi replied, having already checked.

"'Many Milinover chassidim from Eretz Yisrael and the world over will be attending the wedding," Aziz continued reading from the American-Jewish newspaper, "as well as numerous students and admirers of the Rosh Yeshivah. The wedding will take place in Eretz Yisrael, as the Rebbe's health does not permit him to fly to America.'"

Leaning back in his chair, Aziz asked, "What exactly is a 'rebbe'? Would that be the equivalent of a sheik? Or a *khadi*?"

The professor swiveled in his chair to face his research assistant. "Yousuf has done a bit of research for us."

The student was nervous at the prospect of lecturing his two honored companions. With his first words, his voice shook slightly.

"Yesterday, I spoke with Dr. Jimmy Trobski," he began. "He's an anthropologist and a comparative-religion researcher. I got most of my information from him. I also found a bit of material in the library. And I finished by interviewing a medical student, Leiby Klein, who's a chassid himself.

"Anyway, *Rebbe* refers to someone who is the leader of a religious Jewish group called a 'Chassidus.' It's sort of like one of our tribes — Hamullah or something like that.

"We're talking about a group of scores, hundreds, or even thousands of families under a Rebbe's leadership. Most of them prefer living near him, too. There are a large number of these groups, and each one is named for its town of origin in Eastern Europe: Satmar, Pupa, Bobov, Milinov, and so on. By and large, these are ultra-Orthodox Jews, extremely religious people who tend concentrate in areas like New York's Williamsburg and Boro Park. You can tell them apart from other religious Jews by the way they dress: a black silk coat that's called ..." Yousuf ran his eye down his notes until he came to the item he wanted. "... called a '*kapoteh*.' On their heads the men wear a fur hat called ... just a second ... a '*shtreimel*.' The Rebbe who heads the group is well-versed in 'Torah,' the Jews' holy book, and he has the power to draw his chassidim after him by the power of his personality.

"The position is hereditary — usually, father to son. Membership in a chassidic group is not usually based on geography, but on a family and tribal connection, so that someone who marries or moves far away still belongs to the group. He will seek the Rebbe's advice before taking any important step in his life, and will come see him at certain set times: the Jewish holidays, the anniversary of the death of a previous Rebbe in the dynastic chain, and family celebrations of the Rebbe, who serves as a sort of spiritual father to them all. All of his chassidim participate in his happy occasions."

Yousuf studied his notes a moment longer, and then continued. "A wedding like this one is an opportunity to invite and honor the leaders of other sects — that is, the rebbes of other chassidic groups — as well as local political figures and public officials. These weddings are enormous events that usually take place in the group's large neighborhood synagogue or a nearby catering hall. The emphasis is not on food or style, but rather on the ingathering of all the chassidim — a collective rejoicing."

"How do these gatherings work? What happens at them?" the professor asked.

The student flipped some pages in his notebook. "Okay. The ceremony actually begins a couple of days before the wedding. On a day that's called … I hope I'm pronouncing this correctly … the 'Shabbis oifrief.'"

"That's when all the guests fly in from abroad?"

"Leiby Klein, the medical student, explained that it's not always the same. The 'Shabbis oifrief' takes place on a Saturday. If the wedding will be on Sunday or Monday, then it makes sense for everyone to come before then; religious Jews, as you know, don't fly on their Sabbath. But if the wedding is to be held on, say, a Wednesday or Thursday, some of the guests will prefer to come right before the wedding and to stay through the following Saturday, which also has a strange name …." Once again, he rifled through his papers. "It's called the 'Shabbis sheva bruches.'"

"Okay," Aziz pressed. "What's the first event that *everyone* attends?"

"On the day of the wedding — in the afternoon or early evening — there's something called a 'kabulas poonim.' That's the ceremony that kicks off the wedding. It's characterized by singing melancholy songs from the chassidic musical repertoire, and there's a speaker/poet who talks about the importance of the wedding ceremony in the Jewish faith, about the exalted lineage of the families involved, and so on."

"And how long does all that take?"

"About an hour to an hour and a half. Afterward, there's the 'chippah,' which is the official wedding ceremony. Immediately after that, a dinner is served to the multitudes of people — in completely separate locations, by the way: one for the men and another for the women.

"The evening reaches its climax at about ten or eleven p.m. The orchestra breaks into a lively tune, and the Rebbe enters the hall and is seated at the head table along with the groom and the two fathers. A throng of chassidim fills the hall. The older or more honored men are seated at long tables, and the younger ones, whether married or single, come together in specially constructed bleachers; they sing and dance until dawn."

"Good job," Majdi said, though he was well aware that there was one other event in the wedding week — a very significant event — that Yousuf had failed to mention.

Yousuf inclined his head bashfully in the face of the professor's praise.

"And what of these chassidim — the Milinovers? Have you found out anything about them?" Majdi asked.

"Yes, of course." Yousuf hastened back to his notes. "The Milinover dynasty was founded in Eastern Europe about 180 years ago. The present leader, or Rebbe, has been serving in his position for over 40 years now — since 1962. Until about twenty years ago, he lived in Los Angeles and led his group from there. Then, in the '80s, he immigrated to Palestine and built a large synagogue in … just a second … Bnei Brak. That's not far from Tel Aviv. The Rebbe is old and weak today, and has spent the past few weeks in a vacation flat in the north of Palestine, in a city called Tzefat.

"The Milinover Rebbe has many chassidim throughout the United States. When he was younger, he would often travel from state to state, speaking in public and trying to bring secular Jews into the fold. When that happened, they would become his chassidim as well. He also has followers in Great Britain, Australia, France, Belgium, Switzerland, and even in Argentina. Most of them hope to be present at the wedding this summer …."

"And to return to their respective homes afterward," the Imam said, with an evil grin. He threw a meaningful glance at the Professor.

"Now, about the heir," Yousuf continued. "Undoubtedly, the oldest son is considered by all to be most deserving of the role. But there are also —"

"All right. That's enough," the professor broke in. He turned to Aziz. "How does it sound so far?"

"Not bad. Not bad at all …" answered Bashir Abdul Aziz. Then, as though struck by a sudden recollection, he added, "Tell me — the wedding is to be held in an enclosed area, right? It won't be an open-air event?"

Yousuf shrugged. Neither the chassidic medical student nor Dr. Trobski had addressed that point, but it should not be too hard to find out.

"Check it out. It's very important. I want to know if that wedding hall — Ganei HaSimchah — is an enclosed hall."

Yousuf jotted the question down in his notebook.

"Ah .... Because of the air conditioning," the professor said in a tone of comprehension.

"Yes. Because of the air conditioning," the imam replied with a smile.

Yousuf looked from the imam to the professor, curious to know what was so important about the air conditioning. Naturally, he did not dare to voice the question aloud. He was an obedient young man who would faithfully carry out what he was ordered to do. In time, he would know everything.

Professor Majdi gazed dreamily down at the floor, nodding his head with the ghost of a smile.

"The air conditionering," he said slowly. "The air conditioning. Simply ... perfect. It couldn't have been better."

31

Grayston, Texas — 5721 / 1961

As it turned out, John and Eddie Lowinger were not bad students at all. They were extremely bright. Even their tireless mischief abated to a degree. The two brothers were both friends and enemies. They were bound to each other all day long. They played together and did their homework together. But they never stopped quarreling and fighting.

They completed first grade successfully, and moved on to second grade. It was in 1964, during third grade, on the day the new Town Hall was inaugurated, that John's life took a significant turn.

Grayston was growing by leaps and bounds. No longer a tiny settlement, it was now a town worthy of the name. New cattle ranches had been established in the area, the narrow streets had been widened and paved, and a plethora of new homes had been built. A number of oil rigs, producing respectable quantities of oil, had been erected within the town limits.

The entire town turned out in honor of the big day. The three-story building that had been erected in the lot between the bank and the train station was decorated with Texas and United States flags. A platform had been set up in the square in front of the new Town Hall, with a table for the guests of honor, a podium for speakers, and sufficient space for a band.

Ben wasn't interested in the event, and stayed home to watch his favorite shows in the company of a six-pack of beer. Barbara piled John, Eddie, and Manuela into her truck and drove into Grayston.

When they arrived in town, the band was already in place on the stage, playing a medley of patriotic American tunes. Eddie and some of his classmates plotted together to sneak into Town Hall before the VIPs cut the ribbon. But John, uncharacteristically, did not join them. He stood facing the stage, staring openmouthed at the musicians. The sight mesmerized him.

This was the first time he had ever seen a live band up close. The musicians were so near that he could almost have touched their instruments. His eyes drank in the sights. The drummer, in the rear, was a skinny young man with long hair, a cigarette dangling from his lips. The drumsticks in his hands seemed to have a life of their own. Near him stood three trumpeters in identical uniforms, their cheeks puffing out like big balloons as they played their shiny golden trumpets. Another young musician stood to play an instrument that resembled a giant violin.

There were other musicians and other fascinating instruments. But the one who interested John most of all was the black saxophone player.

He was elderly and wore sunglasses; his grizzled hair was completely white. Sitting at the edge of the stage, with the saxophone to his mouth, his fingers raced with dizzying speed across the numerous keys. All the other musicians, John noted, had a book of music open on the stand in front of them. Only the saxophone player played from memory. He never consulted any notes or turned a single page.

Throughout the ceremony, John stood near the stage with his gaze fixed on the band. They didn't play the entire time. Between songs, men in suits and ties stood up and made long, boring speeches. At the end, the band played the "Star-Spangled Banner" and each individual present stood silently with his right hand over his heart. After the mayor cut the red-white-and-blue ribbon with a pair of shiny scissors, everyone streamed into the new Town Hall.

"John, you coming?" Eddie yelled. The boys had not yet managed to get into the building, but now that the doors had been opened, they could slip past the adults and be among the first to enter.

John didn't even hear him. He was mesmerized by the old black musician, who removed the saxophone from around his neck with a sigh, tucked it between his knees, opened a bottle of beer, and gulped down the contents. Then he slowly bent over and began taking the saxophone apart, cleaning each piece with a rag before setting it in its place in a long black case. The other musicians began leaving the stage. To John's surprise, the saxophone player stayed where he was until one of the trumpet players came over and led him by the hand to the band's small bus. Only then did John comprehend that the saxophone player was blind.

That night, young John's dreams were filled with melodies played on a host of complex and shining instruments. He dreamed that he was seated on a tall stage with a huge orchestra all around him. In his dream, no one managed to produce a single sound — except John, playing the saxophone that belonged to the blind musician. As the melody grew louder and louder, John began floating in the air until he was perched on the roof of the new Town Hall, his musical notes scattering to the four winds.

Three months elapsed. On the Fourth of July — Independence Day — Grayston celebrated again. And, once more, the Lowinger family went into town to join in the festivities.

Even from a distance, John noticed the band's bus parked near the Town Hall. His heart nearly lifted right out of his chest in sheer joy. As soon as his father parked the truck, John raced to the stage. Many boys and teenagers were already gathered around the band members, who were warming up for their performance. John wormed his way closer and soon found himself in the front row, standing very close to the musicians.

The old black saxophone player with the white hair and sunglasses was already in place in a corner at the rear of the stage. He withdrew parts of his saxophone from the elongated case at his feet and reassembled the instrument. Fascinated, John watched him pass a long, thin stick of wood through the saxophone's mouthpiece. Then the strap went over the musician's head and he placed his fingers on the keys running down the length of the instrument.

From that moment, John lost all sense of where he was. He was completely hypnotized by the saxophonist's playing. Hours passed; various performers came and went onstage, speeches were delivered, and the skies erupted in fireworks, but John never moved his eyes from the saxophone player. He was mesmerized by those nimble fingers, racing so energetically over the keys. He was fascinated by the old musician's cheeks, rounded as balloons, and by the lips puckered around the mouthpiece. At one point, an older boy lifted John onto the stage, where he sat cross-legged, just a few feet away from the object of his admiration. At the fringe of the Town Hall square there was candy to be bought and booths filled with carefree children playing the games on offer. But John did not budge from his place all evening long.

The band wound up the show and the crowd began to disperse. Stagehands began dismantling the lighting and sound system. John inched a little closer to the saxophonist, hoping to see how he took apart and cleaned the instrument before returning it to its case.

Suddenly, the old man turned his head in John's direction. "Hey, little boy."

Startled, John stepped back.

"Hey, little boy," the musician repeated with a smile. He had a thick voice, low and hoarse. His eyes, behind the sunglasses, were facing John.

"Do — do you mean me, mister?" John asked, after a hasty glance convinced him that there were no other children around.

"Yeah, boy," the musician said. "Did you like the music?"

John took a half-step closer, still finding it hard to believe that the saxophone player was actually addressing him. "Yes, mister. It's pretty. You play nice ...."

"Come a little closer. Do you want to play?"

John was excited. "Me? Play on the saxophone?"

"Sure. Why not?"

John practically ran to him. The blind man put out a hand and measured the boy's height. "How old are you, boy?"

"I'm ten."

"Okay. Let's try." The musician bent over the case at his feet, took out another long stick of wood, and replaced the one that was inside the saxophone. He handed John the instrument. "Come on, put the mouthpiece into your mouth and blow hard."

John grasped the saxophone and encircled the mouthpiece with his lips. He blew a mighty breath. At first, there was no sound at all. Then, when he relaxed his lips at the musician's suggestion, a thin note emerged.

The saxophonist smiled with satisfaction. "Nice, little boy," he told John. "But that was just a note. Now, put three of your fingers on these three keys." He placed the index, middle, and ring fingers of John's left hand on the three keys at the top of the saxophone. "Now, press on those keys and blow again."

John blew with all his might. The note he produced was different from the first one.

"That was a 'G,'" the black musician told John. "Now, lift up one finger and blow again."

John lifted his ring finger, leaving only his index and middle fingers on the keys. He blew, and made another sound. In some indefinable way, he sensed that this note was higher than the one before.

"You just played an 'A,'" the old man said. "Now lift up another finger and try again."

John did as he was told. Only his index finger remained pressed to the key as he blew. Once again, this note was different than the others — even higher than the two previous notes.

"That was a 'B,'" the old man said. "Now, play all three notes in a row: G, A, B."

John played the three notes over and over: G, A, B ... G, A, B .... Some of the other musicians paused in the course of packing their instruments to smile at the impromptu music lesson.

"Hey, boy, want to play my trumpet?" the trumpeter called.

John shrugged his refusal. The musicians laughed. The trumpeter tousled John's hair and said something the boy didn't understand: "The kid has a black soul."

"Okay, Christopher. Time to go," the young trumpet player told the elderly saxophonist. The blind man quickly disassembled his saxophone and placed it in its case. He held the thin wooden stick out to John.

"Here. If you ever want to play, you'll already have this; it's called a reed," he said with a smile.

The young trumpet player took Christopher's arm and began leading him to the bus. "All you need," the blind man called back over his shoulder, "is a saxophone."

"Thanks a lot, mister!" John cried.

"Good-bye, little boy," Christopher said, and continued on toward the bus.

At that moment, John knew exactly what he wanted to be when he grew up.

The next day, Sunday, the Lowinger family sat down to dinner.

"So, how was the Independence Day celebration?" Frankie asked the boys. He had stayed home with Sam and missed the fun.

"It was great!" young John said enthusiastically. "There was a blind musician there, and he let me play his saxophone!"

"It was great," Eddie mimicked. John kicked him under the table.

"When I grow up, I'm going to play in a band," John told Frankie.

"Very nice," the veteran stableman said. "Music is good for the soul."

"Nonsense," Barbara announced. "Musicians don't make any money. At most, you'll be an old man traveling from place to place on a bus and earning a few measly dollars."

"That musician was an old black man," Eddie said conversationally, ready to start trouble. "And his fingers were all crooked."

"You can't play music with crooked fingers," Barbara said acidly. "And stop talking to black folks, or they'll kidnap you and take you to Alabama, and cook you up to feed their black kids!"

John spread his fingers and studied them carefully. "My fingers aren't crooked," he said, affronted. "And, anyway, he was very nice. He doesn't eat kids."

Eddie, on the other side of the table, grimaced at him. Crooking his fingers into claws, he began mockingly to play an imaginary saxophone. John threw his fork at him. Eddie countered by hurling the remaining juice in his cup at John.

"You can't play the saxophone," Barbara repeated firmly.

"But I want to play," John said, blinking back tears.

"There's lots of things that *I* want," Barbara said in a hard voice. "For example, I want the principal of your school not to call me every couple of weeks to complain about the new antics the two of you have been up to."

"If he wants to play — let him play," Ben said suddenly.

Barbara turned her head angrily. Ben met her stare with one of his own. "He wants music lessons? Let him have them," he said. "What difference does it make to you?"

John leaped up from his chair, both fists over his head in a gesture of victory. "Yes! Yes!" he crowed.

"Do what you want. He's your son," Barbara snapped at her husband. With that, she stood up and went into the kitchen.

"I'll find out where you can take music lessons," Ben told John, and returned his attention to his plate.

John was happy. But Barbara's last sentence diluted his joy. How many times had he heard his mother tell his father, "He's your son"? Wasn't he her son, too? Was it possible that he had a different mother? For some time now, he had noticed that she loved Eddie much more than she loved him. She always looked at John differently.

He had no one to ask, no one with whom to share these troubling questions. But as he lay in bed at night, he would ask himself — *Was his mother really his mother at all?*

Tall Willy, their neighbor from the ranch down the road, knew someone who knew the saxophone player. Two days later, he got the man's address in Port Stockton and jotted it down for young John to take to his father.

John was excited. His school was in Port Stockton; he would be able to have music lessons after school. Ben put the paper into his pocket and said that he'd take care of it. But he seemed in no hurry to keep his promise. He had more important things on his mind, such as vital baseball games, rodeo championships, or even just lounging around the Drunken Ox draining the contents of one bottle after another.

Two weeks later, on a spring afternoon, Ben — annoyed by the child's incessant pestering — loaded John into his pickup truck and drove to Port Stockton.

The saxophone player's street was a poor one, but his house was neat and clean. A few flowerpots were ranged near the front door, and in the small window high in the door itself hung a delicate lace curtain.

Ben knocked. A black woman opened the door and looked at him inquiringly. He said that he was looking for the saxophonist.

"Christopher! It's for you," the woman called. An armchair with its back to the door moved slightly.

"Who is it?" the musician asked from the chair, in the rich, low voice that John remembered from his brief lesson on the Fourth of July.

"My son wants to learn to play the saxophone," Ben said from the doorway.

The chair swung around, and John saw the blind musician with the ever-present sunglasses covering his eyes. The man was smiling.

"Oh, the little boy's come, has he?" he asked.

"Yes, mister. It's me, John" John said. He took a step into the house.

"Oh, little boy," the saxophonist drawled. "So three notes weren't enough for you, eh?"

"No. I want to play like you, mister."

The black man threw back his head and laughed joyfully. "To play like me, little boy, you'd have to practice eight hours a day for ten years. Are you ready to do that?"

John's answer was decisive. "Yes, sir."

"Your fingers will hurt, your lungs will burn, your lips will bleed, and your eyes will tear from reading all those notes. Are you ready for that, little boy?"

"Yes." John nodded vigorously.

"Okay." The blind man thrust out a hand. "In that case — you're accepted."

Young John hastened forward to shake his hand.

Ben discussed payment, but he didn't bargain too hard. This was the first time he had ever done anything special for his son, and he was surprised at how good it felt. John's lessons were set for four p.m. every Tuesday.

"There's a bus from here to Grayston," the blind musician said. "John can take it home. I once had a student from Grayston. He stopped coming. But little John, I'm sure, will stick to his lessons."

"Why?" Ben asked curiously.

"Oh, it's simple," the musician said with a smile. "That other kid came here because his parents dragged him. But little John, I understand, is the one who dragged *you* ...."

The saxophonist's wife set out coffee, cookies, and a newspaper for Ben in a nearby room. This first time, Ben had decided, he would stay till the end of the lesson and bring John home himself. In the future, John would go home by bus — together with the saxophone that his father promised to buy him the very next day, in the big music store in El Paso.

"And now," the blind musician said to young John, "Go get Sam, and we'll start our first lesson."

"Sam?" the boy asked in astonishment. "You want me to bring my uncle?"

"Oh, no!" The musician threw back his head and laughed heartily. "Is your uncle named Sam, too? I didn't know that. I meant him." He pointed at the corner. The familiar saxophone case stood propped up there.

John lugged the case over, still surprised. "Do all instruments have names, mister?" he asked naively, laying the saxophone at the man's feet.

"First of all, little John, you can call me Christopher. That's what my friends call me."

John nodded. Then, remembering that the man couldn't see, he said aloud, "Okay, mister ... uh ... Christopher."

"Well, then, little John, the answer is 'no': Not all instruments have names. My saxophone has a name because it's my best friend. The first time we met — some thirty-eight years back, in a little music store in Alabama — I told it, "Hi, there. My name's Christopher, and I want to be your friend ...."

John sat openmouthed, staring at the blind man in complete fascination. "And what did the saxophone say?"

The musician leaned close to John and whispered, "He told me, 'Hi, Christopher. My name's Sam, and I'd like to be your friend, too.' Since then, we've been inseparable. To this very day."

As he spoke, Christopher took out the various parts of his saxophone and began to assemble them. This was the instrument that John had seen onstage, at the Town Hall inauguration and on the Fourth of July. The same instrument on which John had played his first three notes: G, A, and B. John studied the saxophone up close. It was old, its patina marred by many tiny dents and scratches. All along the length of the instruments he saw a series of small levers and valves. At the tip of each one — where the finger pad rested — was a mother-of-pearl button. Christopher pulled a new reed from a narrow tin box, wet it in his mouth, and mounted it on the black mouthpiece.

"But ... how can a saxophone talk?" At long last, John found the words to express the wonderment he had been feeling. And how was it that Christopher had seen him on that stage in Grayston? How had he come to call out so suddenly, "Hey, little boy?" Wasn't he blind? He couldn't see anything. He wore dark glasses, and the young trumpet player had to guide him back to the bus. What a mysterious man, capable of seeing although he was blind, and talking to musical instruments ....

Christopher didn't respond. He brought the mouthpiece to his lips, lifted his head slightly, and began to play a slow tune. Low, soft notes filled the room. Christopher moved with the saxophone to the rhythm of the melody, wrapping both hands around the gilded metal and embracing the instrument with his fingers as they moved incessantly: rising and falling, pressing and releasing, squeezing and letting go.

There was no other sound in the house except the saxophone's music. Even Ben, in the dining room, stopped turning the pages of his newspaper. As the sorrowful melody echoed through the house, John felt a great sadness welling up inside him. Suddenly, he wanted to cry. Christopher's saxophone was telling a very sad story — a story without words, but one that was filled with tremendous pain and endless longing. Perhaps he was telling of the light in his eyes, which had been extinguished. Or maybe he missed his own little boy, who had traveled away to a far-off land. Or maybe ... maybe he was crying for the years of his own youth, which would never return. The song expressed a profound grief, as though the saxophone was mourning and in pain. Tears filled John's eyes.

Christopher finished playing and slowly removed the saxophone from his lips. For a moment, total silence reigned in the room.

"People think," the blind musician said quietly, "that you need a mouth to talk with. But they're wrong. People think," he added, tapping his dark glasses, "that you need eyes to see with. But that's a big mistake. You hear that, little John? It's not the mouth that speaks, but the heart. Eyes don't do the seeing — the heart does. And how does the heart talk? Do you know that, little John?'"

John was silent.

Christopher tapped lightly on the saxophone. "Through music, little John. Music can tell a sad story or a happy one. It can express joy, anger, pain, or disappointment. Music comes straight from the heart, without anything holding it back. That's why it's called the language of the heart. It's a very special kind of language. Everyone can hear it; some can understand it; a very, very few can speak it.

"You can, little John. I can sense your little heart beating in time to the music. You can speak this language — the simplest kind of language there is. It's such a human language that only the good L-rd up above could have created it.

"You have it, John. It's that simple. You have what it takes. All you have to do is pull it out of you. It won't be easy. It will be hard work, hours and hours of practice, going over a piece any number of times. But, in the end, one day you'll manage to produce one genuine note. One pure note that comes straight from the deepest part of you.

"And then, little John, you'll know that you managed to speak your first word in the language of the heart."

Um-el-Facham — Iyar, 5766 /May 2006

An unexpected heat wave assailed the city of Um-el-Facham. Though the sun was about to set, the heat was still intense.

Three border-patrol jeeps were parked in the main square. They were there as a reminder of yesterday's riots. Youthful Arabs had hurled rocks at the highway; several of the young men were arrested. Then the real ruckus had begun, one side throwing incendiary bottles while the other responded with rubber bullets.

This morning things had calmed down, and the day had passed peacefully. But the calm was very tenuous. Passersby eyed the soldiers with hatred, but kept their distance. An Egged bus drew into the square and a large group of young people coming home at the end of the workday emerged. The border police tensed as the group passed them, but the Arabs were too tired and hungry to instigate trouble. A small barefoot boy ran toward them from the sidewalk.

"Turk! Turk!" the boy cried, waving to a tall, thin young man wearing a smudged cotton shirt too big for him. "You had a phone call from America. He said he'd call back later."

Turk Majdi lifted his nephew in his two strong arms and glanced in alarm at the Jewish soldiers. If they had overheard the boy's shout, it was all over for him. The G.S.S. (General Security Service) would come for him in the night and interrogate him.

"Quiet, you little fool," he hissed. The child had no idea what he had done wrong.

Turk's mother placed his dinner in front of him and sat down with a sigh. She was elderly, ill, and always dressed in the same traditional Arab

THE MEXICO FILE / 279

garb made of coarse black cloth and embroidered with colorful threads that had frayed in places. The patchwork of lines on her face was partly due to age and partly to pain. She was missing several front teeth, and those that were left ached.

"My brother-in-law was looking for you," she said.

Turk nodded as he chewed. The boy had already told him.

"I hope he's finally going to do something useful and take you to America," his mother went on, wiping a tear away with the edge of her sleeve. "Maybe, over there, you'll succeed in life more than your poor brother did."

Turk tore off a piece of pita and heaped it with rice. "My brother is a *shahid*," he said. He did not like it when his mother mourned his brother. That showed that she did not believe with all her heart in Mohammed and in the Koran. "Ishmael was a hero who fought the Zionist Satan."

"Enough, enough! One *shahid* in the family is enough." His mother buried her face in her hands and burst into tears. Ishmael, her firstborn son and Turk's older brother, had blown himself up in Kfar Saba three years earlier. He had taken five Jews with him and wounded dozens more. But he had blown a painful gap in her heart.

When the reporters and photographers had been brought to her tent of mourning, she had repeated exactly what they told her to say: that she was proud of her son and hoped that all her sons would become *shahids*. But there wasn't a day when she did not shed tears for him, or curse those who sent him out with a belt of explosives around his waist.

Those men had taken advantage of the fact that Ishmael had been jobless and depressed, that he had not managed to find a bride, and that he was always butting heads with the G.S.S. Those men didn't send *their* sons off to be suicide bombers. *Their* sons were sent to school in Jordan or Egypt. It was only her poor son whom they had turned into a *shahid*. And now Turk was talking the way his big brother used to talk, before he went and blew himself up among the Jews.

"Mohammed wants me to have at least one living son," she told Turk, as she stood up in tears.

"Mother, Mother," he called after her in a placating tone. "Maybe Uncle Barak really will find me a job in America."

His mother walked, weeping, toward the yard to pick a few figs. She kicked away the two black goats that had wandered near. In her imagination, the kicks were aimed at her brother-in-law, living peacefully in Los Angeles.

"If he's so devoted, my dear brother-in-law the professor," she said, spitting out the word "professor" as though it were a curse, "he can send some money now and then to his poor sister-in-law in Palestine."

Turk didn't hear her. He was completely focused on the call from his uncle, Professor Barak — Barry — Majdi, and filled with excited speculation as to what his uncle might have to tell him.

Grayston, Texas — 5724 / 1964

The music lessons carried John away. He spent all his free time practicing and made very rapid progress. Each afternoon, he would return home on the yellow school bus, do his homework at the dining room table, and then hurry to his room to play the saxophone.

Barbara was beside herself. "I can't stand that noise!" she told her husband night and day. "He'd better stop playing, or I'll toss that 'shofar' off the roof!"

Barbara was none too pleased that Ben had taken John into El Paso to buy the most expensive saxophone available. Even Christopher was surprised when John brought it with him at his next lesson. "Wow! That's a real Selmer," he said, stroking the saxophone with his hands. "It's a very expensive instrument, made in Paris, France. I hope you'll take good care of it."

Ben never took Eddie shopping, Barbara fumed. He never spoiled *her* son. He only showered money on John. He found interesting hobbies for John, while her dear, sweet Eddie walked around bored, with no one to play with. *All of a sudden*, she thought venomously, *Ben and little John had become the best of friends* .... Out of the blue he was laughing with his son and listening to how far along he had advanced in his lessons with that "shofar" ....

She used the word "shofar" deliberately, to anger her husband. Ben had no idea where she had learned what a shofar was, but her use of the word was a poisonous dart aimed at the Jewish roots he tried so hard to deny. And it was a sharp reminder that John was the son of Devorah, his first wife — his Jewish wife.

Eddie, too, was suffering from his brother's new hobby. The hours that John spent practicing the saxophone — hours that they had once spent playing together — hung heavy and lonely on his hands. He had nothing to do ... except disturb John's playing.

The moment John started practicing was the precise moment that Eddie remembered to play records on his father's new stereo, or raise the volume on the big radio near the dining-room table. When John came in to lower the volume, Eddie would use the opportunity to slip into his brother's room and start "playing" the saxophone, or else kidnap the instrument and run out into the yard, with John in hot pursuit, screaming and crying. More than once, John's practice sessions ended with the saxophone being tossed onto the bed or into a bush, and the two brothers going at each other with clenched fists — hitting, scratching, and kicking until blood flowed, or one of the adults intervened to separate them.

It was at the age of eleven, on the last day of school, that John's secret fears were confirmed.

The yellow school bus was late, and everyone waited impatiently for it to take them home. A group of boys from Port Stockton began to taunt the Grayston children, and soon a melee filled the sidewalk. Everyone hit everyone else. Noses bled, clothing was torn, glasses were bent, and knapsacks were hurled to the ground. John initially stayed out of the fracas, but when a couple of boys attacked Eddie, he hurried forward, fists at the ready.

The fight ended only with the arrival of the school bus. The Port Stockton boys remained on the pavement while the Grayston youngsters scrambled aboard. The two Lowinger brothers were last to climb the steps. Eddie seized the chance to get in one last kick at a red-haired kid, while

John pulled another boy's hair a moment before the driver closed the door.

The bus had not yet started on its way as the Port Stockton kids stood on the sidewalk, waving their fists in the air as they outlined what they planned to do to the Grayston boys when school started again in the fall. The boys on the bus heartily returned their curses and threats.

"Go to the same place your mother went!" one of the boys yelled at John.

"What did you say?" Eddie narrowed his eyes through the window. He took a handy rock from his pocket and aimed it at the boy outside. The boy wailed in pain when the rock hit his shoulder.

"If you curse my mom one more time, I'll kill you!" Eddie screamed.

The bus started moving, making for the main road.

"I wasn't talking about *your* mother!" the Port Stockton boy shouted back. "I was talking about *his*!" He pointed at John.

John and Eddie took their seats, still breathing hard from the fight.

"Did you hear what he said?" John asked after a few minutes.

"What?" Eddie was busy scrutinizing the cuts and scrapes on his arms and legs.

"That my mom isn't your mom," John told his brother. "Listen. Could it be true?"

Eddie shrugged and continued inspecting his wounds. Setting his knapsack down between them, John gazed out the window, lost in thought. If the kid from Port Stockton was right, it would explain all the times that his mother had told his father, "He's your son." She never said that about Eddie.

The more he thought about it, the more the idea took hold of him. His mom ... that is, Eddie's mom ... was not a mother to be proud of. More than once, he had noticed people wrinkling their noses behind her back, and whispering about her. Everyone in Grayston hated her because she refused to let the ranch owners buy on credit in her brother's store. She was loud, harsh, and irritable. Maybe his real mother was a good, gentle woman who read her kids stories before they went to bed. Maybe his real mother was someone who greeted her children with a smile on her face and asked them how their day at school had been.

He would ask his father. He would find a time when his mother — or rather, Barbara — was not around and his father was not in a bad mood, or drunk, or upset over losing a horse race, and ask him then.

Young John walked around for the next few weeks gnawed by doubt. His chance came during the big transportation strike. The bus to Port Stockton wasn't running. At breakfast that day, John asked how he was supposed to get to his music lesson.

"You can miss one lesson," Barbara said. "Anyway, your playing is getting on my nerves. One day I'm going to break that 'shofar' in half."

Ben, uncharacteristically, was in a good mood — or maybe he was just looking for a reason to get out of the house. He volunteered to drive John to his lesson and back home afterward. When it was time to go, John placed his saxophone and his music folder behind the seat and climbed up front with his father.

"So how's the music going? Are you enjoying yourself?" Ben asked, as they pulled onto the main road.

"Very much," John answered enthusiastically. "I already learned five major and minor scales, including arpeggios."

"Very nice," Ben said, though he hadn't the foggiest notion what John meant.

"And I also learned 'The Lonely Foal,' by Patrick Kargeill. Do you know it?"

"Ah-hem," Ben cleared his throat evasively. "I heard of him."

Most of the ride went by in silence. Father and son did not share many topics of conversation. After ten wordless minutes, John mustered his courage.

"Dad," he said hesitantly. "A kid once told me something, and I want to know if it's true."

"What?"

"That ... that Barbara is not my mother. Is it true?"

"Yep," Ben said casually.

"So Barbara's not my real mother?" John felt tears welling up in his eyes.

"Didn't I just say that?"

"Where is she?"

"Who?"

"My mother."

"She's nowhere," Ben said. "She's dead."

Now the tears overflowed, unstoppable. John's disappointment was deep. The possibility that Barbara was not his mother had given rise to a flood of mixed emotions — chief of which had been the hope that another, kinder mother awaited him some place. Now he learned that he had had a mother, but she had died.

"Stop blubbering like a girl," Ben snapped, with a sideways glance at John. "She died before you even knew her. And she wasn't such a great mother anyway."

John knew what death was. Teddy Whitman, in his class, had lost his father in Vietnam, and the whole class had gone to the Port Stockton cemetery for the funeral. Teddy and his mother had cried the whole time, but the ceremony had been very impressive. Uniformed soldiers had carried the coffin, draped in the Stars and Stripes; trumpets had blared and then played the American anthem. Finally, the coffin had been placed in the ground and the principal of their school, Mr. Gardiner, explained to them that Teddy Whitman's father had returned to his Father in Heaven.

"So — my mother is in the ground? They buried her?" he asked.

"If you need to know, they buried her in the graveyard behind the Grayston church," Binyamin said, already regretting his offer to drive his son to Port Stockton. "But take a lesson from me: I've never gone there. When a person's dead, she's dead. They put her in the ground and that's that."

Silence filled the pickup until they reached Christopher's house. John grabbed his saxophone case and music and climbed out. His father told him that he would get a drink and be back in an hour.

The lessons started off as usual. Christopher went into the kitchen to fix himself a cup of coffee, calling to John, "Start from G, D, A, F — chords and arpeggio." John finished assembling his saxophone and began to play.

"Very good, John," Christopher called. "Just pay a little more attention to the beat. You always move faster as you get near the end. Now, play 'The Lonely Foal' for me."

John began to play the song about the little lost foal in the desert whose mother had galloped away with the rest of the herd, across the river where the grass grew green, the water flowed, and there were no Indians to trap wild horses. John knew the song by heart and didn't look at the notes. This time, he identified more than usual with the young abandoned horse, a foal that no one loved and that wandered the great desert, hungry and tired ....

Christopher felt his way back to his chair. He sat with a sigh and sipped his coffee.

"You sad today, little John?" he asked gently.

John nodded his head. Then, remembering that Christopher was blind, he said, "Yes. A little."

The old saxophonist smiled in understanding. "It's okay to be sad sometimes, little John."

"My mother died," John said.

"Ah. That's very sad. When did it happen?"

"About ten years ago ..." John whispered.

"But you just found out today," Christopher said, as though completing John's sentence.

John nodded. Swallowing his tears, he asked, "How did you know?"

"You told me," Christopher said with a smile.

"I did?" John hadn't said a word.

"You told me — not in words, but in the language of the heart. Your music, little John, is what told me that you're feeling sad today."

Summer vacation dragged on. John was filled with a burning desire to find the place where his mother was buried, but he wanted to do it on his own, without Eddie. He had to wait for his chance, for a time when Eddie was busy elsewhere.

Then Eddie's surgery was scheduled, and John knew that his chance had come.

Eddie's frequent sore throats had led his doctor in Port Stockton to send him to the hospital in Austin for a tonsillectomy. Barbara was to travel with him, and to stay for the several days that he would be hospitalized, even though Tony, her brother, would have a hard time coping with the seasonal business on his own.

Early one afternoon, a week and a half before the start of the new school year, Barbara and Eddie set out for Austin in her truck. The rest of the family stood on the porch waving them off. Even Ben managed to detach himself from his stupor in order to say good-bye to his frightened son and to wish him a speedy recovery. Big, tough Eddie suddenly looked very small and scared. Barbara had frightened him by saying that the doctors were going to cut his throat and that it would heal back together afterward. But, she had warned, if he didn't stop weeping and wailing she would ask them to stitch up his mouth at the same time, so that he couldn't cry anymore.

That night, John had a hard time falling asleep. This was the first time he had ever slept alone in his room, without his brother. The house seemed quieter and somehow scary. From outside he heard the howls of wild coyotes. But he was kept awake more by his great excitement in the knowledge that, very soon, he would be able to visit the graveyard behind the church to see the burial place of his real mother.

The next morning, John got up very early — something he hadn't done all summer. His father wasn't up yet, but he could hear the pickup truck start.

John ran out. Frankie was in the truck, preparing to leave. "Are you going to Grayston?" John called.

"Yes," said Frankie. "Want a lift?"

John scrambled into the truck.

"What do you need in town?" Frankie asked.

"I want to buy a present for Eddie," John said, conjuring up the pretext on the spot. "Something small, to give him when he gets back from the hospital."

The pickup was already bumping along the gravel road toward the road that ran among the ranches. "Do you have cash?" Frankie asked.

"Yes. Mom gave me some yesterday." He turned his head to the window, to watch the passing scenery — and to avoid further questions.

Frankie was humming along with the tune on the radio. John had a feeling that the old stableman was well aware that he was lying. Frankie knew everything. You couldn't pull the wool over *his* eyes. He knew that Barbara never doled out money, and especially not for buying gifts ....

But Frankie, apparently, had more important things on his mind. He was silent for the rest of the drive, and they were soon traveling along Grayston's main street. He let John out near Norman Chambers' bakery, rummaged in his pockets, and pulled out a few coins.

"Here, he said, handing John the money with a wink. "Buy yourself something to eat."

John took the coins and thanked him.

"I'll be going back to the ranch in about two hours," Frankie said. "If you want, you can ride back with me."

John went into the confectioner's shop and bought a donut. Norman put it into a paper bag and handed it to him.

"And where's your brother?" he asked, looking around suspiciously. He wasn't accustomed to seeing John on his own. The Lowinger brothers always arrived together, and generally disappeared together, along with a couple of jelly donuts.

"Eddie went to Austin," John said.

"Austin?"

"Yes. They're taking his tonsils out."

"Really?" Chambers looked worried. "Poor kid. Will you be going to visit him?"

"Yes," said John, seeing where the questions were heading.

Norman Chambers placed two jelly donuts into a fresh bag and gave it to John. "That's for Eddie," he said compassionately. "Tell him that we all wish him a speedy recovery."

Carrying the bags of donuts, John strode toward the graveyard behind the church. He approached it cautiously, standing on tiptoe to peek over the wooden fence. Row upon row of headstones stretched from the church wall, all the way down the hill to the riverbank. It was a little scary to walk into a cemetery all by himself. Maybe it would have been better if he had brought Eddie with him ....

The wooden gate creaked when John pushed it open. To his relief, he saw that each headstone bore the name of the person buried there. He had almost two hours before Frankie would be returning to the ranch. He would search among the rows until he found her .... But wait a minute. What was her name?

He didn't even know his real mother's name.

He would search until he found the name "Lowinger," he decided, and hope that she hadn't been known by another name.

Half an hour passed as John moved among the rows of headstones, occasionally dwarfed by their size. He saw simple graves and ornate ones. There was a stone in the shape of a broken branch, and a short poem saying that this was the grave of Emily Busch, who had been taken by the river when she was only four years old. Another marker, on a poet's grave, depicted a feather and scroll.

On and on. Another thirty minutes had gone by and he had not yet located his mother. John continued moving among the headstones. One section held the older graves: Matthew Cornwall, Grayston's first sheriff, lay beneath a large stone etched with the municipal logo; Isabella Stanson, devoted wife, mother, and grandmother, who had used a gun to chase off five robbers and died of her injuries a week later, at the age of 74; Anthony Garcia, a kind-hearted Mexican who had drowned while trying to save little Emily Busch from the river.

And then, suddenly, at the end of a row, his eyes glimpsed a familiar name: Lowinger.

He caught his breath in excitement. Was this his mother? Quickly, he moved closer. The headstone was extremely plain, made from ordinary stone and engraved with only a few words:

Devorah Lowinger
1917-1954

Above the words were some unclear embellishments — and that was all.

Tears welled up in John's eyes. Devorah. His mother's name was Devorah. He had never known her, but at least now he knew her name. Devorah. What an odd name. He didn't know anyone else with that name.

John bent down and touched the headstone. It felt cold and damp with the morning dew. What should he do now? What did a person do at his mother's grave? What did other people do when they visited their loved ones in the cemetery? John looked around. The cemetery was deserted.

He sat on the grass, his back against another stone, and gazed at his mother's grave.

Devorah Lowinger
1917-1954

His mother had been born in the year 1917 and had died in 1954. How many years had she lived? John tried to figure it out in his head, but became confused. He picked up a twig and wrote the figures on the ground. He wasn't fond of math but this was an easy one: 1954 minus 1917 came to 37. His mother had died at the age of 37.

That was very young to die. What had she died of? Sickness? An accident? The headstone didn't tell him. She had died in 1954 — and he had been born in 1953. He'd been one year old when she died.

Why was her headstone so plain? Why didn't it have any adornment or parting words like, "Our dearly beloved mother"? Other stones held lines and lines of warm sentiments. But nothing extra had been inscribed on his mother's stone.

John sat on the grass for half an hour, lost in thought. When he grew hungry, he took out the jelly donut he had bought at the confectioner's and ate it. He placed the empty paper bag into the larger bag with the two donuts for Eddie. It wasn't proper to litter a cemetery, especially when your own mother is buried there ....

Why wasn't he crying? Usually, people cried when they visited a cemetery. Why did he feel a kind of happiness instead, because he had found his mother? Was there something wrong with him?

The Town Hall clock told him that he still had ten minutes before it would be time to go. Frankie would be waiting outside the confectioner's at ten-thirty, and John had no other way to get home. He prepared to take his leave.

He looked around, committing everything he saw to memory so that he would be able to find the spot more easily the next time he came. The grave was under the old pecan tree, almost directly opposite the church's back entrance. He stood up, brushed off his pants, and checked to make sure he hadn't left any litter on the ground.

Just then, he realized that there was something else on the headstone. What was it? He had thought at first that it was only some sort of decoration — but now, looking more closely, he thought that maybe they were letters. Not English letters — certainly not English — but, yes, what he was looking at was definitely some kind of lettering.

There were two words, with an unfamiliar symbol above them: a six-pointed star formed by two triangles, one upside-down over the other.

This new discovery interested John. There was a clue here. These letters would tell him more about his mother. He had to copy them down — but how?

John looked around. All he had was the donut bag in his hand. He reached in and pulled out the smaller bag he had placed inside earlier. Tearing it along one side, he now had a large square of paper. He placed it on the headstone, and to his joy the paper covered both the words and the symbol above them. He wished he had a pencil.

Then he remembered the coins that Frankie had given him. A coin would do the job. He pressed the coin against the paper and began moving it rapidly across the page. The impression of the letters transferred itself to the paper. The minute he got home, he would go over the tracing with a pencil. It would have to do.

John folded the page and put it in his pocket. Then he ran toward Main Street. Frankie was already waiting in his truck.

"Ready to go home?" he asked.

All was quiet at the ranch house. Barbara phoned from the hospital in Austin to say that the operation had gone well. Eddie was feeling fine and they should be home in a few days. Ben, with his usual facetiousness, said there was no need to hurry. She could stay in Austin as long as she liked.

The housekeeper had prepared a tasty dinner and Ben was in a good mood. John decided that this was the right moment to finally find out what was written on his mother's gravestone.

"Dad, can I ask you something?" John ran up to his room and returned with the donut bag on which he had taken the impression of the words from the stone.

Ben was relaxing in his chair, reading the newspaper. John spread out the paper bag and placed it on the arm of his father's chair. "What does this say?" he asked.

In his worst nightmare, he could never have anticipated his father's reaction. Ben shot up in his armchair. "What's that?" he yelled. "Who gave this to you?"

John turned rigid with shock. Then he burst into tears.

"Answer me!" Ben got to his feet, cheeks burning. "Where did you get this?"

John had never seen his father so beside himself. He was terrified. Apparently, he had done a very bad thing. It was probably forbidden to copy things from headstones in cemeteries. He began to bolt from the room, but, shaking with fury, his father raced after him and caught him before he got very far. "*Who gave this to you?*" he bellowed, grabbing John and shaking him with all his might.

John's tears intensified. Frankie and Manuela stood by, helpless in the face of Ben's wrath.

"Answer me!" Ben yelled, pushing John's back up against the wall. "Where did you get it from?"

John couldn't utter a word. He blubbered inarticulately, deeply frightened and confused.

"Talk to me," Ben insisted, shaking John hard. "Who gave this to you?"

"It was ... on ... on the ... gravestone," John finally managed to say between his tears.

"On the gravestone? What gravestone?"

"The stone," John wailed, "on my ... mother's grave."

Ben stepped back. His face wore a look of menace that John had never seen before.

"You went to the cemetery?" he half-whispered. Then, gathering his strength, he yelled, "I told you not to go there!"

John hid his head between his hands, trembling and sobbing.

"I *told* you not to go there, didn't I?" He suddenly noticed Frankie and Manuela staring at him in horror.

"What are you two gaping at?" he roared. "Get back to the kitchen!"

His two employees turned silently and left the room.

Ben picked up the paper with the words John had copied from the headstone and in a rage ripped it in half.

"Don't you dare go back there again! Understand?" He loomed over the boy, who was still cowering on the floor. "Now get up and stop blubbering like a baby."

Ben stalked out to the front porch, kicking a chair on his way. *Gravestone?* he thought furiously. *Who had put up a stone for Devorah?* He climbed into his truck and started it with jerky, angry movements. He would drive into Grayston and have a drink to calm down. Who had the gall to interfere in his life? Who had decided what to inscribe on his wife's headstone? And who had dared write something in Hebrew?

Old Sam. It must have been he. When Devorah was killed, the old man had still had his wits about it from time to time. He must have ordered the stone.

And the "Chief Rabbi of Grayston" — the combination *mohel*-funeral director — must have been involved as well. The sheriff's father had three Hebrew words engraved on his stone: Yoel Ze'ev Abramson, with a *Magen David* over them. At the time, the sheriff had learned the proper words from that ridiculous rabbi. Apparently, the rabbi had stuck his dirty hands into Ben's business, too.

Old Sam was completely senile now. But if Ben ever caught up with that crazy rabbi, he would know what to do ….

Ben never came home that night. He went to the Drunken Ox, ordered himself a full bottle of Black-and-White for starters, and drank it down, glass after glass.

Within two hours, he had been kicked out of the bar, reeking with alcohol. He crouched on the sidewalk, crying and laughing by turns, and then rose, swaying on his feet, to try and buy another drink. The burly bartender shoved him roughly out the door.

Ben rolled on the pavement before hauling himself up with difficulty so that his back was against the wall. His head lolled tiredly to one side. He vomited all over himself. But he still tried to stop passersby, holding out a fifty-dollar bill and begging them to go inside and buy him a bottle of something strong.

In the end, he fell asleep right there on the sidewalk, in a puddle of his own vomit. He woke the next morning, filthy and aching, and crawled back to his pickup with a sandpaper mouth and a pounding headache.

It was late morning by the time he returned to the ranch house, driving slowly. Barbara, he remembered with relief, was away from home. She and Eddie were still at that hospital in Austin. At least he would be able to avoid her sharp tongue.

John hid when he saw his father's truck approaching. He was afraid of being shaken and hit again. Escaping through the window of his room, he moved surreptitiously toward the stables. He saddled a horse, tied his saxophone case onto the pommel, and galloped away from the house.

Fifteen minutes later, he dismounted and tied the reins to a tree with grass growing around it. John took out his saxophone, assembled it, and began to play.

He felt peace stealing into all his limbs. In the notes that emerged from his instrument and floated across the hills, he found release from his sad and difficult reality. He played for half an hour, reviewing what he had learned in his last lesson with Christopher. And then he began playing his own compositions — melodies that, in his opinion, were no less beautiful than "The Lonely Foal." He was embarrassed to play these pieces for his teacher, lest he incur a scolding for wasting his time on nonsense instead of practicing his scales.

After two hours of playing, John rode home. He hesitated before going inside but his father had already collapsed in his chair, absorbed in a baseball game and a six-pack of beer.

Ben didn't speak about what had happened the night before, and neither did John. Two days later, Eddie came back from the hospital, and school started a few days after that. John returned to his routine: school in the morning, saxophone in the afternoon.

It was Frankie, the veteran stableman, who told John how his mother had died.

They were sitting together on the front porch, watching a big crane erect an oil rig on Tall Willy's ranch in the wake of an oil discovery on the property. Old Sam sat near them in his wheelchair, staring expressionlessly into space.

"She was a good woman," Frankie told John. "She was so happy when you were born, and she loved you very much."

Frankie omitted to mention the fact that Devorah had been depressed from the day she set foot in Texas to the day of her death. He also prudently concealed the fact that John's mother had scarcely acknowledged his existence, handing him over to Manuela to raise. Why destroy the boy's dreams? Let him believe she was a wonderful, caring mother ....

"And how did she die?" John asked.

Frankie gnawed at a plug of tobacco and spat the juice out onto the grass. "How did she die?" He jerked his thumb over his shoulder, at the military compound behind the house. "One of the soldiers from the compound shot her."

John jumped up in childish fury. "Really? A soldier killed my mother?"

"It was an unfortunate accident. She was looking out the window at the off-limits area, and one of the soldiers shot her by mistake."

"No one shoots by mistake," young John declared. "You have to aim before you shoot."

"Well, that soldier's in jail now," Frankie lied. As far as he knew, the man had never been tried for Devorah's death. Life was cheap in Texas.

"Where did it happen?" John asked. "Which window was she at when he shot her?"

"Leave it alone." Frankie was sorry he had provided any details. "It happened a long time ago. I have to get Sam to bed now."

"Tell it quickly. Just tell me where it happened."

"All right," Frankie sighed. "If you insist ...."

Frankie helped Sam get ready for bed, covered him with a blanket, and went back out to John.

"Bring a flashlight," he told the excited boy.

The stableman went to the hidden door behind the bedroom and opened it. John's eyes widened in astonishment at the sight of the narrow spiral staircase behind it. The house seemed filled with secrets he had never been aware of.

"Want to go up?" Frankie asked doubtfully.

John had already begun climbing, squeezing his way between the cardboard boxes and broken furniture that filled the lower stairwell.

With a sigh, Frankie started after him. If Ben ever found out about this, he would have his head.

"Where does this lead?" John asked eagerly. "What's up there?"

"Once," Frankie said, "a long time ago, this was a watchtower."

The upper part of the staircase was free of rubbish. John skipped rapidly up the steps, with Frankie following more slowly behind. Dust motes danced in his flashlight beam. He coughed and blinked back tears when dust entered his throat and eyes.

The door at the top of the staircase was detached from its top hinge and hung crookedly from the door frame. Frankie carefully moved it aside to reveal a small room beyond. A flock of birds that had been roosting in the room burst into flight and fled through the window with a great flapping of wings. The window glass was shattered, and a portion of the tower roof had collapsed with the passage of time.

Frankie watched John as the boy stood in the doorway, gazing inside with a mixture of surprise and emotion.

"That's where your mother was standing." Frankie pointed to the south-facing window. "She opened the window, and the sentry shot at her."

John went to the window and peeked out. Alarmed, Frankie darted forward, grabbed him by the arm, and dragged him back. "Quit that! Do you want to die?"

"There are no soldiers. Only a big cloth," John said. "Take a look."

Frankie advanced cautiously and peered through the broken window. Indeed, the military watchtowers were no longer visible. A huge camouflage net stretched several meters above the compound's wall.

"Back then, that net wasn't there," he said. "They must have added it later."

Frankie urged John to go back downstairs. All he needed was for Ben or Barbara to come home and catch him spilling all the family secrets to the boy. But John was in no rush to leave. As he inspected the room curiously, an idea began to percolate in his brain.

"I think I want to move into this room," he announced.

Frankie thought his heart would explode.

Jerusalem — 5724 / 1964

A single bare bulb cast its pale light on the narrow room. Around the old table sat four aging Jewish men, their faces tense with worry. The *"chalukah,"* or distribution of funds, for the month of Nissan was fast approaching — a time when many large, poverty-stricken families in Jerusalem waited anxiously for the bit of money that would rescue them from the ravages of hunger. But the coffers were nearly bare.

R' Shmerel, head administrator of Kollel Tzidkas Yerushalayim, had gone to the post office that morning to retrieve several envelopes that had come from across the ocean. Among them, he hoped, were some generous contributions. But a handful of grain will not satisfy a lion's hunger. There were many needy families in Israel.

The kollel was experiencing hard times. There was no trace now of the former golden age, when R' Shmerel's father and grandfather had administered the kollel with a lavish hand. In those far-off days, the kollel had built new neighborhoods throughout the city, generously supported hundreds of indigent families, and served as the primary channel through which donations from Diaspora Jewry were funneled into the Holy City.

Hard times. In order to have something to distribute on the previous Erev Rosh Hashanah, R' Shmerel had gone to Barclay's Bank, spoken to Mr. Holtzman, the branch manager, and received a large loan. The kollel had not yet managed to repay this loan — and the Nissan "*chalukah*" was coming. Without the money, how would families be able to buy matzos and wine for the Seder? How would they sew their children new clothing to replace those that were falling into tatters? How to buy new shoes, to replace the worn-out pair that was pinching a little girl's toes?

R' Shmerel took out the bundle of envelopes that he had fetched from the post office and removed the string that held them together. R' Aharon Sherman, the kollel's veteran treasurer, opened his heavy ledger, revealing page after page filled with rows of figures in his precise handwriting.

"Chatzkel Rosenberg, from England," R' Shmerel announced hopefully, when he saw the name printed on the back of the first envelope in bold English letters. This thick, costly envelope usually brought good news. Chatzkel Rosenberg in England had once been one of the kollel's foremost supporters. A survivor, he had made his fortune in construction in Europe even before the war. As he grew old, he remembered that he was a Jew. He donated a sizeable sum for the construction of a Talmud Torah building and continued sending generous checks from time to time.

When the business had passed to his sons — all of them, *r"l*, married to gentile women — the donations had dwindled. However, they were still respectable sums. *Maybe this time*, R' Shmerel thought hopefully, *the amount would be a bit larger than usual.*

R' Aharon, the treasurer, craned his neck in anticipation. But, to the disappointment of all present, the envelope contained no check at all. Instead, it held a letter from Chatzkel Rosenberg's son, informing them that on January 13, 1963, their father had died in the hospital. Two days later, he'd been buried in London's Jewish cemetery. He had indicated in his will that he wanted Kollel Tzidkas Yerushalayim to be informed of his passing. Hence, the letter.

R' Shmerel sighed from the depths of his heart. *The merit of the charity he had given in his lifetime would serve Chatzkel Rosenberg well*, he thought — *but the man's sons could be struck off the contributors' list.* They had not even had the wisdom to include a nice donation for the elevation of their father's soul. R' Tzvi Hirsch HaLevi, the kollel fundraiser responsible for keeping track of donors' *yahrzeits*, would check the Jewish date of Rosenberg's death and make a note of it in the kollel's big record book. During the first year, *Kaddish* would be said for him every day, and a *minyan* of Torah scholars would learn *Mishnayos* for the elevation of his soul. They would do the same on each *yahrzeit*.

"Martin Klapholtz, from Los Angeles," R' Shmerel intoned, opening the next envelope. This one did contain a check. R' Aharon, the treasurer, jotted the details down in his thick ledger. Several more contributors had sent respectable sums, but the total still fell far short of what was needed.

The atmosphere in the kollel office was glum. Berel Margolis, the fourth man in the room, suggested that they send letters to contributors who had sent donations in the past, but whose contributions had petered out with time.

"Who, for instance?" R' Shmerel asked.

"There are a number of them," R' Aharon said. "For example, Kalman Levinger's brother. He's a wealthy man in America. He used to send us regular donations, but these past few years hardly anything has come from him."

"Kalman Levinger's brother?" R' Shmerel wrinkled his brow.

"Shmiel. Shmiel Levinger," the treasurer said. He began flipping through the pages of his account book, scanning them for the details he sought. "In America, he's known as Sam Lowinger. He owns a huge cattle ranch in Texas."

"Maybe he already passed away?" R' Tzvi Hirsch wondered aloud. "Does he have any children?"

"He's not married," R' Aharon replied. "Binyamin Levinger, his nephew — Kalman's son — went to him in America years ago. They say he runs the whole ranch, but he's cut all ties with his family here."

"We'd better write him a letter," R' Shmerel decided.

R' Aharon took out a piece of the kollel's stationery, with its familiar logo of the Western Wall and the *Har HaBayis*. The stationery contained a form letter to all past contributors who no longer sent donations, with the details changed for each. R' Aharon opened the letter to Sam Lowinger in a pleasant vein:

"To our esteemed friend, a man who pursues charity and loving kindness, the respected philanthropist R' Shmuel Levinger, of the city of Grayston in the state of Texas, and to his entire exalted family."

34

Grayston, Texas — 5724 / 1964

Y ou want to move into this room?" Frankie repeated incredulously. "I don't think that's a very good idea."

But John thought it was a wonderful idea. He would convert this tower room into his bedroom! It would be exciting. He planned to go ask his father if he could, right now, this very day. He was sure his father would give his consent. Why should he care where John slept?

The man and the boy descended the stairs from the tower and re-entered the house proper. All the way down, Frankie tried to dissuade John from pursuing his plan. Ben would blame *him* — and rightly so. He should never have told the boy how his mother had died. Ben was capable of flying into one of his rages and throwing Frankie out on his ear. And if that happened, where would he — an aging stableman who had spent the past several years caring for a senile old man — find another job?

But all his efforts at persuasion fell on deaf ears. When John wanted something, he knew how to be stubborn about it. He had decided that he wanted to move into the tower room, the very room where his mother had met her death. And that was what he intended to do.

He waited with childish impatience on the front porch. Night fell, bringing with it enormous mosquitoes that clustered around the light bulbs in the warm air, but still John kept his vigil. It was nearly nine before he heard the truck in the distance, and saw the twin headlight beams on the road. The green pickup truck pulled up in front of the house and parked on the gravel.

Ben was at the wheel, and Barbara was sitting beside him. This complicated John's plan. He had forgotten that she would be coming back with his father. He clenched his jaw. It was now or never ....

The moment Ben and Barbara stepped out of the truck, John ran over to greet them.

"What happened?" his father asked anxiously.

"I want to move into the tower room!" John announced.

At first, Ben didn't understand. "What do you want?" he asked, striding toward the house.

"I want to start sleeping up there from now on." John pointed at the tower jutting up from the side of the house.

Ben stopped suddenly. He studied his son's flushed face for a moment, and then turned to glare at Frankie, standing abashedly in the doorway. A few seconds' thought put all the pieces together: John had recently discovered that he had a different mother, he had found her grave, and now he knew where she had met her death.

"Stop talking nonsense," he snapped. "What's wrong with your bedroom?"

Prudently, John refrained from bringing his real mother into the conversation — certainly not in front of Barbara. He followed his father across the porch and into the house.

"I want to move there," he persisted, with the first signs of tears in his voice. "It's a great room and I want it to be mine. I don't want to share a room with anyone anymore."

Ben sat down at the table and roared that he was hungry. Barbara and Frankie came inside, too. She went to the kitchen, while he remained near the door.

"There are all kinds of things up there," Ben warned. "Howling winds, and owls, and bats. You'll be shaking with terror all night long." He glanced again at the stableman, seeking support. "Right, Frankie?"

Frankie shrugged and stepped out, refusing to play the part that Ben had assigned him.

"In short, there's nothing to talk about. You're staying in your room, with Eddie!" Ben thrust a fork into the juicy steak that Manuela had set down in front of him.

Suddenly, to his surprise, Barbara intervened.

"If he wants it so much, let him have the room," she called from the kitchen.

Ben lifted his head in astonishment.

"Let him play that 'shofar' of his up there," she continued. "I can't stand that deafening noise."

"No one goes up there," Binyamin said, though less decidedly than before. "John's staying where he is."

Barbara, as usual, ignored him. She emerged from the kitchen and addressed the housekeeper. "Manuela, prepare the upstairs room," she ordered, throwing a challenging look at Ben, as if daring him to contradict her. "John will be sleeping there starting tomorrow night."

Ben made a face and muttered into his mustache.

"I don't think there's any glass in the windows. And the roof leaks," Manuela said in a low voice.

"I'll take care of that," Frankie volunteered, reappearing suddenly in the doorway.

"Very good," Barbara said, and returned to the kitchen.

"The soldiers in that compound are going to shoot him," Ben told Frankie. "The second he looks out the window, they'll kill him — just like that." He snapped his fingers.

"They made the wall higher," John broke in. "They put a kind of cloth on top that covers everything."

"I'll go talk to them," Frankie told Ben quietly.

"And anyway," Barbara stated in a loud voice, "if they shoot him, no one will be too upset. We'll finally have a little peace and quiet around here!"

It took a few days to ready the room for John. Manuela cleaned it over the course of long, backbreaking hours. Frankie repaired the roof, replaced the missing shingles, painted the walls, and cleared out the junk that had accumulated in the stairwell over the years. He also fixed the door and installed new panes of glass in the windows. But before the boy took possession of the room, there was one more thing that Frankie had to do.

He walked around to the rear of the house and approached the main gate of the compound. The sentry asked him, pleasantly enough, what he wanted. Frankie asked to speak to the compound's security chief or the person in charge of military personnel.

The officer who appeared ten minutes later was a tall man of about thirty. He shook Frank's hand vigorously. "You're from the house next door, right?" he asked. "How can I help you?"

The veteran stableman was slightly confused by the warm reception. "Where is the officer that used to be here?"

"Arrogant fellow? Liked to yell a lot?"

"Yes."

"He's gone. He was court-martialed and dishonorably discharged from the army after he caused a soldier's death."

"Caused a soldier's death?" Frankie repeated. "Are you aware that, on his orders, a woman was also killed here?"

"I am well aware of that," the officer said. "Those were different times." There was a brief silence.

"Well, then. How can I help you?" the officer asked again.

"The son of that woman wants to move into the tower room. I notice that you've put up a camouflage net, so that it's impossible to see into the compound. But I still wanted to let you know."

The officer raised his eyes to the tower at the side of the Lowinger house, and then looked at the compound's encircling wall.

"Okay," he said. "No problem. These days, we're not so quick to shoot. But thanks for letting me know."

Los Angeles — Iyar 5766 / May 2006

It had been one of the most frustrating days in Professor Barry Majdi's life.

A host of procedural and bureaucratic demands converged on him all at once: a meeting with the chancellor and the faculty vice provost about the upcoming semester, a scholarship committee meeting, a training conference requiring his presence — and, on top of everything else, there was a power outage on the laboratory floor and several of the refrigerators and incubators had stopped functioning. There was a great deal of racing around the faculty corridors, and various tubes and flasks had been transferred to emergency refrigerators, but numerous scientific experiments were ruined. Professor Majdi returned to his office in a state of exhaustion, his jacket over his arm.

"Any messages?" he asked his secretary. Without looking up from her keyboard, she told him that there weren't.

He paused at the door of his office, as if struck by a thought. "By the way, Jeanne, how late will you be staying today?"

"Till five," she said. "Why?"

"An air-conditioning expert is supposed to be coming here to check something," the professor said, his eyes raking the air vents above her desk. "I hope that won't disturb you."

"Would you like me to leave earlier?" the secretary asked hopefully.

"No, no, don't bother. It'll only take a few minutes."

"But Professor," she protested, "if there's a problem with the air-conditioning, you can call the university's maintenance department."

"No," said Barry Majdi. "This fellow's just a consultant. He's helping me with an experiment that I'm running by him."

"Okay," the secretary said indifferently, and returned to her typing.

The man arrived at 4:15. The secretary, who had expected a fellow in a suit and tie, carrying a briefcase, was surprised to find a simple air-conditioning repairman. He was thirtyish, with a Mediterranean complexion, wearing a red coverall featuring the logo of a local air-conditioning company. He wore heavy work boots and lugged a big toolbox.

Yousuf, the professor's research assistant, began chatting amiably with him and discovered that the repairman, like himself, belonged to the big Los Angeles mosque. Yousuf's eyes shone when Imam Aziz's name came up, and the repairman agreed wholeheartedly with his assessment. The Imam Bashir Abdul Aziz was definitely head and shoulders above the rest, having built a towering religious edifice for Islam right in the heart of the infidel city.

The professor greeted his visitor warmly and shook his hand. "Thanks for agreeing to come," he said. "I really appreciate this."

"That's okay," the man murmured. The revered imam had asked him, as a personal favor, to help his friend the professor, so he was happy to be here.

"If my friend Bashir Abdul Aziz sent you," Professor Majdi said, lowering his voice, "I'm sure we can count on your discretion."

"Of course, of course," the repairman said hastily.

"I am developing something in the field of multi-sensory strategic triggers," the professor began. "Or, in simpler terms: marketing through fragrances."

The repairman sipped noisily from the cup of coffee that Yousuf had handed him, eyes darting in surprise at the cabinets filled with research equipment and experimental tools. He was still trying to figure out why he had been asked here.

"Research has shown that certain aromas can create an atmosphere," the professor continued. "A fragrance can influence a customer's feelings and mood. A scent can have an impact on his decision-making ability, turning his innate caution switch on or off. An aroma can cause him to linger in a store and even want to return to it. In short, if we can control the aromas in a store, we can increase sales."

"Are you talking about a specific smell?" the repairman asked.

"Nature has more than 10,000 scents, and each one has its own function. This is a field for serious research in the sciences of neurology, sociology, and biology. For our purposes, however, let's talk a little about techniques for disseminating the fragrance."

"Okay."

Yousuf gave the professor a baffled look. What, exactly, was going on here? This was no new idea. It was a registered patent and there were companies that already made millions from disseminating scents.

"Let's take this office, for example," the professor said. "Pretend that this is a clothing store, and I'd like to spread a certain fragrance ... coffee, say, or vanilla, or strawberry — anything. Okay? I could put a small dispenser on every shelf, but we want something high-efficiency and concealed from the customers' view. I'd prefer to do it by way of the air conditioner."

"Very logical."

The professor returned to the outer room, Yousuf and the repairman at his heels. "This air conditioner here, for example, has two vents: one in my office and another here in the secretary's. All along this floor of the building, there are dozens of other air vents. It would not, of course, be cost-efficient to mount a disseminator in each individual vent. The question is whether it is possible to release a concentrated scent at one point within the unit, and rely on the air-conditioning system to spread it throughout the area."

"Well, why not?" The repairman scratched his head. "Stores usually have a large, central unit made up of two parts: a compressor and a fan. The compressor doesn't interest us. It's the fan that cools the air and spreads it through the ceiling duct or ducts before it passes out through the air vents. If you were to spray your fragrance into the fan, at the entrance of the first duct, there's no reason why it wouldn't reach every vent."

"The problem is that the fragrance might lose its potency," the professor said. "At what temperature does the air leave the fan?"

"Between 55 and 70 degrees."

"And it flows out into the room at the same temperature?"

"It may heat up slightly on the way, but not to any significant degree."

"Ah," the professor said thoughtfully. "And those ducts in the ceiling — what are they made of?"

"There are rectangular ducts made of metal, and others made of round, flexible tubing."

"And is there any insulation around them?"

"Sure — rock wool."

The professor turned to Yousuf. "Remind me to look into the subject of rock wool. If I'm not mistaken, it's made from basalt and mineral rock." He returned his attention to the repairman. "What are the ducts in *this* building made of?"

The man climbed onto the secretary's desk, removed the cover of the air vent, and peered inside. To the secretary's consternation, several plaster chips drizzled down onto her desk.

"This one's made of metal," he called down to Majdi. "But you would need to check out the actual store where they want to install the system."

The professor had several more questions; the air-conditioning technician answered them all to his satisfaction. At the end of half an hour, Majdi sent him on his way with thanks.

"He messed up my whole desk," the secretary complained, shaking out some papers. She was disgruntled over the fact that all of this had taken place in her office instead of Majdi's. Why should *she* suffer if the professor preferred not to have dirty shoes planted on his fancy desk?

The professor walked back into his inner office, wearing a small, sly smile.

Yousuf accompanied the repairman outside. They wandered around the university parking lot for a while, as the latter was having a hard time recalling where he had parked his car, until they spotted his red truck in a corner, its sides emblazoned with the company logo.

Yousuf was excited. Though the professor hadn't said anything, Yousuf was beginning to understand what was happening. He began putting all the pieces together: a Jewish wedding with numerous participants, the dissemination of some invisible material by way of the air-conditioning ducts; a professor of Biology who had once worked for the CDC, where the United States kept its most dangerous germs and viruses — and an imam who mocked Bin Laden and said that thousands of corpses were just small change.

It seemed to Yousuf that Majdi did not intend to disseminate any fragrance to encourage customers to buy. He had something much more lethal in mind.

Grayston, Texas — 5725 / 1965

The fateful decision that was to save their lives was made by John and Eddie Lowinger in the snowy winter of 1965.

Even after John moved out of the bedroom they shared, the two brothers continued quarreling over everything, including Eddie's right to enter John's room. Eddie was jealous of his older brother for finding an isolated room of his own so far from the center of all the unpleasantness on the main floor. Not much comforted by the fact that he, too, now had a room of his own, Eddie spent a great deal of time in his brother's — much to John's dismay.

Fortunately for John, it was at around this time that Eddie discovered the joys of reading. While sitting and reading for hours on end, he was unusually quiet and focused. Eddie devoured books, increasing his breadth of knowledge and broadening his horizons, but that did not prevent him from being as wild and mischievous as ever. On the contrary: the books he read provided new ideas for even more clever and sophisticated pranks.

However, as the principal said of him during a faculty meeting: "At least while he's reading he's engaged in an activity that's useful and harmless." Eddie had cards at two different libraries, borrowed books from his classmates, and even dragged Barbara to the bookstore from time to time to buy new ones.

John continued to make progress in his music, until Christopher laughingly said that he would soon be ready to perform in New Orleans. "That would be a real attraction: a white saxophonist," the blind man told his fellow band members with a chuckle. Most of the wind instruments used in performance halls in New Orleans — the jazz capital of the United States — were wielded by black musicians, who imbued their music with rhythms and motifs retained despite centuries of slavery.

One Sunday, Barbara returned home from Grayston with John and Eddie. Turning off the main road, she paused for a moment to take several letters from the mailbox and then drove on. There was a figure sprawled on the front porch steps. The boys leaned forward to see who it was. Barbara knew at once.

"It's your father," she said in disgust. "Once again, he's 'had a little something to drink.'"

As the truck pulled into the clearing in front of the house, Frankie came out, went over to Ben, and lugged him inside. Ben was totally out of it after a night of drunken revelry.

Barbara walked into the house with a quick, nervous stride, and the boys followed with long faces. A rich, fragrant meal waited on the table,. The aroma drew the children like magnets, but they never got to eat. Barbara began shrieking at their father, pouring out all the vitriol that was in her heart. Frankie and Manuela remained out of sight in the kitchen, and the boys disappeared into John's tower room. For ten full minutes Barbara's voice shrilled on, eliciting no reaction at all. Ben sat slumped in the armchair where Frankie had deposited him, listening sluggishly as his wife ranted. The alcohol sloshed in his veins, but he needed more. The screaming was getting on his nerves .... He thrust a shaking hand into his pocket and pulled out a flask of Black-and-White.

"What are you doing?" Barbara yelled. "You want to drink *more*?"

Ben did not respond. He tilted the flask up to his mouth right under his wife's furious eyes.

"Go ahead!" Barbara shrieked. Losing control, she yanked the table-cloth right off the table. Everything that was on the table fell to the floor with a deafening crash and shattered to bits. The tomato soup in the big earthenware tureen spilled onto the wooden floor, mixing with an over-turned bean dish to form a reddish-brown puddle. Roasted chicken rolled off its platter, followed in rapid succession by the potatoes.

The earsplitting noise brought everyone hurrying to the dining room. The boys stared in shock from the foot of the stairs, Frankie stood gri-macing in the kitchen doorway and Manuela began to wail. Everything she had cooked that day was ruined.

"Go ahead — eat!" Barbara screamed at her drunken husband. Wheeling around, she stalked out of the house.

Ben sat in his chair and roared with laughter. With his feet planted in the puddle of spilled food, he tipped back his head to get at the last drops in his flask.

John and Eddie did what they always did when the situation exploded at home. They slipped quietly out the back door, went to the stables, saddled their horses, and galloped away.

For a long time they rode silently side by side, each lost in thought. This time, they were riding along the length of the compound wall, trying to get as far away from the house as possible.

"I'm hungry," John said, breaking the silence after half an hour.

Eddie scanned the plain until he saw what he wanted. Spurring his horse on, he took a homemade slingshot from his pocket. A quarter of an hour later, a spitted prairie hen was roasting slowly over a small campfire.

John's eyes rested on his brother, filled with a mixture of contempt and admiration. His own fingers were good for only one thing: playing the saxophone. He could not do any of the things his brother had learned from his Mexican and Indian friends. Eddie knew how to hunt down a prairie hen and then clean it with the aid of his pocketknife. John could never have done that. In fact, the idea turned his stomach. But Eddie enjoyed every minute. Meat, it seemed, tasted a lot better to him if it had quivered and convulsed in his hands first.

The evening was silent. John could hear only the soft nickering of their tethered horses, the crackle of twigs in the fire, and the sound of a truck rumbling past on the other side of the compound's security wall.

Clouds covered the sky, but they were not rain clouds. A Mexican had taught Eddie that, too. There were no storms expected that night; they would be able to get home easily.

"I don't think I'll drink alcohol ever again," John announced suddenly.

In his imagination, he kept seeing his father dead drunk, devoid of the slightest shred of dignity or self-respect, sprawled on the porch steps in front of his wife and sons.

"Yeah, I'd like to see that," Eddie jeered in open disbelief. Both boys were in the habit of stealing a little whiskey from their father's liquor cabinet from time to time, enjoying the pleasant warmth that spread through their limbs after they had had a taste.

"You'll see," John said decisively. "I'm through with that stuff."

"I know you," Eddie laughed. "Next week, you'll sneak back into Dad's drinks cabinet."

John's answer was a derisive snort.

"You know what?" Eddie said. "Let's see. Let's see how long your good intentions hold out."

The boys' longstanding hostility flared up at once. Once again, they were like a couple of roosters squaring off in the farmyard.

"Okay," John snapped. "But only on the condition that *you* don't drink, either."

"That's fine with me!" Eddie grinned wickedly. "You'll see — I'll hold out longer than you. You're gonna break first."

"Wanna bet?'

"Sure."

Over the course of the next few months, both John and Eddie were determined not to lose the bet. Each refrained from touching a drop of whiskey, while at the same time keeping an eagle eye on his brother and fervently hoping to catch him in the act.

Though neither of them had any way of knowing it, within eighteen months it would turn out that their childish bet had saved them both from a painful death.

Los Angeles — Iyar 5766 / May 2006

Yousuf parted hurriedly from the air-conditioning repairman and rushed to the faculty parking lot. Professor Majdi had mentioned earlier that he had a business meeting to attend in Yousuf's neighborhood and could give him a lift home. Yousuf didn't want to miss his ride. Maybe, over the course of the drive, he would be able to glean some more information about the professor's mysterious plan.

Barry Majdi waited in his office exactly five minutes, and then headed for his car. He dialed a number on the cell phone he held in his hand — a model that was similar to that of his personal cell phone, but with one important difference. This was a pre-paid phone that he had purchased in a small store in a remote area. He had paid for the phone and the accompanying minutes neither by check nor by credit card, but with cash. There was no way to trace it to him. Nowhere was Barry Majdi registered as its owner. He could safely use it to contact Aziz.

"Mosque of Los Angeles, *salaam aleikum*," said the voice on the answering machine. The voice went on to offer an array of options: "Dial 1 for prayer times, 2 for the executive offices, 3 for the *madrasa*, or 4 for the imam's office." Barry pressed 4. Aziz answered just as Majdi entered his car.

The professor inserted the phone into its holder, switched on the engine, and headed for the parking-lot exit.

"Everything went according to plan," he reported with satisfaction. "The air-conditioning man came and explained everything to me."

"I'm glad to hear that," the imam said. "A dimwit like him was just who we needed."

"Without a doubt," the professor chuckled. "Ah, here's the boy. Wait a second. I'll let him into the car."

The Jeep Cherokee gradually slowed and came to a stop beside Yousuf, who was waiting by the gate. As the young man climbed into the car, the professor raised a finger to indicate that he was in the midst of an important phone call.

"I'll try to reach him again at Um-el-Facham," he said into the speaker phone.

"Just remember the time difference between here and Palestine." The imam's voice filled the car and Yousuf straightened respectfully.

"Yes — ten hours. It's early morning there now."

"May Allah bless you," the imam's voice boomed.

The professor ended the call.

"That was the imam, right?" Yousuf asked in excitement. The professor nodded his head with a smile and continued driving in silence.

"Have you ever heard of Um-al-Facham?" he asked Yousuf suddenly.

"That's in Palestine, isn't it?"

"Correct. A pleasant city, until the Zionists took over."

Yousuf uttered a spirited curse aimed at the Jews, the Zionists, and infidels in general.

"Did you know that I have a sister-in-law there?" Majdi went on. "In fact … you know my nephew, Turk. You met him when he came to visit me last year, didn't you?"

"Yes," Yousuf recalled. "He told me a lot about the struggle against the Zionist oppressors. We're sitting here peacefully while they're spilling their blood …."

Majdi drove on, a small smile on his lips. Presently, he remarked, "It sounds as if you'd like to help them."

Yousuf jumped in his seat and turned to face the professor. "Of course!" he exclaimed. "I'm dying to do something."

"In the near future, you may get your chance," Barry Majdi said mysteriously.

"I hope so! I can't wait." Yousuf felt a little closer to the heart of the professor's secret. He was gripped by an overwhelming eagerness.

"It's no big thing," the professor said, throwing cold water over the younger man's excitement. "But what is it the imam always says? Mohammed appreciates every small step in the right direction."

Yousuf looked happily out the window. His eyes took in the shop displays, but his thoughts were someplace else entirely.

At the end of a brief ride, the professor pulled up in front of Yousuf's parents' house — a handsome estate surrounded by a tall fence.

"In a few weeks' time, I'll need to send something to my nephew," Majdi told Yousuf before the latter stepped out of the Jeep. "What do you say to a short trip to Palestine?"

"Sounds amazing," Yousuf said, eyes gleaming.

Grayston, Texas — 5726 / 1966

Andrew entered John's life on a Sunday early in 1966.

That morning, neither of John's parents was home. Ben had driven into Grayston; it was anybody's guess when he would return. Barbara had climbed into her pickup and called out that she was going to visit her brother, Tony, and then do some shopping in El Paso.

Eddie, as usual, brought an armload of books into John's tower room, collapsed onto the bed, and settled in for a few hours of reading. John did not appreciate the way his brother made himself at home in his room, but in the interests of peace decided to let it go this time. He took out his saxophone, played some warm-up finger exercises, and then began playing, "Cry, Arkansas" — the sad song that described the way an entire country mourned the death of a single American soldier on the battlefield.

At this stage, he still needed to read the notes in order to play the piece well. He was concentrating hard, when he suddenly stopped. "Quit it, Eddie," he said. "You're disturbing me."

Eddie didn't even hear him. He was completely absorbed in his book. He was near the end of an adventure novel, and the tension was at its height.

John shrugged and went back to his song. The saxophone played the notes while he sang the words in his heart:

> Stop the trees from growing
> Put out the sun
> Teddy went off on two legs
> And came back in a box with a flag around it.

He had been having some difficulty with that part, but it went smoothly this time. He continued:

> Cry, Arkansas, cry
> For a life cut off
> Cry for Teddy's ten children
> Who will never be born ....

Once again, John stopped playing. "Eddie, stop that!"

This time, his brother lifted his head. "What?"

"Quit disturbing me. Or else just go to your own room."

Eddie sat up on the bed. "What's your problem?" he asked angrily.

"Stop humming. It bothers me," said John.

"It's your head that's humming," Eddie retorted. "If you want me to go, just say so. Don't make things up."

Suddenly, they both heard the refrain again:

> Stop the trees from growing
> Put out the sun ....

Eddie glanced at John in triumph. "You mean — that?"

John stared around in all directions. "What is that? Who's playing?" he asked. "It sounds like a trumpet. Where's it coming from?"

John and Eddie went to the door and opened it. No, the music was not coming from anywhere inside the house.

They went to the window and looked out. They saw the camouflage net stretched over the compound wall. Looking down at the space between the wall and the house, they could not see anyone. But the melody had definitely originated at some point beyond the house. It was coming from somewhere within the sealed compound.

John picked up his saxophone, brought his music book to the window, and continued the song:

Cry, Arkansas, cry
For a life cut off ...

He stopped. From the other side of the wall, a trumpet took up the melody:

Cry for Teddy's ten children
Who will never be born ....

So it *was* someone from inside the compound. John and Eddie exchanged a startled glance. Then John and the unknown musician started playing together. They played the first verse, which was also the song's concluding one:

Stop the trees from growing
Put out the sun
Teddy went off on two legs
And came back in a box with a flag around it.

They repeated the refrain slowly, as John's music book instructed, and ended on a long note.

For a moment, all was silent. Each of the boys waited for the other to speak first.

"Hey, who *is* that?" Eddie called at last.

"Andrew," came a voice from beyond the camouflage net. "You play wonderfully."

"Thanks a lot," John said.

"Hey — you're a kid!" the voice said in a surprised tone. "This is the first time I've seen you. I usually only hear you play."

"I'm not a kid," John said, affronted. "I'm twelve and a half."

"Okay, sorry," the invisible Andrew laughed. "I actually meant it as a compliment. You play much better than I'd have expected of someone your age. What's your name?"

"John. John Lowinger. But — where are you? How can you see me?"

"I'm standing on the watchtower just opposite you," Andrew replied. "But you can't see me because of the camouflage."

"Are you a soldier?" John asked.

"Yes." Andrew paused. "Want to keep playing?"

"Sure. Do you know 'The Lonely Foal'?"

"Sure. What key?"

"Whatever you want," John said, and brought the saxophone to his lips.

They continued playing for another thirty minutes. John felt like his blind teacher, playing without being able to see the other members of his band. Sometimes, Christopher had told him, it was better not to see with whom you were playing. That might just spoil it ....

Andrew did not man the watchtower every day, but whenever he was on duty he would join in John's playing and they would make music together.

Sometimes they would also talk.

"Are you allowed to play?" John asked.

"Yes," Andrew answered. "This place is not Vietnam. There's not much danger. I don't know if anyone's ever used a rifle around here!"

"They did use one, once," John said.

"Really? They shot at someone?"

"Yes," John said. "They shot someone ... dead."

"Who was it?"

"It doesn't matter," John said. "Come on, let's play some more."

"Hey, want to come over for a visit?" the soldier asked John one day, at the end of another musical session. "We have a drummer and a bass player. Interested in playing together?"

"I'll have to ask my father."

"And I'll have to ask my commander."

"See you."

"Bye."

The next time they spoke, Andrew informed John that his commander had given his approval. "Go ask your father!"

John raced down the spiral stairs. His father was on his way out and John caught him at the door. Ben couldn't believe his ears.

"You're sure they're allowing you in there?" he asked in astonishment. "That's a very secret place."

"Yes," John said eagerly. "He said that, if you agree, he'll be waiting for me at the gate."

"I wanna come, too!" Eddie said.

Barbara backed her son up: "It's not fair for only John to get in. Let them both go."

"Ask if you can bring your brother," Ben said, ending the discussion. He climbed into his truck.

On Sunday afternoon, the boys approached the sentry booth near the compound gate. John was carrying his saxophone case while Eddie held the music books. They were very excited.

A soldier of Puerto Rican descent awaited them at the booth. He walked over to the brothers with a broad smile that exposed his very white teeth. "Hey, John!" He shook the boy's hand. "Hi there, Eddie."

As he ushered them inside the compound, he remarked, "You are now in one of the most securely protected places in the United States."

"What do they do here?" Eddie asked curiously.

"You mean, besides making music?" Andrew chuckled. "Well, apart from music, we're busy preparing all kinds of nasty surprises for America's enemies: bombs to drop on Communists, traps for Red rats, that kind of thing. But we're not allowed to talk about that stuff."

John wanted to know about the other musicians. Eddie walked beside them, hardly listening to a word. His excited eyes devoured everything he saw. Wow! All of this was hidden right near their house, and he hadn't even known. He had to check out every inch of this place.

This was not the last time he was going to set foot in this compound. Definitely not!

Um-el-Facham — Iyar 5766 / May 2006

It was very early in the morning when the phone rang in the Majdis' home again.

"It's for me!" Turk said, and sprinted to the phone.

"*Keif chalaq* (How are you?)" Professor Barry Majdi asked from Los Angeles.

"*Ana bachir* (I'm fine)," Turk answered.

"Do you remember what we talked about when you visited here?" the professor asked.

Turk's blood began to pound in his veins. So this was no friendly call.

It was not about a job in America. This was something bigger than that.

"I remember, Uncle," Turk said. "I remember it well."

"Did you do what I told you to do?"

"Yes. I've been working for Najid for the past five months."

"And you've made progress?"

"Yes, sure. At first I only hauled air conditioners and pipes. Now I can install an air-conditioning unit by myself. Today, for example, I have a big installation job in Tel Aviv."

"Tel Aviv?"

"Yes. Those Jews built themselves a nice city."

"When you perform that installation in Tel Aviv, Turk, make sure you do an excellent job."

"Why?"

Laughter bubbled up in the professor's throat in L.A., and reached Turk's ears in Um-el-Facham. "Because it's soon going to be ours. All the Jews' houses and cities will belong to us. One of the brothers will undoubtedly live in that house in Tel Aviv, and we install good air conditioners for the brothers, right?"

Turk nodded eagerly. He noticed that his hands were shaking slightly.

"Do you enjoy the work?" his uncle asked abruptly.

"Yes, very much."

"Okay. But after that installation job in Tel Aviv, you're going to quit and find another line of work."

"Another line of work? Why?"

"I'll explain later on."

"What kind of work?"

The professor paused a moment before he spoke the next sentence. He knew that his young nephew would not like his answer.

Turk's mother, peeking at her son from the kitchen, saw his face fall. Barak must have failed to get him a job in America. Curse him!

"But Uncle Barak, I finally know what I'm doing with air conditioners. Why leave?"

"Because that's the plan," Majdi said firmly.

"All right," Turk said submissively. It was a tone that only the three hundred dollars a month that his uncle transferred regularly into his bank account could justify.

The installation job in Tel Aviv was conducted with ease. The job was "bakshish" that Najid, Turk's boss, had secretly given a senior bureaucrat in the financial division of the Ministry of Education. A "bonus," as the Jews liked to call it. It was a profitable business on both sides: the bureaucrat made sure that Najid won a tender of hundreds of thousands of shekels for installing air-conditioning units in the schools in the Arab sector — and received, in exchange, central air conditioning installed in his private home, for free. A fair deal ....

Turk worked with a two-man crew, cursing silently in his heart all along. He hated the woman of the house when she didn't offer him a drink; he hated her when she poured him a glass of Coke; he hated her when he was hungry and he hated her when she served him cake. Covertly studying the house, he decided that he wanted it for himself. He still had no idea exactly what his Uncle Barak was planning, but two things were clear: First, after the plan was set in motion, the world would look very different from the way it did today. And, second: He, Turk Majid, was going to live in this beautiful, spacious house.

On his return to Um-el-Facham at the end of the day, Turk informed his surprised boss that he was quitting his job. Najid was distantly related to the Majdi clan, but even without the relationship he would have been pleased with Turk's work. He offered Turk a raise in salary or a promotion, but the young man was adamant. His decision was final. His boss gave him the last of his pay and shook his hand in parting.

"Do you have another job?" he asked suspiciously.

Turk stuffed the wad of bills into his pocket. "I'll find something," he said.

"I had no trouble getting accepted," Turk reported to his uncle some ten days later.

At first, he had gone to the Ganei HaSimchah wedding hall just to sniff around. But he discovered two Arab brothers there whom he knew from Um-el-Facham. They introduced him to the manager, a red-faced, irritable Jew named Motke who barked out that he didn't need any new workers. The wedding season was not due to begin for another two weeks; maybe then he would need an extra pair of hands in the kitchen. Turk should leave his information and they would call if he was needed.

The need arose just three days later. One of the two brothers was hit near the eye by a Zionist rubber bullet — and what had he done to deserve it? Nothing but hurl a rock at a car and injure a few Jews! After he was arrested, his brother phoned Turk, who was still jobless.

"What are you doing today?" he asked.

"Nothing special," Turk replied with a yawn. "Any ideas?"

"My brother can't come in today. Maybe this is your chance for a couple of days' work."

The wounded brother was released from the hospital the following day, only to be taken in for questioning by the Israeli G.S.S. In the meantime, Turk was employed at the wedding hall, where he did everything that was asked of him: washed floors, cut vegetables for salad, set tables, arranged chairs. The red-faced manager was satisfied with him, and by the end of the week offered him a steady job.

Professor Majdi was happy. Turk's entry into the place had been easier than he had expected. Aziz would be pleased. "But Turk, you'd better make sure to hang onto that job through the summer. Is that clear?" Majdi warned. "Do whatever they tell you. Be the best worker in the place. Don't you dare get the boot a minute before the time."

"Don't worry, Uncle. I'll stay as long as you want."

"And let the manager know that you understand air conditioners," said the professor. "If there's a problem with the air conditioning, offer to fix it."

"Fine."

"The goal — now, listen well, Turk — the goal is for it to look very natural for you to be hanging around in the area of the air conditioner ...."

Grayston, Texas — 5726 / 1966

John and Eddie walked beside Andrew, the trumpet-playing soldier, on a footpath that ran alongside the road. Trucks with cloth-enclosed cargo areas drove on the road, followed by a military jeep. There were soldiers as well as men in civilian clothes walking among the various buildings and structures. It was an entire bustling city, hidden behind concrete walls and open now to the boys' staring eyes.

"Here's where we play," Andrew said. He pointed at a low white-painted building, which faced them across a large lawn. Over the door was a sign proclaiming, "Cultural Center." A nearby building bore a similar sign, reading "Sports Center," and a sign on a yet smaller structure announced: "Mess Hall."

In the ten years since Ben and the sheriff had looked out at the compound from the watchtower window, the place had developed and expanded. New roads had been paved, along with a parking lot; additional buildings had been erected; trees and gardens had been planted. The air of strict secrecy that characterized the place when it was first built had somewhat mellowed with time. Scores of people worked there each day, the vast majority of them entering in the morning and leaving at night in their private cars or in organized carpools.

Andrew and the two boys crossed the lawn at an angle, approaching the cultural center. While John chatted with Andrew about music, Eddie's glance darted in all directions. Wow! None of his friends had ever entered this secure area. No one would ever have imagined what an active, busy place was hidden so close to sleepy old Grayston.

More than anything, Eddie was surprised at himself. Why had he never even wondered what lay hidden behind these walls? The boy who had hidden out in the bank after hours and set off the alarm; who had slipped into the new Town Hall ahead of practically everyone else; who had more than once sneaked into the school office to steal a copy of an upcoming exam — why had he never even tried to find out what was going on in this secret compound right behind his house? How had he come to miss out on such an adventure, lying under his nose? John was busy playing his saxophone all day long — but he, Eddie, had no excuse at all. He had often ridden with his brother all along the outside of the wall. Why hadn't he wondered what lay behind it?

His wide eyes took in many things at once: a helicopter pad near a large hangar; a long road that seemed to stretch over the horizon; and a large structure that looked like an air traffic control tower at an airport. Shortly before they entered the cultural center, Eddie spotted two additional areas that had been hidden by a row of trees. One looked like a military base, including several huts, army jeeps, and a parade ground. The second was more surprising: a single-story private home, surrounded by a flourishing garden. In the driveway stood a man in a tee-shirt, watering his flowers with a garden hose. He had sloping shoulders and thin arms and appeared to be fairly elderly. Something in his general demeanor strongly suggested that he was not a soldier.

Eddie was filled with curiosity, but one thing was clear: He mustn't ask Andrew any questions. He mustn't show the slightest bit of interest in anything he saw. It was up to him to discover the answers on his own.

John did some of the work for him. "Where's the watchtower where you were playing your trumpet?" he asked Andrew.

The soldier pointed behind him at a building flanked by bushes and a fence, near the compound's main entrance.

"It's over there, in the part of the compound that you're not allowed to enter. That's the most secret section of this place. If a civilian goes in there, our orders are to shoot to kill."

"Really?" Eddie asked.

"Really," Andrew said with a grin. "We call that area 'Texas.' You know: Shoot first, ask questions later."

"Like they did to my mom," John said suddenly.

Andrew stopped short. Stunned, he turned to John. He had asked around, and had been told that someone had indeed been killed here once.

"Your mother was the woman who was shot?" he asked.

John nodded.

"They said she was a Communist spy!" Andrew said in confusion. "They said she tried to sell secrets to the Russians."

"She was no spy," John retorted. "She was just my mom."

"I'm so sorry," Andrew said sincerely. "I really am."

John's mood improved dramatically when they entered the cultural center. This was a performance theater, with a real stage on which were a set of drums and a piano, a sound system, and long rows of seats. A yelp of excitement burst from him. This was fantastic!

Three men stood at the edge of the stage, two of them in uniform and one in civilian clothes. They greeted Andrew and his two young guests happily.

"Hey, Andrew, I thought you were bringing a real musician. This is a kid," the man in civilian clothes chided him. He had a gleaming pate and a large moustache.

"That's no kid — he's twelve and a half," Andrew laughed. "But he sure knows how to handle a saxophone. Believe me. A little pale, maybe — but he's got a black soul."

John assembled his instrument and set his notes on their stand. Andrew held his trumpet, the bald man with the mustache took his place at the drums, one soldier sat down at the piano, and another began tuning a contrabass. Eddie sat in the third row of chairs and watched his brother, mingling so easily among the adult musicians. Suddenly, he was jealous.

John had something that he didn't have. He was smarter and more mature than any other kid he knew. He, Eddie, would never have been able to take his place among five adults and chat with them as an equal.

It was a long while since he had beaten John up properly. High time he reminded his brother that all his talent, intelligence, and maturity could not measure up to a pair of good, strong fists ....

"So, what should we play?" asked the soldier by the piano.

"How about, 'Cry, Arkansas'?'" John suggested. He loved the sad song that he had mastered recently.

The others began laughing. John looked insulted.

"We're not allowed to play that," explained Andrew. "It's a song that protests the war in Vietnam. The army doesn't exactly like us playing it on its own turf."

"But this is not exactly an army base, is it?" grinned the man by the piano. "We're not exactly 'army' here." Eddie filed that snippet away for further study. *We're not exactly 'army' here.*

"Okay," the others agreed, seized by a spirit of mischief. "Let's start with that."

Within minutes, the musicians' amusement had melted away. They began with the main melody, and then each played in turn while the others added their accompaniment. Andrew gave John the honor of the first solo. After only a few notes, the others exchanged looks of surprise and excitement. The kid knew how to play, no question about that. He possessed a true talent.

They played song after song until, about ninety minutes later, the drummer announced that it was lunchtime and they were wanted in the mess hall. The adult musicians applauded John, and he thanked them. It had been fun. He had enjoyed every minute.

Andrew walked the brothers to the main gate. "You'll come again next week?"

"Sure!" John said enthusiastically.

"Can I come, too?" Eddie asked.

"Of course," Andrew said.

They passed the sentry booth and were back on the road behind their house.

"How'd we sound?" John asked his brother.

"I liked it a lot," Eddie said.

"Really? I thought you'd be bored."

"No. It was really nice."

Really nice? It had bored him to tears. Music had never interested

Eddie. But this was his ticket to the sealed compound — the only way he could enter its mysterious precincts for a few hours each week.

On the following Sunday, Andrew was once again waiting for them at the main gate. The same thing happened the next week. Both boys gradually became a part of the scenery. Once a week, like clockwork, they could be seen walking from the main gate toward the cultural center, and back again. Andrew no longer bothered walking them back to the gate. He would merely murmur, "You know your way out, right?" and wave them on their way.

Zurich, Switzerland — 5726 / 1966

The antique porcelain store, Stravinski, had stood in the exact same spot — on Zurich's luxurious *Banhofstrasse* — for close to one hundred years.

The shop resembled a small museum. Its glass shelves displayed delicate handmade porcelain objects, rare and original art work, Czech crystal goblets, and beautiful china dishes. Each object was worth a fortune, and only members of Switzerland's upper stratum, people of culture and nearly unlimited money, were numbered among the shop's regular customers.

The business was owned by Marta Stravinski, a wealthy and respected woman. She had inherited the place from her mother, a member of the Russian nobility who had fled from the Czar's regime to settle in peaceful Switzerland. Even back in Russia, the Stravinski family had dealt in works of art, and they brought their expertise with them to their new home.

Marta's daily schedule never varied: She opened the store at ten a.m. and closed it at seven p.m. Lunchtime found her on her way to the main post office, opening her company postal box and removing a pile of mail: invitations, checks, import-export documents, and other correspondence relating to the business. Then she went to a different section, opened another box, and checked to see if there was anything inside.

In contrast to the business mailbox, which was invariably full, the second postal box was nearly always empty. From the day Marta Stravinski had rented it — twenty-one years earlier, in the year 1945 — no more than seven or eight letters had ever made their way there.

For twenty-one years, she had retained the second box. Faithfully, with Swiss precision, she had paid the rental fees. For twenty-one years she had checked the box daily to see if there was a letter inside. At first, she did so covertly, glancing around in all directions to see if anyone was watching her, and wondering why a good Swiss citizen needed two postal boxes.

The apprehension that she would find a letter waiting assailed her afresh each day. This was because the appearance of a letter in her box signaled the start of a process. She must make an immediate phone call to report its arrival, and then wait for it to be picked up ... just as though she were a spy or a secret agent.

As time passed, the fear diminished and the daily check became routine. She emptied her first box, glanced into the second one, saw that it was empty, and returned to her shop. The most recent letter had arrived in the year 1963, and the previous one five years before that. At this rate — one letter every few years — she could handle the pressure. It was a reasonable price to pay for helping one's unfortunate family.

Her wealthy customers liked to hear the riveting story of the Stravinski nobleman who escaped Russia by the skin of his teeth and managed to take a number of precious artifacts with him. What they didn't know was that Marta Stravinski carried around another, much more painful, family secret. Sometimes she wondered how her customers would react were they ever to discover that the owner of the expensive porcelain shop had a sister in the Soviet Union, behind the Iron Curtain — a sister who was secretary of the Communist Party in the city of Rostov, near Moscow.

She had been eighteen when they parted. Her younger sister, Svetlana, had decided to leave Switzerland and return to Russia. For years, they did not set eyes on each other. They became faithful correspondents, however, and through their letters Marta remained connected to her sister's life.

In one of her letters, Svetlana informed Marta that she had married Boris Matosiev, a good communist who worked in a factory that produced tractors. In another, she informed Marta of the birth of her son, Vladimir, followed two years later by Mikhail, and, three years after that, by Yalena. She sent a picture of her family and described how wonderful life was under their glorious leader, Comrade Joseph Stalin. In her next letter, early in the year 1945, Svetlana surprised her sister with the news that the Communist Party had granted her a two-day visa to visit Switzerland, as a token of appreciation for her work on behalf of the Party and the war effort.

Marta was very excited about the visit. She even closed her store for two days in order to host her sister properly. She was sorry to find that Svetlana had come alone, without her husband or children, and even more disappointed to discover that her sister's faith in the Communist ideology was unswerving. Even here, face-to-face and far from any listening ear, Svetlana painted a rosy picture of life in the Soviet Union. Everyone was equal; everyone worked to the best of his ability and received everything he needed from the State. Passionately, she declared that Western reports of constant hunger, a regime of terror, secret police, and political purges were nothing more than a tissue of lies — wicked, anti-Soviet propaganda. Marta preferred not to poison the atmosphere by entering into debate with her. She wanted to enjoy these two days in her sister's company to their fullest. But she could see that Svetlana appeared tense rather than liberated. Something was weighing her down with sorrow.

It was on the second morning that Marta learned the real reason behind the Communist Party's generous gesture in granting the brief visit — and the reason for her sister's sadness.

"I need a small favor from you," Svetlana said, as they plied a motorboat along the peaceful waters of Lake Zurich. "Before I traveled here, I was summoned to the NKVD office in our city. They asked if I could request a favor from you."

"From me?" Marta asked in surprise. "What?"

"They want you to rent a postal box here, in Zurich, and to check it from time to time. If a letter comes, all you have to do is call the Soviet Embassy and ask for Igor. He'll come to take the letter from you."

Marta Stravinski was stunned and shaken. "The secret police know about me?" she asked in shock.

"They know everything," her sister said simply.

Half an hour later, Svetlana's face was blotched and damp with tears, and the games and lies had given way to a desperate plea. Marta now understood the true picture: the NKVD had not requested a "favor" of her sister, but had imposed a mission on her, using the methods it knew best. This trip, ostensibly a reward and a token of esteem, had a single object: obtaining a post-office box in Zurich.

And if Marta refused to cooperate? Much better not to think about that. Her husband would be fired from his job in the factory, which had retooled to produce tanks, and sent to the battlefront to fight Nazi Germany. Svetlana would be demoted from her position as secretary of the Communist Party in her town, and designated "an enemy of the people." Her children would be whisked off to a military academy so that their Soviet education would not be negatively influenced by their mother. On top of all that, she would be forced to stand trial for her family's escape from Russia during the Czar's regime, and made to pay for the objects of art that her grandfather had smuggled to Switzerland seventy years earlier.

The box bore the number 1766, in postal code 8002. During the first few days, Marta opened it in terror, only to find it devoid of any mail. As she grew accustomed to seeing the box empty, she calmed down. And then, one day, she found a white envelope in the postal box. In her panic, she slammed the lid shut and raced back to her store, shaking.

But no miracle occurred. The letter did not disappear of its own accord. The next day, when she opened the box, it was still there waiting for her. This time, she mustered her courage, removed the envelope, and put it into her pocketbook. For three days she kept it in the bottommost drawer beneath the counter in her shop, afraid to even look at it.

Finally, the phone in her store rang. The operator informed her that she had a call from Moscow. Her heart thudded in fear. A call from Moscow? Had something happened to her sister?

The call *was* from her sister, though at first Marta didn't recognize her voice because Svetlana was crying so hard. It was several minutes before she was able to speak. "Marta," Svetlana gasped. "They want to know if a letter arrived."

Marta, in the heart of peaceful, secure Zurich, in her terror could not utter a syllable.

A man came on the line, speaking German with a harsh Russian accent. He didn't bother introducing himself.

"Frau Stravinski," he said in a hard voice. "We do not ask much — only that you call the embassy when a letter arrives. This time, we will release your sister unharmed. But you must know that, in the future, her welfare rests in your hands alone."

Marta clutched the receiver with trembling hands.

"Perhaps you need the number of our embassy in Zurich?" the man asked sarcastically.

"No," Marta managed. "I have it."

A month and a half later, a colorful postcard arrived, filled with lines of writing from her sister. Her husband had been promoted and was now the factory foreman, and they were about to move into a large, spacious apartment. In the meantime, the Party had provided a two-week vacation in a dacha on the shores of the Black Sea. The children were enjoying themselves in the waves and tanning in the sun. The whole family was well and happy — and all because of the just and equitable Communist regime, under the blessed leadership of Comrade Joseph Stalin ....

Since that time, over a period of twenty-one years, several other letters had arrived. They always came from Europe: once from England, several times from France, and once from Switzerland itself. Marta always reacted the same way. She phoned the Soviet Embassy, asked for Igor, and told him that a letter had arrived.

In the beginning, a young, well-dressed man would come to the store, pass among the display cases, and choose a single item: a crystal vase, a set of ivory-handled flatware, or a delicate silver tray. Later, that man was replaced by a heavyset fellow in a gray wool suit. He always paid in cash, waited patiently for his purchase to be wrapped, and then said, "The Ambassador will enjoy this. He knows how to appreciate works of art. By the way, I haven't introduced myself. My name is Igor. Perhaps you have a letter for me?"

Grayston, Texas — 5726 / 1966

Word of the Sunday music fests in the cultural center spread on wings. Civilian workers and soldiers alike came to take a peek, or even to sit down and listen for a while. One day, a tall man in a suit appeared at the door. The musicians became visibly excited. Motioning for them to keep playing, he took a seat in the first row.

John and the others played "The Lonely Foal" and "Boat on the Mississippi." When they were done, the man stood up and approached the stage, applauding.

"Very nice," he said. "I don't know much about music, but that sounded really professional to me."

John looked at the man with respect. He had a long face and wore round glasses. He exuded a quiet authority.

"Can you play the national anthem?" the man asked the drummer, who was senior among the musicians.

"We can try." The drummer looked at his friends as though seeking their agreement.

"No, I don't mean right now," the guest said. "But it would be a good idea if you practiced it. We have an important visitor coming in a few days. I'd like you to be ready."

"Okay," the drummer said, surprised. "We'll practice."

"Who was that?" John asked Andrew, when the man had left.

"His name is Colin Baron," Andrew told him. "He's the top honcho around here."

That day, Andrew requested a jeep so that he could drive into Grayston to shop. John and Eddie were thrilled when he suggested that they accompany him. They had never ridden in a military jeep before.

A few hundred yards before the exit gate, Andrew turned onto a side road and waited for a friend who wanted to go into town with him. The jeep was parked near the fence surrounding the main building — the high-security area called "Texas" that was the beating heart of the compound. While John and Andrew exchanged animated views about a new recording by Patrick Kargeill, their favorite saxophonist, Eddie covertly studied the mysterious building. A tall fence surrounded it, while dense bushes did their share to hide the building from view.

Presently, Andrew's friend arrived. He jumped into the front seat and the jeep started for the gate. At that moment, Eddie glimpsed something he had been seeking for a long time: a small break in the fence. He felt his heart begin to pound with excitement. He had found a way into "Texas"! That small opening was large enough for him to crawl through.

Next Sunday, he resolved, he would enter the sealed area and find out what was happening there. At long last, he would solve the big mystery.

Two hours later, Andrew drove the two happy boys back to the small clearing in front of their house. Barbara sat in her pickup truck, glaring at them. John and Eddie wanted to run to her and tell her about their day, but she waved them angrily away. "Get away from me," she snapped.

She was worried and irritable. Things had spiraled out of her control. Each day, she would stop at the mailbox at the end of the lane where it met the main road, checking to see if any mail had come for any member of the household. Each time an envelope with Hebrew lettering appeared, her heart would skip a beat. Soon, she knew, she could start collecting her supplementary income. Ben would decide to send checks to

Israel — checks that her brother, Tony, would take to El Paso, where he would convert them into cash for Barbara.

But this was not the season of the envelopes, and the letter that had arrived from Israel today looked different from the others. She had a feeling that it would be a good idea for her to open it and read its contents before passing it on to her husband.

Checking to make sure that the boys had gone into the house, she carefully opened the envelope. It contained two pages. The first was written in an incomprehensible language, but the second offered a translation. As she read what it said, her heart sank. This was it. The party was over. In the letter, the Jews were asking why Sam had stopped sending them his usual donations.

She didn't go into the house. Instead, she started the truck again and headed back to Grayston. She had to show the letter to Tony. He was to blame here. He had been the one to convince her to steal the money that Ben sent to orphanages and soup kitchens in Israel. Had he believed those Jews would never notice that the money hadn't arrived? Did her stupid brother think that the Jews would give up a golden goose named Sam Lowinger? It was amazing that it had taken them this long to react.

And now, suspicion would immediately fall on her. Ben knew that she was the one who always took out the mail. They would inform him at the bank that a moneychanger in El Paso had redeemed the checks, and not an Israeli institution. From there, it would be but a short step to Tony ... and her.

Tony read the letter from start to finish, and chuckled. On second thought, Barbara, too, realized that the situation was not as dire as she had thought.

The tone of the letter was neither angry nor demanding; it was rather humble and flattering. The Jews had written that it was a long time since they had had the honor of shaking Mr. Lowinger's hand, and reminded him that his generous contributions helped feed the poor and the orphaned in the holy city of Jerusalem. A postscript mentioned that the kollel obligated itself to commemorate the death dates of all its donors, and to write them down in a memory book. There were some unfamiliar words, such as "Kaddish," "mishnayos," and "yahrzeit," but Barbara was able to get the gist.

"Don't you get it?" Tony grinned. "They don't know if Sam is alive or dead, so they wrote the letter in a way that would suit either possibility. If he's alive, let him please go on sending money. If he's dead — his heirs are asked to let them know the date of his death, so that they can carry out the proper religious rituals in his memory. These are Jews, remember?"

"So what do we do?" Barbara asked, considerably calmer now.

"We tear up the letter and wait to see what happens next," Tony said. "If they don't get an answer, they may just give up."

Tony had not accurately gauged the urgency felt by the kollel administrators. At their next meeting, Sam Lowinger's name came up again. The letter they had sent to Grayston, Texas had not borne fruit, reported R' Aharon Sherman. In fact, he said, it had not even warranted a reply. It would seem likely, therefore, that this important donor had gone the way of all flesh and passed from the world.

This, as they all knew, raised certain problems. Sam Lowinger had no offspring to inform them of his passing. The kollel had explicitly undertaken to mark their donors' *yahrzeits* in perpetuity, and its members prided themselves on faithfully carrying out their obligations. They made sure to ascertain each donor's *yahrzeit*, even if this called for convoluted methods. And this was Reb Shmuel Levinger of Grayston, Texas, who had always responded promptly and generously to their moving pleas for help each Rosh Hashanah and Pesach.

"When I travel to America, I'll try to find out what happened to him." The *meshulach*, R' Tzvi Hirsch HaLevi, suddenly spoke up from his corner of the table.

The others turned to gape at him in astonishment.

"R' Tzvi Hirsch!" exclaimed R' Shmerel, the chief administrator. "Are you planning another trip?"

R' Tzvi Hirsch nodded.

The other three exchanged relieved glances.

"*Nu, baruch Hashem. Baruch Hashem!*" R' Berel Margolis said. "A big *yasher koach*, R' Tzvi Hirsch."

Although he served as one of the kollel's four administrators, R' Tzvi Hirsch was noted mostly for his fund-raising trips. In recent years he had not traveled much because of his health. Now, with help from Above, he felt stronger and was prepared to make another trip. There was no substitute for R' Tzvi Hirsch, the others knew. Contributors in America and Europe opened their doors, their hearts, and their checkbooks to him in a way that they did for few others. R' Tzvi Hirsch, the rich men seemed to feel, did more than merely come for a donation. He came to bring them a whiff of the Holy Land.

He carried with him a bit of the holiness of Jerusalem, bringing it into the palatial residences of San Francisco and the mansions of Los Angeles and New York City. Jerusalem entered wherever he did. Wherever he was, there was the Holy City. In his old caftan and the worn yarmulka he wore beneath his hat, he shone a light into their hearts. They found themselves showering him with money and almost begging him to take more.

Everyone esteemed R' Tzvi Hirsch for his piety and his Torah scholarship, but R' Shmerel was especially solicitous of his honor. He was one of the few who knew the fund-raiser's secret. R' Shmerel's father, the kollel's former head administrator, had told it to him before he died.

"You must be very careful to honor R' Tzvi Hirsch," he'd told his son. "As fine and respectable as he seems — that is only a drop in the ocean of his true greatness. You must know that he is one of the hidden *tzaddikim* in whose merit the world continues to exist."

In years past, R' Shmerel's father had said on his deathbed, R' Tzvi Hirsch had belonged to a group of hidden *tzaddikim* in Jerusalem — a group headed by R' Dovid Leib, *ztk"l*. They would meet every Erev Rosh Chodesh to pray in one of the small shuls in the Shaarei Chesed section of the city, and brought about many salvations in the country. Most of these hidden *tzaddikim* looked like simple people. One was a storekeeper in Petach Tikvah, another seemed to be a blind Yemenite beggar from Tel Aviv, a third was known as the *"Poilisher melamed"* who taught in the Eitz Chaim Talmud Torah, while a fourth cleaned the Shortkov *shtiebel*.

There were also some better-known men in the group, R' Shmerel's father had continued. A *dayan* from Yaffo; the two holy brothers, R' Zalman and R' Zeidel, who learned together in the old Motzah shul; and the Moroccan *chacham* who learned Torah on the top floor of the Zaharei Chamah shul in Machane Yehudah. R' Tzvi Hirsch was the youngest of the group, and the only one still alive today. For the past two years he had been ailing and unable to travel. Now, *baruch Hashem*, his health had improved and he had just announced his intention to go abroad.

"Are you sure the trip won't be too much for you?" R' Shmerel asked R' Tzvi Hirsch.

"*HaKadosh Baruch Hu* gives strength to the weary," R' Tzvi Hirsch replied. "On my next trip to America, I will investigate the fate of our honored friend, R' Shmuel Levinger. Maybe I'll find people in America to help me. If not — I will travel to his hometown myself."

On the following Sunday, John and Eddie went to the cultural center as usual, one holding the saxophone case and the other the music folder. The sentry at the gate did not ask for any authorization for them to enter. The two boys had become familiar faces in the compound, and their presence did not arouse curiosity or apprehension.

The drummer, the pianist, and Andrew were already onstage. The contrabass player joined them a few minutes later. Eddie took a seat in a middle row and listened to them play.

A quarter-hour later, he stood up and waved to John.

"You're going?" John called from the stage.

Eddie nodded.

John was surprised, but soon lost himself again in his music. The drummer suggested that they start practicing the national anthem, as Colin Baron had requested. He had already written the notes and made several copies, which he distributed to the others.

Eddie left the cultural center, crossed the lawn as though heading for the main gate, and quickly reached the compound's main road. As he walked along the right-hand pavement, the "Texas" building with its high fences loomed just ahead. He looked around surreptitiously. No one was looking at him. He turned right, to the side road where Andrew had parked his jeep, hoping that no one had fixed the breach in the fence.

His heart raced with fear and excitement. What would happen if he were caught? What if the soldiers on the watchtower spotted him? Andrew had said that this was a place where they shot anyone entering without permission ....

The minute he saw that the fence had not been repaired, his fears melted away. He was seized by a spirit of adventure. Eddie looked carefully around. There were no soldiers or workers in the area. Crouching low on the ground, he wormed his way through the hole. In seconds, he was swallowed up by the dense bushes in the building's yard. He was in.

He was in the most secret and secure place in the compound. He, Eddie Lowinger, a boy of almost eleven, had eluded all the guards and soldiers.

His heart thudded rapidly in his chest. He closed his eyes and breathed deeply, trying to calm down. The first stage was behind him. He had entered the fenced area. Now he would crawl closer to the building and see what was inside.

39

Eddie slinked through the bushes, moving closer to the "Texas" building. It was a three-story structure, with half the first floor below ground. The barred and reinforced windows were positioned about two feet above ground level.

Eddie peeked cautiously into the first window. He saw a medium-sized room, well-lit but devoid of humanity. Its walls were painted white and the floor shone with cleanliness. The door was made of steel, with a small window set in it. All four walls held a series of strange, glass-fronted cabinets. Above each cabinet — Eddie suddenly realized that they were refrigerators — was mounted a small thermostat. The glass was clouded with condensation, except for one refrigerator whose glass front was clear and permitted Eddie to see what was inside. It was filled with shelves all along its length, and on the shelves were hundreds of minuscule glass vials — like tiny corked bottles.

Eddie continued his prowl around the building's perimeter. The next window exposed to his view another roomful of refrigerator units. This time, however, a long, metal table stretched along one of the walls, bearing glass tubes and vessels of various shapes, a microscope, and other strange pieces of equipment that Eddie had never seen before. One machine, for instance, held a bottle full of dark liquid, which it agitated continuously. There was a familiar symbol on each of the refrigerators: a skull and crossbones.

Eddie recognized it from the Port Stockton pharmacy. In the pharmacy, it was displayed on a cabinet that held poisonous substances. The pharmacist had once explained to him that anyone who drank even a drop of these liquids would die at once. Here, in the most secure heart of the sealed compound, were refrigerators full of death-inducing poisons! Was that the reason why the place was so secret? Were these the anti-Communist weapons that Andrew had talked about? The "traps for the Red rats"?

Eddie continued his slow reconnoiter around the building. The next three rooms looked more like jail cells. Each of them contained a metal bed, table, and chair that were fastened to the floor. Over each bed, a thick chain was attached to the wall, a handcuff dangling from it. *Who were the people who were imprisoned here?* Eddie wondered uneasily. *What were these cells for? Maybe* — he shivered involuntarily — *maybe these cells were meant for people who trespassed on this secret place … and were caught!*

He felt dizzy with fear. Everything here was so mysterious and terrifying. It was like a place out of a nightmare. Strange, frightening rooms, and not a living soul in sight ….

The next window made Eddie gasp. What he saw reminded him of a zoo. It was a very large room filled with cages containing various animals. The cage nearest the window held dozens of white rabbits; small white mice raced about in another; and a host of hamsters frolicked in a third. Eddie's eyes raked the room. An even greater surprise awaited him in the far corner. Here stood two tall cages, one of them enclosing several dogs. Monkeys leaped about in the second.

What was this? Why were all these animals kept here? Was it a zoo for the workers to enjoy? Would the next window reveal lions and tigers? And why were these animals kept in the most strictly guarded part of the compound?

It was the next window that made Eddie realize that the animals were not kept for amusement. In this room was a single, narrow cage holding one monkey. Its head was bound by a round metal ring and there were metal wires attached to its scalp. In an adjoining cage, another monkey lay on a bed, held down with metal loops. Leather straps crossed the monkey's chest, attached to wires that ran to some sort of machine. The animal whimpered, softly and continuously, arms and legs twitching. In its arm was an I.V. needle, like the one the nurse in Austin had insisting on inserting into Eddie's arm before his tonsillectomy. A line from the needle led to an inverted bottle on the machine. Eddie knew what that was. The nurse had explained that the intravenous line allowed medicine to go directly into the patient's bloodstream.

They were putting medicine into the monkey's arm, too. Or maybe it was some of the stuff from the other room — the one with the cabinets bearing the skull and crossbones? This was no zoo. These were laboratory animals. Eddie had read about such experimental labs in a book once, but had never thought he would actually see one with his own eyes.

What an interesting place, Eddie thought. It was hard to tear himself away from the window. And it was all so close to his house! He wondered if those who worked here enjoyed torturing animals as much as he did. The principal of his school was always lecturing him about doing things to animals. Once, for example, Eddie had tied a blindfold around a chicken's eyes and let it loose on the main road, just a minute before a truck was coming. Another time, he had stolen a colt, poured kerosene around it in a big circle, and tossed in a lit match. It had been an unforgettable spectacle, seeing that colt rearing and stamping in the circle of fire, and reading the terror in its eyes. It was too bad that the animal had managed to escape .... Eddie stared into the window. He just *had* to get inside this place.

The laboratories and refrigerated cabinets didn't interest him — but this room, with all the animals connected to machines, was something he wanted to see up close. It was a good thing that John, the coward, hadn't come along. He would probably be quaking all over and begging to get out of here. When it came to these kinds of adventures, John was such a baby. Eddie remembered the way his brother had darted into the street to try and save the blindfolded chicken, so that the truck nearly ran *him* over .... John was not a *real* Texan. He would never be a cattleman or farmer. His delicate fingers were good for nothing but that dumb old saxophone of his.

On the other hand, Eddie thought, it was because of John that he was here in the first place. Suddenly, he wondered how much time had elapsed since he had left the cultural center. Twenty minutes? Half an hour? He had better leave the compound before John did. He had to reach the exit gate before his brother.

But first, to complete the mission. There were still two windows into which he hadn't looked. Who knew what exciting things they might reveal? Eddie continued his cautious circuit, staying close to the wall.

The next window showed him a storage room. There were a few empty cages piled in a heap, cartons of empty test tubes, and some more boxes. That was all. One more window, and he would start back. One quick peek and he would be out of here.

The situation was getting more dangerous. From where he was positioned, Eddie could see the front of the building. Some workers were piling sealed wooden crates onto a truck, while armed guards looked on.

With his thoughts on the way home rather than on the present danger, he lifted his head recklessly to peer into the last window. He recoiled at the unexpected sight that met his eyes.

The room was the same size as the others, with scores of shelves laden with books and binders covering two of its walls. There was a desk in the center of the room. A man sat typing at the desk.

Eddie stopped breathing. His heart hammered. This was the first person he had seen in his entire tour of the building. Very carefully, he peeked again from a corner of the window. The man sat with his back to Eddie. He was wearing a crisply ironed shirt, his hair was gray, and his back was slightly hunched. Despite the thick window pane, Eddie heard the tapping of the typewriter keys. The man was typing rhythmically, using two fingers instead of all ten, as the secretary at Eddie's school did.

Suddenly, Eddie understood something: This was the man he had once seen on their way to the cultural center, watering his garden. The man lived inside the compound. Who was he? What did he do here? Why had they built him a house inside the compound?

The man sat at the desk, working diligently. There was a pile of handwritten pages near his elbow, which he was apparently transcribing. Every time he finished copying a page, he placed it onto a second pile on the other side of the typewriter. A third pile held the typed pages. The three piles were arranged with extreme precision, as were the table's other contents. A pen, a cup of tea, three books, and a stapler were lined up like soldiers.

Eddie was fascinated. The rhythmic typing all but hypnotized him. He knelt and peered inside. The man stopped typing and sat motionless for several minutes, looking at his papers. Then he crossed his arms behind his neck and rocked slightly in his chair, lost in thought.

Eddie glanced away for a moment. When he looked again, he caught his breath and turned pale. The man had apparently seen him. He had swiveled his chair around and was staring directly at the window.

Eddie froze in panic. He stared at the man, longing to run away but unable to move a muscle. He was finished. He was dead. They had caught him. Any second now, the man would summon the armed guards — and they, as Andrew had predicted, would shoot first and ask questions later.

Los Angeles — Iyar, 5766 / May 2006

Majdi's call to update Aziz was brief. The conversation took place over Majdi's untraceable phone. He told the imam that his nephew had succeeded in obtaining a job at the wedding hall in question. Bashir Abdul Aziz voiced his approval of this positive development. Both of them spoke quietly, taking every precaution. Although no one else knew of their great plan, they would continue to be careful. If they did that, they anticipated no problems at all.

They did not know that they had already made their one fateful mistake, many weeks before ....

From their first conversation about the great plan, both had known that they would not be able to carry it out unless they received "fatwah," authorization, from a senior Islamic religious authority. In the year 2002, the imam had traveled to Egypt, where he returned to their childhood neighborhood to meet with old Imam Mohammed Tahe Abu-Samir — the man's whose vision they hoped to turn into a reality.

To Aziz's great surprise, the aged cleric had behaved evasively, and refused to issue the requested *fatwah*. He said he must consult with religious authorities higher than himself. The imam should return to America, he urged; he would send his reply at a later date.

Aziz was sorely disappointed. The imam whom he had admired since childhood had been exposed as a weakling. He knew how to make lofty speeches and incite children with his talk of destroying the infidels. But when it came to action, he had turned into a frightened rabbit.

Aziz couldn't bring himself to tell Majdi that when he had outlined their plan to Abu-Samir, the old man had begun to tremble. He had been too frightened to sign the *fatwah*. He could not and would not take a responsibility of such magnitude on his own frail shoulders.

Then, a few weeks ago, the old imam had passed away. It went without saying that the professor would stay away from the funeral, and only Aziz would attend. Barry Majdi must remain free of any taint of connection to radical Islam. A single trip to Egypt could spell disaster.

The funeral of Imam Mohammed Tahe Abu-Samir was large and well attended. Heading the procession was the mufti of Egypt, followed by other *khadis*, mullahs, and Islamic religious figures. Egyptian government officials were in attendance as well, despite the fact that the old cleric had not been an enthusiast of the regime.

At the funeral's conclusion, the *muzzein* of the local mosque approached Bashir Abdul Aziz. "Are you the imam of Los Angeles?"

Bashir inclined his head modestly.

The *muzzein* drew a sealed envelope from his robe and handed it to the startled imam. "Imam Abu-Samir signed this document two days before his death," he whispered. "He asked me to give it to you."

Aziz's heart missed a beat. Though he had already guessed what the envelope contained, his pulse pounded wildly as he opened it.

He had guessed right. It was the *fatwah* he had been awaiting for four years, written on the mosque's official stationery. The document contained no less than ten lines in Arabic, authorizing the implementation of the plan. There were three signatures at the bottom of the paper: those of two relatively insignificant religious figures flanking the shaky but ornate signature of the old imam himself.

Aziz couldn't wait. He rushed back to his hotel room and with shaking hands dialed the Los Angeles number.

A secretary answered and transferred the call to the professor.

"Professor Majdi?"

The professor recognized his friend's voice immediately. He knew that the imam was calling from Cairo.

"This is Brian, from BioSystems, London branch." Aziz introduced himself before Majdi could utter a word. "I am happy to be able to inform you that we've finally received confirmation of your patent. If you have a fax machine handy, I can send you a copy. The document is highly classified and for your eyes only. Please read it immediately and then destroy it. You must be aware of our company's strict policies with regard to privacy and information security."

Barry Majdi took the advice of "Brian of Biologic Systems." He locked his office door and waited with pounding heart as the paper emerged from his personal fax machine. When he saw the *fatwah*, he nearly shouted with joy. He read it over and over, proud and elated, until his secretary's knock on the door reminded him of "Brian's" next directive: to destroy the fax. He fed it into the shredder and watched it turn into confetti, which he flushed away in the men's room.

From there, it was a short hop to choosing the Milinover affair as the focal point for carrying out the imam's great vision. The lethal Mexican fever virus, so efficient in wiping out the Chuma tribe, would be no less effective when set into operation at a Jewish wedding.

There was just one thing that he and Aziz did not know. Shredding the fax and flushing it away had not been as effective as they both believed. Professor Majdi's office was under surveillance by a special CIA unit — a small force that reported directly to one of the agency's senior members. Though this unit was not aware of Majdi's untraceable phone, his office telephone and personal fax machine had been bugged for several months.

Which was why, as Majdi stood exulting at his office window in the aftermath of the *fatwah's* arrival, that same document was sitting on the desk of a senior official on the seventh floor of the CIA building at Langley. The desk belonged to Assistant Director Walter Child.

Grayston, Texas — 5726 / 1966

Eddie felt tears well up in his eyes. He didn't want to die at the tender age of eleven. He wished he had never come to this place.

To his astonishment, the man smiled.

True, it wasn't an especially warm smile, but the thin lips framed by a trimmed beard had definitely curled into the semblance of one. The man also raised his hand and waved at Eddie.

Stunned, Eddie lifted his own hand and waved weakly back.

The man's lips moved. He said something, but no sound was heard. The window was closed and a thick pane separated them.

"I can't hear you," Eddie tried to explain with gestures.

The man got out of his chair, went to the window, and opened it. Eddie could now see him up close. The man's eyes were cold and gray.

"What's your name?" the man asked, trying for a friendly note.

"E-Eddie."

"Eddie?"

"Eddie Lowinger."

"Do you live here?" the man asked. "Are you the son of one of the workers?"

He had, Eddie noticed, a distinct accent. He was certainly not a Texan. Maybe he came from a different part of the United States, or even from a foreign country. He pronounced English words in the oddest way.

"I live near here," Eddie said. "In the ranch house near the gate."

"Ah, you're from the family that once owned this whole property?"

Eddie nodded.

"You look like a fine young man," the man said. "With your permission, I will close the door so that no one will disturb our getting-acquainted talk."

He went to the door, locked it, and returned to his chair. All this took a long minute, during which Eddie could have bolted. By this time, the idea didn't even occur to him.

"So, how did you get in here?"

"I slipped through a hole in the fence," Eddie admitted.

"A hole?" The man was genuinely surprised. "Fools. They call this place 'Texas' and guard it so carefully — and now we see that a small child can slip right in. But how did you get past the gate?"

"My brother plays in the band," Eddie explained. "I come to the cultural center with him every week. Today, I left before him and sneaked in here."

"Ah — the boy with the saxophone." The man nodded. "I have heard of him. But I don't like that kind of music. It is loud and crude. I prefer Wagner, Beethoven, Bach, Strauss. Genuine music."

Eddie had never heard any of their music, but he had read enough in his short life to know that these were German composers.

"Are you German?" he asked nervously. Maybe that was the reason for the man's strange accent. Eddie had never met a German before. He only knew that Norman Chambers, who owned the bakery shop, always cursed the Germans for killing his brother during World War Two. Once, it was rumored, he'd put a sign in his shop window reading, "No Germans or dogs allowed," but Sheriff Jack Abrams had come in and persuaded him to take down the sign. How, then, could a German be working in a secure American compound? There were a great many mysteries hidden behind these concrete walls ....

"It does not matter what I am," the man said. "But the Germans do have fine music. Certainly better than the Americans."

Eddie shrugged. He had no opinion on the matter. He only noticed that the man had said, "the Americans," as though he was not one.

Suddenly, Eddie panicked. Time was passing. He must get out through the gate. If John and Andrew discovered that he hadn't left, that was when the real problems would start.

"I — I have to go," he blurted. "I don't want anyone to notice that I'm not with my brother."

The man stood up, moved to the window, and thrust his hand through the bars. "It has been a pleasure to meet you. My name is Dr. Henry Reiner," he said formally.

Eddie shook his hand. Dr. Reiner's hand was cold and clammy, and Eddie quickly withdrew his own. There was something about the man that repelled him, though he couldn't put his finger on what it was.

"You are invited to return here," Dr. Reiner said. "Are you interested in science?"

"Yes," said Eddie. "I read a lot of books."

"I can teach you things that you won't find in any books," the man said with the same chilly smile. "I am nearly always in this room. You may come whenever you can."

"Okay. Uh ... so long," Eddie said.

He pushed his way into the bushes and began crawling back toward the hole in the fence.

"I've been away from the band for two weeks," John said, almost skipping in his excitement. "It feels like a long time."

"But it was worth it," Eddie replied, not without a twinge of envy. "Your party was great."

On the previous Sunday, they had missed their session at the compound because of John's birthday party. All the kids in his class had come to the ranch house. Even their parents had been, for once, perfectly well behaved: Ben wasn't drunk, Barbara wasn't irritable, and Frankie had tucked Sam away in an inner room because he sensed that John and Eddie would be uncomfortable having their classmates see their ailing old great-uncle.

"I wonder if they played a new piece last week," John mused aloud. He held his saxophone and Eddie, as always, carried the music. The pair walked along the main compound road, John lost in his musical musings and Eddie surreptitiously scanning the fence around "Texas." Two weeks, he guessed, was enough time to repair the broken fence.

Eddie exhaled in disappointment. From now on, he assumed, he'd no longer have access to the building. Too bad. There were a number of questions he wanted to ask Dr. Reiner, such as why they kept rabbits, mice, and monkeys in the big room with the cages. What sorts of experiments were being conducted on the animals in the next room? And what was kept in all those refrigerators with the glass fronts? The short time that he had spent in "Texas" had supplied him with two weeks' worth of questions.

Why hadn't Dr. Reiner been angry at him, even though he had penetrated the most secure part of the compound? Who were the "fools" he had referred to with such contempt? Where did he live? Was it in the house where Eddie had seen him watering the garden? Eddie felt like a junior detective — the kind he read about in books. There was a mystery here, and he longed to get to the bottom of it.

The brothers left the pavement and cut diagonally across the lawn to the cultural center. Maybe it would be worth his while to make a little detour in the direction of the private home he had seen, Eddie thought. With any luck, Dr. Reiner would be watering his garden again.

When they entered the cultural center, the other musicians were already seated onstage. Andrew held his trumpet, the mustachioed drummer sat behind his drums, and the other musicians were in their places.

The minute John appeared in the doorway, the drummer gave the signal. All the musicians burst into a rousing rendition of "Happy Birthday to You." On a small table in the center of the stage was a large cake, courtesy of Norman Chambers' bakery, with a large chocolate "13" at dead center.

John's face split into a huge smile. His grown-up friends hadn't forgotten him. It must have been Andrew who organized this birthday celebration. It was just like him.

Andrew cut the cake, handed out slices, and gleefully announced that John Lowinger was the best thirteen-year-old saxophone player in the United States. The festivities were soon over, and the band settled down to practice. The drummer reported that the director, Colin Baron, had asked if they had a solid repertoire yet, and if they had practiced the national anthem. "There's a scent of an important visitor in the air," the drummer said. "Maybe even the president. Who knows?"

Eddie sat in one of the last rows of chairs and opened the book that he had brought with him. John, absorbed in the music, hardly noticed him. Fifteen minutes later, Eddie slipped out of the cultural center and crossed the lawn.

This time, he did not go toward the main road, but toward the row of trees in front of Dr. Reiner's house. Behind the trees were tall bushes that effectively concealed the single-story home. Eddie glanced over his shoulder. No one even glanced his way. He penetrated the hedge and pushed his way through.

The strip of bushes was no more than five feet thick. Eddie traversed it quickly — and felt his heart lift with joy. He had made it. Dr. Reiner was sitting on a wooden bench, in the same place that Eddie had once seen him watering his garden. Tied to a slat at the back of the bench was a tall, thin dog on a leash. The dog was crouching and occasionally wagging its tail.

The sound of music could be heard clearly from here. The scientist certainly heard it, Eddie thought, judging by the way he kept looking at the cultural center. Or — Eddie was startled by the idea — was it possible that it was not the music that interested Dr. Reiner ... but Eddie himself? Eddie had told him that he always came to the compound with his brother when the band practiced. Could Dr. Reiner be sitting here waiting to meet him again?

On his knees, Eddie stuck his head through the bushes. The scientist caught the movement and he smiled. He glanced around cautiously, and then waved to the boy. Eddie was afraid to leave his hiding place. Dr. Reiner untied the dog's leash, stood, and strolled over to Eddie, leading the animal.

"How are you?" he asked with same cold, falsehearted smile. "I see that you have returned."

"I ... I'm fine." Eddie had been imagining this meeting for two weeks, but now he found himself tongue tied. He was suddenly afraid. Not of the dog that was rumbling in its throat in a friendly way, but of the soldiers. They might catch him at any moment, and evict him from the compound. This was not "Texas," but it was surely not okay for him to be talking to Dr. Reiner ....

A sudden thought struck the boy. Dr. Reiner had looked around before waving to him. Could he be a prisoner here, too?

"So, why have you returned?" the doctor asked.

"I wanted to know ... why are those animals in the room?"

"You are interested in animals?"

"Yes," Eddie said eagerly. "Very interested."

"But those mice and monkeys are used in medical experiments," Dr. Reiner said. "They are not pets."

"I know," said Eddie. "Laboratory animals. We learned about them in school."

"Does this interest you? I have a book on the subject. I can lend it to you, if you like — but no one must know. Do you know how to keep a secret?"

"Sure!" Eddie answered.

"When you leave, do they inspect you at the gate?" Dr. Reiner asked.

"No. They never check my brother or me."

Eddie remembered one afternoon when he and John had headed out at the same time as Steven Chambers, Norman's son, who had once been a ranch hand at Tall Willy's place and now worked in the compound as part of the landscaping crew. Steven had asked in surprise and a touch of anger what they were doing here. They had explained that John played with the compound's band. As they had neared the gate, Steven had broken away from them to stand in front of a small booth, where soldiers ordered him to empty his pockets and checked him from head to toe.

"What do they think?" Steven had grumbled as he rejoined the boys. "That I'll try to smuggle some flowers out of here? Or maybe a plant or two?" That was when Eddie noticed that all the workers underwent a similar search as they came and went. But no one ever checked him or John. The soldiers just grinned at them, and sometimes cracked a joke or two. The boys came and went unchallenged.

Eddie didn't know it, but Steven was not really angry at being inspected at the gate. On the contrary — it was proof that his cover was still good, and that no one knew about the important job he was doing in the compound. It had been six months since his CIA handler had recruited him. Until now, his mission had been to keep working as a gardener and await further instructions. Most important, he was to maintain absolute silence about the fact that he was a CIA agent.

The day one of the guards let him pass without checking him, his handler had said, would be the day he would know that his mission had failed.

"Wait here," Dr. Reiner told Eddie. He walked into the small house and returned a few minute later carrying a slim volume.

"Thanks a lot," said Eddie. "See you ...."

He headed for the bushes and began crawling back toward the cultural center.

The scientist and his dog returned to their bench. Dr. Reiner's thin lips bore a curious expression. He had been waiting all year for a chance like this. For a full year he had been waiting for the right moment to fall into his hands — ever since a random encounter in the Department of Agriculture building in El Paso.

The encounter had taken place at the beginning of 1965. One day, Colin Baron had come into Reiner's room and told him that he had a special job for him. Department of Defense officials in Washington wanted a report on what was being accomplished at the compound. For two decades, they had provided the compound with a huge budget via the Department of Agriculture, and they were now demanding a progress report.

Actually, the secretary of agriculture himself had been planning to visit the compound in person. By pulling strings among his contacts on the Hill, Baron had managed to postpone that visit to an undetermined date. In its place, a preparatory lower-level meeting was arranged outside the compound, for the purpose of providing general information about the program.

"We have to throw the dogs a bone," Colin Baron had explained to the doctor. "Spread around a lot of technical jargon to thoroughly confuse them. But let them leave feeling that they've understood the whole thing perfectly."

The meeting's venue was, of course, the Department of Agriculture building in El Paso — the project's all-purpose cover.

The Department of Defense sent three senior men to El Paso. The Grayston contingent was made up of Colin Baron, his assistant Richard Eastwood, and the project's chief scientist, who was introduced by the Americanized version of his name: Dr. Henry Reiner.

The doctor remembered the trip well. He remembered every occasion that he had had the chance to pass through the compound's gates, because they were so infrequent. He longed for the sensation of freedom, to roam about the streets of a city at will, to walk into a store and buy something. But that was impossible. He was a prisoner in a gilded cage. He lived alone in a private home within the compound, where he read the books in his extensive German-language library, listened to his classical music, walked his dog, and tended to his flower garden. Officially, he did not exist. He had no passport or driver's license, no bank account or Social Security number.

Colin Baron had promised him that, at the end of eighteen years, he would be granted his freedom. But that deadline was behind him and nothing had changed. The director kept finding new excuses for extending the period of the Nazi's atonement for his war crimes and postponing the granting of American citizenship. Heinreich von Reiner was an angry and embittered man — but also a helpless one. He had no recourse to the police or the courts. He did not exist.

Each of his infrequent forays outside the compound gates filled him with excitement, but that particular trip became unforgettable. It was a day that changed his life and gave it a whole new meaning.

Colin Baron opened the meeting with a few brief introductory remarks and then handed the proceedings to "my esteemed colleague, Dr. Henry Reiner." The scientist presented a host of impressive facts, and the Washington bureaucrats received satisfactory answers to all their questions. About an hour later, Colin Baron introduced his assistant, who spoke about budgetary matters. Dr. Reiner seized the opportunity to step out to the restroom. Baron was calm, knowing that the entire floor was under secure surveillance. One of the Department of Defense officials excused himself and left as well.

A guard followed Dr. Reiner down the hall, but let him enter the restroom unaccompanied. A few minutes later, as the scientist stood washing his hands at the sink in front of the big mirror, the senior DOD bureaucrat from Washington entered and took his place at the sink next to his.

"Do you miss Germany, Dr. Reiner?" the American asked, without turning his head from the water running over his hands. "Would you want to return to your native country?"

The scientist threw the bureaucrat an icy look in the mirror. No one was supposed to know that he was German or that he had a "native country." Only a handful of people knew what he had done in Nazi Germany; even fewer knew that he was in the United States.

"Do you miss your old name, Dr. Heinrich von Reiner?" the American continued.

The scientist froze. His nostrils widened in fear. Was this a trap? Or was this man one of those who were privy to the secret and merely making small talk?

"Yes," he said finally, still washing his hands. "Sometimes I miss it."

The DOD man drew a long breath before speaking his next words. He was about to take a big personal risk — but, if he was successful, it would be a great coup. He glanced over his shoulder. All the cubicles were empty. Only the two of them were in the restroom at the moment and the door was closed.

"General Sergei Petroshov is still waiting for you," he said softly, almost in a whisper.

He saw the blood drain rapidly from the German's face.

"Dr. Reiner?" The guard knocked on the door.

"Post Office Box 1766, Zurich, zone 8002," the man from Washington said quickly, and left the restroom.

Heinrich von Reiner washed his face over and over, until he had regained his equilibrium. Then he walked out of the restroom and strode down the corridor toward the conference hall. At the meeting, the DOD official behaved no differently than before. He acted as though nothing had happened; it was Dr. Reiner who found himself completely unable to focus. He could not stop thinking about what had just happened.

"General Sergei Petroshov is still waiting for you." That simple sentence sent him reeling twenty years back in time, to Nazi Germany in 1945.

The war situation was deteriorating and the end was already in sight. As the Red Army advanced rapidly on Berlin, the atmosphere inside the Berlin Institute for Medical Research was rife with panic. It was obvious to all that either the Russians or the Americans would lay claim to the Institute and all its secrets. The institute's director prepared a plan for the methodical destruction of their programs and equipment. More and more staff members began disappearing from the labs, and those who remained realized that they were living on borrowed time.

One morning, in the cafeteria, the institute's director was seated at von Reiner's table, quietly eating. He waited until the others had gone, and then leaned toward the scientist. "A KGB general by the name of

Sergei Petroshov has been appointed by the Soviet leadership to find you and bring you back as a present for Stalin. Beware of him."

Heinrich von Reiner had continued his meal without any overt reaction. Rising to his feet, the director thumped the scientist's shoulder in a friendly way. Von Reiner had no way of knowing if the man's warning had been genuine, or if the director was himself a Soviet agent, trying to recruit him.

The next morning, he sat down beside the director and waited until they had the table to themselves. "Those Russians have always been idiots," he said with feigned amusement. "Let's say I did want to turn myself in to the Russians. How in the world do they expect me to do it?"

The director smiled at his plate. "Yes, it appears that the gang at the KGB are nothing but dolts," he agreed, playing along. "They'd expect you to send a letter to Post Office Box 1766 in Zurich — zone 8002. And then they'd show up with their Red Army to rescue you."

"So that's how they work, over there at the KGB?" Von Reiner chuckled, memorizing the numbers.

"Yes." The director joined in his laughter. "How primitive they are ...."

Post Office Box 1766, Zurich 8002. Russian mortars thundered around Berlin. The American Army advanced from the opposite direction. Dr. Heinrich von Reiner had committed the numbers to memory.

He had other questions to ask the director, but the next day he was found shot to death in his apartment near the Institute. No one knew, at the time, whether he had done the deed himself or had some help in exiting this world. Now, two decades later in the heart of an American government building, von Reiner had encountered a senior bureaucrat from the Department of Defense who reminded him that General Sergei Petroshov was still waiting for him.

A full year had passed since that day. The bureaucrat who had delivered the message in the restroom was no longer among the living. Six months after the El Paso conference, Colin Baron told Dr. Reiner that one of the DOD men they had met there had committed suicide by swallowing a capsule of cyanide, after falling under suspicion of being a Soviet spy. "He was a Soviet mole for the past twenty years," Baron had told him. "The KGB had a code name for him: Black Sheep. That describes him, all right!"

The Nazi scientist removed his dog's leash and let it run free in the yard. General Petroshov, then, had made two attempts to recruit him:

the first through the Berlin Institute's director in 1945, and the second through a senior DOD official — alias Black Sheep — in 1965. Both recruiters had paid with their lives.

Maybe that nice American youngster with the mop of blond hair, so typically Aryan, would finally be able to help him reach the general who was so anxiously awaiting him.

Don't think that I don't see you leaving in the middle of our re-hearsals," John told Eddie as they walked to the cultural center on the following Sunday. "What are you up to? Where do you go?"

"Nothing. Nowhere. I just sit on the grass," Eddie said nonchalantly. "There's not much else to do around here."

John grinned. He knew his younger brother very well. Eddie was incapable of sitting still for five minutes without getting into some sort of mischief.

"Well, just remember this," he snapped. "If they don't let you in again — *I* won't care."

"Neither will I," Eddie retorted. "There's nothing to do here anyway. I only come to keep you company."

"Thanks a lot," John said sarcastically.

Fifteen minutes after this exchange, Eddie was slipping through the bushes toward Dr. Henry Reiner's house. Beneath his shirt was the book the scientist had loaned him the previous week. Eddie had found the book both frightening and fascinating. It had pictures of various medical experiments, in which students had been photographed as they dissected monkeys and frogs. Beside each photo was some text, but Eddie hadn't understood all of it. There were many scientific terms that he wanted to ask the doctor to explain.

But all that was only a means to an end. What Eddie really wanted to do was ask Dr. Reiner about himself. Who was he? What was he doing here? In his mind's eye, Eddie could see himself as the hero of a book: *The Grayston Gang and the Mysterious German Scientist*, or *Eddie Lowinger, Boy Detective, in the Secret Compound*.

The doctor was seated on the bench again, his dog beside him. Eddie had learned that the dog was a greyhound, and had jotted this new piece of information down in the back of his history notebook, along with everything else he had unearthed about the compound.

Dr. Reiner noticed Eddie's head protruding from the bushes, but — as on the previous occasion — he did not react immediately. Instead, he looked around, first right and then left, before approaching his young visitor.

"How was the book?" he asked.

"It was super!" Eddie said. "But I didn't understand some things."

"Such as what, for example?"

Eddie opened the book and pointed to a photograph of a dog connected to electrodes and running on a treadmill.

The scientist sighed. "It's complicated," he said. "If you want, I will write down the explanation and give it to you next week."

"Sure! That would be great," Eddie said eagerly.

"Very good. And now, I must get back to the laboratory building."

Eddie's face fell. He was disappointed that the encounter had been so brief.

Once again, the doctor looked cautiously around. Looking down at the boy, he said, "Could you do me a small favor, Eddie?"

"Sure. Be glad to."

Dr. Reiner looked around for the third time. Lowering his voice still more, he said, "I have a letter that needs to be mailed urgently. The mail here in the compound is very slow. Could you throw this envelope into a mailbox in town?"

"Of course!" Eddie said. "Why not?"

The doctor took an envelope out of his pocket. It bore a number of stamps.

"It's a letter to my cousin in Zurich," he said. "That's a city in Switzerland. Have you ever heard of it?"

"Yes. They make watches there. The principal of my school, Mr. Gardner, has a real Swiss watch."

"My cousin has a watch factory," Dr. Reiner told him. "If you mail the letter for me, I will ask my cousin to send a watch for you."

Zurich, Switzerland — 5726 / 1966

Marta Stravinski waited until there were no customers in the store. She opened her telephone book. Under the name "Svetlana" was listed the number of the Soviet Embassy in Zurich. She dialed the number and asked for Igor.

This time, a woman answered the call. "You can speak with me," she said, when Marta asked for Igor again. "Igor isn't here at the moment."

"Please tell him that a letter has come to Post Office Box 1766," Marta said.

The woman at the embassy froze in momentary astonishment. Then, recovering from her surprise, she said, "Someone will come at once."

A quarter of an hour later, a diplomatic car pulled up in front of the shop. Marta looked at it apprehensively. The entire procedure was different this time. The car's doors opened and an elderly woman alighted, accompanied by two bodyguards. Her cold eyes were devoid of the slightest spark of emotion.

"You are the one who phoned for Igor?" she asked abruptly as soon as she entered the shop.

"Yes. Here's the letter." Marta held out the envelope that had arrived that morning.

"Thank you." The woman turned around and left, followed by her two faithful guards.

The woman slit open the envelope as soon as she was back in the car and read the letter. The call from the owner of the fine-porcelain store had surprised her. Until now, all mail that had come to the post-office box had been intended merely to ensure that the system was working. All the letters, for the past 21 years, had been sent from Soviet embassies in various European capitals. But no instructions had been issued for a letter to be sent today. For the first time, the stamps on the envelope were

American. This could mean only one thing: the purpose of the box had been fulfilled. Heinrich von Reiner had finally made contact.

The moment the car entered the Soviet Embassy compound, the woman hurried into her office. She told her assistant to call General Sergei Petroshov immediately. She would tell the general the good news over the phone, and send the letter to Moscow via diplomatic courier.

She looked again at the page that had been tucked into the envelope. The message was clever. If it fell into the wrong hands, it would look like a simple, friendly message to a relative.

The page held only a few sentences:

> To my dear cousin, Sergei,
> Greetings! Do you still miss me? I am working hard. Perhaps, in the near future, I may be able to send you a small gift.
>
> Heinrich
> Grayston, Texas

The call reached KGB headquarters in Moscow at a late hour of the evening. "Zurich Embassy, calling General Sergei Petroshov."

The Moscow operator said that the general had already left for the night. Upon being told that the matter was urgent, the operator transferred the call to Petroshov's home.

General Sergei Petroshov was approaching his sixty-fifth birthday. He had survived the numerous changes of leadership in his country, and — unlike some of his colleagues, who had ended their careers facing a firing squad or doing hard labor in Siberia — he was about to retire with honor. Years ago he had given up his dream of heading the KGB, but he had no reason to complain. He lived in a multistory building designated for senior academics and military personnel near Taganka Square, several hundred meters from the Kremlin. His wife did not have to stand in line for a loaf of bread or a kilo of potatoes, and his daughters had been accepted into the musical academy without taking entrance examinations. The Soviet government knew how to reward its faithful with a lavish hand.

The house was quiet. The general's wife set out his usual dinner, reminiscent of his peasant background: black bread, boiled potatoes, Russian sausage, and a bottle of vodka. Sergei Petroshov ate in brooding silence. For the past week, he had been meeting with the young officer who was slated to replace him. Ilya Orchenko was considered a rising star in the

KBG training academy. The general was ordered to instruct the younger man and introduce him to the various matters under his jurisdiction. He felt as if he were attending his own funeral and being asked to provide the eulogy.

He had informed Ilya about all the important operations he had conducted in the decades he had served, about the spies he had planted, and about the spies he had apprehended. He felt as though his life were passing before his eyes — as though it were all happening on a stage. When he retired in a few weeks' time, the curtain would come down with finality. Getting old was a sad thing. It was sad to be discarded in favor of other, younger men — but that was the way of the world. He had served the Party with all his heart. Though he had witnessed his beloved country undergoing fluctuations and revolutions, he had always, always been a faithful son to Mother Russia.

A call transferred to his home from KGB headquarters was a not infrequent occurrence, but when the general heard that this particular call had originated in Zurich, his heart missed a beat.

His conversation with the woman at the Zurich embassy lasted less than a minute, but it left the general feeling twenty-five years younger. His fatigue vanished in an instant. The blood began flowing vigorously through his veins again.

"I'm going back to headquarters," he told his wife.

His wife nodded in resignation, as she had been doing for the past forty years.

The general donned his coat and rode the creaky elevator down to street level. He strode briskly toward Dzerzhinsky Square, his heart swelling in excitement. The seeds he had planted a quarter-century ago had begun to bear fruit. Decades of patience and diligence were beginning to prove themselves. This would be a marvelous going-away gift before his retirement.

In sharing the details of his career with the young officer who was to replace him, Petroshov had found himself recalling incidents long forgotten. The incident concerning Heinrich von Reiner, however, had required no prompting. He remembered every detail: In the year 1944, near the end of the Second World War, Stalin had ordered the capture of a brilliant young Nazi scientist by the name of Heinrich von Reiner. In 1945, with Germany floundering and near defeat, the scientist had vanished as though swallowed by the earth. Only nine years later, in 1954, had their mole in Washington, Black Sheep, stunned the KGB leadership with his report that Heinrich von Reiner had not died, but was alive and well in the United States. The Nazi scientist was working for the Americans in a secret complex that had been built near a small Texas town on the Mexican border.

Three years later, in 1957, Black Sheep had reported that von Reiner had developed an unprecedented biological weapon known by its code name, "Mexico A." General Petroshov could recite by heart the spine-tingling message that had been passed on, word for word, to Nikita Khrushchev, the Soviet leader at the time, and to the entire Politburo: *"It is a long-lived airborne fever virus, which penetrates through the respiratory tract. The virus causes immediate illness and leads to death within 24 to 72 hours. The death rate is nearly 100 percent. We surmise that this is a virus that began to be developed in Germany via experiments on Jewish subjects in labor camps, as well as on prisoners of war. Experimental subjects in the final stages were Indian tribes in the jungles of Mexico, near the city of Juarez. Unconfirmed rumor has it that Von Reiner is developing a second version of the virus, code-named 'Mexico B.' While its characteristics are still unknown, it is said to be both more sophisticated and more controllable than its predecessor."*

In the year 1965 — eight years after this report — Black Sheep succeeded in making first contact with Heinrich von Reiner at a conference of Department of Defense officials and the Grayston contingent. He told von Reiner that General Petroshov was still waiting, and reported that, in his estimation, the scientist had understood the message. A year had passed since then — a year in which Black Sheep had been exposed by the CIA and chose suicide rather than interrogation and standing trial.

And now, all the effort was bearing fruit. Heinrich von Reiner had sent a letter to the post-office box in Zurich, in which he had stated that he wanted to give his cousin Sergei "a small gift" ....

When the general returned home in the early hours of the morning, his wife nearly didn't recognize him. It was impossible to tell that he had just spent the entire night working. The sad, brooding man had disappeared, replaced by one who was alert and energetic. The sparkle had returned to his eye.

"Find me a suitcase," he requested.

"A suitcase?" she repeated, astonished.

"Certainly. A suitcase!" he said blithely.

His bewildered wife took a suitcase down from the top shelf of their big closet. It had been years since the general had last traveled. Once it had been a common occurrence. He would come home, sometimes in the middle of the day, and ask her to pack his bag. She would cram a suitcase with clothes and some good Russian food, and he would fly off to some corner of the world on one of his secret missions.

"I'm going to Mexico," the general told his wife. "I'll try to bring back something nice for you."

"Have a pleasant trip," she said, swallowing her surprise. They had been married more than forty years, and this was the first time he had told her where he was going.

At 10 a.m., General Petroshov drove to Moscow's Sheremetyevo Airport. Ilya Orchenko, the man he was training to replace him, would be waiting for him there. Together they would fly to Mexico City and from there to Juarez, the Mexican city closest to Grayston, Texas. It would be an opportunity to show the young officer how an operation was conducted on the ground. An opportunity to prove to the younger generation that the older one was still worth something.

General Sergei Petroshov, and none other, would bring Heinrich von Reiner's "small gift" home to the Soviet Union: a resounding final chord in the symphony of an illustrious career.

On the other side of the world, in America, R' Tzvi Hirsch HaLevi, faithful fund-raiser for the Tzidkas Yerushalayim kollel, was traveling toward Grayston.

He was finding the journey particularly arduous. For weeks, he had been crisscrossing the country, from New York to San Francisco and from Chicago to Los Angeles. It had been a successful trip. He had raised a respectable sum of money and sent it to Israel. Near the end of his tour, R' Tzvi Hirsch planned to take the train to Dallas, Texas, where the kollel had several benefactors, and then head for the remote town of Grayston to see what he could learn about their longtime supporter, R' Shmuel Levinger. Was the man no longer alive? In that case, he must find out the date of the *yahrzeit* so that the kollel members could mark it in perpetuity.

Or perhaps Levinger was still alive in a hospital or a nursing home somewhere. If that were the case, R' Tzvi Hirsch would pay him a visit and see how he was faring.

A third trip to Grayston was also being planned — this one from Washington, D.C. One day recently, Colin Baron had walked into the compound's cafeteria and officially announced what rumor had been claiming for some time: in just three weeks' time, a CIA assistant director was planning to pay a visit.

The level of activity within the compound's walls accelerated. There was a feverish burst of cleaning and beautification. Steven Chambers and the other gardeners worked overtime, painting buildings, pruning trees, repairing fences, and clearing away what minimal litter could be found. The landing strip was widened; at one end a large, square open area was paved, with a narrow road leading from it directly to the complex's central laboratory building.

An advance CIA contingent arrived from Washington, along with a large official car. Lengthy meetings were held with Colin Baron and his staff, deciding where the military honor guard would be positioned, where to place the speaker's podium, and where the workers and locals would be permitted to gather.

The drummer with the balding head and luxurious mustache told his fellow band members that the project commander had decided that they were to play the national anthem along with three other songs: "The Lonely Foal," "Look up to America's Skies," and "The United Way" — all of them, of course, melodies with no political overtones.

Like everyone else, Dr. Henry Reiner — who had privately reverted to thinking of himself by his original name, Heinrich von Reiner — was excited about the chief's upcoming visit. He hoped with all his heart that his efforts had not been in vain: that General Petroshov still worked for the KGB, that the post-office box whose number he had been given twice in the past twenty years was still active — and, most of all, that the Russian general would manage to contact him sometime in the next three weeks, prior to the CIA director's arrival.

R' Tzvi Hirsch HaLevi's arrival at the Grayston train station attracted a great deal of attention.

The time was past when the place was so isolated that any strange face created a stir of excitement. The construction of the government complex had led to rapid development and had turned Grayston into a hive of activity. The train depot, which had once been little more than a wooden shack beside the railroad track, was now a proper stone building, and even boasted a hotel: Norman Chambers, owner of the bakery, had added two stories to the station building, thereby providing ten guest rooms. Nevertheless, no one in Grayston had ever laid eyes on someone like *this*.

Passersby stared at the fund-raiser from Jerusalem in open amazement. What was he, exactly? He was not a priest, nor a cattleman, nor a bureaucrat. He bore a vague resemblance to the Amish, in his long black coat tied with a silken sash and the low, broad-brimmed black velvet hat worn over a white-bearded face.

For his part, R' Tzvi Hirsch took stock of his surroundings. Noticing a number of people seated around a table at the corner, he approached them. This was the bakery. On sunny days, Norman Chambers placed two or three tables on the pavement, and customers could order coffee and cake, a milk shake, or cold lemonade. Mornings found the city's old-timers gathered here, discussing town business.

This group, dubbed the "Grayston Senate," included Tall Willy; Dennis Half-Tooth and his handicapped brother, Jack; Bobby Follett from the ranch up the river; and Jack Abrams, pensioned from his long-held position as the town sheriff. Their ranches were now run by their sons or sons-in-law, or leased to oil companies in exchange for a percentage of the profits on each barrel of oil that issued from the ground. The group spent the morning hours drinking coffee, chewing tobacco, gossiping about the latest community news, and bemoaning days gone by.

Not infrequently, the "Grayston Senate" served as an informal information center. Its strategic location, in front of the bakery and near the railroad station, brought any traveler in need of directions right to that knot of old-timers. They would explain how to reach his destination and, in exchange, be the first to know what was happening in the neighborhood. They turned their heads now toward the outlandish-looking newcomer slowly approaching them.

"He looks like a holy man," Bobby Follett whispered. He was an ardent Christian who never missed a Sunday service. "Could they have sent us a new priest?"

"He's a rabbi," Jack Abrams declared, sitting up excitedly.

"Rabbi?" Tall Willy repeated in surprise. He knew the "Chief Rabbi" of Grayston, rotund and energetic — that ludicrous figure who served as *mohel*-cum-*chazzan*-cum-funeral director. This fellow didn't look much like him, but if the sheriff said so, he should know. Everyone knew that Jack Abrams was a Jew.

The aging sheriff stood up. He didn't remember much from his distant childhood, but he still knew how to introduce himself to a fellow Jew.

"*Shalom aleichem*," he said, sticking out his hand.

R' Tzvi Hirsch's face lit up. To meet a Jew the moment he came into town — what *siyata d'shmaya*!

"*Aleichem shalom*," he replied. "*Vus macht ah Yid?*"

Though the sheriff did not speak Yiddish, he recognized the word *"Yid"* and nodded eagerly. "I *Yid*. I *Yid!*"

"What is your name?" R' Tzvi Hirsch asked, switching to English. He was a generations-old Yerushalmi, but when he undertook to travel the world on behalf of the kollel he had studied English with Dr. Brandhoffer, the veteran language teacher at the high school. Dr. Brandhoffer, an observant Jew of German extraction, had been astounded at his elderly student's quick grasp. Over the course of a number of lessons, R' Tzvi Hirsch learned the English alphabet and rules of grammar. Then, using a dictionary, he began teaching himself words. Within an astonishingly short time he was able to speak the language passably well.

"My name is Jack Abrams," the old sheriff said. His Jewish name, he added, was Yaakov Abramson. His father, Yoel Zev Abramson, had come to America from White Russia. He was buried right here in town, and there was *Magen David* on his tombstone.

"I have three sons," the sheriff ended proudly. "All of them had Jewish circumcisions."

R' Tzvi Hirsch listened with interest, but his heart constricted in pain. *Oy, oy, oy, how deep is the galus .... How far Your children have wandered ....* This Jew, standing before him now, looked indistinguishable from his gentile friends. Had he ever donned a pair of *tefillin*? Did he know what Shabbos was? Had he ever *davened*, even once in his life?

And yet, the Jewish spark was still there. It had not been extinguished. He had introduced his sons into the covenant of Avraham Avinu, he had given his father a Jewish burial — and how happy he was to see a fellow Jew! How eagerly he had spoken those two words, perhaps the only two that he knew in the Holy Tongue: *"Shalom Aleichem ...."*

"How can I help you, rabbi?" asked the elderly sheriff.

"I'm looking for a Jew by the name of Shmuel Levinger," said R' Tzvi Hirsch. "I don't know if he's still alive, but he used to live in Grayston."

"Shmuel Levinger?" the other men repeated, shaking their heads. They didn't know anyone by that name.

"He means Sam," the sheriff said suddenly. "Sam Lowinger."

The others sighed, and shook their heads again, sadly this time.

"Do you know him?" R' Tzvi Hirsch asked. "Is he still alive?"

"What can I say, Rabbi?" the old sheriff said. "He's alive — but very sick. He's completely senile. It's impossible to talk to him."

R' Tzvi Hirsch's expression was sorrowful. "Where does he live?"

"Just opposite my house," Tall Willy said. "Right near the compound."

The sheriff shot the rancher a scornful look. What a fool! As though the rabbi, here in town for no more than a few minutes, would know what he was talking about.

"If you want, Rabbi, I can take you there," Abrams offered.

"I thank you for that, very much," the *meshulach* from Jerusalem said with a smile.

The former sheriff still drove his old Chevy, though the five-pointed white star had long since faded from its doors. He rapidly left the town behind, taking the road that led to the ranch. The road, normally quiet and nearly deserted, bustled now with preparations for the official visit. CIA vehicles drove back and forth, bearing men in dark suits and sunglasses to and from the compound.

Grayston's current sheriff drove by. Jack Abrams beeped "hello" with a sense of bitterness. The entire district was in a frenzy over the upcoming visit, but he was a pensioner now, out of the loop. Once, he had controlled the whole area; now he sat with his old friends, gossiping outside the bakery. Yes, those were the days ....

Back then, he had had power and had known how to use it. Maybe he hadn't always done the right thing. As far as the government complex was concerned, he had to admit that his darkest fears had not materialized. The place had become a simple fact in their lives, and a number of young people from the town were employed there.

"Does Shmuel have any children?" R' Tzvi Hirsch asked, rousing the sheriff from his thoughts.

"No," Abrams said. "He has a nephew who lives with him. His name's Ben. Ben Lowinger."

Binyamin Levinger, R' Tzvi Hirsch said to himself. He knew that a nephew by that name had traveled across the ocean to visit his uncle many years before.

"And what does Ben do?"

The sheriff chuckled uncomfortably. "Well, one thing's for sure: He's no rabbi. He tells me that, back in Jerusalem, he used to wear a long black coat, like yours." He gestured at the fundraiser. "Here, though, he looks just like everyone else."

"What does he do? How does he earn a living?"

"He managed his uncle's ranch until Sam got sick. Then he sold it. Rumor has it that he's still living on the money from that sale. I'll tell you the truth, rabbi — Ben is not so well thought of around these parts. He hasn't given Jews a good name."

"Is he married? Does he have children?"

"Yes, sure. He has two boys."

"And his wife's name is Devorah?"

"Oh, no. Devorah died many years ago. Today, Ben's married to a woman named Barbara. His older son is from his first wife, and the younger boy's from the second."

"Is she ... Jewish?"

"I'm sorry, rabbi. But she isn't."

R' Tzvi Hirsch stifled the heartbroken groan that rose up in his throat. How could a son of Yerushalayim have sunk so low as to marry a gentile woman? *Ribono shel Olam!*

The sheriff's car approached the ranch house. A huge tarpaulin tent stretched along the side of the road, near the house. This was advance headquarters for all branches of security. Dozens of CIA agents were scurrying around, making their final preparations. Two deputy sheriffs sat in their cars, ready to lend a hand where needed. CIA agents in tailored suits clustered around someone who seemed to be a senior official, listening intently as instructions were issued. Off to one side stood a stretch limousine, ready to transport the guest of honor. United States flags waved and fluttered in every available breeze. The open area in front of the compound gates sparkled with cleanliness.

The sheriff parked near the small square in front of the Lowinger house. "This is where Sam lives," he said, pointing at the house.

R' Tzvi Hirsch lifted his suitcase and prepared to exit the car. Suddenly, Jack Abrams looked at him with concern. He knew how much Ben Lowinger hated his Jewish past, and with what disdain he talked about the people of Jerusalem. Once, seeing a picture of a rabbi dressed the way this man was dressed, Ben had torn it up in a rage. Abrams couldn't let this rabbi go in there on his own. If Ben was at home, the encounter would not end peacefully. Ben would lose control — and then anything could happen. The sheriff shook his head with determination. He simply could not let the rabbi go in there alone.

"Rabbi," he said, "it may be a good idea for me to go in with you. Come to think of it, it's been a while since I've been over to see Sam."

Dr. Heinrich von Reiner completed his day's work in the laboratory building and walked slowly home. He planned to take Rudy for a walk and then listen to a new recording of classical music that he had ordered from Germany.

As he walked up the path to his house, he noticed something tucked under his door. He came a little closer. It was the edge of an envelope. Someone had pushed an envelope under the door of his home. Had his experiment succeeded? Was the post-office box in Zurich still active? Had General Petroshov sent a reply?

Reluctant to bend down and pick up the envelope for fear that he might be observed, he kicked it gently into the house and closed the door behind him. He quickly toured the small house, checking to see that no window was open and no uninvited visitors were present. Only then did he return to the door and pick up the envelope.

It contained a single page, bearing a few simple words:

What do you propose? What do you want?

Your cousin, Sergei

Von Reiner did not hesitate. For a fleeting instant, he wondered if this were a trap. Perhaps the Soviet general's letter had somehow been intercepted, and the CIA was trying to catch him in the act.

He didn't care. He had already made his decision. His life was forfeit in any case. He would try, at least, to end it with a resounding act of vengeance against America.

The scientist did not give much thought to the question of how the envelope had come to be under his door, or how the Soviet intelligence establishment had managed to plant an agent in the most secret compound in the country. Turning over the page, he wrote on the back:

I have someone who will be able to smuggle a vial out of the compound tomorrow or the next day. After that, you're on your own.

He returned the page to its envelope, which he replaced under the door, leaving one edge visible. Then he left the house and walked his dog through the compound. He ambled slowly around the cultural center and the helicopter hangar. In the distance, he observed the bustle in preparation for the official visit, but he preferred not to go too near. On his return home forty minutes later, the envelope was gone.

So, someone *had* been watching him. Someone had taken the envelope. His answer was now wending its way back to General Sergei Petroshov.

Near dusk, Steven Chambers passed through the compound gates. The security check he underwent was far more rigorous than usual. Steven was planning to stop in at the bakery to celebrate his successful day with a couple of donuts. The gardening crew had been working at full throttle, but that was not the main reason for his celebration. That was reserved for his role as a secret agent.

Two days earlier, his handler had informed him that the complex's chief scientist, Dr. Henry Reiner, was under heavy suspicion of being a covert agent for the Soviet Union and of trying to find a way to pass samples to KGB agents sniffing around the place.

"The higher-ups have decided to run a loyalty test," the handler told Steven. "We're going to offer temptation in the form of a written message from General Sergei Petroshov, and see if the good doctor swallows the bait." Steven had taken a sheet of paper from the compound's administrative office, written what he was told to write, and pushed the envelope under the door of the scientist's home.

It turned out that the suspicion was well founded. Dr. Reiner had quickly replied to the message, writing, "*I have someone who will be able to smuggle a vial out of the compound tomorrow or the next day. After that, you're on your own.*"

Steven had reread this answer until he knew it by heart, and then destroyed the original. He must not take something like this out of the compound. With the stringent security at the gates, he couldn't take the chance. This evening, his handler was scheduled to speak to him; Steven would report that the suspicion of betrayal was true. Dr. Reiner had responded to the Soviets' overtures and had even offered to smuggle a vial out of the compound. The slimy Communist traitor ....

The bus to Grayston departed at last, weaving its way slowly among the myriad security vehicles. Steven sat in the last row, near the window. He was feeling very proud of himself. Finally, he was doing something real. For months, his orders had been merely to keep his eyes open and maintain a low profile. Now, for the first time, he had been handed a mission. He was filled with patriotic zeal, proud of being an American.

Observing the scores of CIA personnel, he smiled to himself. Soon he would be one of their number. His handler had said that, after he proved himself here, he would send him to a course for agents in New York. He was practically there already.

This evening, he would give his report on Dr. Henry Reiner, and await further instructions.

Even before he knocked on the door of the ranch house, the sheriff realized that his fears had been in vain. Ben's green truck was not parked in its usual place. Of course. Today was the day the yearly rodeo championships were held in Houston. Ben would never miss such an important event.

Manuela opened the door to their knocking. "Is anyone home?" the sheriff asked.

"No one," she answered, staring at R' Tzvi Hirsch with frightened eyes. "Mr. Ben, he go to Houston, and Miz Barbara, she is in the store."

The sheriff gestured at the man standing beside him. "This is a friend of Sam's," he said. "He's a rabbi. That's like a priest, but for Jews. He's come from a faraway land to visit Sam. Can we come in?"

"*Si, si*," the housekeeper said, moving aside.

R' Tzvi Hirsch and the aging sheriff entered the house, and Manuela showed them to a small room on the ground floor. Sam was resting in a tall bed with a railing around it. The sheriff, who had not been to see his old friend in some time, was shocked at the sight of him. Sam was alarmingly thin. His protruding ribs gave him a skeletal look. His eyes were glassy and unfocused. A line of drool oozed from his open mouth. Once, the sheriff remembered sadly, Sam would sit in his rocking chair, basking in the sun. Now, apparently, he did nothing but lie in bed and wait for the Angel of Death to come calling.

"I told you, Rabbi," he said. "There's no one to talk to anymore. Sam Lowinger is as good as dead."

R' Tzvi Hirsch stood at a distance from the bed, gazing at Sam in silence. Sam Lowinger might be dead, but Shmuel ben Reb Abraham Levinger was still alive. As long as he was breathing, there existed the possibility of repentance. Every moment that a Jew spent in this world was more precious than pearls.

"I'd like to say a few prayers with him," he told the sheriff. "It will take about half an hour. Can you stay that long?"

"What kind of prayers?" the sheriff asked with interest.

"When a Jew leave this world," R' Tzvi Hirsch explained, "his soul goes up to Heaven and gives an accounting for everything it did. Therefore, every Jew tries to render an accounting on his deathbed — to confess his sins and repent."

The sheriff pointed at Sam and grimaced sadly. "But look at him, Rabbi. He doesn't hear, he doesn't speak. He can't repent."

"Maybe the body doesn't hear," R' Tzvi Hirsch said. "But the soul can hear very well. I'll say the words for him, and even if he is unable to respond, his soul will surely hear me."

"Okay," the sheriff said in surprise. "I'll wait in the living room."

R' Tzvi Hirsch pulled a chair closer to the bed and sat down near Sam's head. This was the biggest favor, the most eternal kindness, that he could do for the kollel's benefactor who had given of his personal wealth to support the families of needy Torah students. Not every Jew had the merit of saying *viduy* before his death. Not everyone knew when his time would come. Who knew what merit Shmuel Levinger had? What great mitzvah he had done, to merit having someone come and recite *viduy* with him before he returned his soul to his Creator, here at the edge of the world ....

"*Modeh ani lefanecha* ... I acknowledge before You, Hashem my G-d and the G-d of my fathers, that my healing and my death are in Your Hands," R' Tzvi Hirsch began. "*Yehi ratzon milfanecha* ... May it be Your will that You grant me a full recovery. And if I were to die, Heaven forbid, let my death serve as an atonement for all the errors and sins and transgressions that I have transgressed and sinned before You ...."

The sheriff sat in the hallway, his mind in turmoil. He sensed that something exalted was taking place behind the closed door of Sam's room. Whatever it was, it drew him as though with enchanted ropes. He felt as if an enormous power uprooted him from the spot and carried him over to the closed door. He put his ear to the door and listened to R' Tzvi Hirsch's voice, coming through clearly from the other side. Though he didn't understand the words, the melody was both mesmerizing and heartrending. R' Tzvi Hirsch sighed from the depths of his heart, and began weeping softly. He paused for a moment, and then continued to recite in a plaintive voice.

To the sheriff, the words sounded like a jumble in an unknown tongue. But his soul heard, and his Jewish soul understood. The aging sheriff, who had for so long been the terror of Grayston — the granite man of the law who was afraid of no one — stood with his ear glued to the door and his eyes inexplicably welling with tears.

Manuela, emerging from the kitchen, stood transfixed in shock. She had never seen the sheriff in such a state. He leaned on the door of Sam's room, shoulders shaking as he wept. Feelings that had been buried beneath thick layers burst forth from him — hidden feelings that he had never even realized he had. He heaved and shook with harrowing sobs such as he had never cried before in his life.

R' Tzvi Hirsch spent the night in Norman Chambers' small hotel on Grayston's Main Street. A seasoned traveler, he had enough dried food with him to satisfy his modest needs, and his bag held all the *sefarim* he required. The long ocean voyage to America and the lengthy train rides crisscrossing the continent were for him a time of spiritual striving, for they left his days entirely free for Torah and *tefillah*. In a train packed with gentiles or on a ship crowded with strangers, he felt like an only son in *HaKadosh Baruch Hu's* household. The world around him might be filled with people who wasted their time with emptiness and vanity, but he used every minute to serve his Creator. In the heart of the ocean or at the edge of Texas, one could always learn another page of Gemara, finish *Sefer Tehillim* again, absorb a deep lesson from the *Zohar,* or sharpen his concentration in prayer ...,

He did not sleep on the bed, for fear of *shatnez*. This was his practice anywhere outside his home. He spread his own sheet on the wooden floor and lay there for the short time he devoted to sleep, his travel bag beneath his head to serve as a pillow.

The train that would take him to California — the next stop on his itinerary — was scheduled to pass through Grayston at two p.m. the following afternoon. The ticket was already in his wallet. But before he went, there were two things he had to do. The old sheriff had asked him to recite a few chapters of *Tehillim* and the *"Keil malei rachamim"* prayer beside the grave of his father, Joel W. Abrams — that is, Yoel Zev Abramson. Also, R' Tzvi Hirsch felt a need to return to Sam Lowinger's house and meet with Sam's nephew.

The sheriff had told him in no uncertain terms that he considered this a terrible idea. Not only was Ben very far from anything pertaining to his faith, the sheriff had said, he also hated and despised his Jewish brothers. But R' Tzvi Hirsch was adamant. He must try. He could not pass up this opportunity to try to influence a Jew to do *teshuvah*. After all, Binyamin, too, had a Jewish soul that had been carved from beneath the Throne of Glory. He, too, had stood at the foot of Har Sinai to receive the Torah. Who knew if R' Tzvi Hirsch would not manage to ignite the Jewish spark in Binyamin, buried so deeply inside? Hadn't Hashem promised that no one would be forgotten?

Had the sheriff been able to hear what was taking place in the Lowinger home that afternoon, he would surely have found a way to prevent the visitor from Jerusalem from returning there next day.

Poor Manuela was unprepared for Ben's outburst. He had actually returned home from Houston in a good mood. The horses he had bet on had won their races and his pockets were filled with his winnings. But when he heard about the rabbi from Jerusalem who had visited his home and prayed with Sam, he saw red. A wild expression crossed his face as he shot up furiously from his seat.

"Why did you let him in?" he screamed at the housekeeper. "Why do you allow strangers in here? I'm going to throw you back into that filthy country of yours!"

Manuela fled into the kitchen and burst into tears.

"Did he say he'd be back?" Ben shouted. "Is he coming back here?"

"I don't know," she managed to answer. "He didn't say."

Ben returned to the living room, still enraged. On the wall were mounted several old rifles. He took one of these down and propped it on a small table near the door.

"If he does come back, I'll shoot him right between the eyes," he announced. He shouted at Manuela, who stood tearful and afraid in the kitchen doorway, "And if you let him in, I'll kill both of you!"

Ben planted himself at the dining-room table. John and Eddie came down from the tower room and joined him. The housekeeper served a meal that was eaten mainly in silence.

"Why do you care so much about that rabbi?" John asked.

His father grabbed a newspaper that lay on the table, and rolled it in his hand. "Shut your mouth," he roared, and smacked the boy's head with the paper.

Juarez, Northern Mexico — 5726 / 1966

KGB General Sergei Petroshov and his young replacement, Ilya Orchenko, took up lodgings in a typical Mexican villa on the outskirts of Juarez. Both were tense and excited. The young officer was about to learn how his older, more experienced colleague functioned in the field, while General Petroshov felt that this was his last chance to fulfill a lifetime's mission.

In days — maybe even hours — he could take possession of the Mexico virus, the nightmare creation of the brilliant Nazi-American scientist, Dr. Heinrich von Reiner. In one fell swoop, he could shift the balance of power in favor of the Soviet Union.

The villa was a single-story house well past its prime, whose rooms were built around a central courtyard. This square space had a neglected look: Wild cactus grew within its bounds, several hens and a pompous peacock strutted freely about, and the small amount of water that remained in the ornamental pond in its center was covered with algae. From the outside, the house appeared equally neglected. The gate surrounding it was rusted and locked with an old metal chain. The front rooms, which could be seen from the street, contained dusty furniture and cracked windows.

The two rooms in the rear, however, were totally different. They had been scrupulously cleaned, their floors washed, and new office furniture introduced. The telephones and communications equipment in these rooms were sophisticated, the most advanced of their kind. Entrance to these rooms was from the villa's back door, through an empty lot piled with old cartons that had once housed various appliances. This door was well disguised to appear rusted and battered, but the key slipped into its lock with surprising ease and the hinges were oiled with regularity.

The many pedestrians who passed through the street each day had no idea that the neglected villa concealed one of the most important western bases of the KGB. It had been established several years earlier, after Black Sheep had reported that Dr. Heinrich von Reiner was living and working in the United States. For the KGB, this village was the closest they could get to Grayston, Texas. The villa was on the Mexican side of the border, outside American jurisdiction. Nevertheless, its distance to the secret American complex was no more than a few score kilometers.

The two KGB officers sat in one of these back rooms now. Facing them were a pair of Mexican policemen known only by their first names: Tomas and Leoro. This, of course, was not an official mission. The Mexican policemen had been secretly working hand in glove with the local KGB agent for several years, and charging an exorbitant fee for each mission — in American dollars.

The usual liaison man was not present at this meeting. He had contacted the two Mexicans some hours before, to inform them that two senior officials had come from Moscow for the express purpose of giving them an important mission. A mission for which they would receive more money than they had ever earned so far.

Tomas and Leoro duly arrived at the empty lot behind the villa, and entered quickly. The two KGB officials, the older and the younger, pored over maps with them and explained what they wanted. The mission did not appear too difficult or complicated. On the table rested a thick pile of dollars, which the Mexicans eyed greedily. The moment they returned with the goods, General Petroshov told them, the money was theirs.

■ ■ ■

On the American side of the border, the frenetic preparations for the official visit drew to a close. A tense, anticipatory silence descended on the compound. Everything was ready and waiting.

THE MEXICO FILE / 379

The band would have only two more rehearsals, the drummer announced. That day's rehearsal would take place at four p.m. in the cultural center; the next day, they would take part in a general rehearsal in the area where the CIA assistant director would be officially welcomed: the large auditorium in the laboratory building.

John and Eddie left home after their dismal mealtime, and hurried off in the direction of the compound. All the musicians were very excited, and Eddie was soon able to slip away to the scientist's house.

Dr. Reiner sat on the bench in his garden, as usual, his tall, thin dog beside him. Catching sight of Eddie, he breathed a sigh of relief. Everything was proceeding according to the plan he had outlined to General Petroshov's unseen messenger. He told Eddie that his cousin in Zurich had been in touch and had sent a genuine Swiss watch for Eddie.

"Really?" Eddie cried. "Thank you!"

"I don't have it with me," Dr. Reiner said. "Right now, it's with someone on the outside. He wasn't granted authorization to enter the gate because of this official visit."

"Can I go get it from him?" Eddie asked eagerly.

"Certainly," said the doctor. From his pocket he took an elongated object made of wood; it resembled a fat wooden pen. "If you're going to see him, please give this to him as well."

Eddie took the object and turned to go.

"Put it in your pocket," Dr. Reiner said in a slightly odd voice. "And be very careful. If it breaks, he won't give you the watch."

"Okay," Eddie said cheerfully, and started for the gate.

The wooden object was a simple protective container used for transporting ampoules and small vials. It was padded with cotton wool on the inside, to safeguard the fragile glass. Taking a sample of the virus from the laboratory building had proved extraordinarily simple. No one bothered to check the doctor as he left "Texas," as long as he remained within the compound. All he had to do now was watch to make sure that the boy got through the gates. Then his plan would be crowned with success. *Unbelievable how easy it all had been*, the scientist thought.

Eddie walked toward the gate with a light step. He wondered what kind of watch Dr. Reiner's cousin had sent him. He hoped it would have a small window that showed the date, like the one Mr. Gardner, his principal, wore to school.

A moment later, he glanced over his shoulder. Dr. Reiner had apparently decided to take his dog for a walk along the main road today. He walked slowly behind Eddie, never moving his eyes from the boy.

Eddie passed through the gate unchecked, as usual. He stood outside for a few minutes, hands in his pockets, but saw no one waiting for him. He moved away from the compound's entrance, until he was standing in the clearing in front of his own house. A car was parked there. Two friendly looking Mexicans were seated in it.

The man beside the driver called out to him. "Hey, Eddie."

Eddie approached the car. Someone, a third passenger, was hunched down in the back seat. Eddie couldn't see him, but his hair was fair.

The Mexican gave him a broad smile. "How are you?"

Eddie shrugged, hands still in his pockets.

"You have something for me from the doctor, right?" the Mexican asked. So the man had been sent here by Dr. Reiner's cousin in Switzerland.

"Yes," Eddie said, and took out the wooden container that Dr. Reiner had given him. He handed it to the Mexican, who took it gingerly.

"Thanks a lot," the Mexican said, his smile growing even broader.

"So where's the watch?" Eddie asked. But the car had already erupted into motion and was speeding away.

Eddie stood rooted on the spot, stunned and disappointed. The smiling Mexican had run away with his watch! He should have demanded it first, he thought, before handing over what the doctor had given him.

Tomas and Leoro's car crossed the U.S.–Mexican border with ease. The two Mexican policemen were wearing civilian clothing, and the third passenger, the blond American, aroused no suspicion either. They drove to Juarez, and soon reached the mysterious villa in the neglected lot.

Ilya Orchenko opened the door for them. The Mexicans entered, one of them grasping the wooden container. The American looked around in wonder. Suspicion began to cloud his eyes. The writing on all the wall maps was in Russian. Nor did the two men waiting in the room look particularly American. What was going on here?

He was a CIA agent in the midst of carrying out a mission — but it looked as if he had stumbled onto a Soviet base. Where was his handler? He had been told to enable the scientist to smuggle out the virus so that he could testify against him in court. So who were these two Russians? And what role did the two Mexicans have in all of this?

Sergei Petroshov did not give him much time to wonder. He signaled the pair of policemen with his eyes. Before the confused young American knew what was happening, the Mexicans had grabbed him and taken him out to the courtyard.

A single gunshot rang out, followed by the splash of a body falling into the nearly empty pool. A smile touched Petroshov's lips. Their first problem had just been solved.

He opened a drawer. There were two pistols inside. *Go outside*, he motioned to his young colleague. *Get rid of them.*

Ilya Orchenko threw a startled glance at the General. Kill the two Mexicans? Ah ... disposing of the witnesses .... But Orchenko didn't move quickly enough to satisfy his superior officer.

Sergei Petroshov snorted with disdain. These spoiled young men. Today's KGB officers had no spine ....

He went outside with a pistol in either hand, and returned two gunshots and thirty seconds later.

"Get the lab people over here," he told his young colleague calmly, his glance falling with satisfaction on the wooden container on the table.

With shaking hands, Ilya Orchenko dialed the number written on a sheet of paper. Within minutes, two Russian lab workers arrived from a nearby house and proceeded to deal with Dr. Heinrich von Reiner's little package. All their equipment was ready for them in the next room. A sophisticated laboratory had been waiting a full six years for the day that the Soviet Union would succeed in laying its hands on one of the products of the secret military complex across the border.

"And now, order the plane," Petroshov told Orchenko.

The General made the return trip to the Soviet Union in a military plane that the KGB had made available to him. Along with the two pilots, the passengers included two lab technicians whose job was to meticulously safeguard the virus sample until it reached its destination: Bacteria Institute #16, the Lenin Briga, where the Soviet Union kept and developed its weapons of biological warfare.

Sergei Petroshov sat on the hard military seat, looking out the window at the blue sky and sipping vodka from a small bottle that his wife had packed in his suitcase. He was happy and satisfied. He still had what it took. Sergei Petroshov still knew his job. The corpses he had left behind had not shaken him. Over the course of his years with the KGB he had initiated the death of many people, to the point where death no longer moved him.

The pool in the courtyard of the Juarez villa now held two Mexican policemen and the naive young American — one of the gardening staff at the compound who, until the last second, had believed he was working for the CIA. And behind Petroshov in the tail of the plane, in a wooden box, lay the body of young KGB officer Ilya Orchenko. He had been killed just before they left the secret house in Juarez, in an "unfortunate accident."

His body would return to the Soviet Union and be buried with honor, as befit a fine KGB officer who had fallen in the line of duty. His family would receive full compensation as provided by the law. To have let him live would have been too dangerous. Every additional person who knew that the Soviet Union was now in possession of the "Mexico virus" constituted a threat to the State's welfare.

44

The next morning, the aging sheriff came to take the Yerushalmi fund-raiser from his hotel. From there, they went directly to the Grayston cemetery to pay a visit to Abram's father's grave.

R' Tzvi Hirsch's heart pained him when he realized that this was a Christian cemetery. The only sign of the sheriff's father's Jewishness was the *Magen David* on his tombstone and the name Yoel Zev Abramson engraved on the marble in Hebrew letters. R' Tzvi Hirsch recited a few chapters of *Tehillim* at the gravesite and then a fervent "*Keil Malei Rachamim*."

Afterward, he visited the graves of several other Jews who were buried in the cemetery — among them, the simple resting place of Devorah Levinger, Binyamin's first wife.

It was nearing ten-thirty when the sheriff and R' Tzvi Hirsch drove back to the Lowinger house. When they were about one hundred yards from the place, soldiers stopped them and announced that the road was temporarily closed due to the impending official visit. Nor were they permitted to continue on foot. If they wished to reach the ranch house, they must wait patiently in the car.

R' Tzvi Hirsch told the sheriff that he could go about his business, but Abrams replied that he would wait with him until the visit was over and then escort him to the train station. The green truck, the sheriff saw, was parked near the house. He was afraid to leave R' Tzvi Hirsch alone with a hostile Ben.

There was also another reason for his decision: The sheriff was immensely enjoying every minute spent in the company of this guest from Jerusalem. Thirstily he drank in the rabbi's every word, as R' Tzvi Hirsch explained some basic concepts in Judaism: There is a Creator Who made the world and Who keeps it running from minute to minute, He gave us a Torah that teaches us how to live, there are 613 *mitzvos*, prayer, faith, and the expectation of ultimate redemption. R' Tzvi Hirsch promised to send him books about Judaism and an English-language *siddur*, but the sheriff insisted on hearing more and more from the rabbi's own lips.

There was a great deal of movement on the road ahead of them. The official car was driven into the compound proper, along with equipment and additional cars for the staff members. From the window of their car, the sheriff and R' Tzvi Hirsch could see the ranch house, low and broad, flanked by its two towers.

Suddenly, the front door opened. The sheriff tensed — until he saw John and Eddie. They walked the length of the porch, making for the compound gate.

"Those are Ben Lowinger's two sons," the sheriff said.

R' Tzvi Hirsch looked, and his heart constricted.

"The darker one is the first wife's child," the sheriff said. "He's quieter and more gentle. The blond kid — the present wife's son — is a real wild one."

"*Ai, ai, ai!*" A deep sigh burst from R' Tzvi Hirsch's aching heart. A lost and unfortunate Jewish soul. A Jewish boy who probably didn't even know he was Jewish. And his brother was no less unfortunate. He had a Jewish father, but was a complete gentile.

"What are their names?" he asked.

"The older one is called John," the sheriff said. Suddenly, he remembered. "By the way, it was old Sam who insisted on having a circumcision ceremony for him. The boy's father wasn't interested ...."

R' Tzvi Hirsch sighed again. He realized that his conversation with Binyamin was not going to be easy. Nevertheless, he was committed to trying.

"The other one's Eddie," the sheriff added.

Inside the house sat Ben, wreathed in alcoholic fumes. He toyed with the hunting rifle on the table in front of him. He was waiting. If that accursed rabbi showed his face here again — if he tried to come back and visit Sam — he, Ben, would deal with him the way you dealt with any intruder in Texas ....

For the first time in history, John and Eddie were stopped at the gate. The CIA agents had taken charge of the entrance, as they had done of the entire compound, and they shouted at the two boys marching right past the security booth.

The regular guards hastened to explain that the boys played in the compound's orchestra and had come for the big general rehearsal. The men in the crisp suits and sunglasses relaxed their stance, but John and Eddie were still subjected to a search — another first for them. One of the agents opened John's saxophone case and his folder of music. Only when it had been established beyond all shadow of a doubt that the Lowinger boys were not plotting an attack were they permitted to enter the compound.

John was dressed in his best and extremely excited. At only thirteen, he was slated to play before an important government official. Christopher, his saxophone teacher, told him that the most exalted personage he had ever played for had been the governor of Texas.

Eddie was excited, too, but for a different reason. This was the first time that he would be entering the "Texas" building in an open and aboveboard manner — the building with the laboratories, so securely guarded that only a privileged few were permitted to walk inside.

He was not only excited; he was angry. Eddie couldn't wait to meet Dr. Reiner again and give him a piece of his mind. This wasn't right. It wasn't fair. That messenger, the smiling Mexican, had taken the wooden container from Eddie and then fled before giving Eddie his promised Swiss watch. Did Dr. Reiner think he could treat him this way? Just because he was a kid, was it right to promise something and then not deliver it? If Dr. Henry Reiner thought so, then he didn't know Eddie Lowinger very well. A deal was a deal. Dr. Reiner owed him one Swiss watch. If not — he would pay the price.

Andrew, the trumpet-playing soldier, was waiting for them beside the door of the laboratory building. He wore his dress uniform and looked more solemn and more excited than the boys had ever seen him. He hung special passes around their necks to show that they were authorized to enter the restricted area on this single occasion, and ushered them into the building.

Eddie looked around with interest. Though no one knew it, he was already quite familiar with this building — from the outside. He knew that it held a well-stocked menagerie, including dogs, monkeys, and mice; that medical experiments took place on the lab animals; that there were rows upon rows of rooms containing refrigerators filled with poisonous substances. This was the first time that he was seeing the place from the inside, and he had to admit that it looked like any ordinary building.

The front door opened onto a small lobby with staircases on either side. John and Eddie followed Andrew one flight down. Here, too, they saw corridors branching off on both sides. They turned left, and after a short walk reached a large festooned auditorium filled with rows of chairs. At the front of the auditorium was a stage draped with American flags, a speaker's podium positioned in its center. The band was already waiting at one side of the stage. The musicians greeted John and Andrew enthusiastically.

"Let's go, let's go!" cried the drummer. He, too, was wearing his dress uniform, and for the first time Eddie realized that he was a fairly high-ranking officer. There were stripes on his shoulders and numerous medals on his uniform.

John climbed onto the stage, while Eddie took a seat in one of the back rows, near the door. He kept an eye on the hallway, and was relieved to see no one pass by for five whole minutes. That was a good sign. His sense of direction told him that Dr. Reiner's office was on this floor, but on the other side of the building. To find him, Eddie would have to return to the stairs and continue down the entire length of the corridor.

A CIA agent sat in the last row. He was very impressive in his crisp suit and crew cut, though his eyes looked tired. His head kept falling forward onto his chest and then jerking up again. The waking moments were becoming fewer and farther between.

John and his fellow musicians began their rehearsal. After two or three songs, when everyone was completely focused on the music, Eddie slipped out of the auditorium. No one — including the dozing agent — saw him go.

The corridor was deserted. Eddie walked quietly, very conscious that he, an eleven-year-old boy, was in the most securely guarded place in the country. If anyone caught him, he thought, he would say that he was looking for the bathroom. He passed the staircase and continued down a long hall with numbers on the doors. One door was wide open. It was one of the refrigerator rooms, completely empty now. The many vials that had filled the appliances were gone.

Finally, on the door of the last room, he saw a sign that read, "Dr. Henry Reiner." Eddie clenched his fists and set his jaw tensely. Here he was, that thieving scientist who promised Swiss watches and then didn't deliver.

He looked around. There was no one in the hall. Placing his hand on the doorknob, he twisted it cautiously. His heart skipped a beat as he realized that the door wasn't locked.

Without hesitation, he pushed the door slowly. It moved silently on its hinges and began to open.

Meanwhile, the sheriff and R' Tzvi Hirsch sat patiently in the sheriff's car. It was eleven a.m.; there was still plenty of time before the train was due to depart from the Grayston station. A quarter-hour later, the roadblock was finally lifted. The sheriff drove up and parked in the clearing in front of the house, behind Ben's green pickup.

"Rabbi, I'll wait here," he said. "Afterward, I'll take you to your train."

"I thank you very much," said R' Tzvi Hirsch.

The Yerushalmi *meshulach* got out of the car and slowly approached the house. His lips moved in silent supplication to Hashem, asking for success in his endeavor. The sheriff watched him, heart pounding.

R' Tzvi Hirsch climbed the three steps to the porch and knocked on the front door.

The door was opened by Manuela. Seeing him, she panicked and tried to shut the door in his face. "Mister, get away from here," she said, waving her hands. "Mr. Ben, he is very angry. Go from here. He will kill you!"

From his vantage point behind the wheel of his car, the sheriff saw that something was happening. He was about to get out when the front door burst open again and Ben's figure appeared behind Manuela. He was drunk — that much was easy to see at a glance.

R' Tzvi Hirsch retreated a step. The sheriff got out of his car and began running toward the ranch house. Then he saw the hunting rifle in Ben's hand.

Instinctively, his hand went to his hip. His gun! It wasn't in his belt! He'd left it in the car …. He whirled around and hurried back in the direction he had come. Behind his back, he heard Ben Lowinger bellow like a madman.

Eddie thrust his head into the room. Dr. Reiner was sitting at his desk in the center of the room, in the same position as Eddie had seen him when spying through the window: facing a typewriter and flanked by piles of typed pages. The room was very quiet. The doctor was not typing; he was absorbed in reading a thick book.

Eddie quickly scanned the room. Directly opposite him, in a spot that had been hidden from him at the window, was a long marble counter with a few pieces of laboratory equipment. Slender test tubes sat in a special holder. Nearby stood several bottles filled with various fluids. Under the counter was mounted a glass-fronted refrigerator containing a few small vials.

But he hadn't come here to look around, Eddie reminded himself. He was here to get what the scientist owed him.

He cleared his throat.

Dr. Reiner slowly raised his eyes from his book. When he saw who was standing there, his face registered alarm. "What are you doing here?" he blurted.

"I want my Swiss watch," Eddie said.

The doctor regarded him calmly, but his sharp scientist's mind was hard at work, rapidly assessing the situation. Something had gone wrong. This must be a CIA plot. Otherwise, how would the boy have gained entry here? Also, if General Petroshov of the KGB had been involved, the boy would no longer be among the living. Of that, Dr. Reiner had no doubt at all. He had heard a great deal about the general's ruthless efficiency. In all honesty, that was the real reason he had not responded to Petroshov's blandishments in the waning days of World War Two. The general would have brought him back to the Soviet Union, extracted the information he wanted, and disposed of him the minute he was no longer useful. Sergei Petroshov was not in the habit of leaving footprints behind.

So it had all been a clever American trap. The mention of General Petroshov had been nothing but bait. It had been the CIA that had left the envelope under his door — and now they had sent the boy to win an explicit confession from him. In the corridor, behind the door, were probably armed American security men, listening intently to every word.

Well, he would not give them what they wanted. He would not make their job easy for them. They were not going to hear a single admission from him.

"Boy, what are you doing here?" the scientist asked again, injecting surprise and anger into his voice.

"'Boy'?" Eddie jeered. "Suddenly you forgot my name?"

"What do you want?"

"I want my watch," Eddie said, raising his voice. "The Swiss watch that you promised me."

The boy's tone was something new to the scientist. Until now, Eddie had seemed like a harmless youngster. Suddenly, he was showing a new firmness and strength. Obviously, there was someone behind this. He was drawing confidence from the agents who had prompted him.

"I don't understand. What do you want?"

"You don't know what I want?" Eddie's face twisted with scorn. "That Mexican took what you sent with me, and then ran away without giving me my watch. And anyway ... what was that about? What did you give me to smuggle out? Maybe I should tell the army about it."

The scientist studied Eddie for a long moment. The boy was threatening him. Eddie was trying to get him to admit to smuggling out the vial. He had been well trained, this accursed young American.

"How did you get in here?" he asked, continuing the farce. "Children are not allowed to wander around this building."

"I already told you — my brother plays in the band," Eddie said angrily. "They're having their last rehearsal in the auditorium. But don't change the subject, and stop pretending that you don't know me!"

The scientist tilted his head. "I don't hear anything. Where is the band?"

Eddie listened, too. The band was not playing. Maybe they were taking a short break.

"They're rehearsing in the auditorium at the end of the hall," he said. "But, doctor, I'm in a hurry. Give me the watch and I'll leave. You used me to get that thing to the Mexicans, and you didn't pay me what you promised."

Dr. Reiner thought for a long moment. The picture was very clear. He had no choice.

"You know what?" he said finally. "I do have something for you. Wait here a moment."

He stood up and went to the marble counter beneath the window. Eddie waited. A few seconds later, the scientist turned to face Eddie. He had both hands behind his back and a mysterious smile on his face.

"Close your eyes and hold out your hands," he told the boy.

Eddie stood in the doorway, looking at the doctor suspiciously. Why couldn't he just give him the watch without all this fuss?

Dr. Reiner still had both hands behind his back. He walked slowly toward Eddie, stopping in the center of the room. "Boy, do you want the present or not?"

"'Boy'," Eddie repeated with disdain. "Are you really trying to tell me you don't recognize me? You know very well what my name is."

Dr. Reiner winced. The boy was trying to get him to admit that he knew him. In the corridor, past that door, waited all those American agents — quiet, tense, ready for action. They were waiting for the slightest utterance on his part, the smallest fragment of an admission that he knew the boy and had used him to smuggle something out of the compound. Then they would burst inside, grab him, and arrest him.

No, he wouldn't let them do that. He would attack them before they could fire off a single bullet. That would be his greatest revenge! His revenge against all of America, this despicable land of immigrants, swarming with Jews and blacks, this land that had destroyed his beloved Germany and degraded his homeland. It would be his vengeance for the freedom that had been stolen from him for decades, for his robbed name and identity, for his imprisonment behind tall walls of concrete.

The hatred that had been brewing inside him through the long years had intensified on the day Black Sheep had made contact with him in the

Department of Agriculture building in El Paso. Feelings of abasement, so long suppressed, had burst forth with renewed strength. The urge to give the virus to the Soviet Union was not derived from any love he bore toward the Russians or from any identification with the Communist ideal. It was solely from a desire to avenge himself on America.

The moment had come. Dr. Henry Reiner had died — and Dr. Heinrich von Reiner had returned from the dead to restore Nazi glory. He, a member of the exalted Aryan race, a loyal officer of the Third Reich, Nazi Germany's stellar scientist, would repay the United States as she deserved.

Eddie, in the doorway, turned his head and looked over his shoulder. The corridor was still deserted. John and his fellow musicians were still in the auditorium, the CIA man was probably still nodding in his chair. He looked back at Dr. Reiner, who was waiting for him to extend his hands.

Heinreich von Reiner saw Eddie glance over his shoulder. For him, this was the final proof that there was someone there, behind the boy, issuing instructions. He broke out in a cold sweat. He felt the adrenalin pour through his veins, filling him with courage. His heart thudded wildly.

Eddie held out his hands. "Okay, give me the watch," he said impatiently. "But I just want to say that I don't like this. You know my name very well. Now, suddenly, you're pretending that you never sent me out with something for those Mexicans."

The doctor's lips began to tremble. This was the moment of truth. It was now or never. If the agents sensed that the boy wasn't getting the job done, they would burst into the room — and then it would be too late. It was time to act.

He quickly drew his hands from behind his back.

Eddie just had time to think: *That's not a watch. It's a little glass bottle filled with liquid ....*

He tried to break away and run back to the door. But the doctor was too quick for him. In one rapid motion, he threw the contents of the vial directly at the boy.

"What are you doing?" Eddie sputtered in shock. His shirt was all wet. Some droplets had landed on his face, entering his mouth and nose.

Terrified, he looked up at the scientist. He didn't recognize the man. Dr. Reiner's face had twisted, distorted in sudden madness. His entire body shook and his hands were clenched into fists as he howled, "This is for all of you! This is for rotten America!"

He stood with both legs planted on the floor, his head raised and both arms spread wide. "Come in!" he screamed. "Come in and arrest me!"

The doctor's shouts could be heard throughout the floor. Jerking awake, the CIA agent sprinted from the auditorium, drawing his gun as he ran. All he saw was a young boy standing at the far end of the corridor. He was too far away for the agent to see that he was wet, but his posture unquestionably indicated that he was in distress.

Heinrich von Reiner suddenly fell silent. Nothing had happened. No team of American agents had burst into the room with weapons drawn. From elsewhere on the floor there erupted the melodic wail of a trumpet. He froze in place as the realization slowly dawned on him that he had made a fatal error. His overactive imagination and his fears had misled him.

"You're crazy," Eddie said. Now he had no chance of getting away unseen. The CIA agent was racing toward him down the hall.

"What are you doing here, kid?" the man shouted as he came.

Dr. Reiner recovered quickly. There had not been any security team waiting beyond the door, but he couldn't undo what had been done. The missile of his revenge had been launched, and it was unstoppable.

He walked into the hallway, a stern expression on his face. "Why is this boy wandering around in here?" he demanded. "See what has happened to him? Take him away at once."

The CIA agent came closer and grasped Eddie's arm. "Why are you wet?" he demanded.

"A dangerous substance has spilled on him. Take him up to the lobby," the scientist thundered. He began hurrying toward the stairs.

The CIA agent hesitated. Over his shoulder, Heinrich von Reiner shouted, "I know how to treat him. Bring him upstairs!"

The man hurried after him, scooping a protesting Eddie into his arms. The lobby was empty. Outside, Heinrich von Reiner saw Colin Baron, the compound's director, standing at the center of a large security detail as they held a final conference before the CIA assistant director entered. A large contingent of workers and soldiers were gathered nearby, awaiting orders. Not far away, a helicopter waited for the signal to lift off.

"Let's take him to the director," the scientist shouted to the CIA agent behind him.

The group's attention was immediately drawn to the spectacle of two men bursting out of the building, one of them carrying a boy. What was happening?

"What's going on, Dr. Reiner?" Colin Baron called.

The two men and the boy reached the group in seconds, breathing hard.

Eddie was the first to speak — or rather, yell. He pointed at the scientist. "He gave me something to give to two Mexicans. He asked me to take it out through the gate!"

The scientist appeared to be calm. He stood with arms crossed, looking directly at Colin Baron.

"Dr. Reiner, what's going on?" Colin Baron asked again.

"He's pretending he doesn't know me," Eddie continued furiously. "He's a liar!"

"Boy, be quiet," Baron barked. Again, he addressed himself to the doctor. "Can you explain what is happening here?"

The German scientist spread his hands, wearing an oddly sinister smile.

Baron suddenly noticed that the boy was wet. "What happened to you?" he asked Eddie. "What spilled on you?"

Eddie pointed again at the doctor. "It was him. He threw this stuff onto me."

Colin Baron's eyes moved slowly back to Dr. Reiner. The smile on the scientist's face widened. He shrugged apologetically, like a child caught in a prank. A horrible suspicion began to sneak into Baron's mind. The blood drained from his face.

"What did you spill on him?" he asked Dr. Reiner, moving menacingly closer.

"You know ..." the scientist murmured. "Something I had in my room."

"Is it ... Mexico?"

The change that came over the scientist's face was instantaneous. The mask of normalcy that he had worn for the past few minutes vanished in a flash. A yelp of insane laughter burst from his mouth. Lifting his hands, he raised his head and shouted mockingly, "Code 33! Code 33!"

The security men and CIA agents watched in astonishment as Baron pulled his walkie-talkie from his belt, pressed a button, and shouted hysterically, "Code 33! Code 33!"

The senior CIA agent realized that something serious had transpired. "What's going on?" he snapped. "What is it?"

"Toxic leak," Colin said tersely. "The stuff that spilled on the boy has infected all of us. It's an airborne virus. Everyone put on your gas masks. I just hope it's not too late."

A strident siren sounded. At the same moment, the nearby helicopter began whirling its propellers, stirring up a breeze in the warm air.

"Stop the helicopter!" Colin Baron screamed hoarsely. "He's spreading the virus!"

Someone ran over to warn the helicopter pilot, but Baron knew it was too late. He was all too familiar with the properties of the "Mexico virus"....

"Just a second," said the head of the CIA detail. "There's nothing here, remember? We evacuated all toxic materials yesterday."

This had been one of the CIA's first demands: The assistant director would not set foot in the compound until all dangerous substances had been removed. Agents had checked all the refrigerators to make sure that nothing had been left behind.

Baron's face was gray. He gestured at the scientist who now stood with his back to them, watching the helicopter.

"He had a few vials in his room," he said. "He was finishing up an experiment."

The CIA agent flushed with anger. "You're going to pay for this," he hissed. "You're going to be held accountable."

Colin Baron gave him a strange look. "I'm going to be held accountable?" he repeated. "A few hours from now, we'll all be dead."

A scene no less stormy was taking place at the front door of the Lowinger place. Ben burst out of the house in a rage, and butted his head into the fund-raiser from Jerusalem.

The sheriff moved away from his car, gun in hand. "Leave him alone!" he yelled as he ran toward the house. "Don't touch the rabbi!"

Ben's thrust had hurled R' Tzvi Hirsch violently backward. He hit the porch railing and sprawled down the stairs, his thin body slamming painfully into each step. His black hat flew through the air and landed beside a low bush. The *meshulach* himself came to rest on the gravel at the foot of the stairs, blood gushing from his head even as both hands held tightly onto his yarmulka.

At that precise moment, the sound of a siren blared from the adjacent compound. The wail rose and fell with frightening intensity.

Ben stood up breathing heavily, his face twisted with loathing as he prepared for a renewed assault on the Yerushalmi. Alcohol and the turmoil of his own emotions had so muddled his senses that he didn't even register the siren. Leveling his hunting rifle, he advanced on R' Tzvi Hirsch with a roar of fury — a bloodthirsty beast about to pounce on his prey.

It was the announcement over the loudspeaker that stopped him in his tracks.

"Warning — toxic leak. Put on your gas masks immediately," the metallic voice repeated over and over. "Warning — toxic leak. Put on your gas masks immediately."

Ben sobered up with lightning speed. As the siren wailed again, spreading its fearful message, he stopped two feet from R' Tzvi Hirsch, still lying on the ground. Then, abruptly, he whirled away and began racing toward the house.

Sheriff Abrams froze, the gun still in his outstretched arm.

"Warning — toxic leak. Put on your gas masks immediately."

The sheriff's arm sank slowly back to his side. He felt an icy shiver run up his spine. He stared accusingly at the compound's concrete walls, at its watchtowers and steel gates. He had predicted this from the start. He had known it would happen — a leak of toxic chemicals that posed a fatal threat to everyone in the area. Was he breathing the stuff in even now? Was he going to die? And would the toxic cloud waft over Grayston, to spell the end of its hundreds of inhabitants?

Nearby, a spate of frenetic activity began taking place. Dozens of cars started their engines at once. With a squeal of tires, CIA agents headed for the main road, the assistant director bundled into the first vehicle. Their first order of business was to put some distance between them and the toxic leak.

The soldiers on the watchtowers were stunned. There were no gas masks on the towers, and they began shouting for the protective masks. The stunned silence that had dominated the first seconds of the crisis had given way to pandemonium. Senior officials shouted orders, but their voices were drowned out by the cries of the soldiers.

Frankie and Manuela came running out of the house, wild eyed with fear. "The boys are in there!" Frankie yelled at the sheriff, pointing at the concrete walls surrounding the compound. "John and Eddie are inside!"

R' Tzvi Hirsch lifted himself off the ground and sat up with a groan. Blood trickled from the gash on his head, staining his white shirt and his coat. When Binyamin had charged him, he had lost consciousness for a few moments. He had woken to this huge commotion. *What had happened? What was going on?*

The sheriff saw that he was awake and began walking his way.

R' Tzvi Hirsch closed his eyes, fists clenched. His thoughts were not on his aches and pains. *Everything that Hashem does is for the good,* he reflected over and over. He would accept his suffering with love. Let the blows and humiliation he had just been dealt serve as atonement for his many sins.

Abruptly, the siren stopped. There was a moment's silence, followed by a voice on the intercom system — a voice that was trying, without much success, to sound calm. "This is Colin Baron, commander of this compound," the voice said.

The sheriff paused, listening.

"A state of emergency exists. It encompasses a radius of one kilometer from the laboratory building. There is a suspicion that a dangerously toxic substance has been leaked. We are conducting an investigation and will shortly be in a position to identify the substance. All security forces, the FBI, the CIA, and the local police — whether outside the gates or on the road — are requested to remain where they are. No one will be leaving until it can be ascertained that he has not been infected. That's an order!"

The sound of whispering followed on the intercom, as the speaker held a hasty conference with some other person next to him. A few seconds later, Colin Baron spoke again.

"Our primary concern is the spread of an unknown strain of fever virus. The virus is airborne, has a long half-life, and is highly contagious. We have a sufficient stock of vaccinations and medications for anyone who is presently within the compound. However, if anyone were to leave and begin spreading the virus in the region, there would not be enough medicine for the local citizens. Standing beside me is William Perisher, field director of the CIA. This order has been issued with his knowledge and consent. I repeat: No one is to leave the confines of this compound without authorization. Please behave responsibly, and remember that you are under oath to protect the United States of America."

The sheriff spat on the ground in anger. How afraid he had been of just this contingency! How naive he had been, when he told that black officer long ago that he was going to make sure to close down the government complex. Only later had he begun to comprehend the powerful forces that were at play here. This was not the CIA proper, but a secret, hidden branch appointed through the Department of Agriculture. Behind these concrete walls, the director of the compound had unlimited power.

The sheriff was well aware of the rumors. He had listened to what the local workers had to say when they had had their fill of whiskey at the Drunken Ox: There was some weird scientist in the compound who never left its precincts; there was a whole building that no one was allowed to enter; Congressional committees had voiced a desire to visit, but Colin Baron had managed to torpedo their plans; things happened behind those walls that came straight out of the Third World, behind the Iron Curtain.

And now, it was all blowing up in their faces. This was Judgment Day for all the long years of secrecy.

The two security men made sure that the microphone was off before they spoke.

"You're lying," William Perisher said flatly. "There are no vaccinations and no medicines. I can see it in your face. We're all going to die!" he exploded.

They were in Colin Baron's office on the first floor of the laboratory building. They had made their way here as fast as they could, in order to supervise and control developments. There were a dozen things that had to be done at once, including the need to summon medical help. But most vital of all was isolating the area and preventing anyone from stepping outside.

Colin Baron looked at them both in distress. "What did you want me to say? That we're all doomed to die? That in just an hour or two the bodies are going to begin piling up?"

The two security men exchanged a terrified look.

"I already have the results of our investigation," Baron continued. He pointed at a device that stood at one end of his office. "There was a dissemination of a virus known as 'Mexico A.' No one must be allowed to leave these premises. Each and every one of us is a walking biological time bomb. Each of us is spreading millions of virus germs into the air. I don't mind lying bald-faced to the people. The important thing is for everyone to remain here, within these confines. Otherwise, we can say good-bye to all of Texas ... and maybe even to the entire southwest United States. Is that clear enough for you?"

At four in the afternoon, five hours after the outbreak, the FBI disaster investigator who had been summoned from El Paso summarized what he knew. He and the rest of the medical team in the area were clad in full protective gear, including sealed suits and gas masks. Oxygen tanks were strapped onto their backs. The compound's scientists were all dead and there was no one to check whether or not the area was still contaminated. The experts from the Centers for Disease Control — the CDC — in Atlanta were not due to arrive until late that night. Until then, their orders were to continue wearing full protective gear.

In summary, 216 people had contracted the virus.

To date, the number of dead was 168.

Forty-eight of the victims were unconscious. The doctors predicted that all were expected to die within 24 to 48 hours.

Most of the victims, the FBI investigator said, were security men and government workers: soldiers who had been guarding the compound, as well as scientists, administrators, and other compound personnel. The rest included members of the CIA and local sheriff's deputies from Grayston. Also, some citizens had succumbed: the residents of the ranch house located near the compound gates.

In addition, the investigator continued, one citizen by the name of Benjamin Lowinger had been shot and killed by soldiers while trying to escape the infected area in his truck. He had been headed in the direction of Grayston, which was outside the affected perimeter. He had begun speeding away and refused to heed police orders to halt. After the officers shot out his tires, the man began to flee on foot. There had been no option but to bring him down with a bullet.

Only quick action on the part of the soldiers had prevented the spread of the virus outside the area adjacent to the compound, which would have led to an uncontrollable spread of the disease, sowing enormous tragedy.

Something above him dazzled and blinded John by turns. His eyes were open just a slit. He was so weak that he couldn't even turn his head.

He was lying on a hard army cot, under a thin striped blanket. The noonday Texas sun was scorching, its rays showing no pity for him or the other patients lying in long rows beside him. John's mind briefly cleared, as though a bank of heavy cloud had parted for just a moment to let a beam of sunlight bathe the earth below. His head burned with fever, and there wasn't a part of his body that didn't ache.

Where am I? he wondered in confusion. *Where is everyone?*

He sank again into a stupor, only succeeding in rising above the fog for brief intervals. Fragments of memory, images in flashes, rose to his mind and sank immediately into the murk. Sometimes he felt as lost and frightened as a little child, and at others supremely apathetic, staring straight ahead with his mind blank.

What had happened? Where was Eddie? Where was his father? Where was everybody?

All around him, he heard sick people sighing and groaning. The sounds they made mingled with the bustle of the rescue personnel. Doctors shouted orders, nurses issued reports, and orderlies carried out stretchers. Men in army uniforms circulated continuously among the beds. John didn't recognize anyone, as all the faces were concealed by gas masks.

"Where am I?" he said aloud. *Where were Andrew and the rest of the band?* Once, when John woke, he heard the sound of a zipper rapidly closing. He managed a sideways glance, and saw a large black bag on the bed next to his own. Four men in gas masks lifted it up and placed it on a stretcher. *Someone's died*, John thought in alarm. Was he going to die, too? Would they soon be putting *him* in a bag like that and zipping it closed?

Sleep descended gently on him again — only to vanish with another sudden waking to pain and fear. His body was bathed in perspiration. He shivered constantly and uncontrollably. Several rubber-covered faces with round glass lenses instead of eyes gathered around his bed, peering into his eyes with a small flashlight and holding low-voiced conferences. They pried open his mouth with the aid of a flat wooden stick and spoke words he couldn't understand. Where was he? What was this place? How had he come here?

He remembered that he had been in the auditorium of the laboratory building for the band's final rehearsal. They had stopped playing for a few minutes because Andrew suggested that they add a bit of music to one of the songs, and everyone had paused to write down the notes. Suddenly, from the corridor, there had come a strange shouting. The CIA agent sitting in the last row had raced out, ordering them to stay where they were. John had sensed that this was somehow connected to Eddie, who had been sitting in the auditorium but was now nowhere in sight.

Thirty seconds later, they heard screaming and someone running up the stairs. It was Eddie. He was fighting with someone, yelling and hitting. The drummer peeked out of the auditorium door but saw nothing. He tried to get the rest of the band to continue the rehearsal, but they were interrupted by the siren's wail. Then came the terrifying announcement about a leak of some dangerous substance.

Everyone had stared at everyone else in alarm. Abandoning their instruments, they stampeded up the stairs. From every office and room came a stream of people trying to flee the building. John remembered that everyone had searched, panic stricken, for gas masks. He recalled Andrew yelling, "I need two masks for children!" He remembered everybody racing around with fear-filled eyes, and the soldiers shouting from the watchtowers, and the officers looking helpless ....

He also remembered a group of people standing around outside. He had never known that so many people worked in the compound. He saw Eddie, alone and miserable, with everyone keeping their distance from him. John wanted to go to him, but someone grabbed him with strong arms and held him back.

So where *was* Eddie? Had he died? John saw two more bags being borne along on stretchers. What had happened to his father? And Frankie? And old Sam, and Manuela? Were they all dead? Was he the only one left? If that was the case, he would rather be dead, too ....

Once again, he felt his body burning up. He sank into another fever dream. When he woke, the sun was setting. The large room was strangely silent. The commotion had stopped. The sighs and groans that had filled the air were no more. The doctors and nurses who had been moving endlessly around the room were gone, too. With an effort, John managed to lift his head slightly and look around. He was lying in a huge tent that had many dozens of cots lining its walls. Most of them were empty. Only a few of the beds still held patients, hooked up to I.V. lines.

The silence was eerie. John wanted to ask where Eddie was, and Andrew, and his father. But he was afraid to ask. He knew the answer. It was easier to just close his eyes and let the lassitude overcome his body, carrying him back to a place where he didn't feel anything at all.

Near midnight, there was an excited stir among the medical team. As the news spread, relief came to lighten the heavy atmosphere: The team from Atlanta had arrived. The CDC experts had landed in El Paso an hour before, and their buses were even now parked in the nearby town of Grayston.

An advance team of six experts, dressed in protective gear and armed with sophisticated equipment, fanned through the tent that had been set up as a field hospital, and then through the laboratory building. Over the span of the next twenty minutes, they conducted precise investigations to determine whether there were any remaining biological contaminants in the air.

"The danger has passed. You can now remove your gas masks," came the announcement over the intercom. With sighs of relief, scores of soldiers, military physicians, and other personnel removed the constricting rubber masks that they had been wearing for long hours. Now the larger CDC crew could enter the compound without fear. The buses that had been waiting in Grayston now came rolling through the compound gates: a regiment of epidemiologists, virologists, and other experts in related fields who would try to determine what, exactly, had gone wrong and caused this disaster.

The doctors began conducting exhaustive examinations of the surviving patients. At this point, twelve hours after the accident, only 29 of these remained. Most of them continued to deteriorate, with only a few in stable condition. Reigning over the entire operation was Dr. Patrick Braithwaite, director of the CDC, whose primary concern was not the fate of the survivors but the extent of his own group's authority.

Patrick Braithwaite was a formidable expert in biology; he was also no mean politician. For years now, he had been demanding that the Grayston complex be placed under his own supervision. Instead, the U.S. government, through the secret team in the CIA, had concealed the whole thing behind a jungle of bureaucratic red tape, attaching it to a remote division of the Department of Agriculture and thereby eliminating all supervision by any outside body.

The present situation, while sorrowful indeed in terms of the many casualties it had claimed, now played right into the CDC's hands. Of the entire administrative and scientific strata at the Grayston compound, no one had survived. To the last man, they had all died in the catastrophe. Dr. Patrick Braithwaite intended to step into the vacuum that their deaths had left behind.

He instructed his investigators to move rapidly through all the offices and labs and read every written document, every research paper, every lab report. He ordered them to take samples of every identifiable substance and transfer it all to Atlanta. Hours earlier, he had phoned various senators and men of influence in the capital and had been assured that, in light of the terrible and unprecedented tragedy, the complex at Grayston must be placed immediately under his jurisdiction. Colin Baron had stepped out of the picture under painful circumstances — leaving the field clear for Dr. Braithwaite to step in.

Of course, the CIA assistant director's visit had been canceled. By special order, a communications blackout was placed on the entire area. No American newspapers published so much as a word about the catastrophe in southwest Texas — just as, for years, they had not breathed a word about the existence of the secret government complex.

The reason for this secrecy was soon clear. The CDC experts were stunned by what they discovered in the laboratories. The developments had been extremely advanced and the research mightily impressive. But the biggest surprise was the unfamiliar name that appeared everywhere: that of a brilliant scientist by the name of Dr. Henry Reiner.

He was a genius. His work was far ahead of anything being done by other scientists elsewhere. He had signed off on all the experiments and research reports. The entire complex, it seemed, had been built to suit his needs and purposes. *What a pity that he died in the accident*, thought Dr. Braithwaite. *His death is a true loss to science in general and to the United States in particular. The mysterious Dr. Henry Reiner could have done great things for the CDC.*

John woke up as he felt his bed moving. Startled, his eyes flew open. The sky was dark, but floodlights lit the entire area. He felt better now — but what was this? Two men in white were carrying him on a stretcher. Who were they? Where were they taking him?

One of the orderlies saw that he was awake, and smiled at him. "Welcome back, kid. How do you feel?"

"What happened?" John asked fearfully. Now that the bad feeling had gone away, he was alert enough to be afraid. He tried to lift his head, to look around, to seek a familiar face ....

"Relax," the orderly said. "They're taking you to the infirmary."

Infirmary! The terrible memories flooded John's brain again. There had been an accident. A lot of people had died. Maybe even people that he knew.

"Where's my father?" he asked, tears beginning to trickle down his cheeks. "Where is everyone?"

"They'll tell you everything in the infirmary," the orderly said reassuringly. "Anyway, you'll have a friend there. Another kid your age. You can play together."

John beseeched him with his eyes. "A boy? My age? Could it be my brother?"

The man looked at John doubtfully. "Your brother? I don't think so."

The other boy had blond hair and blue eyes and didn't look at all like this dark-haired boy. And anyway, his mother had already arrived. She had been searching for him hysterically and threw a tantrum when she wasn't allowed in to see him. When they finally put a gas mask on her and brought her to the hospital tent, she had flung herself at the boy with hugs and tears. She had said nothing about another son.

"His name's Eddie," John said hopefully.

"Yes!" the orderly said in surprise. "Are you two really brothers?"

John's heart thudded. "Are you sure he's okay?"

"More than okay. While you were still burning up with fever, he was already jumping around in his bed."

The infirmary was located in the auditorium where the welcoming ceremony was to have been held. Now it was partially filled with hospital beds. Eddie was lying on one of them, not quite as lively as the orderly had described him, but definitely alive and fully alert.

He told John that most of their family had died in the catastrophe. Their father and old Sam, Frankie and Manuela — none of them had survived.

"My mother was saved because she was at work," Eddie said. John reflected that Eddie at least had a mother, while he was completely alone. His mother had died, and now his father was dead, too.

Eddie, in fact, was the only living relative he had in the world.

As the doctors had expected, the victims' condition continued to deteriorate. The number of beds in use decreased hourly, as additional corpses were carried away. On the morning of the third day, less than 48 hours after the accident, only three survivors remained: the two Lowinger boys, and a person officially dubbed "John Doe 7" but informally known as "the old man." He was a slender, elderly man with a white beard. At the start, his condition was not critical and it looked as though he would emerge from the ordeal intact. As time passed, however, he lost consciousness and sank into a coma.

Nobody knew who the anonymous man was. No one could identify him. He carried no papers and no one remembered whether he had been picked up inside the compound or just outside it, at the Lowinger place.

Grayston's sheriff was summoned to the infirmary; he confirmed that the man was not a local. The bartender at the Drunken Ox, who knew most of the people who worked at the government complex, was unable to solve the riddle. An exhaustive check confirmed that the fellow was not a member of either the CIA or the Texas police.

John and Eddie were released and sent home, leaving the third survivor, the anonymous old man, as the sole remaining patient in the infirmary. The doctors described his condition as stable and said that his life was not in danger, but they had no idea how long the present situation would last. He might wake at any moment and tell them who he was — or he could remain in a vegetative state for months, or even years.

Grayston was sorely hit. The small cemetery behind the church saw a series of painful, tear-soaked funerals for the dozens of young people who had held low-level jobs at the government facility. All had died in the disaster.

Contrary to Dr. Braithwaite's fears, the citizenry did not vent their anger against the compound. They viewed the catastrophe as a national tragedy. Supporting this idea was the long row of army trucks, bearing flag-draped coffins, that drove along Grayston's Main Street on their way to the Austin airport, where the bodies would be flown to every corner of the country.

Frankie was buried in his native town in South Dakota. Manuela's family took her remains to her village in northern Mexico. A double funeral was held for Sam and Ben, just hours after former sheriff Jack Abrams was laid to rest.

Barbara and the two boys received the mourners at the funeral. John and Eddie, who were still weak, attracted a great deal of attention. They had survived the epidemic, people whispered. Eddie was happy to see his entire class from the Port Stockton School, led by their principal, Mr. Gardner. John was moved when Christopher, his blind saxophone teacher, appeared at the funeral as well.

There was one other person who attended: the odd little *mohel*-cum-*chazzan*-cum-funeral director — the fellow who popped up whenever a Jew died or was born in the region. He appeared before noon for Jack Abrams — the person who had originally dubbed him the "Chief Rabbi of Grayston" — and remained for the funerals of the Lowinger uncle and nephew. For Ben alone, he would not have lingered. He still remembered the humiliating drive that Ben had forced him to take in the back of his pickup truck on the way to his son's *bris milah*. But old Sam surely deserved a few Jewish words to speed him on his last journey.

The local priest, as was his habit, stood back to make way for the Jewish rabbi, who mumbled a few verses and recited the *"Keil Malei Rachamim,"* followed by the Mourner's *Kaddish*. Barbara gave him a few dollars, and he disappeared the way he had come.

The next morning, Barbara woke the boys early and urged them to go to school. "You have to get back to normal life," she told them. "Your father's dead, but the world goes on."

She was not planning to go to the store today, she told the boys over breakfast. She would stay home to try and put things in order. Her brother, Tony, had told her that she could take the day off.

Barbara was telling the truth when she said she would not be at work that day. But she had no intention of tidying the house. She had a much more important agenda. Her first stop would be the bank on Main Street, where she planned to find out how much money Sam and Ben had left her. She was now a wealthy woman.

The hard times were over. From now on, life was going to be much easier and a lot more fun. She had not had much joy from her marriage to Benjamin Lowinger. Now, at last, she would be compensated for everything.

Her visit to the bank ended in bitter disappointment.

After murmuring some words of condolence, the bank manager warned her not to build up her hopes. "We both knew Ben," he said, lowering his voice as though reluctant to speak ill of the dead. "He didn't work, and he spent money all the time. Twelve years ago, a check for one million dollars was deposited into his account. Today ... I don't know if enough is left to put up a headstone for him."

Barbara's face registered complete shock.

The manager spread his hands out as though in self-justification. "Believe me, Mrs. Lowinger. I tried speaking to him more than once. I advised him to invest the money, to start a business, to do anything rather than use up Sam's money until it was gone. But, as you know, he was not very good at taking advice ...."

Barbara was too stunned to speak. She simply stood up, turned, and left the bank. That miserable husband of hers! Ben was lower than a worm. Squandering a million dollars in twelve years? Throwing it all away on drinking and gambling? A million dollars! Why, you could buy half of Grayston with that kind of money. He could have died a rich man!

She drove recklessly homeward, moaning in frustration. Why did life always disappoint her? Her first husband had robbed banks, and her second was a drinker and a gambler. And now he had died without a penny to his name, leaving her saddled with two brats!

Well, she would just see about that. John wasn't even hers. She had no responsibility toward the boy. She could not go on feeding him and paying his tuition until the end of her days. She had always hated him, always been furious at the way Ben favored him — that little Jew with his "shofar." This was her chance to get rid of him, once and for all. She would send him to some orphanage and never have to see his Jewish face again.

She flew along the road between the ranches. Tall Willy's wife waved. She wanted to tell Barbara that the funeral had been lovely and not to hesitate to call if she needed help. But Barbara didn't stop. She had nothing to say to her, or to anyone in Grayston. It was too bad they had not all been killed in that outbreak.

As she turned onto the gravel road, an encouraging thought popped into her mind: At least she had the house. The ranch house should be worth something. She could sell it and move into a smaller place.

As she neared her home, she saw an unfamiliar car parked in the small gravel clearing fronting the porch. The car door was open and the driver, wearing a suit and narrow-brimmed hat, was knocking on the front door. When there was no response, he walked along the porch and peered through one of the windows.

He must be a real estate agent, Barbara thought. *He is wasting no time in checking out the house.* She wondered how much he would offer for it.

The man noticed the approaching pickup truck. He climbed down the porch stairs and was waiting as she pulled up beside him.

"Good morning. Are you Mrs. Lowinger?"

"Yes."

"My condolences on your loss," the man said, placing a hand on his heart and inclining his head slightly. "Please permit me to introduce myself. My name is Patrick Braithwaite, director of the CDC in Atlanta and charged by the United States government with heading ... whatever is left of this complex."

So he wasn't a real-estate man after all, Barbara thought. But — hey! Just a minute! What about compensation? She was in a position to demand enormous damages from the U.S. government. She would tell them that her dear husband, the household's primary breadwinner, had died in the disaster. Old Sam, the head of the family, had died. All their employees had died. And what about the psychological trauma to the two precious boys — especially poor John, who was now orphaned of both his mother and his father? It could come to millions ....

"I believe you are aware of the legal standing of this house?" Dr. Braithwaite said.

"Uh ... more or less," Barbara replied cautiously.

"We will meet you halfway," the man said, his tone compassionate. "But I'm afraid you will have to leave soon. Say, no later than two weeks from now."

Barbara stared at him, stunned. This was not at all what she had expected to hear. "Leave the house?" she sputtered, when she could speak. "Why?"

"You don't know?"

"Don't know *what?*" Barbara almost screamed.

"Your husband didn't tell you about the contract?"

Barbara sighed, and looked at the man with bitter resignation. "My husband didn't tell me anything. Maybe you can just spit it out."

As Dr. Braithwaite explained the situation, Barbara was treated to her second shock of the day: The ranch house had not actually belonged to the family for some time now. Ben had sold it, along with the rest of the property, to the United States government, with the proviso that he and his family could continue living there as long as Sam was alive. Now that Sam had tragically succumbed to the virus, she and the boys could no longer call this place home.

Dr. Braithwaite's next words dashed her last remaining hope. "It is important the I mention that your husband also signed a rider — I can show you the document if you wish — stating in advance that there would be no financial demands should any future damage incur to his family as a result of his choice to continue living adjacent to the complex, which, as you know, dealt with dangerous substances."

Barbara was still sitting in her truck, staring numbly into space. What a horrible day. A triple whammy had descended on her: no money, no house, no compensation. That miserable Ben had died, leaving her with nothing.

47

The CDC director had one piece of good news for Barbara amid all the bad. The department responsible for the complex had decided, he told her — in a spirit of compassion far removed from the spirit of the law, and in light of the special circumstances of the case — to provide a measure of compensation to the two children. The government would fund John and Eddie's education and underwrite their medical insurance until they reached the age of 21. They would also receive subsidies toward renting an apartment, along with a monthly stipend for basic necessities.

Barbara stared at the man through eyes blurred with tears. This was the first ray of light in an otherwise black, black day.

"Really?" she said eagerly. "I don't know what to say. Thank you!"

"That's all right," Patrick Braithwaite said. "The children shouldn't suffer for something that is no fault of their own."

The first item on the agenda, he explained, was for the boys to visit the Centers for Disease Control in Atlanta. They had just lived through a complicated medical event, and they must undergo a battery of tests far more comprehensive than the on-site military doctors had been able to carry out. The boys would be undergo X-rays, blood work, and other testing procedures. It might be determined that they required medication for a period of time. A hospital in Atlanta specialized in these kinds of diseases.

The CDC director suggested that Barbara and the two boys move to Atlanta, Georgia for a period of time. The boys' education would pose no problem: He would enroll them in the same school that his own sons attended. This was an expensive private school, with fine teachers and a beautiful campus. The children would certainly enjoy it there, no less than they did the public school they had attended in Port Stockton until now. His wife, Braithwaite continued, would help Barbara find an apartment and a job, and assist her to acclimate herself to her new home.

Though Barbara insisted that she needed time to think it over, the idea appealed to her already. She was tired of Grayston and ready to start a new chapter in her life. As for John and Eddie, they received the proposal joyously. Just one week later, the Lowinger family had moved into their new quarters in Atlanta.

Most pleased of all was Dr. Braithwaite himself. The money that had been allocated for the children's upkeep and education was a drop in the bucket compared to the enormous benefit that the country could expect to reap from them. These two valuable commodities must not be allowed to disappear into the vastness of the United States. After all, John and Eddie Lowinger were two out of the only three survivors of the Mexican virus. Their blood now carried antibodies against the lethal germ. If there was a chance to examine the virus and devise a countermeasure against it — those boys were the answer.

Grayston was licking its wounds. Many of the houses in town had an empty place at the table — a place where a father, son, or brother had once sat, lost now to the general catastrophe. Most of the families had fresh graves to visit, leaving flowers and tears. Only one family had a lingering mystery to contend with: Steven Chambers, son of Norman Chambers of the bakery on Main Street, was missing. His body had not been found within the walls of the compound — or anywhere else. His parents told the Missing Persons unit of the FBI that Steven had not slept at home on the night before the outbreak. He had gone to work the day before as usual, and had never returned.

At first, the Chambers were hopeful that Steven had merely driven off somewhere without telling anyone. Perhaps he was lying injured in some hospital. Or perhaps he had become drunk and been arrested in a neighboring town.

But time passed, with no sign of life from their son.

Soviet Union — 5726 / 1966

Already well decorated, General Sergei Petroshov was in line to rake in the coveted "Hero of the Soviet Union" medal for his role in obtaining the Mexico virus. The government newspaper, *Isvestia*, had printed an article filled with praise for the general, without revealing the details of his most-recent secret mission. But, for him, the biggest prize was having his retirement postponed for a full year. The aging general was afraid of the long, empty days that would follow his retirement. With his experience and expertise so indispensable now, he had been "requested" by the Party leaders to remain in the ranks of the KGB, and he had been glad to obey.

The military plane carrying the general and the priceless virus flew directly from Mexico to Riga, in Latvia. There, in the Bacteria Institute #16, the Lenin Briga, the scientists would take over. They would identify the virus, study it to understand its properties, and use it to create a mighty biological arsenal for the state.

Back in Juarez, the two scientists he had brought along on the mission pointed out that the vial was labeled "Mexico B." This seemed to imply that there existed a "Mexico A," probably a more primitive and less effective version of the virus.

An entire laboratory at the institute was made available for the project — an expensive and sophisticated facility whose cost would easily have fed the thousands of hungry Riga citizens who stood in long lines to receive their daily bread.

"Welcome, Comrade General. My name is Nikolai Krakov," the director of the lab introduced himself to Petroshov. The next morning, he said, fifty mice would be infected with the virus. The mice would then be carefully studied to determine the virus's course. If the general was interested, he could watch the process from the safety of the observation room, behind thick glass.

Infecting the mice was the job of a technician, dressed from head to toe in protective gear, who introduced the virus into the subjects' glass-enclosed cage. The mice appeared unaffected. They continued to race around their cage, just as though they had not been exposed to a biological time bomb that the Soviets had taken such pains to acquire. The general left, bound for an important meeting at KGB headquarters. Three hours later, when he returned to the lab, he found the mice apparently still in possession of their good health. They darted around the big cage just as before. The same held true in the evening and — to Petroshov's disappointment — on the following morning as well.

The lab workers, on the other hand, were pleased. Their examinations showed that the virus was multiplying in the mice's bodies. Fifty additional mice were introduced to the cage three days later, and were quickly infected. The conclusion was clear and encouraging: The virus spread through the respiratory system during its incubation period, moving from mouse to mouse even before a single symptom was observed. This, the general knew, would be a definite advantage in terms of biological warfare. Should the virus be let loose in a city — say, for example, New York or Washington — the carriers would be spreading the disease even before the authorities were aware of its existence. The circle of infection would grow rapidly before any measures could be taken to isolate the affected area. Heinrich von Reiner had done his job well.

On the tenth day, excitement filled the lab. "There's been an outbreak," a young scientist cried. The others clustered near the glass windows. Three of the mice from the first round of contagion were lying in a corner of the cage, their bearing weak and their breathing labored. They were clearly near death.

General Petroshov rubbed his hands in anticipation. The great moment had arrived. Now the virus would demonstrate its true strength. Would it really guarantee a 100 percent mortality rate? Had the German scientist succeeded in creating the perfect germ, one that was capable of wiping out entire human populations? Did the Soviet Union at last own the ultimate weapon — a biological broom capable of sweeping whole American cities clean without touching its buildings or infrastructure?

A day passed, but none of the affected mice died. By this time, the cage was filled with trembling, feeble rodents clinging to life. The small creatures continued crouching in place, breathing with difficulty, on the second day as well — and on into the third. It was near dusk on that day that the general was summoned to the lab. As he entered, he noted the discouragement on the scientist's faces. There was a sense of failure in the air.

"What happened?" he asked sharply.

Nikolai Krakov, the lab director, cracked his knuckles unhappily. "Comrade General, I don't know what to say ...."

The general strode over to the cage. He was shaken by what he saw. At noon, the entire cage had been filled with sick mice. Three hours ago, they had still been lying motionless and apathetic. But now, several of them appeared to be recovering. They lifted their heads and sniffed the air. Two of them even began dragging themselves toward the food and water.

"What is the meaning of this?" Petroshov said without turning his head. The anger in his voice was palpable.

"They're recovering, Comrade General," Krakov said in trepidation.

"How can this be?" Petroshov roared. "They're supposed to die!"

Krakov paled. The general grabbed him by the nape of the neck and shook him. "They're supposed to die! What's going on here? Can you explain that to me?"

The other lab technicians lowered their heads industriously to their work, trying not to make a sound. The director was on the verge of tears. He was well aware of what the KGB general could do if he was not satisfied with the results.

"Comrade General," he whispered humbly, "we will make every effort to figure out why the mice are not dying."

The general left the lab in a fury.

By the following morning, the extent of the catastrophe had grown. The first fifty mice were in various stages of recovery. General Petroshov simmered with rage. His thunderous comments shook the windows when Krakov nervously suggested that the smuggled vial had been no more than a CIA ruse, and the virus nothing but a short-lived tropical bug.

"Don't try to distract me!" Petroshov bellowed. "Where did you come up with such an idea? Perhaps *you* are an American agent! You are undermining the Soviet Union!"

That night, Nikolai Krakov was arrested by the KGB. A large black Volga sedan pulled up in front of his house and carried him off to the organization's headquarters in Riga. He was placed on trial for the crimes of treachery and sabotage and sent away to serve ten years' hard labor in Siberia.

The next two weeks were ones of terrible frustration for Sergei Petroshov. The Kazakhstani scientist selected to take Krakov's place did not produce the desired results. A fresh crop of mice was introduced to the cage. All of them eventually showed symptoms of the disease, and then miraculously recovered and were restored to health. *Maybe this fellow ought to be sent to Siberia, too,* the general thought angrily.

After a month of disappointment, Petroshov returned to Moscow in disgrace. But he did not cease his efforts. Each day he phoned the lab in Riga, asking for a progress report on the virus. The new manager's answer, though worded in various different ways, was always essentially the same: This was a violent and particularly hardy bug, but all efforts to turn it into a lethal one had so far been in vain.

The first clue to help unravel the riddle was a fragment of information that reached the Soviet Union regarding the mysterious incident at Grayston.

The information arrived through an American journalist who worked for *The New York Times*. He had heard from a reliable source about the catastrophe that had taken place at the Texas biological facility, but had been ordered by government decree not to share the news with his readers. The newspaperman, who harbored secret Communist sympathies, initiated a covert meeting with his regular contact at the Soviet Embassy in New York. In this way, the closely guarded secret made its way, via diplomatic pouch, from America to KGB headquarters in Moscow.

General Petroshov exploded. Over and over again he checked the calendar to make sure his eyes were not deceiving him. The accident in Texas had taken place one day — *one day!* — after Heinrich von Reiner had passed the virus along to Juarez. *This juxtaposition of dates could not be a coincidence*, the general thought. *There must be an explanation.*

Petroshov threw himself into solving the mystery. An urgent message was sent out to every Soviet agent and spy in the United States: Find the investigative report on the incident at Grayston. Top priority!

In the end, it was money that talked. The start of 1967 ushered in the annual international biology convention in Paris. Scientists from across the

globe were invited to attend, to update and be updated on the latest discoveries in the field of biological research. The Soviet scientists, as was
customary at such affairs, had an additional mission thrust on them by
the KGB: to establish contact with American scientists and extract every
possible morsel of information from them. Another four Soviet spies were
present in disguise, posing as tourists staying at the hotel. Their job was to
form a support system for their scientific compatriots, and watch over them
lest they fall into a trap — or try to sell Soviet secrets to the Americans.

On the morning of the third day, the phone rang in General Petroshov's
Moscow office. It was one of his men in Paris, with news: He had met an
American scientist who worked for the CDC in Atlanta. The fellow was
willing to provide interesting information about the accident at Grayston
— for a price. A steep price.

That same night, a meeting took place between the American scientist, the head of the KGB Paris station, and an envelope filled with green-
backs. The information the scientist provided was worth every dollar.

Thirteen hours later, the spool of tape was on Sergei Petroshov's desk.

He listened carefully to the interview that had taken place the night
before, and which had been brought to Moscow by special messenger.

"I was a member of the team that investigated the accident in Texas,"
the American scientist's voice blared. "I left the CDC a few weeks later,
but I can describe what we found up until that point."

"Tell us everything you know," the KGB man ordered.

"There were three survivors: two boys — brothers — from a family that
lived nearby, and an unconscious patient, an old man who was known
only as 'John Doe 7.'"

"Why did they call him that?"

"He was anonymous. No one knew who he was," the American scientist replied. "The kids were taken to Atlanta for a series of tests, while the
old man stayed behind in the Grayston infirmary. Our director, Patrick
Braithwaite, urged us to find the key to the trio's survival. The two brothers underwent a battery of tests to determine their antibodies they had
produced to fight previous illnesses, genetic characteristics, a surplus or
lack of vitamins and minerals, and so on. Then, one day, they happened to
mention that they had not touched a drop of alcohol in two years. Their
father was a drunkard, and the two boys had made a bet about who could
last longer without drinking at all.

"That was the moment of truth. From that point on, our progress was rapid. Once we had that clue, we discovered that imbibing alcohol causes the body to discharge an enzyme that we called 'whiskeyose' —"

"Whiskeyose?" the KGB man repeated, mystified.

"An inside joke. The names of enzymes usually take a form ending with 'ose': lactose, amylose, and so on. We called this one 'whiskeyose' — the whiskey enzyme. In layman's terms, you might say that the Mexico virus works slowly and with diminishing strength, so that the immune system generally manages to overcome it. But the presence of this enzyme, which is found in a body that has become needful of alcohol, speeds up the virus's action many times over, strengthens its effects, and ends by causing death."

That same night, in the Bacteria Institute #16, a fresh crop of mice received a mixture of water and vodka. While they may have enjoyed the change in diet, it sealed their fate. The next morning they were infected with the "Mexico B" virus — and, a few days later, all of them had closed their eyes forever.

General Petroshov received the news with an explosion of joy. At long last, the mystery was solved. The Mexico virus worked. The problem had been the experimental subjects. "They were not true Russian mice," he said laughingly to the Kazakhstani doctor who now ran the institute. "The proof: They didn't drink!"

Among the human population, however, who didn't indulge in a glassful of wine now and then? Who refrained from the occasional shot of whiskey or vodka?

The big question was whether von Reiner had handed the Soviet Union the virus as an exclusive gift, or if the United States possessed it as well. Did the two superpowers now both own this mighty weapon — or had the Nazi scientist, consumed with hatred for the America that had robbed him of his liberty, granted the Soviet Union the deciding edge in its longstanding, bitter rivalry?

48

The bad news reached the Chambers family two weeks after their son disappeared.

The man who called late one night introduced himself as a Texas state trooper. He told Norman that his son, Steven, had been found lifeless in a nearly empty ornamental pool in the courtyard of an abandoned villa on the outskirts of Juarez, Mexico. His driver's license had been in his pocket, allowing the police to ascertain his name and address.

Shocked and heartbroken, Norman answered all the officer's questions. Steven was 28 years old, he said, and unmarried. He had never been involved in criminal activity and had no enemies. For the past few years he had had steady work as a gardener in a local government complex.

The anonymous caller was actually not a state trooper but a member of the Mexican secret police, and the purpose of his call had not really been to inform a grieving father of his loss. In Mexico, it was not all that unusual to find a young American who had died under suspicious circumstances. What had shaken the Mexican security service were the two additional corpses that had also been found in the ornamental pool — corpses that had been quickly identified as two missing policemen, Tomas and Leoro. That was enough to justify a full-scale investigation.

There were signs that the house had been used for an indeterminate period of time by the KGB. While the Soviet agents had attempted to cover their tracks, impressions of Russian letters could be made out on the blank page of an abandoned notepad. In a trash can nearby, the police had also found blank tape spools used with a recorder manufactured in the Soviet Union.

What, the Mexican intelligence men wondered, *had the Russians been seeking in the northern tip of Mexico? What had they been plotting so close to the U.S. border? What had they considered worth the deaths of two Mexican police officers?*

They hoped that the identity of the third corpse, the young American, would shed light on the mystery — and they were not disappointed. According to his father, he had worked at a secret government compound. The picture suddenly became very clear.

Word was passed up to the topmost echelon of Mexican intelligence. This was not merely a matter of three individuals who had lost their lives, but something with the potential for a deal between intelligence services. The Mexicans now had information that could be traded to the Soviet Union for a nice price.

The Mexican secret service sent a message to the KGB, requesting an explanation for the operation that its agents had conducted in Juarez, in the course of which two local policemen and an American citizen who worked in the highly classified U.S. compound in Grayston had met their deaths.

The implicit threat was clear: The Mexicans were not actually requesting an explanation, but rather hinting at their willingness to keep the Americans from knowing that the Soviets had been sniffing around their secret compound. And they were demanding a stunning recompense in exchange for their silence.

The reply from Moscow came quickly. The Soviets offered the Mexican secret service a real treasure: intelligence on illegal activities that the U.S. had carried out on Mexican soil within the framework of that same government project — deeds that ran counter to both American and international law. Information that Mexico could well use in its dealings with its wealthy neighbor to the north.

The material from Moscow arrived in Mexico City in a cardboard file brought by special messenger. The file, as promised, contained political dynamite with the power to cause an international scandal. Thirteen years earlier, the file said, in the year 1953, the United States had completed development of a new biological weapon, a lethal virus with widespread effectiveness. The virus had functioned well under laboratory conditions, but its developers wanted to know if it would work just as efficiently on humans. The U.S. had found its human test subjects in the Chuma, an ancient and isolated Indian tribe that had dwelled in the dense Mexican jungle for centuries.

The experiment had taken the form of disseminating the virus by means of a helicopter hovering over the native village. And it had been crowned with success. The entire tribe had been wiped out. Several bodies — possibly some still-living natives among them — had been brought by helicopter to the secret CIA laboratories in Grayston, Texas. Then all trace of the crime was erased by means of a conflagration in the jungle, ignited by hurling a fire bomb from a military plane.

The Americans had treated the Chuma as experimental guinea pigs. And, to add insult to injury, they had had the audacity to label the new virus, "Mexico."

This information was duly passed up to the president of Mexico, but nothing was done with it. The heads of the Mexican intelligence community had no idea that the Russians had handed them old news. The incident was already known in the highest government circles. The United States had closed the account a long time ago. By the end of the fifties, America had paid Mexico an enormous sum of money as compensation, ostensibly for the "accidental" forest fire, but actually for the destruction of the Chuma tribe.

The cardboard file, on which someone from the President's office scribbled, "Juarez Incident," was sent for storage to the government archives, located in the basement of a beautiful building on El Zócalo, Mexico City's central square. There it stayed, in a cabinet crammed with other files in one of the archives' more remote corners. For the next forty years it gathered dust there. No one opened it or glanced through its yellowing pages. For forty years, not a soul in Mexico took the slightest interest in the Juarez incident or its unfortunate victims.

It was only on a winter's day in 2006 that a bored clerk named Octavio

Solarz rummaged through that particular cabinet and came upon the cardboard file. When he opened it and saw what was inside, his eyes opened wide in shock. The file contained the kind of material that topples governments. There were many people who were interested in the file. Some of them were prepared to pay a great deal for the documents it contained.

The middleman was Jorge Diaz, a bureaucrat in the Juarez municipality. He put the archivist in touch with Romero Alameda, a scrawny, passionate Indian activist. Romero paid the fantastic sum of 4,000 pesos for the file, and passed it on — through a student by the name of Munzio Rodriguez — to Professor Costa, noted anthropologist at the University of Mexico City. For the professor, it was pure gold.

The file contained proof of his thesis concerning the criminal genocide of the Chuma tribe. The yellowed pages filled out the picture that he had arduously constructed over the course of years. With the "Juarez Incident" file he now had final and definite confirmation. He could now complete his work and publish a scientific article that would shake the world. At long last, he would tell the story of the great crime that the United States and Mexico had perpetrated against the Indian population.

That was when Walter Child, assistant director of the CIA, stepped in.

The group intent on publicizing the Juarez incident was a threat to many vital interests. Interests more important than freedom of speech. More important than free scientific expression. More important, even, than their lives. The assistant director ordered one of his field agents — no ordinary agent, but one who was capable of carrying out this sort of order — to silence the Mexicans at any price.

And they had been silenced, along with several other people in Mexico who were in possession of information about Juarez. An American also paid with his life: Lenny Brown, assistant manager of the toxins supervisory unit at the Department of Agriculture in Houston — the man who, unluckily for him, had naively supplied the professor with material about the Chuma affair. Right now, the only person who knew about Juarez was Jacob Stern, Lenny's boss. The pale agent longed to finish him off, too, but Walter Child had decided that his threatening phone call to Stern's home would do the job just as effectively. Silence in exchange for his life — that was the deal he had proposed in that call. Jacob Stern, of course, had grabbed it with both hands.

And now, Child thought, *there was nothing standing in the way of Professor Barry Majdi and Imam Bashir Abdul Aziz.* They could carry out the biological attack they were plotting, undeterred. Should the existence of the Mexico virus become public at this time, there was no telling how their plans might be affected. He was not prepared to take any chances.

He had removed all obstacles from their path. All that was left was to wait patiently for the wedding of the Milinover Rebbe's grandson.

The Bnei Brak-Ramat Gan Border — Iyar 5766 / May 2006

Pandemonium reigned in the Ganei HaSimchah catering hall. Enormous trays of chicken were inserted into the oven and removed again, appetizingly brown and crispy; huge bowls of salads were assembled and tossed; and giant vats of soup bubbled on the burners. The cooks and kitchen staff did not rest for a moment — a fact that did not prevent the red-faced manager from scolding everyone for everything, everywhere. Since it was the period of *Sefiras Ha'Omer* there were no weddings to be catered, but babies continued being born, *baruch Hashem* — either eight days or thirteen years earlier — and *bris milah* or bar mitzvah celebrations were in full swing.

"Turk, Mahmoud, Jibril!" the manager roared. "Start putting on the tablecloths."

Turk Majdi finished doling fruit salad out of a large can onto melon halves and passed from the kitchen to the dining room. His two co-workers began dragging chairs, and he joined them with a mass of tablecloths draped over his arm.

"Just a minute. There's been a change in the order," the manager grumbled as he peered into a large book. "Set up thirty tables: eighteen for the men and twelve for women."

The trio of workers began moving tables and partitions across the large room, while the irate manager observed them.

When the tablecloths had been spread and Turk and his colleagues were setting out the plates, a side door opened. Five men emerged from the office behind that door: the hall's owner — R' Anshel — and four visitors in chassidic garb.

Turk peeked at them as he worked. In the short time he had been here, he had come across a brand of Jew that he didn't know at all. They were dressed in long dark coats, usually wore black hats, and had long white strings dangling from their belts. He learned that they were called "*chassidim.*" As Jibril explained, these were ultra-religious Jews. "Not exactly like our Hamas," he added, "but they're the genuine article. They're not acting a part."

The discussion between R' Anshel and the four *chassidim*, begun in the office, continued as they spilled out of it. "For the men, let's connect Halls A and B," one of the visitors said. "The women will be in Hall C. That will certainly be enough."

"What about the '*seudas aniyim*' [feast for the poor]?" another man asked.

R' Anshel stopped and stared at the speaker in surprise. "*Seudas aniyim*? What are you talking about? When does that take place?"

One of the four men — the senior member, in Turk's opinion — stared back at the hall's owner in no less astonishment. "One day before the wedding," he said. "On 28 Av. Didn't we tell you about it?"

"No," R' Anshel said firmly. "We didn't talk about it. We only spoke about the wedding itself, on 29 Av — the 23rd of August. Do you have to make the *seudah* here?"

"Really, R' Yoel," one of the other men tried to persuade the other in a low voice. "Do we need the hall? Other chassidic groups hold the *seudas aniyim* in shul."

"I know," R' Yoel said patiently. "But, in Milinov, the *seudas aniyim* has always taken place where the wedding is held. We spoke about this at the previous wedding, and the Rebbe instructed us not to change the custom of our forefathers. Don't you remember, R' Anshel? We held Yisrael Moshe's wedding here — and the *seudas aniyim* as well."

The hall owner spread his hands in resignation. He had forgotten. "How many people?" he asked.

"About 250 to 300 portions," R' Yoel replied. "Only the poor themselves actually sit at the tables. But we need a large hall because there will be just as many people all around them. *Bachurim* come, and a large number of the married men, and of course the guests from abroad. The Rebbe would like the *seudah* to be the same as a wedding meal — the same menu, a band, many guests, and so on."

"I don't think the date is free," R' Anshel muttered in visible distress. He turned to his work manager. "Motke, bring the book."

The manager began looking around the room. Turk, who had noticed the book lying on a chair, handed it to him. The relief on the chassidim's faces was apparent as R' Anshel discovered that the date was still open.

"I'm writing it down," he said as he scribbled. "28 Av — August 22nd — Milinov — Hall A — *seudas aniyim*. All right?"

"Very good. Now, let's get back to the wedding itself," R' Yoel said with a sigh of satisfaction.

R' Anshel and the others sat at a table for a long time, going over the details for the upcoming affair. Turk Majdi tried to hover in the area and glean as much information as he could. He knew where the band would be stationed, and where the cameras that would transmit the spectacle by closed-circuit video to the women's section would be set up. He knew that the *chuppah* would take place outdoors, in the open garden, and that the meal itself would feature long, rectangular tables rather than round ones. He knew the planned menu and gathered that the affair would last till dawn's early light.

Despite his adequate Hebrew, there were some words he did not understand, such as "*Shekiyah*," "*Mizrach*," and "*mitzvah tantz*." But he would keep his eyes open and write down every detail. He would continue gathering information until the picture was complete.

In two weeks, when he called his uncle in Los Angeles, he would have much more to report.

49

Turk Majdi stood in the hall's parking lot, his face twisted with hatred. *I wish Motke would die*, he thought with venom. The work manager had just fired him without cause. The Jew had simply tossed him out. Well, he would pay dearly for that.

It had been a couple of days, Turk knew, since Motke had begun to have it in for him. With the man he had replaced — the one under interrogation by the G.S.S. — back at work now, Turk had become superfluous. And today — it had to be today! — Turk had dropped a tray of chicken quarters at the precise moment that sponge cakes were in the oven. Usually, when things dropped like that, the waiter would simply pick up the food and replace it on its tray. Motke usually joked about it, once saying that, after such a mishap, the client remarked that the chicken had been especially good! But today, Motke became angry. He ordered Turk into his office, calculated how much he was owed in pay since the beginning of the month, and told him to go.

Turk tried to argue, but the Jew had been adamant. Turk took the money and left quietly, but as the hours passed his rage mounted. The manager had ruined his whole plan. His uncle would be furious, and he would put a stop to Turk's monthly allowance. He had warned Turk to hold onto the job until the end of August. Uncle Barak had depended on him. Now everything was ruined.

The next stages of the operation were ready to be implemented. In two weeks, Turk was supposed to rent a small apartment near the wedding hall — preferably in Yaffo, where no one would hesitate to rent to a young Arab. Then he was to get hold of a good refrigerator, along with a generator in case there was a power outage. His uncle had told him that he planned to send him something very important, something that must remain refrigerated.

And now, that accursed Jew had gone and fired him.

Visions of vengeance swirled through Turk's brain, especially after Motke saw him in the parking lot and stridently ordered him to leave the premises and wait outside the fence. Humiliated, Turk walked over to the pavement, where he stood sweating and tense, imagining how he would kill the manager, the hall's owner, and all Jews everywhere.

It was noon. Cars began turning into the parking lot for a *bris milah* that was due to take place shortly. As though to underscore his failure, some of the guests were the very same group of ultra-Orthodox Jews who were planning the August 23rd affair — the wedding he just *had* to be here for.

At two p.m., Turk circled the parking lot, careful not to run into Motke or any of the *chareidim* he had seen. He sneaked in among the bushes, dug into the soil near the gate, and found the plastic bag he had hidden there a while back. Inside were two screwdrivers and a sharp Japanese knife. He put them in his pocket, glanced furtively around to make sure he was not seen, and began stealing toward the hall's back door.

Turk Majdi was gone no more than ten minutes. It was 2:15 when he left the place where he had been standing since he was fired, and only 2:25 when he was back on the spot. Sweat was pouring off him, his breathing was shallow, and his heart thumped erratically.

Turk checked himself: his shoes, pants, and shirt gave no indication of what he had done. No one had witnessed him entering or leaving the hall. He had tossed the screwdrivers and the Japanese knife into the huge rubbish bin behind the kitchen, then raced around the building to the spot in front where he had been seen standing all morning.

A moment passed, and then another and another. He watched the hall tensely. Had they sensed nothing? Hadn't they noticed yet?

Ten minutes later, two men — Motke and R' Anshel — burst out of the hall. They scanned the parking lot anxiously, until Motke's eyes fell on Turk. "There he is," he called out to his employer. They began advancing on the young Arab.

"So, you want to know what I did?" Turk asked his uncle with pleasure some two weeks later. He had already rented the apartment in Yaffo, close by the hall, and had bought a new refrigerator in an upscale appliance store in Tel Aviv. In his biweekly phone call with Professor Barak Majdi, Turk had begun by telling his uncle that he had been fired.

The professor had sucked in his breath. Then he bellowed, *"You lost your job?"*

"Yes," Turk said eagerly. "There's a fat Jew there named Motke. He got upset with me because I dropped a tray of chicken, and he told me to go home."

"Just a minute. You don't work there anymore?"

"Listen to what I did," Turk chuckled, ignoring the ominous note in his uncle's voice. "I got the work tools that I had hidden ahead of time, entered through the back door, went up to the roof and disconnected the air-conditioning. Then I ran back to the place where I had been standing all morning, ever since he fired me. There was some sort of affair going on at the hall and people started feeling the heat. A few minutes later, Motke came out with the owner of the hall, and they asked me if I could figure out the problem. He knew that I had once worked with air conditioners."

The professor heaved a sigh of relief. "And ... did you manage to fix it?"

"Not right away," Turk laughed. "I spent fifteen minutes up there before I reconnected the wire that I had detached in the first place. He wanted to hug me! Of course, he gave me my job back right away — especially when I said that the air-conditioning system had a serious problem that could cause it to go on the blink again at any time."

"So you're still working at the place?"

"Of course!"

"Good," the professor said. "Then we can move on to the next stage. Do you know Yousuf Nadir? The student who works with me? My research assistant?"

"Of course I know him. When I was in Los Angeles, we went sightseeing together and went to the mosque."

"Okay. He'll be arriving in Palestine in a few weeks. You are to meet him at the airport."

"Is he bringing something with him?" Turk asked. "Something that needs to be kept in the refrigerator that I bought?"

"Stop asking so many questions," his uncle snapped. "Call me after he landed and passed through passport control. You'll get your instructions then."

Motke was in a good mood when Turk walked into his office. He leaned back in his executive chair, talking in Yiddish to someone on the phone. Removing the receiver from his ear for a moment, he asked Turk what he wanted. To his surprise, the young Arab asked for a two-day leave of absence from his job.

"You want a vacation?" Motke asked, laughing loudly enough to let the man at the other end of the phone hear. "What's the matter? Do you have another holiday coming up?"

"No. But we're expecting guests from abroad," Turk said hesitantly. "And I thought that ... if it's possible ... I could take a couple of days off."

"Okay," Motke said. He wagged a warning finger. "But stay in the area, in case we have a problem with the air conditioning."

Ever since Turk's short-lived bout of unemployment, Motke had begun to notice the Arab's assets. Turk made sure to do a good job in every area, along with his expertise in his specialized field. Three times, in the middle of a wedding, the air conditioning broke down, and Turk stepped in and saved the day. *A kitchen hand who is also an air-conditioning technician*, Motke thought. *Who could ask for anything more?*

Once, he called Turk at the apartment when the young man was not slated to be working, to tell him that the air conditioning had gone on the blink again. *Strange*, Turk thought. *Apparently, air conditioners could break down all on their own, too ....*

Two days later, Turk rented a car from a lot in Yaffo, bought a road map, and carefully studied the route to Ben-Gurion Airport. He also acquired a large cooler and found out where he could buy bags of ice cubes. He armed himself with a can opener from his kitchen drawer and bought a second one as insurance. By all appearances, he was preparing for a big picnic.

But the operation he was involved in was no picnic. Not by a long shot.

The day of Yousuf Nadir's night flight to Palestine was a festive one at the university. The eminent French microbiologist, Professor Francois Collagi, had arrived in Los Angeles for a scientific convention, after which he was scheduled to deliver a speech to the UCLA faculty. The halls hummed with activity as students, professors, and biologists streamed in to hear the noted scientist. The visiting professor spent the last half-hour before his speech visiting with his old friend, Professor Barry Majdi.

Yousuf did not want to miss this significant event. He had packed his bags the night before and brought them along to the university. Professor Majdi had promised to give him a ride to the airport after the lecture. Yousuf reviewed the list in his mind to make sure he had everything he needed: his passport, airline ticket, and the envelope that contained the most important thing of all — the letter that he was to deliver to Turk Majdi, the professor's nephew.

Professor Collagi's lecture was a rousing success. The audience was riveted, and the question-and-answer period at its conclusion lasted a long time. By the time Professor Majdi parted from his French guest, evening was beginning to fall over Los Angeles.

The professor drove Yousuf to the airport, where he helped him pull his bags from the trunk of the car. Then he took something from his own briefcase. It was a small rectangular package, covered in handsome gift wrap from a prominent department store and sealed with a small paper-flower sticker.

"This is a small gift for my nephew," he said. "Put it into your briefcase. I don't want it to get lost."

"What is it, cologne?" Yousuf asked as he struggled to insert the package into his overloaded briefcase.

"Yes," the professor said carelessly. "Turk loves that kind of nonsense. So, do you have everything? Passport, ticket ...."

"Everything's here," Yousuf said.

"And the envelope?"

Yousuf tapped his briefcase. He would faithfully deliver the letter to Turk the moment they met.

"Have a pleasant trip." Barry Majdi shook Yousuf's hand warmly. "Call me the minute the two of you meet up in Palestine."

Yousuf endured the long flight from Los Angeles to Israel — a journey of approximately 15 hours — in a state of tension and trepidation. He hardly tasted the meals, couldn't sleep, and was unable to concentrate on the book he had brought with him. He sat unmoving in his seat, keeping close watch on his briefcase, and terrified to death of the moment he would land in Israel.

His briefcase contained the all-important letter to Turk from his uncle, the professor. If it was lost or damaged, Professor Majdi would go berserk with fury. More than that: Yousuf had no way of gauging the damage that such a thing might do to the Muslim world as a whole. He had no idea what was in the letter, but from the broad hints that he had been given he believed it was something that would help his Palestinian brothers free themselves from the yoke of the Zionist oppressor — and help Muslims everywhere to be rid of Western dominance at last.

He had been awaiting this moment for a long time — ever since his trip to the village in Afghanistan where his father had been born, and ever since his return to the States, where he had embraced the faith of Islam. Ever since he had begun attending Imam Bashir Abdul Aziz's mosque in Los Angeles. And, especially, ever since he had been included in the professor and the imam's secret plot. How he had longed for the day when he could take part in the war against the great Satan, America, which regularly degraded the Arab world, and the smaller Satan, the Zionist entity that had conquered the Palestinian people's holy land. And now — it was here. It was happening.

As the hours passed and their arrival drew nearer, Yousuf became even more frightened. He transferred the envelope from his briefcase to his jacket pocket, then back to his briefcase again. Which was preferable? Where would the envelope be safer? He had heard a great deal about the strict searches that the Israelis conducted on every Arab or tourist from a Muslim country. They persecuted anyone who was not a Jew or an American. They went through suitcases, checked clothing, and conducted humiliating body searches. They would spot the envelope at once, and then — who knew what they would do?

At one point, as panic overcame him, Yousuf seriously considered tearing up the envelope and throwing it away. He nearly stood, pale and perspiring, before the wave of fear passed and left him a bit calmer. Actually, he realized, he had no reason to be afraid. He appeared in his passport as "Joe," and he looked completely American. No one even knew that he was of Muslim extraction. Apparently anticipating this situation, the Imam had stopped him from wearing a Muslim skullcap or holding the *misbaha* — the string of beads used in prayer. Besides, he could count on the professor: If there was anything in the letter that the Israeli security forces wouldn't approve of, it was doubtless presented in hints, code, or some sort of secret writing.

The curiosity that had been gnawing at him throughout these final days returned with full intensity. What was it? What could the envelope contain? What required personal delivery by hand — something that could not be transmitted via fax, mail, or over the phone?

Maybe if he opened the envelope and saw that it contained nothing special, he would be able to calm down. What he had managed to see back home, when he had held the envelope up to a strong light, was that the letter was handwritten and was comprised of two pages. From the few words he had been able to decipher, it appeared to be an ordinary family letter. Could there be some sort of hidden instructions or message between the lines?

Why send someone all the way from Los Angeles to Palestine? Why buy him a round-trip ticket for the sole purpose of having him deliver the letter? Maybe Turk Majdi, the professor's nephew, would reveal the secret. Maybe he knew something.

When the steward announced that the plane was approaching its destination, another wave of fear convulsed Yousuf. He pictured the Israeli security service stopping him and interrogating him ruthlessly. Would he be able to withstand the torture? Would he break and give everything away? He must be strong! For Mohammed's sake! For his Palestinian brothers! For the whole Arab world!

Yousuf would doubtless have been many times more afraid had he known that, just three seats behind him, sat a passenger who had been keeping a close eye on him all through the flight. The man's appearance was enough to frighten anyone. His face and hair were strangely pale; his eyes were colorless and devoid of emotion.

This passenger, too, waited impatiently for the plane to land. His job was to make sure that Yousuf brought the lethal package to Israel. He was supposed to report to Assistant Director Walter Child the moment the research assistant successfully passed through passport control — and another stage in the operation had been successfully completed.

The plane passed over the Israeli coastline and began its descent. Yousuf stared out the window, feeling his hands tremble with suspense. The moment the plane's wheels touched the tarmac, a group of Israelis burst into song, while the non-Jews on board looked on in astonishment. The plane rolled up to the terminal and its doors opened. Yousuf stayed in his seat.

While he didn't leave in the first exodus of passengers, he did not wait to be among the last, either. He had heard that if a person wants to smuggle something, it's important for him to walk in the midst of a stream of passengers, where the customs inspectors are apt to be less vigilant. It was also important to do his best to conceal his inner tension, which meant preventing his eyes from gazing fearfully about and his legs from walking too rapidly. He must force himself to behave like a person who has nothing to hide. He was just an ordinary tourist, arriving in Israel for a routine visit.

Passport control came and went with ease, and his luggage arrived promptly on the baggage carousel. Yousuf placed his suitcase on a cart and tried to fix his features into nonchalant lines, though his heart was hammering wildly as he approached customs. If they stopped him, he thought, he would give them his suitcase but not his briefcase. Maybe, if they found nothing in his big bag, they would be uninterested in the small one ....

Another thirty seconds, another twenty steps, just ten more yards and he would be at the longed-for exit. Don't run, don't hurry, don't look around ....

The moment Yousuf stepped through the doors and entered the central part of the terminal, he heaved an enormous sigh of relief. He had done it! He was in Palestine with the professor's letter!

Pushing his cart ahead of him, he scanned the crowd of people waiting for the new arrivals. A slender young man standing at the barrier waved to him. Yousuf recognized Turk and hurried up to him. They shook hands and then embraced.

"How was the flight?" Turk Majdi asked.

"I was terrified all the way over," Yousuf admitted. His hands were still shaking and his stomach was clenched after the hours of nonstop tension. "Don't ask. The entire plane was full of Jews."

"You're telling me? I live with that all the time!" Turk grinned.

Yousuf didn't answer. His legs could barely support him, his throat felt parched, and his heart was still beating far too rapidly.

"All right, I'm supposed to call my uncle the minute I meet you," Turk said. Yousuf sank onto a bench as Turk pulled out his cell phone and punched in a number in Los Angeles. The call was picked up after one ring.

"Uncle Barak? It's Turk."

"Where are you?"

"At the airport. Yousuf just came out."

Turk fell silent as the professor began issuing instructions. As he listened, he smiled slightly to himself, his nostrils quivering with visible excitement. Finally, he hung up.

"Okay, let's go," he told Yousuf.

They headed for the parking lot, where Turk's rental car was waiting. Turk put the suitcase on the backseat. With a thankful groan, Yousuf collapsed into the passenger seat, leaned his head back, and closed his eyes. He felt sick to his stomach and could think of only one thing: sleep.

The moment the car left the airport and started down Highway One, Turk asked if the professor had sent him something.

"Oh, right. The letter." Yousuf roused himself and began to open his briefcase.

"No," Turk laughed. "Not the letter. The present."

Yousuf grimaced in surprise. Turk wanted the present? Had he no patience? Couldn't he wait until Yousuf unpacked in the apartment?

"Hurry up!" Turk urged. "Give it to me."

Now Yousuf understood why his host had not placed the suitcase in the trunk — he thought the gift was in the large bag. What an impatient fellow he was!

"What's the rush?" Yousuf grumbled, curling up in his seat. "I'll give it to you at the apartment."

"Forget it!" Turk snapped. "Just give it to me now!"

Yousuf stared at him, stunned. When he realized that Turk was serious, he swiveled in his seat, silently opened the case, and felt around in it until he found the professor's package.

"Here — take it," he said, thrusting the gift at Turk with an irritation he made no attempt to conceal.

"In case you hadn't noticed, I'm driving," Turk said. "You open it."

"What?" This kid had no manners to speak of. How different from his uncle ....

"Come on, open it already. It's late!" Turk yelled.

Utterly bewildered, Yousuf stumbled over an apology. Why was it late? What was going on?

He tore open the wrapping paper and opened the cardboard box. Inside were two items: a glass bottle of after-shave lotion and an aerosol can of the same brand of spray deodorant.

"He sent you cologne," he told Turk mockingly.

Turk threw a quick glance at the two items in Yousuf's hands. "It's in here," he said, pointing at the deodorant. "Start emptying it."

Yousuf gaped at him. "What are you talking about?"

"Tell me, are you mentally deficient or something?" Turk snatched the can. With one hand on the wheel, he used his other hand to spray deodorant out the window. A long stream of aerosol spray streamed out behind the speeding car, rapidly dissipating in the wind created by their movement.

"What are you doing?" Yousuf shouted. "Are you insane?"

Turk stopped for a moment to give Yousuf a long, slow look.

"What?" he asked in genuine surprise. "Didn't my uncle tell you what was inside?"

Yousuf narrowed his eyes. Was there something in the can besides deodorant? He had thought this was merely a gift from the professor to his nephew, a small token that he had purchased at the last minute.

"What ... what's in there?" he asked apprehensively.

Turk Majdi continued driving toward Tel Aviv, steering with his right hand while his left held the quickly depleting can. He gave his guest from Los Angeles a mysterious smile. "What's in there?" he echoed. "You'll know soon. Patience."

The student's exhaustion had vanished. He sat erect in his chair, eyes wide with fear. If what he had brought from L.A. was not deodorant — then what was it? And why was Turk spraying the stuff while he drove?

He sent Turk a questioning look, but his companion was gazing straight ahead at the road. The shadow of a smile lingered on his lips. Turk was enjoying the situation. He knew something that this university student, his uncle's assistant, did not.

Yousuf ground his teeth but said nothing. He refused to degrade himself by begging. But ... just a second! What about the letter? He still hadn't given that to Turk.

"Is the letter also connected to this?" he asked, taking the envelope from his briefcase even as he began to entertain the glimmering of a notion as to its true purpose.

Turk burst into raucous laughter — laughter that confirmed Yousuf's theory.

"The letter?" Turk said. "You can toss that out the window."

Yousuf was insulted. The professor hadn't trusted him. Barry Majdi had pulled the wool over his eyes. He had given Yousuf a letter for his nephew, pretending that that was the important thing — while, all along, what he had really wanted to give Turk was the can of deodorant. The professor trusted his infantile nephew more than he did his faithful assistant.

Turk saw the offended look on Yousuf's face and decided to soothe his ruffled feathers.

"It's not that my uncle doesn't trust you," he said. "But you've got to understand one thing: If anyone had stopped and questioned you, you had to honestly believe that you were bringing an important letter. Believe me, the Israeli security people are trained to read body language. They notice the slightest involuntary movement. I know them. The minute they would have come near that envelope, you would have started sweating — no matter how hard you tried to look calm. On the other hand, if they had opened the gift box you would have really been calm, because you 'knew' that it was just a present for me. That kind of calm can't be faked. My uncle had no choice. He had to send this with you — without your knowledge."

"Okay," Yousuf said, still angry. Turk's words were logical, but the insult still rankled. It might have been necessary, but he had still been made to feel like an idiot. Remembering how he had safeguarded that letter so frantically, how terrified he had been that someone would open it, how he had transferred it from his briefcase to his pocket and back again, he felt an utter fool.

"Listen," Turk said. "My uncle told me to tell you three words that will explain what he did."

"Three words?"

"Yes: 'Weaken and destroy.'"

"'Weaken and destroy'? What's the connection?" Yousuf was very familiar with the concept, a biological mechanism in the immune system that the professor had been researching for many years.

"No clue," Turk shrugged. "But my uncle said you'd understand. 'Tell Yousuf that I employed a strategy of "weaken and destroy," and he'll understand.' That's what he told me."

Yousuf thought a moment, and finally smiled. "Okay, okay," he said. "Let it go."

The rental car passed the eastern outskirts of Holon. On the horizon sprouted the first tall buildings of Tel Aviv. The stream of deodorant grew weaker and finally disappeared. The can was empty.

"Now can I know what was inside?" Yousuf asked.

"Gladly," Turk said. He pointed at the glove compartment. "Give me the can opener."

"The can opener?"

"Yes. You'll find one in there." Turk slowed down and turned off the main highway onto a short dirt road that led to an Israeli electric-company plant. Everything was going according to plan. This was the place he had decided on when he checked out the territory yesterday. In a radius of ten kilometers on every side were clustered hundreds of thousands of residents of greater Gush Dan. He enjoyed the thought that the thing he held in his hand was capable of killing them all.

These last few days, he had not been able to stop thinking about the professor's great plan, and he was glad that he had a part to play in it. He frequented the mosque in Yaffo, sitting with folded legs on the prayer rugs and ruminating about the huge privilege that had fallen to his lot. He, Turk Majdi from Um-el-Facham, was a participant in the greatest *jihad* in human history — the *jihad* that would change the face of the world — the *jihad* that would raise the nation of Islam to greatness and destroy every infidel on the planet.

Turk looked around. The coast was clear. The electric-company plant seemed devoid of humanity. He gripped the can and began opening it with the aid of the can opener. The professor had chosen a deodorant that could be opened with such an implement.

Yousuf watched him in wonder. Turk had already dispensed the contents of the can all the way from the airport. Why, then, was he opening it now?

The opener completed its circle and the top portion of the can could be lifted off. It was now a hollow cylinder, open at one end.

"Look," Turk said excitedly. He flipped the can over so that its open end faced Yousuf, and urged him to peer inside. Inside the hollow space was a small cylindrical rod in the shape of a miniature thermos. It looked like a narrow test tube and was screwed into the bottom of the can. Reaching inside with two fingers, Turk gave a few gingerly turns and freed the small tube from the deodorant can.

"This is what you brought from America," he said, holding it up. "Not a letter, and not cologne ...."

Yousuf recognized the device. It was one of the oldest inventions of Biologic Systems, the company the professor owned: a small device containing ampoules of liquid nitrogen, used for storing frozen blood samples or vaccinations doses for approximately twenty hours. Concentrated liquid nitrogen, kept at a temperature of 196 degrees below zero, was useful for refrigeration and freezing in the fields of medicine and industry. The professor had succeeded in producing a miniaturized version of the device, and then sold the patent to a large medical-equipment firm.

How clever of him, Yousuf thought. The refrigeration device was attached to the center of the can, around which the professor had inserted deodorant. Should any security personnel at the airport have harbored suspicions, he would have checked and tested the sprayer, which would have emitted nothing but ordinary deodorant. The metal container also prevented the device inside from showing up on an X-ray. Genius. That Barry Majdi was simply a genius!

Turk opened the tiny freezer, to reveal a test tube filled with a frozen yellow substance. Holding it very carefully, he exited the car, walked to the rear, and opened the trunk. He hid the test tube in a mound of ice cubes in the cooler he had brought with him. Then he returned to the driver's seat, exhaling in relief.

"What I'm about to tell you is top secret," he told Yousuf. "The stuff in that little tube that is now in the trunk is capable of wiping out every infidel on earth. It's a deadly virus ... and I'm going to set it loose in a few weeks."

"How?" asked Yousuf, infused with his companion's excitement.

"Through the air-conditioning system in the catering hall where I work."

"Just a minute .... You're going to spread it at the wedding of some big 'rebbe,' or whatever they call him?"

"Right. How do you know that?"

"And his name is ..." Yousuf tried to recall. "His name is ... the Milinover Rebbe?"

"That's right! How'd you know?"

Yousuf glowed. *He* was the one who had done the research for Majdi and Aziz. He had managed to locate the anthropologist, Dr. Jimmy Trovsi, as well as the chassidic medical student, Leiby Klein, who had described the way chassidic weddings worked. At the professor's request, Yousuf had also looked into specific details about the Milinover dynasty.

Yousuf chuckled to himself. The last traces of his anger at the professor were gone. Of course Majdi trusted him. Of course he had respect for him. After all, Yousuf had been present in the office when the professor had invited the imam for a conference and consulted with an air-conditioning expert.

There was no question about it: The professor trusted him implicitly. He had allowed Yousuf to share the most secret details of the great and glorious plan.

The hum of passing traffic from the nearby highway reached them. A power-plant employee left the building and walked into the parking lot. He peered at the rental car parked on the shoulder of the road, with two young Arabs sitting inside it.

"Let's get out of here," Turk told Yousuf, "before someone gets suspicious."

He started the car and headed back toward the Jerusalem-Tel Aviv highway. The windows were closed and the air-conditioning worked at full blast as the scenery flowed past. For a long time, neither of them spoke.

Yousuf was lost in thought. He, unlike Turk, knew exactly what havoc the substance in that little glass vial was capable of perpetrating. A sudden memory flashed into his brain: a snippet from one of his earliest university lectures. "Nature has created some extremely cruel substances," the lecturer — an expert in viral research — had said. "But man has gone one better."

The lecturer had told his students that the CDC labs contained samples of the most lethal viruses on earth, from anthrax and the plague through the Ebola virus. Moscow's Center for Viral Research was also in possession of a respectable collection of these minuscule but lethal germs. The governments of both countries purportedly encouraged their scientists to find cures for these diseases, while in actuality ordering them to devise ever more deadly strains of them.

"There are viruses," the lecturer had added, "whose very existence is a state secret. These are engineered viruses, of which a minuscule amount, set loose in the air or water supply, would be enough to destroy every living creature for miles around ...."

Yousuf shivered. *Was the substance in the vial resting in the trunk of this car,* he wondered, *one of those viruses?* Was he traveling in the company of a virus that represented the seeds of a worldwide epidemic capable of wiping out half of humanity? Would the vial he had just brought from the States spell the agonizing deaths of tens or hundreds of millions?

As they approached Netivei Ayalon, traffic began to slow. Yousuf gazed in surprise at the tall office buildings, colorful billboards, and an up-to-date railroad terminal. This was not the way he had imagined the oppressed land of Palestine. The Jews had established a modern, Western-style country — on land that had belonged to Arabs. The infidels lived in sumptuous cities, while Muslims crowded into refugee camps and crumbling huts without running water or electricity. Yousuf's heart overflowed with rage at this perceived injustice, outraged at what he had been taught to see as the degradation of his brothers and the trampled honor of the Muslim nation as a whole.

His trepidation over the consequences of his actions was abruptly transformed into an overweening pride. He would have his share in changing the world. He was an important part of the great plan to restore Muslim dominance, as in the glorious days of Tzalach-a-Din.

Suddenly, an icy chill gripped him. Had Barry Majdi taken everything into consideration? If a deadly outbreak started in Palestine, it would quickly move on to the neighboring countries with their crowded population centers — and millions of Muslims would pay with their lives. How could the professor and the imam be certain that only infidels would die in the biological *jihad* they were plotting? Was the virus, sophisticated as it might be, capable of differentiating between Muslim, Christian, and Jew?

51

Turk's voice brought Yousuf back to the present reality.

"What does 'weaken and destroy' mean?" he asked.

Yousuf smiled. "Never mind. It's a biological concept. You wouldn't understand."

"So explain it to me in words that I *can* understand."

"All right," Yousuf sighed. "If you insist …. 'Weaken and destroy' is a biological mechanism in the immune system that the professor has been studying for years. I'll spare you the technical terms, like 'lymphocytes,' 'cytotoxic T-cells,' and 'antigens' — but, in a general sense, the immune system, whose job it is to overpower foreign bodies such as germs, viruses, or cancerous cells, sometimes employs a double strategy. Its first step is to kill off the affected cells by spreading a deadly protein called proporin. The second is to activate the destructive mechanism of those very cells, causing them to 'commit suicide' in a process known as 'epiptosis.' Clear so far?"

"More or less."

"Actually, this is an ongoing process. If you've ever had the flu and recovered, that's a sign that your immune system used one of these two methods — or both of them together."

"Okay."

"But the biological mechanism known as 'weaken and destroy' is even more sophisticated. It was discovered several years ago, and your uncle has studied it in depth. In such a case, the immune system exudes 'dummy' receptors that *look* like the lethal cells that attack an infected cell. The attacked cell recruits all its energy in order to fight off the attacker, thereby weakening itself. Then — from a completely unexpected direction — along comes another protein, truly deadly, that subdues and overpowers the already weakened cell.

"In short: 'Weaken and destroy' is a clever decoy mechanism used by the immune system to overcome infection and disease."

"And that's what the my uncle did to you!" Turk exclaimed in sudden comprehension. "He made sure you were focused on keeping the letter safe, but that was just a decoy. He made you concentrate all your energy on the letter — until you suddenly discovered that the really important thing was the gift box with the deodorant."

"Exactly," said Yousuf.

"I see that my uncle turns his research into a philosophy of life," Turk laughed.

"You could say that."

Another silence fell. Turk's car had reached the outskirts of Yaffo. It passed the watchtower and the local mosque, then turned at the flea market, moving toward his rental apartment.

Yousuf looked around with a mixture of surprise and disappointment. The neighborhood where Turk lived was very different from the modern, Western-style areas he had seen on the way here — starting with the lavish terminal at Ben-Gurion Airport, through Netivei Ayalon and the adjacent office towers, to Rechov HaYarkon with its line of hotels, embassies, and restaurants. If he had felt as though he were still in America until now, here he had definitely stepped into the Middle East. The houses were ugly and crowded, their walls sooty and peeling, the courtyards serving as repositories for piles of rubbish.

"We're here," Turk announced, parking the car. "Let's get the cooler upstairs."

They climbed a dim, narrow flight of stairs to the second story. Turk opened the door — and Yousuf recoiled. He had never seen an apartment like this even in the worst neighborhoods of Los Angeles. The floor was filthy and the walls were urgently in need of a paint job. A single exposed lightbulb hung from the ceiling, and the bed linens had not been changed for many weeks. Yousuf glanced with disgust into the kitchen. Moldy leftovers littered the countertop, while the sink held a stack of dishes that had not been washed since dinner the night before — or the day before that, or perhaps even all week.

Against this dispiriting backdrop stood a gleaming new refrigerator. It seemed to be an expensive model.

"So, what do you think of my place?" Turk asked, smiling. This apartment in Yaffo was a definite cut above his mother's home in Um-el-Facham. He had two large rooms here, all for himself, with no sisters or brothers to share it, no shrill mother who wept and cursed by turns, and no goats wandering in from the yard. There was no one to tell him to clean up his mess, and he had all of Yaffo's kiosks and restaurants at his disposal. He could go to the beach or stroll on the boardwalk. Even America couldn't offer a better life.

Yousuf didn't answer. He was glad now that he had been too lazy to bring his suitcase up from the car. He was not going to stay under this roof for even a single night. He would not eat at that dirty table — and he didn't even want to imagine what the bathroom might look like. Turk's living conditions reminded him of the primitive villages he had visited when he had flown to Pakistan after graduating high school — the trip that had roused his Islamic consciousness. The trip that had led him to change his name from Joe to Yousuf and to begin attending services at the imam's huge mosque.

Here in Israel, the Jews lived comfortable lives, while Yaffo — an important Arab city with an illustrious history — was neglected and decaying. It was not enough that the infidels had deprived his brothers of their land, Yousuf thought angrily; they were also compelling them to live in conditions that were degrading in the extreme.

Turk, meanwhile, had opened the cooler. He rummaged around among the ice cubes until he found the still-frozen vial, which he quickly placed into the freezer compartment of his new refrigerator.

He had use of the rental car only until the following morning, and he still had one more task to accomplish: picking up a package that had been sent from abroad and that was waiting for him at the delivery office near the central train station. The sender: Biologic Systems, 6114 Mercury Street, Los Angeles, California, U.S.A.

He retrieved the package without any problems. Turk Majdi showed the clerk his identity card and the documents that his uncle had faxed him, and was handed a rectangular package about the size of the average book.

Turk and Yousuf couldn't resist opening the package in the car. Inside the cardboard box, securely wrapped, was an elongated metal device that resembled a digital book reader. Turk turned the object over and over, trying to figure out how it worked.

Yousuf, meanwhile, was busy reading the instruction booklet that came along with the device; the pamphlet described methods of disseminating fragrances through a large area. An ampoule of the desired aroma was introduced into the long, narrow opening at the top of the device — made exclusively by Biologic Systems, of course. By pressing the keys found at the side of the disseminator, one could select the preferred time delay, up to sixty minutes. At the end of that time, a small hammer would break the top of the glass vial, releasing the fragrance inside. The fragrance would then travel through the air, preferably through an air-conditioning system, although it would work to a limited degree even in the open air. Biologic Systems thanked its customers for choosing its high-quality products.

As Turk gripped the device in his hands, his heart quailed. A quick glance at Yousuf's face showed him that they both realized they were not dealing with fragrances. This was the device meant to spread the substance in the vial now lying in the freezer in his apartment. Turk was to insert it into the air-conditioning system at Ganei HaSimchah on the 23rd of August, at the Milinover Rebbe's grandson's wedding. Afterward, the professor had told him, he was to call him immediately for further instructions.

Yousuf took the device from Turk and replaced it in its box. Turk started the car and, at Yousuf's request, began driving in the direction of the hotels on Rechov HaYarkon. The inside of the car was charged with suppressed excitement.

"What do you think is in that vial?" Turk asked Yousuf, hoping that his voice would not betray his jitters.

"What's in the vial?" Yousuf echoed. "How should I know? Maybe some Black Death germs, or a Bolivian paralytic virus, or Lhasa fever. There's no shortage of diseases that can cause mass death. Diseases that no medicine or vaccination can protect against. Diseases that, from the minute they are set loose, are difficult or impossible to control."

Neither expressed it aloud, but the same bloodcurdling thought was going through both of their minds: Were they marching toward their own doom? Would spreading the toxin at the Milinover wedding on August 23rd seal their own fate? How, exactly, did the professor and the imam plan to ensure that only infidels would die from the outbreak, while all true believers survived?

Had the young Muslims known what the professor was planning to release at the wedding, their fears would have been calmed. The Mexico virus developed by the Nazi prisoner might have been custom made for the Islamic *jihad*. Only a person who drank alcohol could be harmed by it.

A good Muslim who refrained from imbibing wine might become slightly ill, but he would eventually recover. Only infidels who regularly indulged in wine and alcohol would die amid great suffering. Only in the infidel's bodies, which produced a special enzyme after drinking alcohol, would the virus become lethal. It was not for naught that Aziz and Majdi had nicknamed the virus, "The Sword of Mohammed." Like that legendary weapon, the Mexican virus would kill all the infidels — Jews and Christians — while leaving alive all faithful Muslims who followed in Mohammed's footsteps.

Standing in the lobby of the David Intercontinental Hotel near the Tel Aviv boardwalk, they paid no attention to a strange-looking man with a very pale face and hair, seated on one of the sofas and speaking into his cell phone. No one would have taken him for a CIA agent in conversation with one of the senior men at Langley.

The pale agent, who had sat three rows behind Yousuf on the flight from L.A., reported to Assistant Director Walter Child that the mission had been accomplished. The vial had arrived safely in Israel and was resting safely in Majdi's freezer. All they had to do now was to wait patiently for the wedding date.

How was he to know that it was entirely possible that the wedding would never take place?

How could he guess that, just a week and a half before the appointed date, a serious halachic problem would arise — a problem that would threaten to postpone the happy day and leave the entire body of Milinover chassidim stunned and abashed?

Who knew that, on August 23rd — the 29th day of Av, the day the wedding was scheduled to take place — it was wholly possible that the Ganei HaSimchah hall would be standing dark and empty, with a note on the door for those who had not yet heard the bad news, announcing that the wedding had been put off to an indeterminate date in the future?

Who knew then, two months before the wedding was slated to take place, that the only way to avert an unprecedented biological attack would be a halachic muddle that would lead the *mechutan* to fly, crestfallen, back to the United States just days before the *chuppah*?

Jerusalem — Av 5766 / August 2006

Troubles tend to cluster in the month of Av, thought R' Shammai Lederman sadly, as he traveled by bus to Jerusalem.

All the terrible destructions in the Jewish nation had taken place in that month. And the *churban* that was fast approaching now was happening in the same month, when *simchah* was diminished. In just a week and a half, the great wedding was slated to take place: the marriage of Zalman Leib, the Rebbe's beloved grandson. But R' Shammai was on his way to Jerusalem to bring the young bridegroom some bitter news.

The Milinover Rebbe's chief *gabbai* focused on the *Sefer Tehillim* that had been open before him from the moment he had left the Rebbe's apartment in Tzefas two hours earlier. He had been chief *gabbai* for 25 years — a quarter of a century — but never remembered such misery. Such a terrible thing had never occurred before. Unquestionably, the Satan was at work here. It was precisely at this great hour, in these emotional and exalted moments, that catastrophe had struck.

The memory of the painful phone conversation was etched in his mind. Tears kept filling his eyes. R' Shammai was a deeply emotional man; when he led the *davening* at Shacharis on Yom Kippur, the congregants were quickly brought to tears. He felt as though it were Yom Kippur now. It was the awesome hour when the gates are shut, when one's fate is sealed for life or death. The haunting melody of *"U'Nesaneh Tokef"* began running through his thoughts. He hummed the tune through a throat choked with tears: "Who will live in tranquility and who will be distraught; who will enjoy serenity and who will suffer ...."

He arrived in Jerusalem in the early afternoon. The taxi left him in front of the yeshivah building and R' Shammai climbed the broad steps to the front door. The *beis midrash* was packed to the rafters with *bachurim*. For a long time the *gabbai* stood at the door, scanning the noisy room in search of Zalman Leib. Several young men in chassidic garb paused in passing to ask if they could help. A few recognized his aristocratic face and knew that he was the Milinover Rebbe's *gabbai*. In that case, he must be seeking the Rebbe's grandson. "Shall we call him?" they asked.

At first, R' Shammai declined. He would allow Zalman Leib a few more moments of peace before imparting the bad news. He would let him have a bit more pleasure in his carefree learning, before he told him what had been said in that difficult telephone conversation from the United States — the call that had plunged them all into a hornet's nest of trouble.

But there was no choice. The thing must be done. R' Shammai asked one of the *bachurim* to summon Zalman Leib, who was learning at the front of the vast room. He saw the question on the Rebbe's grandson's face. Someone was waiting for him at the door? Who could it be?

Telling his *chavrusah* that he would be right back, the young chassid began walking toward the door. He saw R' Shammai from afar, and noted instantly that the *gabbai's* face was downcast. Zalman Leib's heart missed a beat. Walking faster now, he hurried over to R' Shammai.

"*Shalom aleichem*." The *gabbai* extended his hand.

Zalman Leib didn't even hear him. "What happened?" he asked hoarsely. "Is the Rebbe all right?"

"The Rebbe is well," R' Shammai said. He sensed the younger man's relief. "But a difficult problem has arisen this morning."

R' Zalman Leib looked at him questioningly.

"It a problem with the *mechutan*, R' Yom Tov Padlinsky."

"What's happened?" Zalman Leib asked in sudden anxiety.

"Is there a quiet place where we can talk? A classroom or something?" R' Shammai didn't want the young *chasan* exposed to the eyes of the curious when he was given the bad news.

"Zalman Leib," R' Shammai began, when they were seated opposite each other in a small room near the library. "This morning, a call came from the United States. A difficult halachic problem has arisen concerning your *mechutan*, R' Yom Tov Padlinsky. Actually, not just with him, but with the entire family ....

"It began in the Bnei Brak *Beis Din*, with regard to the divorce of R' Yom Tov's nephew. The other side was trying to find a way to harm the family — and they succeeded. In short, Zalman Leib, without going into detail right now, a serious question has surfaced regarding the family. It is possible, *r"l*, that two generations ago a woman was permitted to marry after her husband's death ... but it has now come to light that the husband was still alive.

"That woman was R' Yom Tov's mother — the *kallah's* grandmother. If the story is true, then we have a big problem."

Not a muscle in Zalman Leib's face moved. He had not yet absorbed the import of the news. "What does this mean?" he asked.

R' Shammai threw an agonized look down at the table, and then lifted his eyes to the young *chasan*. "It means that there's a chance that the wedding will not be able to take place," he whispered.

"But — but the wedding is in just a week and a half!" R' Zalman Leib stammered in bewilderment.

"It ... is *supposed* to take place in a week and a half," R' Shammai said. He compressed his lips in pain.

"So what do we do?"

R' Shammai spread his hands and heaved a deep sigh. "I don't know," he said. "I simply don't know what to do."

Tel Aviv — Av 5766 / August 2006

The first signs of the approaching catastrophe were picked up by Israel's intelligence network at the height of the second Lebanese war.

The I.D.F., G.S.S., and other security arms were busy with the battle in the north. All efforts were being bent toward subduing Hezbollah and halting the Katyusha rockets aimed at Haifa, Tzefas, Nahariya, and Beit She'an. Still, it was impossible to ignore the worrying information that was slowly trickling in, information about an upcoming terror attack on an unprecedented scale. All indications pointed to the end of the summer.

The intelligence arrived in several waves. The first intimation was included in a report from the CIA under the umbrella of a routine information exchange, but additional details quickly came to light. The attack, it appeared, would be biological in nature. In ensuing talks between G.S.S. leaders and their American counterparts, the latter said that the source of their information was classified. They could not expose their source — but the level of reliability was extremely high. Further indications seemed to imply that the attack would not come from a recognized and established organization, but rather from a dormant terrorist cell that could be operating independently. This only complicated the situation: The fewer people in on a secret, the more intelligence gaps existed.

What sort of biological attack? Plague? Anthrax? No one in either the Israeli G.S.S. or the broader intelligence network had an answer. No one knew anything except the tidbits that the CIA was willing to divulge, but no one was prepared to take any chances. The threat was treated as a red-hot item based on solid information. The war in Lebanon had made the nation edgy. Every day more soldiers were being laid to rest; every day brought its share of bad news. And now, to top it all, was this newest piece of intelligence, many times more menacing.

In total secrecy, under heavy blackout conditions, a state of emergency was declared in the highest echelons responsible for dealing with biological threats. A steering committee for hospital preparedness in the event of a biological attack met at the Hillel Yaffe hospital in Chadera. An elite police team, including specialists trained in unconventional weapons, was placed on high alert. The Ministry of Health's epidemic division convened an urgent meeting.

Far from the public eye, feverish activity was taking place. In the biological institute at Nes Tziona, lights burned till the wee hours; trucks laden with immunization kits lumbered through the nights, from the central emergency warehouses to various distribution points; a special shipment of thousands of protective suits with sealed breathing units arrived from a factory in Germany. Israel prepared blindly for a huge terror event. No one knew what they were about to face. No one knew which devious and industrious enemy the State might be coming up against this time.

The atmosphere in the prime minister's office was tense. As it had done daily throughout the war, the inner security cabinet was meeting to discuss developments. The prime minister, who had slept less than two hours in the last forty-eight, listened to the various ministers while battling off a wave of intense exhaustion. One of his aides handed him a note. It was from Uri Arbel.

"The U.S.," Arbel had written, "is sending a senior agent about the biological threat."

The prime minister's face relaxed slightly. Officially, Uri Arbel was one of his three military advisers. In reality, Arbel was one of the most important figures in the prime minister's office. His special domain was the "unconventional warfare" menace.

Uri Arbel was also one of the few people in the State of Israel whose name was routinely kept out of newspapers by the military censors. His picture had never appeared in print — despite the fact that, should his photo ever have appeared in connection with the prime minister, no one would have given his nondescript face a second glance.

Arbel was considered one of the top experts in his field, which was perhaps the reason he had retained his post under four consecutive prime ministers. His analytical mind was a treasure trove of information and connections. At night, he dreamed about Ebola and anthrax. He ate, drank, and breathed "dirty" radioactive bombs, poisoned water sources, and ballistic missiles with chemical warheads. The prime minister's staff knew this: When Uri Arbel wished to speak to their boss, or to have a note delivered to him in the middle of a high-level meeting, his wishes were to be carried out at once.

Ben-Gurion Airport was relatively quiet for early August. Most years, this was the peak of the season, but the war in the north had slowed tourism and the planes were coming in half empty. The El Al flight from the U.S. landed right on time. The few people waiting behind the waterfall-railing to greet the disembarking passengers knew from experience that it would be at least thirty minutes before the first of the travelers walked through the sliding doors. Passengers must first pass through passport control and then find their luggage. A select few would also submit to a luggage search by the customs crew.

There were a few individuals, however, who received special treatment. The American special agent was first off the plane and was moved rapidly along the VIP route. Just ten minutes after the plane's wheels touched down, Uri Arbel's cell phone rang as the agent let him know that he had arrived.

Arbel, waiting at the perimeter of the arrivals terminal, saw the American first. Though not tall — just slightly above average in height — the agent was impressive looking. About fifty, he was slim and muscular, with an energetic walk that radiated good health. His skin was slightly sunburned and his hair was still black, with only a touch of silver at the temples. He carried a medium-sized suitcase.

Uri Arbel strode over with outstretched hand. "Welcome to Israel."

The agent shook the proffered hand, his grip strong. The flight had been excellent, he replied to the courteous question.

A car from the prime minister's office awaited them. Quickly leaving the airport behind, the driver took them onto Highway 1, toward Jerusalem. Uri Arbel tried to engage the agent in casual conversation, but the latter said dryly that he had some work to complete that he had begun on the plane. He opened his laptop, tilting it so that the Israeli could not see the screen. The man, Arbel thought, was not even trying to be pleasant.

The ride passed in an oppressive silence — at least, from Uri's perspective. The American agent worked with remarkable diligence, barely lifting his eyes from the monitor. Mostly, he read, occasionally typing in a few brief lines.

As they entered Jerusalem, he switched off the laptop, stretched in his seat, and studied the streets and pedestrians through the window. Uri Arbel had the distinct impression that this was the man's first visit to the city. As they approached the government plaza, the agent prepared to exit. He slipped the computer into its case, buttoned his suit jacket, and straightened his tie.

Representatives of many security branches were at the meeting taking place in one of the conference rooms in the prime minister's complex: the minister of defense and his military aide, as well as the directors of the G.S.S., the Mossad, and the police. Each was accompanied by several assistants. Uri Arbel thanked them all for coming on such short notice.

"First, I'd like to welcome Agent Scott, from the Special Operations Branch of the director of the American D.N.I., or Department of National Intelligence," he said, yielding the floor to the visitor.

The director of the D.N.I., as they were all aware, was the man with overall responsibility for coordinating American intelligence, directly answerable to the president himself. He oversaw all information and intelligence services, from the CIA, FBI, Secret Service, and NSA to the DEA, Treasury intelligence, Coast Guard, and more. But what was the Special Operations Branch?

The Israelis were not alone in being in the dark here. Even within the United States government, there were not many people who knew about the new, half-secret branch that had been established just a few months earlier. The division was made up of a small, select group of top intelligence people. These individuals were obligated to be free of any constraints on their time, and ready to fly out at a moment's notice to any point on the globe. The Special Operations division was, in effect, a vigorous and effective intervention arm for solving crises. It existed on a plane outside the usual gray cloud of bureaucracy and interagency bickering that had each organization scrambling for budgetary gains and honor.

Agent Scott certainly fit the bill. He had begun his career in an elite commando unit — an outstanding soldier who became an outstanding officer — and then moved into the shadows. For the next two decades he served as a Defense Department intelligence analyst and participated in several covert operations that were never made public. Along the way, he earned two degrees in political science, passed a course in the art of negotiation, and specialized in the field of biological terror. At one point, he had worked with a branch established to combat terror in Los Angeles. He had been brought in to help compensate for a leadership vacuum in the branch, and had been responsible for getting it back on its feet.

Inclining his head, Agent Scott thanked Uri Arbel. He reviewed everything that was known up to that point, and said that his goal was to heighten communication between the Israeli intelligence community and that of the United States with regard to this specific threat. He formulated various methods by which the two could work in cooperation, and ended by saying that each new development or piece of information would be brought to the forum's attention.

To Arbel's disappointment, Scott had brought no new information with him.

Analysts from all federal intelligence agencies had been diligently at work over the past 24 hours, sifting data for any sort of clue. The position of Director of the D.N.I. — Agent Scott's direct superior — had been created in the wake of September 11, which had highlighted glaring flaws in the transmission of classified information between the various intelligence agencies. A tidbit of information presently in the hands of naval intelligence, for example, might be exactly the missing piece that the Secret Service or NSA was feverishly seeking. All organizations in the American intelligence community, therefore, were advised to ascertain whether they had any concrete information regarding a biological attack on Israel, due to take place toward the end of the summer.

So far, nothing had come to light. The only thing that was known was that an attack was expected — but where, and how, and by whom, were still one big mystery.

Jerusalem — Av 5766 /August 2006

An anguished silence fell over the small room adjoining the *beis midrash* library. Zalman Leib gazed wordlessly at R' Shammai for a long moment, and then bowed his head.

Everything had happened so suddenly, so inexplicably. His tranquil life had exploded with a bang, leaving him solitary, sad, and filled with questions: Would the wedding simply fail to take place? How could that be? Just ten days before he was supposed to stand beneath the *chuppah* — was it all to go up in smoke? What would he do now? How could he go on?

And how had such an awful thing happened? How was it possible that R' Yom Tov Padlinsky's mother had been permitted to remarry while her husband was still alive? Was that a proven fact or only a concern? And did that mean that the Rosh Yeshivah and his entire family were, Heaven forbid, disqualified from marrying?

Zalman Leib stared out the window, trying to blink back the tears that threatened to overcome him. Why had this happened to him? Why should such a painful thing be visited on his dear parents? What sorrow it would cause his grandfather, the elderly Rebbe, and the entire *kehillah* ....

His anguish was not only for himself and his family, but also for his esteemed teacher, R' Yom Tov Padlinsky. After all, apart from being his future father-in-law, R' Yom Tov had also been his Rosh Yeshivah. Zalman Leib had learned in his yeshivah, Knesses HaTorah, for five years. A beloved student, he had ended by being chosen for R' Yom Tov's daughter. This honor had come as a surprise: Though R' Yom Tov came from a chassidic family, he had deep roots in the Litvishe world. In general, he had not made *Rebbishe* shidduchim for his children. But in R' Zalman Leib's case, he had made an exception.

At Pesach, R' Zalman Leib had come to Israel, planning to stay until after the wedding. He attended the yeshivah in Jerusalem, traveling to Tzefas on Fridays to spend Shabbos with his illustrious grandfather.

"Who knows about this?" he asked the *gabbai*.

"Only a few people," R' Shammai said. "Very few. Only those who need to know."

"My father?"

"Of course. He called me from New York and asked me to tell the Rebbe."

Zalman Leib fell silent for a moment, imagining the painful scene in which the *gabbai* had given the Rebbe the bad news.

"What did the Rebbe say?" he asked at last.

"The Rebbe wants you to come to him," R' Shammai said gently. "He wants to talk to you."

The trip from Jerusalem to Tzefas afforded Zalman Leib plenty of time to think. He detoured to Meron to daven Minchah and Maariv at the Rashbi's grave, the tears pouring like water for himself and his family. It was early evening when the taxi arrived in Tzefas's Old City. The *hoiz bachur* welcomed him warmly and ushered him in to see the Rebbe.

Zalman Leib knew this room well. It was a narrow space, with its decorative windows, a bookcase full of *sefarim*, and a low dresser near the bed holding a tray of *yahrzeit* candles. But this time felt different from his previous visits. Always before, he had come here in joyful anticipation. Now he had come in mourning and humiliation.

The Rebbe appeared unchanged. He sat at the head of the table, a *Maseches Kiddushin* open in front of him and another volume lying unopened beside it.

"Come. Let's learn," the Rebbe said. This was his custom with every grandson who was engaged to be married: Between the engagement and the wedding he would learn *Maseches Kiddushin* with them, from beginning to end — a spiritual preparation for the great day when the young couple would marry. He and Zalman Leib were nearing the end of the tractate. How ironic, thought Zalman Leib, that the *perek* they were learning dealt in part with the status of the offspring of forbidden unions ....
He tried to concentrate, but this proved to be a feat that was beyond him. After several minutes, overcome with emotion, he put his head on his hand and wept bitterly. The Rebbe was learning *Kiddushin* with him, as though he were an ordinary *chasan* on the brink of the *chuppah*. But the Rebbe must know that the wedding was about to be canceled! All

this learning was for naught. He was no longer a *chasan*. He was just an unfortunate *bachur* whose happiness had turned to ashes.

The Rebbe didn't move. For a few long minutes he sat with eyes closed, waiting for his beloved grandson's weeping to abate.

"Let me tell you a story that happened to my holy grandfather, Rebbe Azriel," he said.

Zalman Leib lifted his head and focused, his eyes still brimming with tears, on the Rebbe.

"When R' Azriel was about to marry off his son, R' Tuvia, some evil people spread slander about the *kallah's* family, in the hopes of breaking the shidduch. Those who were close to the Rebbe were worried and upset. It was very near the time for the wedding, and *chassidim* had already begun to arrive from the neighboring towns. Wagon after wagon made its way toward Milinov — while no one knew if the wedding would even take place.

"To their surprise, in their Rebbe's countenance they saw not the great apprehension and misery that they had expected, but the opposite. The holy R' Azriel's face shone with joy. He showed no sign of worry. The day of the *aufruf* came and went. The wedding day — slated to take place that Wednesday — came closer. Just one day before the wedding, it came to light that it had all been nothing but a totally false aspersion without any basis in fact. The wedding took place on time, amid great joy and good cheer.

"When they asked my grandfather, R' Azriel, why he had been so confident that the wedding would take place, he answered that a person's forebears come from the Next World to attend their descendant's *simchah*. As all the *chassidim* began coming in on their wagons and trains, he saw his own holy ancestors arrive, joyful and elated, to participate in the happy occasion. 'I knew that they would not have arrived for nothing,' he said. 'Heaven would not have troubled them to come in vain. Therefore, I was confident that the wedding would take place.' And so it did."

Zalman Leib listened to his grandfather intently, trying to understand what he was trying to tell him. But the Rebbe had no more to say.

"Go back to yeshivah," he told his beloved grandson. "Immerse yourself in Torah and *tefillah*, and *HaKadosh Baruch Hu* will help us."

R' Shammai sighed with relief when Zalman Leib told him what had transpired in the Rebbe's room.

"I have no idea how," he said, trying to encourage the young *chasan*, and perhaps himself as well, "but the wedding will take place on time. Don't worry."

There were three other people who would have been equally thrilled to hear the Milinover Rebbe's words to his grandson about the upcoming wedding. They, of course, had no inkling of the halachic threat to the proceedings — but any change or delay in the scheduled event would have upset their plans. Two of the three lived in Los Angeles: Professor Barry Majdi and Imam Bashir Abdul Aziz. The third was CIA Assistant Director Walter Child.

None of the three had any interest in witnessing the establishing of a new Jewish family or in preventing gloom among the Milinover chassidim. They looked forward to the wedding for one reason alone: as a necessary backdrop for their great act of terror.

Tel Aviv — Av 5766 / August 2006

T he armed marine ordered the American special agent to place his hand on a small square glass surface near the doorframe.

The United States Marines are charged, among other things, with embassy security across the world. Security in this secret portion of the American Embassy in Israel was tight. No ordinary ID would serve here; biometric identification was standard procedure. Only after computerized systems "recognized" the special agent's fingerprints did the buzzer sound to allow the marine to open the door for him.

"Good morning, Agent Scott," the marine greeted him from behind his desk in the lobby. "The communications room will be available to you in five minutes."

There was a row of chairs nearby, but Agent Scott chose to stand at the window — made of bulletproof glass — and look outside. The Tel Aviv coastline was spread before him in all its glory. The sea was calm and filled with beachgoers. It was the end of August, the war in the north had ended, and Israelis had come out in force to take full advantage of the bit of freedom remaining before the new school year began.

The agent felt the calmness that descended upon him each time he walked into American territory in a foreign country. It had happened to him in Yemen, the Ukraine, Slovenia, and other hot spots to which he had been sent in the course of his career. Always, the American Embassy was an island of safety and security. A place where, for a few moments, he could let down his guard and relax. Where he was free of the fear of capture, of the need to notice every detail, of an alertness that kept him in a constant state of readiness — for anything and everything.

The embassy was like a small taste of home. Here, he could see American faces, hear English spoken minus the heavy Mediterranean or Middle-European accent, and drink an American brand of coffee, in American disposable cups, with American sugar, mixed with American-made teaspoons ....

Here in the U.S. Embassy in Tel Aviv, he felt the same. He had been at G.S.S. headquarters, near Tel Aviv, when the White House had phoned to inform him that the president wanted an update on the situation. Agent Scott had hastened to Tel Aviv. This was one conversation that would not take place on an ordinary telephone, but rather on a secure satellite hookup from the embassy's communications room.

There are those who are of the opinion that issuing visas is the primary occupation of the American Embassy in Tel Aviv. Others believe that the fortress like complex on Rechov HaYarkon is the work hub of diplomatic teams and people from the U.S. State Department. But the forest of antennae and satellite dishes situated on the embassy roof serves as evidence that far more than basic diplomatic chores are carried out here.

It is an open secret that the two upper stories of the embassy building are devoted to intelligence activities. Or, in more explicit terms, to spying on Israel. Disguised as embassy personnel were a large contingent of CIA staff — headed by a senior member of that organization — representatives from every branch of the U.S. military, and an FBI office. The embassy also hosts members of the Pentagon and its own intelligence agency, as well as NSA — the National Security Agency responsible for tracking electronic transmissions. While Americans do not hesitate to eavesdrop on those around them, they exert every effort to prevent others from eavesdropping on *them*. The entire embassy building is fashioned from a combination of concrete, steel, and other materials impermeable to tapping. And most secure of all is the communications room, equipped with secure lines and garbled by special state-of-the-art computer programs.

Agent Scott leaned against the window and continued looking out while he organized his thoughts. His preoccupied gaze followed an Israeli patrol boat speeding through the surf on a parallel course to the beach. Not many people were aware, he thought, that the location of the embassy near the coast was not a coincidence. In the event of a war that spiraled out of control, government chaos, a biological or chemical terror attack, or the closing of local airports, American naval forces would be able to swoop in and rescue diplomatic personnel quickly via the sea.

Was that going to happen here in the near future? Was Israel going to be subjected to an unconventional attack on an unprecedented scale? That, in essence, was the question the president was going to ask him in a few moments' time. The president had requested a situational update. After spending nearly a week in this country and meeting with all the senior people involved, Agent Scott would be expected to have formed an opinion.

The heads of all intelligence branches gathered in the Situation Room in the basement of the White House's western wing. Also seated around the elliptical table were the Joint Chiefs of Staff, the National Security adviser, and several senior military officers.

One of the wall clocks was set to Washington time. The two others — as was the custom in the Situation Room — reflected local time in whatever spot on the globe the current crisis had mushroomed. Today, Israel had that dubious honor.

The door opened. The president, accompanied by the White House chief of staff entered. Everyone stood up in his place, taking their seats only after he had taken his at the head of the table. From this room, equipped with sophisticated communications equipment, the president — who was also the commander in chief of the United States armed forces — could command all of his forces in real time. This was where the president and his advisers adjourned when important events were taking place, whether inside America or beyond her borders. The threat of a biological attack on Israel definitely fell into this category. Such a catastrophe would have very significant consequences for the United States. The president gestured for the director of National Intelligence to take the floor.

"I'm raising Agent Scott, from Special Ops," the director said. Automatically, every head turned toward the monitors on the wall facing the President. Such conversations generally took place via a satellite feed, so that those present could see the speaker sitting somewhere at the ends of the earth.

"Agent Scott will report over the telephone," the Director said dryly.

The men around the table shifted in their seats and prepared to listen, each in his own way. Two out of three turned their heads and creased their brows indicating of ferocious concentration. Others folded their arms or leaned their heads on one hand. Only Walter Child, assistant director of the CIA, choked back a sigh of disappointment. He had very much wanted to see the man who had been sent to observe the attack on Israel.

For three days now, Child had been trying to discover that man's identity. "Agent Scott" didn't mean a thing. That was clearly not the man's real name. In the Special Ops department of the D.N.I., one does not use his birth name. Walter Child very much wanted to at least have a peek at the fellow, but the director was apparently holding his cards very close to his chest, refusing to expose his agents even to those who headed the agencies under his supervision.

Faint electronic sounds filled the room, followed by the voice of the agent in Tel Aviv: "Hello, Mr. President."

Over the course of the next five minutes, he summarized his findings from the previous few days. In his estimation, there was no indication that the threat was still relevant. There was no supporting information, no chatter from the worldwide intelligence community to back up the thesis that an attack was pending. It was possible, Scott said, that the news they had had concerned an old conspiracy, dating from before the outbreak of Israel-Hezbollah hostilities — a plan that had gone sour because of the war. Perhaps that plan had involved spreading a biological contaminant.

Israel's own security network had, he said, come to the same conclusion. The G.S.S. and the I.D.F. were contenting themselves with basic protective countermeasures: tightening security at the airports, putting the Air Force on special alert to prevent any unauthorized incursion into

Israeli air space, and checking for the transport of hazardous materials between Israel and the occupied territories.

"In short, we can relax a bit," the D.N.I. director concluded. "The situation appears calm right now."

"Certainly."

"You are to remain in Israel for the time being. We'll wait and see what happens next." The director ended the call.

The president looked as though a heavy stone had just been rolled off his shoulders.

"Do we step down completely from the state of alert?" asked the CIA delegate, Walter Child. "We don't want to fall asleep on the job, and suddenly get slapped in the face with a couple of thousand dead."

The head of the FBI added his own warning to that of his colleague. It was not yet time to rest on their laurels, he said. With all due respect to Agent Scott's assessment, they must conduct themselves as though the threat was still in force.

The president threw them a meaningful look. "I hope, for the Arabs' sake, that this attack does not take place," he said. "Otherwise, they will face immediate forceful retaliation."

His chief of staff compressed his lips. He did not like the president's outburst, but there was one thing he knew: If such an attack did take place against an ally of the United States, it would mark the end of diplomatic appeasement and of all attempts to draw the Arab world closer.

He very much hoped that Agent Scott's assessment was accurate. He also hoped that, if there had ever been such a plan afoot, it was indeed no longer in play. Otherwise, the world would soon find itself poised on the brink of a third World War — with Islam assuming the enemy status formerly occupied by Nazi Germany.

New Jersey — Av 5766 / August 2006

Yeshivas Knesses HaTorah and the adjacent yeshivah community were in a furor. Preparations for the big wedding were at their peak, with hundreds of the Rosh Yeshivah's students and community members set to fly to Israel to participate in the wedding of R' Yom Tov Padlinsky's eldest daughter to his esteemed student, the Milinover Rebbe's grandson.

The fact that the wedding had been scheduled in the month of Av, which fell in August, substantially increased the number of participants. It was vacation time, and many were able to take advantage of the discounted tickets that the yeshivah had managed to obtain despite the busy season. Bulletin boards in the yeshivah itself and in the nearby supermarket displayed a plethora of announcements pertaining to the trip: times for picking up airline tickets, *Hachnassas Orchim* centers in Israel, plans for policing the neighborhood while so many of its residents were absent, and even a special sale on sturdy suitcases.

No one had an inkling about the specific anguish that had beset the Rosh Yeshivah, R' Yom Tov Padlinsky. His daily schedule had changed hardly at all in the wake of the terrible blow that had befallen him and his family — a blow of which only a select few were aware. His faith was powerful. Everything that Hashem does is for the good: That was what he taught his students, and that was the tenet he lived by.

But there were things that needed to be done. Steps that must be taken. There were complex halachic questions to be unraveled. Decisions that would have a profound impact — and specifically the laws of *lashon hara*, gossip and slander ....

As soon as the first details had come to light on Sunday morning, R' Yom Tov summoned two loyal and responsible men, both former students of his. They were R' Eliyahu Gorman, a *dayan* of the New York *Beis Din*, and R' Shlomo Direnberg, one of the most important *maggidei shiur* in the yeshivah's kollel.

He briefly outlined the problem for them. His mother, may her memory be a blessing, who had resided in Jerusalem, had been widowed over 40 years earlier. Thereafter, she had married again. Her second husband was R' Moshe Padlinsky. The couple were blessed with twins: R' Yom Tov and his brother, R' Eliezer, currently living in Chicago. Someone had just come forward, claiming to have proof that in truth his mother's first husband had not been deceased at the time, and that the *beis din* that had permitted her to marry his father had acted in error. It had, in essence, authorized a married woman to remarry. In which case, both he and his brother, r"l, were disqualified for most marriages and they and their offspring were forbidden to marry anyone of pure Jewish lineage.

R' Eliyahu and R' Shlomo heard the Rosh Yeshivah's words with impassive faces, though both understood the horrific significance of what he was saying. The fate of an entire Jewish family hung in the balance. The Rosh Yeshivah had five children; his brother, R' Eliezer, had seven, two of whom had already married. If the *beis din* had indeed erred forty years before, allowing a married woman to take another husband, this would constitute a tragedy of major proportions. It would spell the destruction of an entire family, branded with an eternal halachic stigma.

There was no need for words. It was clear that their rebbi had summoned them to his room in order to ask them to drop everything else and devote all their time and energy to uncovering the truth. Time was running out. The clock was ticking. The Rosh Yeshivah's daughter was due to wed on Wednesday of the following week. It would not be possible for the wedding to be performed with such an awesome doubt hanging over their heads.

A heavy silence filled the room. R' Yom Tov sat lost in thought, eyes closed in anguish. His two veteran students sat facing him, stunned and shaken by what they had just heard, unsure whether to leave or if the Rosh Yeshivah wished to add something further to what he had told them.

"My parents, *z"l*, were G-d-fearing Jews," the Rosh Yeshivah finally said in a low voice. "I'm certain they would never have been the instruments of such a terrible thing. We often see a person who's worried and anxious about one thing or another, and after some time discovers that there was never any reason for concern. Sometimes Hashem's salvation does not come in the blink of an eye, but only after a period of time. Sometimes a person is sentenced to a period of great pain and anguish.

"I have no doubt that my parents' marriage was performed according to halachah. The question is only how long it will take to prove that beyond the shadow of a doubt. And how much bitter suffering we will be forced to bear before we merit Hashem's salvation."

The Rosh Yeshivah heaved a deep sigh as his students parted from him. *How shortsighted a man's vision was,* he reflected sadly. But all he had was what his eyes could see .... His two faithful students would do everything in their power to disprove the slander and enable his daughter's wedding to take place as scheduled.

But would they have done so, had they known that that same wedding was poised to bring agonizing death to all who participated?

Would the Rosh Yeshivah have decided to exert any and all efforts to clear his family's name, knowing that letting the marriage go forward as planned would trigger unimaginable tragedy, killing thousands upon thousands of Jews?

Would he not have been prepared to suffer any degree of pain and sorrow, had he known that evil men were planning to use his daughter's wedding to spread one of the cruelest and most deadly viruses ever developed by humanity ... that is, if a cold-blooded Nazi criminal could even be classified as human?

54

The calm and relief from tension in the American intelligence community exploded suddenly on the following day.

The Baltimore FBI branch office was quiet on this Sunday afternoon. There were no burning issues to attend to this weekend.

At 4:05, an agent burst into the supervisor's office. "There's someone on the phone with information about a biological attack," he gasped.

"Put the call through to me," the FBI supervisor called to his secretary, pressing two buttons on his desk at once. The buttons read "Intercom" and "Record."

"Yes, sir?" he said into the phone. "You wanted to tell us something?"

The caller sounded agitated and confused. His voice was that of a simple and elderly man.

"Uh ... yes ... I want to let you know about this."

"About what?"

"About what those two fellows were saying at the mall. In — in a coffee shop." The man drew an emotional breath.

"Sir, please calm down. What, exactly, were they talking about?"

"About an attack that he wants to carry out. The professor."

"Which professor?"

"I don't know. The other guy kept calling him 'professor' all the time. He said that the professor's going to attack with germs in a distant country."

"Germs in a distant country?"

"Yes. Yes, that's what he said."

"When?"

"I don't know! He didn't say."

"What did he look like? Would you be able to identify him?"

"They were sitting behind me ... in a coffee shop ... I was terrified. I ran out of there. I decided to call you people ...."

"Where are you now?"

"In a public phone booth. In the mall. Near the coffee shop."

"Which mall?"

"The big one. Near McDonald's."

"Are they still there?"

"Who?"

"The men who were talking about the professor and the terror attack."

"I don't know. That was before. I'm not ...."

"How long ago?"

"It just happened .... Look, I have to go to work now."

"Sir, please wait for us. We want to talk to you."

"But I'm already late for work. I'm in a rush ...."

"Wait by the phone. We're coming to you. It's very important that we speak with you."

"But my boss will fire me!" the caller protested. "I have to clean all the rooms." The phone went dead.

The supervisor suddenly realized that six agents had crowded into his office. "Call headquarters. Tell them to pinpoint the source of the call!" he shouted to his secretary.

Twenty minutes later, dozens of police officers and FBI agents descended on one of the malls on the outskirts of Baltimore. The public phone booth from which the call had been made was inspected, centimeter by centimeter, but no one hoped to find useful fingerprints in a place where hundreds of people passed in the course of a day. There were no other signs: no folded note, no cigarette butt, or anything else that might offer the slightest clue to the caller's identity.

The mall featured three coffee shops. Two of them, on the other side of the sprawling complex of stores, were covered by security cameras. The one nearest the public phone booth — as well as the booth itself — had not been captured by any camera.

The FBI questioned the workers in the coffee shop, but most of them were incapable of remembering whom they had served sixty seconds earlier. It was a self-service place: Customers came, paid for their coffee or light meal, and sat at a table. The detectives took a list of all credit cards that had been used in the hours before the call. Perhaps they could use it to compile a partial customer list. But many others — the majority, in fact — had paid with cash.

The anonymous phone call was played and replayed hundreds of times over the rest of that weekend, and analyzed by various experts. Detectives maintained surveillance on the coffee shop 24 hours a day, in case the caller should return. Others sought any person in the area who worked as a janitor. Fingerprints were taken from the phone booth, hoping for a match.

The new information was quickly passed along to all interested parties — including Special Agent Scott in Israel. Someone in Baltimore had spoken about a professor who was planning a terror attack using a virus in a distant country. Investigations were reinstated. Detectives and scientific experts went back to work at full throttle.

They now had two new items to work with. First, they had an indication that the threat was still in force. Second — and more important — they had the beginning of a trail. Something they could hold onto. A clue to kick off their investigation: a professor, germs, Baltimore, a distant country, a man who cleaned rooms.

Sooner or later, something would come up that they hoped would take them a step further in the investigation.

Jerusalem — Av 5766 / August 2006

Rabbinical adjudicator Zevulun Katzenbaum's crowded office was situated in a tiny, two-room apartment in the Geulah section of Jerusalem, not far from Zichron Moshe.

The office was a mess. Hundreds of loose-leaf binders, filled with documents, were crammed onto the bookshelves. An ancient computer wheezed in a corner of the room, where a frustrated secretary attempted to make some order out of the chaos on her desk.

But his most valuable possession, Zevulun Katzenbaum liked to say, pointing at his own forehead, was his head. Others, burned by bitter experience, had their own versions: his wickedness, his craftiness, and his utter ruthlessness.

The seasoned rabbinical adjudicator dealt with everything: divorces, business conflicts, wills, inheritances — in short, anything that might add thousands more to his already overflowing bank accounts. He knew how to make witnesses break down in tears in front of *dayanim*, and how and when to brandish a contradictory document or incriminating verdict they had once written. His reputation went before him. No one liked him, but they hired his services because he usually won. And, more important, no one wanted to face him as their adversary if the other side hired him first.

The pair of dignified-looking yeshivah men who stood at his door had not made an appointment ahead of time. They had hoped that Heaven would help, and that they would find him in his office — and so it was. They were R' Eliyahu Gorman and R' Shlomo Direnberg, here on behalf of R' Yom Tov Padlinsky.

On the flight to Israel, the two had spent a long time discussing and analyzing what they knew. It was hard to come up with a plan of action, but their first step, they decided, was to see the person responsible for the entire painful episode — the man who was threatening to bring proof to the *beis din* that the Rosh Yeshivah's mother had been given permission to remarry some forty years before, while her first husband had still been alive.

Zevulun Katzenbaum had nothing against the Rosh Yeshivah. As a matter of fact, he had never even met him. His quarrel was with R' Yom Tov's twin brother, R' Eliezer Padlinsky, in Chicago.

Three months earlier, R' Eliezer's son — R' Yom Tov's nephew — had married. The marriage was a mistake from the outset. The matter could have been resolved quietly, had the *kallah's* family not enlisted the services of Zevulun Katzenbaum. He poured more fuel on the fire, insisting that a large sum of money could be extorted from the Padlinsky family in exchange for accepting a *get*.

As always, he preferred having additional weapons in his arsenal. He began digging around in the Padlinsky family's past, and quickly came up with his big find: There was a halachic problem regarding the *chasan's* grandmother's marriage. A problem with the power to tarnish the entire family and declare them unfit for proper Jewish marriage. In that case, the young couple's marriage would be nullified at the source.

However, he was prepared to forget the whole thing if the *chasan's* side would agree to meet the *kallah's* family's modest demand of $150,000 ... to begin with. If they did, he was ready to set aside his proofs and burn the evidence, and the Padlinskys could go on being a highly respected Jewish family until the end of time.

Katzenbaum was on the phone, pacing to and fro across his office and talking at the top of his voice, as was his usual practice. His two visitors — one a member of *beis din* and the other an important figure in the kollel — stood in the doorway waiting for him to notice them.

He spotted them while speaking into the phone, and sized them up to see whether they were charity collectors or potential clients. Deciding on the latter, he quickly terminated his call and turned to them with a jovial greeting.

"Yes, *rabbosei*? How can I help you?"

A half-hour later, R' Eliyahu and R' Shlomo left the rabbinical adjudicator's office. They were still in shock.

"I think I'll go to the mikveh," one of them said. The other nodded in complete understanding. He felt the same way: a need to purify himself after the contaminating encounter with Zevulun Katzenbaum.

The thirty minutes they had spent in his company had hurled them into another world: a reprehensible one, filled with plots and strategies, lies and trickery. Both of them knew that not all rabbinical adjudicators were lily white. But this man had raised the level of despicable behavior to an entirely new level.

They had not introduced themselves as R' Yom Tov Padlinsky's representatives. That much they decided the moment they saw him and grasped the kind of person they were dealing with. Had they told him who had sent them, he would undoubtedly have sent them packing at once.

Instead, they said they were seeking his services in relation to a complicated divorce case, while privately counting on his characteristic volubility and lack of discretion to give them what they wanted.

Katzenbaum did not disappoint them. A bit of flattery easily loosened his tongue. While he did not mention the name Padlinsky or reveal any identifying details, he told them about a case he was "putting together" for one of his clients, in which the evil young husband refused to give his modest and unfortunate bride a divorce. Delving into the *chasan's* history, he had uncovered a dark blot on his family's past. "They don't want to give her a *get* on our conditions?" he chuckled. "They're going to regret it ...."

The fact that he was prepared to ruin the name of a well-respected Jewish family did not particularly bother him. In fact, he seemed to actually derive a measure of enjoyment from the destruction he was about to wreak.

R' Eliyahu Gorman and R' Shlomo Direnberg walked in the direction of Kikar Shabbat and on into Meah Shearim. Their visit to Katzenbaum had not been encouraging. On the contrary, they now knew the kind of cruel and ruthless enemy they were facing. He had told them nothing new.

It was time to move on to the next step: Rechov Chevras Shas 58, second floor, second door on the right. On the door, they'd been told, you'll see a small sign on which *"Kollel Tzidkas Yerushalayim"* was written. No need to knock; just open the door and walk right in.

The furniture in the kollel office was very old, with the ambience of a time long past. The walls were painted from the floor upward until the halfway mark, after which the paint gave way to faded yellow wallpaper. Many memorial plaques dotted those walls, a testament to generations of generous donors. The older plaques were made of marble, with engraved lettering; the newer ones were aluminum, each with its flickering electric memorial light. The man sitting behind the battered desk also belonged to a previous generation. He was elderly and pleasant looking.

R' Eliyahu and R' Shlomo felt like explorers returning from the jungle and its ravenous beasts back into the society of men. The old-timer turned to them with a gentle smile and asked what they wanted. Here, they could introduce themselves by name and state who had sent them — without giving away, of course, the real reason for that visit.

"Oy, R' Yom Tov Padlinsky!" the elderly clerk said admiringly. "How can I have the privilege of helping him?"

For anything relating to the kollel's past, the clerk said after hearing what they wanted, it was best to turn to Yanky Sherman, a young yeshivah man who loved history; he had made a study of many of the kollel's tomes and knew them well. "He writes all sorts of articles for the newspaper," the clerk said. "He'll certainly be able to help you."

The two men paid a visit to Yanky Sherman's home immediately. He was a grandson of Aharon Sherman, the kollel's legendary treasurer, and he knew the kollel's history like the back of his hand. In his home were copies of the kollel's books going back generations. Within a short while, the picture became a little clearer.

R' Yom Tov Padlinsky's mother, Yanky Sherman told them, had been married to R' Tzvi Hirsch HaLevi, one of the kollel's four original "trustees." R' Tzvi Hirsch had served as the kollel's fund-raiser and traveled on its behalf. His last trip, from which he never returned, had been to America in the year 5726. One year later, the kollel's administrator donated a *Sefer Torah* in his name, as he had died without leaving any living offspring behind.

The two Americans made a rapid calculation: R' Yom Tov was not yet forty, which meant that his mother had indeed married his father some time after her first husband, R' Tzvi Hirsch HaLevi, failed to return from his mission in America. All they had to do now was find out if the fund-raiser had died there — or whether, Heaven forbid, he had still been alive when she married a second time.

That evening, a flight from New York landed in Ben-Gurion Airport. One of the passengers was a CIA agent. This time, however, airport personnel had not been instructed to let him off the plane first, no official car was waiting for him outside, and no one was there to escort him to a meeting with the heads of Israeli intelligence.

The man's passport indicated that he was called Jeffrey Sieberg, and it got him through passport control without a hitch. Had he been asked the purpose of his visit, he would have answered that he was an advanced-electronics distributor representing a cartel of American and Canadian interests. His last visit to Israel had taken place several months before. Then, as now, he had stayed at the David Intercontinental near the Tel Aviv boardwalk.

The man approached a car-rental desk and hired a car. Here, too, his passport and driver's license raised no red flags ... even though the real Jeffrey Seiberg, a law-abiding citizen from Oklahoma, had died in a traffic accident years earlier.

Once past the maze of airport access roads, the traveler headed for Tel Aviv. He smiled to himself. These past few months had been, one way or another, one big costume party. Today he was Jeffrey Seiberg from Oklahoma; three months ago, he had been an American landowner of Latin-American extraction who had invited several guests to his hotel suite in the heart of Mexico City. His present mission was chockful of adventure: One day he was in Houston, ramming his car into African-American bureaucrat Lenny Brown and preparing a lethal ambush for Mexican Jorge Diaz, and the next he was following a Muslim-American student as he penetrated Israel with a vial containing a dangerous virus. Now he was back in Israel, on the heels of yet another American — a member of a quasi-covert agency that went by the name of "Special Operations Division, Office of the Director of National Security."

The agent with the pale face and light hair texted a message while driving — "Arrived safely" — and sent it to CIA Assistant Director Walter Child. He would check into his hotel and await further instructions. And this time, he admitted, he would be waiting impatiently. He had been doing a number of unconventional things of late — but acting against a fellow American agent? That was something that happened only once in a lifetime, and he intended to do it right.

Bnei Brak — Av 5766 / August 2006

R' Shammai sat in his room in the Milinover building in Bnei Brak with drawn face and downcast mood. The more he listened to the voices from next door — voices filled with energy and enthusiasm — the lower his spirits descended.

He had not yet recovered from his talk the previous day with the *chasan* whose future had just come apart. Over and over he saw Zalman Leib's shaken face as the young man absorbed the fact that the wedding due to take place in just ten days was about to be canceled. The terrible transition from joy to anguish, the shining eyes filling with sudden tears, the radiant face turning suddenly gray — it had been a heartbreaking moment that still held R' Shammai fast in its grip.

And, right next door, the head of the Milinover institutions and the rest of the preparatory committee were poring over plans of the catering hall together with a representative of the firm contracted to supply the bleachers and to set up the dais. None of them had a clue that all their work would be for nothing.

The dais with the head table would be positioned on the eastern wall, R' Yoel explained. That side had a separate entrance for Rebbes and *rabbanim*, with a spacious parking lot behind it. The remaining three walls would be lined with bleachers where *bachurim* and married men would stand, while the large space in the middle held tables for the older chassidim and honored guests.

"The band will be here," R' Yoel said, drawing a small rectangle in the hall's southwest corner. "I spoke to the bandleader, and he said that eight musicians would need a platform measuring at least four by eight meters."

"And it all has to be ready on the morning of Tuesday, August 22nd," one of the other committee members cautioned. "There's to be an additional event before the wedding, called 'seudas aniyim.' It will be as similar as possible to the wedding itself: in the same hall, with the same band, with the participation of all the chassidim."

"Like a sort of dress rehearsal?" the man asked.

Everyone chuckled. "You could call it that," R' Yoel said, amused.

But R' Shammai, in the next room, wasn't laughing. How could he laugh, when a real likelihood existed that the wedding would never take place? How was even a smile possible, when that dais and all those bleachers might, Heaven forbid, be in a dark and deserted hall on the night that had been designated for such a joyous occasion?

These past two days, he had been walking around torn by anxiety. He could not sleep at night and was unable to concentrate during the day. The wedding date was fast approaching. Today was Monday. On Shabbos, the *chasan* would be called up to the Torah — and still no solution to the difficult problem had been found. One day had passed, and then another, with no light at the end of the tunnel.

He listened to the feverish discussions next door, as preparations were made to host the many guests and to serve meals to the enormous crowd. In a day or two, chassidim from abroad would begin flying in to take part in the festivities. They were coming from all over: America, Europe, even Australia. What was going to happen? Would they unexpectedly be informed that there was to be no wedding? That everything was canceled? That they should all turn around and go home?

What heartbreak. What terrible pain and bewilderment. What an unspeakable tragedy ....

So far, fortunately, the secret was still well kept. Hardly anyone, including the planning committee in the next room knew that the wedding was under a dark cloud. But when the story surfaced, it would be like a second Tishah B'Av this month.

Half an hour earlier, R' Shammai had finished a painful phone call with the *mechutan* in New Jersey. They had each hung up with tears in their eyes.

These were supposed to have been happy days for the Rosh Yeshivah, R' Yom Tov Padlinsky. His eldest daughter was about to marry one of his top students — a fine and fitting match in every respect. The whole household should have been caught up in a whirlwind of joyous bustle. Preparations for the flight would be nearly complete, the children's clothing ready, the bridal gown hanging in the closet, and suitcases in the process of being packed — with the rebbetzin still managing to find time to help other women in the community, less organized than she, cope with it all.

The terrible question mark, the sudden shadow cast on his family's halachic status, gave the Rosh Yeshivah no rest. Despite the inner strength that he had built over the course of many years' hard work, despite the monumental refinement of his *middos* and his unshakeable faith in his Creator, he felt his strength ebbing. This was one test that just might be beyond him.

His two faithful students, R' Eliyahu Gorman and R' Shlomo Direnberg, had phoned from Israel two hours earlier to report their findings. They had spoken with the rabbinical adjudicator, Zevulun Katzenbaum, the source of the evil tidings, but had not succeeded in prying any new information from him. They had gone to the Kollel Tzidkas Yerushalayim, after learning that his mother's first husband had been connected to that institution, and had learned that he had indeed been one of its administrators and a fund-raiser for the Kollel. His name had been R' Tzvi Hirsch HaLevi.

Here, however, they had run into the proverbial brick wall. They had not been able to access the *beis din's* decree pronouncing his mother a widow and granting her permission to remarry. They tried the Israeli Ministry of the Interior, but had found no proof there, either.

Time was pressing; the wedding day was advancing with giant steps. The Padlinsky family's flight to Israel was scheduled for two days hence, on Wednesday. The moment was fast approaching when he would have no choice but to share the terrible news with his family. How would his wife, the rebbetzin, react? And his daughter, the *kallah*, whose whole world would collapse in a single instant? How would the entire community cope with the crisis? And how would the catastrophe impact him, personally?

Though R' Yom Tov Padlinsky did not go into the halachic details of the case with R' Shammai, he had been delving deeply into the *sugya* these past few days. He had not left a stone unturned, from the earliest of the *Rishonim* to the last of the *Acharonim*. He studied all the Responsa dealing with similar cases, and had come to the conclusion that, under present circumstances, according to the letter of the law, the wedding could go forward as planned. No *beis din* would have prevented the marriage, because his family had a kosher standing and were permitted to enter the congregation of Israel.

However, R' Yom Tov was determined to take the more stringent line — like some of the *Rishonim*, who were of the opinion that, in such a case, the wedding should not take place. In their words: "Let all sides of the question be well looked into, and [doubt] removed completely .... It is best to postpone the wedding for a period of time until the matter has been thoroughly investigated and all doubt erased."

R' Yom Tov, as the *gabbai* knew, was a man thoroughly immersed in Torah. Considerations of honor or status meant nothing to him. He had always been scrupulous in his halachic observance, and he had decided not to rely on leniencies in this matter as well. He was prepared to "postpone the wedding ... until the matter has been thoroughly investigated and all doubt erased." And if it was decreed that the wedding be canceled? Well, he did not run the world. He would do his part: learn Torah, pray from the depth of his heart — and make every effort to get to the bottom of the matter.

"I informed the Rebbe," the Rosh Yeshivah had told R' Shammai over the phone, "that if we do not learn with certainty that there is nothing wrong, we will simply not have the *chuppah*. Unless we have clear proof, there will be no wedding. How can we ask the young couple to start life with a black cloud suspended over their heads? I won't be a party to that. I will not take such a terrible responsibility on myself. If things are not clarified beyond the shadow of a doubt — the wedding will not take place."

"And what did the Rebbe say?" R' Shammai asked.

The *mechutan* was silent for a long moment. "The Rebbe hardly said anything at all," he answered in a voice choked with tears. "'There is still time before the wedding,' he said. '*Yeshuas Hashem k'heref ayin* — Hashem's salvation can come in the blink of an eye. But I ....'" He drew a quivering breath. "It's not easy," he finished simply.

R' Shammai raised his eyes heavenward in mute prayer, and sighed from the depths of his pain-filled heart.

"I'll tell you this, R' Shammai," the Rosh Yeshivah said. "If it is Hashem's will that the wedding not take place, I will accept it with love. I hereby accept all the suffering and the humiliation. May they serve as an atonement for me and for all of *Klal Yisrael* ...."

The streets around the Milinover Rebbe's *beis midrash* wore a festive air. Colorful signs reading "*Simchas Beis Milinov*" hung in all the institutional buildings. A huge cloth banner was stretched across the street: "*Kol rinah v'yeshuah b'ohalei tzaddikim.*" For the residents of the community, it felt like a holiday eve. The wedding was not slated to take place until Wednesday of the following week, but there was already feverish excitement in the air.

The men who had been designated to serve as ushers and organizers at the various events held meetings, the children and yeshivah students watched all the preparations with intense curiosity, and even the municipality gave the neighborhood a thorough cleaning, repairing several fences and railings that had been in need of service for years. The Milinover enclave was all set to greet the great day: the marriage of the Rebbe's beloved young grandson.

By the middle of the week, the first of the guests from abroad began to arrive. The familiar faces were seen throughout the neighborhood streets or driving to shul in their rented minivans. From time to time, a hearty "*Shalom aleichem!*" resounded, as two old friends met again after a monthlong separation. Apartments in the area were at a premium. Many young couples took advantage of the situation to rent their homes to visitors for a week or two, at a price that would cover their rent for the next half-year.

The Stern brothers flew in as well, one from Houston, Texas and the other from Los Angeles, California.

Jacob Stern came with his wife and three children. Using the vacation days he had accrued at work, he planned to stay in Israel until the beginning of Elul. The toxins supervision unit at the Department of Agriculture could survive without him for two-and-a-half weeks. Admittedly, he would have left with an easier conscience had Lenny Brown, his former assistant, been there to keep an eye on things in his absence. But Lenny Brown was unfortunately no longer alive. He had been hit by a car and subsequently died. When? Back in Iyar. Wow! Had it really been three whole months ago?

Don't think about Lenny, Jacob scolded himself. That would only bring back the horror of the pale man who had visited his office, of Jorge Diaz, lying bullet riddled near the Museum of Nature and Science, all the Mexicans so cruelly murdered, and — the worst moment of all — when he had seen the pitiless killer climbing the fence of his own backyard, just as his wife and children were coming home ….

Baruch Hashem, that nightmare was behind him now. That senior fellow at the CIA had called his home and they had made a deal. On that day, Jacob had decided not to breathe a word of the episode to anyone — including his wife and his brother. He would not give anyone a reason to harm him or his family.

So far, *baruch Hashem*, it had worked. Three peaceful months had gone by since then. Now he was in Israel with his entire family, all of them looking forward to the Rebbe's great *simchah*. Life had returned to normal. The episode was over.

David Stern had brought his family from Los Angeles as well. He was fortunate in having a good man to leave in charge of the winery. George Bellini, his head winemaker, had postponed his annual vacation in order to allow David to fly off to Israel with peace of mind.

David trusted George implicitly. Not a day went by that he didn't congratulate himself for choosing him. The winery was thriving because of George Bellini, with more and more Stern Family wines winning honors and prizes. George had dealt effectively with the contamination crisis, when mold in the bottle corks had threatened the winery's reputation. *A good man*, David thought again now, as he had done so many times in recent years. In fact, George was the one responsible for the fine wine that they had chosen for the Rebbe's wedding: a very special, half-dry Zinfadel 2004.

One of the first things the Stern brothers did on their arrival was to check on the wine that had been sent for the wedding. They found everything in order. The wine had arrived in good shape. The cardboard cartons had been piled on a wooden platform in a dark corner of the catering hall basement. The brothers removed one bottle and examined it.

Perfect. It was a magnum — a large bottle containing a liter and a half of wine, with the wedding logo emblazoned on the label along with the information that this wine had been donated to the Milinover *simchah*, with gratitude, by the Stern Family Winery in Los Angeles. The bottle had an elegant shape and metal wiring covered the cork, which featured the Stern Family Winery stamp. David and Jacob were faithfully continuing a family tradition handed down from generation to generation. Like their father, grandfather, and great-grandfather before them, they had sent wine to grace a wedding in the Milinover Rebbes' family. Please G-d, their sons and grandsons would pursue the tradition after them.

"By the way, I brought ten special corkscrews," David said, as he replaced the bottle.

Jacob laughed out loud. At the previous Milinover wedding, things had become complicated because of the inordinate length of time it had taken to remove the corks from the numerous bottles before they were brought to the table. Now, with the help of these automatic corkscrews, the waiters would be able to pop them out in minutes.

"For pity's sake, make a simple metal bottle-top," R' Yoel had begged David. "Make a top like the ones on bottles of grape juice. This is a *chassidishe* wedding, not a gourmet restaurant!"

David, of course, had resisted this idea. He would bring the finest wine and present it in the most honorable way: an elegant bottle, a classic cork, and a handsomely lettered label. He had told R' Yoel that he would make sure all the wine was opened half an hour before serving.

"Why half an hour?" R' Yoel had asked.

"To let the wine breathe. Exposing it to oxygen for about thirty minutes, my winemaker tells me, releases all the flavors."

"Oy, do me a favor," R' Yoel had said. "Milinover chassidim are not experienced wine tasters. What are you doing bringing us Cabernet, Shmabernet, all those fancy names? Believe me, they wouldn't know the difference if you give them sweet *kiddush* wine at 15 shekels a bottle!"

But David Stern had refused to back down. And he had won over the opposition.

"All right," R' Yoel sighed to his fellow committee members. "Do I have a choice? He's insisting that the wine be served to the Rebbe the way he would serve it to a king. The rich have some eccentric notions ...."

Tuesday arrived. It was exactly one week and a day before the wedding; four days before the *chasan* would be called up to the Torah; two days before the Padlinsky family was due to touch down in Israel.

R' Eliyahu Gorman and R' Shlomo Direnberg were back at the airport in Lod, headed back to the U.S. this time. They had exhausted all investigative avenues in Israel. In essence, they were leaving empty-handed — but perhaps there was still hope. Two days after their visit to Yanky Sherman, he had phoned them at the number they had provided in the event he found something else. They hurried back to his house.

"I've discovered something peculiar," he said, showing them several handwritten lines in the kollel book. "It says here that the kollel received word from one of their benefactors in Dallas, whom R' Tzvi Hirsch had visited, that he learned that R' Tzvi Hirsch HaLevi had definitely died in an accident at a secret army base. Doesn't that sound strange to you? What was he doing there? It's interesting that I never paid attention to that until now."

"And where is this base?"

"It says here: 'In the town of Grayston, Texas,'" Sherman answered.

R' Eliyahu Gorman and R' Shlomo Direnberg stared at one another in astonishment. Grayston? In Texas? They had never heard of the place.

It wasn't easy finding Grayston, Texas. They finally located it as a tiny dot that didn't even appear on most maps. It was near the American border city of El Paso and, directly facing it on the other side of the Rio Grande, the Mexican industrial city of Juarez.

So they were flying to New York today, where they would catch a domestic flight to Houston, Texas. There they intended to rent a car and drive west until they were almost at the Mexican border.

Maybe in Grayston, the last place R' Tzvi Hirsch HaLevi had visited, Hashem would help them find the clue that would finally unravel the tangled web of riddles.

56

Time was pressing. Every minute was precious. But it seemed as if everything was conspiring against R' Yom Tov Padlinsky's two messengers.

Every possible delay occurred. Their nonstop flight was scheduled to land in New York after an eleven-hour flight; two hours into the flight, the stewardess announced that the plane would be making a forced landing in Portugal due to a faulty engine. Passengers were instructed to disembark and were taken to a hotel in Lisbon. It was only the next morning, after the problem was repaired, that the interrupted flight to the U.S. was resumed.

Of course, R' Eliyahu and R' Shlomo missed their connecting flight to Houston. It was another half day before they managed to board another flight. They used the time to purchase basic provisions, in the event that they were be stuck in a distant city over Shabbos. The way things were going, that eventuality seemed entirely possible.

They bought a bottle of wine, loaves of challah, a jar of gefilte fish, and some vacuum-packed cold cuts. Not exactly a king's feast, but at least they would have something with which to mark the day. More time passed until they obtained a rental car at the Houston airport. It was nearly noon on Thursday when they set out on the road to Grayston.

Both men were tired and drained after nearly a week of continuous disappointments. These were no adventurous private eyes, but serious Torah scholars, and this mission — important as it undoubtedly was — had been difficult and exhausting for them. They decided that one of them would drive while the other tried to sleep, and then switch places in a couple of hours. Unless something went wrong — and that was a definite possibility — they would reach Grayston in five or six hours.

It was a tedious and fatiguing journey, through monotonous scenery under a burning sun. The weather was scorching and the air-conditioning in the rental car was not up to par. The men's mood was not optimistic. They were doing the best they could, exerting tremendous effort, but the chances of success were slim.

Near evening, they came to a crossroads with a sign: Grayston — 10 miles. The mood inside the car lightened slightly. Perhaps the wheel of fortune would somehow start turning their way. Maybe *HaKadosh Baruch Hu* would shine a light to guide them in the proper direction.

Both were tense and silent. Now that they were so close to their destination, they were struck by a horrible thought: What if their visit to this town did not dispel their fears — but the opposite? What if the investigation actually ended by confirming the terrible suspicion raised by the rabbinical adjudicator in Jerusalem?

What if they discovered, for example, that R' Tzvi Hirsch HaLevi had not died in that accident at the secret base, but passed away at a later date? It was very possible that they were about to make the situation many times more difficult. Until now, only a doubt had been raised. It was possible, Heaven forbid, that they would find the proof here that the fund-raiser from Jerusalem had been alive when his wife was granted permission to marry the Rosh Yeshivah's father.

In that case, there would be only one stark conclusion: The Padlinsky family was disqualified for marriage. R' Yom Tov and his entire family would be forbidden to enter the pure congregation of Israel.

Grayston, Texas stood revealed in all its stark simplicity.

It was a typical cattle town, situated right on the highway. For the space of a few hundred yards the interstate ran through the town's main street, after which it continued on through barren hills and grazing pastures until it reached the next town.

There were few houses at first, some shops and small businesses scattered among them. Not many vehicles moved through the narrow streets that branched off the main highway. Most of them were old pickup trucks. Near one home two horses were tied to a hitching post, munching from a heap of hay in front of them.

As they penetrated deeper into the town the picture improved, but not by much. In the central square they found the Town Hall, long past its prime. Nearby was a bank, looking equally ancient and nondescript.

The sun-baked streets were nearly deserted. The few people to be seen looked very Texan: cowboy boots, leather hats, and tanned faces. There was a small crowd in front of a single-story building that looked like a saloon, judging by its name, which made the two yeshivah men smile: The Drunken Ox. The building that stood out most prominently was the church. Some distance away was another building, whose first floor served as a bakery and coffeehouse, while the two upper levels were the property of a roadside inn called Norman Chambers' Place. It all looked old and dusty, as though everything had been crouching in that same spot for decades. Time seemed to have passed by the town.

The car rolled slowly on. Once past the bar and the coffee shop — the sole points of interest on Main Street — the place became deserted again. The two Jews drove straight through the town and out the other end under the hot sun, now dipping down toward the horizon. They must find that army base. That would be the starting point for their investigation. The base was apparently located either in the town or close by. Since they hadn't seen it as they drove through Grayston, it must lie farther down the road.

They traveled another twenty miles. Evening fell over Texas, but to their disappointment no army base was in sight. R' Shlomo was so tired that he nearly fell asleep at the wheel.

"Let's go back," he suggested to R' Eliyahu. "We'll continue searching tomorrow."

The small inn they had noticed in town seemed providential to them. They would rent a room and get a good night's sleep. Tomorrow morning, everything would look brighter.

Norman Chambers' inn, like the rest of the town, had been built many decades earlier. The reception desk was made of ancient, scarred wood and the sofas in the tiny lobby had been in style in the fifties. A few wall sconces emitted a doleful jaundiced light.

A ring of the desk buzzer summoned a young reception clerk. She seemed a bit surprised to see two such unusual-looking visitors, but managed to contain her curiosity. She accepted their payment and gave them the key to their room.

"Do you live in the area?" R' Eliyahu asked. "Were you born here?"

"Yes," she answered. "I was born in Grayston — and looks like I'll die here, too."

"We're looking for the army base," R' Eliyahu said.

"Army base? There's nothing like that around here."

"Maybe something connected with the army. There was some sort of big accident here, forty years ago."

"An accident at an army base? I haven't heard about it."

"It was a long time ago," R' Shlomo said. "Maybe someone older will remember."

"Maybe," the girl said doubtfully.

The two men went upstairs, disappointed. They *davened* Maariv, recited the *Kriyas Shema,* and were sound asleep in seconds.

The next morning, they woke early. The new day and the beaming sun infused them with fresh energy. After Shacharis and a quick breakfast from the supplies they had brought, they went downstairs to continue their investigation.

The same girl was waiting behind the reception desk. As though determined to sour their mood, she informed them that she had spoken to several of her fellow townspeople the night before. No one had ever heard of such a thing. There had never been an army base in Grayston — nor had there been any accident.

While it was still Friday morning in the United States, the sun was sinking over the Israeli sky and the Shabbos Queen stood poised to spread her wings over the city of Bnei Brak.

The large Milinover shul was packed to capacity. The last of the latecomers hurried in, *peyos* still damp from the mikveh. Youngsters in white shirts stood in long lines, while the men and older boys clustered in the areas designated for them. An air of muted excitement filled the *beis midrash*. This was no ordinary Shabbos. This was the Shabbos of the *aufruf*, when Zalman Leib — the Rebbe's grandson and son of the head of the Milinover community in New York — was to be called up to the Torah.

Apart from the guests from abroad, who continued to arrive daily, chassidim had come from every corner of Israel: from Jerusalem, Beitar Illit, Haifa, Petach Tikvah, and other chassidic enclaves.

All eyes were on the shul's rear entrance. In minutes, the door would open to reveal the Rebbe, making his first public appearance in a long time. Throughout summer he had been absent from Bnei Brak, staying in a vacation apartment in Tzefas. Not since Pesach had the Milinover chassidim prayed with their Rebbe, or stepped up to him to wish him a "*Gut Shabbos*" and be blessed in their turn, or sat at his holy *tisch* on Friday night or at *Shalosh Seudos*.

This Shabbos, it was all going to happen: *davening, tischen*, saying "*L'chayim*" ... The Rebbe had returned to Bnei Brak reinvigorated. Though he had returned from Tzefas two days earlier, he had yet to be seen in public. Now they all waited impatiently for his entrance.

A hush fell over the *beis midrash*. The door opened. As if by magic, an aisle formed in the center of the throng, leading from the door to the Rebbe's seat beside the *Aron Kodesh*.

The *gabbai*, R' Shammai Lederman, came through the door first, holding the Rebbe's *siddur*. He stood aside, and in a few seconds the long-awaited figure of the Rebbe appeared. He was thin and bent, but a glow seemed to emanate from him.

The excitement in the large room was palpable. An electric current seemed to pass through the crowd as they were seized with reverence. The chassidim gazed admiringly upon their Rebbe, who returned their gaze with a loving smile. The Rebbe nodded slightly in each direction, as he acknowledged the wordless good wishes that flew at him from all sides.

Standing beside the Rebbe was the young *chasan*, resplendent in a shining *kapote* and tall *shtreimel*. Zalman Leib's eyes were fixed shyly on the ground as grandfather and grandson made their way along the aisle that the chassidim had created toward the *Aron Kodesh*.

Behind them came the *mechutanim*: the *chasan's* and *kallah's* fathers. Hands were extended to them amid cries of "*Shalom aleichem*" and

"Mazel tov!" The men returned the greetings with smiles before taking their places at the front of the shul.

"*Hodu la'Hashem ki tov, ki l'olam chasdo*," began the *chazan*, launching the Erev Shabbos Minchah service. Hundreds of worshipers joined in. Hearts swelled in exaltation. Another link in the holy chain of the Milinover dynasty was about to be forged. Another descendant of the ancient and venerable house was about to establish a home of his own. Another joyous milestone for their esteemed Rebbe and his venerable family.

No one in that packed shul dreamed of the enormity of the tragedy about to be perpetrated upon their community. No one knew of the horrific plot being secretly woven by evil men. No one imagined that, in just a few days, every participant at the wedding was slated to become a martyr in a violent and deadly attack by one of the most effective germs man had ever devised. A virus developed by a Nazi scientist, originally meant to be used in cruel experiments on their own fathers and grandfathers in the death camps, was now in the hands of Arabs who, raised on a diet of anti-Semitism since birth, intended to finish the job.

Hundreds of chassidim — family men, yeshivah men, *bachurim*, and young boys — rose for *Shemoneh Esrei*, never dreaming that their only chance for salvation from the death sentence hovering over their heads was something no less cruel or terrible. The act of biological terror being planned against them would be canceled only if the wedding itself was canceled.

The lives of the wedding guests would be spared only at the cost of declaring an entire Jewish family disqualified from ever marrying into the pure congregation of Israel.

57

The Milinover chassidim, locals and guests, sat down to their Friday night *seudah* in good cheer and high spirits. The sound of *zemiros* wafted through the windows of every home, spreading into the well-lit streets. Around R' Shammai's Shabbos table sat his entire extended family: Both his married sons had come from Beit Shemesh and Jerusalem respectively, along with their wives and children, to join his recently married daughter and her husband, who were living nearby, and the *gabbai's* two teenaged sons.

Shortly after the soup was served, there was a knock at the door. One of R' Shammai's grandchildren ran to open it. In the doorway stood two bareheaded men, one slightly plump and wearing a checked shirt, the other thinner and dressed in an elegant tan jacket.

"Is your father home?" the plumper one asked.

"*Zeide*, someone wants you," the boy called into the dining room.

R' Shammai stood up and went to the door. "*Shabbat shalom*," he greeted his two visitors in surprise.

"*Shabbat shalom*, Rabbi," the stranger said. "Do you speak English?"

R' Shammai said that he had served as the Rebbe's *gabbai* during the period when the Rebbe had lived in Los Angeles, and his English was fluent.

"I'll speak English, then, so that my colleague will understand," the man said. "I was told that you are the Milinover Rebbe's *gabbai*."

"That is correct."

"My name is Uri Arbel. I'm aide to the prime minister's military secretary, and this is Special Agent Scott, a representative of the United States' intelligence community. Can we speak privately?"

"Please — come in," R' Shammai invited. He led the men into his study. As they passed the dining room, the visitors looked around curiously at the long table set with fine dishes, a silver candelabra shining in the center, and the whole family sitting around it. For their part, the grandchildren threw curious looks at the uninvited guests. It was strange to see their grandfather, in his Shabbos garb, together with two bareheaded men in weekday clothes.

R' Shammai closed the study door and sat down in his chair. His visitors took seats facing him.

"First of all, everything that is said here is a state secret. You may not speak about it to anyone," Uri Arbel began. "I will not make you sign a paper to that effect, because you are a religious man and today is Shabbat. But I am counting on your word."

"Certainly," R' Shammai replied.

"I understand that your chassidic group will be celebrating an important wedding this week," Arbel said.

R' Shammai heaved a sigh before answering, "Yes, *b'ezras Hashem*. On Wednesday."

Uri indicated the man sitting next to him. "Agent Scott," he said, "was sent to Israel by the U.S. government after a serious threat came to light, concerning a massive biological terror attack in the near future. We're talking about the spread of deadly germs by some method as yet unknown." He paused. "We have reason to believe that your wedding will be the site of the anticipated attack."

R' Shammai paled. *Ribono shel Olam,* as if they weren't coping with enough trouble already! Here was yet another problem hanging over this affair that had more than its share of hard knocks ....

"Because of the war in Lebanon," Arbel continued, "many events have been canceled throughout the country. However, according to the information we've put together, the event targeted for the terror attack has not been canceled. There are several possibilities — but your wedding seems the most appropriate for what is termed a 'high profile' attack. We are turning to you, as one of the senior members of the community, because we're going to have to enlist your cooperation over the next few days."

Silence fell as R' Shammai contemplated what he had just been told.

"We are people of faith," he finally said. "We know that the One Who runs the world is *HaKadosh Baruch Hu*. We will pray and hope that whatever wicked men are plotting against us will fail, and that their plans will be foiled. Of course, we will be at your service in any way you need, and hope that Hashem will help you."

Agent Scott withdrew a laptop computer from its case and opened it on the desk. R' Shammai watched him bleakly as the sanctity of his Shabbos was about to be profaned.

"With your permission, I'd like to ask you a few questions," the American said, speaking for the first time.

"Please."

"When exactly is the wedding scheduled to take place?"

"This Wednesday. On August 23rd."

The agent typed on his keyboard. "Where?"

"In a catering hall, Ganei HaSimchah."

"And where is that?"

"I don't recall the street name right now, but it's not far from here. On the Bnei Brak-Ramat Gan border."

"Please make sure to get me the street address later," Scott instructed.

R' Shammai gazed at the American in visible distress. Then he looked at Arbel. "Is this necessary? It's Shabbos today."

"Listen to me, Rabbi," Arbel said. "I know this situation is not pleasant, but we didn't come here by chance. Let's be very clear about this: Every minute may be critical. We have only partial information and we don't know whom we are up against. Any detail, any fragment of information, even a word dropped inadvertently, may supply the clue we need. You tell us the name of the street, for example, and maybe somewhere in the American intelligence network there is a piece of data that will hook us up with potential suspects. Right now, we have nothing except a general warning that an attack is expected. So don't hold back the details.

Tell us everything you know. Maybe that will give us something we can latch onto."

R' Shammai spread his hands in resignation. He would do everything in his power to help. Danger to life took precedence over the Sabbath.

"I understand that guests from all over the world will be attending the wedding," Agent Scott resumed his questioning. "Can you list the places they'll be coming from?"

"Mostly the U.S.," R' Shammai replied. "But also from England, Belgium, Australia. There will be a few guests from France, one family from South Africa, a large group from Switzerland, two families from Argentina ...."

"I take that it the fact that people will be flying in from all over the world is well known. And also, that the wedding date was set in place ten months ago."

"Correct."

Agent Scott threw Uri Arbel a glance and compressed his lips in several moments of focused thought.

"It's here," he said at last, stabbing a finger into the desk. "It's going to happen here."

The blood froze in R' Shammai's veins. Abruptly, the awful realization truly penetrated. He suddenly realized what these two men were talking about. A terrible danger was headed for the Milinover community, for the city of Bnei Brak — for the entire country. A biological attack, germs, a deadly outbreak. *Oy, Ribono shel Olam!* In his naiveté, he had thought that the *mechutan's* halachic problem would ruin the *simchah*. He had felt despondent, near despair. But all of that seemed dwarfed now in comparison to the dimensions of the tragedy that hovered over the community as a whole. It was no longer a matter of shame or unpleasantness. Now it was a question of life and death.

The two agents wanted more details about the logistical side of the wedding. For those technical details, R' Shammai told them, they would have to speak with the head of the Milinover institutions.

"Can you get him for us?" Uri Arbel asked.

One of R' Shammai's sons, without being given a reason for the summons, was sent to fetch R' Yoel from his home.

R' Yoel was surprised to find R' Shammai in his study in the company of two strangers. He was given a brief explanation and asked to remain in the room to answer a few questions.

After twenty minutes, R' Yoel noticed R' Shammai repeatedly glancing at the wall clock in mounting distress. He knew why. The *tisch* would be starting soon and R' Shammai must be in his place behind the Rebbe's chair.

He explained the situation to Uri Arbel. R' Shammai's absence would raise questions, he said, and secrecy was paramount right now. R' Yoel stayed behind with the two intelligence men while R' Shammai set out for the *beis midrash*.

He walked as rapidly as he could. He wanted to catch the Rebbe before he went out to the *tisch*. R' Shammai must consult with him.

When he arrived, agitated and out of breath, he found the Rebbe still seated at his table, learning, as he did every Friday night before the *tisch,* from an old *Chumash* he had inherited from his father, and his grandfather before that. The *Chumash* was said to have originally belonged to the Baal Shem Tov.

R' Shammai leaned slightly toward the Rebbe, to catch his attention. The Rebbe paused for a moment, lifted his head, and motioned for the *gabbai* to speak.

In a turmoil, R' Shammai told the Rebbe about the two agents who had come to his home, and informed him of the frightening news they had brought with them. He added that they were presently talking to R' Yoel, questioning him about the logistical details of the wedding preparations.

The Rebbe nodded several times, and then returned to his learning. No change was discernable on his face. He continued perusing the *Chumash* as though he had not just been informed that life-threatening danger was speeding toward him and his entire *kehillah*.

Earlier, in far-off Grayston, because of the time difference it was still daytime on Friday. Here, too, the outlook was bleak.

The receptionist's words had hit home — hard. R' Eliyahu and R' Shlomo had been away from their families for a week already, traveling continuously in an attempt to solve this mystery. They had hoped that the answer would greet them here. But this young woman, a native of Grayston, Texas, had asked other people and confirmed what she knew: There was no army base near this town, or any story of an accident that had occurred in the area.

After they checked out of the inn and loading their belongings into their rental car, the two men set off down the street on foot. There were still a few hours before it would be time to start for Austin, where they would be spending Shabbos. They would walk around and try to engage people in conversation. Perhaps Hashem would help them in the short time that remained, and give them some information that would help them.

The morning, sunny but cooler, showed Grayston in a more sympathetic light. Several large trucks were parked near a busy store featuring cattle feed and ranch equipment. Other commercial concerns appeared to be doing a livelier business as well. People came and went at the bank, the town hall, the train station, and the Sheriff's office.

R' Eliyahu and R' Shlomo attracted more than their share of curious looks. If strangers in general were a rarity in this remote southwestern town, the sight of two Jews with large skullcaps, long beards, and white strings dangling from their belts was many times more so. They peeked into the front window of their inn's ground floor, which bore a sign that read, "Norman Chambers' Confectioner's." People were seated at the counters, eating quickly or gulping coffee as they read their newspapers. *There is no help for us here*, the two men thought. *Maybe we will have better luck at the two round tables set out on the sidewalk.*

At these tables sat a group of elderly cowboys who seemed to have all the time in the world. They sipped coffee at their leisure as they watched the world go by — including, of course, the two odd-looking strangers.

"Let's ask them," R' Eliyahu suggested to his friend, and headed toward the group. The men appeared to be in their sixties and seventies and even older. If some sort of accident had indeed taken place some forty years before, they would be the ones to remember it.

"Good morning," R' Eliyahu greeted them.

"'Mornin'," some of the locals replied.

"Nice place," R' Eliyahu tried again.

"Nice?" One of the ranchers, with a sunburned face and enormous mustache, guffawed. "There are nicer places in America."

"Where are you fellas from?" asked another, much skinnier, Texan.

"From New Jersey," R' Shlomo volunteered.

"Ah. That's a long way off."

"Yes. A long way."

"So what does Grayston have that New Jersey doesn't?" the first old-timer asked.

"We're looking for details about a person who died here in an accident forty years ago."

"Forty years? That's a long time."

"Yes. We were told that there was once an army base near here, and that's where the accident happened. The man we're inquiring after was one of the people killed in that accident."

The old men suddenly fell silent, exchanging glances.

"Accident? Here?" the skinny man said. "Are you sure?"

"Positive. We were told that there was an army base near Grayston."

The old man looked at his friends, his eyes moving from one to the next. "Anyone remember an army base?"

All of them shook their heads.

"You must be mistaken, gentlemen," a third rancher said. "There was no accident around here."

"But we were told ..." R' Shlomo began.

"People say all kinds of things," said a fourth old-timer, both hands resting on the curved top of a cane. He was older than his companions. If the others were elderly, this man was positively ancient.

R' Eliyahu realized that the conversation had gone as far as it was likely to go. "Thank you," he told the men with a pleasant smile. "Have a good day." He turned to leave.

"You, too," the man with the cane called after them. "Go back to New Jersey!"

R' Shlomo followed R' Eliyahu, shoulders slumped. Despair engulfed him. This whole trip had been useless. Even the town's oldest residents knew nothing about a military base or an accident that was supposed to have occurred there forty years ago. They had reached a dead end. They would have to go home empty-handed. What would they tell the Rosh Yeshivah? What *could* they tell him?

Only the most sharp-eyed of the men seated around the Rebbe's *tisch* sensed that there were currents beneath the surface. The Rebbe behaved as usual, with no change from his usual conduct. But anyone who looked closely could see that the chief *gabbai*, R' Shammai Lederman, was experiencing great inner turmoil. Some of the men wondered where R' Yoel was tonight. It was unusual for him to be absent from such an important *tisch*.

No one dreamed that he was in R' Shammai's study, conversing with two secret agents, one American and the other Israeli. Their conversation with him was most productive. However, R' Yoel's English was weak, which forced Uri Arbel into the role of interpreter and slowed the pace of the interrogation.

Scott's agenda included screening the guest list and running a security check at the door of the catering hall. As R' Yoel sought to bring to mind the building's layout and the number of entrances and exits, the agent decided that he wanted to see the place for himself. R' Yoel, unlike the *gabbai*, knew the hall's address and offered to fetch the key from the owner, R' Anshel, another Milinover chassid who lived nearby.

The two agents exchanged a quick glance.

"That won't be necessary," Uri Arbel said. "We'll find our own way in. The fewer people who know about this, the better." At this point, the matter was still secret. The moment it became public, it was liable to give rise to mass panic. That was the last thing they wanted.

The *beis midrash* was crowded. The *tisch* was at its height. Rows upon rows of men and *bachurim* stood on the bleachers, swaying to the rhythm of the song. The Rebbe had already made *kiddush*, recited the *motzi* on the challah, and tasted the fish. Now everyone was singing *"Menuchah V'Simchah."* After *"Mah Yedidus,"* the Rebbe would give a *dvar Torah*. R' Yoel entered and stood close to the head of the table, behind several others. R' Shammai noticed him immediately. After all, he had been anxiously scanning the room for him these past forty minutes ....

The Rebbe's "Torah" lasted nearly twenty minutes. Though everyone else listened attentively, R' Shammai — for the first time in his life — found himself unable to focus for as long as sixty seconds. His thoughts leaped from one scenario to the next, painting nightmarish scenarios that he tried, in vain, to banish. When the Rebbe finished speaking, the chassidim launched into another song. R' Shammai left his place behind the Rebbe's chair and hurried away to a corner of the room. R' Yoel followed.

"They asked dozens of questions about the setup of the wedding. Now they've gone to have a look at the hall," R' Yoel updated the *gabbai* briefly.

"Good. I'll tell the Rebbe after the *tisch*."

"They asked me to let you know that they'll be back tomorrow morning. The American agent said that he needs to observe the community and form an impression of them with his own eyes."

"What do they plan to do? Come to shul?" R' Shammai asked in surprise.

"No. They don't want to step out into the open. They were thinking about watching from the window of your house."

"Let them come," R' Shammai said.

58

At seven a.m. the next morning there was a firm knock on the Ledermans' door. R' Shammai hurried to open it and welcomed his guests: "*Shabbat shalom*. Please come in."

"Yoel told you we'd be coming?" Uri Arbel asked.

"Yes, certainly. It's fine," said R' Shammai. "My house is at your disposal. Would you like a cup of coffee?"

"Coffee would help," Arbel admitted. "We didn't sleep much last night."

R' Shammai returned a few minutes later with two cups of coffee and a plate of home-baked cookies. "So what's going to be happening here in the next few hours?" Uri Arbel asked.

"At eight o'clock, everyone will come to shul for Shacharis."

"For how long?'

"*Davening* ends at about eleven-thirty. Then everyone goes home to make *kiddush* and eat."

"Good. That'll be enough for us," Uri said. Scott nodded agreement. From the window of R' Shammai's room they could observe the shul entrance and even take a peek inside — which was exactly what they wanted.

"Of course, you're both welcome to join us for the Shabbos meal," R' Shammai said.

"No, thanks. We couldn't impose."

"What's the imposition? You're staying," R' Shammai insisted. "My married children and my grandchildren won't be eating here today. Even my teenagers will have their *seudah* in yeshivah. It'll be just my wife and myself. You'll feel right at home."

"Okay, thanks. We'll see later," Uri said.

At noon, the two intelligence agents were at the Shabbos table with R' Shammai and his wife.

Throughout the morning, the agents had been watching the worshipers at shul through the slats in the window shutters. Uri Arbel, who had grown up on a kibbutz, was secretly moved at the sight of hundreds of chassidim wrapped in their prayer shawls, and the boys in their black coats and velvet hats. It reminded him of the one and only time his parents had taken him to visit his religious grandfather in Jerusalem during a Jewish holiday. Agent Scott maintained his professional demeanor, trying to read faces, study characteristics, and become acquainted with this closed community, so different from the ones he knew, which some unknown assailant seemed intent on harming.

When R' Shammai returned from shul, he reiterated his invitation to the *seudah*. The American agent was happy to accept, which left Uri Arbel with little choice but to do the same.

R' Shammai made *kiddush* on a small glass of whiskey and the Rebbetzin served homemade cakes. They chatted for a few minutes, then R' Shammai washed, made the *motzi*, and cut the challah, offering brief explanations for what he was doing. Scott was interested in everything. Uri Arbel was less receptive, becoming animated only when the food arrived. "Wow, gefilte fish!" he exclaimed. "I haven't eaten this in years."

The men found the rest of the food to their liking as well, especially Mrs. Lederman's famous cholent. As they ate, Scott asked many questions about the structure and character of the chassidic community.

The meal proceeded pleasantly. R' Shammai found Scott a man after his own heart. He was down to earth, serious, interested, and open-minded. It was Uri Arbel who started off with a closed attitude.

"Hey!" Uri suddenly laughed, as though he had caught the *gabbai* in an error. "Why didn't you use wine for *kiddush*? Did you use whiskey because Agent Scott is a non-Jew?" he said, his tone amused.

"What are you talking about?" R' Shammai asked. "You know that under Jewish law, if a non-Jew or a non-observant Jew—like yourself, Uri—should touch the wine, an observant Jew isn't permitted to drink it."

"Interesting," Scott remarked. "I'd never heard that before."

"Let me tell you something even more interesting," R' Shammai said. "A good friend of mine owns a big vineyard in the United States. Stern Family Winery — perhaps you've heard of it? The wine produced there is kosher, of course, despite the fact that the head winemaker is not a Jew. That winemaker is not permitted to touch the wine. When he wants to taste wine from one barrel or another, the Jewish supervisor opens the tap, pours a little wine into a glass, and hands it to him. And all this, by the way, does not seem to prevent him from creating superb wines that win top prizes in every competition they enter."

"Are you serious?"

"Absolutely. That winemaker knows that, were he to go down into the wine cellar without a Jew there to supervise, all the wine would become forbidden to Jews."

"Really?"

"Yes. That's what Jewish law states — and he's fine with it."

The atmosphere at the table had taken a serious turn. In order to lighten it somewhat, R' Shammai told an old, favorite joke: "You know, I come from a long line of vinegar manufacturers. Although my sons have expanded the business to include numerous other food products, we are essentially proud vinegar-makers. Every time I meet my friend the vineyard owner, I tell him that he's simply wasting all that precious raw material. We could have made the finest vinegar out of his wine ... but instead, he sells it before its time ...."

"If that head winemaker manages not to touch the wine," Agent Scott said, laughing, "I guess I can restrain myself, too."

The rest of the meal passed in an amicable atmosphere. When the *seudah* was over, the two intelligence men thanked the *gabbai* and his wife for an excellent meal and stimulating conversation.

"We'll be in touch by phone tonight," Uri Arbel said. "We're going to keep working and see how things develop. I'll update you as necessary."

■ ■ ■

R' Eliyahu Gorman and R' Shlomo Direnberg walked away from the group of aging cowboys in front of the bakery shop and continued down Main Street. R' Shlomo had a long face. But when he glanced at his friend, he was astonished to see him smiling broadly.

"What happened?" he asked in surprise.

"Didn't you notice? They're hiding something. It's clear as day."

"Hiding something?"

"Of course! Didn't you see how hostile they became the minute we mentioned the accident? In a split second, their whole attitude changed. There's some big secret here that they're hiding."

They walked on in pensive silence. Across the street, they saw the local church. A wooden fence ran alongside the building, its gate standing half-open to reveal rows of tombstones.

R' Eliyahu quickened his pace. "Come on, let's go over there!"

"What do you mean?"

"If the living won't talk to us," R' Eliyahu said with the glimmer of a smile, "perhaps the dead will have something to say."

Grayston's cemetery was sprawled at the foot of the church, with the earliest graves literally touching the stone walls and the rest sloping down to the riverbank. The cemetery was dotted with religious symbols, but they spotted a Jewish grave in the second row. English lettering identified the grave as that of one "Joel W. Abrams." A Star of David was etched above and three Hebrew words beneath: Yoel Zev Abramson.

R' Shlomo took out his camera-phone and snapped a picture of the monument, and they continued along the rows of graves. Not far away, they found Joel Abrams' son. His name had been Jack Abrams — or Yaakov Abramson, according to the Hebrew words engraved beneath his Star of David. He had been the sheriff of Grayston, the tombstone announced, and had died on October 25th, 1966.

Over the course of the next thirty minutes, the two men found no further sign of anything Jewish. They went from grave to grave, reading the stones. There were a few interesting ones, such as the burial place of a girl who had drowned in the river, not far from the grave of the Mexican who had jumped into the water in an effort to rescue her ... and the 74-year-old grandmother who had chased five robbers from her home with a shotgun before dying of her wounds. But they found nothing that gave them a further clue about the mystery they had come to solve.

It was after eleven. Their feet hurt, and the Texas sun was beginning to sap their energy. Both men were thirsty and perspiring as they came to the end of the first section of the cemetery.

R' Shlomo looked around. "We've hardly even covered half this place," he said in discouragement.

R' Eliyahu didn't answer. He rubbed his eyes and stared at the two next graves in the row. "Look at this," he said excitedly.

As R' Shlomo studied the pair of headstones, his gloomy face brightened in a real smile. "*Oy, baruch Hashem*," he said with relief. "At last, a familiar name!"

The right-hand grave belonged to Sam Lowinger — or, as the stone was inscribed, Shmuel Levinger. Beside it was the final resting place of Binyamin Lowinger.

Yanky Sherman, the young history-lover whom they had met in Jerusalem — grandson of R' Aharon Sherman, the kollel's legendary treasurer — had continued his research after the Americans left. Just hours after they flew off to Texas, he phoned them to say that he had found something that might be helpful to them.

R' Tzvi Hirsch's final trip, to Grayston, he had discovered, had been made with the goal of meeting a longtime supporter of the kollel by the name of Shmuel Levinger, and his nephew, Binyamin. As was customary at that time, the kollel had signed an agreement to commemorate its donors' *yahrzeits*, reciting *Kaddish* and learning *mishnayos* for the elevation of their souls. Studying the protocol of the kollel's meetings, Yanky Sherman had found one from the year 5724 in which R' Shemerel, then the head trustee, had stated that Shmuel Levinger, a generous contributor from Grayston, Texas, had stopped sending his usual donation despite the many reminders the kollel had sent. R' Tzvi Hirsch HaLevi later announced his intention, on his next trip to the States, to put Texas on his itinerary. His mission: to ascertain whether Shmuel Levinger was ill or, Heaven forbid, no longer among the living.

And now, R' Eliyahu and R' Shlomo were standing in the Grayston cemetery, looking at graves of Sam and Benjamin Lowinger. The circle was beginning to close.

"But look when they died," R' Shlomo exclaimed in surprise. "Both exactly on the same day as that other Jew — the one who was sheriff."

"Are you sure?" R' Eliyahu's brows lifted in amazement.

"Yes. October 25, 1966," R' Shlomo said, after flipping through the pictures on his camera.

"All three men died on the same day? Don't you think that's a rather strange coincidence?"

"Very strange. Maybe it's connected, somehow, to the accident?"

R' Eliyahu nodded slowly as he thought out loud. "Is this an indication that, apart from the *meshulach* — whose grave we haven't found yet — Shmuel Levinger, his nephew Binyamin, and the former sheriff all died in the same accident? It's certainly feasible."

The next section of graves gave them the proof they were seeking. A long row consisted of more than twenty graves of young men, all of them between the ages of 22 and 28. All the headstones implied, in one way or another, that they had been cut down in the flower of their youth, and that their lives had been stolen through some cruel or tragic means. The dates on each of the markers ranged from October 25 through October 27, 1966.

"So there was no accident, huh?" R' Shlomo said ironically, feverishly snapping pictures. "Twenty-five men die within three days — and no one around here knows anything."

It was obvious now that they had stumbled upon a conspiracy of silence. It was impossible that an accident of these dimensions had already been forgotten by the townspeople. Judging by the long row of graves, hardly a family had been spared in the tragedy. Someone was trying to hide something.

The name on the last headstone in the row electrified R' Shlomo.

"Look who's buried here," he called to R' Eliyahu. He read the name out loud: "Steven Chambers, son of Norman Chambers."

"So?'

"Where did we sleep last night?"

"Ah, that's right. Norman Chambers' inn."

The two men stared at each other. "Then the Chambers family also lost someone in the accident," R' Eliyahu said. The receptionist had not shared this, either.

"We'd better go back there," R' Shlomo said.

"Let's finish here first," R' Eliyahu suggested. He still hoped to stumble across R' Tzvi Hirsch's grave and put an end to all their questions.

It was a vain hope. Another hour spent touring the second half of the cemetery brought no headstone with the fund-raiser's name, or any indication that an anonymous Jew had been buried there. They found one more Jewish grave, that of a woman by the name of Devorah Lowinger — yet another member of Sam Lowinger's family.

It was past noon. The air had become scorching again. R' Eliyahu and R' Shlomo returned to Norman Chambers' small inn and the rental car they had left in his parking lot. Word of the two strangers who were digging into the town's past had apparently spread. Hostile glances were hurled at them from every side. When they entered the lobby, it was empty.

"Hello? Anybody here?" R' Shlomo called, pressing the bell.

No one answered.

"Miss Chambers?" R' Eliyahu tried.

The young receptionist popped out of an inner room. "Yes? What's the problem?" she asked coolly.

"Oh, nothing. We're leaving now. We just wanted to say thank you," R' Eliyahu said.

The girl's face thawed slightly. "Okay. I hope you enjoyed yourself."

"Certainly, certainly." R' Eliyahu started for the door, and then turned. "By the way," he said pleasantly, "Who's Norman Chambers?"

"He's my grandfather. He built this place years ago."

"Is he still alive?"

"Sure," the girl said with a proud smile. "Still alive and on the job, though he's past ninety."

"Wonderful! I hope he stays healthy and strong for many more years to come."

"And who is Steven Chambers?" R' Shlomo asked suddenly.

The smile vanished from the girl's face. "St-Steven?" she stammered.

"Yes, Steven Chambers. Norman's son."

"He's ... my uncle. My father's brother."

"He died young," R' Eliyahu said, his tone sympathetic. "We saw his grave in the cemetery."

"That must have been very hard for your grandfather," R' Shlomo said, with no less empathy. "To lose a son ...."

"But he died in Mexico," the girl blurted. "It had nothing to do with the accident."

"Accident? What accident?" R' Eliyahu pounced on the word.

The girl bit her lip, turning pale.

"You mean the accident that never happened? The accident that no one ever heard of?" R' Shlomo pressed.

The girl's eyes filled with tears. "I don't know anything!" she wailed. "Leave me alone. Go away. I don't know anything!"

That's enough! Leave her alone," came a hoarse cry from behind them.

R' Eliyahu and R' Shlomo turned. In the doorway stood the old man with the cane to whom they had spoken that morning. He raised his stick threateningly. "Get out of here. Go on — get out!" he yelled.

"Grandpa," the girl called. "It's fine."

"Leave my place," Norman Chambers shouted. "Where are you from? The FBI? The CIA? What do you want with us? We never said a thing. We've kept the secret all these years. So just leave us alone!"

The two Jews stared at him in stupefaction.

"We're not from the FBI or the CIA," R' Eliyahu said, when he had found his voice. "We are simple people who are just looking for a Jew who died here forty years ago. To this day, no one knows what happened to him."

Norman Chambers' aged eyes rested on his tearful granddaughter. "Jews, Jews," he grumbled. "Our minister says that you people always bring trouble with you."

A tense silence filled the lobby. The only sound was the old man's ragged breathing. Chambers studied them for a long moment; he turned to look again at his granddaughter and then back at the two men. He seemed to be pondering something. Finally, he came to a decision. His shoulders drooped, his eyes fell, and a resigned expression came over his face. Leaning on his stick with both hands, he suddenly looked every day of his ninety-plus years.

"If Ben Lowinger hadn't sold his ranch, none of it would have happened," he said sadly.

R' Eliyahu and R' Shlomo stood frozen.

The old man nodded slowly. "He took advantage of the fact that Sam was sick, and sold the land right out from under him. The government poured millions into that piece of property. A high wall, an iron gate, buildings and watchtowers ...."

He smiled bitterly. "At first, they spun us a tale: The compound belonged to the Department of Agriculture, which was erecting a factory to turn manure into commercial fertilizer. It wasn't until later that we found out they were really incubating dangerous viruses there. They told us that the viruses were weapons against Communism — that our little town was going to save America from the Soviets. But in the end ... look what happened ...."

His granddaughter stared at him in astonishment. This was the first time she had ever heard him speak of that painful episode in their family's history.

"At least Ben Lowinger got his just desserts," Norman Chambers continued, eyes sparkling with anger. "One of the guards at the compound shot his wife." He waved a contemptuous hand. "Not that he cared. He went ahead and married himself a new wife pretty quick ...."

The two Jewish men had many questions. There was a great deal about Chambers' story that they did not understand. But they were afraid to break into the stream of his reminiscences, as he unburdened himself of memories that had apparently been weighing on him for decades.

He continued, "Lots of young folks from the town had jobs inside the compound. They thought it was a fine place to work: a government salary, full benefits, possible room for promotion. Ah! How naive we were. My Steven, he got a job there, too. He was a gardener. I told him, 'Steven,' I said, 'come work with me in my bakery shop.' That was just around the time we opened up this inn. But he wanted to work inside those high walls. That's what he wanted. What could I do?"

The old man's voice broke. His eyes filled with tears.

"And then the accident happened, and everyone died: the sheriff, old Sam, Ben — not that I care a snap about *him* — and the soldiers. So many soldiers .... Every day, convoys of trucks left with coffins, headed for every corner of America. And twenty of our own boys died, too. There were twenty graves dug in Grayston's cemetery that week. Twenty boys who paid with their lives ...."

He took a faded handkerchief from his pocket and mopped his eyes.

"Steven was the only one they couldn't find. He had simply disappeared! We went among the dead and checked every one. He wasn't there. We hoped that he had been spared. We wanted to believe that he was still alive. But two weeks later they informed us that they had found him in Mexico — dead — down in Juarez ....

"Then the CIA men came. 'What was Steven looking for in Mexico?' they asked. 'Why did he go to Juarez without telling a soul?' I told them that I didn't know. Maybe he had gone traveling with friends. Maybe he wanted a vacation. He was a grown man. I didn't keep him on a leash."

R' Eliyahu peeked at his watch. Twelve-thirty. The old man could ramble on till nightfall. It was Friday, and soon they had to start out for Austin.

"Were there any survivors?" he asked.

"I don't know," Norman Chambers replied. "All I know is one thing: my son could have been a husband and father today. Instead, he's buried in the cemetery, back of the church."

"Where was the compound?" R' Shlomo asked. "Is it still around today?" The "army base" mentioned in the kollel ledgers, they understood now, referred to that secret government compound.

"The compound? It's right where it's always been: behind Sam's place."

"How do you get there?"

"You have to drive along the road between the ranches," the girl answered in her grandfather's stead.

"The highway?"

"No. It's a back road that starts behind the train station."

"Is there a sign on the compound? How will we recognize it?"

"No need for a sign. You'll see it. It's impossible to miss."

On either side of the road, pastures and fields stretched to the horizon. Every few miles brought another isolated ranch, featuring a large house, a barn and a stable or tractor shed. Dotting the landscape here and there were tall oil wells, their pumps rising and falling slowly as they sucked the precious fluid from the ground. Texas is cattle land, but oil men also do fine there.

The road began climbing a series of low hills. They had already been driving for a quarter of an hour, and the two men had begun to wonder whether the girl had deliberately misled them. Then, rounding the next bend, they saw something that left no room for doubt: They had reached the compound.

They rode downhill until they reached a narrow lane leading to a large ranch house. Two towers rose at either side of the house, and a porch stretched along the front. In front of the house was a small clearing. R' Shlomo parked the car.

It was obvious that the house had been neglected for many years. The peeling wooden walls had been bleached by the sun; the window panes were shattered, with gaping wide spaces in their place. Grass and weeds had sprouted everywhere and even rose through cracks in the wood floor. There was no sign of life. The house was silent as a graveyard.

The strange thing — no, more than just strange, actually frightening — was the huge concrete wall that surrounded the house on three sides. The ranch house was situated in a sort of large niche created for it by the wall, which continued along both sides until it disappeared from view behind the hills.

The two men stepped from the car. They walked across the overgrown grass and climbed the three steps to the front porch. Neglect was everywhere. The front door had been loosened from its hinges. The old wooden floorboards creaked beneath their feet. Peeking into the house, they surprised a flock of birds, which flew up to the ceiling with squawking and a great flapping of wings. Broken furniture lay strewn in fragments and a powerful odor of dust and mold permeated the interior.

In the center of the front room they saw signs of transient life, where vagabonds had passed a night or two: old newspapers and empty cans. A big lizard peered up at them with its strange eyes, as though wondering what they were doing here.

"There's nothing to see here," R' Shlomo said, and shivered. He felt as if he were looking into an open grave. A cold wind seemed to crawl up his spine. Instinctively, he retreated a step.

"Let's go see the compound," R' Eliyahu suggested.

They walked back down the porch steps and headed for the concrete wall. Here, too, the touch of a human hand had clearly been absent for a long time. Large bushes grew wild and tall; an uprooted tree lay on its side, its withered branches pointing at the sky. An ancient rusty Ford pickup truck stood abandoned nearby, its tires flat and dried rubber disintegrating from the rims.

The iron gate in the concrete wall was locked with a heavy chain. An impressive sign stated that this was the property of the United States Army and there was to be no unauthorized entry. Even the sign was old and faded.

The asphalt in the open area in front of the gate had cracked with the years, and there were pieces of equipment scattered haphazardly about. Not only had the Lowinger house been abandoned, but the secret compound seemed to have stood deserted for decades as well.

To their surprise, the guard booth beside the gate boasted a gaping hole. They would be able to pass right through it, into the compound proper.

"Shall we go in?" R' Shlomo asked.

R' Eliyahu considered the question. First of all, it was against the law. And, secondly, who knew what kind of dangerous substances might still be lying about inside?

However, now that they had come this far, they must explore all possibilities — at least have a look at the place. Maybe they would find a clue inside.

"Yes," he decided finally. "Those on a mission to do a mitzvah are not harmed."

R' Shlomo, the nimbler of the two, squeezed through the hole in the guard booth first. R' Eliyahu followed, with a little help from his friend. The two were standing inside the complex — the secret compound.

It was clear that no one had set foot in this place for many years. The area had been built up along a broad road that started at the main gate and stretched to the horizon. Here, too, were skeletons of old trucks and rusty jeeps that appeared to have been rooted in their places for the past four decades. Untrimmed bushes lined the roadside, their roots pushing up the nearby pavement. Weeds flourished unhindered everywhere.

To the left of the road, near the gate, stood a long, multistoried building, surrounded by a forest of undergrowth and many layers of barbed wire. They also saw a large hangar with a collapsed roof; several broad, low buildings; and, in the distance, another single-story structure. All the buildings were neglected and in a state of sad disrepair. There was not a sign of life anywhere.

"It's as if they all picked up one day, went away, and left this place behind," R' Eliyahu said in a hushed voice.

"You're right," R' Shlomo agreed.

They walked around for a few minutes, but soon agreed that there was no purpose to be served by lingering. They would drive back to Grayston and continue on from there to Austin. On Sunday, they would return to resume their investigation.

They went out the way they had entered, through the breached guard booth. R' Shlomo turned the car around in front of the gate and began driving carefully along the narrow road, toward the larger one that connected the area ranches.

"What's that?" he suddenly asked in alarm. A car was advancing toward them from the other end of the lane.

The two men exchanged a worried look. Another car at the abandoned compound? For forty years no one had remembered the place — and now, on the very day they had come here, someone else had suddenly appeared?

The car approached slowly and stopped in front of them. A wide Chevrolet, it completely blocked the narrow access lane.

The car doors opened, and two men got out.

"The sheriff and his deputy," R' Eliyahu murmured, seeing their uniforms.

"We're in trouble," R' Shlomo said, just as quietly. "We shouldn't have trespassed on government property."

The two lawmen came closer, approaching the car from two sides. R' Shlomo and R' Eliyahu rolled down their windows.

"License and registration, please," the sheriff said.

R' Shlomo, at the wheel, handed over his papers.

"You're from New Jersey," the sheriff stated. "What are you doing here?"

His voice was hard and his glance unfriendly.

"We're looking for information about a person who died here in an accident, forty years ago."

"You his relatives?"

"Not exactly."

"You related to the Lowinger family?" the sheriff asked.

"No, but ...."

"Get out of the car."

The Jews obeyed, throwing each other despairing looks.

"You've been going around disturbing the peace in this town," the sheriff said, raising his voice. "You're poking your noses in places where they don't belong and asking too many questions."

"We're just —" R' Shlomo tried to explain.

"Quiet!" the sheriff yelled, whipping out his gun.

R' Eliyahu and R' Shlomo froze. They both smelled the scent on the lawman's breath: alcohol. He was apparently an experienced enough drinker to hide the fact that he had been drinking, but the smell could not be disguised.

Slowly, the sheriff lowered his arm and replaced the gun in its holster. "Arrest them!" he barked at his deputy.

The Jews held their breath. The situation was rapidly going from bad to worse. Would they be spending Shabbos in a jail cell in this forsaken little town at the edge of Texas? They had heard about arrogant southern sheriffs ruling their domains with no holds barred. Justice, in this part of the country, could be very flexible and open to interpretation.

The deputy took two pairs of handcuffs from his belt. He was older than his boss. "Turn around, please."

R' Eliyahu and R' Shlomo shuddered at the sound of metal rattling behind them. Seconds later, they were both securely handcuffed. The sheriff faced them, red-faced and angry.

"Do you know what the punishment in Texas is for trespassing?" he asked, thrusting his face near theirs. "The death penalty! I know you people make fun of us. You say that we shoot first and ask questions later. What you don't know ... is that it's true."

The Jews stared at the sheriff. Was he serious? Was he simply going to shoot them in cold blood? R' Eliyahu began reciting a silent prayer. The hearts of kings and officers — and even drunken sheriffs — were in Hashem's hands.

For the next ten minutes, the sheriff treated them to a harangue on the severity of their crime and the punishment they deserved.

"But I'm going to be good to you two," he said at last. "I'm going to take into consideration the fact that this is your first offense." His voice rose to a scream again: "I want you to get out of here. And don't show your noses in Grayston again — *ever!*"

He nodded at his deputy, who seemed to take this drama in stride. The deputy walked silently over to the two prisoners and removed the handcuffs.

The sheriff was already halfway to his car. With his back to them, he took a swallow from a small bottle plucked from the door pocket.

He turned back. "If I see you two out here again, I'm going to arrest you and set the law on you," he warned them before getting behind the wheel. "Now, get in your car. We're going to escort you out of this district. This is the last time I ever want to see your Jewish faces around here again. Is that clear?"

The sheriff led them to his office in the center of town. Once there, he disappeared into his inner room — no doubt in need of another swig — leaving his deputy to deal with the pair. The deputy was calmer and more genial. Offering them chairs, he wrote their names and license numbers down in his police log.

"I'll escort you to the edge of the district," he said, starting for his car.

All of Grayston was outside to see them off. The silence was deafening. While no one cursed them or threw stones, R' Eliyahu and R' Shlomo could feel the scores of eyes piercing their backs. Youngsters and grownups, men and women, stern-faced ranchers in cowboy hats — all stood and watched the best show in town: the two snooping Jews being driven out of town like beaten dogs.

R' Shlomo and R' Eliyahu drove silently behind the deputy. They were very close to solving the riddle. They had been nearly there when again, at the eleventh hour, something had happened to halt them in their tracks.

Had they been able to return to Grayston on Sunday, perhaps they could have spoken to more people. Maybe the circle of old-timers would have revealed something, or Norman Chambers would have added to his tale. One more visit to this town might have unraveled this whole terrible tangled web.

But none of that would happen. They were now *persona non grata* in Grayston: undesirables. They had been chased out of town and could not come back any time in the foreseeable future — and it was the near future that mattered. The wedding was scheduled to take place in just four more days.

If they did not succeed in answering the questions before that — the marriage was simply not going to take place.

R' Shlomo and R' Eliyahu drove obediently along behind the deputy. As they approached an intersection, the lawman pulled over onto the shoulder of the road and motioned for them to come closer. R' Shlomo parked alongside, window to window.

"This here's Highway 10," the deputy said, pointing to his right. "You can go on alone from here." He hesitated. "Listen, I want to apologize for my boss. He can get a little … carried away."

"Thank you, sir," R' Eliyahu said. "We appreciate that."

"What were you guys really looking for over there?" the deputy asked curiously.

R' Eliyahu sighed. "All we want to do is save an entire family from a terrible tragedy."

Shabbos was coming, and Austin was still a long way off. But this could be their last chance to glean something from their trip to Grayston. R' Eliyahu began telling the deputy about the Rosh Yeshivah and his daughter, the *kallah*, and the complication that had suddenly come to light just ten days before the wedding. And the answer to the mystery seemed to be right here in Grayston, Texas — the town from which they had just been banished.

"Well, as you can see," the deputy said, "around these parts people don't like talking about that episode. The compound and the big accident — they're kind of a secret pressing down on our town. Some folks blame Steven Chambers for having something to do with that whole mess, and that doesn't help folks feel any better about it."

"Were there any survivors of the accident?" R' Eliyahu asked.

"A few. There were the two Lowinger boys. They were called John and Eddie. I knew them well. We went to school together."

"And where are they today?"

"No one knows. They disappeared along with their mother a few days after their father and uncle were buried. Far as I recall, they went off to Atlanta."

"Atlanta?"

"Yes. No one's heard from them since. By the way, if you ask me, Eddie is probably some kind of crook today. He had a criminal mentality even as a kid. I remember more than once when he beat me up and I came home crying. I wouldn't be surprised to hear that he's sitting in some jail somewhere."

"And the other son?"

"John? The older boy? He was a different type altogether. More gentle-like. He got dragged into his brother's shenanigans, but he was always more restrained. I guess it's all about the genes."

"What do you mean?"

"They were actually only half-brothers. They had the same father. They didn't like to talk about it, but John was the son of the Jewish wife who came here from Israel with Ben Lowinger. She was killed when John was just a baby, and then his father married Barbara, a native of Grayston. Her brother owned the feed store. His son runs the place today."

"You say that John, the older boy, was the son of the Jewish wife, and Eddie was the son of … a local woman?"

"Exactly. By the way, if you're looking for John, you might start with the music world. He took saxophone lessons and spent all his free time practicing. If folks predicted that Eddie would turn out to be crook, they said that John was going to grow up to be a great musician. Look for a saxophonist by the name of John Lowinger. Who knows? He may be famous."

"Were there any other survivors?"

"There was one more," the deputy said. "Come to think of it, he just might be your man. No one knew who he was. He was in a coma for a long time, in the local infirmary set up in the compound. They waited for him to regain consciousness, but he never did. He died."

"And why do you think this is the man we're looking for?"

"Because he had a beard, just like you guys. I never saw him, my-self, but everyone in Grayston called him 'the old man' or 'the man with the beard.' He was a mystery that I still remember from my childhood. Everyone wondered who he was."

R' Eliyahu's heart missed a beat. R' Shlomo broke out in a cold sweat.

"How long did you say the bearded man was hospitalized?"

"At least four years," the deputy said. "Maybe longer. He was in hos-pice care in a local facility. I remember the grown-ups saying that it was the one good thing Grayston got out of the accident, because several families earned their livelihood taking care of him for such a long time."

R' Eliyahu and R' Shlomo parted from the lawman with heartfelt thanks, despite the fact that his story had thrown them into a turmoil. The information he had so innocently proffered only thickened the fog surrounding the Padlinsky family. Until now, there had been a possibil-ity that the whole thing was no more than a wicked rumor started by a heartless rabbinical adjudicator. Now, the rumor had sprouted legs and taken off.

They knew that R' Tzvi Hirsch, the kollel's fund-raiser, had planned to visit the Lowinger family. Now they had learned that a bearded man had survived the accident — a man who had lain in a coma for at least four years afterward. Had the *beis din* actually made a horrific mistake in al-lowing R' Tzvi Hirsch's wife to remarry when she did? When she married R' Moshe Padlinsky and gave birth to her twin boys, Yom Tov and Eliezer, had her first husband still been clinging to life — comatose, bedridden in a remote corner of the U.S. — but nevertheless alive?

It was still a full hour before Shabbos when they reached Austin, where they were to be the guests of the local rabbi. On the way there, they contacted a top private detective in New York who specialized in locating missing persons. A non-Jew, he was highly regarded in his profes-sion and had been recommended by reliable friends. With his experience

520 / THE MEXICO FILE

and connections, he should certainly be able to locate the two Lowinger boys, who would be in their fifties now.

R' Eliyahu provided the detective with all the facts he had, along with various clues they had garnered along the way — such as the speculation that Eddie Lowinger might be active in the criminal underworld and that John probably moved in musical circles, that the boys had relocated to Atlanta after the accident, that the local feed store belonged to Eddie's mother's brother and was now under his son's management. The detective would have resources at his command that they did not. He would be able to dig through data banks and connect to the worldwide computer network. He had his sources in various military, quasi-military, and government bodies. Surely he would be able to track down those two brothers, wherever they might be.

"And maybe," R' Shlomo quipped in a lighthearted moment, "it'll be just like in the books, and the Jewish brother will turn out to have done *teshuvah* and is now living in Bnei Brak or Yerushalayim!"

"The question is, what can he tell us?" R' Eliyahu said, bringing his friend back down to earth with a thud. After all, locating one of the Lowinger brothers might be the final nail in the coffin: the final confirmation that the bearded man had been the kollel's *meshulach*, R' Tzvi Hirsch HaLevi.

That information would serve a death blow not only to Wednesday's wedding, but also to the Padlinskys' family status within the Jewish community — until the end of time.

The *"aufruf"* Shabbos passed in a joyous blur for the Milinover chassidim. The *Shalosh Seudos "tisch"* went on for a long time — as though the Rebbe, like the large crowd, was reluctant to part from this special Shabbos and its aura of exaltation.

Hardly anyone noticed the weighed-down spirits of some of their leaders. R' Shammai and R' Yoel managed to hide their worry, though their eyes met several times over the course of the day before looking away with a sigh.

The two men were not the same age; a full generation divided them. Yet both knew the meaning of responsibility. They shared a terrible secret and were carrying an almost unbearable burden. Looming before them were events of fateful significance. The coming days could shower tragedy on them, their families, the broader Milinover community, and perhaps the nation as a whole — but they had no one with whom to share their feelings. Not even their nearest and dearest could share their gnawing anxiety.

Their source of strength was the Rebbe. He conducted himself all Shabbos without any change from the norm. R' Shammai was very familiar with the Rebbe's daily schedule and habits: prayers, *tischen,* and the time he spent alone in his room, absorbed in his Torah study and spiritual devotions. Everything played out today just as on any other Shabbos. All through the day, R' Shammai provided updates on the situation; each time, the Rebbe merely nodded. He betrayed no concern. Instead, he lifted his eyes heavenward and repeated, *"Yeshuas Hashem k'heref ayin. Yeshuas Hashem k'heref ayin."* Hashem's salvation can come in the blink of an eye.

And if R' Yoel was worried, R' Shammai was doubly so. In contrast to R' Yoel, he was aware of the additional menace hovering over the *simchah* and threatening to obliterate it: the slander that had been raised regarding the Padlinsky family. Though not fully updated on the progress of the investigation — he had no idea, for instance, that R' Yom Tov's two "detectives" had flown to Texas — he knew from the *mechutan,* the Rebbe's son, that all efforts to come at the truth had not yet borne fruit.

Knowing all this, R' Shammai was in a position to admire and be moved by R' Yom Tov's extraordinary self-control. As the Rosh Yeshivah *davened,* partook of the Shabbos meals, and sat near the Rebbe at the *tischen,* R' Yom Tov evinced no sign at all of the inner turmoil he must surely be experiencing. His face never betrayed a hint of the family drama that was poised to destroy his life.

R' Shammai had spoken with him over the course of the week, and knew how truly anxious he was. But the moment the Shabbos descended, R' Yom Tov had detached himself from all his worries. His face seemed to grow brighter and his posture more erect. As the Gemara says, Shabbos is not a time to cry out for help — and salvation is near ....

The private eye told them at the very start that he would require a minimum of 48 hours for an investigation of this magnitude. He promised to phone R' Eliyahu late on Sunday afternoon.

When the call came, he was able to report that he had, indeed, managed to track down the two Lowinger brothers who had been born in

Grayston. He had found a record of their attendance in a school in near-by Port Stockton some forty years earlier, as well as medical records of Eddie's tonsillectomy in an Austin hospital. In ensuing years they had moved to Atlanta, where they attended elementary and high school. Both were good students and earned good marks, though Eddie seemed to have had some behavioral issues. Each had joined the army immediately after high school.

The problem, said the investigator, was that from that point on, all trace of the brothers simply disappeared. He had been unable to find a sign of them anywhere — to this very day. Not in the prison system, not in university, not in the medical network system. Nothing. Perhaps they had been killed, or had left the United States, or changed their names. But even these things usually left a trail; not in this case. There was no saxo-phonist by the name of John Lowinger. No one in Grayston had kept in touch with them, including the cousin who today ran the local feed store.

"In short," the investigator concluded, "no John or Eddie Lowinger ex-ists today. They've both vanished, as though swallowed up by the earth."

The American intelligence community also had a busy weekend. The various groups assigned their best men to try and glean additional details about the forthcoming terror attack — without much success. At CIA headquarters, the tape of the phone call from that anonymous Baltimore man was listened to again and again, in an effort to learn something from the background noises, from his accent, from his vocal tones. No useful conclusions were reached.

CIA computers spat out a list of professors in various virus-related fields: doctors in a spectrum of specializations, medical scientists, mi-crobiologists, chemists, researchers, and lecturers. The list was useless. Its tens of thousands of names did not advance the investigation by a millimeter.

The breakthrough came at 7:50 on Monday night, when the same caller from Baltimore phoned again. He had run down for a minute to make the call, he hurriedly told the switchboard operator at the local FBI field office, because he had remembered something important. His boss would kill him if he found out he had gone to make a call, but as a patriotic American he felt an obligation to report that the two men in the coffee shop near the mall had said something else. They had mentioned the imam of Los Angeles. They had said that the professor had to first talk to the imam of the Los Angeles mosque.

Twenty seconds after the call — which was terminated as abruptly as the first one had been — word had been passed along to FBI headquarters. From there, it was quickly transmitted to all the other relevant intelligence branches. Adrenalin began coursing through the system again. Listlessness vanished and renewed energy flowed into the investigation. A spark lit the discouraged eyes of hundreds of agents and investigators. Los Angeles! A Muslim imam! At last, a significant clue that could be probed.

Thirty minutes later, at 8:20, scores of troops from the special unit against terror surrounded the large mosque in the heart of Los Angeles presided over by Imam Bashir Abdul Aziz. Well disguised, they drew no attention from pedestrians. Perhaps the local residents were surprised at the sight of so many commercial vehicles with tinted windows and the three closed trucks parked on a nearby street. But no one dreamed that waiting inside was a small army, well armed and just waiting for the signal to attack.

It was a sunny, happy day in the Milinover community. Excitement was mounting. In just two days, on Wednesday, the big wedding would take place. Tomorrow, Tuesday afternoon, would see the start of the festivities, with the *seudas aniyim* slated to take place in the Ganei HaSimchah catering hall,.

The last of the guests from abroad landed in Eretz Yisrael during the course of the day. These were businessmen and others who were unable to get away for a lengthy period. They had not come early enough to be present for the Shabbos *aufruf* and would not be staying for the Shabbos *Shevah Berachos*, but would have to content themselves with attending only the wedding itself. They could have arrived on Wednesday and lifted off again on Thursday morning, but nearly all chose to arrive in time to participate in the *seudas aniyim*.

Everyone knew the importance with which the Rebbe regarded this *seudah*. He insisted that it be as beautiful and sumptuous as the wedding itself. The Rebbe frequently spoke of the wonderful benefits to be accrued by including the poor and downtrodden in the wedding celebration. As a result, all Milinovers were careful to attend, including the wealthier chassidim: It was well known that participating in this *seudah* was a *segulah* for prosperity. After all, he who has one hundred will always hunger for two ....

But not everyone was looking forward with anticipation. Late that night, shortly after midnight, R' Yom Tov Padlinsky entered the Rebbe's room looking very sober. The latest news from his two messengers had been worrying in the extreme. What had begun as an unfounded rumor about his family history had slowly taken on the form of actual fact. It was no longer just a suspicion, but practically a certainty. Vigorous investigation had led to the chilling conclusion that the story was probably true.

It was time to face reality. Time to announce the painful news that the wedding was being postponed, perhaps permanently. And the sooner it was done, the better. In R' Yom Tov's opinion, the *seudas aniyim* should be canceled as well, and he and his family should return home to New Jersey.

The Rebbe rejected the suggestion out of hand. First of all, he told the agitated Rosh Yeshivah, even without a wedding one was still obligated in the mitzvah of giving charity. The poor were anticipating the *seudah* and there was no justification for canceling it. As for postponing the wedding — should the need arise, Heaven forbid, it could be done then.

And anyway, the Rebbe reiterated, *yeshuas Hashem k'heref ayin*. Even if a sharp sword is resting on a person's neck, he must never despair of Heavenly compassion.

The Ford parked opposite the Los Angeles mosque was about four years old: neither too new and sparkling, nor too old and dusty. The vehicle was not likely to attract any special attention. The two people inside looked like a father and son, or perhaps a businessman and his driver.

The passenger, about 50, was chatting on a cell phone, his forearm resting casually on the armrest. The driver, a young man under 30, tilted his head back and closed his eyes as though indulging in a catnap. But the picture was misleading. The older man was not feeling casual and the younger one was not asleep. This was a stage setting that the two had perfected over the course of a long career conducting stakeouts. In reality, both were as tense as coiled springs.

The older man was Ted Cone, the head of the Los Angeles antiterrorism unit. The driver who appeared to be dozing was his second in command, Ralph Simon. The seemingly ordinary Ford was equipped with several improvements that the manufacturer had not included in the original. Ford Motors had not, for example, planned to have the trunk serve as a storage area for a mobile arsenal of pistols, submachine guns, stun grenades, and a large quantity of ammunition. Nor was the option of pushing a button to turn all the windows instantly opaque offered to just any customer.

Ted Cone's cell-phone conversation was another part of his disguise. He had no need of such old-fashioned devices. He was in direct communication with his unit's headquarters via a tiny microphone hidden in a flap of his bulletproof vest and a minuscule earphone in his ear. He reported on the situation on the ground, while his staff updated him with new information that was constantly coming in.

The mosque's marble-and-glass facade had been designed with a Middle Eastern motif. Soft lighting illuminated the facade of the building as well as the open space in front. Additional agents were in position opposite the mosque's rear entrance and in the yards of both adjoining houses. More operatives had surrounded the imam's personal residence, several blocks away, despite the fact that his present location — pinpointed by his cell phone — put him inside the mosque.

The imam had neither made nor received any calls within the past hour, and the reason for this was clear: According to the mosque's website — a very active and thriving site — he was delivering his daily class on the Koran. The lecture was scheduled to end at nine.

"The *madrasa* has three classes every evening," Ted Cone repeated to his assistant as the information reached him from headquarters. "There's Conversational Arabic, History of Islam, and, of course, the Koran. About thirty to forty people attend each class." Indeed, through the windows on the ground floor the outlines of many people could be seen inside the building.

"So, we wait," Ralph Simon said. Both of them understood that entering the mosque and interrupting the popular imam in the presence of scores of Moslems was a recipe for certain disaster — and for immediate broadcasting over the news networks, coast to coast.

"Absolutely," Cone agreed. The imam never left the mosque before nine p.m. They would not make their move for another thirty or forty minutes.

The time was put to good use for any number of feverish intelligence-gathering activities. Updated photos of Bashir Abdul Aziz were transmitted to the forces in the field. An agent visited the offices of the company that provided security services for the mosque, armed with a federal writ requiring it to provide any and all help requested by the counterterrorism unit. Surprisingly, the imam had a clean record with both the CIA and every other security agency. He had never been sighted at meetings held by quasi-legal Islamic organizations devoted to raising funds to liberate the "holy lands" or for the families of security internees in Israeli prisons; he did not travel to Arab countries on the terrorism blacklist, and was not chummy with extreme Muslims on the CIA's radar. No extremist Islamic or pro-terrorist views had ever been heard being promulgated by the imam. He delivered eloquent speeches about the supremacy of the Islamic nation, fanning the flames of his listeners' national feeling and urging them to take pride in their roots and their faith. He told his audiences that the true believers were meant to dominate the infidels, and not the other way around. But he had never crossed the fine line dividing a legitimate religious discourse from support or encouragement of terror. Bashir Abdul Aziz always remained within the letter of American law, which has sanctified the right to free speech and freedom of expression.

"Tell you what I think?" asked the analyst updating Ted Cone on Aziz's profile. "He looks like someone who's deliberately worked to keep his nose clean. These may not be his true positions. He's too much a Muslim to be free of any trace of incitement."

It was a little after nine when the first of the *madrasa* students began emerging from the mosque. They parted from one another with handshakes and some friendly talk before getting into their cars and driving away — completely unaware that the unit's photography crew, concealed behind a car facing the entrance, was snapping pictures of them. Later, decisions would be made as to which of them to question in their homes.

By 9:15, the sidewalk in front of the mosque was deserted. The lights in the classrooms had been turned off and an elderly man with a mustache and an Islamic head covering, clearly a mosque employee, stepped outside and locked the front door. He walked slowly across the yard and locked the gate as well. The building's facade was still illuminated, as were the windows in the administrative wing. The operatives watching the back door affirmed that Aziz was still inside.

"Unit One — go!" Ted Cone said into his communications device, from the Ford that had become the operation's command center.

Six counterterrorism agents, headed by Ralph Simon, slipped over the fence into the mosque's yard and, under cover of the darkness, stole around to the rear. Ralph Simon gently turned the doorknob; as expected, the door was locked. Under other circumstances he would have resorted to explosives — but here, in the heart of Los Angeles, other means were preferable. One of his operatives, an expert locksmith, had the door open within seconds. The agent at the mosque's security service on the other side of the city had done his job well: no alarm sounded, and the video monitors in the mosque's security room did not receive a live feed from its cameras, but only a replay of the previous few minutes. If Aziz or one of his people sought to view what was happening behind the back door, they would see nothing but an empty path.

The door opened onto a long corridor. At the end of it, they had been instructed, there would be a right turn, another door, and then a staircase leading up to the administrative wing and the imam's office.

The six agents covered the corridor in absolute silence. They were well trained in the art of silent ambulation in much more difficult terrain than this — a floor covered by a soft Persian rug.

The door at the end of the corridor was open. Ralph Simon peeked cautiously around the corner. There was no one on the stairs. The six climbed silently and were soon ranged around the imam's door, three on each side.

Ralph Simon burst through the door with a single swift kick. His companions entered right behind him, assuming a battle-ready stance — only to find themselves in an empty room. There was no imam seated behind the big desk.

It took no more than a few seconds to confirm that the man they wanted was not hiding elsewhere in the room. Quickly and methodically, the armed operatives checked the closet and large cabinets, behind the heavy drapes, under the desk, and even the adjoining restroom.

"Clear," one of them announced.

Most of the time, this word signals a success: The territory is clear of hostile forces. This time, it was a statement of failure. Aziz was not in his office.

More agents streamed into the mosque, where they began combing every room to make sure Aziz was not hiding in one of them. A third team — plainclothes investigators — hurried into the office and pounced on the computers and bulging paper files.

"The building's clean," came the report to a very disappointed Ted Cone. He repeated the message briefly to the rest of the unit: "Aziz is not in the building and was not seen leaving it in the past hour." They had wasted precious time staking out the mosque. The man they wanted had eluded them.

After a pause of two seconds for thought, he added, "Check that with the people who were here tonight."

"Will do."

Three additional teams set out from headquarters, with the task of asking members of the Koran class if anyone had taken Aziz's place as teacher that evening.

There was still another possibility: Perhaps the imam *had* been in the building but knew of a secret exit. Perhaps he had sensed the unusual activity and managed to slip out at the last minute.

"Where's his cell phone?" Ted Cone barked into his communicator. He had exited the car and was racing toward the mosque.

Someone in the unit several miles away glanced at the computer screen near him. "In the mosque," he said. The cell phone's locater told them that it was still in the same place.

"Call him," Cone ordered.

He reached the imam's office, where his detectives were poring over files and folders. One of them copied the contents of the entire hard drive onto a flash drive, while another went over the walls with a device that resembled a vacuum cleaner, trying to flush out a safe or other hiding place.

A muffled telephone ring froze the investigators in their places. The ringing was coming from one of the closed desk drawers. Ted Cone kicked the desk in a fury. "The phone's here," he said between his teeth.

Ralph Simon went to the desk and removed the phone from its drawer. Quickly, he checked the list of incoming and outgoing calls. The lists were empty. Someone — most likely, Aziz himself — had made sure to erase all sign of his most recent telephone conversations.

"Get the list of calls," Ted ordered. This was a mistake that amateurs often made. They thought that erasing the call list from the phone itself made it impossible to know to whom they had spoken. What they forgot was that the same list was available from the phone provider. Still, this would lead to a delay of ten or fifteen minutes that they could ill afford to waste. Who knew what Aziz would be doing in that precious space of time?

"Unit Five, enter the house," he ordered through his communicator.

The team of operatives, several blocks away, burst into Aziz's house only to discover that no one was there. It was a large private home surrounded by a garden. In the three children's rooms they found clear indications of a hasty departure. Closets and toy cupboards were gaping open and partially empty. On one of the beds lay a pile of folded clothes, as well as a suitcase and two smaller bags that had apparently been left behind as unnecessary. Though there had not been enough time for a thick layer of dust to settle on the floor or the furniture, this was clearly a home that had been abandoned by its dwellers days earlier.

The kitchen, in contrast, showed signs of being lived in more recently: several dirty cups in the sink, a jar of coffee and a sugar bowl on the counter, and an open box of cookies that had attracted a convoy of ants. Within minutes, confirmation was found via airline records: The imam's wife and five children had left the United States four days ago. They had made their way to Italy, continuing on from there to Saudi Arabia.

The word that came in ten minutes later surprised no one: Aziz, too, had left the U.S. He was also on his way to Saudi Arabia — this time on a direct flight, with no stops.

"When?" Ted Cone asked.

He had his answer in seconds: "He lifted off from Los Angeles at 7:43 this evening."

Cone ground his teeth in frustration. He looked at his watch: 9:55 p.m. The imam had been beyond U.S. airspace for two hours.

What a mess up. What a disappointment.

What a failure.

As the hands of the clock inched up to ten p.m. in Los Angeles, it was early Tuesday morning in Israel.

Special Agent Scott had been at G.S.S. headquarters since the evening before, along with Uri Arbel and two other senior intelligence officers. In the course of a lengthy discussion, several differences of opinion had arisen among them.

While the Israelis had locked in on the Milinover wedding and were certain that it was to be the target of the expected terrorist attack, the American was no longer sure. Doubts had begun to creep into Scott's mind. Could he have fallen prey to a false perception? Was his intuition failing him in this instance?

At this point, there were still no concrete indications to support the supposition — no intelligence pointing specifically to this event as the terror target. They had arrived at the Milinover wedding by process of elimination: All the other possibilities had been discarded, leaving this wedding as the default target. But Scott had suddenly begun to wonder if they weren't all making a huge mistake. Suddenly he was beginning to feel that, while they focused all their attention and energy in this one limited area, the actual matter might be getting away from them.

What they needed to do, Scott insisted, was start over again. They must reevaluate, without any prior considerations. They had to begin looking into other possibilities — and not only in Israel.

They were still deep in discussion when the cell phone at his belt vibrated. Reading the message on the screen, he stood up. "I have to run over to the embassy," he said. "Let's be in touch over the course of the day."

The roads were fairly empty this early in the morning, and Scott put his foot down hard on the gas pedal. In less than a quarter of an hour, he was passing through the American Embassy gates in Tel Aviv. He hurried up to the secure communications room where, as requested, he established contact with his headquarters back home.

"I'm going to connect you with Ted Cone, head of counterintelligence in L.A.," the operator in Washington told him.

In seconds, the connection was made between the embassy building in Tel Aviv and Bashir Abdul Aziz's office in the heart of Los Angeles.

"Hi, Ted," the special agent said in greeting. "This is Agent Scott, in Tel Aviv. I was looking for you."

"Hello, sir," Ted grinned.

The two knew each other well. The man speaking from Rechov HaYarkon in Tel Aviv had been Ted Cone's boss in the counterterrorism unit, and the one who had recommended him as his successor when he had stepped down and moved into his present position. Ted was very familiar with his former superior officer. He knew of his practice of switching identities, and his insistence — amusing but also exasperating — that his acquaintances call him by his current name. Ted, an underling but also a friend, would never give him the satisfaction. While he did not use his boss's real, hidden name, he refused to play the game. He would simply call him "sir," thus elegantly sidestepping the little trap.

Ted Cone gave Scott a detailed report about the latest developments in L.A.: the stakeout at the mosque, the fruitless break-in, and the fresh news that Aziz and his family had left the U.S., bound for Saudi Arabia — the others by prearrangement, he apparently in a panic.

"When did you say his plane lifted off?" Scott asked from Tel Aviv.

"At 7:43."

"And when did the call from Baltimore reach the FBI?"

"At 7:50."

"Has anyone checked the coincidence?"

Ted Cone smacked his forehead, stunned. "I'm an idiot!" he said slowly. "Simply — an idiot."

"Check to see if Aziz had any calls from Baltimore."

"Of course."

Cone had his answer in minutes. As he had expected, it was positive. At 5:45, Aziz had received a call from a public telephone booth in Baltimore — from roughly the same area from which the anonymous caller had contacted the FBI on both occasions. And the phone company's list of calls brought to light another fact: Immediately after that call, Aziz had initiated a series of calls to airlines and travel agencies until he acquired a seat on the first flight out.

"He must have had another ticket waiting, for a later date," Scott guessed.

"Exactly," Cone concurred. "He already had a ticket, dated for tomorrow. But he took an earlier flight."

"Do you understand what's happening here? Someone has thrown us a bone. He let the FBI in on it, like a good citizen — but only after warning Aziz and giving him a chance to escape the country."

"So our boy in Baltimore seems to be playing a much more pivotal role than we thought," Ted Cone mused aloud.

"Absolutely," Agent Scott said. "He's not just any anonymous tipster. This changes the whole picture."

By the time the American agent walked out of the embassy building, the morning was already well advanced and the Tel Aviv street had filled with people. He stretched tiredly and looked around for a nearby coffee shop. His eyes were red with sleeplessness and all his muscles ached from sitting in the communications room for so long. In the past four hours, he had conducted several important — perhaps even fateful — conversations.

First, he had spoken with the head of the FBI Baltimore office who had taken the first anonymous call two days before. Then he had held long consultations with the director of the CIA, after which he had spoken with his direct superior, the head of U.S. national intelligence.

There had been, he learned, no additional progress in their investigation. While Aziz's precipitous flight to Saudi Arabia had certainly aroused suspicions, so far no one had managed to find any way to link him to terrorist activity. On the contrary, the deeper the investigators dug into the material confiscated from the mosque, the more Aziz stood revealed as a measured leader who had distanced himself from anything that smacked of illegality. His profile was not that of the typical terrorist. All efforts to find a link between him and the man described by the Baltimore caller as a "professor who dealt with viruses" had so far come to naught.

Counterterrorist investigators looked into the mosque's correspondence, at all incoming and outgoing phone calls, and at the list of those who had visited its website. Some were brought in for questioning, but not one provided the connection to a biological terror attack. Aziz certainly appeared to be one of the "good" Moslems, a moderate who does not allow his religious beliefs to threaten the peace and welfare of his host country. If it turned out that Bashir Abdul Aziz *was* one of the bad ones, a top security adviser declared, he would lose faith in all Moslems everywhere in America.

In a parallel investigation, the CIA tried to link Aziz to the Milinover wedding. Special Agent Scott had already received a list of all invited guests — including, of course, those who had flown in from abroad. Computers were put to work seeking some sort of connection, however faint, between one of these guests and Aziz. The attempt bore no fruit.

At the same time, the Israeli G.S.S. was running a discreet check on all the catering hall's personnel. Here, too, no red flags were raised. All the employees seemed to be clean. About ten Arab workers were employed at the Ganei HaSimchah wedding hall. Some lived in Um-el-Facham, one in Yaffo, and another three shared an apartment in southern Tel Aviv. None of them had any sort of connection to Aziz. None of them was linked to anything relating to a biological terror attack.

Agent Scott finished his cup of coffee and immediately ordered another. The menace now seemed a great deal less urgent and much less focused. Apparently, his initial instincts had misled him. The Milinover wedding was not the focal point. In fact, he was beginning to doubt the existence of the terror attack completely.

The Baltimore caller had lost his trustworthiness; without him, the entire story did not hold water. He was not the classic concerned citizen who called the police in order to prevent a crime. Definitely not. His motives were entirely different. What were they? That was something he planned to look into when he got to Baltimore. He was finished here. Israel, it seemed, was not the main player in this drama. The real action was taking place in Baltimore. Something was cooking there. Someone out there had initiated a surprising and inexplicable chain of events.

Uri Arbel was taken aback when he received Scott's call. They had parted early that morning, before dawn, in the midst of their meeting with the two additional analysts, and the American had not been in touch since then. So Arbel was astonished to hear his news: "I'm flying back this afternoon."

"What happened?"

"A reassessment of the situation, based on new information, has reduced the threat to a low level," Agent Scott said. "I'm booked on a flight to the U.S. at two p.m. If you want to meet me and hear the details, I'll be at Ben-Gurion Airport before that."

"Okay," Arbel said. "I'll be there at one." He was eager to hear about the American intelligence community's "reassessment" and the "new information" that had led to it. Scott had said something about a reduction in the official threat level. If only he was right about that!

Arbel called the prime minister and told him that the Americans had lowered the threat level.

"I'm glad to hear that," the prime minister said in open relief. "Please continue to keep me updated."

Tuesday, the eve of the big wedding, began happily in the Milinover community. Hundreds of worshipers participated in Shacharis in the big *beis midrash*, guests from all four corners of the world standing side by side with the locals. Everyone was interested in the schedule of events surrounding the wedding and the *Sheva Berachos*, and kept careful track of the announcements posted by the organizing committee.

One sign on the bulletin board at the shul's entrance, for instance, announced that buses to the *seudas aniyim* — to take place today, Tuesday (double "*ki tov*") at the Ganei HaSimchah hall — would be available to the chassidim starting from 2 p.m., in front of the Talmud Torah building.

Logistical preparation for the wedding itself were also at their peak. Workers erected the raised dais on which the *chuppah* was to take place outdoors in front of the shul, while a small knot of curious passersby looked on. Copies of the newest CD of Milinover melodies — which had been released, as usual, at the last minute — were snatched up like fresh-baked rolls, and its joyous strains could be heard emanating from many homes.

Uri Arbel drove toward Ben-Gurion Airport, whistling a cheerful tune. His mood had definitely improved. He had not slept for at least 24 hours, and his body was screaming for sleep after the tension of the past few days. But Agent Scott's words had filled him with a sense of hope and vast relief. He longed to know what new and dramatic information had changed the situation, at least in the Americans' opinion. If Scott was permitting himself to leave Israel and return home, it was a sign that the situation had indeed taken a turn for the better.

As he entered the terminal, Scott waved to him from one of the tables in front of a coffee shop. He, too, had been on the go for a day and a night. He was surviving only on the strength of a nonstop river of coffee, and planned to use the flight to catch up on his sleep.

"Would you like something to drink?" he asked his Israeli colleague as Arbel dropped into an adjoining seat.

"Yes. The strongest coffee they have."

Even before the coffee arrived, Scott's cell phone vibrated. The name that appeared on the caller screen caused him to lift his brows in surprise. Ted Cone, from Los Angeles? What did he want?'

He quickly took the call.

"Where are you?" Cone asked his former boss, dispensing with the pre-liminaries. He knew that Scott had intended to travel to Baltimore, and exhaled in relief when he heard that Scott had not yet boarded his flight.

"Listen, we're on to something," Cone said.

"Do you want to talk from the communications room?"

"No. Let's talk now." The trip from the airport to the embassy would take at least half an hour, and he wasn't sure they had the time. Their cell phones were fairly secure. In a pinch, they would have to do.

"What's going on?" asked Scott.

"It's like this. Aziz's original flight to Saudi Arabia was supposed to take place today. Naturally, he wasn't on it, because he's been in Saudi Arabia since yesterday. What we found out is that someone else made a reservation on the same flight, and he also failed to take his seat. The man in question is a professor and lecturer in the field of biology at UCLA. And guess what? He also left a day early, grabbing a flight to Saudi Arabia at the last minute."

"What's his name?"

"Barry Majdi. Professor Barry Majdi. He looks perfectly clean, American as apple pie, but he's Egyptian by birth and grew up in the same Cairo neighborhood as Aziz."

"Were they in contact with each other?"

"Nothing that we know about — yet. But we're still checking."

Something lit up in Scott's brain.

"Barry Majdi, you said? Wait a second." Scott opened his laptop and rapidly booted up. The file he wanted was on the screen in seconds. When he saw the name, he shook his head and compressed his lips.

"Listen," he said, with a trace of excitement in his voice. "There are a number of Arab workers at the hall where the wedding's supposed to take place. The Israeli G.S.S. checked them out, and they're all okay. But guess what? One of them is named Turk Majdi."

"Do you think this is the link we've been looking for?"

"If they're related, it's a clear indication."

"We can find that out easily enough," Ted Cone said.

Ten minutes later, Special Agent Scott knew that he would not be boarding his flight. Baltimore would have to wait. Israel had just jumped back into the game — in a big way. The Milinover wedding, the Ganei HaSimchah hall: That's where it was going to happen.

Professor Barry Majdi was apparently the one who had planned it, his nephew Turk Majdi had been elected to carry it out, and Bashir Abdul Aziz was the spiritual adviser who had lent the project its religious support.

The wedding was to take place on the following night. He had just thirty hours left to foil the plot.

63

What happened?" Uri Arbel asked. He had been privy to only one side of the phone conversation — Agent Scott's — but it didn't take a genius to realize that something dramatic had transpired.

"There have been developments," Scott said. Briefly, he outlined the events of the past few hours to his Israeli colleague: the second communication from the anonymous Baltimore caller; the foray into the Los Angeles mosque; Aziz's premature flight to Saudi Arabia. He withheld his suspicions about the Baltimore caller. That was an internal affair calling for investigation by the American intelligence community.

"What's become clear now," the American agent said, "is that Aziz originally planned to fly with a second person, who likewise left the U.S. a day early: a lecturer in biology at UCLA by the name of Barry Majdi. On the face of things, he's a respected American scientist, free of any connection to terrorism or to Islam. But he's Egyptian by birth, grew up with Aziz, and attended the same school."

"And ...?" Uri prompted. He knew there was more.

"What we've just discovered," Scott continued, "is our first link between Aziz, the professor, and the Milinover wedding. One of the kitchen staff at the wedding hall is a young man named Turk Majdi — originally from Um-el-Facham, now living in Yaffo. We noted the similarity in their family names, and quickly received confirmation from the CIA: Turk Majdi is Barry Majdi's nephew."

Uri Arbel reached for his cell phone.

"What are you doing?" Scott asked.

"Calling the G.S.S. I want them to send in a unit to pull him out of the hall."

"Good," Scott said. "And let's make tracks in that direction ourselves. I'd like to get a look at that kid."

UCLA's biology department was empty and quiet. It was the height of the summer break and the hour was late. Most of the students, lecturers, and staff members had departed, leaving only the odd few who had research to complete or were following up on an experiment or writing articles.

From Ted Cone's perspective, the fewer people in the area, the better.

Updates from headquarters came at him in an almost incessant stream, as agents and investigators broke into the professor's apartment and the office adjoining it, subjecting both to a thorough search. Barak Majdi's profile was run through the agency's computers and emerged completely clean. Majdi's biography seemed emblematic of the American dream: the child of immigrants attaining an honored position in the land of unlimited opportunity, serving as a university lecturer, liked by his students and esteemed by his fellow scientists. The professor owned a private company called Biologic Systems, which developed and marketed medical and pharmaceutical patents. In this role he had appeared in the American media more than once — most recently for the development of Klistemprol, a wonder drug intended to fight the common cold, which had been the subject of a coast-to-coast advertising blitz. The drug had made him a very rich man.

All the data pointed to a man completely detached from terror-related activity. He was possessed of a sound Western orientation, never attended the mosque, and did not identify with any Islamic organizations. Simply in the light of the dry facts, Ted Cone concluded, Professor Majdi was above suspicion.

But his sudden departure for Saudi Arabia, in startling conjunction with Aziz's hasty flight, was a clear indication that the two were plotting something together. Perhaps that was why they had taken such care to stay apart and avoid communicating openly. Both had succeeded, deliberately, in distancing themselves from anything that smacked of terror — until the last minute.

Until zero hour, when the evil plot they had been brewing stood ready to come to fruition.

The counterterrorist unit that burst into the professor's office found only a middle-aged secretary typing on a computer. She looked up and shrieked in alarm as the door was thrown open and a group of men entered, shouting, "FBI! Don't move!"

Two men faced her with weapons drawn, while four others moved rapidly through her office and that of the professor, next door. The secretary watched them with wide, stricken eyes. She couldn't believe what she was seeing: armed men in the heart of Los Angeles ... drawn weapons in the biology department ... submachine guns in Professor Majdi's office ....

"What do you want?" she screamed. Her face was white.

"Where is Professor Majdi?" asked one of the men at her desk. It was Ted Cone.

"Who are you people? What do you want?" Signs of panic were beginning to show. Her eyes filled with fear and her hands shook.

"I asked where the professor is," Ted Cone asked, hardening his voice slightly.

"Who are you? What do you want?" she wailed again.

Ted Cone pointed at the identity tag on his chest. "L.A. counterterrorism unit. We don't want to hurt you. I just want to know where Professor Barry Majdi is."

"I don't know," the secretary gasped.

"What do you mean, you don't know?" Ted Cone shouted. "You're his secretary! You make his appointments."

"I don't know where he goes during semester breaks. What do you want from me?" She was on the verge of tears.

"He's a suspect in a terrorist operation."

Shock pulled her back from the edge of hysteria. She was, Cone thought, genuinely surprised.

"What kind of nonsense is this?" she snapped. "Do you know who Barry Majdi is? He develops drugs for contagious diseases. He does so much for humanity. He can't be involved in terrorism. It's simply ... impossible!"

"Are you aware that he's run off to Saudi Arabia?"

"Saudi Arabia?" She was astonished. "Why there?"

"Have you spoken to him within the last 24 hours?"

The secretary lowered her eyes. Then, in a low voice, she admitted, "I've been trying to reach him since yesterday. This is the first time since I've started working for him that he's been out of touch for such a long time."

"Listen, miss," Ted Cone said. "I know this will come as a big shock, but the man you've been working for is suspected of being a clever and dangerous terrorist. He has stayed faithful to his Muslim roots, though he's managed to hide it from the whole world — even from you. He is undoubtedly a member of a group that's planning to murder thousands of people tomorrow night. If you don't cooperate and tell us everything you know, you will be as responsible for the slaughter as he is!"

She closed her eyes for a long moment of silence. When she opened them, they held a different expression. "You know what? Maybe you should talk to Yousuf," she said quietly.

"Yousuf?"

"Yousuf Nadir. Professor Majdi's research assistant."

"Yousuf? Is he involved?"

"All I know is that he recently changed his name. He used to be called 'Joe,' but now he's 'Yousuf.'"

Ted Cone signaled to the agent beside him, who stepped aside and established communication with headquarters. "Run the name Joe or Yousuf Nadir," he said. "See what we have on him."

"What do you know about him?" Cone pressed. "Where does he live? Who are his parents? Is he a devout Muslim? Does he attend the mosque?"

The secretary started shaking again. All at once, she grasped the enormity of the situation. Her teeth rattled, making it hard to speak.

"His f-father came here from Afghanistan. Today, he owns a chain of electronics stores."

"Is Yousuf here at the university now?"

"I think so. The professor gave both of us a number of assignments to take care of this week. That's why I'm in the office so late. Yousuf said he might have to sleep in the faculty room because he has so much to do. He could be in the library, or perhaps in the lab."

"Does he have a cell phone?"

"Yes."

"Okay," Cone said. "Calm down, miss. You can help us. I want you to phone Yousuf and ask him to hurry back to the office. Don't tell him we're here; just tell him it's urgent. We need to talk to him."

Ralph Simon, Cone's second in command, brought the agitated woman a cup of water. She took it with thanks. "I never liked that Yousuf," she said in a trembling voice. "I never understood what the professor saw in that ... that Arab."

The Ganei HaSimchah kitchens hummed with activity. Workers carried trays of food toward the dining hall, while others quickly set additional tables as the number of guests waiting outside rose to higher-than-expected levels. Motke, the red-faced manager, rose to each new challenge, stridently hurrying his staff along. The morning's *bris milah* celebration had ended late, and the hall had to be prepared for the *seudas aniyim* at top speed.

It was right then, with the pressure at its height, that one of his men decided to do a disappearing act.

When three strangers walked into his kitchen, Motke exploded. "Who are you and what are you looking for?" He had no time to be pestered now.

One of the men took out his G.S.S. identity card and showed it to him. Motke glanced at it quickly, and subsided.

"We're looking for a worker of yours by the name of Turk Majdi."

"Turk? I'm looking for him myself."

"What do you mean?"

"Half an hour ago, he suddenly disappeared," Motke complained. "Can you find him for me?"

The G.S.S. men exchanged an expressionless glance.

"Did he say where he was going?" the team leader asked.

"No. He simply walked out, without any advance notice. His phone isn't turned on, either. I'm furious! When he gets back, he's going to hear from me — but good."

Uri Arbel got the news from the G.S.S. man while on his way to the hall. He smacked the steering wheel in frustration.

"We missed him," he told Scott.

Those people were always one step ahead of him. First Aziz escaped, then Majdi vanished — and now, Turk Majdi had disappeared just minutes before his men appeared on the scene. The G.S.S. and the police had instituted a manhunt, for all the good it would do now ....

They were nearing the hall. The car turned left and sped along Rechov Jabotinsky. "Get me one of our Milinover contact men," Agent Scott requested.

Uri Arbel punched in R' Shammai's number. The *gabbai* was on another call and didn't pick up. Arbel tried R' Yoel next, but was immediately transferred to his voice mail.

The car flew through one traffic light after another. It sped through the Rabbi Akiva-Jabotinsky intersection and approached Ramat Gan. Subsequent attempts to reach either R' Shammai or R' Yoel were equally fruitless.

"We're very close to the hall now," Uri Arbel said. "We'll be there in a minute."

They were on Rechov Ben Gurion. A large sign, proclaiming "Ganei HaSimchah," was evident over the low, long building at the end of the street. Near the building was a sight that made Arbel's eyes cloud with sudden anxiety. "What's that about?" he wondered aloud.

The hall's parking lot was swarming with chassidim — just like those he had seen from R' Shammai's window last Shabbos. What were they doing here? Agent Scott watched them with the same surprise, which quickly turned to apprehension.

"Don't tell me we made a mistake, and the wedding's really today." For the first time, Arbel heard a note of alarm in the American's voice.

He tried R' Yoel's number again. This time, it was picked up at once.

"The wedding is tomorrow," R' Yoel said, calming his fears. "Today we have a preliminary event that we call the '*seudas aniyim.*'"

"What's that?"

"It's a mitzvah to include the poor in one's happy occasion, so we prepare a special feast for them, one day before the wedding. The Rebbe will be there, and all his chassidim."

Arbel passed this information along to his colleague.

"Agent Scott and I are in the area right now," he said. "Maybe we'll look in on the party."

"Please do," R' Yoel said. "You're invited."

Arbel hung up. His car was positioned to give them a view of the hall's parking lot.

"Wait here a minute," Scott said. His narrowed eyes moved slowly across the lot. His forehead was creased and his face gradually grew taut with tension. The new idea that had burst in on him was horrifying. He felt his blood begin to race, filling him with a sensation of near-panic.

Uri Arbel sensed that something was happening, but asked no questions. He knew by now that the American would talk only when he was ready and not a minute before.

"Who are they?" Scott asked, gesturing at the crowd that had gathered near one of the doors. "Are those the men who've been invited to the feast?"

"Apparently," Arbel said.

Scott closed his eyes in concentrated thought. After a few seconds, he turned to face Arbel. "Is the *seudas aniyim* a routine affair with this type of wedding?" he asked. "Is it publicized ahead of time?"

"Apparently," Arbel said again. "That's what Yoel told me."

Scott's tips tightened. The pieces of the puzzle suddenly joined in his mind, creating a terrifying picture. He looked directly at his Israeli colleague, and there was an expression in his eyes that Uri Arbel had never seen before.

"Listen," Scott said. "The attack is not going to take place tomorrow. That was a deliberate decoy. The terror attack is about to happen — here and now."

64

Professor Barry Majdi's secretary took a deep breath and mustered her courage. Rapidly, she dialed Yousuf's number, activating the speaker phone for the benefit of Ted Cone and his men.

Yousuf answered right away.

"Where are you?" the secretary asked. Her voice did not betray the slightest tremor.

"In the library," Yousuf said.

"Please come to the office for a minute. Professor Majdi has just sent a fax."

"Can it wait? I'm in the middle of something."

"Not really," she said. "He asked that you read it and send him an answer immediately."

"By the way," Yousuf said, "He hasn't been reachable since yesterday. I tried to reach him several times, but couldn't get through."

"Right," the secretary said, quickly improvising, much to Cone's delight. "His phone got lost. He left me another number that will reach him."

"Okay, I'm on my way." Yousuf hung up.

The secretary replaced the receiver and exhaled in relief. She took another sip from her cup of water, her hands still shaking.

"Thank you. Good job," Ted Cone said. "Now, I want you to go into the other room and stay there. We may still need you."

Yousuf's footsteps could be heard coming down the hall. He tapped lightly on the door and opened it. Two operatives set on him without a sound, dragged him farther into the room, and threw him onto the floor. Within seconds, he was bound hand and foot.

Yousuf Nadir demonstrated remarkable self-control — much better than the secretary's. After his initial resistance to capture, he submitted in silence. He was seated and handcuffed to a chair . He sat hunched over but shed no tears, begged for no mercy, and asked no questions. He simply sat in silence and waited to see what would happen next.

Ted Cone recognized this behavior. It was taught in underground workshops run by extremist Muslim group for their "brothers" in the United States — training them to stand firm under arrest and interrogation.

Running Yousuf's name through the CIA computers elicited a host of interesting information, all of which made its way in a steady stream to Ted Cone's earpiece.

Yousuf looked up and studied his surroundings. By the look of the soldiers' uniforms, he concluded that these were counterterrorist commandos. In the special course that he and his friends had taken, they had been taught to distinguish between the various units of their enemy, America, the great Satan. These commandos were the most dangerous of all: the most ruthless, most intelligent, and least merciful. Yousuf's heart began to pound in terror, though he tried not to betray his fear to the infidels surrounding him. Clenching his jaw, he focused his thoughts on the great bliss that Mohammed had promised all *shaheeds* who were ready to lay down their lives in the cause of spreading Islam throughout the world.

Ted Cone pulled up a chair and sat directly facing the prisoner. "Why did you fly to Israel three months ago?" he asked.

Yousuf became a little confused. This was not the way the course had taught him to expect an interrogation to start. Usually, the questioner avoided the main point, leading up to it indirectly. And besides, how did his questioner know about the flight to Israel?

Quickly, Yousuf summoned up the lesson he had learned from his instructor, an Islamic activist and a veteran of numerous interrogations by both the CIA and the FBI: *Deny everything*. Never admit to a thing. Don't volunteer one iota of information to the infidels.

"I did not fly to Israel," he said.

Ted Cone smiled apologetically. "You left the U.S. on your own passport and returned on your passport. It's all registered and recorded. There's no point in denials. I repeat: Why did you fly to Israel? What were you looking for there?"

Yousuf weighed his options. "America is a free country," he said. "I'm allowed to travel whenever and wherever I want."

"Who sent you?"

"No one sent me. I wanted to take a trip."

"Why Israel?"

A shrug. "It's a nice place."

"Who paid for your ticket?"

"I did. I wanted to travel a little."

Ted Cone knew he was lying. According to the reports coming in from headquarters, the ticket had been charged to Barry Majdi's credit card. However, Cone chose not to reveal this information immediately. Instead, he pursued his line of questioning: "Why didn't you go to Europe? Do you have relatives in Israel?"

"I told you, I just wanted to see it."

"And you didn't feel like seeing any other countries?"

"You know what?" Yousuf raised his voice slightly. "I wanted to visit the Islamic holy places, okay?"

"So why didn't you travel to Mecca and Medina?"

"Maybe I'll get there one day."

"So you just happened to decide to go to Israel, to pray at the Temple Mount?"

"Yes. Is that against the law?"

"Certainly not. Where did you stay?"

"At the Tel Aviv Hilton. You can check to see if my name appears in their register."

"And where else did you go?"

By this time, Yousuf had realized that the American didn't have much to work with. He listed several places he had visited, including Ramallah, Gaza, and Tel Aviv. He did not, of course, mention Yaffo or Um-el-Facham. He stayed away from any information that might hint at the real reason Professor Majdi had sent him to Israel.

For the next ten minutes, Ted Cone and Yousuf chatted in an almost casual way, with Cone asking innocent questions about the student's impressions of Israel, his job at the university, and his relations with his family.

Yousuf grew calmer by the minute. Their talk was almost pleasant. At one point, Cone offered him a drink of water, which Yousuf accepted. The interrogator softened him up with considerable skill — in advance of the blow. He lulled the suspect into a sense of security. Ted Cone was very familiar with this type of dabbler in terror, spoiled American kids playing at being *shaheeds* and *jihadists*, but quickly folding up under a little neat psychological handling.

"Okay," he said to one of his men, stretching in his seat with a sigh. "Let him go. Take off the cuffs."

A smile rose to Yousuf's lips. He had successfully undergone his first interrogation. His instructor would have been proud of him.

The counterterrorism operative brought his key ring over to Yousuf. He crouched at Yousuf's feet and began dealing with the restraints.

"Just tell me one more thing," Cone said. "When you were in Israel, why did you meet Turk Majdi?"

Shock immobilized Yousuf. The blood drained away from his face and his entire body froze in fear. The question had come at the moment he had least expected it. Cone's man, of course, left him shackled and bound. The farce was over.

"T-Turk?" Yousuf stammered. "Who's that?"

"Barry Majdi's nephew." Ted Cone moved closer, his voice raised to a threatening pitch. "Why did you meet him?"

"I don't know any Turk."

Before Yousuf's stunned eyes, the formerly polite and urbane interrogator turned into a beast of prey. He attacked, grabbing Yousuf's shoulders and shaking him menacingly. "You don't know any Turk?" he roared. "Do you think I'm stupid? That you can pull the wool over my eyes? Do you think I don't know that Barry Majdi paid for your ticket? Why did you fly to Israel? *Why did you meet Turk?*"

Yousuf cowered in his seat, terrified. "I don't know any Turk," he repeated feebly.

"What were you doing in Israel?" he yelled. "Why did you meet Turk?"

Yousuf's eyes filled with tears of rage.

Ted Cone raised the volume. "*What were you doing in Israel? Why did you meet Turk?*"

Yousuf doubled over in fear. It was hard to breathe.

Suddenly, Cone subsided. He sat back down in his chair. His voice went down a full octave.

"Yousuf, why did you fly to Israel?" he asked quietly, looking directly into the young man's eyes. "I'm going to get the answer out of you one way or another. It'll be better for you if you tell me now, before you suffer any further. You have no idea what I can do. There hasn't been a suspect that has not talked to me in the end."

Yousuf's breath came back. He clenched his teeth as his nostrils flared and sparks of hatred flew from his eyes. He was not afraid of this infidel American. What could he do to him? Kill him? He was not afraid of death. On the contrary, he longed to die for Islam. Death, said Mohammed, belonged to the brave. To the heroes.

Ted Cone knew exactly what was going through Yousuf's mind. He knew the brainwashing that fundamentalist Moslems underwent, including the depiction of a *shaheed's* death as a sure key to Paradise. He smiled, a cold, wicked smile, as he began to explain to Yousuf that he did not intend to kill him. Not at all. Instead, he intended to put him through a series of tortures that the best minds at the CIA had developed specifically to persuade men like him to talk.

"You'll be screaming in pain. You'll beg me to stop. You'll be left with no teeth and no fingernails, crippled and blinded for the rest of your life. You'll suffer so much that you'll *beg* me to kill you."

A heady commotion filled the Ganei HaSimchah hall, as the gates were thrown open and the crowd began pouring in.

Young chassidim politely ushered the invited guests over to the sumptuously set tables, where the hungry throng started on the rolls and salads. The chassidim themselves stood around, the older men hovering near the dais where the Rebbe and the *mechutanim* would shortly be taking their places, while the younger ones sat on the bleachers surrounding the tables. On a special platform in a corner of the hall, the band that would be playing at the wedding on the following night was poised to begin. At a signal from the bandleader, the musicians broke into a lively rendition of "*Siman Tov U'Mazel Tov.*"

Uri Arbel and Agent Scott sat in their car, a short distance from the hall. The spacious parking lot was now devoid of humanity. Strains of merry music wafted clearly out into the street, though the two men in the car were feeling neither merry nor cheerful. If Scott's guess was right and the attack would be coming today, the situation looked hopeless.

Turk Majdi had managed to slip right through their fingers. According to reports from Israeli antiterrorist units who had hastened to the spot, his apartment in Yaffo had revealed nothing significant. G.S.S. men had gone over the entire place with a fine-tooth comb and questioned his neighbors, but had found no sign of any biological substance.

A large police force had descended on Turk's home in Um-el-Facham as well. His mother had no idea where her son was, but under vigorous questioning had admitted that he had recently been in close contact with her brother-in-law, Professor Majdi. On what subject? She hadn't a clue.

"What are we waiting for?' Uri Arbel asked. "Let go in."

Scott compressed his lips and shook his head "no." Absolutely not. They were not going anyplace before they knew exactly what they were getting into. When you walked in the dark, the chances were high that you would fall right into the very trap of which you were afraid.

A biological attack could be carried out in any number of ways: introducing a toxic substance into the food, polluting the water, dispersing a powder in the air, pouring a liquid from a vial, spraying something from an aerosol can, or spreading a poisonous material over areas that people came in contact with, such as door handles and sink faucets.

Terrorists had wide-ranging options. They could set loose a swarm of virus-carrying mosquitoes or burst into the hall on a vehicle bearing lethal biological material. Or perhaps one of the guests was actually a carrier, previously infected with some sort of disease that he was now spreading with every cough and sneeze?

Which biological threat were they dealing with? Here, too, the list of possibilities was long — and nightmarish. Anthrax, black death, ricin, and on and on. Scott was not about to walk in with his eyes closed. Right now, Ted Cone was interrogating the professor's research assistant, who

THE MEXICO FILE / 551

had taken part in the plot. Ted knew how to do his job. He was an expert in forcing subjects who were not afraid of dying to confess. If the young American-Islamic student knew anything at all, Ted would soon get it out of him.

At the same time, other operatives were working on refreshing the secretary's memory, in the hopes of gleaning important details about Professor Majdi. Additional investigators were going through every paper and electronic file found in the professor's home and on his office computers.

Meanwhile, the Israeli security services were not sitting idle. They had set in motion a series of well-rehearsed emergency measures, including mobilization of a huge medical team and search-and-rescue crews. These personnel had gathered in two predetermined areas: the Ramat Gan Stadium parking lot, and the eastern section of the Yarkon Park. Both were located a short distance from the Ganei HaSimchah hall, though not within sight. Direct orders were not to expose their feverish preparations until an additional indication of the impending attack surfaced. In other words, no sirens or flashing lights.

The heightened activity in the area had, of course, been accompanied by a news blackout. Media reporters, requesting an explanation from the usual official sources, found themselves facing a military-mandated brick wall. Nothing, not the tiniest hint, was permitted to leak. A special military unit was set in position in the event that the area would need to be sealed off, to prevent the spread of a terrorist-induced disease beyond the first circle of exposure. Preparations were also underway to spirit top government figures to a secure location, the moment the need should arise.

The Ministry of Health, too, was getting ready to meet the threat. Every hospital in the region — Bellinson, Tel HaShomer, and Ichilov — had been instructed to free up a sizeable space to be used as a biological emergency room. Field cots and decontamination showers were distributed, along with protective gear for the medical crews. Hospital labs were provided with increased personnel and all vacations for doctors and nurses were canceled. The ministry's Disease Control Team opened a situation room, from which it updated the relevant parties in the Biological Institute at Nes Tziona.

Music continued to blare from the hall. "*Od yishoma b'arei Yehudah ...*" played the band, as the large throng of chassidim joined in. Everyone was waiting expectantly for the Rebbe and his entourage to appear. No one had the faintest notion of the involved preparations secretly under way outside. No one guessed that the commercial GMC that had parked near the hall's entrance was actually equipped with sophisticated laboratory equipment, designed to detect toxins used in biological warfare. It was manned by two officers from the army's engineering division, who sat inside the mobile lab keeping a steady eye on the dozens of dials and gauges in the rear of the vehicle.

As of now, nothing out of the ordinary had registered. The sensitive instruments had not identified any deadly organism or toxic substance. Another technician was checking samples from the hall's kitchen. The fact that Turk had worked in the kitchen placed food poisoning at the top of the list of possibilities. But the food was found to be free of any taint.

"Why don't we go in?" Uri Arbel asked again. He was in continuous contact with both the prime minister and the minister of defense. Both were insistent that he take some action. What was he waiting for, a pile of corpses? Uri's explanation — that they were waiting for information from one of the agents on the case in the U.S. — failed to soothe either minister.

"If you want to go in, go ahead," Scott said. "I'm staying here."

"Okay," Arbel said. "I'm going in. Stay in phone contact."

Agent Scott sat in the car, anxious and troubled. He couldn't share with Uri Arbel the reason he had chosen to remain outside. It was an internal American affair. He had suddenly realized that he was not alone in this theater of operations. There was another American on the scene, as interested as he was in the Milinover wedding — but not for the right reasons. Someone else was intent on dancing at this wedding, and Scott had no idea where his interest really lay.

It was the anonymous caller from Baltimore who had led him to this conclusion. Just a few minutes earlier, as Scott listened for the umpteenth time to the FBI recording of the two calls to their field office, Scott had suddenly come to grips with what it was that had been bothering him all along. In the second conversation, in which the caller had "remembered" to report that the Los Angeles imam was involved, he had spoken from a clear understanding that the FBI operator would know what he was talking about. This was not the behavior of an ordinary citizen.

Not a word had appeared in the American press. Any reasonable caller would have checked first to see if the operator knew to what he was referring. This fellow had not done so — because he had known that she knew. The caller from Baltimore was well aware that all U.S. intelligence agencies were in an uproar after the first call. Why?

Because he was someone on the inside. Because he was privy to the most classified information. He might even be an official government representative.

The Israeli, Uri Arbel, had only one enemy inside this catering hall: radical Islam and its crazed messengers. Scott had another: an American enemy.

And that enemy just might have a reason to stab him in the back.

A gent Scott stayed in Arbel's car, trying to figure out his next step. *I have to get inside*, he thought in rising frustration. He had to be inside the hall. He couldn't just sit here on the outside.

On the other hand, he needed more information before he went in. He had to know whom he was up against.

Sounds of celebration emanated from the big hall. The band began playing a rhythmic song that drew the entire crowd into a lively vocal rendition. They continued singing the song — "*Kol rinah v'yeshuah b'ahalei tzaddikim*" — with great enthusiasm, as the Rebbe and the main players in the *simchah* entered the hall: the *chasan* himself, his father — the Rebbe's son, leader of the Milinover community in New York, — the *kallah's* father — R' Yom Tov Padlinsky — and their families.

"*Der Rebbe zuhl haben ah mazel tov, alleh mechnutanim ah mazel tov!*" sang the hundreds of men on the bleachers as they danced in place to the music. Agent Scott stared at his cell-phone screen in tense expectation, but no calls came in — neither from Ted Cone in L.A. nor from the Washington division that was working on his behalf, coordinating all incoming information from the CIA, FBI, and other intelligence organizations.

The music played on, and despite his tension Scott found himself humming along. *This is no time to be singing*, he scolded himself. But the music drew him in. He could discern drums, a keyboard, an electric guitar, a bass guitar, and at least three wind instruments: a trumpet, a saxophone, and a trombone. He found himself reflecting with admiration on a chassidic sect that brought such extensive musical accompaniment to a party meant essentially for the indigent.

The inspiration flashed into his head with startling abruptness. For a minute he wrinkled his brow, weighing the notion from every angle. Then his fist clenched in triumph. Yes! He had found a way to get inside. He phoned Uri, who was already in the hall, and outlined his idea in a few terse sentences.

He didn't see his Israeli counterpart's grimace. "Are you sure that's necessary?" Uri Arbel asked doubtfully.

"Absolutely," Scott said. "Organize it for me — quickly."

"I think we'll need to get authorization from above."

"So what are you waiting for?"

Uri Arbel quickly tracked down R' Yoel, head of the Milinover institutions. He was standing in a corner of the hall, surrounded by several active young men and talking into two phones at the same time. Although Arbel had a secular appearance, he did not attract much attention. He blended in with the band, the hall employees, and other nonchassidic workers.

"What happened?" R' Yoel came over to him at once.

"You won't believe this," Uri grinned. "But the American's had a bizarre idea."

R' Yoel shared Uri's surprise, but acceded to Scott's request. He spoke to the necessary parties, persuaded whoever needed to be persuaded, and then gave Arbel the thumbs-up sign from across the room, signifying that all was arranged.

Three minutes later, Agent Scott was inside the hall and enjoying the best view of all, right up on the stage. He scanned the crowd with a pounding heart. The sight was a moving one. And the head table, at which men of noble bearing sat devoting their time to those less fortunate than they in their hour of rejoicing, was memorable.

For the first time, he set eyes on the Milinover Rebbe, about whom he had heard so much from R' Shammai at the Shabbos meal. The Rebbe's countenance was regal. His eyes radiated goodwill and boundless wisdom.

But Scott had not come to gather his impressions of the Milinover chassidim. He had a job to do. He had a biological terror attack to circumvent.

Motke, the catering hall's red-faced manager, was under pressure. Until a few minutes ago he had had to contend only with the mysterious disappearance of Turk Majdi. Now he was missing five other employees: all his Arab kitchen staff had been taken away for questioning by G.S.S. agents in Tel Aviv, leaving him decidedly shorthanded.

Luckily, the custom at the Milinover *seudas aniyim* was for the elder chassidim and the *mechutanim* to serve the food themselves, in order to physically fulfill the mitzvah of giving charity and honoring the poor.

Through the open kitchen doors came a number of chassidim, ranging in age from forty to fifty and even older, bearing laden trays. They moved along the passageways between tall bleachers before dispersing among the tables and beginning to dole out portions of fish. One of them was Dr. Jacob Stern — or, as he preferred to be called here, Yaakov Meyer Stern.

The time he had spent among the Milinover chassidim had been happy and useful. All year long he lived in Houston, a place almost devoid of Jewish warmth. He worked as a senior administrator for the Department of Agriculture in Texas — the only Jew in his division. It was only natural that, when the opportunity arose to be near the Rebbe, he exerted himself to squeeze every drop of spiritual richness from the experience.

Jacob tried to do his job properly, to give each and every guest a sense of well-being. He set the plates down before each one with a smile and a friendly word. This was the third wedding at which he had actively participated in the *seudas aniyim*, and each time he was surprised anew to see the different reactions to his warm attention. There were those who thanked him volubly and showered him with blessings, others who offered a faint smile of appreciation, and those who turned away in discomfort.

When Jacob reached the seventh man at the table, their eyes met for an instant. The man inclined his head at once, absorbing himself in his food. He didn't see his chassidic waiter's face turn white. Jacob thought he was going to faint on the spot. His arms felt suddenly weak. He had to rest the tray on the table before it crashed to the ground.

The next three men did not get the friendly treatment. Jacob Stern set down their fish rapidly and started back for the kitchen. He did not look back. Was the man looking at him? Had he recognized him? His heart thudded with fear. The nightmare was back.

The man who had made his life a misery three months early had returned — showing up, in all places, here at the Milinover feast. What was that … that killer looking for at a *seudas aniyim*? What was he plotting? Why was the man with the pale hair and light, expressionless eyes sitting here, among all the *aniyim*?

Jacob walked stiffly, as though there were a gun pointed at his back. The minute he was out of sight of the tables, he stopped, placed a hand on his chest, and breathed deeply. What was he supposed to do now? Who would help him? He had to tell someone — but who?

"Yankel Meyer, are you all right?" Jacob heard someone call. It was one of the chassidim, who had observed him breathing heavily, as though after a race.

Jacob nodded and pulled himself together. He was all right. He was just fine. He had to be strong to cope with this new threat to his safety and that of his family.

But — just a minute. Were only he and his family at risk? Perhaps this was not a personal matter at all. The man had appeared in disguise at a Milinover event. Maybe he ought to tell one of the senior chassidim.

The fellow was up to something — that much was certain. He hadn't come here for a piece of chicken or the 200 shekels that the Rebbe would hand out at the end of the meal ….

R' Shammai Lederman stood at attention behind the Rebbe's chair at the head table. The band was playing a lively tune and everyone was singing along, but the *gabbai* did not share in the general air of celebration. He was feeling more anxious and troubled than he ever remembered feeling before.

Tomorrow night was the wedding, but everything seemed to be conspiring against it. First, there was the warning of a possible terror attack, Heaven forbid. He had glimpsed both Arbel and Scott in the hall, but the looks on their faces had not inspired him with confidence. He had heard that G.S.S. men had come to arrest one of the kitchen staff, and that other Arab workers had been pulled in for questioning. What was happening? What sort of bad fortune was dogging this wedding?

And that was not all — not by a long shot. There was also the terrible fear hanging over the heads of the entire Padlinsky family. The chassidim singing and dancing so joyously today had no idea that they were preparing for a wedding that was most likely not going to take place. R' Yom Tov had said explicitly that, as long as there was no solid information to remove the blot on his family name, he was not going to allow the *chuppah* to go forward. *Ribono shel Olam*, how was this all going to end?

His only source of strength and comfort during these difficult moments was the Rebbe. *"Yeshuas Hashem k'heref ayin,"* the Rebbe had repeated, and it was clear that he believed every word. Indeed, he was behaving as if he hadn't a care in the world. The Rebbe was conducting himself as if he had no doubt that the wedding would take place the next day. *How*, the *gabbai* wondered, *did a person reach such a height of emunah during such a terribly painful time?* He had thought that he knew the Rebbe. He had stood at his right hand, serving him for the past twenty-five years. But only now did he truly witness the level of pure faith that the Rebbe had attained.

R' Shammai noticed Jacob Stern, trying to catch his eye from the edge of the dais. At first, he ignored him. What did the American want? What could be so urgent in the middle of the *seudas aniyim? No doubt the wine that he and his brother had brought had become either warmer or cooler than the perfect temperature*, he thought cynically. They made far too great a fuss over that wine of theirs.

But Jacob was persistent. Clearly agitated, he signaled urgently: *Come now! It's important!*

What can I do? I can't leave, R' Shammai signaled back.

Jacob refused to accept this answer. He headed toward the stairs at the side of the dais, as though to indicate that, if R' Shammai didn't come to him, he would go to R' Shammai.

With no choice, the *gabbai* abandoned his post for a moment and walked to the edge of the dais. "What's the matter?" he asked in annoyance. But now that he was closer, he sensed that the American was in an extraordinary state of distress.

"Do you remember when I came to see the Rebbe in Tzefas a few months ago?" Jacob asked.

"Of course."

"And do you remember that I asked you to add the words, 'and protection' to my *kvittel*?"

"Certainly." Such things were not easy to forget.

Jacob lowered his voice to a fearful whisper. "He's here."

R' Shammai didn't understand. "Who's here? What are you talking about?"

"The man who was after me."

"Where was he after you?" R' Shammai was still bewildered. "And where is he now?"

"He tracked me down in my office, at work," Jacob answered tensely. "He came to my house, he threatened my children, he killed my assistant ...."

"Where? In Houston?"

"Yes, yes!"

"And where is he now?" the *gabbai* repeated.

"He's right here, sitting with the other guests. I served him the fish, and we made eye contact."

"Are you sure?"

Jacob gestured discreetly. "There — at that table. He's seventh in the row, on the right."

R' Shammai did not glance in that direction. If there was someone suspicious sitting there, it would not do to have him know they were onto him.

"Listen to me," he told Jacob, after brief thought. "There's a senior American intelligence agent here in the hall. I think you need to talk to him."

"Is he from the CIA?" Jacob asked apprehensively. "I don't know whom to trust anymore!"

"I don't think so. I think he's higher up than that."

"Okay," Jacob said. "I'll talk to him."

R' Shammai walked quickly behind the bleachers, Jacob Stern at his heels. They reached a remote corner of the hall, behind the band's raised platform.

This area was hidden from the view of the invitees at their tables. Long electric cables snaked across the floor, along with various instrument cases and covers. A staircase led to an upper level. At its foot, on a folding chair, sat a blond young man, Russian by appearance, spiffily dressed and temporarily wearing a *kippah* on his head. He sat idle, and didn't seem to be enjoying it much.

R' Shammai turned to him. "Can you get him, please?"

The young man hurried up onto the stage, to return a moment later with someone else. The newcomer was a man in his fifties with dark hair, thin and wiry. His face radiated strength and determination. He glanced from R' Shammai to Jacob Stern, questioning.

"This is Agent Scott," R' Shammai told Jacob. He turned to the American. "This is Dr. Jacob Stern, a Milinover chassid and an American citizen who works for the U.S. Department of Agriculture in Houston. He has something to report."

The idea of sitting with the band had occurred to Scott when he heard the music emanating from the hall.

"Listen," he had told Uri Arbel on his cell phone, while still sitting in his car. "I know how to play the saxophone. Go to the bandleader and tell him what's going on. Tell him that I want to take his saxophonist's place from time to time. That way, I'll be able to watch the hall without drawing attention to myself. No one will pay attention to the band members."

At first, the bandleader had strenuously objected. Boris, his regular saxophonist, was an excellent musician, and he saw no reason to replace him. He also had no idea how good the replacement would be; he could ruin their sound and negate all the time spent in rehearsal. But he quickly learned that this was not a request, but an order. The Russian-born saxophonist was no happier than he, but was not offered a choice in the matter.

One minute after Agent Scott began to play, the bandleader realized that he had gotten the best of the bargain. The replacement saxophonist was outstanding. This man knew how to play! He knew how to hold the instrument, how to produce his notes, and — most important of all — how to blend in with the other musicians in the band. The leader had never seen a musician join an existing group and, within minutes, become so much a part of it. And he had loads of experience in the music world ....

Nor did he fail to observe the fact that the saxophonist's eyes were constantly roving the hall. R' Shammai had explained that the man had not come here in a spontaneous desire to launch a new musical career. He was a senior security man who wanted to observe the hall from a convenient location.

Nevertheless, the bandleader thought, *the fellow was one of the greats.* He wondered what the man's story was. What was his name?

It was, of course, impossible for him to know that the musician's real name — the name he had been given at his *bris* in a small town in Texas — was John Lowinger.

66

R' Shammai returned to the head table, leaving the American agent and Jacob Stern behind the stage.

"What is your position at the Department of Agriculture?" Scott asked.

"I'm ... a department head," Jacob answered hesitantly.

"Which department?"

"The one in charge of supervising toxins." Jacob was uneasy. Despite R' Shammai's assurances, he was afraid to trust this government agent. Who knew if he wasn't part of the great conspiracy? Who knew if he wasn't working hand in hand with the pale-faced killer?

The agent noted Jacob's trepidation. "Let me introduce myself," he said, in an attempt to calm him. "My name is Scott. I work for the Director of National Intelligence. Our mission, in essence, is to oversee and coordinate the various intelligence agencies in the United States."

Jacob felt slightly better. If Agent Scott worked on a supervisory level above the CIA, perhaps he *was* the right person for him to talk to.

"Well," he began with a sigh, "a few months ago, I got a call from an anthropologist at the University of Mexico City. His name was Gustavo

Costa, and he was interested in a spate of deadly epidemics that had attacked and wiped out an Indian tribe near Juarez in the fifties. I didn't suspect that anything was wrong, as the information was not classified and readily available in our office's archives. I passed the file on to my assistant, Lenny Brown, who gave it to Costa.

"One afternoon, a few weeks later, Lenny came to me in a panic. He said that a stranger was waiting for him in the lobby. He was terrified, because just that morning he had learned that the Mexican anthropologist and a group of Indian-rights activists had died, under mysterious circumstances, within a period of two or three days. A Mexican police officer who had decided to investigate the strange chain of deaths was also killed. Lenny hurried out of the building, despite the fact that I, at the time, thought he was imagining things.

"A few minutes later, a stranger came into the department, looking for Lenny. He had a very pale face and hair, and light eyes. When he heard that Lenny had gone out, he left as quickly as he came. But Lenny's fears turned out to be well grounded. That night, as he walked down a street in Houston, he was hit by a speeding car. He died of his injuries two days later."

"Did you report this to anyone?" Agent Scott asked.

"To tell the truth — no," Jacob admitted. "I didn't know who was who. I had a feeling that the pale guy was a CIA agent himself."

"Why?"

"Because the United States has the strongest reason to cover up the incident at Juarez. I found out that the epidemics had not been natural disasters, but experiments in biological warfare conducted by members of a secret compound located in a small town in southwest Texas. The Indians had been deliberately infected with a virus developed by the United States Army, in order to test its effectiveness. Apparently, it was highly successful: The entire tribe was wiped out."

"And how is that connected to your section?"

"The department that I head — toxins supervision — was created at that time by the CIA, in conjunction with the Defense Department, as camouflage for the secret project. That way, the project could receive a generous budget without any oversight by Congress. Later, after the project ended, it turned into a permanent division within the Department of Agriculture. For some reason — perhaps someone was careless — the documents from that period remained in our archives, and were not even marked as classified."

Agent Scott — a.k.a. John Lowinger — listened in astonishment. Only with monumental effort was he able to hide his inner turmoil from the other man. It was simply unbelievable. The reality surpassed any flight of the imagination. Jacob Stern didn't know it, but he wasn't telling Scott anything new. He was already in full possession of the facts — not through his present career, but because he had *been* there. He had grown up in Grayston. He'd spent his entire childhood in the shadow of the secret compound that Stern was talking about.

He had never been much interested in religion, but he had the strange sensation that he was seeing the Finger of G-d. While he still had no idea what Jacob Stern had seen that had so frightened him, too many circles were closing here. Too many things were happening to be mere coincidence ....

"Of course, I was afraid for my own life," Jacob Stern continued his story — omitting an account of his panicked flight to Israel to seek the Rebbe's blessing. "The next Shabbos, my phone rang all day. Being a religious man, I didn't pick up. But the caller wouldn't give up. That night, he came to my house.

"At first, I chased him away with a gun. I was terrified that he had come to kill me. Then, on second thought, I realized that he didn't look threatening. On the contrary, he seemed pitiful. I agreed to meet him the next day, Sunday morning, right after Lenny Brown's funeral, in front of the Museum of Science and Nature.

"The man's name was Jorge Diaz. He was a municipal worker in Juarez, the only survivor of the group of Mexican activists. He told me how he, Professor Costa, and three others were invited to a hotel suite in the heart of Mexico City by a man who said he had additional details about the episode they were investigating. At the start of the meeting, their host poured a glass of tequila for them all, and offered a toast. The drink was poisoned. Within minutes, they were all sprawled on the floor — dead. Jorge Diaz was the only one who'd been suspicious of the man's intentions. He didn't drink the tequila, and lived."

"What did he want from you?" Agent Scott asked.

"He had made his way from Mexico City to Houston in order to meet Lenny Brown. When he learned that Lenny had died, he started looking for me. He wanted me to get the incriminating file from our archives, so that he could take it to the media. Of course, I didn't agree, but since he was on the run and he was in such bad shape, I wanted to at least give him a little money. Asking him to wait a few minutes, I went over to a nearby ATM. When I came back, there was an ambulance and police car in front of the museum. Someone had just shot him at close range."

"Interesting," the American agent exclaimed, shaken. *If this was the handiwork of the CIA, it was not commendable.*

"Naturally, I panicked," Jacob continued. "I drove home as fast as I could, feeling as if a noose were tightening around me. I thought I was going to be the next in line. And then, two hours later, I looked through the window of my house and saw the pale man — the one who'd been looking for Lenny in my office just hours before he was hit by a car. You can imagine how I felt: deathly afraid. I took my wife and kids — who'd just come home from school — and was about to run. At that moment, the phone rang, and a man with an authoritative voice came on the line. He said that he wanted to offer me a deal: If I'd forget everything about Juarez and never tell another soul about it, he promised not to hurt me."

"Who was he?"

"He didn't introduce himself. There was no need. It was obvious that he was a senior man in one of the intelligence services. For some reason, I believed he worked for the CIA."

"What happened after that?"

"For the next few months — nothing. I thought I'd put the whole thing behind me. But just now, as I was walking among the tables, serving the food, I suddenly saw him — the pale man. He was sitting with all the other poor people, eating, just like them. I don't think he recognized me in my suit and hat, but I have no doubt that it's him. He has eyes you can't forget."

The American agent looked at Jacob for a moment. His expression was stern. "Where is he?" he asked. "Can you show him to me?"

"Seventh in the row, last table," Jacob said. "On the right side."

"Okay. I'm going back up to play. I want to see him." Scott turned toward the stage stairs. "Wait for me here." He had a strong feeling that the uninvited guest — the one Jacob Stern had dubbed "the pale man" — was tied up in some way with the anonymous caller in Baltimore. There was an inexplicable riddle running through this whole episode, and he had to unravel it. The first step was to have a look at the mysterious pale fellow.

He climbed onstage. This time, he let the Russian saxophonist stay where he was and sat down behind him, picking up an extra saxophone and joining in the music. He did not look immediately at the place Stern had indicated. It was only twenty seconds later that his eyes reached the person seated in the seventh seat on the right side of the last table. His blood froze in his veins.

He knew this man — knew him well. He had not seen him in over five years. The light hair had grown lighter, the pale face had become paler — but it was he.

Of all the people in the world, the man sitting among the paupers was none other than his own brother — rogue CIA agent, Eddie Lowinger.

67

Even in his state of shock, John Lowinger continued playing. Seated near the rear of the stage behind Boris, he was partially hidden from the guests' eyes in general, and from his brother's in particular.

The band leader signaled for the musicians to turn to page 31 in their scores, which held the song *"Machnisei Rachamim."* John played the notes two or three times, until he knew the melody by heart, then closed his eyes and played with tremendous concentration. He didn't know the song or its lyrics, but it was a slow, haunting melody that evoked the emotions. He needed time to think, and he did his best thinking while playing.

It had been the same back in his far-off childhood in Grayston, when his father would return drunk after another day at the racetrack, when his stepmother battered him verbally and physically, when old Sam wandered around the ranch house like a ghost, when Eddie inflicted one of his wicked pranks. At times like those, John would take a horse from the stables, bind his saxophone case onto the pommel of his saddle, and go galloping off into the wilderness.

There, far from humanity, after tying his horse to a solitary tree, he would take out his instrument and play for hours. His thoughts would roam freely and touch on many important things. He had no one to ask for advice, so he would advise himself. "Your heart, Little John, is your most faithful adviser," Christopher, his blind music teacher, had told him repeatedly. "If you listen well to your heart, you'll never go wrong."

Machnisei rachamim
Hachnisu rachameinu
Lifnei Ba'al HaRachamim.

[Those who gather in mercy
Gather in our mercy
Before the Master of Mercy.]

He needed time to think. As in his younger days, he had no one to ask. He had no choice but to listen closely to the sage counsel of his own heart.

His next steps must be weighed very carefully. He was in the throes of the greatest conflict of his life — the great mission for which he had been recruited, and for which the agency he worked for had been created. And it was right here, at this critical juncture, that he found himself face-to-face with his most dangerous enemy: his own brother.

This was no longer about childish pranks or careless antics. This was not about swiping donuts from Norman Chambers' bakery or setting off the burglar alarm at the bank in town. This would be a war of Titans. A fateful and uncompromising encounter between powerful forces. A battle for life or death. Two brothers had been sent out into the battlefield — but only one of them would survive.

What had, until now, been no more than conjecture, had suddenly become a force to be reckoned with. Over the past few years, his brother Eddie had been considered one of CIA Assistant Director Walter Child's rising stars. In the intelligence world Child was a hawk, advocating a militant line against radical Islam. Child's clique — which had limitless power in both the Capitol and the Pentagon — demanded complete freedom of action in the war against terror. They claimed, in internal debates, that the imams and other extremists were trying to attain gradual dominance over America, at which point the infidels were eventually to be reduced to the status of unwanted guests.

They protested the way the leaders of the Arab community took advantage of American freedom-of-speech statues to strengthen their grasp in the country. Only a vigorous and ruthless war, they insisted, could halt this dangerous trend. The state of emergency that had been declared in the aftermath of the attack on New York's World Trade Center was not over yet.

Walter Child was once heard, in closed session, saying that the West would wise up and declare all-out war on Islam only after a second strike. Thousands of deaths at the Milinover wedding, a pile of corpses in Ganei HaSimchah, would be the final straw — the one additional incident of terror that he hoped for, to allow him to demand that the government take off its gloves and launch a war of destruction against all Muslims.

Walter Child was prepared to sacrifice thousands of lives in Israel — including those of United States citizens — in order to prove to the world how dangerous and ruthless Islam really was. He had been well aware of the attack that Bashir Abdul Aziz and Barry Majdi were plotting. But instead of using the information to stop them while there was still time, he was utilizing it to turn the American intelligence community in the right direction — and to whip up some passion in the hearts and minds of the decision-makers.

With Eddie's presence pointing an accusing finger at Walter Child, it also served to throw a spotlight on another fact that Scott had not yet viewed as significant: Child was a native of Baltimore. He knew every street and alleyway. The anonymous Baltimore caller — who had been fully aware, during his second call, that the first had stirred up a storm in all the intelligence agencies — had known exactly where to call from, both to the FBI and to Aziz, without being caught by a single security camera. That anonymous caller had, apparently, been none other than the CIA assistant director himself.

Child was anxious to turn all heads toward the Islamic threat — but not before he had warned Aziz and given him and Professor Majdi time to flee the country. He intended to use the planned mass slaughter here as a political tool with which to influence the White House. He had sent his man here, not to thwart the attack, but to make sure it took place. Eddie Lowinger was here, at the Milinover wedding, to see to it that the spark meant to ignite a Third World War between East and West, between the Islamic world and the Christian one, would duly burst into flame.

Hishtadlu v'hirbu techinah
V'hirbu techinah u'bakashah
Lifnei Melech Keil ram v'nisa
Melech Keil ram v'nisa.

[Make your efforts, and increase your supplication
Increase your supplication and pleading
Before the King, the high and exalted G-d
The King, the high and exalted G-d.]

As the band played the tune over and over, and the crowd joined in with a mighty swelling of voices, the American agent was lost in thought. *Walter Child could not have found himself a better agent than Eddie Lowinger,* he reflected. Jacob Stern's bloodcurdling descriptions fit his brother's personality like a glove. The cruelty, the pleasure of playing cat-and-mouse with helpless victims — these were traits that had been observable in Eddie when he was still a boy in Grayston and a student in Port Stockton. When their family — or what was left of it after the catastrophe — had moved to Atlanta, things had not changed for the better.

Both boys had attended the same high school and graduated with equally good grades. The major difference between them had always been in their behavior. Eddie had not let slip an opportunity to get in trouble. He would participate in street-gang fights and had been arrested on more than one occasion. His rescuer had always been their patron and benefactor, Dr. Patrick Braithwaite, director of the CDC in Atlanta. In fact, John thought now, the person responsible for their both taking up a career in the military, and then in the field of intelligence, had, beyond doubt, been Dr. Braithwaite himself.

Any beginner in psychology could explain that, after the dismal role model their biological father, Ben Lowinger, had provided, both boys had been eager to find a substitute in Dr. Braithwaite. Essentially, they went on to embrace his path in life.

The move from tiny Grayston to the bustling metropolis that was Atlanta had been a significant change in their lives. Dr. Braithwaite had enrolled them in the same upscale boarding school that his own sons attended, hosted them frequently at his home, and sometimes even included them in his vacations. He saw to it that their medical needs were provided for, in the wake of the accident that had exposed them to the

THE MEXICO FILE / 571

toxic virus. John had been a source of nothing but pride to the scientist. Eddie had been the exact opposite.

Time after time, Dr. Braithwaite was summoned to the principal's office, to submit to a blistering scolding about his ward's conduct. "Why can't he be like his brother John?" The question was asked over and over again in a thousand different variations. "How can two brothers be so different?"

So what was he to do now? Arrest his brother? Call someone for advice? Wait for Ted Cone to report new developments? How would Eddie react to the sight of him, and to the fact that they would be pitted against each other? They had not maintained much contact in recent years. In the army, which they had joined almost as a matter of course after completing their education, each had chosen a different direction.

Eddie had joined an antitank regiment, gone on to take an officers' course, and quickly been recruited by the CIA. He, John, had started out in an elite commando unit that generally operated behind enemy lines. Later, he became a senior analyst in the DOD's intelligence arm, and spent twenty years in the corridors of the Pentagon. Just a few years ago, he had been activated to restore the crumbling Los Angeles counterterrorism unit, which was suffering from an acute leadership crisis. After handing the unit, now back on a solid footing, to his second in command, Ted Cone, he had been assigned his current mission.

The brothers did not meet often in their personal lives, either. At first, they would get together once a year at Barbara's grave. Eddie's mother and John's stepmother had died of cancer a decade after the move to Atlanta. It wasn't long, however, before John stopped coming. During her illness, he had cared for Barbara devotedly — certainly more so than Eddie, who had a tendency to disappear for prolonged intervals. But he never forgot that the woman had no familial ties to him. His real mother, spurned and rejected, lay buried in Grayston, beneath a simple concrete tombstone on which were etched only her name, the years of her birth and death, and a Jewish symbol: the six-sided star made of two inverse triangles that someone had once told him was called a *Magen David*.

So what was he to do with his brother now? The list of his crimes, according to Jacob Stern, was long and varied. He had begun by taking the lives of a series of Mexicans, most of them in Mexico City and one in the heart of Houston, and ended by killing Lenny Brown, an American citizen and government employee, in cold blood.

John wondered why Eddie and the man who had sent him to do his dirty work had decided not to kill Jacob Stern. Stern's removal from the scene would certainly have been desirable: Jacob was the last keeper of the secret who was still alive. Apparently, Walter Child had realized that there was a limit. Impossible to murder — within a single week — both the head of a government department and his immediate subordinate. Who, more than Child, would know that the coincidence of these two deaths would bring them to the instant attention of the FBI for exhaustive investigation?

What to do about Eddie? His brother had no sentimental feelings toward him. He would wipe John out without blinking an eye, if those were his orders. Eddie was here at the behest of people who were prepared to close their eyes to the deaths of thousands of innocent people, as long as those deaths advanced their agenda. One victim more or less would not alter the balance at all.

Suddenly, the phone vibrated at his belt. Taking advantage of a brief lull in the music, John Lowinger glanced at the caller screen. It was Ted Cone, from L.A. Perhaps he had finally succeeded in getting something out of the professor's research assistant.

He was right. Yousuf Nadir had begun to talk. He had been removed from Professor Majdi's office and taken to counterterrorism headquarters in the center of town. Interrogation can be noisy work, and messy, too — quite unsuited to the elegant corridors of academia.

The young Muslim was a tough nut to crack. Even the most rigorous questioning failed to elicit from him a confession of his participation in either planning or executing a terror attack. The imam had inculcated in him a fierce belief in the supremacy of the Islamic nation, along with a burning hatred of America and its infidels. It was clear to Ted Cone and his crew of interrogators that Yousuf knew something, but he refused to open his mouth.

"I don't like using torture," Cone told him. "But you're leaving me no choice." If, as suspected, the young man had information that could save the lives of thousands of innocent souls, any means of getting him to sing were kosher. He gestured meaningfully at a table covered in sharp, gleaming implements that he had no intention of actually using.

Yousuf wept in despair and suddenly blurted, "Air-conditioning."

"What's in the air-conditioning?" Ted Cone demanded.

Yousuf clenched his teeth together and didn't answer.

"Come on, you know you want to tell me before …," Cone trailed off, knowing that the fear of torture was often enough.

"He's fainted," said the doctor who was standing by for this phase of the interrogation.

Cone stood. "Call me when he regains consciousness," he said. "I'm going out to make a phone call."

Majdi's secretary was still in her office at the university, stunned and tearful. She was having a hard time digesting the sudden change in her perception of the professor. Barry Majdi — an Islamic terrorist? If that was true, then she could trust no one. As a good American, she did her best to help by answering all the questions put to her, but in her heart of hearts she still hoped that the whole thing would turn out to be a huge mistake.

A cell phone rang. The counterterrorist operative assigned to guard the secretary listened for a moment, and then handed her the phone. On the line was Ted Cone, calling from headquarters.

"What does the term 'air-conditioning' mean to you?"

"Air-conditioning?" The secretary's eyes lit up as a light flashed on in her brain. "One day, the professor said he was bringing an air-conditioning expert into the office. I told him that if there was a problem with the air-conditioning, we could call the university maintenance department. But he said there was no problem — he was just consulting someone with regard to a new innovation of his. So a technician came … as I recall, he was a Muslim. Yousuf knew him. They kidded around and laughed together. The air-conditioning technician checked our system, and the professor talked to him about his invention."

"What was it?"

"A way to disperse fragrances in stores using the air-conditioning system, or something like that."

Ted Cone slammed the phone shut without even saying "thank you." He dialed Israel with frantic speed, trying to reach the person he was not permitted to call "John Lowinger" but whom he would never call "Agent Scott" or any of his other temporary names. "Sir," Ted said urgently, "apparently, it's the air-conditioning. Check for dissemination through the air-conditioning system."

Within two seconds, the message had been transmitted from the American agent to Uri Arbel, standing near the kitchen. He contacted the team waiting outside the hall, and raced over to Motke, the work manager. "Turn off the air conditioners!" he shouted.

"Are you crazy? Why?"

"No questions. Do it!"

The air-conditioning control box was affixed to a wall in the office. Motke and Uri Arbel hurried there.

"You know something?" Motke suddenly remembered. "Turk Majdi, the guy the police were looking for earlier, took care of the air-conditioning here. He was an a/c technician before he started working for me."

"Why didn't you tell us that before?" Arbel asked furiously.

"I still don't know why you're looking for him," Motke reminded him. "You people just walked in and took over the hall. If R' Shammai hadn't told me to give you any help I can, I would have thrown all of you out a long time ago."

The special military engineering team had already climbed up to the building's roof from the rear. The air-conditioning system was located in a small room on the roof. Finding the door open, they stepped inside. At that precise moment, Motke lowered a lever in his office, and the compressor fell silent.

The officer in charge of the team knew how the system was put together. He was interested in neither the compressor nor the condenser. If there were to be a dispersal of biological material through the air-conditioning system, it would take place from the fan and outward. Three large, rectangular metal tubes led down into an opening in the catering hall's roof. There, between the concrete ceiling and the decorative one, they expanded into a plethora of thinner tubes that carried the chilled air to vents throughout the hall.

Abandoning Motke in his office, Uri Arbel raced to the rear of the hall. He waited at the foot of the ladder, chewing his lower lip in suspense. Three minutes later, he heard a muffled shout from the roof: "We found it!"

The officer, in full protective garb, hurried back down the ladder. He hurried over to the mobile lab equipped to identify toxic substances, still parked near the hall, and motioned for Arbel to join him. Something in his body language announced that all was not well. His gas mask had a large, glass viewplate, and the face peering out through that plate was twisted with anxiety and fear. In one hand he held a plastic bag with something metallic inside.

"What happened?" Uri called as he ran.

The officer didn't stop. Opening the rear door of the GMC, he rushed inside and placed the bag on the technician's table. Uri Arbel entered behind him. When he saw what was on the table, he gasped. His eyes passed from the officer to each of the two technicians manning the van. Nobody spoke. They all saw what he had seen.

Inside the plastic bag on the table lay a device used to disseminate the weapons of biological and chemical warfare. It was shaped like a long, metal flashlight. The pointed side was meant to be inserted into a hole drilled in the wall of the air-conditioning tube. At the other end was a space for attaching a glass vial. A small electronic gizmo in the center was designed to break open the vial at a prearranged time, allowing its contents to flow into the a/c channel.

But that time was already past. The vial was broken, its interior empty. The red digital readout showed -07:54, and continued advancing with breathtaking speed:

-07:55

-07:56

-07:57

And then, three seconds later: -08:00.

The clock was moving backward. Zero hour had already come and gone. The virus had been set loose in the hall eight full minutes earlier, while the air-conditioning was still working at full strength.

There could only be one, horrifying conclusion: The biological material had already been disseminated in the hall and drawn into the lungs of all those who were inside.

Uri Arbel picked up his phone and rapidly punched in a number. It was a number known to only a select few: the prime minister's red telephone.

Without anyone in the hall being aware of it, a radius of several hundred meters around the Ganei HaSimchah wedding hall was cordoned off from the outside world. No one would be permitted to enter or leave.

The decision was made by the prime minister himself, and within seconds was passed along to the combined security and emergency forces that had been established on the western side of Abba Hillel Street, not far from the hall. The rescue teams, waiting in the Ramat Gan stadium and the eastern side of Gan HaYarkon, came to life. Scores of military jeeps and police vehicles began moving as one. Hundreds of soldiers and police officers began fanning out to take up the positions they had been assigned in advance, creating a human ring — still sparse at this stage — around the perimeter, always at a distance to remain beyond the hall's line of sight.

Each security employee was provided with protective gear, including a thick plastic suit impermeable to liquids, an evaporation suit over the plastic, to cool the body underneath, rubber boots, two pairs of gloves, and, of course, a gas mask. At this stage, they were not asked to wear the gear; only when they received the signal would each team member open the sealed package and put it on.

Traffic was halted on streets adjoining the hall, the drivers redirected to alternate routes. All roads leading to the area were set off limits with red-and-white tape stretched across the width of the street. Policemen on foot and horseback kept pedestrians at bay with the well-known drill used for a suspicious object. Other teams prepared to clear the routes to the nearest hospitals, which were being readied for the first victims.

For the moment, the extensive mobilization was in a state of limbo. No step had yet been taken in the open. The heads of the various security factions waited tensely for the results from the mobile lab parked near the hall. A trace of residue had been found in the broken glass vial, and this was now undergoing a rigorous check. The moment they knew what sort of germ, virus, or poison had been spread throughout the hall — along with the degree of danger involved, and any neutralization options — a decision about the next steps would be taken.

The easiest and least critical part was preventing additional people from entering the "hot zone" — the area containing a hazardous concentration of toxic material. The greatest risk was that one of those exposed to the toxin would decide to return to Bnei Brak, spreading the epidemic through ever-widening and impossible-to-supervise circles of the population. Orders were issued to security forces inside the perimeter: Stop anyone who tried to leave the circle, and bring him to a special area to undergo medical testing to gauge his condition.

Until now, to everyone's relief, no one had tried to leave the hall. The Milinover *seudas aniyim* did not attract many people outside chassidic circles, and anyone who had come was prepared to remain until the end of the meal — until the climactic moment when they sang "*Niggun HaParnassah*" ("The Livelihood Song"), composed by R' Tuvia, the present Rebbe's great-grandfather. This song was sung by Milinover chassidim on one occasion only: just before *bentching* at the *seudas aniyim* held on the eve of the marriage of a scion of the chassidic dynasty. Afterward, all the guests would pass before the Rebbe and the *mechutanim*, offering their good wishes and receiving a generous donation. Then the rest of the chassidim would pass down the line, receiving wine from the Rebbe's "glass of blessings" — a *segulah* for prosperity.

"What's happening?" Uri Arbel asked the technician in the mobile lab.

"I'm still checking."

"How long will it take?" The hardest part still lay ahead of Arbel. The moment the substance was identified and its properties known, he would have to enter the hall, climb onstage, stop the music, and take the microphone. He would introduce himself as a representative of Israel's security service, and inform those present that an unidentified substance had been disseminated in the hall. The substance, he would say, was not dangerous; nevertheless, cautious steps had been decided upon. In a few minutes, army medical personnel would be entering to examine the guests, after which they would allowed to return to their homes.

All of this, of course, would be a blatant untruth. No one would be leaving the hall for the next 48 hours — except in a body bag.

Then the panic would ensue. He knew the scenario. Soothing words and reassurances would be useless. People would attempt to at least send their children outside. They would be unable to phone their relatives, because the area would be sealed to cell communication. This would only fuel the general air of alarm. Many people would start feeling ill, despite the fact that, from a physical standpoint, the virus would not begin to affect them for several hours yet. And, as always, there would be a few who would rush to the doors in a panic and try to escape. There would be no choice: His men would be compelled to use force or even to shoot. That was the only way to control an increasingly agitated crowd trapped in a sealed environment.

"Let me know the second you know something. I'm going back inside," Uri Arbel said. He had to update Agent Scott on the situation.

"Are you crazy? You're not protected," the other man said.

Uri shrugged. He had been inside the hall when the material was released. Whatever it turned out to be — he had already been exposed.

He went from the parking lot into the hall, walked to the rear of the stage, and climbed the stairs to reach the band. The American was playing the saxophone with his back to the Israeli. Arbel called his name quietly.

The special agent looked stricken — as though he had been kicked in the stomach. He had not yet recovered from the revelation that his brother Eddie was in the hall.

"Are you all right?" Arbel asked anxiously.

"I'm fine." The American pulled himself together. "What's new?"

"Bad news," Arbel sighed. He reported to his colleague that the information blurted by Yousuf Nadir had been accurate. The material had been disseminated through the hall's air-conditioning system. Unfortunately, they had discovered it too late. By the time they came upon the vial, it was already empty.

The American received the news that he had been exposed with a calmness that surprised even Arbel.

"What was it? What was disseminated?" he asked.

"We don't know yet. They're working on it."

"It's taking a long time, isn't it?"

Arbel shrugged. He was going back out, to the mobile lab. He very much hoped they had made some progress.

"Keep me posted on new developments," the special agent said, ending the conversation — partly because he saw Jacob Stern standing at the foot of the stairs, waiting for him.

"Did you see him?" Jacob asked.

"I did," John Lowinger replied. "I'm checking out the situation. It's a good thing you came to me."

John did not believe there was a link between a Department of Agriculture employee and this terrorist attack. Nevertheless, for safety's sake, he wanted to eliminate several possibilities.

"Tell me, does the name 'Barry Majdi' mean anything to you?" he asked.

Jacob wrinkled his brow, and then shook his head. He had never heard of the man.

"What about 'Bashir Abdul Aziz'?"

"No. Who are they?"

"The first is a biology lecturer at UCLA and owns a medical-development company. The second is an imam who heads a large mosque in Los Angeles."

Jacob shrugged. He had no idea who they were.

"Okay," the special agent concluded. "In the meantime, keep your distance from the 'pale guy,' as you call him. And stay in contact with me."

Bits and pieces of information assembled themselves in John's mind, forming one big puzzle. While many of the pieces joined together seamlessly, the picture was not yet complete. There were details missing. He must learn more about the man called Barry Majdi.

From a quiet corner, he called Ted Cone and asked him to pass on, immediately, everything he had on the professor.

The contents of the dense file, transmitted to his mobile device within minutes, was fascinating. Majdi appeared to be a solid American in every way. There was nothing at all in his background to indicate that he would involve himself in the kind of evil plan he had concocted. He was a popular lecturer at the university, had often appeared in the media, and had held several minor public roles as well. Barry Majdi was actively involved with several research teams developing drugs for pharmaceutical firms. And then there was his own company, Biologic Systems, which had come up with some developments beneficial both to mankind and Majdi's bank account. On and on ... more details, more information. Professor Barry Majdi, astonishingly, had actually represented the United States government as a member of a scientific delegation sent to Russia after the dissolution of the USSR, to assist in the organization and transfer of its viral laboratories. He had earned lavish praise for his devoted work in Bacteria Institute #16, in Riga.

On and on .... The file was comprised of hundreds of pages, with links to other sources. The American agent sat on the stage steps, scanning it with his eyes and lingering over details that seemed important, though he would have needed hours to carefully go through it all. One of the links took him to a media interview that Barry Majdi had done with a major U.S. network, to launch his wonder drug, Klistemprol. The new drug made use of a biological mechanism that he had studied for many long years, he told the enthralled talk-show host. He called the mechanism, "weaken and destroy."

The idea, Majdi had explained, was based on the fact that the immune system sometimes makes use of a dual strategy in order to fight off attackers: killing infected cells via lethal proteins, and, at the same time, activating a self-destruct mechanism in the cells themselves.

The "weaken and destroy" strategy, the professor said, causes the body to hurl attackers at the deadly cells, causing those cells to waste their energy trying to fight off the attackers and survive. This weakens the cells.

And then, along come the truly lethal weapons, to subdue and destroy the already enfeebled cells.

"It's an interesting philosophical approach," Majdi had said in the interview. "This dual strategy may be used in struggles between nations and faiths as well. If you direct a decoy weapon at the enemy, so that it fights back, sapping all its strength — you can then, when he is at his weakest, come back and conquer him with a single sweep of your sword."

With a sigh, John Lowinger returned to the original file. Reading on, he came to the section of the file that contained documents from Majdi's early years at the university. Until the year 1992, he had not resided in Los Angeles. He had lived in … *What*? John sat up. Barry Majdi had lived in Atlanta, and worked for — the CDC! He had been employed at the national center for the study and prevention of disease. How had this small fact managed to elude them all? This was the missing piece of the puzzle.

The picture was clear now. It was complete.

He called Uri Arbel immediately in the mobile lab. As he had expected, the Israeli experts were having a hard time identifying the virus.

"Listen closely," John said. "What was disseminated here is a rare virus by the name of 'Mexico A' — and don't ask how I know. It won't turn up on the standard spectrum of tests, which may be why your people aren't having any luck identifying it. It's something that exists only in the CDC laboratories in Atlanta, Georgia. Contact them at once and ask for help."

The picture was complete, and it was clear. If Walter Child was so anxious to keep the Juarez episode a secret — to the point that he had systematically executed everyone who wished to publicize it in detail — and if the same agent-killer who had disposed of the Mexicans had been sent to a site designated for a terror attack, that meant they were dealing today with the very virus that had affected Juarez: the Mexican virus developed at the secret compound in Grayston, and used experimentally on that Indian tribe.

The only place Mexico A existed was in the CDC labs in Atlanta, where it had been transferred, along with everything else in the Grayston compound, after the tragic accident in the fifties. There had been a suspicion, at the time, that a sample of the virus had been stolen from the labs. Anyone familiar with the subject knew that in 1992, an exhaustive investigation was conducted at the CDC after signs of a break-in were found in the refrigeration unit that held samples of the virus. No proof was ever found.

The circle had closed. Barry Majdi was the one who had stolen the sample, when he had been employed at the institute. He had held onto it all these years — until he deemed the time ripe for the great *jihad*.

"What do you know about the properties of the virus?" Arbel asked.

"They're not particularly encouraging. The virus is transmitted by air, is capable of retaining its lethal properties for a relatively long time, and reaches a 100 percent death rate. The first symptoms of the outbreak appear an hour or two after contagion."

"How do you know all this? And what else can you tell me?"

"Nothing. But trust me — we're dealing with Mexico A."

While John Lowinger was speaking to Uri Arbel, a "call waiting" signal flashed onto his phone screen. He read the caller's name — and his heart skipped a beat.

He did not return the call. Of course not.

Ten seconds later, the phone rang again. John stared at the number with clenched teeth. He would not take the call. It could still be nothing but a bizarre coincidence.

When the third call came, he still did not pick up. He knew what would happen next: The persistent caller would send him a text message.

And that was precisely what happened. No more than fifteen seconds later, his phone emitted a shrill sound, signaling that a new message had come in.

The special agent held the phone and read, *"Hey, John. As always, you play great music. But why don't you come over and say hi to your little brother?"*

John gazed at his phone with rising bitterness. His glorious career, it seemed, was about to end in resounding failure. Not only had he failed to prevent the dissemination of the virus by a few critical minutes, but his cover had just been ripped away. Eddie knew he was here. He had scored a knockout blow in the first round.

How had he known?

Had he noticed John by accident — or was there a mole busily reporting to Walter Child from what was purportedly the most close-lipped agency in the intelligence community?

It didn't really matter, John thought, turning his focus back on the reason he was here. He still had an incredibly important mission to carry out. And if he had indeed been placed at risk due to the virus, he did not have much time. He must expose the assistant director of the CIA and obtain proof of his crimes.

It was time for a few critical decisions. Should he report the latest developments to Washington? No. He would not inform them that another agent, of doubtful loyalty, was in the theater of operations — and certainly not that it was his half-brother. He would also not report that the virus had already been set loose.

And what about Eddie? Acknowledge his message, or ignore it?

Not only would he acknowledge it, he decided; he would go over and talk to him. A face-to-face encounter with Eddie was liable to be the most productive step he could take at this juncture.

He texted a brief reply: *"I must talk to you."*

Eddie's answer arrived within seconds: *"The lobby. Five minutes."*

Special Agent John Lowinger set his saxophone in its stand and began descending from the stage. His expression was troubled and stern, his forehead creased in thought. What was his brother plotting? Why had Eddie contacted him? It had to be more than mere mischief. There was some purpose behind it.

Maybe Eddie simply wanted to neutralize him in some dark corner. He was certainly capable of shooting his brother in cold blood. Eddie was devoid of human emotions — or, if he did possess them, they were twisted and evil. Well, there was one thing that he, John, could be confident about, he thought as he checked the gun in his belt and his two additional concealed weapons. No one could beat him in a gunfight. When he had headed the counterterrorism unit in L.A., he had been the fastest draw and the most unerring shot.

New updates from the investigation kept streaming into his mobile device. Yousuf Nadir, Professor Majdi's research assistant, had regained consciousness and begun to spill what he knew. He described the after-hours meeting between Majdi and Aziz at the university, in which he first learned of the powerful bond between the two men and their dream of executing a huge act of terror. He repeated what he had learned, at the professor's request, about chassidic weddings in general and the Milinover dynasty in particular. He also told of the air-conditioning repairman's visit to Majdi's office, and his own flight to Israel, when he brought the lethal vial inside an innocent-looking can of deodorant.

Meanwhile, Turk Majdi was captured by the G.S.S. as he tried to enter Um-el-Facham. He broke after just a few minutes of interrogation, and began to sing. According to his story, he had drilled a hole in the side of the air-conditioning tubing the day before and had inserted the device.

That same morning, he rented a car in Yaffo and then, at noon, after putting the glass vial in its place and setting the timer for one hour, slipped out of the hall and traveled toward his mother's house, where he planned to stock up on provisions and continue north. He never stopped cursing the professor, who had promised to provide him with a safe house where he could hide for a few days. But the minute he had let his uncle know that he had inserted the vial, Majdi had broken the connection, ignoring all of Turk's pleas for directions to the promised refuge.

The information supplied by Yousuf and Turk, the first in Los Angeles and the second in Tel Aviv, jibed perfectly and completed the picture. *A fine interrogation*, John Lowinger thought bitterly. If only it had taken place half an hour earlier ....

He looked at his watch. Five minutes had passed. Leaving his place of concealment behind the stage, he started for the lobby, scanning the crowd as he went. For now, all was fine. No one had collapsed, lost consciousness, or begun suffering from shortness of breath. The band continued playing, and the singing grew louder. The poor, who had finished their salads and first course, were waiting impatiently for the main course to appear.

John moved closer to the door that connected the hall with the lobby. To his surprise, he realized that his heart was beating rapidly. Was he afraid? Was he worried about what was going to happen? Strange — that had never happened to him before. He had carried out missions no less dangerous in the past, and always maintained total composure. Even at times when he had been cornered and at life-threatening risk, he had known how to hold onto his professional cool. Death didn't frighten him. It was not fear that was making his knees weak. Could these be the disease's first symptoms? Or maybe ... maybe a confrontation with his brother Eddie scared him more than he was prepared to admit, even to himself ....

The lobby was not empty. Three men stood near the door, chattering animatedly. John was not conversant in Hebrew, but he saw from the men's body language and gestures that they were worried about someone who had left the hall and had not been heard from. The son of one of the men had left to return to his yeshivah. When the father tried to phone him to make sure he had caught his bus, his call had not gone through.

Neither did a call from his friend's phone, which used a different cellular service.

When the father went out to the lobby, he had noticed the flashing lights of a distant patrol car, and panicked. Was his boy all right? Had something happened to him, Heaven forbid? Something about the way the street looked set off alarm bells in his mind. After a moment, he realized why: The street was completely deserted. There was not a single pedestrian or vehicle to be seen. It was a frightening and apocalyptic scene.

The distraught father and one of his friends hurried out to the parking lot, and continued on to the street. John Lowinger watched them go with compassion. He knew what would happen next. The minute they were out of visual range of the hall, they would be stopped and taken away to be placed in isolation in one of the hospitals — probably not far from the worried father's son, who would not be returning to yeshivah any time soon.

The third man went back inside the hall. The lobby was now empty. John stood in the small entrance foyer, waiting for his brother. Or for a bullet?

"Hey, John." He heard a familiar voice.

His brother stepped out from behind a folding screen. Eddie had put on weight and grown paler since John had last seen him, five years earlier. And there was another strange thing about him: His clothes were not in the pristine condition he usually affected. He obviously had intended to be accepted as one of the poor guests.

A wide, mocking smile curved Eddie's lips. He approached his brother, arms outstretched to embrace him. "How are you, my dear brother?" he asked cynically.

John did not return the hug, nor did he evince any particular sign of friendliness. He stood woodenly, waiting for his brother to release him. "What are you doing here?" he asked.

"Me?" Eddie smiled cheerfully. "I was in the area and they said there'd be free food, so I dropped in."

John responded with a scornful look.

"What about you? What are *you* doing here?" Eddie asked, an edge in his voice.

"If you came to eat — I came to play the saxophone."

Eddie burst into raucous laughter, as if he had heard a great joke.

"So how are you, John?" he said, thumping his shoulder. "Haven't seen you in a while."

John's eyes narrowed as he studied his brother. "Tell me something. Do you think I'm an idiot? Do you think I don't know what you're looking for in this place?"

Eddie assumed an innocent expression. "What do you mean? Is it against the law to eat?"

"Eddie. I know about the series of killings in Mexico. I know about Lenny Brown's 'traffic accident' in Houston, and I know about the threats to Jacob Stern. I know all about Walter Child's plan."

"I have no idea what you're talking about."

John snorted. Suddenly, he had an idea. There was one thing that his brother might not know. Something that Walter Child had apparently not seen fit to share with him. Eddie did not know that Child, who'd been glad to make use of his murderous talents, planned for him to die together with all the Milinover chassidim, and thus bury the last witness to his crimes.

"So you have no idea that the Mexico A virus has been set loose in this hall?" he asked.

Eddie laughed dismissively.

"Eddie," John said, "I don't know what story your boss has sold you, but the virus has already been disseminated through the air-conditioning system. Everyone in the hall is going to die within 48 hours — including you and me."

An odd look crossed Eddie's face. For a brief moment he gazed at John in shock, but quickly recovered. With a genial smile, he said, "John, you really ought to see a doctor. You're imagining things. How in the world did you come up with such a story?"

"You know," John remarked, "I have a powerful urge to punch you in the face."

"Look, I'm sorry," Eddie spread his hands apologetically, "but I think they're serving the main course. I'm going back to my seat. You can return to your saxophone. I've been enjoying every minute. It takes me right back to the good old days in Grayston."

Still laughing, Eddie turned away and walked into the dining hall.

John stayed where he was, wondering. What did Eddie really want from him? What was the meaning of their strange encounter just now? It had been a mistake on his part. He should not have responded to Eddie's text message. He had not profited from the meeting in any way ... while Eddie was doubtless on the phone right now, reporting to Walter Child that his brother, John Lowinger of National Intelligence, suspected that he was involved.

Jacob Stern sat in a corner of the hall, terrified and helpless. He could not take this pressure any longer. He felt as if he was losing his mind.

R' Shammai had sent him to talk to one of the musicians in the band, saying that he was a senior American agent who could be trusted. So he had spoken to the fellow, laying all his cards out on the table — including his suspicion of the pale man.

Now, just seconds ago, as he had wandered restlessly near the lobby, what had he seen with his own eyes? The trusted agent, talking to — and even embracing — none other than the pale-faced killer!

It was a lucky thing he had seen him. And lucky, too, that Jacob had managed to slip back into the dining room without being spotted. It was obvious that the two agents knew each other well. They were on the same side. The American agent and the man who had been hounding and threatening his life were good friends.

Enough. He could not take any more. He had no one to depend on, no one he could trust. He had hoped that salvation would come through R' Shammai — but the *gabbai* had sent him straight into the lion's den.

70

When John rejoined the band onstage, he looked out at the hall to gauge the crowd's mood. The outbreak had not yet begun. Everyone was still hale and healthy. How long had it been since the vial was broken? He calculated rapidly: just over half an hour. How long before the first chassid started feeling ill? If his estimation was correct, within thirty minutes the first symptoms would begin to make themselves felt. After that, the picture would change completely.

Uri Arbel had reported over the phone that a complete description of the virus's properties had come in from the CDC in Atlanta. The file had gone directly to the mobile lab parked outside the hall, where technicians were testing the residue in the vial at that very moment. They would have the answer within minutes, after which all emergency and rescue teams would converge on the hall.

He had to think. He had to focus. The fate of the guests in the hall was already sealed. He could not help them. He was neither a doctor nor a rescue worker. His sole mission was to find proof of Walter Child's criminal involvement in all of this. The Assistant Director must pay the price for not stepping in to prevent this attack. Such a ruthless and un-principled man could not be permitted to remain at his post.

It might be useful to play the saxophone. He would return to the bandstand and make some music. Maybe an idea would occur to him.

John went back to his place at the edge of the stage, behind the other musicians. He grabbed the waiting saxophone and thumbed through the score to the page the others were on: Page 103. He would let all the facts sort themselves out in his mind. There must be something he had failed to notice.

> *V'hayah k'eitz shasul al palgei mayim*
> *Al palgei mayim*
> *Asher piryo yitein b'ito*
> *V'aleilu lo yibol.*

> [He shall be like a tree replanted by streams of water
> By streams of water
> That yields its fruit in due season
> And whose leaf never withers.]

The band played on. John played along with them, but he found his mind wandering in other directions. Bashir Abdul Aziz had succeeded in portraying himself as an enlightened and moderate man of faith, while beneath the surface he had been a not-inconsiderable ideologue and fanatic. In this way, he had managed to survive for years without bringing himself to the attention of the authorities. Turk Majdi and Yousuf Nadir were probably puppets on a string, manipulated by men far more clever and sophisticated than they.

Professor Majdi: Here was the true enigma. If he had, indeed, stolen the virus sample during his stint at the CDC at the beginning of the nineties, that meant he had been planning this *jihad* for nearly fifteen years. All that time, he had kept his image squeaky clean, in spite of the evil plot he was secretly brewing.

Aziz and Majdi had grown up together in Egypt and had maintained their friendship, while making sure not to leave behind a scrap of evidence that they were so much as acquainted. In fact, the CIA had been unable to find any evidence of a connection between the two despite all their digging. The two men had never called each other on their phones or met in public — until that night at UCLA, when they'd met in the presence of Yousuf Nadir, the professor's research assistant.

"'*V'chol asher, asher ya'aseh yatzliach … asher ya'aseh yatzliach … asher ya'aseh yatzliach,*'" John Lowinger played along with the band. *What had been the real purpose of that meeting?* he wondered. Why had they drawn another person into their big secret? For fifteen years they had maintained absolute secrecy — and suddenly, one night, they decide to meet in the presence of a third party?

There had to be some purpose to the meeting, John thought. Then, in quick succession, other questions rose up in his mind.

Why had the professor invited the air-conditioning repairman into his office at the university — also in Yousuf's presence?

Why had he made sure that his longtime secretary was also present when the repairman — a Muslim — came to the office?

Why had he abandoned his nephew, Turk, cutting off all contact and failing to provide the safe house he had promised?

The professor was too calculating. He did not make these types of mistakes. He had invested too much time in planning this escapade; it wasn't like him to leave loose ends dangling. Had … had he done it all on purpose?

Had he had some ulterior motive in all of these things? It seemed as if he had left a clear trail of footprints behind, leading directly back to him. Why?

> *V'hayah k'eitz shasul al palgei mayim*
> *Al palgei mayim*
> *Asher piryo yitein b'ito*
> *V'aleilu lo yibol.*

Something sparked suddenly in John's brain. The faintest whisper of an idea skittered past the edges of his mind, refusing to be caught. It was connected to something he had read in the professor's file. Something he ought to remember about him …. But what?

> *V'chol asher, asher ya'aseh*
> *Asher ya'aseh yatzliach, asher ya'aseh yatzliach*
> *V'chol asher, asher ya'aseh*
> *Asher ya'aseh yatzliach, asher ya'aseh yatzliach.*

[Everything that he will do will be successful]

As John was pulled along by the melody, he heard someone calling him from behind: "Scott! Agent Scott!"

He stopped playing and turned around. It was Uri Arbel, wearing a look of vast relief.

"We've stepped down from our state of red alert," the Israeli told his American colleague. "There was nothing in the vial."

"*What?*"

"There was no biological material in the vial — unless you count water mixed with a bit of food coloring."

"I don't understand!" John set the saxophone down on its stand and shot to his feet.

"Come see for yourself. It's just colored water. There was no toxic substance there at all."

"So they tricked us?"

"Apparently."

John Lowinger made a skeptical face. "Do you think Barak Majdi sent Yousuf to Israel with a bottle of plain water? Do you think this whole mess was for nothing?"

"I don't know, Scott. But the only thing dispersed here today was water."

"How can you explain that?"

"The only explanation is that someone got cold feet and switched the vial. All the tests that were run on people who left the hall were negative. All of them are healthy. There was no toxic matter in their bloodstream."

John looked at Arbel in utter incomprehension. The inchoate idea that had sprouted in his brain a few minutes earlier began to take shape and form.

"We've opened all the roadblocks," Uri Arbel continued. "There's no point keeping the hall isolated any longer."

The American glanced out at the crowd. A few men who had apparently been held up in the surrounding streets were now entering through the front door.

Suddenly, he knew exactly what was happening.

"Don't step down from anything," he said urgently. "The vial was only a decoy."

Arbel stared at him. "What do you mean?"

"Majdi wanted to pull the wool over our eyes," John said. "That vial was meant to be a distraction, nothing more. The material will be dispersed by different means."

"Forgive me, but what are you talking about?" Arbel simply couldn't believe it. Professor Majdi had constructed a carefully laid plan for getting the vial to Israel. He had rented an apartment in Yaffo for Turk, bought him a brand new refrigerator, put Yousuf on a plane to Israel, and had his company manufacture a special deodorant can for Yousuf to take along. Under separate cover, he had sent a package to Israel, with a device and precise directions to Turk describing how and when to insert the vial into it. Had all this been a smokescreen? All of it meant to distract them ... from what?

"Do you know what 'weaken and destroy' is?" John asked Uri. "It's what Majdi is doing to us. Weaken ... and destroy."

"What on earth ...?"

"Majdi is a bit more clever than you think," John said. "He's referencing a sly 'weaken and destroy' biological mechanism that he's been studying for years. Apparently, he has also found it a useful philosophy for life. He's caused the entire security network to focus entirely on chasing down and analyzing that vial — while the real attack is going to take place another way. He left clear footprints, through Yousuf, Turk, his secretary, and that Islamic air-conditioning technician. He cut off contact with his nephew because he wanted Turk to be arrested and to spill the beans, under interrogation, about the vial in the a/c system. But it's all been one big smoke screen. The real attack is going to be carried out in a completely different way."

"How?" Uri Arbel asked, in open skepticism.

"That's what we need to find out."

"Forgive me, Agent Scott. It seems to me that you've gone completely mad."

Jacob Stern felt a friendly hand on his shoulder. Lifting his head, he saw his younger brother.

"What's the matter?" David Stern asked. "Don't you feel well?"

Someone had apparently noticed Jacob, shaken and fearful, at the precise moment that he had witnessed the encounter between the federal agent and the murderer. His face was pale and he was slumped in a chair at the side of the hall, trembling. The observer had gone over to David, who had been standing near the head table, enjoying every minute. "Your brother isn't well," he had said. David had immediately raced over to Jacob.

His brother did look ill. He sat hunched in his corner, gray faced and woebegone.

"Should I call an ambulance?" David asked anxiously.

Jacob stood up and tried to pull himself together. "Never mind, it's nothing," he said, trying feebly to calm him. "I feel fine."

David was not reassured. His brother looked as though he had just received some bad news. "What happened, Jacob? Is everything all right back home?"

"David, everything's all right. Leave me alone."

"Everything's not all right, and I'm not leaving you alone." David raised his voice. "What happened?"

Jacob's eyes darted frantically in every direction. David grabbed his shoulders and forced Jacob to look at him. Fear was not something he associated with his big brother. *What in the world was going on here?*

"Jacob, talk to me," he pleaded. "What's going on?"

"Not here," Jacob said, after a moment's hesitation. Once again, his eyes began roving, as though he was afraid that someone was watching him.

"Let's go into the wine room," David suggested. "I have the key."

The special Zinfandel 2004 that the Stern Family Winery had sent for the Rebbe's wedding was being stored in a room near the hall owner's office — a room usually used as the *cheder yichud* for the newly married couple. Half an hour before *bentching*, three or four young men would be sent in to remove the corks from the bottles and leave them free to "breathe" — in accordance with the Sterns' capricious (in R' Yoel's opinion) demand. At *bentching* time, the bottles would be loaded onto metal rolling carts and brought to the table. The Rebbe would pour some wine into a silver goblet and recite the *Birkas HaMazon* over it, after which he would pour out some wine for every participant present, to the refrain of R' Tuvia's song, "*Niggun HaParnassah.*"

The two brothers hastened toward the wine room. David unlocked the door, with Jacob continually glancing around in every direction.

"Now, calm down," David ordered, after he had locked the door behind them again, "and tell me what happened."

Jacob gazed at him for a long moment. He was still hesitant, but it seemed to him there was no other way. He had to trust his brother. He could not cope with this thing alone.

"Okay," he said with a sigh. "It all started three months ago ...." He began his story with the Mexican anthropologist who asked for information about the epidemic near Juarez, continued with the series of systematic killings carried out by the pale man, and reached the threatening phone call to his home by a senior CIA man after the death of Jorge Diaz — a conversation that forced him to keep absolutely silent about the Juarez affair.

"I remember now," Jacob said, "that, just before the CIA fellow called me, I tried to call you. The call was transferred to your voice mail. Afterward, you got back to me and asked what I'd wanted. I said that maybe one of the kids had dialed your number by mistake."

"That's right. I remember that conversation," David said. "You sounded strange, but I didn't want to probe. But tell me — why are they going to such lengths to keep the story under wraps?"

"Why?" Jacob repeated bitterly. "Because the episode exposes one of America's darkest secrets. First of all, no country would admit that it's been developing biological weapons — and certainly not that it used human guinea pigs in the process. The epidemic that wiped out the Chuma tribe was an experiment conducted with the government's knowledge and consent, by American scientists. Do you have any idea of the damage to America, if it became known?

"And that's not the only secret," Jacob continued. "Only a handful of people were aware of the identity of the scientist who headed the research project. He was an outstanding microbiologist, a genius in his field, by the name of Dr. Henry Reiner. But that wasn't his real name. His real name was Heinrich von Reiner. He was a German scientist who had been an important figure behind the Nazi military machine. He reported on the progress of his work directly to the Fuhrer — Adolf Hitler himself. When World War II ended, the U.S. sent secret agents into every prisoner-of-war camp until they found him. Then they made him an offer he couldn't refuse: He would be brought secretly to Texas, where he would be pardoned for all his crimes against humanity and would complete the work he hadn't managed to finish in Germany: creating the ultimate virus, to serve as a powerful weapon in the hands of his adopted country."

"Unbelievable!" David murmured, clearly shaken.

"Do you see? The sacrificed Indian tribe was only the tip of the iceberg. Most of Heinrich von Reiner's work was performed on Jews in the Nazi concentration camps. He had an unlimited number of experimental subjects there, and he inflicted all sorts of tortures on them. He infected Jewish inmates with various diseases that caused them to die in agony. He tried out all sorts of biological weapons on them. The Chumas represented just the final stage in his scientific work. I'm not surprised that they killed off anyone who even *thought* of publicizing all of this. Believe me, David, what I don't understand is why they let *me* live ...."

David was shocked to the core by what he had just heard. "But ... what's happening today?" he managed to ask.

Jacob's chest heaved with another deep sigh. David's question had restored him to the present.

"What happened was that I was handing out the fish, when I suddenly saw the pale man right in front of me, sitting among the *aniyim.*"

"Here? Today?"

"Yes."

"Wow! What did you do?"

"I went over to R' Shammai. I never told you that back then, when I was feeling terrified, I made a special trip to the Rebbe, who was staying in Tzefas, and wrote a *kvittel* asking for protection. Seeing the pale man today, I thought that if he's come to an event connected to the wedding, maybe it has something to do with the Milinovers in general."

"And ...?"

"R' Shammai said that there's a senior American agent in the hall, and urged me to talk to him. He's called Agent Scott. I did it. I trusted him, and told him everything I knew. And then, just a few minutes later, as I was walking around the hall, I suddenly saw them talking together and even giving each other a hug."

"Who? The pale guy and Agent Scott?"

"Yes."

"So that means — they're working together?"

"Yes."

"Just a minute," David said. "I don't get it. Why did Agent Scott come here?"

"I have no idea. R' Shammai didn't say."

"And Scott didn't tell you himself?"

"No."

"So what *did* he tell you? Did he just listen to what you had to say?"

"Pretty much. At the end, he asked me some questions about a few people I might know."

"Who?"

"What difference does it make? I didn't know them. Some imam in Los Angeles, and a scientist."

"What are the names? Do you remember?"

"Not really .... One of them was Bashir ... Aziz .... And I think he also said Majdi. I can't remember exactly."

"Majdi? Barry Majdi?" David asked.

"Yes, that's it. Barry Majdi."

Now it was David who turned pale.

"What did he tell you about him?" he asked.

"That he's a lecturer in biology and has a private company that develops medical patents."

"And why was he interested in him?"

"How should I know?"

"Jacob, I have to talk to him."

"To who?"

"Agent Scott."

"Why?"

"Because I know Professor Barry Majdi very well. Let's just say that we have a certain ... business relationship."

71

Y ou know him?" Jacob asked in surprise. "How?"

"From the winery," David said. "Our head winemaker is a pro-tégé of his."

"George?"

"That's right. Professor Majdi was the one who introduced George to the field of winemaking. Seems George started his college career as a bi-ology student — and was failing. The professor realized that he had been blessed with an extraordinary sense of smell and taste, and recommended that he transfer to Davis University and study winemaking. He even got him a generous scholarship from some foundation in California. George became, as you know, an excellent winemaker."

"So what's your business relationship with Majdi?"

"It's not exactly business .... George consults with him frequently. There's been an experimental project that they've been involved with in these past few months, to prevent cork decay. Have you ever opened a bottle of wine and it simply reeked? That smell is caused by a bacterium called T.S.A. that can develop in cork and cause the wine to spoil. Last year, many of our bottles were returned to us from restaurants and stores, and we didn't know what to do. George put me in touch with Professor Majdi, who developed a special tasteless and odorless cleanser. When the corks are rinsed with the cleanser before insertion in the bottle, it prevents the bacteria from developing."

"And you've found that it solved the problem?"

"We'll know that in a couple of months. The first bottles with corks that have undergone the cleansing process have already been sent out into the market; we'll soon see if there's a drop in the return rate. If the process proves itself, it can bring in plenty of money. Cork rot is a well-known problem in the wine-making industry."

"So why would Scott be interested in him?"

"That's exactly what I'm going to ask him," David rejoined.

Jacob was alarmed by this idea. "Are you crazy?" he hissed. "You're going to talk to Agent Scott?"

"Certainly."

Jacob strode to the door and stood with his back to it, as though determined to prevent his brother from leaving. "David, you're not going to him. He's working with the pale man."

"Excuse me," David said. "He's a government agent; R' Shammai said he can be trusted; I think it's my duty to tell him that I know the man he's been asking about."

"You're making a mistake," Jacob warned.

"Jacob, I'm a big boy now," David said. "Let me do as I see fit. Just point him out to me."

Jacob grumbled and shook his head, but David was adamant. The brothers left the wine room, locking the door behind them.

"He's the fellow playing the saxophone," Jacob said, nodding at the bandstand. "But, David — it's dangerous. I'm not happy about it."

"Is he an agent or a musician?" David asked in astonishment.

"That's just his disguise." Jacob noted that there were now two saxophonists onstage. "He's the one sitting in the back. The dark-haired man with the bigger saxophone .... David, why are you being so stubborn about this? You're putting yourself at risk."

Ignoring his brother's warning, David began walking firmly toward the edge of the hall, to the stairs leading up to the bandstand. Back here, concealed from the public eye, were piles of equipment, empty instrument cases, and stacks of additional tables and chairs.

Jacob was beside himself with anxiety. His brother was walking right into a trap, and he couldn't stop him. David was in danger. Perhaps Jacob himself was at fault for telling him that Agent Scott had been interested in Barry Majdi. He felt restless and agitated.

The best place to be, he decided, was near the Rebbe. He walked to the front of the hall and took up a position near the dais. From time to time, he sent fearful glances toward the bandstand, where he estimated that his brother should now be arriving.

David climbed the stairs to the stage. The saxophonist's back was to him, but Scott caught David's movement in the corner of his eye and turned questioningly.

"Can I speak to you?" David asked.

"Let's go down." The agent gestured. The music was making it difficult to hear.

"I understand that you're Agent Scott," David said, when they reached the foot of the stairs.

"That's right."

"I'm Jacob Stern's brother. The one who spoke to you earlier?"

"Ah — the Department of Agriculture fellow," John said.

Jacob Stern did not remain long near the head table. Restless with worry over his brother, he began roaming the hall. Horrific scenarios crossed his mind in quick succession. Suddenly, he froze where he stood. The worst possible scenario was happening right before his eyes: The pale man was walking rapidly just a few yards ahead of him. He hadn't noticed Jacob, because he was facing ... the rear of the stage, where David had gone just minutes before.

Jacob clenched his fists. He wanted to scream out a warning to David — to tell him to run while there was still time. But the pale-faced killer had already disappeared behind the bandstand.

"What's your name?"

"David. David Stern."

"Yes, David? What did you want to tell me?"

"My brother told me that you asked him if he knows certain people in Los Angeles."

"Correct."

"I live in L.A. I hear that one of the people you asked about was Professor Majdi."

David saw an instantaneous change come over the other man's face. Up to this point, the agent had been paying close attention to him. All at once, his face became shuttered as his eyes moved to something — or someone — that was moving toward them behind David's back.

David's surprise did not last long. A stranger entered his field of vision from behind. The man walked over to Agent Scott and placed a hand on his shoulder. "What's going on?" he asked genially. Then he glanced at David: "What have we here?"

The pale man! This had to be him. It couldn't be anyone else. The nickname that Jacob had given the man suited him to a tee. His face was oddly pale and his blond hair was bleached nearly white. Even his eyes were curiously colorless.

David did not see the gun that the pale man thrust into Agent Scott's back. From where David was standing, it looked like a gesture of friendship. But John felt the gun very well.

"So you say you know Professor Barry Majdi," John said, picking up their talk where it had been interrupted. "Where from?"

David hesitated. He didn't understand what was happening here. Jacob had warned him against this pale fellow, who now seemed to have joined the conversation.

John Lowinger noticed his hesitation. He also felt his brother's pistol boring into the small of his back.

"It's okay. You can talk," he said with a smile. "We're working together."

"Well .... You asked about Professor Majdi," David said, much less confidently than before. "And I thought it only right to tell you that he works with me."

"Works with you — at what?"

"I have a winery. Stern Family Winery, Los Angeles."

Shammai's friend, John thought at once. "And what does Professor Barry Majdi do at your winery?" he asked.

"He doesn't have an official job. He actually serves as a consultant to our chief winemaker, George Bellini, who was a student of his at UCLA.

Majdi encouraged him enter the winemaking field and they've maintained a professional connection ever since."

The agent considered this. Then he said, "Okay. Thank you for coming to tell me."

"If you need me, I'll be in the hall," David said.

"Certainly. Thank you very much."

David turned and walked away, sensing the eyes of both men on him as he went. The situation struck him as very strange. There had been a clear current of tension between the agent and the pale fellow. Scott had clearly not enjoyed the fact that the other man had joined in the conversation. On the other hand, he had urged David to speak freely in front of him.

His puzzlement had prevented David from providing too many details. Maybe Jacob was right. Maybe he ought not to have spoken to that agent — if he really *was* an agent ....

The brothers waited until David Stern had moved out of hearing range. Eddie backed away from John, still pointing the gun at him.

"So, you came here for a good meal, eh?" John said cynically.

Eddie grinned with undisguised pleasure. "I came to eat — and also to make sure *you* don't do anything stupid."

"Like what, for example?"

"Anything that would run counter to the interests of the United States government."

"Or do you mean anything that runs counter to the interests of Walter Child?"

Eddie retreated an additional few steps, moving at a diagonal. A tall wooden crate now separated them; it had been used in transporting microphones and amplifying equipment. "I just want you to know that I have the authority to stop you by any means — *any* means — from harming American interests. And I'll gladly do it."

"I have no doubt of that," John said dryly.

"First of all, give me your weapons," Eddie said, his gun still pointed directly at his brother.

John removed his gun from its holster and placed it on the crate. Eddie picked it up and stuffed it into his pocket. "The others, too," he ordered.

John pulled another gun from a shoulder holster, and a third that had been strapped to his calf. He placed these, too, on the crate. Lifting both hands into the air, he said, "You can frisk me if you like."

Eddie did not rely on his brother's word. He executed a quick search, and pulled from John's belt a can of knockout spray and an electric prod. In John's shirt pocket he discovered another treasure: his cellular phone.

"With your permission," Eddie grinned mockingly, "I'll borrow this. Okay?"

John trembled with fury. Eddie had left him helpless, confiscating his weapons and his means of communication. But it was crucial that he maintain his self-control. The struggle between him and Eddie — between what he stood for and what his brother represented — was a battle of wits. The one who was smarter would win. Strategy, not force, would determine the outcome of this war. Eddie had tied his hands, but he had not taken away his ability to think.

"And now," Eddie Lowinger said with theatrical humor, gesturing at the stairs. "If you'd like to go on playing — be my guest."

Without a word, John turned around and climbed back onstage. He ground his teeth and clenched his fists tightly. He would not give in. He would never surrender. He was minus a weapon and a phone, but he would win. He would beat his brother and Eddie's evil superior — even if he was armed with nothing but his saxophone!

The saxophone was waiting beside John's chair. He picked it up and quickly joined the other musicians. The band was playing a slow, soulful tune; John didn't know the melody or understand the lyrics, but the song suited his mood perfectly.

Think, think, he urged himself. Now he really had no one to consult. He was truly alone. There was no one to listen to except his own heart.

What had he gleaned from the brief conversation he had had with David Stern, before Eddie interrupted them? First of all, the fact that Professor Majdi had an interest in a Jewish winery. And not just any winery, but one whose owners belonged to the greater Milinover community — the very group selected as the target for a big terror attack. That fact ought to set off some very loud alarm bells.

How in the world had no one stumbled across it until now? How had this piece of information eluded the dozens of investigators and analysts working on the Majdi file? How was it possible that there was no hint of this problematic connection, in the vast wealth of material they had amassed on the professor?

The answer was simple: The professor had concealed it.

Barry Majdi had hidden his connection with the Stern Family Winery, just as he had covered up his longtime connection to Bashir Abdul Aziz. Majdi took his responsibilities seriously. He was an expert at concealment. Even if Eddie hadn't taken his phone, even if he could have called Ted Cone right now and asked him to search for a link between the two, John had no doubt at all that no such link would be found — not a single phone call or document or letter between Majdi's home or office and the winery. He probably used an untraceable number, one that could be purchased in a store without any ID, as his sole method of communication with the winery and its chief winemaker.

Despite himself, John had to admire Majdi's efficiency. The man was a professional. He had done a thorough job. Just as he had been able to scatter the misleading clues that had deceived everyone into chasing the vial in the air-conditioning system, he had also managed to avoid leaving footprints in the actual direction: poisoned wine.

Here was the professor's famous "weaken and destroy" — his life's philosophy — in action. He had certainly weakened the force arrayed against him, causing it to invest all its resources into fighting an empty threat. Now he would strike the decisive blow from a totally unexpected direction.

But there was a much larger question here. David had said that Majdi had encouraged his student to enter the wine field, and had maintained contact with him to this day. How was that possible? Alcohol was forbidden to Muslims. If Majdi was so faithful to the Koran and its commandments — what was his connection to wine? What was his interest in the winery? The whole business of creating an intoxicating drink was loathsome in the eyes of a true believer in Mohammed.

The only explanation was that this, too, had been planned in the most calculating fashion, in order to give Majdi access to a place that made wine. Here, too, Majdi had not presented himself as a Muslim or mention the fact that he had been born in Egypt.

There was no doubt in John's mind that the true dispersal of the toxic virus was meant to be carried out, somehow, through the wine. That was why the professor was in such close contact with a Jewish winery. And it also explained why he had kept that connection such a closely guarded secret.

Wine ... wine ... wine .... Had wine been served at the meal? As an intelligence professional, John had developed his skills of observation to allow him to absorb and remember the minutest and seemingly most trivial of details. He reviewed the progress of the meal in his mind, and concluded that no wine had been served during the time he had been in the hall. Of that, he was certain. And when he had entered the hall, about half an hour after the event began, there had been no empty wine bottles on the tables.

In that case, when was the dispersal expected to occur? Tomorrow, perhaps, at the wedding itself? This was difficult for him to believe. If the "weaken" portion of the program had taken place today, then the "destroy" part should occur today as well.

All he needed now was another few words with David Stern.

Still playing, John glanced back over his shoulder. That brief talk, he saw with dismay, was not going to be possible. His brother, Eddie, had taken up a position right behind the bandstand. John couldn't go down there. He was a prisoner here onstage. All he could do was keep on playing with the band. Playing — and thinking.

There was still a hole in his theory, an important detail that cut the ground out from under the foundation of assumptions he had constructed. Mexico A was contagious only through the respiratory system. The toxins in the virus attached themselves to the lungs, and proceeded from there to infiltrate the rest of the body. It was impossible to spread Mexico A through the medium of wine or anything else that entered the digestive system. John knew this for a fact. If there was one person in the American intelligence community who was an expert on the weapons of biological warfare, it was John Lowinger. That, of course, was one of the reasons he was here right now.

He was well versed in the properties of all the various diseases and germs and lethal viruses. There was no way to disseminate the Mexico A virus in wine, period.

Again, the questions came back to haunt him: What was Professor Barry Majdi's plan? What was his connection to David Stern's winery? *And how was the terror attack going to be carried out?*

"Page 153," the conductor announced. There was a sudden stir of excitement onstage. This, the musicians knew, was one of the highlights of the entire event. For most of them, this was not the first time they had played at a Milinov affair.

The conductor lifted his baton, and the band broke into the next song:

Te'hei hasha'ah hazos
She'as rachamim
V'es, v'es ratzon
Milfanecha.

[May this be a favorable hour
A time of mercy
A time of mercy
Before You.]

The Rebbe and *mechutanim* stood up all along the length of the head table, clasped hands, and began dancing in place. Around them, the enthusiastic crowd danced on their bleachers with great devotion. The entire hall shook with emotion and fervor.

Te'hei ha'sha'ah hazos
She'as rachamim
V'es, ve'es ratzon
Milfanecha ...

It was impossible not to be affected by the tremendous fervor. The tune drew one inexorably in. The members of the band felt their spirits being elevated as their playing was filled with feeling and focus. Only John's mind continued chasing the answer to the elusive riddle that gnawed at him. Once again, he went over all the facts he knew, trying to view them in a fresh light. He found no way out of the maze. After a strong start, he had reached a dead end.

The conductor waved his baton, and the band played on:

Te'hei ha'sha'ah hazos
She'as rachamim
V'es, v'es ratzon
Milfanecha.

Te'hei ha'sha'ah hazos
She'as rachamim
Ve'es, ve'es ratzon
Milfanecha ...

Oh, no! The new thought froze his blood.

No! It couldn't be possible! Could it be that the virus the Professor intended to spread throughout the hall was not Mexico A at all, but — he was afraid to even entertain the awful possibility — Mexico B?

In his shock, John stopped playing. All the air whooshed out of his lungs, and his fingers felt nerveless and numb.

For a full thirty seconds he sat rigidly in place, his face devoid of expression. The hall around him roiled and churned with ecstatic emotion, but he was detached from it all. He was in another world entirely. Again and again, he went over everything he knew.

Mexico B ... Mexico B ....

This form of the virus *did* work through the digestive system, he reflected. The question was: How had the professor obtained a sample? Mexico A was available at the CDC labs in Atlanta, where Majdi had once worked. A person with evil intentions and an ingenious mind would have been capable of smuggling some out. But Mexico B? That virus did not exist anywhere in the United States, despite the fact that it had been developed within its borders. The only viral lab in the world that contained a sample of Mexico B today was Russia's central laboratory in Moscow, which had inherited it from the former Soviet Union.

The answer was obvious. The solution had been hidden in the mountain of material that Ted Cone had passed on to him. The relevant sentence rose up in his mind: *As a CDC employee, Professor Majdi was a member of a delegation of researchers and scientists sent from the U.S. after the dissolution of the Soviet Union, to help reorganize the collapsing Soviet viral labs. Majdi earned much praise for his devoted work in Bacteria Instituute #16 in Riga.*

Here it was — the last piece of the puzzle to complete the picture. Barak Majdi had taken advantage of his job in Russia to steal a sample of the lethal virus and smuggle it into the United States. That was it. They were dealing with Mexico B. That was the germ that Majdi intended to use to infect the Milinover wedding guests in this hall. This was the "destroy" segment of his plot.

And what an ingenious and Satanic plot it was! How deliberately cruel and wicked .... The professor had fooled the whole world. He had organized the classic wild-goose chase — a scenario even Walter Child had accepted without suspicion — in which everyone was convinced that they were after an airborne Mexico A virus. But, in the end, he had made use of a more sophisticated form of the virus, Mexico B, which could be ingested by mouth.

As a boy in Grayston, John had had no idea what was taking place in the secure compound, behind the concrete walls and watchtowers. He had been happy when Andrew, the trumpet-playing soldier, had obtained permission for him to enter the compound and play with the band. Even after the terrible catastrophe that took so many lives, including those of his father, old Uncle Sam, Frankie the ranch hand, and Manuela the housekeeper, he had not sought an explanation for the event. He had had the perspective of a young boy of 13. His biggest concern back then was finding a suitably challenging musical framework in which to play the saxophone in his new home, Atlanta.

It was only when he grew up and his life took a turn into the arena of biological warfare that he realized what had really happened. Only decades after he left Grayston did he discover that an entire complex of laboratories had been built around a single individual, a brilliant scientist whom the U.S. had located after World War II, just minutes before the Soviets would have snatched him up. Only after John achieved the highest security classification did he learn what that scientist, Dr. Heinrich von Reiner, had been doing while under the protection of the Americans, and with the full consent of some senior government officials.

He remembered how hard it had been for him to believe his eyes, the first time he was permitted to read about von Reiner's work. He had been incredulous at learning that the United States, that noble protector of human rights and liberty, had participated in such heinous crimes against humanity.

The information had been stark and incontrovertible. The first experiment took place on October 18, 1953. The helicopter lifted off from the Grayston compound at 11:07, headed for the experimental ground in the Juarez region of Mexico. It sprayed 600 ml. of the Mexico A virus over a group of about 30 experimental subjects.

The "subjects," as Heinrich von Reiner had dubbed them, had not volunteered for the job. They were valiant warriors of the Chuma tribe, who naively believed that they were battling a huge, predatory hornet. They hurled poisoned arrows at the helicopter, trusting in their old shaman's enchantments to help them chase away the terrorizing enemy.

A visual check of the area two days later showed a 100 percent death rate among the subjects. Every single one of the warriors who had breathed in the material that the helicopter had sprayed had fallen ill and then died. The rest of the Chuma tribe was not harmed. The results of this human experiment accorded with those obtained using lab animals: Mexico A destroys only those in the first circle of contagion, but progressed no farther.

The second experimental run, according to Dr. von Reiner's handwritten log, was a complete success. This time, he wanted to explore the effects of Mexico B, which enters the body via the digestive tract and then passes from person to person by way of their breathing. The helicopter dumped several ampoules of the toxic material into the stream that ran near the subjects' village. Those who drank from its waters in the thirty minutes after contamination were the first circle of contagion. Afterward, the material dissolved and was washed away. There was now a group of several dozen carriers from the first circle of contagion who began suffering cold or mild flu symptoms. They had no way of knowing that, with each sneeze or cough, they were spreading the disease in all directions, infecting more and more of their fellow tribesmen.

The first outbreak occurred ten days later. The first to succumb to the symptoms were, naturally, those in the first circle of contagion: the tribesmen who had drunk from the contaminated water. Within just two or three days, however, the rest of the tribe joined them: the second and third circles. By the fifteenth day, the death toll had risen to 100 percent. The remote Chuma tribe had been destroyed — or in Dr. Heinrich von Reiner's enthusiastic version, as recorded in his scientific journal: The experiment was crowned with unprecedented success.

This, then, was Professor Majdi's brilliant plan. He had weakened the intelligence communities of both Israel and America in their futile pursuit of Mexico A, the basic virus with limited contagion that spread through the air. But, in actuality, his plot involved disseminating the Mexico B virus through the medium of wine, causing an uncontrollable outbreak with ever-widening circles of contagion.

All the wedding guests would become carriers. The Milinover chassidim and the other participants in the celebration would become thousands of walking biological time bombs. As each one returned to his home, he would help spread the disease to the four corners of the earth.

After the ten-day incubation period, the first victims would show symptoms of the disease in different parts of the world. The authorities would try to help, but it would be too late. The epidemic would engulf many countries. It would be impossible to isolate it — or control it. The lethal Mexico B virus would rampage across the globe, unhindered.

John sat in his place on the bandstand, the saxophone cold and silent in his hands. The band continued playing rhythmically as the atmosphere in the hall grew more heated. John's eyes scanned the crowd dancing with increasing animation, completely unaware of the cruel and bitter fate that awaited them.

Did Walter Child realize what kind of porridge he had helped cook up? Did he have any idea of the kind of horror he was about to impose on America and Europe? Was he aware that the "small" terror attack he had been willing to let the professor and the imam perpetrate, with "only" a few thousand dead, had swung out of control and was about to turn into a worldwide pandemic that could claim *millions* of lives?

Oh, Walter, Walter, thought John. *You think you run the world. You think that you're manipulating the professor and the imam from afar. You think you control them, that you're allowing them to operate according to your agenda. But it's all slipping through your fingers. You're about to lose any control you ever had. By your irresponsible actions, you stand poised to destroy the world.*

There was one thing that the assistant director certainly did not know. It was one of the most carefully guarded secrets in the biological-warfare industry. The Mexico virus had one property that made it dangerous and destructive on an unparalleled scale. It was a property that played right into the imam's and the professor's hands: The virus harmed only those who drank alcohol.

It had taken a long time for the CDC scientists in Atlanta to figure out why he and Eddie had survived. At first, they tried to credit their survival to their youth, but that notion was quickly rejected, since there had been another survivor, an elderly man. The real reason was found by accident. In one of their interviews with the scientists, the boys innocently revealed that one day, after seeing their father humiliate himself while in a drunken stupor, they had made a bet to see which of them could abstain from liquor the longest. From there, it was a quick jump to understanding the reason for their recovery.

The virus, as the CDC scientists determined, turned deadly only in the body of a person who had consumed alcohol in the months before exposure. The toxins in the virus attached themselves to an enzyme that the body produced in reaction to the alcohol. Every one of the victims of the accident in the government compound had consumed alcohol to one degree or another. Only John and Eddie, who had sworn off liquor on a bet — and the anonymous old man as well, apparently — had not touched a drop. It was this abstention, the scientists said, that had saved them.

And it would be that same fact, John mused, *that would finish off the Western world.*

The Mexico B virus would spread everywhere, but faithful Muslims, who didn't touch alcohol even secretly, would sicken mildly and then recover. Only Christians, Jews, and the rest of the "infidels" — anyone who had had so much as a beer, a shot of liquor, or even meat cooked in wine — would die.

In your arrogance and the intoxication of power, Walter Child, you've led radical Islam to a truly unprecedented victory. In your wickedness, you've unsheathed the sword of Mohammed. That sword will now be free to rampage freely through the world, destroying the "infidels" and sparing only the lives of faithful adherents to Mohammed's teachings. Is this what you wanted?

Was this the outcome you anticipated: that, while America and Europe bury their dead, exulting hordes of radical Muslims with their extremist and pitiless beliefs will rule the entire world?

73

John threw another glance at Eddie, still seated at the foot of the stairs behind the stage. His brother was exploring, with great interest, the phone he had confiscated from him. This didn't worry John, as the device demanded biometric identification designed specifically for times like this. Without John's fingerprint, Eddie would never be able to read the classified material inside.

The problem was that Eddie had virtually made him a prisoner here. He was keeping a close eye on John and denying him the chance to operate freely. John urgently wanted to speak with either Jacob or David Stern. They had no idea of the evil motives that lay behind the professor's affable assistance to their head winemaker. Alternatively, he could whisper in the ears of his chassidic liaison men, R' Shammai and R' Yoel, who knew that a terror attack was expected.

But Eddie was not about to let him talk to anyone. Initially, he had tried to conceal his presence at this banquet; now that his identity had been exposed, he was making very sure that his brother did not leave the bandstand.

John's saxophone had been silent for long minutes now. He sat still, clutching his instrument while his mind was busy with his thoughts. He had to try to get inside Eddie's head — to see the situation through his eyes. Why, for instance, was Eddie sitting down there right now? What was he waiting for? If, as John assumed, his brother was here to make sure the terror attack took place as planned and to protect Walter Child's reputation, Eddie was apparently just waiting for the outbreak to begin. He was waiting for the first guest to feel ill. And then — what?

He had probably already reported that "Agent Scott" suspected that Child knew about the attack in advance and had done nothing to prevent it. What instructions would Child issue regarding John? To kill him? How, exactly, did Eddie plan to stop him from "harming American interests"?

At a signal from the conductor, the band moved on to the next song.

> **Vayimalei mishaloseinu**
> **B'middah tovah yeshuah v'rachamim**
> **B'middah tovah yeshuah v'rachamim**

[May He fulfill our requests
In good measure, with salvation and mercy
In good measure, with salvation and mercy.]

The enthusiasm in the big room flared up again, even more powerfully than before. Some of the chassidim continued dancing jubilantly on the bleachers. Others stepped down and pulled some of the *aniyim* into a joyful dance.

Actually, John suddenly realized, Eddie had no idea that there had been no biological material in the vial — nothing but plain tap water. Eddie — and, of course, his handler Walter Child — did not know that the dispersal of the virus by means of the air-conditioning system had been a mere smoke screen, intended to distract attention away from the true dispersal by means of the wine. How much longer could this party go on? Another quarter of an hour? Half an hour? The guests were already finishing their main course. Dessert would be served soon. What would happen when Eddie realized that no outbreak was taking place? How would he and his boss react when they understood that the original plan had not been carried out?

The band launched into the second stanza:

Vayimale mishaloseinu
B'middah tovah yeshuah v'rachamim
Vayimale mishaloseinu
B'middah tovah yeshuah v'rachamim.

The dance lasted even longer this time. Despite his visible weakness, the old Milinover Rebbe continued dancing, on and on to the limits of his strength, eyes closed in devotion and face tilted up toward the heavens. The *chasan* was on his right and the *mechutan*, R' Yom Tov Padlinsky, on his left, with the rest of the crowd joining voices in a powerful plea:

Vayimale mishaloseinu
B'middah tovah yeshuah v'rachamim
Vayimale mishaloseinu
B'middah tovah yeshuah v'rachamim.

Long minutes later, the Rebbe resumed his seat at the head table, and the *mechutanim* followed suit. All around, the chassidim continued dancing, though their enormous fervor was gradually lessening. Now they'd sing another two or three songs, until dessert was served to the guests. And then came the most important and emotional portion of the entire affair, the thing they'd all been waiting for: R' Tuvia's *Niggun HaParanassah*. The song that was sung on one occasion only: at the *seudas aniyim* preceding the wedding of a scion of the Milinover dynasty.

The marked change in the guest musician's manner had not escaped the conductor's notice. When R' Shammai had whispered to him that the fellow was an intelligence agent who required a vantage point from which to observe the hall, the conductor had been resigned — and glad that this was not taking place at the wedding itself, but at the *seudas aniyim*. Within just seconds, however, the uninvited visitor had been revealed as an outstanding musician who equaled, or even surpassed, anyone else in the band.

Then suddenly, in the past quarter of an hour, the man had simply stopped playing. He sat quietly, looking worried and at a loss. Who was he? The conductor made a mental note to ask R' Shammai for the story later.

The guitarist, sitting closest to John, also noticed his neighbor's lowered spirits. He was about thirty, not religiously observant but a veteran of this band, who had already played at three Milinover weddings before this. In the distant past, he had played at a few jazz clubs in New York and had dreamed, as they all did, of making it big one day. He, too, had noted that the American saxophonist was extraordinarily talented. He had tried striking up a conversation with the newcomer, but the saxophonist hadn't been interested. Perhaps now, the guitarist thought, when he seemed to be fretting about something, was a more propitious moment. Taking out a flat whiskey bottle, he held it out to John.

"You look worried. Want some?" His English was not Oxford level, but he could express himself clearly enough.

"I'm more interested in wine," John heard himself say.

"Wine?" The guitarist chuckled. "If you wait just a bit longer, you'll have some."

John tilted his head questioningly.

"At the end of the meal, the Rebbe hands out wine to everyone," the musician said. "That's how it always goes at these feasts for the poor. I hope they do it today, too."

"Really?" Suddenly, John was very, very interested.

"Sure. The wine at most chassidic weddings are usually so-so, but the Milinovers always have something special. Something from the United States."

John digested this information in silence.

"Tell me something," the guitarist said, moving on to a really important topic. "Have you ever played in any serious clubs? You're not bad."

"Quiet!" John barked. "I can't think ...."

The guitarist subsided in affront.

There was no time for politeness. Unwittingly, the guitarist had just given him a piece of vital information. The dispersal of the virus would take place during this meal. The "weaken" and the "destroy" portions of the program were to happen at the same time. He had perhaps a quarter of an hour, perhaps less, to stop the nightmare. He would have to go down to Eddie and try to neutralize him. If he got close enough, perhaps he could overpower his brother even though Eddie had a gun.

He must let David Stern know that the wine he was about to serve was poisoned.

He must halt the mass slaughter that Barak Majdi and Bashir Abdul Aziz were plotting.

Eddie saw John coming down the stairs. He shot up to his feet and blocked his brother's way, one hand on the gun in his belt.

"Get back up there," he ordered, his voice hard.

"Eddie, just a second."

Eddie tugged the gun slightly out of its holster. "If you don't go back, I'm going to shoot. I have my orders, and they were very clear."

"I need to talk to you."

"No more talk," Eddie said. There was about three yards between them: too far for John to leap forward with any confidence and subdue Eddie, but close enough for him to see the silencer screwed onto the gun.

"Eddie, you don't understand what's happening here."

"I don't have to understand anything. Get back up!"

"Eddie." John raised his voice. "The Israelis found the vial that Turk Majdi left here. There was nothing toxic in it. It was filled with plain water."

He saw Eddie's slight hesitation as this hit him.

"You're waiting for the virus to break out," John continued rapidly. "But it's not going to happen. Majdi tricked us all. There was nothing in the vial that Yousuf brought to Israel."

For an instant, Eddie was stunned. Then he recovered. "Get back up there!" he yelled, and whipped out his gun.

John retreated slowly. "Majdi tricked you and Walter Child. The vial in the air-conditioning was only a decoy. He deliberately left a trail of clear footprints for us to follow. He caused us to arrest Turk and Yousuf. The dispersal is going to happen a different way."

Eddie was becoming furious. "Do you *want* me to kill you?" He waved his gun in his brother's direction.

John continued moving slowly back toward the stairs. He saw the confusion in his brother's eyes. As Eddie continued threatening him, making sure to keep a safe distance between them, he was also trying to figure out whether there was anything in what John was saying. He, Eddie, had followed first Yousuf and then Turk. Had it all been for nothing?

"The dispersal is going to take place in a quarter of an hour," John pounded his message home. He was already standing on the first step. "And it's not going to be Mexico A — but Mexico B."

Eddie's shock was impossible to miss. The hand pointing the gun at John shook with rage.

John continued his retreat, shouting down to his brother, "Majdi has a contact in the winery that provided the wine for this affair. He introduced the virus into the wine that's going to be handed out in just fifteen minutes!"

He was now on the fourth step up. His brother stood under him, his attitude arrested. Something in his body language told John that he could yank the rope a little tighter.

"Who knows about Mexico B better than you?" he asked. "You have to warn Walter Child. This is not the way he planned it. Maybe he wanted a few thousand corpses to promote his cause. He certainly didn't intend to wipe out thirty million people! Mexico B only affects alcohol drinkers. All the Christians, Jews, atheists, and even secular Arabs will die. And who'll be left? Only extremist Muslims. Is that what he wanted to achieve?"

Eddie awoke from his trance and waved the gun. "Get up on that stage right now!" he screamed. "I have no time to listen to your nonsense."

John took another backward step. "I can get you together with Uri Arbel, Israel's senior intelligence man. He'll show you the empty vial."

"*Will you be quiet?*" Eddie let off a single shot at the stair under John's feet. The silencer ensured that the shot was not heard, but John felt the step shudder beneath him.

"The next bullet will be in your head," his brother warned. "Now, get up there!"

John turned around and sadly went back to his place on the bandstand.

There's no chance, he thought in despair. The situation was hopeless. Eddie refused to listen to him — justifiably, from his perspective. He didn't believe that the professor had led them all on a wild-goose chase. He was convinced that the attack would take place via the Mexico A virus. His brother's comments about Mexico B were, to his mind, aimed only at obtaining evidence against him and Walter Child. John — so Eddie thought — was trying in any way he could to extract an admission from Eddie that he knew something about the impending attack. Well, he was not going to get *that* by any means!

What to do? John wondered in anguish. In just a few minutes, wine would start to be poured for the guests. If he tried to warn anyone from here on the stage, Eddie would shoot him on the spot. What to do?

How could he possibly halt this biological attack? How could he prevent the worst pandemic in human history?

Ten minutes passed.

John cast about desperately for a way out, but nothing occurred to him. Minute by minute, his despair grew. Time was passing.
The dispersal of the biological toxin was drawing ever closer. Any moment
now, the tainted wine would be served to the guests, spelling unmitigated
triumph for Barak Majdi and Bashir Abdul Aziz.

Every now and then, he glanced secretly behind him. Perhaps Eddie
would relax his vigilance, turn around, give John a chance to leap down
and subdue him ....

These were vain hopes. Eddie was very tense as he engaged in a long
phone conversation without once removing his eyes from John's back.
The conversation seemed to be a stormy one, filled with differences of
opinion, though Eddie tried to conceal this by restraining his gestures.
It was clear to John that he was arguing with someone. The argument
gradually abated, until Eddie finally ended the call with a more relaxed
manner and even a satisfied smile. He had been talking to Walter Child,

John guessed; by the look on Eddie's face, the assistant director had fully convinced him that his brother was talking nonsense.

The band moved on to the next song. The picture had not changed: John was stuck on the bandstand, Eddie was still on guard below, time was passing, and the wine would shortly appear on the tables.

Another five minutes ticked past. Zero hour was coming.

"The *Niggun HaParnassah* — page 197," the conductor announced.

A stir of excitement passed through the group of musicians. The conductor, a chassidic Jew, had explained to them the significance of this tune to the Milinover chassidim.

The guitarist, who had been sulking since the saxophonist had behaved so uncivilly toward him, decided to forgive and forget. "After this song, they start pouring the wine," he winked at John.

"Really? Thanks for telling me," John said, a little more friendly this time.

Immediately, from below, came Eddie's warning whistle. Turning his head, John saw his brother pass a finger warningly across his throat, and then put the same finger to his lips. *Careful! Stop talking to the other musicians! I see everything!*

The moment the band started playing R' Tuvia's *niggun*, the atmosphere in the hall changed dramatically. The spirit of rejoicing gave way to a serious, almost solemn air. The chassidim who had been rollicking along with the music calmed down, swaying slowly and fervently to the melody's rhythm.

At the head table, where the elderly Rebbe and the *mechutanim* sat, an air reminiscent of the *Yamim Noraim* reigned, for all were aware that this was a holy and exalted moment. It was a time for *teshuvah mei'ahavah*, for returning to one's Creator with love; a time for closeness and devotion to the Almighty. In fact, this song represented the transition from the celebration of the *aufruf* to the day of the *chuppah*, whose greatness and holiness, as brought down in the holy books, are unbounded.

John was overcome with a powerful urge to pick up his saxophone and join in the music. R' Tuvia's *parnassah* song was designed to pierce the heart. There was something terribly moving about it .... But this was no time for making music. The moment required his full and total concentration. His eyes scanned the hall. He was not the only one who had been touched by a sense of exaltation. The same emotion suffused the entire crowd. The Rebbe swayed with devotion, eyes closed and hands raised heavenward. The *chasan*, with his young and noble demeanor, sang with feeling as tears trickled from his eyes. The *mechutanim* felt the same. As for R' Shammai, the chief *gabbai*, he stood behind the Rebbe's chair singing along with his eyes closed, waving a clenched fist from time to time in fervent punctuation.

John's eyes remained fixed on R' Shammai. The memory of the wonderful Shabbos meal he had had at the *gabbai's* home, just three days before, rose up in his mind: R' Shammai's pleasant talk, his radiant face, the tasty traditional dishes, and even the argument begun by Uri Arbel, meant to annoy, but answered by the *gabbai* with wisdom and warmth. Was that going to be the last pleasant experience in his life? Was he, John, along with Uri Arbel and R' Shammai, the Rebbe and his entire family, the groom and all the chassidim in this big hall, doomed to die an agonizing death — the first in an ever-widening circle of bereavement and loss that would eventually span the globe?

John began to move. He moved like a robot, as though someone greater than he was guiding his movements and telling him what to do. The idea had popped into his head very suddenly. He felt a wave of emotion beating inside his chest and, without thinking much, simply stood up and began walking down the stairs toward Eddie.

He had nothing to lose. In any case, he was about to lose his life. Let his death at least serve a purpose. At least let him know, with his final breaths, that he had halted the murderous chain that began in Nazi Germany, moved on through the wicked Soviet empire, and was on the brink of being brought to fruition by bloodthirsty, death-embracing radical Islamists. With his last heartbeats, he would know that his death had spared many, many people throughout the world, starting with the Milinover chassidim — his brothers and his people. After all, he was just like them. He was a Jew.

His father, Ben Lowinger, had become enraged when he learned that John had been to see his mother's grave in the Grayston cemetery. He had beaten John when he saw the Hebrew letters and the Star of David above them that young John had traced from his mother's headstone. His father had wanted to keep from him the knowledge that he was a Jew. But a person, it seemed, could never outrun his destiny. His father, estranged from his faith, had sought to cut off his son from his roots. Now, John was about to die for the sake of his Jewish brethren.

His life was forfeit. His brother — the son of his father, but not his mother — was about to take it from him. Let him at least save his people through his death. Let him save the lives of this amazing group, the chassidim of Milinov who, in their generosity of spirit, did not forget the poor and the unfortunate even in their moment of greatest joy.

"What is it this time?" Eddie snarled. Once again, he stood at a safe distance from John, his gun ready.

"Eddie, I have to talk to you."

"Okay, talk. But make it fast."

John took a long breath. *Progress*, he thought. At least Eddie was willing to hear him out.

"Eddie," he began. "I know that you took the lives of a number of people in the course of this affair. You ran over Lenny Brown in your car, shot Jorge Diaz at point-blank range in Houston, served poisoned tequila to a group of Indian activists in Mexico City. And I'm personally aware of some other CIA operations in which you eliminated more than a few people."

Eddie tried to hide it, but a small, self-satisfied smile crept onto his lips. To his ears, John's words sounded like praise.

"I don't get excited about things like that," John continued. "My own hands are not clean either. I'm no saint. Like everyone who works for United States intelligence, we sometimes have to dip our hands in blood. We don't do it for pleasure. We have a country to protect. We have a democracy to preserve. Anyone who knows the history of the CIA knows how much loss of life we've been responsible for. Africa, Asia, South America — our long arm has reached everywhere. We've supported military uprisings, helped establish corrupt governments, and backed tyrants — all in the name of American interests. And it's all been accomplished with a great deal of spilled blood and an appalling loss of life."

Eddie listened to his brother without expression, betraying no sympathy for what John was saying, but no impatience, either.

"But what's about to happen today, Eddie, is not CIA. It's only *you*. The mass murder of millions that's about to start here today touches *you*, Eddie Lowinger, and no one else. There's something that only the two of us know about. A secret that, forty years ago — just one day after the catastrophic accident in Grayston — we swore we'd keep forever. I've kept my word. To this day, I've never told a soul.

"We both know that, on the day before the accident, you took something out the compound for Dr. Heinrich von Reiner. We both know that you gave that something to those two Mexicans in a car that also held poor Steven Chambers, Norman's son — who was found several days later in an empty pool in the yard of a Juarez house. We both know that KGB agents were staying in that house. One of them was General Sergei Petroshov, whom the Soviet Union had put in charge of pursuing Dr. von Reiner. And we both know that the thing that was passed on to the Soviets was a vial filled with a liquid, labeled in von Reiner's handwriting, 'Mexico B.'"

Eddie continued listening, his face still devoid of expression. Not a muscle moved.

"Von Reiner," John continued, "apparently wanted to take his revenge on America for, as he felt, stealing his freedom. He wanted to give the Soviet Union a biological weapon that was more sophisticated and efficient than anything America had. The official version has it that Steve Chambers was responsible for passing the vial — but the reality, Eddie, is that *you* were the one to transmit Mexico B to the Russians. In reality, if you hadn't taken the vial out of the compound — in exchange for the Swiss watch the good doctor promised you — the Russians would not have the virus now."

"What's the point of all this?" Eddie asked in open disdain.

"It's connected to our present situation — because Majdi got Mexico B from Russia. After the collapse of the Soviet Union, he was sent there with a U.S. scientific delegation to help organize the Soviet viral labs, which were in terrible shape. On his return home, he smuggled a sample of the Mexico B virus into the United States — the same way he had stolen a sample of Mexico A from the CDC labs in Atlanta."

Eddie remained unperturbed. If John had hoped that his brother would exhibit remorse or shock, he'd been deluding himself.

"Eddie," John said. "You've killed many people, but there was some justification for those deaths. You were working on behalf of your government. You were following orders issued by your superiors. You were a soldier of sorts. But are you prepared to be responsible for the deaths of tens of millions of people? Will you be able to live with the knowledge that your actions led to the destruction of the whole Western world? You're poised to sign the death sentence of entire nations. You are about to become the man who brought about the collapse of Western civilization.

"You, who are well aware of the properties of Mexico B, know that it has the ability to change the face of the world in just a few weeks' time. You'll be leading radical Islam to a historic victory. You, Eddie Lowinger from Grayston, Texas, a CIA agent who's sworn to protect the United States, will be added to the list of Arab heroes — right up there with Osama bin Laden ...."

Angrily, Eddie cut him off. "Tell me, who are you trying to fool? There's no Mexico B here. That's just something you made up."

"Not that dispersing Mexico A is any less a crime," John said at once.

"You and your nonsense. There's no Mexico A or Mexico B here. You're just confused."

John's chin jerked toward Eddie's hand. "Then why the gun? Why are you threatening me? Why won't you let me get down off the bandstand?"

"I told you. I'm making sure you don't harm American interests."

"Which interests?"

"I don't have the authority to tell you that."

John looked long and hard into Eddie's eyes.

"What if I'm right, and not Walter Child?" he asked. "What if you find out, too late, that Mexico B was released here today? By the way, is *he* aware that you're responsible for the fact that the Russians possess Mexico B? Did you bother telling him that? Does he know that Majdi helped rehabilitate Soviet labs? Does he have that information?"

Eddie's nostrils quivered. His jaw worked almost unconsciously. For a brief instant, he lowered his gaze.

Then he looked up again. "You're just trying to scare me."

"I'm not trying to scare you. Mexico B is about to be dispersed in this hall — and you'll be responsible."

"What do you want from me?" Eddie screamed in frustration.

"I'll tell you exactly what I want," John said. "I want to walk around this hall."

Eddie glared at him. "Forget it."

"What are you afraid of? That I'll talk to someone? I promise not to speak to or contact anyone."

Eddie snorted contemptuously.

"How can I harm American interests if I don't talk to anyone?" John pressed.

Eddie weighed this for a long moment.

"Eddie, listen to me. You can walk right behind me. You can stick to me like glue. Keep your gun pointed at me under your jacket. The minute I say a word to anyone — I give you permission to shoot me."

Eddie grinned. "I don't need your permission!" he laughed.

"I'm serious," John said. "This is no time for jokes. If I say a word, or pass a message to anyone — kill me."

Eddie grinned slyly. "You know something?" he said. "That might not be such a bad idea. I wasn't intending to kill you myself .... Well, never mind that."

His meaning did not escape John. Eddie had other operatives in this room. The knowledge only increased John's conviction that this was the only way.

"So — shall we go?" he asked.

Eddie compressed his lips in thought, his fingers playing with the gun. "What are you up to, John?"

"If I'm 'up to' something, it's only to make sure that my brother does not turn into the biggest mass murderer in history."

Eddie gave the matter one more minute's thought. "You know what?" he said at last. "I'm going to do this — just to prove that you're talking nonsense. There's no Mexico B here."

"All right then. Let's go." John turned his back. "I'll lead, and you follow. If I speak a word or pass a message to anyone, you can shoot me without warning."

"With pleasure," Eddie said. And he meant it.

John emerged from the concealed area behind the stage and moved along the edges of the hall, behind the bleachers. The *Niggun HaParnassah* was still playing, so it was reasonable to assume that he would meet neither Jacob or David Stern, R' Shammai, or R' Yoel. If anyone else tried to talk to him, he would simply ignore them.

John remembered the layout of the hall from the tour he had taken with Uri Arbel on Friday night. He went to the kitchen first, hoping to find the wine stored there. Eddie, fuming, followed at his heels.

The kitchen looked the way all catering-hall kitchens look at the end of an affair: leftover food, dirty trays, and half-filled pots. There was no one there. The Arab workers had been taken away by the G.S.S. for interrogation, and all the chassidim who had served as waiters were in the dining hall.

The wine wasn't there.

John's next guess proved luckier. The wine was in a small room near the office, not far from the lobby. As he, followed by Eddie, approached it, they were both assailed by a powerful fragrance of fine wine. The door was open. John peeked inside.

In the room were several institutional metal carts used to transport food. On the top surface of each, one-and-a-half-liter magnum bottles of wine were arranged, their corks already freed. John moved closer to the door. Now he could see some of the details on the label. While he could not make out the name of the winery, he saw that the wine was a Zinfadel and that the Milinover wedding logo was emblazoned on the upper half.

A quick look around the well-lit room gave him an accurate idea of the position. Along one wall was a haphazard arrangement of cartons in which the wine had presumably been brought from the U.S. Each carton was clearly stamped with the words: "Stern Family Winery, Los Angeles." On a nearby table was a pile of corks, newly released from their bottles.

A young man in chassidic garb was in the room, holding a large ring of keys. After a last look around, as though to make sure that all was in order before he left, he moved toward the door.

Zero hour was fast approaching, John knew. The bottles were already open and ready to be served. The minute the signal was given, the carts would be rolled out into the main hall.

Eddie was close behind him, his gun pointed at John's back.

The young chassid came to the door and selected the correct key from his ring.

"What are you two doing here?" he asked irritably. "Go back to your tables." As far as he was concerned, they were just two of the many paupers at the feast.

John didn't answer. Not only because Eddie might shoot him, but because he didn't understand what the man had just said in Hebrew.

He began turning his head slightly, to say something to Eddie. Suddenly, he felt the gun grind into a spot right between his shoulder blades.

"Don't turn around," Eddie ordered. "The minute you turn — I shoot."

75

John froze.

He was dangling Eddie at the end of a very slender rope, he knew. Eddie was torn between two opposing but powerful drives. On the one hand, he suspected John of trying to obtain proof that Walter Child was involved in the attack, and to that end of concocting a fantastic tale of the Mexico B virus. On the other hand, John had succeeded in planting a seed of doubt: that Mexico B might really be about to be dispersed; that Majdi had indeed managed to fool them all, including the assistant director; and that Eddie's reckless deed as a child in Grayston could bringing about the collapse of the free world.

Eddie's dilemma was a difficult one. He was afraid to disobey his boss's orders, especially since Child had other operatives in the vicinity. But he was equally afraid of discovering, when it was too late, that his brother had been right.

John believed he had only a few moments' grace. At any time now, Eddie could become angry and force him to return to the bandstand.

THE MEXICO FILE / 629

How much longer could he tighten the rope? How much more patience did Eddie possess? John needed just half a minute, no more. Maybe even less.

The young chassid in the wine room had finally found the right key. He went out and locked the door behind him. John noted that it was a wooden door with a simple key.

Before he left, the chassid turned back to them, this time more politely, and asked if they wanted something to eat. Receiving no answer, he shrugged and returned to the hall. He had to return the key ring to R' Yoel, who was doubtless to be found alongside the other dignitaries.

They were alone. Just the two of them. The entire hall resounded with R' Tuvia's haunting song. No one noticed the two brothers standing, one behind the other, near the office.

"The wine contains Mexico B," John said without turning around. He gestured with his head at the closed door three yards in front of him. "They'll be serving it in a few minutes."

"You're lying," his brother said behind his back. But his voice shook slightly.

"I'll prove it to you," John said.

Eddie was quiet for a long moment.

"Let's see," he challenged at last.

With complete suddenness, John shot forward at the closed door and kicked at the lock with all his strength. Under the forceful thrust, the door broke. John hunched his shoulders and stood perfectly still, his back still to Eddie.

"What are you doing?" Eddie yelled.

John breathed a sigh of relief. That had been a dangerous moment — the critical point of his plan. Eddie could have instinctively shot at John's unexpected movement. He had been counting on the fact that his brother, a seasoned killer, would realize within a fraction of a second that John was moving not toward, but away from him, and would restrain the automatic impulse to pull the trigger.

For two more seconds he stood there, shoulders hunched, allowing Eddie to calm down. Then he permitted himself to straighten slightly.

Slowly, with his back still turned to Eddie, John walked forward, into the wine room. There was no one inside now — just five metal carts, each of them bearing tens of bottles arranged in tidy rows.

"What are you doing?" Eddie stood in the doorway, the gun trained on John.

John didn't answer. He pushed the carts, scattering them to different points of the room as though seeking something. Then he picked up two bottles, one in each hand, held them up to the light, and placed them on an empty table standing nearby.

"What are you doing?" Eddie asked, louder now.

John hesitated before answering. Quickly, he picked up two more bottles, this time from two other carts.

"I'm looking for proof that there's Mexico B here," he said, as he moved additional bottles.

"Don't play games," Eddie snapped. "You're trying to buy yourself some time."

"Why do you think that?" John looked up in surprise.

Eddie's patience was at an end.

"That's it. Go back to the bandstand!" he yelled.

The bottle in John's hand slipped and crashed to the floor. Shards of glass flew in every direction and a large puddle of wine spread across the floor.

"Get back to the stage!" Eddie bellowed, pointing his gun at John's head.

John nearly slipped. He grabbed a cart for balance, which rolled to the edge of the room as all the bottles on it rattled and fell on their sides. The second bottle fell out of John's hand and followed the first to the floor.

"Come back to the bandstand with me right now!" Eddie shouted.

John moved slowly, sending his brother a serene look. "Calm down, Eddie."

"John," Eddie said between his teeth. "You're taking advantage of the fact that I don't want to kill you now. But if you don't get out of here this instant, I'm going to call on some guys who'll drag you outside and put a bullet right between your eyes."

John sobered at once. Picking up one bottle, he held it by the neck and walked toward the door.

Eddie retreated a few steps, letting John pass through the door while keeping a safe distance between them. His face was twisted with rage and frustration. He had admitted his weakness, blurting out to his brother that he was incapable of killing him. But why was John taking that bottle with him? What was he planning to do with it? Use it as a weapon? Throw it at him?

John, to Eddie's vast surprise, began walking rapidly in the direction of the bandstand.

"What are you doing?" Eddie called, rushing to follow. "Where are you going?"

"Come with me, and you'll see that there's Mexico B here," John called back over his shoulder.

"John, if you speak to anyone, I'm going to shoot!"

Holding the bottle in both hands, John advanced at a rapid clip. "Absolutely!" he said. "Our deal is still on."

"No, John. I demand that you stop!"

John didn't stop. The stage was too close now.

He didn't see Eddie punch in the number, but he certainly heard him say breathlessly, "Get over to the area behind the stage. Now!"

Ten more steps to the foot of the staircase. John covered the distance in seconds. He felt no fear now. He was doing the right thing. He was acting according to plan. Eddie couldn't hurt him anymore.

He leaped up the steps, taking them three at a time. Eddie hurried after him, but John was already onstage. As he passed his seat, he snagged his saxophone. Instead of sitting down, he stood in front of the guitarist. He didn't have to look over his shoulder to know that his brother's gun was aimed right at his back.

"Hey, I see you've already got yourself a bottle of wine!" The guitarist grinned.

John ignored him.

Arrogant, ungrateful so-and-so, the guitarist thought with a scowl.

The band was now playing the *parnassah* song for the seventh or eighth time. The conductor noticed that the saxophonist had returned and was holding his instrument. The event was nearing its conclusion. He was determined to catch him later, for a little talk.

In his wildest dreams, he could never have guessed what that talented musician would be doing in just one minute.

Still holding the open bottle of wine in his right hand, John lifted the saxophone with the other. He placed the mouthpiece at his lips and blew with all his might.

The sudden piercing note silenced the entire hall. It was a shriek of sound that had nothing to do with the music being played. The members of the band glared at John furiously. The conductor looked ready to explode. Many eyes in the crowded hall turned in surprise toward the bandstand to see what had caused the discordant sound. The spectacle that met their eyes was extremely odd: The saxophonist was standing at center stage, drinking from the bottle of wine.

A few seconds later, John lowered the bottle. With an apologetic wave at the conductor, as though to say, *Sorry, I don't know what came over me,* he glanced at his notes and began playing along with the band.

Many of the chassidim resumed their singing immediately, ignoring the slight disturbance and forgetting it in seconds. But there were a few men whose eyes remained riveted on the saxophonist in astonishment.

Jacob and David Stern thought they would faint on the spot. *What!* How had Agent Scott managed to get hold of one of the bottles they'd sent for the Rebbe's wedding? The wine had not even been served yet! And why was he drinking from it up there on the stage? What in the world was going on?

R' Shammai, too, stared at the American agent from his place behind the Rebbe's chair. What was Scott doing? This whole day had been one long chain of strange occurrences. At the start of the *seudas aniyim,* Agent Scott had insisted on climbing onto the bandstand and playing along with the rest of the band. Now he was drinking, in front of everyone, the special wine that the Stern brothers had sent for the wedding. What was happening? The whole world seemed to have gone crazy. Everything that could go wrong seemed to be doing just that.

Eddie, on the top stair at the rear of the bandstand, stared at his brother. What, exactly, was John up to? Why did he drink from that bottle? Now he had resumed playing his saxophone. What was going on?

When the two men — local hired thugs — that he had summoned by phone came running breathlessly up to him, he sent them back to their places with a wave of his hand.

David and Jacob hurried over to the wine room. A quarter of an hour before, they'd left the room with four young chassidim inside, all of them busy popping the corks off the bottles and arranging them on carts preparatory to rolling them out into the hall. One of the young men had been given the key to the door and was supposed to return it to R' Yoel afterward. So what had happened? How had the agent gotten hold of that bottle of wine?

Their apprehension spiked dramatically as they approached the room. The door was open and the lock splintered. Inside, they found carts scattered in every direction, bottles rearranged, two of the magnums shattered on the floor.

"Oh, no!" David cried.

Jacob raced back toward the head table and waved hysterically at the Rebbe's chief *gabbai*.

This time, R' Shammai responded to his signal at once. Abandoning his position behind the Rebbe's chair, he hurried to the wine room with Jacob.

"What is this?" he asked in shock, staring at the upheaval in the room.

David was on the verge of tears. "The wine was ready to go. The room was locked. And look what happened ...."

"Who did this?"

"It was that Agent Scott of yours," Jacob fumed. "He must have broken open the door to steal a bottle of wine."

At this point, they were joined by the young man who had been the last to leave the room. He testified that the saxophone player had indeed been prowling in the vicinity, along with another strange character, as he had locked the door.

R' Shammai gazed around at the mess. He tightened his lips for a few moments, and then lifted his eyes to the two Stern brothers.

"I'm afraid we won't be able to serve this wine," he said. "All of it is *yayin nesech* — impermissible. The gentile was here alone, and he moved and touched all the bottles. We'll have to find some other wine."

David's face turned gray. He grabbed his head with both hands.

Jacob reacted with uncontrollable anger. "I'll show him!" he shouted, and darted at the door.

R' Shammai ran after him and stopped him. "Wait a minute," he ordered. "Just wait a minute."

"What do you mean, 'wait'?" Jacob cried, gesturing at the topsy-turvy room. "Look what he did! He's cut off a beautiful family tradition lasting generations. Our father, grandfather, and great-grandfather all sent wine to the dynastic Milinover weddings. The Rebbe always *bentches* over Stern wine at the *seudas aniyim*. And now, because of that drunkard — that ... despicable creep ... there's no wine!"

"It's your fault," David turned on R' Shammai. "You said he could be trusted. You sent Jacob over to talk to him."

"And you know what?" Jacob added, shaking a finger at the *gabbai*, "Afterward, I saw him in the lobby, talking to the murderer who chased after me in Houston. Scott and the pale killer are working hand in hand."

In the heat of the discussion, no one noticed another person standing in the doorway and listening to every word. It was Uri Arbel.

The things that R' Shammai and the Stern brothers were saying had just filled out the picture for him. Agent Scott had apparently stood by his conviction that the vial found in the air-conditioning system had been nothing more than a clever decoy. He had also figured out that the dispersal was to take place through the medium of the wine. For some reason, he had been neutralized and unable to pass this information on to Arbel or anyone else. He, Uri, had been trying unsuccessfully to reach Scott on his cell phone for the past twenty minutes. Now he knew why.

There was a hostile force in this hall. Someone whom this agitated fellow had just called "the murderer who chased after me in Houston." The young chassid who had locked the door had said that Scott was seen in the area with "another strange character." The only way open to Scott to prevent the terror attack had been to disqualify all the wine for the religiously observant guests, by turning it into *yayin nesech*.

What a brainstorm! Arbel marveled. *What quick thinking.* He, himself, had been at the same Shabbat meal at R' Shammai's home. In fact, it was he who had raised the topic of a non-Jew or even a Jew who did not observe the Sabbath being alone with wine. R' Shammai had said that even if there was a possibility that he had touched it, religious folk would not drink from it. Scott had remembered this, and used it to prevent the great attack.

"Gentlemen. Please stay where you are. Nobody move," he ordered.

Everyone in the little room swung around in surprise.

"It's all right," R' Shammai told the others. "He's with Israeli intelligence."

"You'll have to be checked before you leave this room," Uri Arbel said. "Apparently, there's a deadly toxin in this wine."

"*What?*" the Stern brothers screamed in shock.

A smile of relief and understanding filled R' Shammai's face. A vast sensation of released tension swept over him. For some reason, he was not surprised. He suddenly entertained a vision from three months before: Jacob Stern appearing in Tzefas unexpectedly and in a state of agitation ... going into the Rebbe's room with a request for protection ... and the Rebbe "mistakenly" calling him "Dr. Polanski" ....

Uri Arbel used his phone to summon the team from the mobile lab parked outside. The lab that specialized in the identification of hazardous biological materials.

"This time, it's for real," he told his men.

R' Shammai's heart skipped a beat. If Agent Scott had drunk from the bottle of wine, he had exposed himself to the virus.

Agent Scott — there was no other way of putting it — had sacrificed his life to prevent the attack. He had infected himself with the virus in order to prevent the death of thousands of people.

76

A technician from the mobile lab entered the hall, dressed from head to toe in a protective suit and wearing a gas mask. Once again, a direct link was established between the joint security forces on Abba Hillel Street and the CDC Situation Room in Atlanta, Georgia.

It was quickly determined that the bottles of wine did contain a dangerous toxin: not Mexico A, but the rarer and more dangerous Mexico B virus. According to the information transmitted from Atlanta, the virus penetrated the body through the digestive system. As nobody in the storage room had drunk the wine, they were released with a recommendation for a follow-up, just to be on the safe side.

The decontamination crew isolated and sealed the room. Then they began the job of gathering up the wine and transferring it to a safe location, where it would later be destroyed under supervision. R' Anshel, the hall's owner, was asked to bring up several hundred bottles of inexpensive Israeli wine from his storage cellar.

Jacob and David Stern hovered nearby, deeply shocked and confused. The rapid sequence of events had left them reeling. So far, no one had explained to them what exactly was going on. But they had heard enough: The wine that they had sent to the Rebbe's wedding was capable of spreading a lethal virus. Only one person had intervened between the Milinover community and a massive tragedy.

Later, they would then learn to their relief that winemaker George Bellini had had no knowledge of Barry Majdi's plot. Majdi, apparently, had closely followed the entire cork-cleansing process, making sure to introduce the virus at the stage when the corks designated for the wedding wine was treated with the special cleanser.

One thing was beyond dispute: The person who had averted the horrible catastrophe was American Special Agent Scott. In an unparalleled act of self-sacrifice, he had imbibed the wine and infected himself with the disease in order to make the wine impermissible to religious Jews. He had been willing to give up his life — to save not a single life, but the lives of thousands, perhaps millions.

"I want you all to go back into the dining room and behave as usual," Uri Arbel ordered. "No one is to know about the near-tragedy that took place here today. I know that you're all shaken and upset, but this business is not over yet. The threat still exists."

With all due respect, Arbel knew that the danger that still threatened the State of Israel was named Agent Scott. He had had time to take a rapid glance at the properties of Mexico B, and had learned that it was an especially virulent virus. While the first victim was infected via the digestive system, about ninety minutes after exposure he began spreading the germ to others through his breathing.

There was a very short time left before Agent Scott became a threat. He must be neutralized.

The band continued playing R' Tuvia's *niggun*. John Lowinger played with feeling — and, this time, with no mistakes or squealing notes. The conductor watched the hot tears trickle down the saxophonist's cheeks as he plied his instrument. The bandleader had seen his share of emotional musicians, but never one affected this powerfully.

He had no way of knowing that John was weeping over his life. He was mourning himself. John didn't need Uri Arbel to tell him that he was not long for this world. In just an hour and a half, a biological explosion would begin.

The first symptoms would be those of an ordinary cold. But with each breath, each cough, millions of tiny germs would scatter in all directions, spreading the disease farther afield. He just wanted to be sure that his strategy had succeeded. He wanted to see, with his own eyes, that he had prevented the infected wine from being served.

To this end, he had done everything that he could. The details of the conversation at R' Shammai's Shabbos table were fuzzy in his memory, and he had not known the exact criteria needed to disqualify wine for Jews. Therefore, he had moved the bottles, poured wine onto the floor, shattered a couple, remained in the wine room with Eddie, and — as a grand finale — he drank from the bottle in front of everyone, so that there would be no question in anyone's mind as to who had been inside that room.

He hoped it hadn't all been in vain. He hoped that another wine would be served instead. Then he would be able to leave the hall in peace, find an isolated place, and perform his last act on behalf of mankind: end his life. The minute the victim died, John knew, the deadly virus died as well.

He was weeping, but he had no regrets. Never. He had made his decision wholeheartedly. It had been the only way to save millions of people from certain death. He would die with his head held high, and with the absolute conviction that he had done the right thing.

There was a stir at the front of the hall. John narrowed his eyes. Cardboard boxes were being carried up to the head table — boxes filled with wine. And ... yes! Thank G-d! They were different bottles. They were not from the Stern Family Winery. They were not toxic.

He had succeeded. He had prevented the great attack.

As his emotion increased, tears choked his throat. It was hard to play the saxophone. His death, then, would not have been in vain. The lives of millions had been saved through his action. He saw R' Shammai leaning earnestly over the table and talking to the Rebbe. The Rebbe lifted his eyes and gazed across the room at John.

Closing his eyes, John played for another minute. Then he turned around so that he faced his brother. Eddie still stood on the rear steps leading down from the bandstand. John looked at him over the rim of his saxophone and gave him a broad smile. It was a smile that radiated joy and freedom.

And Eddie understood. He understood that somehow — he didn't know how — John had managed to best him. Though he hadn't a clue as to how John had done it, his brother was celebrating his victory.

Eddie's lips thinned. His features sharpened and his eyes burned with fury. John was very familiar with this expression. It was the way Eddie had often looked in Grayston — and, later, in Atlanta. There was nothing that infuriated Eddie more than John's triumph. Eddie's strength lay in his wily, ruthless nature. People stood helpless before his cruelty and his stony heart. There was only one thing that that shook Eddie: having John outsmart him, suddenly realizing that his big brother, in some clever way, had managed to ruin his plans and paint him a loser.

At such times, Eddie's rage was monumental. He was seized by an uncontrollable, destructive spirit, all too reminiscent of his own drunken father, Ben Lowinger.

Eddie leaped down the stairs and raced for the wine room. Even from a distance, he was able to see Israeli soldiers in protective gear hanging a thick plastic curtain over the doorway. Another group of men came in, blocking his way back to the area behind the bandstand. He didn't understand how John had done it — but John had won. Once again, his brother had managed to triumph over him. And he didn't even know how ....

A roar of rage erupted from his chest. Something inside him exploded. He broke into a furious run toward the front of the bandstand, pushing people aside, jumping over benches, toppling tables. His brother saw him coming, fists doubled, eyes flashing, and teeth bared. John continued playing. Maybe, he thought, Eddie would pull out his gun and do the job for him ....

"Come here, John!" Eddie yelled from in front of the stage. "Come here if you've got an ounce of courage!"

John didn't budge. He stayed where he was, high above Eddie's head, and played on. People were still unaware of what was happening. The loud music and powerful singing drowned out Eddie's shouts so that only those nearest could hear him.

Eddie shook a clenched fist. "You're always right, eh, John?" he screamed hoarsely. "You always know best. You know better than anyone else."

At the conductor's signal, the band played the concluding notes of R' Tuvia's melody.

"You always have to ruin everything!" Eddie continued at the top of his lungs. Wrapping his hands around the metal bars that supported the stage, he shook them with all his might.

In the quiet after the song, his voice thundered through the hall. Everyone looked to see what the drama was about. It seemed as if one of the guests was standing at the foot of the stage, hurling epithets at the musicians.

"John Lowinger!" Eddie bellowed. "The great John Lowinger always has to have the last word!"

Two well-built chassidim broke free of the crowd and approached the disruptive "pauper" from behind, grabbing his arms. Eddie struggled and thrashed out with his arms and legs, eyes bloodshot and lips flecked with foam.

"You were always the smarter one," he shrieked at his brother. "Even as a kid. John Lowinger — the better student! John Lowinger — more successful! I'm going to kill you. I'm going to wipe you out!"

Total silence reigned. It was as if time had stopped moving inside that hall. John didn't say a word. He closed his eyes, hugging his saxophone; the tears on his cheeks had not yet dried. Suddenly, Eddie collapsed in the arms of the two young men holding him. A strange noise emerged from his throat: a kind of mad whimper. They put him on a chair, where he leaned back, arms dangling limply from his sides.

At that moment, from the entrance to the hall, into the total silence came the sound of excited voices. All eyes turned toward the speakers. They were recognized as the two dignified-looking chassidim who had traveled to Israel with the *mechutan*, R' Yom Tov Padlinsky, on his first visit to the Rebbe. As everyone watched, the pair walked quickly toward the knot of people at the foot of the bandstand. There was a stir in the air: Something extraordinary was about to happen, right before their eyes ....

"Are you John Lowinger?" one of the men asked, looking up at the saxophonist.

The two chassidim were R' Eliyahu Gorman and R' Shlomo Direnberg, whom R' Yom Tov Padlinsky had appointed his investigators. They were exhausted from two weeks of searching in vain for a clue in the matter of the Yerushalmi *meshulach*, R' Tzvi Hirsch HaLevi, R' Yom Tov's mother's first husband. The wedding was scheduled to take place tomorrow, and their despair had been growing exponentially with each passing day. They had been turning over the world to find John and Eddie Lowinger, the sole witnesses who might be able to shed light on their quest — when they had suddenly heard one of those names shouted out in the middle of the *seudas aniyim!*

John didn't answer. A secret agent never reveals his true name.

Eddie answered for him. "Yes!" he cried, amid wild laughter. "That's my big brother, John Lowinger — the wise, the successful, the one who knows it all!"

Jacob and David Stern, on the other side of the hall, looked at one another in astonishment. Agent Scott and the pale man ... brothers?

"Does that mean that you are Eddie Lowinger?" R' Eliyahu Gorman asked.

"Yes. Why do you want to know?"

John, onstage, moved closer in his curiosity. How did these two chassidim know him and his brother — and by their real names?

"You're both from the town of Grayston, Texas?" R' Eliyahu asked.

"We sure are!" Eddie bellowed again with inexplicable laughter.

"And you were there at the time of the horrific accident in the secret compound?"

"Sure!" Eddie giggled. "There were hundreds of dead. Hundreds!"

"And is it true that there were only three survivors?"

"Yup!"

"Who were they?"

"Who were they?" Eddie repeated. "John Lowinger, the great musician ... Eddie Lowinger, his pathetic kid brother who wanted to be a secret agent ... and —"

"Eddie!" John broke in warningly. "That's a state secret."

Eddie stood up and threw a glassy look in John's direction. Two men gripped his arms as he staggered and swayed. "State secret?" he screamed. "I don't care about the State! Let the U.S. burn, together with Walter Child. I'll tell whatever I want!"

"Eddie, you can't!"

Eddie laughed wildly. "I can't — but I will. The third survivor was Dr. Heinrich von Reiner, the celebrated Nazi scientist!"

The two chassidim exchanged a swift glance.

"There was another person — a Jew with a long beard. What happened to him?" R' Eliyahu Gorman asked tensely.

With another insane laugh, Eddie screamed, "What happened to him? He died, that's what! He died! He died like the rest of them. Like Lenny Brown! Like Jorge Diaz! Like I should have made sure Jacob Stern died — but that fool, Walter Child, wouldn't listen to me!"

There was a deathly silence in the hall.

"The Jew died right away," John spoke up suddenly.

The two chassidim lifted their eyes to him. "How do you know?"

"Because I was with him when he died," John said. "Both of us — along with many other patients — were in the same tent. I began to recover, but he was already dying. I remember him to this day. It's impossible to forget a person like that. I saw scores of people die during those days — but no one died the way he did.

"Everyone knew that their fate had been sealed. All of them — soldiers and civilians alike — knew they were not coming out of there alive. They cried, they cursed, they tried to kick the doctors. There were many who had to be tied down ... and that's the way they were when they died. Only he, that Jew, was quiet and peaceful. He suffered and was in pain, but he never let out a groan. He kept on murmuring prayers, with such devotion. It was hard for him to breathe, he was coughing up blood, but never for a moment did his serenity leave him.

"I was a curious child. I asked him why he was so quiet, when everyone else was weeping and wailing. And he explained to me that this world, the world that we're all living in, is only a corridor. It leads us through a hard, long road to another world, the world of truth, a beautiful palace that is our true life. 'Soon, I will be going to the World to Come', the old Jew told me. 'Soon I shall reach my destination — the beautiful palace. So I have no reason to be sad.'

"The next morning, he asked me, for the first time, to do something for him. He asked me to bring him a glass of water. I brought it to him. He closed his eyes, fervently said prayers for a long time, and drank a little water. Then he lay down on his bed and peacefully passed away.

"He passed from the corridor into the beautiful palace, with a wonderful smile on his face ...."

From the other side of the stage, where the stairs were, came Uri Arbel. He approached John.

"We have to go," he said quietly.

John glanced at his watch. "I still have an hour," he whispered. He wanted to report to his superiors and tell them what had transpired here today — the last report of his career.

"I'm going to take you to the hospital, where you'll be put in isolation, okay?"

John leaned closer. "Uri, I'll finish the story myself," he said, forming a gun shape with his fingers. "An hour from now, I'll no longer be with you. I think that I, too, am about to pass from the corridor into that beautiful palace."

Uri Arbel nodded his head. His eyes were filled with tears. He shook John's hand powerfully.

"I'll have to be near you when ... it happens," he said apologetically.

John nodded in agreement.

R' Shammai came up to the bandstand. "The Rebbe wants to speak to you," he told John. "Can you please come with me?"

This was the first time John had ever seen the Rebbe up close. He was very old, his face lined with years, but his alert eyes gleamed with life. John's breath caught with emotion.

He had met many of the world's movers and shakers. He had conversed with presidents and heads of state. But he had never felt the reverence that swept over him now. Something about the Rebbe radiated greatness and power. It had nothing to do with his physical appearance, but rather with a spiritual essence that came from within.

The conductor, in an unrehearsed move, signaled to his band to play a slow, quiet tune.

The Rebbe seated John beside him. Uri Arbel stood behind them, with Jacob and David Stern, R' Shammai, and the *mechutanim* clustered around. R' Yom Tov Padlinsky was beside himself with happiness. At long last, Heaven in its mercy had burst the bubble of doubt that had been hovering over him and his family. In the eleventh hour, the terrible suspicion had been removed. It was now clear to everyone that his mother's first husband had died in the days immediately following the tragic accident in Grayston. His parents' wedding had been a kosher one. Hashem's Hand in all of this was almost tangible.

Yeshuas Hashem k'heref ayin.

The young couple could now proceed to the *chuppah* in joy and confidence. The Rosh Yeshivah longed to discuss the whole affair with his two students/investigators, but the Rebbe asked them all to move closer and listen to what he had to say.

"I would like to tell you a story that happened about seventy years ago," the Rebbe began. "In the Meah Shearim section of Yerushalayim, there lived a fine, modest girl named Toivy Lederman. Her father, Chatzkel Lederman, died young, and her mother supported the family to the best of her ability from the proceeds of a tiny vinegar store.

"When it was time for Toivy to marry, the girl became engaged to a boy from a respected family in Shaarei Chesed. A wedding date was set and preparations were nearly finished, when a terrible rumor suddenly began to circulate about the *kallah*. People said that she had been seen coming out of a convent near the Old City. They said that she had been chatting with the nuns, and that she wanted, *rachmana litzlan*, to convert to Christianity.

"The *chasan's* family decided to break off the *shidduch*. A respected *rav* in Yerushalayim told them that the *kallah* was innocent. She went to the convent each week, he knew, in order to bring food to her unfortunate younger brother, who'd been born with serious birth defects and whom her father had taken to the monastery to be tended. Toivy's mother didn't know that the deformed child even existed: She believed that he had died at birth. Just before his death, Chatzkel Lederman revealed the secret to his daughter, and instructed her to continue caring for her hidden brother in his place.

"But the *chasan's* family closed their hearts and stiffened their necks. The *chasan* and his relatives refused to listen to the *rav's* pleas or to accept his assurance that the *kallah* was free of all wrongdoing. They broke off the match and did not restrain their tongues from wagging maliciously about the girl and her unfortunate family. They slandered her throughout the city. Not long afterward, the girl's widowed mother died of a broken heart, leaving behind a houseful of orphaned children.

"Above, the *kallah's* tears and her widowed mother's suffering created a great stir. In the Heavenly Court, a harsh decree was imposed on the Jewish people. A very harsh decree. Death and destruction ...."

The Rebbe closed his eyes for a moment, heaving a sigh from the depths of his heart.

"At that time," he continued, "there was a holy group of hidden tzaddikim headed by the holy R' Dovid Leib, *ztk"l*. He knew about everything that had happened. He and his group *davened* and fasted, pleading that the decree be averted — in vain. The Heavenly anger was not appeased and the decree remained in effect.

"Just one thing could sweeten the harsh decree. One of the hidden tzaddikim — the youngest of them all — privately went over to R' Dovid Leib at the widow's funeral and told him that he was willing to accept a personal death sentence. The deaths of tzaddikim, as we all know, are considered equal to the burning of the *Beis HaMikdash* and can atone for the generation. R' Dovid Leib tried to dissuade him, but the tzaddik stood firm.

"The leader of the hidden group asked a *she'eilas chalom*, seeking guidance in a dream, and Heaven let him know that this would not be enough. There is awesome power in the death of a tzaddik — but the sin would find true atonement only in conjunction with a simple Jew's self-sacrifice. Only then would the terrible decree be removed from the Jewish nation."

Again, the Rebbe's eyes closed. His weakness was visible. After a moment, he went on:

"That hidden tzaddik — that righteous man who was taken from this world and did not even merit a Jewish burial — was the *meshulach* of the Tzidkas Yerushalayim Kollel, R' Tzvi Hirsch HaLevi: former husband of the mother of our esteemed *mechutan*, R' Yom Tov. He was the man who gave his life for his people, praying that he be taken from this world to atone for the tears of the orphan girl and her widowed mother.

"But that was not enough. Many years ago, the head of that hidden band of tzaddikim knew that the sacrifice of that one tzaddik would not suffice. You, my dear John, are a Jew. You have sacrificed yourself to save the lives of thousands of your fellow Jews. You tossed away your life for the sake of others. In so doing, you completed the exalted act of that tzaddik, whom you actually had the privilege of meeting, speaking with, and serving in the short time before his passing.

"It was this act that has prevented the terror attack and averted a terrible tragedy. There were no exalted, mystical intentions — just a simple act of self-sacrifice. This has atoned for the sin and erased it. It has atoned for the great prosecution and sweetened the decree."

The Rebbe fell silent. Around him, nobody spoke a word or lifted his eyes. It was not every day that the Rebbe revealed that which was hidden. Not every day that he spoke of things that took place in the rarefied spheres. Not every day that he removed the curtain of concealment that he kept wrapped around him, and allowed a glimpse of his holiness and greatness to show. Not every day that the Rebbe, in simple, explicit terms, spoke of things that were taking place in the Heavens above ....

The Rebbe opened his eyes and looked at the American agent, who was crying with emotion.

"You, John," he continued, "have merited something precious and rare. In our *Tachanun* prayer, we say, 'But we and our fathers have sinned.' Not every man has the privilege and the merit of rectifying the things that his fathers perpetrated. That young man in Yerushalayim who cruelly abandoned his poor bride was your father, Binyamin Levinger. His sin was too great to be borne — and he died still not having repented. But you, today, have accepted the possibility of repairing a little of his wickedness. You, today, can merit the forgiveness that he was not wise enough to seek."

John Lowinger was crying like a baby. His shoulders shook and his eyes streamed with tears.

"I knew nothing about this story," he managed to say. "I knew that my father wasn't perfect, but ...."

"None of us is perfect," the Rebbe said. "We come to this world imperfect, and our job here, in this long corridor leading to the beautiful palace, is to repair and rectify our actions."

"I don't have much time," John said. "But I would like to repair the evil. The bride herself is certainly not alive anymore — it all took place so many years ago. But maybe her sons or daughters ...."

Suddenly, R' Shammai broke down in sobs.

John stared at him in astonishment. He? R' Shammai? Yes! How had he not realized it? His last name was Lederman, and his family owned a thriving vinegar business ....

"Was she your mother?" he asked.

R' Shammai only nodded, too charged with feeling to speak. His mother had been Toivy Lederman, who'd later married her widowed cousin from Warsaw. Because his name was also Lederman, she had never changed her name.

"You knew about all of this?" John asked.

R' Shammai shook his head. He, too, was hearing the story for the first time.

"I don't know how it's done," John said. "But I'd like to ask your forgiveness on behalf of my father."

"I also don't know how it's done — but I forgive you in my mother's name," R' Shammai said, a smile mingling with his tears.

And the two men — Binyamin Levinger's son and Toivy Lederman's son — fell into each other's arms and embraced.

It was Uri Arbel who cut short the emotional scene. Time was pressing. By the book, there was nearly an hour to go before John would become contagious — but they needed a safety margin.

"That's right, we have to go. There's no choice," John said. "I didn't live as a Jew, but at least I'll die knowing that I am one. I've been here among all of you for several days. I thought to myself that, had I lived, I'd want to get to know my people and their Law a little better. But I have only an hour. That's all I have to live."

"An hour is a very long time," the Rebbe said. "A person can do *teshuvah* in a single moment."

"What does that mean — to 'do *teshuvah*'?"

"It means to repent of the bad deeds that we've done, to confess them, and to undertake never to repeat them," the Rebbe said.

"I want to do it," John declared. "At least, I'll try to repent before ...."

The Rebbe held out his hand to John Lowinger.

And John did what he had seen the chassidim do. He bowed his head — and kissed the Rebbe's hand with reverence.

"Shall we go?" Uri Arbel asked.

"Yes," said John.

But a commotion had begun at the hall entrance. Uri Arbel and John Lowinger gazed in that direction. Eddie was in handcuffs and in the firm grasp of two security men. Why had he returned? He had been taken away, to be handed over to U.S. authorities. What had happened now?

"He wants to tell you something," one of the security men shouted at John. "He insisted that we come back here."

Eddie was wild eyed; his hair was ruffled and his clothing torn as a result of his thrashings. John stared at his brother in surprise. Eddie looked like a man in the throes of a nervous breakdown.

"What do you want?" John asked.

"Listen, John," Eddie panted. "You ruined my plans, you ruined my life; you were always the best and the smartest and the most successful. But there's still one thing I know that you don't."

"And what is that?"

"That you don't have to kill yourself."

"What? Why not?"

Manic laughter burst from Eddie's mouth. "Because you're immune, John. You — are — immune!"

John was astounded. Was Eddie right — or was he trying to put something over on him?

"That's impossible," he said forcefully. "There is no vaccination or medicine for the Mexico virus."

"Idiot!" Eddie howled. "They didn't manage to create a vaccine. But we are the only ones who are immune to it. We are the only two people in the world who once had the Mexico virus and then recovered. It was Mexico A, and we were saved because we didn't drink alcohol, but our bodies developed antibodies against both Mexico A and B."

"Are you sure?"

"Absolutely. Why do you think the head of the CDC, Patrick Braithwaite, took such pains over us? Why do you think he gave us a place to live and paid our tuitions in Atlanta schools? Do you think he was just a generous man? Do you think the government felt guilty about what it had done to our family? Don't make me laugh, John. The real reason — and I've only recently found this out myself— was an attempt to use us to obtain antibodies for the Mexico virus.

"For the CDC, we were a valuable asset: two walking specimens for scientific experimentation. All those blood tests and treatments were not meant to heal us. They lied to us, John. We were perfectly all right. Dr. Braithwaite and his staff tried — with our help — to develop a vaccine for the Mexico virus. They didn't succeed. The only two people in the world who are immune to the virus, John, are we two. You and me."

John was still skeptical. "Why are you telling me this now?" he asked his brother.

Again, a mad smile glinted in Eddie's eyes. "I realized earlier that you didn't realize you were immune," he said. "At first, I wanted you to go ahead and kill yourself. But believe me, John — it's worth my while to keep you alive ... if only to hear you admit, for the first time in our lives, that I knew something that you didn't!

"Just once, Eddie Lowinger is smarter than John. Just once, John will be forced to admit that even his pathetic little brother is worth something."

"Page 68 — 'Yodu LaHashem,'" said the conductor.

As the band burst into the song of joy and thanksgiving, the crowd began to dance again on the bleachers. At the head table, the Rebbe got to his feet. He gave one hand to the happy *chasan* and the other to his *mechutan*, who was wiping tears of joy from his eyes. John Lowinger and R' Shammai Lederman grasped hands. And they danced, their hearts pounding with gratitude to the Creator of all worlds.

> *Yodu laHashem chasdo*
> *Yodu laHashem chasdo*
> *Yodu laHashem chasdo*
> *V'nifleosav livnei adam.*

> [Let them thank Hashem for His kindness
> And His wonders to mankind!]

The band played energetically, and the huge throng sang along. John Lowinger danced with tear-blurred eyes. He didn't understand the Hebrew words. He had never lived as a Jew or seen a written verse, but the powerful emotions that filled his heart exactly fit the words of the song:

> *Yodu laHashem chasdo*
> *Yodu laHashem chasdo*
> *Yodu laHashem chasdo*
> *V'nifleosav livnei adam.*

John closed his eyes — and suddenly, from somewhere, other figures joined the dance. There was the righteous *meshulach*, R' Tzvi Hirsch

HaLevi, rising from his sickbed in the infirmary tent in the Grayston compound, wearing the same happy smile with which he had departed this world. He was dancing with John ....

And here was old Sam, getting up from his rocking chair on the porch, approaching the circle and joining hands with the other men as he pulled his nephew, Ben, after him ....

And now came the veteran sheriff, Jack Abrams — or rather, Yaakov Abramson — with a gold badge on his shirt ... and the *chazan-mohel*-funeral director known as the "Chief Rabbi of Grayston," jumping on the table in his strange clothes, and apologizing for coming late ....

And, off to the side — who was standing there? It was his mother, Devorah Lowinger. He had never seen her or even her picture, but it was she. Beyond a doubt, he knew that she was his mother.

Was he dreaming? Hallucinating? Not at all. They had all come to rejoice with him. They had all descended from the beautiful palace where they lived, in the World to Come. They were all smiling, their faces radiant, as they held him close to their hearts.

All of them whirled and danced around him in the circle, their lips singing along with him, along with the band, along with the Milinover Rebbe and his chassidim: "*Yodu laHashem chasdo, v'nifleosav livnei adam ...!*"